WORDS OF
RADIANCE

BRANDON SANDERSON

WORDS OF RADIANCE

PART ONE

Book Two of

THE STORMLIGHT ARCHIVE

Illustrations preceding chapters 22 and 49 by Dan dos Santos

Illustrations preceding chapters 3, 17, 30 and 45 by Ben McSweeney

Maps and illustrations preceding chapters 5, 11, 14 and 35 by Isaac Stewart

The right of Brandon Sanderson to be identified as the author of this
work has been asserted by him in accordance with the
Copyright, Designs and Patents Act 1988.

First published in Great Britain in 2014
by Gollancz
An imprint of the Orion Publishing Group
Orion House, 5 Upper St Martin's Lane, London WC2H 9EA
An Hachette UK Company

This edition published in Great Britain in 2015 by Gollancz

15 17 19 20 18 16 14

A CIP catalogue record for this book is available
from the British Library

ISBN 978 0 575 09331 7

Typeset by Input Data Services Ltd, Bridgwater, Somerset

Printed and bound in Great Britain by Clays Ltd, Elcograf S.p.A.

www.brandonsanderson.com
www.orionbooks.co.uk
www.gollancz.co.uk

For Oliver Sanderson,

Who was born during the middle of the writing of this book, and was walking by the time it was done.

ACKNOWLEDGMENTS

As you might imagine, producing a book in the Stormlight Archive is a major undertaking. It involved almost eighteen months of writing, from outline to final revision, and includes the artwork of four different individuals and the editorial eyes of a whole host of people, not to mention the teams at Tor who do production, publicity, marketing, and everything else a major book needs in order to be successful.

For some two decades now, the Stormlight Archive has been my dream – the story I always wished I could tell. The people you'll read about below quite literally make my dreams a reality, and there aren't words to express my gratitude for their efforts. First in line on this novel needs to be my assistant and primary continuity editor, the incumbent Peter Ahlstrom. He worked very long hours on this book, putting up with my repeated insistence that things which did not fit continuity actually did – eventually persuading me I was wrong far more often than not.

As always, Moshe Feder – the man who discovered me as a writer – did excellent editorial work on the book. Joshua Bilmes, my agent, worked hard on the book in both an agenting and editorial capacity. He's joined by Eddie Schneider, Brady 'Words of Bradiance' McReynolds, Krystyna Lopez, Sam Morgan, and Christa Atkinson at JABberwocky in the US, and John Berlyne at Zeno in the UK. At Gollancz, Simon Spanton put up with me delivering a book even longer than the last one when I promised to make it shorter. In the US, Terry McGarry did the copyediting, Greg Collins the interior design, and Brian Lipofsky's team at Westchester Publishing Services the compositing. In the UK, Charlie Panayiotou in editorial and Paul Hussey worked really hard to get the book into production on time. Jo Carpenter and her team in home sales and Mark Streatfeild and his team in export worked tirelessly selling the novel to booksellers with amazing results. Jennifer McMenemy, Hannah Atkinson and Sophie Calder were responsible for the marketing and publicity effort. A big thanks to all of you.

You may have noticed that this volume, like the one before it, includes amazing art. My vision for the Stormlight Archive has always been of a series that transcended common artistic expectations for a book of its nature. As such, I'm happy to have another excellent cover illustration from Sam Green. His work has graced all of my Gollancz covers, and their enthusiastic reception with local readers has been very humbling.

When I pitched the Stormlight Archive, I spoke of having 'guest star' artists do pieces for the books here and there. We have our first of those in this novel, for which Dan dos Santos (another of my personal favorite artists, and the man who did the cover for *Warbreaker*) agreed to do some interior illustrations.

Ben McSweeney graciously returned to do more brilliant sketchbook pages for us, and he is a pure delight to work with. Quick to recognize what I want, sometimes even when I'm not quite sure *what* I want, I've rarely met a person who mixes talent and professionalism in the way Ben does. You can find more of his art at InkThinker.net.

A long time ago, almost ten years now, I met a man named Isaác Stewart who – in addition to being an aspiring writer – was an excellent artist, particularly when it came to things like maps and symbols. I started collaborating with him on books (starting with *Mistborn*) and he eventually set me up on a blind date with a woman named Emily Bushman – whom I subsequently married. So needless to say, I owe Isaac a few big favors. With each progressive book he works on, that debt on my part grows greater as I see the amazing work he has done. This year, we decided to make his involvement a little more official as I hired him full-time to be an in-house artist and to help me with administrative tasks. So if you see him, welcome him to the team. (And tell him to keep working on his own books, which are quite good.)

Also joining us at Dragonsteel Entertainment is Kara Stewart, Isaac's wife, as our shipping manager. (I actually tried to hire Kara first – and Isaac piped up noting that some of the things I wanted to hire her for, he could do. And it ended up that I got both of them, in a very convenient deal.) She's the one you'll interact with if you order T-shirts, posters, or the like through my website. And she's awesome.

We used a few expert consultants on this book, including Matt Bushman for his songwriting and poetry expertise. Ellen Asher gave some great direction on the scenes with horses, and Karen Ahlstrom was an additional poetry and song consultant. Mi'chelle Walker acted as Alethi handwriting consultant. Finally, Elise Warren gave us some very nice notes relating to the psychology of a key character. Thank you all for lending me your brains.

This book had an extensive beta read done under some strict time constraints, and so a hearty bridgeman salute goes to those who participated. They are: Jason Denzel, Mi'chelle Walker, Josh Walker, Eric Lake, David Behrens, Joel Phillips,

Jory Phillips, Kristina Kugler, Lyndsey Luther, Kim Garrett, Layne Garrett, Brian Delambre, Brian T. Hill, Alice Arneson, Bob Kluttz, and Nathan Goodrich.

Proofreaders for the book include Ed Chapman, Brian Connolly, and Norma Hoffman. Community proofreaders include Adam Wilson, Aubree and Bao Pham, Blue Cole, Chris King, Chris Kluwe, Emily Grange, Gary Singer, Jakob Remick, Jared Gerlach, Kelly Neumann, Kendra Wilson, Kerry Morgan, Maren Menke, Matt Hatch, Patrick Mohr, Richard Fife, Rob Harper, Steve Godecke, Steve Karam, and Will Raboin.

My writing group managed to get through about half of the book, which is a lot, considering how long the novel is. They are an invaluable resource to me. Members are: Kaylynn ZoBell, Kathleen Dorsey Sanderson, Danielle Olsen, Ben-son-son-Ron, E. J. Patten, Alan Layton, and Karen Ahlstrom.

And finally, thanks to my loving (and rambunctious) family. Joel, Dallin, and little Oliver help keep me humble each day by always making me be the 'bad guy' who gets beat up. My forgiving wife, Emily, put up with a lot this past year, as tours grew long, and I'm still not sure what I did to deserve her. Thank you all for making my world one of magic.

CONTENTS

ILLUSTRATIONS

NOTE: *Many illustrations, titles included contain spoilers for material that comes before them in the book. Look ahead at your own risk.*

Roshar

ENDLESS OCEAN

RESHI

Rall Elorim

Kasitor

IRI

RIRA

Kurth

Reshi

Eila

The Misted Mountains

BABATHARNAM

MARABETHIA

SHINOVAR

Panatham

The Purelake

GULAY

Fu Namir

DESH

AZIR

ALM

UEZIER

AIMIA

Azimir

The Valley

STEEN

LIAFOR

TASHIKK

EMUL

GREATER
HEXI

Aimian Sea

Sesemalex Dar

Icewater

TUKAR

MARAT

N

LEEWARD

STORMWARD

S

SOUTHERN DEPTHS

STEAMWATER OCEAN

ISLES

Sea

ATAK

SUML

AKAK

Northgrip

HERDAZ

Mourn's
Vault

Varikev

Ru Parat

Elanar

JAH KEVED

Kholinar

ALETHKAR

Shulin

UNCLAIMED HILLS

TU
BAYLA

Valath

Hornenter Peaks

BAVLAND

Rathalas

Dawn's
Shadow

TU
TRIAX

Silnasen

Vedenar

Dumadari

Shattered
Plains

FALL

Karanak

FROSTLANDS

New Natanan

Kharbranth

Tarat Sea

Longbrow's Straits

The Shallow Crypts

THAYLENAH

OCEAN OF ORIGINS →

FOR HIS ROYAL MAJESTY KING GAVILAR KHOLIN
BY HIS ROYAL HIGH CARTOGRAPHER
ISASIK SHULIN
1167

BOOK

TWO

WORDS OF RADIANCE

SIX YEARS AGO

Jasnah Kholin pretended to enjoy the party, giving no indication that she intended to have one of the guests killed.

She wandered through the crowded feast hall, listening as wine greased tongues and dimmed minds. Her uncle Dalinar was in the full swing of it, rising from the high table to shout for the Parshendi to bring out their drummers. Jasnah's brother, Elhokar, hurried to shush their uncle – though the Alethi politely ignored Dalinar's outburst. All save Elhokar's wife, Aesudan, who snickered primly behind a handkerchief.

Jasnah turned away from the high table and continued through the room. She had an appointment with an assassin, and she was all too glad to be leaving the stuffy room, which stank of too many perfumes mingling. A quartet of women played flutes on a raised platform across from the lively hearth, but the music had long since grown tedious.

Unlike Dalinar, Jasnah drew stares. Like flies to rotten meat those eyes were, constantly following her. Whispers like buzzing wings. If there was one thing the Alethi court enjoyed more than wine, it was gossip. Everyone expected Dalinar to lose himself to wine during a feast – but the king's daughter, admitting to heresy? *That* was unprecedented.

Jasnah had spoken of her feelings for precisely that reason.

She passed the Parshendi delegation, which clustered near the high table, talking in their rhythmic language. Though this celebration honored them and the treaty they'd signed with Jasnah's father, they didn't look festive or even happy. They looked nervous. Of course, they weren't human, and the way they reacted was sometimes odd.

Jasnah wanted to speak with them, but her appointment would not wait. She'd intentionally scheduled the meeting for the middle of the feast, as so many would be distracted and drunken. Jasnah headed toward the doors but then stopped in place.

Her shadow was pointing in the wrong direction.

The stuffy, shuffling, chattering room seemed to grow distant. Highprince Sadeas walked right through the shadow, which quite distinctly pointed *toward* the sphere lamp on the wall nearby. Engaged in conversation with his companion, Sadeas didn't notice. Jasnah stared at that shadow – skin growing clammy, stomach clenched, the way she felt when she was about to vomit. *Not again.* She searched for another light source. A reason. Could she find a reason? No.

The shadow languidly melted back toward her, oozing to her feet and then stretching out the other way. Her tension eased. But had anyone else seen?

Blessedly, as she searched the room, she didn't find any aghast stares. People's attention had been drawn by the Parshendi drummers, who were clattering through the doorway to set up. Jasnah frowned as she noticed a non-Parshendi servant in loose white clothing helping them. A Shin man? That was unusual.

Jasnah composed herself. What did these episodes of hers mean? Superstitious folktales she'd read said that misbehaving shadows meant you were cursed. She usually dismissed such things as nonsense, but *some* superstitions were rooted in fact. Her other experiences proved that. She would need to investigate further.

The calm, scholarly thoughts felt like a lie compared to the truth of her cold, clammy skin and the sweat trickling down the back of her neck. But it was important to be rational at all times, not just when calm. She forced herself out through the doors, leaving the muggy room for the quiet hallway. She'd chosen the back exit, commonly used by servants. It was the most direct route, after all.

Here, master-servants dressed in black and white moved on errands from their brightlords or ladies. She had expected that, but had not anticipated the sight of her *father* standing just ahead, in quiet conference with Brightlord Meridas Amaram. What was the king doing out here?

Gavilar Kholin was shorter than Amaram, yet the latter stooped shallowly in the king's company. That was common around Gavilar, who would speak with such quiet intensity that you wanted to lean in and listen, to catch every word and implication. He was a handsome man, unlike his brother, with a beard that outlined his strong jaw rather than covering it. He had a personal magnetism and intensity that Jasnah felt no biographer had yet managed to convey.

Tearim, captain of the King's Guard, loomed behind them. He wore Gavilar's Shardplate; the king himself had stopped wearing it of late, preferring to entrust it to Tearim, who was known as one of the world's great duelists. Instead, Gavilar wore robes of a majestic, classical style.

Jasnah glanced back at the feast hall. When had her father slipped out? *Sloppy*, she accused herself. *You should have checked to see if he was still there before leaving.*

Ahead, he rested his hand on Amaram's shoulder and raised a finger, speaking harshly but quietly, the words indistinct to Jasnah.

'Father?' she asked.

He glanced at her. 'Ah, Jasnah. Retiring so early?'

'It's hardly early,' Jasnah said, gliding forward. It seemed obvious to her that Gavilar and Amaram had ducked out to find privacy for their discussion. 'This is the tiresome part of the feast, where the conversation grows louder but no smarter, and the company drunken.'

'Many people consider that sort of thing enjoyable.'

'Many people, unfortunately, are idiots.'

Her father smiled. 'Is it terribly difficult for you?' he asked softly. 'Living with the rest of us, suffering our average wits and simple thoughts? Is it lonely to be so singular in your brilliance, Jasnah?'

She took it as the rebuke it was, and found herself blushing. Even her mother, Navani, could not do that to her.

'Perhaps if you found pleasant associations,' Gavilar said, 'you would enjoy the feasts.' His eyes swung toward Amaram, whom he'd long fancied as a potential match for her.

It would never happen. Amaram met her eyes, then murmured words of parting to her father and hastened away down the corridor.

'What errand did you give him?' Jasnah asked. 'What are you about this night, Father?'

3

'The treaty, of course.'

The treaty. Why did he care so much about it? Others had counseled that he either ignore the Parshendi or conquer them. Gavilar insisted upon an accommodation.

'I should return to the celebration,' Gavilar said, motioning to Tearim. The two moved along the hallway toward the doors Jasnah had left.

'Father?' Jasnah said. 'What is it you aren't telling me?'

He glanced back at her, lingering. Pale green eyes, evidence of his good birth. When had he become so discerning? Storms ... she felt as if she hardly knew this man any longer. Such a striking transformation in such a short time.

From the way he inspected her, it almost seemed that he didn't trust her. Did he know about her meeting with Liss?

He turned away without saying more and pushed back into the party, his guard following.

What is going on in this palace? Jasnah thought. She took a deep breath. She would have to prod further. Hopefully he hadn't discovered her meetings with assassins – but if he had, she would work with that knowledge. Surely he would see that someone needed to keep watch on the family as he grew increasingly consumed by his fascination with the Parshendi. Jasnah turned and continued on her way, passing a master-servant, who bowed.

After walking a short time in the corridors, Jasnah noticed her shadow behaving oddly again. She sighed in annoyance as it pulled *toward* the three Stormlight lamps on the walls. Fortunately, she'd passed from the populated area, and no servants were here to see.

'All right,' she snapped. 'That's enough.'

She hadn't meant to speak aloud. However, as the words slipped out, several distant shadows – originating in an intersection up ahead – stirred to life. Her breath caught. Those shadows lengthened, deepened. Figures formed from them, growing, standing, rising.

Stormfather. I'm going insane.

One took the shape of a man of midnight blackness, though he had a certain reflective cast, as if he were made of oil. No ... of some other liquid with a coating of oil floating on the outside, giving him a dark, prismatic quality.

He strode toward her and unsheathed a sword.

4

Logic, cold and resolute, guided Jasnah. Shouting would not bring help quickly enough, and the inky litheness of this creature bespoke a speed certain to exceed her own.

She stood her ground and met the thing's glare, causing it to hesitate. Behind it, a small clutch of other creatures had materialized from the darkness. She had sensed those eyes upon her during the previous months.

By now, the entire hallway had darkened, as if it had been submerged and was slowly sinking into lightless depths. Heart racing, breath quickening, Jasnah raised her hand to the granite wall beside her, seeking to touch something solid. Her fingers sank into the stone a fraction, as if the wall had become mud.

Oh, storms. She had to do something. What? What could she *possibly* do?

The figure before her glanced at the wall. The wall lamp nearest Jasnah went dark. And then . . .

Then the palace disintegrated.

The entire building shattered into thousands upon thousands of small glass spheres, like beads. Jasnah screamed as she fell backward through a dark sky. She was no longer in the palace; she was somewhere else – another land, another time, another . . . *something*.

She was left with the sight of the dark, lustrous figure hovering in the air above, seeming satisfied as he resheathed his sword.

Jasnah crashed into something – an ocean of the glass beads. Countless others rained around her, clicking like hailstones into the strange sea. She had never seen this place; she could not explain what had happened or what it meant. She thrashed as she sank into what seemed an impossibility. Beads of glass on all sides. She couldn't see anything beyond them, only felt herself descending through this churning, suffocating, clattering mass.

She was going to die. Leaving work unfinished, leaving her family unprotected!

She would never know the answers.

No.

Jasnah flailed in the darkness, beads rolling across her skin, getting into her clothing, working their way into her nose as she tried to swim. It was no use. She had no buoyancy in this mess. She raised a hand before her mouth and tried to make a pocket of air to use for breathing, and managed to gasp in a small breath. But the beads rolled around her hand, forcing between her fingers. She sank, more slowly now, as through a viscous liquid.

Each bead that touched her gave a faint impression of something. A door. A table. A shoe.

The beads found their way into her mouth. They seemed to move on their own. They would choke her, destroy her. No ... no, it was just because they seemed *attracted* to her. An impression came to her, not as a distinct thought but a feeling. They wanted something from her.

She snatched a bead in her hand; it gave her an impression of a cup. She gave ... something ... to it? The other beads near her pulled together, connecting, sticking like rocks sealed by mortar. In a moment she was falling not among individual beads, but through large masses of them stuck together into the shape of ...

A cup.

Each bead was a pattern, a guide for the others.

She released the one she held, and the beads around her broke apart. She floundered, searching desperately as her air ran out. She needed something she could use, something that would help, some way to survive! Desperate, she swept her arms wide to touch as many beads as she could.

A silver platter.

A coat.

A statue.

A lantern.

And then, something ancient.

Something ponderous and slow of thought, yet somehow *strong*. The palace itself. Frantic, Jasnah seized this sphere and forced her power into it. Her mind blurring, she gave this bead everything she had, and then commanded it to rise.

Beads shifted.

A great crashing sounded as beads met one another, clicking, cracking, rattling. It was almost like the sound of a wave breaking on rocks. Jasnah surged up from the depths, something solid moving beneath her, obeying her command. Beads battered her head, shoulders, arms, until finally she *exploded* from the surface of the sea of glass, hurling a spray of beads into a dark sky.

She knelt on a platform of glass made up of small beads locked together. She held her hand to the side, uplifted, clutching the sphere that was the guide. Others rolled around her, forming into the shape of a hallway with lanterns on the walls, an intersection ahead. It didn't look right, of course – the entire thing was made of beads. But it was a fair approximation.

She wasn't strong enough to form the entire palace. She created only this hallway, without even a roof – but the floor supported her, kept her from sinking. She opened her mouth with a groan, beads falling out to clack against the floor. Then she coughed, drawing in sweet breaths, sweat trickling down the sides of her face and collecting on her chin.

Ahead of her, the dark figure stepped up onto the platform. He again slid his sword from his sheath.

Jasnah held up a second bead, the statue she'd sensed earlier. She gave it power, and other beads collected before her, taking the shape of one of the statues that lined the front of the feast hall – the statue of Talenel-at'Elin, Herald of War. A tall, muscular man with a large Shardblade.

It was not alive, but she made it move, lowering its sword of beads. She doubted it could fight. Round beads could not form a sharp sword. Yet the threat made the dark figure hesitate.

Gritting her teeth, Jasnah heaved herself to her feet, beads streaming from her clothing. She would *not* kneel before this thing, whatever it was. She stepped up beside the bead statue, noting for the first time the strange clouds overhead. They seemed to form a narrow ribbon of highway, straight and long, pointing toward the horizon.

She met the oil figure's gaze. It regarded her for a moment, then raised two fingers to its forehead and bowed, as if in respect, a cloak flourishing out behind. Others had gathered beyond it, and they turned to each other, exchanging hushed whispers.

The place of beads faded, and Jasnah found herself back in the hallway of the palace. The real one, with real stone, though it had gone dark – the Stormlight dead in the lamps on the walls. The only illumination came from far down the corridor.

She pressed back against the wall, breathing deeply. *I*, she thought, *need to write this experience down.*

She would do so, then analyze and consider. Later. Now, she wanted to be away from this place. She hurried away, with no concern for her direction, trying to escape those eyes she still felt watching.

It didn't work.

Eventually, she composed herself and wiped the sweat from her face with a kerchief. *Shadesmar*, she thought. *That is what it is called in the nursery tales.* Shadesmar, the mythological kingdom of the spren. Mythology she'd never believed. Surely she could find something if she searched the histories well enough. Nearly everything that happened had happened before. The grand lesson of history, and . . .

Storms! Her appointment.

Cursing to herself, she hurried on her way. That experience continued to distract her, but she needed to make her meeting. So she continued down two floors, getting farther from the sounds of the thrumming Parshendi drums until she could hear only the sharpest cracks of their beats.

That music's complexity had always surprised her, suggesting that the Parshendi were not the uncultured savages many took them for. This far away, the music sounded disturbingly like the beads from the dark place, rattling against one another.

She'd intentionally chosen this out-of-the-way section of the palace for her meeting with Liss. Nobody ever visited this set of guest rooms. A man that Jasnah didn't know lounged here, outside the proper door. That relieved her. The man would be Liss's new servant, and his presence meant Liss hadn't left, despite Jasnah's tardiness. Composing herself, she nodded to the guard – a Veden brute with red speckling his beard – and pushed into the room.

Liss stood from the table inside the small chamber. She wore a maid's dress – low cut, of course – and could have been Alethi. Or Veden. Or Bav. Depending on which part of her accent she chose to emphasize. Long dark hair, worn loose, and a plump, attractive figure made her distinctive in all the right ways.

'You're late, Brightness,' Liss said.

Jasnah gave no reply. She was the employer here, and was not required to give excuses. Instead, she laid something on the table beside Liss. A small envelope, sealed with weevilwax.

Jasnah set two fingers on it, considering.

No. This was too brash. She didn't know if her father realized what

8

she was doing, but even if he hadn't, too much was happening in this palace. She did not want to commit to an assassination until she was more certain.

Fortunately, she had prepared a backup plan. She slid a second envelope from the safepouch inside her sleeve and set it on the table in place of the first. She removed her fingers from it, rounding the table and sitting down.

Liss sat back down and made the letter vanish into the bust of her dress. 'An odd night, Brightness,' the woman said, 'to be engaging in treason.'

'I am hiring you to watch only.'

'Pardon, Brightness. But one does not commonly hire an assassin to watch. Only.'

'You have instructions in the envelope,' Jasnah said. 'Along with initial payment. I chose you because you are expert at extended observations. It is what I want. For now.'

Liss smiled, but nodded. 'Spying on the wife of the heir to the throne? It will be more expensive this way. You sure you don't simply want her dead?'

Jasnah drummed her fingers on the table, then realized she was doing it to the beat of the drums above. The music was so unexpectedly complex – precisely like the Parshendi themselves.

Too much is *happening*, she thought. *I need to be very careful. Very subtle.*

'I accept the cost,' Jasnah replied. 'In one week's time, I will arrange for one of my sister-in-law's maids to be released. You will apply for the position, using faked credentials I assume you are capable of producing. You will be hired.'

'From there, you watch and report. I will tell you if your other services are needed. You move only if I say. Understood?'

'You're the one payin',' Liss said, a faint Bav dialect showing through.

If it showed, it was only because she wished it. Liss was the most skilled assassin Jasnah knew. People called her the Weeper, as she gouged out the eyes of the targets she killed. Although she hadn't coined the cognomen, it served her purpose well, since she had secrets to hide. For one thing, nobody knew that the Weeper was a woman.

It was said the Weeper gouged the eyes out to proclaim indifference to whether her victims were lighteyed or dark. The truth was that the action hid a second secret – Liss didn't want anyone to know that the way she killed left corpses with burned-out sockets.

'Our meeting is done, then,' Liss said, standing.

Jasnah nodded absently, mind again on her bizarre interaction with the spren earlier. That glistening skin, colors dancing across a surface the color of tar . . .

She forced her mind away from that moment. She needed to devote her attention to the task at hand. For now, that was Liss.

Liss hesitated at the door before leaving. 'Do you know why I like you, Brightness?'

'I suspect that it has something to do with my pockets and their proverbial depth.'

Liss smiled. 'There's that, ain't going to deny it, but you're also different from other lighteyes. When others hire me, they turn up their noses at the entire process. They're all too eager to use my services, but sneer and wring their hands, as if they hate being forced to do something utterly distasteful.'

'Assassination *is* distasteful, Liss. So is cleaning out chamber pots. I can respect the one employed for such jobs without admiring the job itself.'

Liss grinned, then cracked the door.

'That new servant of yours outside,' Jasnah said. 'Didn't you say you wanted to show him off for me?'

'Talak?' Liss said, glancing at the Veden man. 'Oh, you mean that *other* one. No, Brightness, I sold that one to a slaver a few weeks ago.' Liss grimaced.

'Really? I thought you said he was the best servant you'd ever had.'

'Too good a servant,' Liss said. 'Let's leave it at that. Storming creepy, that Shin fellow was.' Liss shivered visibly, then slipped out the door.

'Remember our first agreement,' Jasnah said after her.

'Always there in the back o' my mind, Brightness.' Liss closed the door.

Jasnah settled in her seat, lacing her fingers in front of her. Their 'first agreement' was that if anyone should come to Liss and offer a contract on a member of Jasnah's family, Liss would let Jasnah match the offer in exchange for the name of the one who made it.

Liss would do it. Probably. So would the dozen other assassins Jasnah dealt with. A repeat customer was always more valuable than a one-off contract, and it was in the best interests of a woman like Liss to have a friend in the government. Jasnah's family was safe from the likes of these. Unless she herself employed the assassins, of course.

Jasnah let out a deep sigh, then rose, trying to shrug off the weight she felt bearing her down.

Wait. Did Liss say her old servant was Shin?

It was probably a coincidence. Shin people weren't plentiful in the East, but you did see them on occasion. Still, Liss mentioning a Shin man and Jasnah seeing one among the Parshendi ... well, there was no harm in checking, even if it meant returning to the feast. Something *was* off about this night, and not just because of her shadow and the spren.

Jasnah left the small chamber in the bowels of the palace and strode out into the hallway. She turned her steps upward. Above, the drums cut off abruptly, like an instrument's strings suddenly cut. Was the party ending so early? Dalinar hadn't done something to offend the celebrants, had he? That man and his wine ...

Well, the Parshendi had ignored his offenses in the past, so they probably would again. In truth, Jasnah was happy for her father's sudden focus on a treaty. It meant she would have a chance to study Parshendi traditions and histories at her leisure.

Could it be, she wondered, *that scholars have been searching in the wrong ruins all these years?*

Words echoed in the hallway, coming from up ahead. 'I'm worried about Ash.'

'You're worried about everything.'

Jasnah hesitated in the hallway.

'She's getting worse,' the voice continued. 'We weren't supposed to get worse. Am I getting worse? I think I feel worse.'

'Shut up.'

'I don't like this. What we've done was wrong. That creature carries *my lord's* own Blade. We shouldn't have let him keep it. He—'

The two passed through the intersection ahead of Jasnah. They were ambassadors from the West, including the Azish man with the white birthmark on his cheek. Or was it a scar? The shorter of the two men – he could have been Alethi – cut off when he noticed Jasnah. He let out a squeak, then hurried on his way.

The Azish man, the one dressed in black and silver, stopped and looked her up and down. He frowned.

'Is the feast over already?' Jasnah asked down the hallway. Her brother had invited these two to the celebration along with every other ranking foreign dignitary in Kholinar.

'Yes,' the man said.

His stare made her uncomfortable. She walked forward anyway. *I should check further into these two*, she thought. She'd investigated their backgrounds, of course, and found nothing of note. Had they been talking about a Shardblade?

'Come on!' the shorter man said, returning and taking the taller man by the arm.

He allowed himself to be pulled away. Jasnah walked to where the corridors crossed, then watched them go.

Where once drums had sounded, screams suddenly rose.

Oh no . . .

Jasnah turned with alarm, then grabbed her skirt and ran as hard as she could.

A dozen different potential disasters raced through her mind. What else could happen on this broken night, when shadows stood up and her father looked upon her with suspicion? Nerves stretched thin, she reached the steps and started climbing.

It took her far too long. She could hear the screams as she climbed and finally emerged into chaos. Dead bodies in one direction, a demolished *wall* in the other. How . . .

The destruction led toward her father's rooms.

The entire *palace* shook, and a crunch echoed from that direction.

No, no, no!

She passed Shardblade cuts on the stone walls as she ran.

Please.

Corpses with burned eyes. Bodies littered the floor like discarded bones at the dinner table.

Not this.

A broken doorway. Her father's quarters. Jasnah stopped in the hallway, gasping.

Control yourself, control . . .

She couldn't. Not now. Frantic, she ran into the quarters, though a

Shardbearer would kill her with ease. She wasn't thinking straight. She should get someone who could help. Dalinar? He'd be drunk. Sadeas, then.

The room looked like it had been hit by a highstorm. Furniture in a shambles, splinters everywhere. The balcony doors were broken outward. Someone lurched toward them, a man in her father's Shardplate. Tearim, the bodyguard?

No. The helm was broken. It was not Tearim, but Gavilar. Someone on the balcony screamed.

'Father!' Jasnah shouted.

Gavilar hesitated as he stepped out onto the balcony, looking back at her.

The balcony broke beneath him.

Jasnah screamed, dashing through the room to the broken balcony, falling to her knees at the edge. Wind tugged locks of hair loose from her bun as she watched two men fall.

Her father, and the Shin man in white from the feast.

The Shin man glowed with a white light. He fell *onto* the wall. He hit it, rolling, then came to a stop. He stood up, somehow remaining on the outer palace wall and not falling. It defied reason.

He turned, then stalked toward her father.

Jasnah watched, growing cold, helpless as the assassin stepped down to her father and knelt over him.

Tears fell from her chin, and the wind caught them. What was he doing down there? She couldn't make it out.

When the assassin walked away, he left behind her father's corpse. Impaled on a length of wood. He was dead – indeed, his Shardblade had appeared beside him, as they all did when their Bearers died.

'I worked so hard ...' Jasnah whispered, numb. 'Everything I did to protect this family ...'

How? Liss. Liss had done this!

No. Jasnah wasn't thinking straight. That Shin man ... she wouldn't have admitted to owning him in such a case. She'd sold him.

'We are sorry for your loss.'

Jasnah spun, blinking bleary eyes. Three Parshendi, including Klade, stood in the doorway in their distinctive clothing. Neatly stitched cloth wraps for both men and women, sashes at the waist, loose shirts with no sleeves. Hanging vests, open at the sides, woven in bright colors. They didn't segregate clothing by gender. She thought they did by caste, however, and—

Stop it, she thought at herself. *Stop thinking like a scholar for one storming day!*

'We take responsibility for his death,' said the foremost Parshendi. Gangnah was female, though with the Parshendi, the gender differences seemed minimal. The clothing hid breasts and hips, neither of which were ever very pronounced. Fortunately, the lack of a beard was a clear indication. All the Parshendi men she'd ever seen had beards, which they wore tied with bits of gemstone, and—

STOP IT.

'What did you say?' Jasnah demanded, forcing herself to her feet. 'Why would it be your fault, Gangnah?'

'Because we hired the assassin,' the Parshendi woman said in her heavily accented singsong voice. 'We killed your father, Jasnah Kholin.'

'You . . .'

Emotion suddenly ran cold, like a river freezing in the heights. Jasnah looked from Gangnah to Klade, to Varnali. Elders, all three of them. Members of the Parshendi ruling council.

'Why?' Jasnah whispered.

'Because it had to be done,' Gangnah said.

'*Why?*' Jasnah demanded, stalking forward. 'He fought for you! He kept the predators at bay! My father wanted *peace*, you monsters! Why would you betray us now, of all times?'

Gangnah drew her lips to a line. The song of her voice changed. She seemed almost like a mother, explaining something very difficult to a small child. 'Because your father was about to do something very dangerous.'

'Send for Brightlord Dalinar!' a voice outside in the hall shouted. 'Storms! Did my orders get to Elhokar? The crown prince *must* be taken to safety!' Highprince Sadeas stumbled into the room along with a team of soldiers. His bulbous, ruddy face was wet with sweat, and he wore Gavilar's clothing, the regal robes of office. 'What are the savages doing here? Storms! Protect Princess Jasnah. The one who did this – he was in *their* retinue!'

The soldiers moved to surround the Parshendi. Jasnah ignored them, turning and stepping back to the broken doorway, hand on the wall, looking down at her father splayed on the rocks below, Blade beside him.

'There will be war,' she whispered. 'And I will not stand in its way.'

'This is understood,' Gangnah said from behind.

'The assassin,' Jasnah said. 'He walked on the wall.'

Gangnah said nothing.

In the shattering of her world, Jasnah caught hold of this fragment. She had seen something tonight. Something that should not have been possible. Did it relate to the strange spren? Her experience in that place of glass beads and a dark sky?

These questions became her lifeline for stability. Sadeas demanded answers from the Parshendi leaders. He received none. When he stepped up beside her and saw the wreckage below, he went barreling off, shouting for his guards and running down below to reach the fallen king.

Hours later, it was discovered that the assassination – and the surrender of three of the Parshendi leaders – had covered the flight of the larger portion of their number. They escaped the city quickly, and the cavalry Dalinar sent after them were destroyed. A hundred horses, each nearly priceless, lost along with their riders.

The Parshendi leaders said nothing more and gave no clues, even when they were strung up, hanged for their crimes.

Jasnah ignored all that. Instead, she interrogated the surviving guards on what they had seen. She followed leads about the now-famous assassin's nature, prying information from Liss. She got almost nothing. Liss had owned him only a short time, and claimed she hadn't known about his strange powers. Jasnah couldn't find the previous owner.

Next came the books. A dedicated, frenzied effort to distract her from what she had lost.

That night, Jasnah had seen the impossible.

She *would* learn what it meant.

PART

ONE

Alight

SHALLAN · KALADIN · DALINAR

SANTHID

To be perfectly frank, what has happened these last two months is upon my head. The death, destruction, loss, and pain are my burden. I should have seen it coming. And I should have stopped it.

—From the personal journal of Navani Kholin, Jeseses 1174

Shallan pinched the thin charcoal pencil and drew a series of straight lines radiating from a sphere on the horizon. That sphere wasn't *quite* the sun, nor was it one of the moons. Clouds outlined in charcoal seemed to stream toward it. And the sea beneath them . . . A drawing could not convey the bizarre nature of that ocean, made not of water but of small beads of translucent glass.

Shallan shivered, remembering that place. Jasnah knew much more of it than she would speak of to her ward, and Shallan wasn't certain how to ask. How did one demand answers after a betrayal such as Shallan's? Only a few days had passed since that event, and Shallan still didn't know exactly how her relationship with Jasnah would proceed.

The deck rocked as the ship tacked, enormous sails fluttering overhead. Shallan was forced to grab the railing with her clothed safehand to steady herself. Captain Tozbek said that so far, the seas hadn't been bad for this part of Longbrow's Straits. However, she might have to go below if the waves and motion got much worse.

Shallan exhaled and tried to relax as the ship settled. A chill wind blew, and windspren zipped past on invisible air currents. Every time the sea grew rough, Shallan remembered that day, that alien ocean of glass beads . . .

She looked down again at what she'd drawn. She had only glimpsed that place, and her sketch was not perfect. It—

She frowned. On her paper, a pattern had *risen*, like an embossing. What had she done? That pattern was almost as wide as the page, a sequence of complex lines with sharp angles and repeated arrowhead shapes. Was it an effect of drawing that weird place, the place Jasnah said was named Shadesmar? Shallan hesitantly moved her freehand to feel the unnatural ridges on the page.

The pattern *moved*, sliding across the page like an axehound pup under a bedsheet.

Shallan yelped and leapt from her seat, dropping her sketchpad to the deck. The loose pages slumped to the planks, fluttering and then scattering in the wind. Nearby sailors – Thaylen men with long white eyebrows they combed back over their ears – scrambled to help, snatching sheets from the air before they could blow overboard.

'You all right, young miss?' Tozbek asked, looking over from a conversation with one of his mates. The short, portly Tozbek wore a wide sash and a coat of gold and red matched by the cap on his head. He wore his eyebrows up and stiffened into a fanned shape above his eyes.

'I'm well, Captain,' Shallan said. 'I was merely spooked.'

Yalb stepped up to her, proffering the pages. 'Your accouterments, my lady.'

Shallan raised an eyebrow. 'Accout*er*ments?'

'Sure,' the young sailor said with a grin. 'I'm practicing my fancy words. They help a fellow obtain reasonable feminine companionship. You know – the kind of young lady who doesn't smell too bad an' has at least a few teeth left.'

'Lovely,' Shallan said, taking the sheets back. 'Well, depending on your definition of lovely, at least.' She suppressed further quips, suspiciously regarding the stack of pages in her hand. The picture she'd drawn of Shadesmar was on top, no longer bearing the strange embossed ridges.

'What happened?' Yalb said. 'Did a cremling crawl out from under you or something?' As usual, he wore an open-fronted vest and a pair of loose trousers.

'It was nothing,' Shallan said softly, tucking the pages away into her satchel.

Yalb gave her a little salute – she had no idea why he had taken to doing that – and went back to tying rigging with the other sailors. She soon caught bursts of laughter from the men near him, and when she glanced at him, gloryspren danced around his head – they took the shape of little spheres of light. He was apparently very proud of the jape he'd just made. She smiled. It was indeed fortunate that Tozbek had been delayed in Kharbranth. She liked this crew, and was happy that Jasnah had selected them for their voyage. Shallan sat back down on the box that Captain Tozbek had ordered lashed beside the railing so she could enjoy the sea as they sailed. She had to be wary of the spray, which wasn't terribly good for her sketches, but so long as the seas weren't rough, the opportunity to watch the waters was worth the trouble.

The scout atop the rigging let out a shout. Shallan squinted in the direction he pointed. They were within sight of the distant mainland, sailing parallel to it. In fact, they'd docked at port last night to shelter from the highstorm that had blown past. When sailing, you always wanted to be near to port – venturing into open seas when a highstorm could surprise you was suicidal.

The smear of darkness to the north was the Frostlands, a largely uninhabited area along the bottom edge of Roshar. Occasionally, she caught a glimpse of higher cliffs to the south. Thaylenah, the great island kingdom, made another barrier there. The straits passed between the two.

The lookout had spotted something in the waves just north of the ship, a bobbing shape that at first appeared to be a large log. No, it was much larger than that, and wider. Shallan stood, squinting, as it drew closer. It turned out to be a domed brown-green shell, about the size of three rowboats lashed together. As they passed by, the shell came up alongside the ship and somehow managed to keep pace, sticking up out of the water perhaps six or eight feet.

A santhid! Shallan leaned out over the rail, looking down as the sailors jabbered excitedly, several joining her in craning out to see the creature. Santhidyn were so reclusive that some of her books claimed they were extinct and all modern reports of them untrustworthy.

'You *are* good luck, young miss!' Yalb said to her with a laugh as he passed by with rope. 'We ain't seen a santhid in years.'

'You still aren't seeing one,' Shallan said. 'Only the top of its shell.' To her disappointment, the waters hid anything else – save shadows of something in the depths that might have been long arms extending downward. Stories claimed the beasts would sometimes follow ships for days, waiting out in the sea as the vessel went into port, then following them again once the ship left.

'The shell is all you ever see of one,' Yalb said. 'Passions, this is a good sign!'

Shallan clutched her satchel. She took a Memory of the creature down there beside the ship by closing her eyes, fixing the image of it in her head so she could draw it with precision.

Draw what, though? she thought. *A lump in the water?*

An idea started to form in her head. She spoke it aloud before she could think better. 'Bring me that rope,' she said, turning to Yalb.

'Brightness?' he asked, stopping in place.

'Tie a loop in one end,' she said, hurriedly setting her satchel on her seat. 'I need to get a look at the santhid. I've never actually put my head underwater in the ocean. Will the salt make it difficult to see?'

'Underwater?' Yalb said, voice squeaking.

'You're not tying the rope.'

'Because I'm not a storming fool! Captain will have my head if . . .'

'Get a friend,' Shallan said, ignoring him and taking the rope to tie one end into a small loop. 'You're going to lower me down over the side, and I'm going to get a glimpse of what's under the shell. Do you realize that nobody has *ever* produced a drawing of a live santhid? All the ones that have washed up on beaches were badly decomposed. And since sailors consider hunting the things to be bad luck—'

'It is!' Yalb said, voice growing more high pitched. 'Ain't nobody going to kill one.'

Shallan finished the loop and hurried to the side of the ship, her red hair whipping around her face as she leaned out over the rail. The santhid was still there. How did it keep up? She could see no fins.

She looked back at Yalb, who held the rope, grinning. 'Ah, Brightness. Is this payback for what I said about your backside to Beznk? That was just in jest, but you got me good! I . . .' He trailed off as she met his eyes. 'Storms. You're serious.'

'I'll not have another opportunity like this. Naladan chased these things for most of her life and never got a good look at one.'

'This is insanity!'

'No, this is scholarship! I don't know what kind of view I can get through the water, but I have to try.'

Yalb sighed. 'We have masks. Made from a tortoise shell with glass in hollowed-out holes on the front and bladders along the edges to keep the water out. You can duck your head underwater with one on and see. We use them to check over the hull at dock.'

'Wonderful!'

'Of course, I'd have to go to the captain to get permission to take one. . . .'

She folded her arms. 'Devious of you. Well, get to it.' It was unlikely she'd be able to go through with this without the captain finding out anyway.

Yalb grinned. 'What happened to you in Kharbranth? Your first trip with us, you were so timid, you looked like you'd faint at the mere thought of sailing away from your homeland!'

Shallan hesitated, then found herself blushing. 'This is somewhat fool-hardy, isn't it?'

'Hanging from a moving ship and sticking your head in the water?' Yalb said. 'Yeah. Kind of a little.'

'Do you think . . . we could stop the ship?'

Yalb laughed, but went jogging off to speak with the captain, taking her query as an indication she was still determined to go through with her plan. And she was.

What did *happen to me?* she wondered.

The answer was simple. She'd lost everything. She'd stolen from Jasnah Kholin, one of the most powerful women in the world – and in so doing had not only lost her chance to study as she'd always dreamed, but had also doomed her brothers and her house. She had failed utterly and miserably.

And she'd pulled through it.

She wasn't unscathed. Her credibility with Jasnah had been severely wounded, and she felt that she had all but abandoned her family. But something about the experience of stealing Jasnah's Soulcaster – which had turned out to be a fake anyway – then nearly being killed by a man she'd thought was in love with her . . .

Well, she now had a better idea of how bad things could get. It was as if . . . once she had feared the darkness, but now she had stepped into it. She had experienced some of the horrors that awaited her there. Terrible as they were, at least she knew.

You always knew, a voice whispered deep inside of her. *You grew up with horrors, Shallan. You just won't let yourself remember them.*

'What is this?' Tozbek asked as he came up, his wife, Ashlv, at his side. The diminutive woman did not speak much; she dressed in a skirt and blouse of bright yellow, a headscarf covering all of her hair except the two white eyebrows, which she had curled down beside her cheeks.

'Young miss,' Tozbek said, 'you want to go swimming? Can't you wait until we get into port? I know of some nice areas where the water is not nearly so cold.'

'I won't be swimming,' Shallan said, blushing further. What would she *wear* to go swimming with men about? Did people really do that? 'I need to get a closer look at our companion.' She gestured toward the sea creature.

'Young miss, you know I can't allow something so dangerous. Even if we stopped the ship, what if the beast harmed you?'

'They're said to be harmless.'

'They are so rare, can we really know for certain? Besides, there are other animals in these seas that could harm you. Redwaters hunt this area for certain, and we might be in shallow enough water for khornaks to be a worry.' Tozbek shook his head. 'I'm sorry, I just cannot allow it.'

Shallan bit her lip, and found her heart beating traitorously. She wanted to push harder, but that decisive look in his eyes made her wilt. 'Very well.'

Tozbek smiled broadly. 'I'll take you to see some shells in the port at Amydlatn when we stop there, young miss. They have quite a collection!'

She didn't know where that was, but from the jumble of consonants squished together, she assumed it would be on the Thaylen side. Most cities were, this far south. Though Thaylenah was nearly as frigid as the Frostlands, people seemed to enjoy living there.

Of course, Thaylens were all a little off. How else to describe Yalb and the others wearing no shirts despite the chill in the air?

They weren't the ones contemplating a dip in the ocean, Shallan reminded herself. She looked over the side of the ship again, watching waves break against the shell of the gentle santhid. What was it? A great-shelled beast, like the fearsome chasmfiends of the Shattered Plains? Was it more like a fish under there, or more like a tortoise? The santhidyn were so rare – and the occasions when scholars had seen them in person so infrequent – that the theories all contradicted one another.

She sighed and opened her satchel, then set to organizing her papers, most of which were practice sketches of the sailors in various poses as they worked to maneuver the massive sails overhead, tacking against the wind. Her father would never have allowed her to spend a day sitting and watching a bunch of shirtless darkeyes. How much her life had changed in such a short time.

She was working on a sketch of the santhid's shell when Jasnah stepped up onto the deck.

Like Shallan, Jasnah wore the havah, a Vorin dress of distinctive design. The hemline was down at her feet and the neckline almost at her chin. Some of the Thaylens – when they thought she wasn't listening – referred to the clothing as prudish. Shallan disagreed; the havah wasn't prudish, but elegant. Indeed, the silk hugged the body, particularly through the bust – and the way the sailors gawked at Jasnah indicated they didn't find the garment unflattering.

Jasnah *was* pretty. Lush of figure, tan of skin. Immaculate eyebrows, lips painted a deep red, hair up in a fine braid. Though Jasnah was twice Shallan's age, her mature beauty was something to be admired, even envied. Why did the woman have to be so perfect?

Jasnah ignored the eyes of the sailors. It wasn't that she didn't notice men. Jasnah noticed everything and everyone. She simply didn't seem to care, one way or another, how men perceived her.

No, that's not true, Shallan thought as Jasnah walked over. *She wouldn't take the time to do her hair, or put on makeup, if she didn't care how she was perceived.* In that, Jasnah was an enigma. On one hand, she seemed to be a scholar concerned only with her research. On the other hand, she cultivated the poise and dignity of a king's daughter – and, at times, used it like a bludgeon.

'And here you are,' Jasnah said, walking to Shallan. A spray of water from the side of the ship chose that moment to fly up and sprinkle her. She frowned at the drops of water beading on her silk clothing, then looked back to Shallan and raised her eyebrow. 'The ship, you may have noticed, has two very fine cabins that I hired out for us at no small expense.'

'Yes, but they're inside.'

'As rooms usually are.'

'I've spent most of my life inside.'

'So you will spend much more of it, if you wish to be a scholar.'

Shallan bit her lip, waiting for the order to go below. Curiously, it did not come. Jasnah gestured for Captain Tozbek to approach, and he did so, groveling his way over with cap in hand.

'Yes, Brightness?' he asked.

'I should like another of these . . . seats,' Jasnah said, regarding Shallan's box.

Tozbek quickly had one of his men lash a second box in place. As she waited for the seat to be ready, Jasnah waved for Shallan to hand over her sketches. Jasnah inspected the drawing of the santhid, then looked over the side of the ship. 'No wonder the sailors were making such a fuss.'

'Luck, Brightness!' one of the sailors said. 'It is a good omen for your trip, don't you think?'

'I shall take any fortune provided me, Nanhel Eltorv,' she said. 'Thank you for the seat.'

The sailor bowed awkwardly before retreating.

'You think they're superstitious fools,' Shallan said softly, watching the sailor leave.

'From what I have observed,' Jasnah said, 'these sailors are men who have found a purpose in life and now take simple pleasure in it.' Jasnah looked at the next drawing. 'Many people make far less out of life. Captain Tozbek runs a good crew. You were wise in bringing him to my attention.'

Shallan smiled. 'You didn't answer my question.'

'You didn't ask a question,' Jasnah said. 'These sketches are characteristically skillful, Shallan, but weren't you supposed to be reading?'

'I . . . had trouble concentrating.'

'So you came up on deck,' Jasnah said, 'to sketch pictures of young men working without their shirts on. You expected this to *help* your concentration?'

Shallan blushed, as Jasnah stopped at one sheet of paper in the stack. Shallan sat patiently – she'd been well trained in that by her father – until Jasnah turned it toward her. The picture of Shadesmar, of course.

'You have respected my command not to peer into this realm again?' Jasnah asked.

'Yes, Brightness. That picture was drawn from a memory of my first . . . lapse.'

Jasnah lowered the page. Shallan thought she saw a hint of something in the woman's expression. Was Jasnah wondering if she could trust Shallan's word?

'I assume this is what is bothering you?' Jasnah asked.

'Yes, Brightness.'

'I suppose I should explain it to you, then.'

'Really? You would do this?'

'You needn't sound so surprised.'

'It seems like powerful information,' Shallan said. 'The way you forbade me . . . I assumed that knowledge of this place was secret, or at least not to be trusted to one of my age.'

Jasnah sniffed. 'I've found that refusing to explain secrets to young people makes them *more* prone to get themselves into trouble, not less. Your experimentation proves that you've already stumbled face-first into all of this – as I once did myself, I'll have you know. I know through painful experience how dangerous Shadesmar can be. If I leave you in ignorance, I'll be to blame if you get yourself killed there.'

'So you'd have explained about it if I'd asked earlier in our trip?'

'Probably not,' Jasnah admitted. 'I had to see how willing you were to obey me. This time.'

Shallan wilted, and suppressed the urge to point out that back when she'd been a studious and obedient ward, Jasnah hadn't divulged nearly as many secrets as she did now. 'So what is it? That . . . place.'

'It's not truly a location,' Jasnah said. 'Not as we usually think of them. Shadesmar is here, all around us, right now. All things exist there in some form, as all things exist here.'

Shallan frowned. 'I don't—'

Jasnah held up a finger to quiet her. 'All things have three components: the soul, the body, and the mind. That place you saw, Shadesmar, is what we call the Cognitive Realm – the place of the mind.

'All around us you see the physical world. You can touch it, see it, hear it. This is how your physical body experiences the world. Well, Shadesmar is the way that your cognitive self – your unconscious self – experiences the world. Through your hidden senses touching that realm, you make intuitive leaps in logic and you form hopes. It is likely through those extra senses that you, Shallan, create art.'

Water splashed on the bow of the ship as it crossed a swell. Shallan wiped a drop of salty water from her cheek, trying to think through what Jasnah had just said. 'That made almost *no* sense whatsoever to me, Brightness.'

'I should hope that it didn't,' Jasnah said. 'I've spent six years researching Shadesmar, and I still barely know what to make of it. I shall have to accompany you there several times before you can understand, even a little, the true significance of the place.'

Jasnah grimaced at the thought. Shallan was always surprised to see visible emotion from her. Emotion was something relatable, something human – and Shallan's mental image of Jasnah Kholin was of someone almost divine. It was, upon reflection, an odd way to regard a determined atheist.

'Listen to me,' Jasnah said. 'My own words betray my ignorance. I told you that Shadesmar wasn't a place, and yet I call it one in my next breath. I speak of visiting it, though it is all around us. We simply don't have the proper terminology to discuss it. Let me try another tactic.'

Jasnah stood up, and Shallan hastened to follow. They walked along the ship's rail, feeling the deck sway beneath their feet. Sailors made way for Jasnah with quick bows. They regarded her with as much reverence as they would a king. How did she do it? How could she control her surroundings without seeming to do anything at all?

'Look down into the waters,' Jasnah said as they reached the bow. 'What do you see?'

Shallan stopped beside the rail and stared down at the blue waters, foaming as they were broken by the ship's prow. Here at the bow, she could see a *deepness* to the swells. An unfathomable expanse that extended not just outward, but downward.

'I see eternity,' Shallan said.

'Spoken like an artist,' Jasnah said. 'This ship sails across depths we cannot know. Beneath these waves is a bustling, frantic, unseen world.'

Jasnah leaned forward, gripping the rail with one hand unclothed and the other veiled within the safehand sleeve. She looked outward. Not at the depths, and not at the land distantly peeking over both the northern and southern horizons. She looked toward the east. Toward the storms.

'There is an entire world, Shallan,' Jasnah said, 'of which our minds skim but the surface. A world of deep, profound thought. A world *created* by deep, profound thoughts. When you see Shadesmar, you enter those depths. It is an alien place to us in some ways, but at the same time we formed it. With some help.'

'We did what?'

'What are spren?' Jasnah asked.

The question caught Shallan off guard, but by now she was accustomed to challenging questions from Jasnah. She took time to think and consider her answer.

'Nobody knows what spren are,' Shallan said, 'though many philosophers have different opinions on—'

'No,' Jasnah said. 'What *are* they?'

'I . . .' Shallan looked up at a pair of windspren spinning through the air above. They looked like tiny ribbons of light, glowing softly, dancing around one another. 'They're living ideas.'

Jasnah spun on her.

'What?' Shallan said, jumping. 'Am I wrong?'

'No,' Jasnah said. 'You're right.' The woman narrowed her eyes. 'By my best guess, spren are elements of the Cognitive Realm that have *leaked* into the physical world. They're concepts that have gained a fragment of sentience, perhaps because of human intervention.

'Think of a man who gets angry often. Think of how his friends and family might start referring to that anger as a beast, as a thing that possesses him, as something *external* to him. Humans personify. We speak of the wind as if it has a will of its own.

'Spren are those ideas – the ideas of collective human experience – somehow come alive. Shadesmar is where that first happens, and it is *their* place. Though we created it, they shaped it. They live there; they rule there, within their own cities.'

'*Cities?*'

'Yes,' Jasnah said, looking back out over the ocean. She seemed troubled. 'Spren are wild in their variety. Some are as clever as humans and create cities. Others are like fish and simply swim in the currents.'

Shallan nodded. Though in truth she was having trouble grasping any of this, she didn't want Jasnah to stop talking. This was the sort of knowledge that Shallan *needed*, the kind of thing she *craved*. 'Does this have to do with what you discovered? About the parshmen, the Voidbringers?'

'I haven't been able to determine that yet. The spren are not always forthcoming. In some cases, they do not know. In others, they do not trust me because of our ancient betrayal.'

Shallan frowned, looking to her teacher. 'Betrayal?'

'They tell me of it,' Jasnah said, 'but they won't say what it was. We broke an oath, and in so doing offended them greatly. I think some of them may have died, though how a concept can die, I do not know.' Jasnah turned to Shallan with a solemn expression. 'I realize this is overwhelming. You will have to learn this, all of it, if you are to help me. Are you still willing?'

'Do I have a choice?'

A smile tugged at the edges of Jasnah's lips. 'I doubt it. You Soulcast on your own, without the aid of a fabrial. You are like me.'

Shallan stared out over the waters. Like Jasnah. What did it mean? Why—

She froze, blinking. For a moment, she thought she'd seen the same pattern as before, the one that had made ridges on her sheet of paper. This time it had been in the water, impossibly formed on the surface of a wave.

'Brightness . . .' she said, resting her fingers on Jasnah's arm. 'I thought I saw something in the water, just now. A pattern of sharp lines, like a maze.'

'Show me where.'

'It was on one of the waves, and we've passed it now. But I think I saw it earlier, on one of my pages. Does it mean something?'

'Most certainly. I must admit, Shallan, I find the coincidence of our meeting to be startling. Suspiciously so.'

'Brightness?'

'They were involved,' Jasnah said. 'They brought you to me. And they are still watching you, it appears. So no, Shallan, you no longer have a choice. The old ways are returning, and I don't see it as a hopeful sign. It's an act of self-preservation. The spren sense impending danger, and so they return to us. Our attention now must turn to the Shattered Plains and the relics of Urithiru. It will be a long, long time before you return to your homeland.'

Shallan nodded mutely.

'This worries you,' Jasnah said.

'Yes, Brightness. My family . . .'

Shallan felt like a traitor in abandoning her brothers, who had been depending on her for wealth. She'd written to them and explained, without many specifics, that she'd had to return the stolen Soulcaster – and was now required to help Jasnah with her work.

Balat's reply had been positive, after a fashion. He said he was glad at least one of them had escaped the fate that was coming to the house. He thought that the rest of them – her three brothers and Balat's betrothed – were doomed.

They might be right. Not only would Father's debts crush them, but there was the matter of her father's broken Soulcaster. The group that had given it to him wanted it back.

Unfortunately, Shallan was *convinced* that Jasnah's quest was of the utmost importance. The Voidbringers would soon return – indeed, they were not some distant threat from stories. They lived among men, and had for centuries. The gentle, quiet parshmen who worked as perfect servants and slaves were really destroyers.

Stopping the catastrophe of the return of the Voidbringers was a greater duty than even protecting her brothers. It was still painful to admit that.

Jasnah studied her. 'With regard to your family, Shallan. I have taken some action.'

'Action?' Shallan said, taking the taller woman's arm. 'You've helped my brothers?'

'After a fashion,' Jasnah said. 'Wealth would not truly solve this problem, I suspect, though I have arranged for a small gift to be sent. From what you've said, your family's problems really stem from two issues. First, the Ghostbloods desire their Soulcaster – which you have broken – to be returned. Second, your house is without allies and deeply in debt.'

Jasnah proffered a sheet of paper. 'This,' she continued, 'is from a conversation I had with my mother via spanreed this morning.'

Shallan traced it with her eyes, noting Jasnah's explanation of the broken Soulcaster and her request for help.

This happens more often than you'd think, Navani had replied. *The failing likely has to do with the alignment of the gem housings. Bring me the device, and we shall see.*

'My mother,' Jasnah said, 'is a renowned artifabrian. I suspect she can make yours function again. We can send it to your brothers, who can return it to its owners.'

'You'd let me do that?' Shallan asked. During their days sailing, Shallan had cautiously pried for more information about the sect, hoping to understand her father and his motives. Jasnah claimed to know very little of them beyond the fact that they wanted her research, and were willing to kill for it.

'I don't particularly want them having access to such a valuable device,' Jasnah said. 'But I don't have time to protect your family right now directly. This is a workable solution, assuming your brothers can stall a while longer. Have them tell the truth, if they must – that you, knowing I was a scholar, came to me and asked me to fix the Soulcaster. Perhaps that will sate them for now.'

'Thank you, Brightness.' Storms. If she'd just gone to Jasnah in the first place, after being accepted as her ward, how much easier would it have been? Shallan looked down at the paper, noticing that the conversation continued.

As for the other matter, Navani wrote, *I'm very fond of this suggestion. I believe I can persuade the boy to at least consider it, as his most recent affair ended quite abruptly – as is common with him – earlier in the week.*

'What is this second part?' Shallan asked, looking up from the paper.

'Sating the Ghostbloods alone will not save your house,' Jasnah said. 'Your debts are too great, particularly considering your father's actions in alienating so many. I have therefore arranged a powerful alliance for your house.'

'Alliance? How?'

Jasnah took a deep breath. She seemed reluctant to explain. 'I have taken the initial steps in arranging for you to be betrothed to one of my cousins, son of my uncle Dalinar Kholin. The boy's name is Adolin. He is handsome and well-acquainted with amiable discourse.'

'Betrothed?' Shallan said. 'You've promised him my hand?'

'I have started the process,' Jasnah said, speaking with uncharacteristic anxiety. 'Though at times he lacks foresight, Adolin has a good heart – as good as that of his father, who may be the best man I have ever known.

He is considered Alethkar's most eligible son, and my mother has long wanted him wed.'

'Betrothed,' Shallan repeated.

'Yes. Is that distressing?'

'It's wonderful!' Shallan exclaimed, grabbing Jasnah's arm more tightly. 'So easy. If I'm married to someone so powerful ... Storms! Nobody would dare touch us in Jah Keved. It would solve many of our problems. Brightness Jasnah, you're a genius!'

Jasnah relaxed visibly. 'Yes, well, it did seem a workable solution. I had wondered, however, if you'd be offended.'

'Why on the winds would I be offended?'

'Because of the restriction of freedom implicit in a marriage,' Jasnah said. 'And if not that, because the offer was made without consulting you. I had to see if the possibility was even open first. It has proceeded further than I'd expected, as my mother has seized on the idea. Navani has ... a tendency toward the overwhelming.'

Shallan had trouble imagining anyone overwhelming Jasnah. 'Storm-father! You're worried I'd be offended? Brightness, I spent my entire life locked in my father's manor – I grew up assuming he'd pick my husband.'

'But you're free of your father now.'

'Yes, and I was so *perfectly* wise in my own pursuit of relationships,' Shallan said. 'The first man I chose was not only an ardent, but secretly an assassin.'

'It doesn't bother you at all?' Jasnah said. 'The idea of being beholden to another, particularly a man?'

'It's not like I'm being sold into slavery,' Shallan said with a laugh.

'No. I suppose not.' Jasnah shook herself, her poise returning. 'Well, I will let Navani know you are amenable to the engagement, and we should have a causal in place within the day.'

A causal – a conditional betrothal, in Vorin terminology. She would be, for all intents and purposes, engaged, but would have no legal footing until an official betrothal was signed and verified by the ardents.

'The boy's father has said he will not force Adolin into anything,' Jasnah explained, 'though the boy is recently single, as he has managed to offend yet another young lady. Regardless, Dalinar would rather you two meet before anything more binding is agreed upon. There have been ... shifts in the political climate of the Shattered Plains. A great loss to my uncle's army. Another reason for us to hasten to the Plains.'

'Adolin Kholin,' Shallan said, listening with half an ear. 'A duelist. A fantastic one. And even a Shardbearer.'

'Ah, so you *were* paying attention to your readings about my father and family.'

'I was – but I knew about your family before that. The Alethi are the center of society! Even girls from rural houses know the names of the Alethi princes.' And she'd be lying if she denied youthful daydreams of meeting one. 'But Brightness, are you certain this match will be wise? I mean, I'm hardly the most important of individuals.'

'Well, yes. The daughter of another highprince might have been preferable for Adolin. However, it seems that he has managed to offend each and every one of the eligible women of that rank. The boy is, shall we say, somewhat overeager about relationships. Nothing you can't work through, I'm sure.'

'Stormfather,' Shallan said, feeling her legs go weak. 'He's heir to a princedom! He's in line to the throne of Alethkar itself!'

'Third in line,' Jasnah said, 'behind my brother's infant son and Dalinar, my uncle.'

'Brightness, I have to ask. Why Adolin? Why not the younger son? I – I have nothing to offer Adolin, or the house.'

'On the contrary,' Jasnah said, 'if you are what I think you are, then you will be able to offer him something nobody else can. Something more important than riches.'

'What is it you think that I am?' Shallan whispered, meeting the older woman's eyes, finally asking the question that she hadn't dared.

'Right now, you are but a promise,' Jasnah said. 'A chrysalis with the potential for grandeur inside. When once humans and spren bonded, the results were women who danced in the skies and men who could destroy the stones with a touch.'

'The Lost Radiants. Traitors to mankind.' She couldn't absorb it all. The betrothal, Shadesmar and the spren, and this, her mysterious destiny. She'd known. But speaking it . . .

She sank down, heedless of getting her dress wet on the deck, and sat with her back against the bulwark. Jasnah allowed her to compose herself before, amazingly, sitting down herself. She did so with far more poise, tucking her dress underneath her legs as she sat sideways. They both drew looks from the sailors.

'They're going to chew me to pieces,' Shallan said. 'The Alethi court. It's the most ferocious in the world.'

Jasnah snorted. 'It's more bluster than storm, Shallan. I will train you.'

'I'll never be like you, Brightness. You have power, authority, wealth. Just look how the sailors respond to you.'

'Am I specifically using said power, authority, or wealth right now?'

'You paid for this trip.'

'Did you not pay for several trips on this ship?' Jasnah asked. 'They did not treat you the same as they do me?'

'No. Oh, they are fond of me. But I don't have your *weight*, Jasnah.'

'I will assume that did not have implications toward my girth,' Jasnah said with a hint of a smile. 'I understand your argument, Shallan. It is, however, dead wrong.'

Shallan turned to her. Jasnah sat upon the deck of the ship as if it were a throne, back straight, head up, commanding. Shallan sat with her legs against her chest, arms around them below the knees. Even the ways they *sat* were different. She was nothing like this woman.

'There is a secret you must learn, child,' Jasnah said. 'A secret that is even more important than those relating to Shadesmar and spren. Power is an illusion of perception.'

Shallan frowned.

'Don't mistake me,' Jasnah continued. 'Some kinds of power are real – power to command armies, power to Soulcast. These come into play far less often than you would think. On an individual basis, in most interactions, this thing we call power – authority – exists only as it is perceived.

'You say I have wealth. This is true, but you have also seen that I do not often use it. You say I have authority as the sister of a king. I do. And yet, the men of this ship would treat me exactly the same way if I were a beggar who had *convinced* them I was the sister to a king. In that case, my authority is not a real thing. It is mere vapors – an illusion. I can create that illusion for them, as can you.'

'I'm not convinced, Brightness.'

'I know. If you were, you would be doing it already.' Jasnah stood up, brushing off her skirt. 'You will tell me if you see that pattern – the one that appeared on the waves – again?'

'Yes, Brightness,' Shallan said, distracted.

'Then take the rest of the day for your art. I need to consider how to best teach you of Shadesmar.' The older woman retreated, nodding at the bows of sailors as she passed and went back down belowdecks.

Shallan rose, then turned and grabbed the railing, one hand to either side of the bowsprit. The ocean spread before her, rippling waves, a scent of cold freshness. Rhythmic crashing as the sloop pushed through the waves.

Jasnah's words fought in her mind, like skyeels with only one rat between them. Spren with cities? Shadesmar, a realm that was here, but unseen? Shallan, suddenly *betrothed* to the single most important bachelor in the world?

She left the bow, walking along the side of the ship, freehand trailing on the railing. How did the sailors regard her? They smiled, they waved. They liked her. Yalb, who hung lazily from the rigging nearby, called to her, telling her that in the next port, there was a statue she had to go visit. 'It's this *giant* foot, young miss. Just a foot! Never finished the blustering statue . . .'

She smiled to him and continued. Did she want them to look at her as they looked at Jasnah? Always afraid, always worried that they might do something wrong? Was that power?

When I first sailed from Vedenar, she thought, reaching the place where her box had been tied, *the captain kept urging me to go home. He saw my mission as a fool's errand.*

Tozbek had always acted as if he were doing her a favor in conveying her after Jasnah. Should she have had to spend that entire time feeling as if she'd imposed upon him and his crew by hiring them? Yes, he had offered a discount to her because of her father's business with him in the past – but she'd still been employing him.

The way he'd treated her was probably a thing of Thaylen merchants. If a captain could make you feel like you were imposing on him, you'd pay better. She liked the man, but their relationship left something to be desired. Jasnah would never have stood for being treated in such a way.

That santhid still swam alongside. It was like a tiny, mobile island, its back overgrown with seaweed, small crystals jutting up from the shell.

Shallan turned and walked toward the stern, where Captain Tozbek spoke with one of his mates, pointing at a map covered with glyphs. He nodded to her as she approached. 'Just a warning, young miss,' he said. 'The ports will soon grow less accommodating. We'll be leaving Long-brow's Straits, curving around the eastern edge of the continent, toward New Natanan. There's nothing of worth between here and the Shallow Crypts – and even that's not much of a sight. I wouldn't send my own brother ashore there without guards, and he's killed seventeen men with his bare hands, he has.'

'I understand, Captain,' Shallan said. 'And thank you. I've revised my earlier decision. I need you to halt the ship and let me inspect the speci-men swimming beside us.'

He sighed, reaching up and running his fingers along one of his stiff, spiked eyebrows – much as other men might play with their mustaches. 'Brightness, that's *not* advisable. Stormfather! If I dropped you in the ocean . . .'

'Then I would be wet,' Shallan said. 'It is a state I've experienced one or two times in my life.'

'No, I simply cannot allow it. Like I said, we'll take you to see some shells in—'

'Cannot allow it?' Shallan interrupted. She regarded him with what she hoped was a look of puzzlement, hoping he didn't see how tightly she squeezed her hands closed at her sides. Storms, but she hated confron-tation. 'I wasn't aware I had made a request you had the power to allow or disallow, Captain. Stop the ship. Lower me down. That is your order.' She tried to say it as forcefully as Jasnah would. The woman could make it seem easier to resist a full highstorm than to disagree with her.

Tozbek worked his mouth for a moment, no sound coming out, as if his body were trying to continue his earlier objection but his mind had been delayed. 'It is my ship . . .' he finally said.

'Nothing will be done to your ship,' Shallan said. 'Let's be quick about it, Captain. I do not wish to overly delay our arrival in port tonight.'

She left him, walking back to her box, heart thumping, hands trem-bling. She sat down, partially to calm herself.

Tozbek, sounding profoundly annoyed, began calling orders. The sails were lowered, the ship slowed. Shallan breathed out, feeling a fool.

And yet, what Jasnah said worked. The way Shallan acted *created* something in the eyes of Tozbek. An illusion? Like the spren themselves, perhaps? Fragments of human expectation, given life?

The santhid slowed with them. Shallan rose, nervous, as sailors approached with rope. They reluctantly tied a loop at the bottom she could put her foot in, then explained that she should hold tightly to the rope as she was lowered. They tied a second, smaller rope securely around her waist – the means by which to haul her, wet and humiliated, back onto the deck. An inevitability, in their eyes.

She took off her shoes, then climbed up over the railing as instructed. Had it been this windy before? She had a moment of vertigo, standing there with socked toes gripping a tiny rim, dress fluttering in the coursing winds. A windspren zipped up to her, then formed into the shape of a face with clouds behind it. Storms, the thing had better not interfere. Was it human imagination that had given windspren their mischievous spark?

She stepped unsteadily into the rope loop as the sailors lowered it down beside her feet, then Yalb handed her the mask he'd told her of.

Jasnah appeared from belowdecks, looking about in confusion. She saw Shallan standing off the side of the ship, and then cocked an eyebrow.

Shallan shrugged, then gestured to the men to lower her.

She refused to let herself feel silly as she inched toward the waters and the reclusive animal bobbing in the waves. The men stopped her a foot or two above the water, and she put on the mask, held by straps, covering most of her face including the nose.

'Lower!' she shouted up at them.

She thought she could *feel* their reluctance in the lethargic way the rope descended. Her foot hit the water, and a biting cold shot up her leg. Stormfather! But she didn't have them stop. She let them lower her farther until her legs were submerged in the frigid water. Her skirt ballooned out in a most annoying way, and she actually had to step on the end of it – inside the loop – to prevent it from rising up about her waist and floating on the water's surface as she submerged.

She wrestled with the fabric for a moment, glad the men above couldn't see her blushing. Once it got wetter, though, it was easier to manage. She finally was able to squat, still holding tightly to the rope, and go down into the water up to her waist.

Then she ducked her head under the water.

Light streamed down from the surface in shimmering, radiant columns. There was *life* here, furious, amazing life. Tiny fish zipped this way and that, picking at the underside of the shell that shaded a majestic creature. Gnarled like an ancient tree, with rippled and folded skin, the true form of the santhid was a beast with long, drooping blue tendrils, like those of a jellyfish, only far thicker. Those disappeared down into the depths, trailing behind the beast at a slant.

The beast itself was a knotted grey-blue mass underneath the shell. Its ancient-looking folds surrounded one large eye on her side – presumably, its twin would be on the other side. It seemed ponderous, yet majestic, with mighty fins moving like oarsmen. A group of strange spren shaped like arrows moved through the water here around the beast.

Schools of fish darted about. Though the depths seemed empty, the area just around the santhid teemed with life, as did the area under the ship. Tiny fish picked at the bottom of the vessel. They'd move between the santhid and the ship, sometimes alone, sometimes in waves. Was this why the creature swam up beside a vessel? Something to do with the fish, and their relationship to it?

She looked upon the creature, and its eye – as big as her head – rolled toward her, focusing, *seeing* her. In that moment, Shallan couldn't feel the cold. She couldn't feel embarrassed. She was looking into a world that, so far as she knew, no scholar had ever visited.

She blinked her eyes, taking a Memory of the creature, collecting it for later sketching.

2

BRIDGE FOUR

Our first clue was the Parshendi. Even weeks before they abandoned their pursuit of the gemhearts, their pattern of fighting changed. They lingered on the plateaus after battles, as if waiting for something.

—From the personal journal of Navani Kholin, Jeseses 1174

Breath.

A man's breath was his life. Exhaled, bit by bit, back into the world. Kaladin breathed deeply, eyes closed, and for a time that was all he could hear. His own life. In, out, to the beating of the thunder in his chest.

Breath. His own little storm.

Outside, the rain had stopped. Kaladin remained sitting in the darkness. When kings and wealthy lighteyes died, their bodies weren't burned like those of common men. Instead, they were Soulcast into statues of stone or metal, forever frozen.

The darkeyes' bodies were burned. They became smoke, to rise toward the heavens and whatever waited there, like a burned prayer.

Breath. The breath of a lighteyes was no different from that of a darkeyes. No more sweet, no more free. The breath of kings and slaves mingled, to be breathed by men again, over and over.

Kaladin stood up and opened his eyes. He'd spent the highstorm in the darkness of this small room alongside Bridge Four's new barrack. Alone. He walked to the door, but stopped. He rested his fingers on a cloak he knew hung from a hook there. In the darkness, he could not make out its deep blue color, nor the Kholin glyph – in the shape of Dalinar's sigil – on the back.

It seemed that every change in his life had been marked by a storm. This was a big one. He shoved open the door and stepped out into the light as a free man.

He left the cloak, for now.

Bridge Four cheered him as he emerged. They had gone out to bathe and shave in the riddens of the storm, as was their custom. The line was almost done, Rock having shaved each of the men in turn. The large Horneater hummed to himself as he worked the razor over Drehy's balding head. The air smelled wet from the rain, and a washed-out firepit nearby was the only trace of the stew the group had shared the night before.

In many ways, this place wasn't so different from the lumberyards his men had recently escaped. The long, rectangular stone barracks were much the same – Soulcast rather than having been built by hand, they looked like enormous stone logs. These, however, each had a couple of smaller rooms on the sides for sergeants, with their own doors that opened to the outside. They'd been painted with the symbols of the platoons using them before; Kaladin's men would have to paint over those.

'Moash,' Kaladin called. 'Skar, Teft.'

The three jogged toward him, splashing through puddles left by the storm. They wore the clothing of bridgemen: simple trousers cut off at the knees, and leather vests over bare chests. Skar was up and mobile despite the wound to his foot, and he tried rather obviously not to limp. For now, Kaladin didn't order him to bed rest. The wound wasn't too bad, and he needed the man.

'I want to look at what we've got,' Kaladin said, leading them away from the barrack. It would house fifty men along with a half-dozen sergeants. More barracks flanked it on either side. Kaladin had been given an entire block of them – twenty buildings – to house his new battalion of former bridgemen.

Twenty buildings. That Dalinar should so easily be able to find a block of twenty buildings for the bridgemen bespoke a terrible truth – the cost of Sadeas's betrayal. Thousands of men dead. Indeed, female scribes worked near some of the barracks, supervising parshmen who carried out heaps of clothing and other personal effects. The possessions of the deceased.

Not a few of those scribes looked on with red eyes and frazzled composures. Sadeas had just created thousands of new widows in Dalinar's camp, and likely as many orphans. If Kaladin had needed another reason to hate that man, he found it here, manifest in the suffering of those whose husbands had trusted him on the battlefield.

In Kaladin's eyes, there was no sin greater than the betrayal of one's allies in battle. Except, perhaps, for the betrayal of one's own men – of murdering them after they risked their lives to protect you. Kaladin felt an immediate flare of anger at thoughts of Amaram and what he'd done. His slave brand seemed to burn again on his forehead.

Amaram and Sadeas. Two men in Kaladin's life who would, at some point, need to pay for the things they'd done. Preferably, that payment would come with severe interest.

Kaladin continued to walk with Teft, Moash, and Skar. These barracks, which were slowly being emptied of personal effects, were also crowded with bridgemen. They looked much like the men of Bridge Four – same vests and knee-trousers. And yet, in some other ways, they couldn't have looked *less* like the men of Bridge Four. Shaggy-haired with beards that hadn't been trimmed in months, they bore hollow eyes that didn't seem to blink often enough. Slumped backs. Expressionless faces.

Each man among them seemed to sit alone, even when surrounded by his fellows.

'I remember that feeling,' Skar said softly. The short, wiry man had sharp features and silvering hair at the temples, despite being in his early thirties. 'I don't want to, but I do.'

'We're supposed to turn *those* into an army?' Moash asked.

'Kaladin did it to Bridge Four, didn't he?' Teft asked, wagging a finger at Moash. 'He'll do it again.'

'Transforming a few dozen men is different from doing the same for hundreds,' Moash said, kicking aside a fallen branch from the highstorm. Tall and solid, Moash had a scar on his chin but no slave brand on his forehead. He walked straight-backed with his chin up. Save for those dark brown eyes of his, he could have passed for an officer.

Kaladin led the three past barrack after barrack, doing a quick count. Nearly a thousand men, and though he'd told them yesterday that they were now free – and could return to their old lives if they wished – few seemed to want to do anything but sit. Though there had originally been forty bridge crews, many had been slaughtered during the latest assault and others had already been short-manned.

'We'll combine them into twenty crews,' Kaladin said, 'of about fifty each.' Above, Syl fluttered down as a ribbon of light and zipped around him. The men gave no sign of seeing her; she would be invisible to them. 'We can't teach each of these thousand personally, not at first. We'll want to train the more eager ones among them, then send them back to lead and train their own teams.'

'I suppose,' Teft said, scratching his chin. The oldest of the bridgemen, he was one of the few who retained a beard. Most of the others had shaved theirs off as a mark of pride, something to separate the men of Bridge Four from common slaves. Teft kept his neat for the same reason. It was light brown where it hadn't gone grey, and he wore it short and square, almost like an ardent's.

Moash grimaced, looking at the bridgemen. 'You assume some of them will be "more eager," Kaladin. They all look the same level of despondent to me.'

'Some will still have fight in them,' Kaladin said, continuing on back toward Bridge Four. 'The ones who joined us at the fire last night, for a start. Teft, I'll need you to choose others. Organize and combine crews, then pick forty men – two from each team – to be trained first. You'll be in command of that training. Those forty will be the seed we use to help the rest.'

'I suppose I can do that.'

'Good. I'll give you a few men to help.'

'A few?' Teft asked. 'I could use more than a few. . . .'

'You'll have to make do with a few,' Kaladin said, stopping on the path and turning westward, toward the king's complex beyond the camp wall. It rose on a hillside overlooking the rest of the warcamps. 'Most of us are going to be needed to keep Dalinar Kholin alive.'

Moash and the others stopped beside him. Kaladin squinted at the palace. It certainly didn't look grand enough to house a king – out here, everything was just stone and more stone.

'You are willing to trust Dalinar?' Moash asked.

'He gave up his Shardblade for us,' Kaladin said.

'He owed it to us,' Skar said with a grunt. 'We saved his storming life.'

'It could have just been posturing,' Moash said, folding his arms. 'Political games, him and Sadeas trying to manipulate each other.'

Syl alighted on Kaladin's shoulder, taking the form of a young woman with a flowing, filmy dress, all blue-white. She held her hands clasped together as she looked up at the king's complex, where Dalinar Kholin had gone to plan.

He'd told Kaladin that he was going to do something that would anger a lot of people. *I'm going to take away their games. . . .*

'We need to keep that man alive,' Kaladin said, looking back to the others. 'I don't know if I trust him, but he's the only person on these Plains who has shown even a *hint* of compassion for bridgemen. If he dies, do you want to guess how long it will take his successor to sell us back to Sadeas?'

Skar snorted in derision. 'I'd like to see them try with a Knight Radiant at our head.'

'I'm *not* a Radiant.'

'Fine, whatever,' Skar said. 'Whatever you *are*, it will be tough for them to take us from you.'

'You think I can fight them all, Skar?' Kaladin said, meeting the older man's eyes. 'Dozens of Shardbearers? Tens of thousands of troops? You think one man could do that?'

'Not one man,' Skar said, stubborn. 'You.'

'I'm not a god, Skar,' Kaladin said. 'I can't hold back the weight of ten armies.' He turned to the other two. 'We decided to stay here on the Shattered Plains. Why?'

'What good would it do to run?' Teft asked, shrugging. 'Even as free men, we'd just end up conscripted into one army or another out there in the hills. Either that, or we'd end up starving.'

Moash nodded. 'This is as good a place as any, so long as we're free.'

'Dalinar Kholin is our best hope for a *real* life,' Kaladin said. 'Bodyguards, not conscripted labor. Free men, despite the brands on our foreheads. Nobody else will give us that. If we want freedom, we need to keep Dalinar Kholin alive.'

'And the Assassin in White?' Skar asked softly.

They'd heard of what the man was doing around the world, slaughtering kings and highprinces in all nations. The news was the buzz of the warcamps, ever since reports had started trickling in through spanreed. The emperor of Azir, dead. Jah Keved in turmoil. A half-dozen other nations left without a ruler.

'He already killed our king,' Kaladin said. 'Old Gavilar was the assassin's first murder. We'll just have to hope he's done here. Either way, we protect Dalinar. At all costs.'

They nodded one by one, though those nods were grudging. He didn't blame them. Trusting lighteyes hadn't gotten them far – even Moash, who had once spoken well of Dalinar, now seemed to have lost his fondness for the man. Or any lighteyes.

In truth, Kaladin was a little surprised at himself and the trust he felt. But, storm it, Syl liked Dalinar. That carried weight.

'We're weak right now,' Kaladin said, lowering his voice. 'But if we play along with this for a time, protecting Kholin, we'll be paid handsomely. I'll be able to train you – really train you – as soldiers and officers. Beyond that, we'll be able to teach these others.

'We could never make it on our own out there as two dozen former bridgemen. But what if we were instead a highly skilled mercenary force of a thousand soldiers, equipped with the finest gear in the warcamps? If worst comes to worst, and we have to abandon the camps, I'd like to do so as a cohesive unit, hardened and impossible to ignore. Give me a year with this thousand, and I can have it done.'

'Now *that* plan I like,' Moash said. 'Do I get to learn to use a sword?'

'We're still darkeyes, Moash.'

'Not you,' Skar said from his other side. 'I saw your eyes during the –'

'Stop!' Kaladin said. He took a deep breath. 'Just stop. No more talk of that.'

Skar fell silent.

'I *am* going to name you officers,' Kaladin said to them. 'You three, along with Sigzil and Rock. You'll be lieutenants.'

'Darkeyed lieutenants?' Skar said. The rank was commonly used for the equivalent of sergeants in companies made up only of lighteyes.

'Dalinar made me a captain,' Kaladin said. 'The highest rank he said he dared commission a darkeyes. Well, I need to come up with a full command structure for a thousand men, and we're going to need something between sergeant and captain. That means appointing you five as lieutenants. I think Dalinar will let me get away with it. We'll make master sergeants if we need another rank.

'Rock is going to be quartermaster and in charge of food for the thousand. I'll appoint Lopen his second. Teft, you'll be in charge of training. Sigzil will be our clerk. He's the only one who can read glyphs. Moash and Skar . . .'

He glanced toward the two men. One short, the other tall, they walked the same way, with a smooth gait, dangerous, spears always on their shoulders. They were never without. Of all the men he'd trained in Bridge Four, only these two had instinctively *understood*. They were killers.

Like Kaladin himself.

'We three,' Kaladin told them, 'are each going to focus on watching Dalinar Kholin. Whenever possible, I want one of us three personally guarding him. Often one of the other two will watch his sons, but make no mistake, the Blackthorn is the man we're going to keep alive. At all costs. He is our only guarantee of freedom for Bridge Four.'

The others nodded.

'Good,' Kaladin said. 'Let's go get the rest of the men. It's time for the world to see you as I do.'

⁘

By common agreement, Hobber sat down to get his tattoo first. The gaptoothed man was one of the very first who had believed in Kaladin. Kaladin remembered that day; exhausted after a bridge run, wanting to simply lie down and stare. Instead, he'd chosen to save Hobber rather than letting him die. Kaladin had saved himself that day too.

The rest of Bridge Four stood around Hobber in the tent, watching in silence as the tattooist worked carefully on his forehead, covering up the scar of his slave's brand with the glyphs Kaladin had provided. Hobber winced now and then at the pain of the tattoo, but he kept a grin on his face.

Kaladin had heard that you could cover a scar with a tattoo, and it ended up working quite well. Once the tattoo ink was injected, the glyphs drew the eye, and you could barely tell that the skin beneath was scarred.

Once the process was finished, the tattooist provided a mirror for Hobber to look into. The bridgeman touched his forehead hesitantly. The skin was red from the needles, but the dark tattoo perfectly covered the slave brand.

'What does it say?' Hobber asked softly, tears in his eyes.

'Freedom,' Sigzil said before Kaladin could reply. 'The glyph means freedom.'

'The smaller ones above,' Kaladin said, 'say the date you were freed and the one who freed you. Even if you lose your writ of freedom, anyone who tries to imprison you for being a runaway can easily find proof that you are not. They can go to Dalinar Kholin's scribes, who keep a copy of your writ.'

Hobber nodded. 'That's good, but it's not enough. Add 'Bridge Four' to it. Freedom, Bridge Four.'

'To imply you were freed from Bridge Four?'

'No, sir. I wasn't freed *from* Bridge Four. I was freed *by* it. I wouldn't trade my time there for anything.'

It was crazy talk. Bridge Four had been death – scores of men had been slaughtered running that cursed bridge. Even after Kaladin had determined to save the men, he'd lost far too many. Hobber would have been a fool not to take any opportunity to escape.

And yet, he sat stubbornly until Kaladin drew out the proper glyphs for the tattooist – a calm, sturdy darkeyed woman who looked like she could have lifted a bridge all on her own. She settled down on her stool and began adding the two glyphs to Hobber's forehead, tucked right below the freedom glyph. She spent the process explaining – again – how the tattoo would be sore for days and how Hobber would need to care for it.

He accepted the new tattoos with a grin on his face. Pure foolishness, but the others nodded in agreement, clasping Hobber on the arm. Once Hobber was done, Skar sat quickly, eager, demanding the same full set of tattoos.

Kaladin stepped back, folding his arms and shaking his head. Outside the tent, a bustling marketplace sold and bought. The 'warcamp' was really a city, built up inside the craterlike rim of some enormous rock formation. The prolonged war on the Shattered Plains had attracted merchants of all varieties, along with tradesmen, artists, and even families with children.

Moash stood nearby, face troubled, watching the tattooist. He wasn't the only one in the bridge crew who didn't have a slave brand. Teft didn't either. They had been made bridgemen without technically being made slaves first. It happened frequently in Sadeas's camp, where running bridges was a punishment that one could earn for all manner of infractions.

'If you don't have a slave's brand,' Kaladin said loudly to the men, 'you don't need to get the tattoo. You're still one of us.'

'No,' Rock said. 'I will get this thing.' He insisted on sitting down after Skar and getting the tattoo right on his forehead, though he had no slave brand. Indeed, every one of the men without a slave brand – Beld and Teft included – sat down and got the tattoo on their foreheads.

Only Moash abstained, and had the tattoo placed on his upper arm. Good. Unlike most of them, he wouldn't have to go about with a proclamation of former slavery in plain view.

Moash stood up from the seat, and another took his place. A man with red and black skin in a marbled pattern, like stone. Bridge Four had a lot of variety, but Shen was in a class all his own. A parshman.

'I can't tattoo him,' the artist said. 'He's property.'

Kaladin opened his mouth to object, but the other bridgemen jumped in first.

'He's been freed, like us,' Teft said.

'One of the team,' Hobber said. 'Give him the tattoo, or you won't see a sphere from any of us.' He blushed after he said it, glancing at Kaladin – who would be paying for all this, using spheres granted by Dalinar Kholin.

Other bridgemen spoke out, and the tattoo artist finally sighed and gave in. She pulled over her stool and began working on Shen's forehead.

'You won't even be able to see it,' she grumbled, though Sigzil's skin was nearly as dark as Shen's, and the tattoo showed up fine on him.

Eventually, Shen looked in the mirror, then stood up. He glanced at Kaladin, and nodded. Shen didn't say much, and Kaladin didn't know what to make of the man. It was actually easy to forget about him, usually trailing along silently at the back of the group of bridgemen. Invisible. Parshmen were often that way.

Shen finished, only Kaladin himself remained. He sat down next and closed his eyes. The pain of the needles was a lot sharper than he'd anticipated.

After a short time, the tattooist started cursing under her breath.

Kaladin opened his eyes as she wiped a rag on his forehead. 'What is it?' he asked.

'The ink won't take!' she said. 'I've never seen anything like it. When I wipe your forehead, the ink all just comes right off! The tattoo won't stay.'

Kaladin sighed, realizing he had a little Stormlight raging in his veins. He hadn't even noticed drawing it in, but he seemed to be getting better and better at holding it. He frequently took in a little these days while walking about. Holding Stormlight was like filling a wineskin – if you filled it to bursting and unstopped it, it would squirt out quickly, then slow to a trickle. Same with the Light.

He banished it, hoping the tattoo artist didn't notice when he breathed out a small cloud of glowing smoke. 'Try again,' he said as she got out new ink.

This time, the tattoo took. Kaladin sat through the process, teeth clenched against the pain, then looked up as she held the mirror for him. The face that looked back at Kaladin seemed alien. Clean-shaven, hair pulled back from his face for the tattooing, the slave brands covered up and, for the moment, forgotten.

Can I be this man again? he thought, reaching up, touching his cheek. *This man died, didn't he?*

Syl landed on his shoulder, joining him in looking into the mirror. 'Life before death, Kaladin,' she whispered.

He unconsciously sucked in Stormlight. Just a little, a fraction of a sphere's worth. It flowed through his veins like a wave of pressure, like winds trapped in a small enclosure.

The tattoo on his forehead melted. His body shoved out the ink, which started to drip down his face. The tattooist cursed again and grabbed her rag.

Kaladin was left with the image of those glyphs melting away. Freedom dissolved, and underneath, the violent scars of his captivity. Dominated by a branded glyph.

Shash. Dangerous.

The woman wiped his face. 'I don't know why this is happening! I thought it would stay that time. I—'

'It's all right,' Kaladin said, taking the rag as he stood, finishing the cleanup. He turned to face the rest of them, bridgemen now soldiers. 'The scars haven't finished with me yet, it appears. I'll try again another time.'

49

They nodded. He'd have to explain to them later what was happening; they knew of his abilities.

'Let's go,' Kaladin said to them, tossing a small bag of spheres to the tattooist, then taking his spear from beside the tent entrance. The others joined him, spears to shoulders. They didn't need to be armed while in camp, but he wanted them to get used to the idea that they were free to carry weapons now.

The market outside was crowded and vibrant. The tents, of course, would have been taken down and stowed during last night's highstorm, but they'd already sprung up again. Perhaps because he was thinking about Shen, he noticed the parshmen. He picked out dozens of them with a cursory glance, helping set up a few last tents, carrying purchases for lighteyes, helping shopowners stack their wares.

What do they think of this war on the Shattered Plains? Kaladin wondered. *A war to defeat, and perhaps subjugate, the only free parshmen in the world?*

Would that he could get an answer out of Shen regarding questions like that. It seemed all he ever got from the parshman were shrugs.

Kaladin led his men through the market, which seemed far friendlier than the one in Sadeas's camp. Though people stared at the bridgemen, nobody sneered, and the haggling at nearby stands – while energetic – didn't progress to shouting. There even seemed to be fewer urchins and beggars.

You just want to believe that, Kaladin thought. *You want to believe Dalinar is the man everyone says he is. The honorable lighteyes of the stories. But everyone said the same things about Amaram.*

As they walked, they did pass some soldiers. Too few. Men who had been on duty back in the camp when the others had gone on the disastrous assault where Sadeas had betrayed Dalinar. As they passed one group patrolling the market, Kaladin caught two men at their front raising their hands before themselves, crossed at the wrist.

How had they learned Bridge Four's old salute, and so quickly? These men didn't do it as a full salute, just a small gesture, but they nodded their heads to Kaladin and his men as they passed. Suddenly, the more calm nature of the market took on another cast to Kaladin. Perhaps this wasn't simply the order and organization of Dalinar's army.

There was an air of quiet dread over this warcamp. Thousands had been lost to Sadeas's betrayal. Everyone here had probably known a man who had died out on those plateaus. And everyone probably wondered if the conflict between the two highprinces would escalate.

'It's nice to be seen as a hero, isn't it?' Sigzil asked, walking beside Kaladin and watching another group of soldiers pass by.

'How long will the goodwill last, do you think?' Moash asked. 'How long before they resent us?'

'Ha!' Rock, towering behind him, clapped Moash on the shoulder. 'No complaining today! You do this thing too much. Do not make me kick you. I do not like kicking. It hurts my toes.'

'Kick me?' Moash snorted. 'You won't even carry a spear, Rock.'

'Spears are not for kicking complainers. But big Unkalaki feet like mine – it is what they were made for! Ha! This thing is obvious, yes?'

Kaladin led the men out of the market and to a large rectangular building near the barracks. This one was constructed of worked stone, rather than Soulcast rock, allowing far more finesse in design. Such buildings were becoming more common in the warcamps, as more masons arrived.

Soulcasting was quicker, but also more expensive and less flexible. He didn't know much about it, only that Soulcasters were limited in what they could do. That was why the barracks were all essentially identical.

Kaladin led his men inside the towering building to the counter, where a grizzled man with a belly that stretched to next week supervised a few parshmen stacking bolts of blue cloth. Rind, the Kholin head quartermaster, to whom Kaladin had sent instructions the night before. Rind was lighteyed, but what was known as a 'tenner,' a lowly rank barely above darkeyes.

'Ah!' Rind said, speaking with a high-pitched voice that did not match his girth. 'You're here, finally! I've got them all out for you, Captain. Everything I have left.'

'Left?' Moash asked.

'Uniforms of the Cobalt Guard! I've commissioned some new ones, but this is what stock remained.' Rind grew more subdued. 'Didn't expect to need so many so soon, you see.' He looked Moash up and down, then handed him a uniform and pointed to a stall for changing.

Moash took it. 'We going to wear our leather jerkins over these?'

'Ha!' Rind said. 'The ones tied with so much bone you looked like some

Western skullbearer on feast day? I've heard of that. But no, Brightlord Dalinar says you're each to be outfitted with breastplates, steel caps, new spears. Chain mail for the battlefield, if you need it.'

'For now,' Kaladin said, 'uniforms will do.'

'I think I'll look silly in this,' Moash grumbled, but walked over to change. Rind distributed the uniforms to the men. He gave Shen a strange look, but delivered the parshman a uniform without complaint.

The bridgemen gathered in an eager bunch, jabbering with excitement as they unfolded their uniforms. It had been a long time since any of them had worn anything other than bridgeman leathers or slave wraps. They stopped talking when Moash stepped out.

These were newer uniforms, of a more modern style than Kaladin had worn in his previous military service. Stiff blue trousers and black boots polished to a shine. A buttoned white shirt, only the edges of its collar and cuffs extending beyond the jacket, which came down to the waist and buttoned closed beneath the belt.

'Now, *there's* a soldier!' the quartermaster said with a laugh. 'Still think you look silly?' He gestured for Moash to inspect his reflection in the mirror on the wall.

Moash fixed his cuffs and actually blushed. Kaladin had rarely seen the man so out of sorts. 'No,' Moash said. 'I don't.'

The others moved eagerly and began changing. Some went to the stalls at the side, but most didn't care. They were bridgemen and slaves; they'd spent most of their recent lives being paraded about in loincloths or little more.

Teft had his on before anyone else, and knew to do up the buttons in the right places. 'Been a long time,' he whispered, buckling his belt. 'Don't know that I deserve to wear something like this again.'

'This is what you are, Teft,' Kaladin said. 'Don't let the slave rule you.'

Teft grunted, affixing his combat knife in its place on his belt. 'And you, son? When are *you* going to admit what you are?'

'I have.'

'To us. Not to everyone else.'

'Don't start this again.'

'I'll storming start whatever I want,' Teft snapped. He leaned in, speaking softly. 'At least until you give me a real answer. You're a Surgebinder. You're not a Radiant yet, but you're going to be one when this is all blown through. The others are right to push you. Why don't you go have a hike up to that Dalinar fellow, suck in some Stormlight, and make him recognize you as a lighteyes?'

Kaladin glanced at the men in a muddled jumble as they tried to get the uniforms on, an exasperated Rind explaining to them how to do up the coats.

'Everything I've ever had, Teft,' Kaladin whispered, 'the lighteyes have taken from me. My family, my brother, my friends. More. More than you can imagine. They see what I have, and they take it.' He held up his hand, and could faintly make out a few glowing wisps trailing from his skin, since he knew what to look for. 'They'll take it. If they can find out what I do, they'll *take* it.'

'Now, how in Kelek's breath would they do that?'

'I don't know,' Kaladin said. 'I don't *know*, Teft, but I can't help feeling panic when I think about it. I can't let them have this, can't let them take it – or you men – from me. We remain quiet about what I can do. No more talk of it.'

Teft grumbled as the other men finally got themselves sorted out, though Lopen – one armed, with his empty sleeve turned inside out and pushed in so it didn't hang down – prodded at the patch on his shoulder. 'What's this?'

'It's the insignia of the Cobalt Guard,' Kaladin said. 'Dalinar Kholin's personal bodyguard.'

'They're dead, gancho,' Lopen said. 'We aren't them.'

'Yeah,' Skar agreed. To Rind's horror, he got out his knife and cut the patch free. 'We're Bridge Four.'

'Bridge Four was your prison,' Kaladin protested.

'Doesn't matter,' Skar said. 'We're Bridge Four.' The others agreed, cutting off the patches, tossing them to the ground.

Teft nodded and did likewise. 'We'll protect the Blackthorn, but we're not just going to replace what he had before. We're our own crew.'

Kaladin rubbed his forehead, but this was what he had accomplished in bringing them together, galvanizing them into a cohesive unit. 'I'll draw up a glyphpair insignia for you to use,' he told Rind. 'You'll have to commission new patches.'

The portly man sighed as he gathered up the discarded patches. 'I suppose. I've got your uniform over there, Captain. A darkeyed captain! Who

53

would have thought it possible? You'll be the only one in the army. The only one ever, so far as I know!'

He didn't seem to find it offensive. Kaladin had little experience with low-dahn lighteyes like Rind, though they were very common in the warcamps. In his hometown, there had only been the citylord's family – of upper-middle dahn – and the darkeyes. It hadn't been until he'd reached Amaram's army that he'd realized there was an entire spectrum of lighteyes, many of whom worked common jobs and scrambled for money just like ordinary people.

Kaladin walked over to the last bundle on the counter. His uniform was different. It included a blue waistcoat and a double-breasted blue longcoat, the lining white, the buttons of silver. The longcoat was meant to hang open, despite the rows of buttons down each side.

He'd seen such uniforms frequently. On lighteyes.

'Bridge Four,' he said, cutting the Cobalt Guard insignia from the shoulder and tossing it to the counter with the others.

Soldiers reported being watched from afar by an unnerving number of Parshendi scouts. Then we noticed a new pattern of their penetrating close to the camps in the night and then quickly retreating. I can only surmise that our enemies were even then preparing their stratagem to end this war.

—From the personal journal of Navani Kholin, Jeseses 1174

R esearch into times before the Hierocracy is frustratingly difficult, the book read. *During the reign of the Hierocracy, the Vorin Church had near absolute control over eastern Roshar. The fabrications they promoted – and then perpetuated as absolute truth – became ingrained in the consciousness of society. More disturbingly, modified copies of ancient texts were made, aligning history to match Hierocratic dogma.*

In her cabin, Shallan read by the glow of a goblet of spheres, wearing her nightgown. Her cramped chamber lacked a true porthole and had just a thin slit of a window running across the top of the outside wall. The only sound she could hear was the water lapping against the hull. Tonight, the ship did not have a port in which to shelter.

The church of this era was suspicious of the Knights Radiant, the book read. *Yet it relied upon the authority granted Vorinism by the Heralds. This created a dichotomy in which the Recreance, and the betrayal of the knights, was overemphasized. At the same time, the ancient knights – the ones who had lived alongside the Heralds in the shadowdays – were celebrated.*

This makes it particularly difficult to study the Radiants and the place named Shadesmar. What is fact? What records did the church, in its misguided attempt to cleanse the past of perceived contradictions, rewrite to suit its preferred narrative? Few documents from the period survive that did not pass through Vorin hands to be copied from the original parchment into modern codices.

Shallan glanced up over the top of her book. The volume was one of Jasnah's earliest published works as a full scholar. Jasnah had not assigned Shallan to read it. Indeed, she'd been hesitant when Shallan had asked for a copy, and had needed to dig it out of one of the numerous trunks full of books she kept in the ship's hold.

Why had she been so reluctant, when this volume dealt with the very things that Shallan was studying? Shouldn't Jasnah have given her this right off? It—

The pattern returned.

Shallan's breath caught in her throat as she saw it on the cabin wall beside the bunk, just to her left. She carefully moved her eyes back to the page in front of her. The pattern was the same one that she'd seen before, the shape that had appeared on her sketchpad.

Ever since then, she'd been seeing it from the corner of her eye, appearing in the grain of wood, the cloth on the back of a sailor's shirt, the shimmering of the water. Each time, when she looked right at it, the pattern vanished. Jasnah would say nothing more, other than to indicate it was likely harmless.

Shallan turned the page and steadied her breathing. She had experienced something like this before with the strange symbol-headed creatures who had appeared unbidden in her drawings. She allowed her eyes to slip up off the page and look at the wall – not right at the pattern, but to the side of it, as if she hadn't noticed it.

Yes, it was there. Raised, like an embossing, it had a complex pattern with a haunting symmetry. Its tiny lines twisted and turned through its mass, somehow lifting the surface of the wood, like iron scrollwork under a taut tablecloth.

It was one of those *things*. The symbolheads. This pattern was similar to their strange heads. She looked back at the page, but did not read. The ship swayed, and the glowing white spheres in her goblet clinked as they shifted. She took a deep breath.

Then looked directly at the pattern.

Immediately, it began to fade, the ridges sinking. Before it did, she got a clear look at it, and she took a Memory.

'Not this time,' she muttered as it vanished. 'This time I have you.' She threw away her book, scrambling to get out her charcoal pencil and a sheet of sketching paper. She huddled down beside her light, red hair tumbling around her shoulders.

She worked furiously, possessed by a frantic *need* to have this drawing done. Her fingers moved on their own, her unclothed safehand holding the sketchpad toward the goblet, which sprinkled the paper with shards of light.

She tossed aside the pencil. She needed something crisper, capable of sharper lines. Ink. Pencil was wonderful for drawing the soft shades of life, but this thing she drew was not life. It was something else, something unreal. She dug a pen and inkwell from her supplies, then went back to her drawing, replicating the tiny, intricate lines.

She did not think as she drew. The art consumed her, and creationspren popped into existence all around. Dozens of tiny shapes soon crowded the small table beside her cot and the floor of the cabin near where she knelt. The spren shifted and spun, each no larger than the bowl of a spoon, becoming shapes they'd recently encountered. She mostly ignored them, though she'd never seen so many at once.

Faster and faster they shifted forms as she drew, intent. The pattern seemed impossible to capture. Its complex repetitions twisted down into infinity. No, a pen could never capture this thing perfectly, but she was close. She drew it spiraling out of a center point, then re-created each branch off the center, which had its own swirl of tiny lines. It was like a maze created to drive its captive insane.

When she finished the last line, she found herself breathing hard, as if she'd run a great distance. She blinked, again noticing the creationspren around her – there were *hundreds*. They lingered before fading away one by one. Shallan set the pen down beside her vial of ink, which she'd stuck to the tabletop with wax to keep it from sliding as the ship swayed. She picked up the page, waiting for the last lines of ink to dry, and felt as if she'd accomplished something significant – though she knew not what.

As the last line dried, the pattern *rose* before her. She heard a distinct sigh from the paper, as if in relief.

She jumped, dropping the paper and scrambling onto her bed. Unlike the other times, the embossing didn't vanish, though it *left* the paper – budding from her matching drawing – and moved onto the floor.

She could describe it in no other way. The pattern somehow moved from paper to floor. It came to the leg of her cot and wrapped around it, climbing upward and onto the blanket. It didn't look like something moving beneath the blanket; that was simply a crude approximation. The lines were too precise for that, and there was no stretching. Something beneath the blanket would have been just an indistinct lump, but this was exact.

It drew closer. It didn't look dangerous, but she still found herself trembling. This pattern was different from the symbolheads in her drawings, but it was also somehow the *same*. A flattened-out version, without torso or limbs. It was an abstraction of one of them, just as a circle with a few lines in it could represent a human's face on the page.

Those things had terrified her, haunted her dreams, made her worry she was going insane. So as this one approached, she scuttled from her bed and went as far from it in the small cabin as she could. Then, heart thumping in her chest, she pulled open the door to go for Jasnah.

She found Jasnah herself just outside, reaching toward the doorknob, her left hand cupped before her. A small figure made of inky blackness – shaped like a man in a smart, fashionable suit with a long coat – stood in her palm. He melted away into shadow as he saw Shallan. Jasnah looked to Shallan, then glanced toward the floor of the cabin, where the pattern was crossing the wood.

'Put on some clothing, child,' Jasnah said. 'We have matters to discuss.'

❖

'I had originally hoped that we would have the same type of spren,' Jasnah said, sitting on a stool in Shallan's cabin. The pattern remained on the floor between her and Shallan, who lay prone on the cot, properly clothed with a robe over the nightgown and a thin white glove on her left hand. 'But of course, that would be too easy. I have suspected since Kharbranth that we would be of different orders.'

'Orders, Brightness?' Shallan asked, timidly using a pencil to prod at the pattern on the floor. It shied away, like an animal that had been poked. Shallan was fascinated by how it raised the surface of the floor, though a part of her did not want to have anything to do with it and its unnatural, eye-twisting geometries.

'Yes,' Jasnah said. The inklike spren that had accompanied her before had not reappeared. 'Each order reportedly had access to two of the Surges, with overlap between them. We call the powers Surgebinding. Soulcasting was one, and is what we share, though our orders are different.'

Shallan nodded. Surgebinding. Soulcasting. These were talents of the Lost Radiants, the abilities – supposedly just legend – that had been their blessing or their curse, depending upon which reports you read. Or so she'd learned from the books Jasnah had given her to read during their trip.

'I'm not one of the Radiants,' Shallan said.

'Of course you aren't,' Jasnah said, 'and neither am I. The orders of knights were a construct, just as all society is a construct, used by men to define and explain. Not every man who wields a spear is a soldier, and not every woman who makes bread is a baker. And yet weapons, or baking, become the hallmarks of certain professions.'

'So you're saying that what we can do . . .'

'Was once the definition of what initiated one into the Knights Radiant,' Jasnah said.

'But we're women!'

'Yes,' Jasnah said lightly. 'Spren don't suffer from human society's prejudices. Refreshing, wouldn't you say?'

Shallan looked up from poking at the pattern spren. 'There were women among the Knights Radiant?'

'A statistically appropriate number,' Jasnah said. 'But don't fear that you will soon find yourself swinging a sword, child. The archetype of Radiants on the battlefield is an exaggeration. From what I've read – though records are, unfortunately, untrustworthy – for every Radiant dedicated to battle, there were another three who spent their time on diplomacy, scholarship, or other ways to aid society.'

'Oh.' Why was Shallan disappointed by that?

Fool. A memory rose unbidden. A silvery sword. A pattern of light. Truths she could not face. She banished them, squeezing her eyes shut.

Ten heartbeats.

'I have been looking into the spren you told me about,' Jasnah said. 'The creatures with the symbol heads.'

Shallan took a deep breath and opened her eyes. 'This is one of them,' she said, pointing her pencil at the pattern, which had approached her trunk and was moving up onto it and off it – like a child jumping on a sofa. Instead of threatening, it seemed innocent, even playful – and hardly intelligent at all. She had been frightened of this thing?

'Yes, I suspect that it is,' Jasnah said. 'Most spren manifest differently here than they do in Shadesmar. What you drew before was their form there.'

'This one is not very impressive.'

'Yes. I will admit that I'm disappointed. I feel that we're missing something important about this, Shallan, and I find it annoying. The Cryptics have a fearful reputation, and yet this one – the first specimen I've ever seen – seems . . .'

It climbed up the wall, then slipped down, then climbed back up, then slipped down again.

'Imbecilic?' Shallan asked.

'Perhaps it simply needs more time,' Jasnah said. 'When I first bonded with Ivory –' She stopped abruptly.

'What?' Shallan said.

'I'm sorry. He does not like me to speak of him. It makes him anxious. The knights' breaking of their oaths was very painful to the spren. Many spren died; I'm certain of it. Though Ivory won't speak of it, I gather that what he's done is regarded as a betrayal by the others of his kind.'

'But—'

'No more of that,' Jasnah said. 'I'm sorry.'

'Fine. You mentioned the Cryptics?'

'Yes,' Jasnah said, reaching into the sleeve that hid her safehand and slipping out a folded piece of paper – one of Shallan's drawings of the symbolheads. 'That is their own name for themselves, though we would probably name them liespren. They don't like the term. Regardless, the Cryptics rule one of the greater cities in Shadesmar. Think of them as the lighteyes of the Cognitive Realm.'

'So this thing,' Shallan said, nodding to the pattern, which was spinning in circles in the center of the cabin, 'is like . . . a prince, on their side?'

'Something like that. There is a complex sort of conflict between them and the honorspren. Spren politics are not something I've been able to devote much time to. This spren will be your companion – and will grant you the ability to Soulcast, among other things.'

'Other things?'

'We will have to see,' Jasnah said. 'It comes down to the nature of spren. What has your research revealed?'

With Jasnah, everything seemed to be a test of scholarship. Shallan smothered a sigh. This was why she had come with Jasnah, rather than returning to her home. Still, she did wish that sometimes Jasnah would just *tell* her answers rather than making her work so hard to find them. 'Alai says that the spren are fragments of the powers of creation. A lot of the scholars I read agreed with that.'

'It is one opinion. What does it mean?'

Shallan tried not to let herself be distracted by the spren on the floor. 'There are ten fundamental Surges – forces – by which the world works. Gravitation, pressure, transformation. That sort of thing. You told me spren are fragments of the Cognitive Realm that have somehow gained sentience because of human attention. Well, it stands to reason that they were something before. Like . . . like a painting was a canvas before being given life.'

'Life?' Jasnah said, raising her eyebrow.

'Of course,' Shallan said. Paintings lived. Not lived like a person or a spren, but . . . well, it was obvious to her, at least. 'So, before the spren were alive, they were something. Power. Energy. Zen-daughter-Vath sketched tiny spren she found sometimes around heavy objects. Gravitationspren – fragments of the *power* or *force* that causes us to fall. It stands to reason that every spren was a power before it was a spren. Really, you can divide spren into two general groups. Those that respond to emotions and those that respond to forces like fire or wind pressure.'

'So you believe Namar's theory on spren categorization?'

'Yes.'

'Good,' Jasnah said. 'As do I. I suspect, personally, that these group-ings of spren – emotion spren versus nature spren – are where the ideas of mankind's primeval 'gods' came from. Honor, who became Vorinism's Almighty, was created by men who wanted a representation of ideal human emotions as they saw in emotion spren. Cultivation, the god worshipped in the West, is a female deity that is an embodiment of nature and nature spren. The various Voidspren, with their unseen lord – whose name changes depending on which culture we're speaking of – evoke an enemy or antagonist. The Stormfather, of course, is a strange offshoot of this, his theoretical nature changing depending on which era of Vorinism is doing the talking. . . .'

She trailed off. Shallan blushed, realizing she'd looked away and had begun tracing a glyphward on her blanket against the evil in Jasnah's words.

'That was a tangent,' Jasnah said. 'I apologize.'

'You're so sure he isn't real,' Shallan said. 'The Almighty.'

'I have no more proof of him than I do of the Thaylen Passions, Nu Ralik of the Purelake, or any other religion.'

'And the Heralds? You don't think they existed?'

'I don't know,' Jasnah said. 'There are many things in this world that I don't understand. For example, there is *some* slight proof that both the Stormfather and the Almighty are real creatures – simply powerful spren, such as the Nightwatcher.'

'Then he *would* be real.'

'I never claimed he was not,' Jasnah said. 'I merely claimed that I do not accept him as God, nor do I feel any inclination to worship him. But this is, again, a tangent.' Jasnah stood. 'You are relieved of other duties of study. For the next few days, you have only one focus for your scholarship.' She pointed toward the floor.

'The pattern?' Shallan asked.

'You are the only person in centuries to have the chance to interact with a Cryptic,' Jasnah said. 'Study it and record your experiences – in detail. This will likely be your first writing of significance, and could be of utmost importance to our future.'

Shallan regarded the pattern, which had moved over and bumped into her foot – she could feel it only faintly – and was now bumping into it time and time again.

'Great,' Shallan said.

4

TAKER OF SECRETS

The next clue came on the walls. I did not ignore this sign, but neither did I grasp its full implications.

—From the journal of Navani Kholin, Jeseses 1174

'I'm running through water,' Dalinar said, coming to himself. He *was* moving, charging forward.

The vision coalesced around him. Warm water splashed his legs. On either side of him, a dozen men with hammers and spears ran through the shallow water. They lifted their legs high with each step, feet back, thighs lifting parallel to the water's surface, like they were marching in a parade – only no parade had ever been such a mad scramble. Obviously, running that way helped them move through the liquid. He tried to imitate the odd gait.

'I'm in the Purelake, I think,' he said, under his breath. 'Warm water that only comes up to the knees, no signs of land anywhere. It's dusk, though, so I can't see much.

'People run with me. I don't know if we're running toward something or away from it. Nothing over my shoulder that I can see. These people are obviously soldiers, though the uniforms are antiquated. Leather skirts, bronze helms and breastplates. Bare legs and arms.' He looked down at himself. 'I'm wearing the same.'

Some highlords in Alethkar and Jah Keved still used uniforms like this, so he couldn't place the exact era. The modern uses were all calculated revivals by traditionalist commanders who hoped a classical look would inspire their men. In those cases, however, modern steel equipment would be used alongside the antique uniforms – and he didn't see any of that here.

Dalinar didn't ask questions. He'd found that playing along with these visions taught him more than it did to stop and demand answers.

Running through this water was tough. Though he'd started near the front of the group, he was now lagging behind. The group ran toward some kind of large rock mound ahead, shadowed in the dusk. Maybe this *wasn't* the Purelake. It didn't have rock formations like—

That wasn't a rock mound. It was a *fortress*. Dalinar halted, looking up at the peaked, castle-like structure that rose straight from the still lake waters. He'd never seen its like before. Jet-black stone. Obsidian? Perhaps this place had been Soulcast.

'There's a fortress ahead,' he said, continuing forward. 'It must not still exist – if it did, it would be famous. It looks like it's created entirely from obsidian. Finlike sides rising toward peaked tips above, towers like arrowheads . . . Stormfather. It's majestic.

'We're approaching another group of soldiers who stand in the water, holding spears wardingly in all directions. There are perhaps a dozen of them; I'm in the company of another dozen. And . . . yes, there's someone in the middle of them. Shardbearer. Glowing armor.'

Not just a Shardbearer. Radiant. A knight in resplendent Shardplate that glowed with a deep red at the joints and in certain markings. Armor did that in the shadowdays. This vision was taking place before the Recreance.

Like all Shardplate, the armor was distinctive. With that skirt of chain links, those smooth joints, the vambraces that extended back just so . . . Storms, that looked like Adolin's armor, though this armor pulled in more at the waist. Female? Dalinar couldn't tell for certain, as the faceplate was down.

'Form up!' the knight ordered as Dalinar's group arrived, and he nodded to himself. Yes, female.

Dalinar and the other soldiers formed a ring around the knight, weapons outward. Not far off, another group of soldiers with a knight at their center marched through the water.

'Why did you call us back?' asked one of Dalinar's companions.

'Caeb thinks he saw something,' the knight said. 'Be alert. Let's move carefully.'

The group started away from the fortress in another direction from the one they'd come. Dalinar held his spear outward, sweating at his temples. To his own eyes, he didn't look any different from his normal self. The others, however, would see him as one of their own.

He still didn't know terribly much about these visions. The Almighty sent them to him, somehow. But the Almighty was dead, by his own admission. So how did that work?

'We're looking for something,' Dalinar said, under his breath. 'Teams of knights and soldiers have been sent into the night to find something that was spotted.'

'You all right, new kid?' asked one of the soldiers to his side.

'Fine,' Dalinar said. 'Just worried. I mean, I don't even really know what we're looking for.'

'A spren that doesn't act like it should,' the man said. 'Keep your eyes open. Once Sja-anat touches a spren, it acts strange. Call attention to anything you see.'

Dalinar nodded, then under his breath repeated the words, hoping that Navani could hear him. He and the soldiers continued their sweep, the knight at their center speaking with . . . nobody? She sounded like she was having a conversation, but Dalinar couldn't see or hear anyone else with her.

He turned his attention to the surroundings. He'd always wanted to see the center of the Purelake, but he'd never had a chance to do much besides visit the border. He'd been unable to find time for a detour in that direction during his last visit to Azir. The Azish had always acted surprised that he would want to go to such a place, as they claimed there was 'nothing there.'

Dalinar wore some kind of tight shoes on his feet, perhaps to keep him from cutting them on anything hidden by the water. The footing was uneven in places, with holes and ridges he felt rather than saw. He found himself watching little fish dart this way and that, shadows in the water, and next to them a face.

A face.

Dalinar shouted, jumping back, pointing his spear downward. 'That was a face! In the water!'

'Riverspren?' the knight asked, stepping up beside him.

'It looked like a shadow,' Dalinar said. 'Red eyes.'

'It's here, then,' the knight said. 'Sja-anat's spy. Caeb, run to the checkpoint. The rest of you, keep watching. It won't be able to go far without a carrier.' She yanked something off her belt, a small pouch.

'There!' Dalinar said, spotting a small red dot in the water. It flowed away from him, swimming like a fish. He charged after, running as he'd learned earlier. What good would it do to chase a spren, though? You couldn't catch them. Not with any method he knew.

The others charged behind. Fish scattered away, frightened by Dalinar's splashing. 'I'm chasing a spren,' Dalinar said under his breath. 'It's what we've been hunting. It looks a little like a face – a shadowy one, with red eyes. It swims through the water like a fish. Wait! There's another one. Joining it. Larger, like a full figure, easily six feet. A swimming person, but like a shadow. It—'

'Storms!' the knight shouted suddenly. 'It brought an escort!'

The larger spren twisted, then dove downward in the water, vanishing into the rocky ground. Dalinar stopped, uncertain if he should keep chasing the smaller one or remain here.

The others turned and started to run the other way.

Uh-oh . . .

Dalinar scrambled back as the rocky lake bottom began to shake. He stumbled, splashing down into the water. It was so clear he could see the floor *cracking* under him, as if something large were pounding against it from beneath.

'Come on!' one of the soldiers cried, grabbing him by the arm. Dalinar was pulled to his feet as the cracks below widened. The once-still surface of the lake churned and thrashed.

The ground *jolted*, almost tumbling Dalinar off his feet again. Ahead of him, several of the soldiers did fall.

The knight stood firm, an enormous Shardblade forming in her hands.

Dalinar glanced over his shoulder in time to see rock emerging from the water. A long arm! Slender, perhaps fifteen feet long, it *burst* from the water, then slammed back down as if to get a firm purchase on the lakebed. Another arm rose nearby, elbow toward the sky, then they both heaved as if attached to a body doing a push-up.

A giant body ripped itself out of the rocky floor. It was like someone had been buried in sand and was now emerging. Water streamed from the creature's ridged and pocked back, which was overgrown with bits of shalebark and submarine fungus. The spren had somehow animated the stone itself.

As it stood and twisted about, Dalinar could make out glowing red eyes – like molten rock – set deep in an evil stone face. The body was skeletal, with thin bony limbs and spiky fingers that ended in rocky claws. The chest was a rib cage of stone.

'Thunderclast!' soldiers yelled. 'Hammers! Ready hammers!'

The knight stood before the rising creature, which stood thirty feet tall, dripping water. A calm, white light began to rise from her. It reminded Dalinar of the light of spheres. Stormlight. She raised her Shardblade and charged, stepping through the water with uncanny ease, as if it had no purchase on her. Perhaps it was the strength of Shardplate.

'They were created to watch,' a voice said from beside him.

Dalinar looked to the soldier who had helped him rise earlier, a long-faced Selay man with a balding scalp and a wide nose. Dalinar reached down to help the man to his feet.

This wasn't how the man had spoken before, but Dalinar recognized the voice. It was the same one that came at the end of most of the visions. The Almighty.

'The Knights Radiant,' the Almighty said, standing up beside Dalinar, watching the knight attack the nightmare beast. 'They were a solution, a way to offset the destruction of the Desolations. Ten orders of knights, founded with the purpose of helping men fight, then rebuild.'

Dalinar repeated it, word for word, focused on catching every one and not on thinking about what they meant.

The Almighty turned to him. 'I was surprised when these orders arrived. I did not teach my Heralds this. It was the spren – wishing to imitate what I had given men – who made it possible. You will need to refound them. This is *your* task. Unite them. Create a fortress that can weather the storm. Vex Odium, convince him that he can lose, and appoint a champion. He will take that chance instead of risking defeat again, as he has suffered so often. This is the best advice I can give you.'

Dalinar finished repeating the words. Beyond him, the fight began in earnest, water splashing, rock grinding. Soldiers approached bearing hammers, and unexpectedly, these men now also glowed with Stormlight, though far more faintly.

'You were surprised by the coming of the knights,' Dalinar said to the Almighty. 'And this force, this enemy, managed to kill you. You were never God. God knows everything. God cannot be killed. So who *were* you?'

The Almighty did not answer. He couldn't. Dalinar had realized that these visions were some kind of predetermined experience, like a play. The people in them could react to Dalinar, like actors who could improvise to an extent. The Almighty himself never did this.

'I will do what I can,' Dalinar said. 'I will refound them. I will prepare. You have told me many things, but there is one I have figured out on my own. If you could be killed, then the other like you – your enemy – probably can be as well.'

The darkness came upon Dalinar. The yelling and splashing faded. Had this vision occurred during a Desolation, or between? These visions never told him *enough*. As the darkness evaporated he found himself lying in a small stone chamber within his complex in the warcamps.

Navani knelt beside him, clipboard held before her, pen moving as she scribbled. Storms, she was beautiful. Mature, lips painted red, hair wound about her head in a complex braid that sparkled with rubies. Bloodred dress. She looked at him, noting that he was blinking back awake, and smiled.

'It was –' he began.

'Hush,' she said, still writing. 'That last part sounded important.' She wrote for a moment, then finally removed pen from pad, the latter held through the cloth of her sleeve. 'I think I got it all. It's hard when you change languages.'

'I changed languages?' he asked.

'At the end. Before, you were speaking Selay. An ancient form of it, certainly, but we have records of that. I hope my translators can make sense of my transcription; my command of that language is rusty. You do need to speak more slowly when you do this, dearest.'

'That can be hard, in the moment,' Dalinar said, rising. Compared to what he'd felt in the vision, the air here was cold. Rain pelted the room's closed shutters, though he knew from experience that an end to his vision meant that the storm had nearly spent itself.

Feeling drained, he walked to a seat beside the wall and settled down. Only he and Navani were in the room; he preferred it that way. Renarin and Adolin waited out the storm nearby, in another room of Dalinar's quarters and under the watchful eyes of Captain Kaladin and his bridgeman bodyguards.

Perhaps he should invite more scholars in to observe his visions; they could all write down his words, then consult to produce the most accurate version. But storms, he had enough trouble with one person watching him in such a state, raving and thrashing on the ground. He believed in the visions, even depended upon them, but that didn't mean it wasn't embarrassing.

Navani sat down beside him, and wrapped her arms around him. 'Was it bad?'

'This one? No. Not bad. Some running, then some fighting. I didn't participate. The vision ended before I needed to help.'

'Then why that expression?'

'I have to refound the Knights Radiant.'

'Refound the . . . But how? What does that even mean?'

'I don't know. I don't *know* anything; I only have hints and shadowy threats. Something dangerous is coming, that much is certain. I have to stop it.'

She rested her head on his shoulder. He stared at the hearth, which crackled softly, giving the small room a warm glow. This was one of the few hearths that hadn't been converted to the new fabrial heating devices.

He preferred the real fire, though he wouldn't say it to Navani. She worked so hard to bring new fabrials to them all.

'Why you?' Navani asked. 'Why do you have to do this?'

'Why is one man born a king, and another a beggar?' Dalinar asked. 'It is the way of the world.'

'It is that easy for you?'

'Not easy,' Dalinar said, 'but there is no point in demanding answers.'

'Particularly if the Almighty is dead. . . .'

Perhaps he should not have shared that fact with her. Speaking of just that one idea could brand him a heretic, drive his own ardents from him, give Sadeas a weapon against the Throne.

If the Almighty was dead, what did Dalinar worship? What did he believe?

'We should record your memories of the vision,' Navani said with a sigh, pulling back from him. 'While they are fresh.'

He nodded. It was important to have a description to match the transcriptions. He began to recount what he'd seen, speaking slowly enough that she could write it all down. He described the lake, the clothing of the men, the strange fortress in the distance. She claimed there were stories of large structures on the Purelake told by some who lived there. Scholars had considered them mythological.

Dalinar stood up and paced as he moved on to the description of the unholy thing that had risen from the lake. 'It left behind a hole in the lakebed,' Dalinar explained. 'Imagine if you were to outline a body on the floor, then watch that body *rip* itself free from the ground.

'Imagine the tactical advantage such a thing would have. Spren move quickly and easily. One could slip in behind battle lines, then stand up and start attacking the support staff. That beast's stone body must have been difficult to break. Storms . . . Shardblades. Makes me wonder if *these* are the things the weapons were truly designed to fight.'

Navani smiled as she wrote.

'What?' Dalinar asked, stopping in his pacing.

'You are such a soldier.'

'Yes. And?'

'And it's endearing,' she said, finishing her writing. 'What happened next?'

'The Almighty spoke to me.' He gave her the monologue as best he could remember while he paced in a slow, restful walk. *I need to sleep more,* he thought. He wasn't the youth he'd been twenty years ago, capable of staying up all night with Gavilar, listening with a cup of wine as his brother made plans, then charging to battle the next day full of vigor and hungering for a contest.

Once he was done with his narrative, Navani rose, tucking her writing implements away. She'd take what he'd said and have her scholars – well, his scholars, which she'd appropriated – work at matching his Alethi words up with the transcriptions she'd recorded. Though, of course, she'd first remove the lines where he mentioned sensitive issues, such as the Almighty's death.

She'd also search for historical references to match his descriptions. Navani liked things neat and quantified. She'd prepared a timeline of all of his visions, trying to piece them into a single narrative.

'You're still going to publish the proclamation this week?' she asked.

Dalinar nodded. He'd released it to the highprinces a week ago, in private. He'd intended to release it the same day to the camps, but Navani had convinced him that this was the wiser course. News was seeping out, but this would let the highprinces prepare.

'The proclamation will go to the public within a few days,' he said. 'Before the highprinces can put further pressure on Elhokar to retract it.'

Navani pursed her lips.

'It must be done,' Dalinar said.

'You're supposed to unite them.'

'The highprinces are spoiled children,' Dalinar said. 'Changing them will require extreme measures.'

'If you break the kingdom apart, we'll never unify it.'

'We'll make certain that it doesn't break.'

Navani looked him up and down, then smiled. 'I *am* fond of this more confident you, I must admit. Now, if I could just borrow a little of that confidence in regards to *us* . . .'

'I am quite confident about us,' he said, pulling her close.

'Is that so? Because this traveling between the king's palace and your complex wastes a lot of my time each day. If I were to move my things here – say, into your quarters – think how much more *convenient* everything would be.'

'No.'

'You're confident they won't let us marry, Dalinar. So what else are we to do? Is it the morality of the thing? You yourself said that the Almighty was dead.'

'Something is either right or it's wrong,' Dalinar said, feeling stubborn. 'The Almighty doesn't come into it.'

'God,' Navani said flatly, 'doesn't come into whether his commands are right or wrong.'

'Er. Yes.'

'Careful,' Navani said. 'You're sounding like Jasnah. Anyway, if God is dead—'

'*God* isn't dead. If the Almighty died, then he was never God, that's all.'

She sighed, still close to him. She went up on her toes and kissed him – and not demurely, either. Navani considered demureness for the coy and frivolous. So, a passionate kiss, pressing against his mouth, pushing his head backward, hungering for more. When she pulled away, Dalinar found himself breathless.

She smiled at him, then turned and picked up her things – he hadn't noticed her dropping them during the kiss – and then walked to the door. 'I am not a patient woman, you realize. I am as spoiled as those highprinces, accustomed to getting what I want.'

He snorted. Neither was true. She *could* be patient. When it suited her. What she meant was that it didn't suit her at the moment.

She opened the door, and Captain Kaladin himself peered in, inspecting the room. The bridgeman certainly was earnest. 'Watch her as she travels home for the day, soldier,' Dalinar said to him.

Kaladin saluted. Navani pushed by him and left without a goodbye, closing the door and leaving Dalinar alone again.

Dalinar sighed deeply, then walked to the chair and settled down by the hearth to think.

He started awake some time later, the fire having burned out. Storms. Was he falling asleep in the middle of the day, now? If only he didn't spend so much time at night tossing and turning, head full of worries and burdens that should never have been his. What had happened to the simple days? His hand on a sword, secure in the knowledge that Gavilar would handle the difficult parts?

Dalinar stretched, rising. He needed to go over preparations for releasing the king's proclamation, and then see to the new guards—

He stopped. The wall of his room bore a series of stark white scratches forming glyphs. They hadn't been there before.

Sixty-two days, the glyphs read. *Death follows.*

⋄

A short time later, Dalinar stood, straight-backed, hands clasped behind him as he listened to Navani confer with Rushu, one of the Kholin scholars. Adolin stood nearby, inspecting a chunk of white rock that had been found on the floor. It had apparently been pried from the row of ornamental stones rimming the room's window, then used to write the glyphs.

Straight back, head up, Dalinar told himself, *even though you want to just slump in that chair.* A leader did not slump. A leader was in control. Even when he least felt like he controlled anything.

Especially then.

'Ah,' said Rushu – a young female ardent with long eyelashes and buttonlike lips. 'Look at the sloppy lines! The improper symmetry. Whoever did this is *not* practiced with drawing glyphs. They almost spelled death wrong – it looks more like "broken." And the meaning is vague. Death follows? Or is it "follow death"? Or Sixty-Two Days of Death and Following? Glyphs are imprecise.'

'Just make the copy, Rushu,' Navani said. 'And don't speak of this to anyone.'

'Not even you?' Rushu asked, sounding distracted as she wrote.

Navani sighed, walking over to Dalinar and Adolin. 'She *is* good at what she does,' Navani said softly, 'but she's a little oblivious sometimes. Anyway, she knows handwriting better than anyone. It's one of her many areas of interest.'

Dalinar nodded, bottling his fears.

'Why would anyone do this?' Adolin asked, dropping the rock. 'Is it some kind of obscure threat?'

'No,' Dalinar said.

Navani met Dalinar's eyes. 'Rushu,' she said. 'Leave us for a moment.'

The woman didn't respond at first, but scuttled out at further prompting. As she opened the door, she revealed members of Bridge Four outside, led by Captain Kaladin, his expression dark. He'd escorted Navani away, then come back to find this – and then had immediately sent men to check on and retrieve Navani.

He obviously considered this lapse his fault, thinking that someone had sneaked into Dalinar's room while he was sleeping. Dalinar waved the captain in.

Kaladin hurried over, and hopefully didn't see how Adolin's jaw tightened as he regarded the man. Dalinar had been fighting the Parshendi Shardbearer when Kaladin and Adolin had clashed on the battlefield, but he'd heard talk of their run-in. His son certainly did not like hearing that this darkeyed bridgeman had been put in charge of the Cobalt Guard.

'Sir,' Captain Kaladin said, stepping up. 'I'm embarrassed. One week on the job, and I've failed you.'

'You did as commanded, Captain,' Dalinar said.

'I was *commanded* to keep you safe, sir,' Kaladin said, anger bleeding into his voice. 'I should have posted guards at individual doors inside your quarters, not just outside of the room complex.'

'We'll be more observant in the future, Captain,' Dalinar said. 'Your predecessor always posted the same guard as you did, and it was sufficient before.'

'Times were different before, sir,' Kaladin said, scanning the room and narrowing his eyes. He focused on the window, too small to let someone slip in. 'I still wish I knew how they got in. The guards heard nothing.'

Dalinar inspected the young soldier, scarred and dark of expression. *Why,* Dalinar thought, *do I trust this man so much?* He couldn't put his finger on it, but over the years, he'd learned to trust his instincts as a soldier and a general. Something within him urged him to trust Kaladin, and he accepted those instincts.

'This is a small matter,' Dalinar said. Kaladin looked at him sharply.

'Don't worry yourself overly much about how the person got in to scribble on my wall,' Dalinar said. 'Just be more watchful in the future. Dismissed.' He nodded to Kaladin, who retreated reluctantly, pulling the door closed.

Adolin walked over. The mop-haired youth was as tall as Dalinar was. That was hard to remember, sometimes. It didn't seem so long ago that Adolin had been an eager little boy with a wooden sword.

'You said you awoke to this here,' Navani said. 'You said you didn't see anyone enter or hear anyone make the drawing.'

Dalinar nodded.

'Then why,' she said, 'do I get the sudden and distinct impression that you *know* why it is here?'

'I don't know for certain who made it, but I know what it means.'

'What, then?' Navani demanded.

'It means we have very little time left,' Dalinar said. 'Send out the proclamation, then go to the highprinces and arrange a meeting. They'll want to speak with me.'

The Everstorm comes. . . .

Sixty-two days. Not enough time.

It was, apparently, all he had.

Freedom   Bridge 4   Kholin   Tanat

I had to spend hours watching
bridgemen to sketch their stupid
forehead glyphs so you could have
them, my friend. I'm pretty sure
this is how they were designed.
—Nazh.

Traditional   Stylized
Year 1173   Year 1173

sas   nahn

shash.

Kaladin's forehead brands   Bridge 4 Uniform Insignia

5

IDEALS

The sign on the wall proposed a greater danger, even, than its deadline. To foresee the future is of the Voidbringers.

—From the journal of Navani Kholin, Jeseses 1174

'On victory and, at long last, vengeance.' The crier carried a writ with the king's words on it – bound between two cloth-covered boards – though she obviously had the words memorized. Not surprising. Kaladin alone had made her repeat the proclamation three times. 'Again,' he said, sitting on his stone beside Bridge Four's firepit. Many members of the crew had lowered their breakfast bowls, going silent.

Nearby, Sigzil repeated the words to himself, memorizing them.

The crier sighed. She was a plump, lighteyed young woman with strands of red hair mixed in her black, bespeaking Veden or Horneater heritage. There would be dozens of women like her moving through the warcamp to read, and sometimes explain, Dalinar's words.

She opened the ledger again. *In any other battalion,* Kaladin thought idly, *its leader would be of a high enough social class to outrank her.*

'Under the authority of the king,' she said, 'Dalinar Kholin, Highprince of War, hereby orders changes to the manner of collection and distribution of gemhearts on the Shattered Plains. Henceforth, each gemheart will be collected in turn by two highprinces working in tandem. The spoils become the property of the king, who will determine – based on the effectiveness of the parties involved and their alacrity to obey – their share.

'A prescribed rotation will detail which highprinces and armies are responsible for hunting gemhearts, and in what order. The pairings will not always be the same, and will be judged based on strategic compatibility. It is expected that by the Codes we all hold dear, the men and women of these armies will welcome this renewed focus on victory and, at long last, vengeance.'

The crier snapped the book closed, looking up at Kaladin and cocking a long black eyebrow he was pretty sure had been painted on with makeup.

'Thank you,' he said. She nodded to him, then moved off toward the next battalion square.

Kaladin climbed to his feet. 'Well, there's the storm we've been expecting.'

The men nodded. Conversation at Bridge Four had been subdued, following the strange break-in at Dalinar's quarters yesterday. Kaladin felt a fool. Dalinar, however, seemed to be ignoring the break-in entirely. He knew far more than he was telling Kaladin. *How am I supposed to do my job if I don't have the information I need?*

Not two weeks on the job, and already the politics and machinations of the lighteyes were tripping him up.

'The highprinces are going to *hate* this proclamation,' Leyten said from beside the firepit, where he was working on Beld's breastplate straps, which had come from the quartermaster with the buckles twisted about. 'They base pretty much everything on getting those gemhearts. We're going to have discontent aplenty on today's winds.'

'Ha!' Rock said, ladling up curry for Lopen, who had come back for seconds. 'Discontent? Today, this will mean *riots*. Did you not hear that mention of the Codes? This thing, it is an insult against the others, whom we know do not follow their oaths.' He was smiling, and seemed to consider the anger – even rioting – of the highprinces to be amusing.

'Moash, Drehy, Mart, and Eth with me,' Kaladin said. 'We've got to go relieve Skar and his team. Teft, how goes your assignment?'

'Slowly,' Teft said. 'Those lads in the other bridge crews . . . they have a long way to go. We need something more, Kal. Some way to inspire them.'

'I'll work on it,' Kaladin said. 'For now, we should try food. Rock, we've only got five officers at the moment, so you can have that last room on the outside for storage. Kholin gave us requisition rights from the camp quartermaster. Pack it full.'

'Full?' Rock asked, an enormous grin splitting his face. 'How full?'

'*Very*,' Kaladin said. 'We've been eating broth and stew with Soulcast grain for months. For the next month, Bridge Four eats like kings.'

'No shells, now,' Mart said, pointing at Rock as he gathered his spear and did up his uniform jacket. 'Just because you can fix anything you want, it doesn't mean we're going to eat something stupid.'

'Airsick lowlanders,' Rock said. 'Don't you want to be strong?'

'I want to keep my teeth, thank you,' Mart said. 'Crazy Horneater.'

'I will fix two things,' Rock said, hand to his chest, as if making a salute. 'One for the brave and one for the silly. You may choose between these things.'

'You'll make feasts, Rock,' Kaladin said. 'I need you to train cooks for the other barracks. Even if Dalinar has extra cooks to spare now with fewer regular troops to feed, I want the bridgemen to be self-sufficient. Lopen, I'm assigning Dabbid and Shen to help you assist Rock from here on out. We need to turn those thousand men into soldiers. It starts the same way it did with all of you – by filling their stomachs.'

'It will be done,' Rock said, laughing, slapping Shen on the shoulder as the parshman stepped up for seconds. He'd only just started doing things like that, and seemed to hide in the back less than he once had. 'I will not even put any dung in it!'

The others chuckled. Putting dung in food was what had gotten Rock turned into a bridgeman in the first place. As Kaladin started out toward the king's palace – Dalinar had an important meeting with the king today – Sigzil joined him.

'A moment of your time, sir,' Sigzil said quietly.

'If you wish.'

'You promised me that I could have a chance to measure your . . . particular abilities.'

'Promised?' Kaladin asked. 'I don't remember a promise.'

'You grunted.'

'I . . . grunted?'

'When I talked about taking some measurements. You seemed to think it was a good idea, and you told Skar we could help you figure out your powers.'

'I suppose I did.'

'We need to know exactly what you can do, sir – the extent of the abilities, the length of time the Stormlight remains in you. Do you agree that having a clear understanding of your limits would be valuable?'

'Yes,' Kaladin said reluctantly.

'Excellent. Then . . .'

'Give me a couple of days,' Kaladin said. 'Go prepare a place where we can't be seen. Then . . . yes, all right. I'll let you measure me.'

'Excellent,' Sigzil said. 'I've been devising some experiments.' He stopped on the path, allowing Kaladin and the others to draw away from him.

Kaladin rested his spear on his shoulder and relaxed his hand. He frequently found his grip on the weapon too strong, his knuckles white. It was like part of him still didn't believe he could carry it in public now, and feared it would be taken from him again.

Syl floated down from her daily sprint around the camp on the morning winds. She alighted on his shoulder and sat, seeming lost in thought.

Dalinar's warcamp was an organized place. Soldiers never lounged lazily here. They were always doing something. Working on their weapons, fetching food, carrying cargo, patrolling. Men patrolled a lot in this camp. Even with the reduced army numbers, Kaladin passed three patrols as his men marched toward the gates. That was three more than he'd ever seen in Sadeas's camp.

He was reminded again of the emptiness. The dead didn't need to become Voidbringers to haunt this camp; the empty barracks did that. He passed one woman, seated on the ground beside one of those hollow barracks, staring up at the sky and clutching a bundle of masculine clothing. Two small children stood on the path beside her. Too silent. Children that small shouldn't be quiet.

The barracks formed blocks in an enormous ring, and in the center of them was a more populated part of camp – the bustling section that contained Dalinar's living complex, along with the quarters of the various highlords and generals. Dalinar's complex was a moundlike stone bunker with fluttering banners and scuttling clerks carrying armfuls of ledgers. Nearby, several officers had set up recruitment tents, and a long line of would-be soldiers had formed. Some were sellswords who had made their way to the Shattered Plains seeking work. Others were bakers or the like, who had heeded the cry for more soldiers following the disaster.

'Why didn't you laugh?' Syl said, inspecting the line as Kaladin hiked around it, on toward the gates out of the warcamp.

'I'm sorry,' he replied. 'Did you do something funny that I didn't see?'

'I mean earlier,' she said. 'Rock and the others laughed. You didn't. When you laughed during the weeks things were hard, I knew that you were forcing yourself to. I thought, maybe, once things got better . . .'

'I've got an entire battalion of bridgemen to keep track of now,' Kaladin said, eyes forward. 'And a highprince to keep alive. I'm in the middle of a camp full of widows. I guess I don't feel like laughing.'

'But things are *better*,' she said. 'For you and your men. Think of what you did, what you accomplished.'

A day spent on a plateau, slaughtering. A perfect melding of himself, his weapon, and the storms themselves. And he'd killed with it. Killed to protect a lighteyes.

He's different, Kaladin thought.

They always said that.

'I guess I'm just waiting,' Kaladin said.

'For what?'

'The thunder,' Kaladin said softly. 'It always follows after the lightning. Sometimes you have to wait, but eventually it comes.'

'I . . .' Syl zipped up in front of him, standing in the air, moving backward as he walked. She didn't fly – she didn't have wings – and didn't bob in the air. She just stood there, on nothing, and moved in unison with him. She seemed to take no notice of normal physical laws.

She cocked her head at him. 'I don't understand what you mean. Drat! I thought I was figuring this all out. Storms? Lightning?'

'You know how, when you encouraged me to fight to save Dalinar, it still hurt you when I killed?'

'Yes.'

'It's like that,' Kaladin said softly. He looked to the side. He was again gripping his spear too tightly.

Syl watched him, hands on hips, waiting for him to say more.

'Something bad is going to happen,' Kaladin said. 'Things can't just continue to be good for me. That's not how life is. It might have to do with those glyphs on Dalinar's wall yesterday. They seemed like a countdown.'

She nodded.

'Have you ever seen anything like that before?'

'I remember ... something,' she whispered. 'Something bad. Seeing what is to come – it isn't of Honor, Kaladin. It's something else. Something dangerous.'

Wonderful.

When he said nothing more, Syl sighed and zipped into the air, becoming a ribbon of light. She followed him up there, moving between gusts of wind.

She said that she's honorspren, Kaladin thought. *So why does she still keep up the act of playing with winds?*

He'd have to ask her, assuming she'd answer him. Assuming she even knew the answer.

⁂

Torol Sadeas laced his fingers before himself, elbows on the fine stonework tabletop, as he stared at the Shardblade he'd thrust down through the center of the table. It reflected his face.

Damnation. When had he gotten old? He imagined himself as a young man, in his twenties. Now he was fifty. Storming *fifty*. He set his jaw, looking at that Blade.

Oathbringer. It was Dalinar's Shardblade – curved, like a back arching, with a hooklike tip on the end matched by a sequence of jutting serrations by the crossguard. Like waves in motion, peeking up from the ocean below.

How often had he lusted for this weapon? Now it was his, but he found the possession hollow. Dalinar Kholin – driven mad by grief, broken to the point that battle frightened him – still clung to life. Sadeas's old friend was like a favored axehound he'd been forced to put down, only to find it whimpering at the window, the poison having not quite done its work.

Worse, he couldn't shake the feeling that Dalinar had gotten the *better* of him somehow.

The door to his sitting room opened, and Ialai slipped in. With a slender neck and a large mouth, his wife had never been described as a beauty – particularly as the years stretched long. He didn't care. Ialai was the most dangerous woman he knew. That was more attractive than any simple pretty face.

'You've destroyed my table, I see,' she said, eyeing the Shardblade slammed down through the center. She flopped down onto the small couch beside him, draped one arm across his back, and put her feet up on the table.

While with others, she was the perfect Alethi woman. In private, she preferred to lounge. 'Dalinar is recruiting heavily,' she said. 'I've taken the opportunity to place a few more of my associates among the staff of his warcamp.'

'Soldiers?'

'What do you take me for? That would be far too obvious; he will have new soldiers under careful watch. However, much of his support staff has holes as men join the call to take up spears and reinforce his army.'

Sadeas nodded, still staring at that Blade. His wife ran the most impressive network of spies in the warcamps. Most impressive indeed, since very, very few knew of it. She scratched at his back, sending shivers up the skin.

'He released his proclamation,' Ialai noted.

'Yes. Reactions?'

'As anticipated. The others hate it.'

Sadeas nodded. 'Dalinar should be dead, but since he is not, at least we can depend upon him to hang himself in time.' Sadeas narrowed his eyes. 'By destroying him, I sought to prevent the collapse of the kingdom. Now I'm wondering if that collapse wouldn't be better for us all.'

'What?'

'I'm not meant for this, love,' Sadeas whispered. 'This stupid game on the plateaus. It sated me at first, but I'm growing to loathe it. I want *war*, Ialai. Not hours of marching on the off chance that we'll find some little skirmish!'

'Those little skirmishes bring us wealth.'

Which was why he'd suffered them so long. He rose. 'I will need to meet with some of the others. Aladar. Ruthar. We need to fan the flames among the other highprinces, raise their indignation at what Dalinar attempts.'

'And our end goal?'

'I will have it back, Ialai,' he said, resting his fingers on Oathbringer's hilt. 'The conquest.'

It was the only thing that made him feel alive any longer. That glorious, wonderful Thrill of being on the battlefield and striving, man against man. Of risking everything for the prize. Domination. Victory.

It was the only time he felt like a youth again.

It was a brutal truth. The best truths, however, were simple.

He grabbed Oathbringer by the hilt and yanked it up out of the table. 'Dalinar wants to play politician now, which is unsurprising. He has always secretly wanted to be his brother. Fortunately for us, Dalinar is no good at this sort of thing. His proclamation will alienate the others. He will push the highprinces, and they'll take up arms against him, fracturing the kingdom. And then, with blood at my feet and Dalinar's own sword in my hand, I will forge a new Alethkar from flame and tears.'

'What if, instead, he succeeds?'

'That, my dear, is when your assassins will be of use.' He dismissed the Shardblade; it turned to mist and vanished. 'I will conquer this kingdom anew, and then Jah Keved will follow. After all, the purpose of this life is to train soldiers. In a way, I'm only doing what God himself wants.'

⋄

The walk between the barracks and the king's palace – which the king had started calling the Pinnacle – took an hour or so, which gave Kaladin plenty of time to think. Unfortunately, on his way, he passed a group of Dalinar's surgeons in a field with servants, gathering knobweed sap for an antiseptic.

Seeing them made Kaladin think not only of his own efforts gathering the sap, but of his father. Lirin.

If he were here, Kaladin thought as he passed them, *he'd ask why I wasn't out there, with the surgeons. He'd demand to know why, if Dalinar had taken me in, I hadn't requested to join his medical corps.*

In fact, Kaladin could probably have gotten Dalinar to employ all of Bridge Four as surgeons' assistants. Kaladin could have trained them in medicine almost as easily as he had the spear. Dalinar would have done it. An army could never have too many good surgeons.

He hadn't even considered it. The choice for him had been simpler

– either become Dalinar's bodyguards or leave the warcamps. Kaladin had chosen to put his men in the path of the storm again. Why?

Eventually, they reached the king's palace, which was built up the side of a large stone hill, with tunnels dug down into the rock. The king's own quarters sat at the very top. That meant lots of climbing for Kaladin and his men.

They hiked up the switchbacks, Kaladin still lost in thought about his father and his duty.

'That's a tad unfair, you know,' Moash said as they reached the top.

Kaladin looked to the others, realizing that they were puffing from the long climb. Kaladin, however, had drawn in Stormlight without noticing. He wasn't even winded.

He smiled pointedly for Syl's benefit, and regarded the cavernous hallways of the Pinnacle. A few men stood guard at the entrance gates, wearing the blue and gold of the King's Guard, a separate and distinct unit from Dalinar's own guard.

'Soldier,' Kaladin said with a nod to one of them, a lighteyes of low rank. Militarily, Kaladin outranked a man like this – but not socially. Again, he wasn't certain how all of this was supposed to work.

The man looked him up and down. 'I heard you held a bridge, practically by yourself, against hundreds of Parshendi. How'd you do that?' He did not address Kaladin with 'sir,' as would have been appropriate for any other captain.

'You want to find out?' Moash snapped from behind. 'We can show you. Personally.'

'Hush,' Kaladin said, glaring at Moash. He turned back to the soldier. 'I got lucky. That's it.' He stared the man in the eyes.

'I suppose that makes sense,' the soldier said.

Kaladin waited.

'Sir,' the soldier finally added.

Kaladin waved his men forward, and they passed the lighteyed guards. The interior of the palace was lit by spheres grouped in lamps on the walls – sapphires and diamonds blended to give a blue-white cast. The spheres were a small but striking reminder of how things had changed. Nobody would have let bridgemen near such casual use of spheres.

The Pinnacle was still unfamiliar to Kaladin – so far, his time spent guarding Dalinar had mostly been in the warcamp. However, he'd made certain to look over maps of the place, so he knew the way to the top.

'Why did you cut me off like that?' Moash demanded, catching up to Kaladin.

'You were in the wrong,' Kaladin said. 'You're a soldier now, Moash. You're going to have to learn to act like one. And that means not provoking fights.'

'I'm not going to scrape and bow before lighteyes, Kal. Not anymore.'

'I don't expect you to scrape, but I *do* expect you to watch your tongue. Bridge Four is better than petty gibes and threats.'

Moash fell back, but Kaladin could tell he was still smoldering.

'That's odd,' Syl said, landing on Kaladin's shoulder again. 'He looks so angry.'

'When I took over the bridgemen,' Kaladin said softly, 'they were caged animals who had been beaten into submission. I brought back their fight, but they were still caged. Now the doors are off those cages. It will take time for Moash and the others to adjust.'

They would. During the final weeks as bridgemen, they'd learned to act with the precision and discipline of soldiers. They stood at attention while their abusers marched across bridges, never uttering a word of derision. Their discipline itself had become their weapon.

They'd learn to be real soldiers. No, they *were* real soldiers. Now they had to learn how to act without Sadeas's oppression to push against.

Moash moved up beside him. 'I'm sorry,' he said softly. 'You're right.'

Kaladin smiled, this time genuinely.

'I'm not going to pretend I don't hate them,' Moash said. 'But I'll be civil. We have a duty. We'll do it well. Better than anyone expects. We're Bridge Four.'

'Good man,' Kaladin said. Moash was going to be particularly tricky to deal with, as more and more, Kaladin found himself confiding in the man. Most of the others idolized Kaladin. Not Moash, who was as close to a real friend as Kaladin had known since being branded.

The hallway grew surprisingly decorative as they approached the king's conference chamber. There was even a series of reliefs being carved on the walls – the Heralds, embellished with gemstones on the rock to glow at appropriate locations.

More and more like a city, Kaladin thought to himself. *This might actually be a true palace soon.*

He met Skar and his team at the door into the king's conference chambers. 'Report?' Kaladin asked softly.

'Quiet morning,' Skar said. 'And I'm fine with that.'

'You're relieved for the day, then,' Kaladin said. 'I'll stay here for the meeting, then let Moash take the afternoon shift. I'll come back for the evening shift. You and your squad get some sleep; you'll be back on duty tonight, stretching to tomorrow morning.'

'Got it, sir,' Skar said, saluting. He collected his men and moved off.

The chamber beyond the doors was decorated with a thick rug and large unshuttered windows on the leeward side. Kaladin had never been in this room, and the palace maps – for the protection of the king – only included the basic hallways and routes through the servants' quarters. This room had one other door, probably out onto the balcony, but no exits other than the one Kaladin stepped through.

Two other guards in blue and gold stood on either side of the door. The king himself paced back and forth beside the room's desk. His nose was larger than the paintings of him showed.

Dalinar spoke with Highlady Navani, an elegant woman with grey in her hair. The scandalous relationship between the king's uncle and mother would have been the talk of the warcamp, if Sadeas's betrayal hadn't overshadowed it.

'Moash,' Kaladin said, pointing. 'See where that door goes. Mart and Eth, stand watch just outside in the hall. Nobody other than a highprince comes in until you've checked with us in here.'

Moash gave the king a salute instead of a bow, and checked on the door. It indeed led to the balcony that Kaladin had spotted from below. It ran all around this upmost room.

Dalinar studied Kaladin and Moash as they worked. Kaladin saluted, and met the man's eyes. He wasn't going to fail again, as he'd done the day before.

'I don't recognize these guards, Uncle,' the king said with annoyance.

'They're new,' Dalinar said. 'There is no other way onto that balcony, soldier. It's a hundred feet in the air.'

'Good to know,' Kaladin said. 'Drehy, join Moash out there on the balcony, close the door, and keep watch.'

Drehy nodded, jumping into motion.

'I just said there's no way to reach that balcony from the outside,' Dalinar said.

'Then that's the way I'd try to get in,' Kaladin said, 'if I wanted to, sir.'

Dalinar smiled in amusement.

The king, however, was nodding. 'Good . . . good.'

'Are there any other ways into this room, Your Majesty?' Kaladin asked. 'Secret entrances, passages?'

'If there were,' the king said, 'I wouldn't want people knowing about them.'

'My men can't keep this room safe if we don't know what to guard. If there are passages nobody is supposed to know about, those are immediately suspect. If you share them with me, I'll use only my officers in guarding them.'

The king stared at Kaladin for a moment, then turned to Dalinar. 'I *like* this one. Why haven't you put him in charge of your guard before?'

'I haven't had the opportunity,' Dalinar said, studying Kaladin with eyes that had a *depth* behind them. A weight. He stepped over and rested a hand on Kaladin's shoulder, pulling him aside.

'Wait,' the king said from behind, 'is that a *captain's* insignia? On a darkeyes? When did that start happening?'

Dalinar didn't answer, instead walking Kaladin to the side of the room. 'The king,' he said softly, 'is very worried about assassins. You should know this.'

'A healthy paranoia makes the job easier for his bodyguards, sir,' Kaladin said.

'I didn't say it was healthy,' Dalinar said. 'You call me "sir." The common address is "Brightlord."'

'I will use that term if you command, sir,' Kaladin said, meeting the man's eyes. 'But "sir" is an appropriate address, even for a lighteyes, if he's your direct superior.'

'I'm a highprince.'

'Speaking frankly,' Kaladin said – he wouldn't ask for permission. This man had put him in the role, so Kaladin would assume it came with certain privileges, unless told otherwise. 'Every man I've ever called "Brightlord" has betrayed me. A few men I've called "sir" still have my trust to this day. I use one more reverently than the other. Sir.'

'You're an odd one, son.'

'The normal ones are dead in the chasms, sir,' Kaladin said softly. 'Sadeas saw to that.'

'Well, have your men on the balcony guard from farther to the side, where they can't hear through the window.'

'I'll wait with the men in the hall, then,' Kaladin said, noticing that the two men of the King's Guard had already moved through the doors.

'I didn't order that,' Dalinar said. 'Guard the doors, but on the inside. I want you to hear what we're planning. Just don't repeat it outside this room.'

'Yes, sir.'

'Four more people are coming to the meeting,' Dalinar said. 'My sons, General Khal, and Brightness Teshav, Khal's wife. They may enter. Anyone else should be kept back until the meeting is over.'

Dalinar went back to a conversation with the king's mother. Kaladin got Moash and Drehy positioned, then explained the door protocol to Mart and Eth. He'd have to do some training later. Lighteyes never truly meant 'Don't let anyone else in' when they said 'Don't let anyone else in.' What they meant was 'If you let anyone else in, I'd better agree that it was important enough, or you're in trouble.'

Then, Kaladin took his post inside the closed door, standing against a wall with carved paneling made of a rare type of wood he didn't recognize. *It's probably worth more than I've earned in my entire lifetime,* he thought idly. *One wooden panel.*

The highprince's sons arrived, Adolin and Renarin Kholin. Kaladin had seen the former on the battlefield, though he looked different without his Shardplate. Less imposing. More like a spoiled rich boy. Oh, he wore a uniform like everyone else, but the buttons were engraved, and the boots ... those were expensive hogshide ones without a scuff on them. Brand new, likely bought at ridiculous expense.

He did save that woman in the market, though, Kaladin thought, remembering the encounter from weeks ago. *Don't forget about that.*

Kaladin wasn't sure what to make of Renarin. The youth – he might have been older than Kaladin, but sure didn't look it – wore spectacles and walked after his brother like a shadow. Those slender limbs and delicate fingers had never known battle or real work.

Syl bobbed around the room, poking into nooks, crannies, and vases. She stopped at a paperweight on the women's writing desk beside the king's chair, poking at the block of crystal with a strange kind of crabthing trapped inside. Were those wings?

'Shouldn't that one wait outside?' Adolin asked, nodding toward Kaladin.

'What we're doing is going to put me in direct danger,' Dalinar said, hands clasped behind his back. 'I want him to know the details. That might be important to his job.' Dalinar didn't look toward Adolin or Kaladin.

Adolin walked up, taking Dalinar by the arm and speaking in a hushed tone that was not so soft that Kaladin couldn't hear. 'We barely know him.'

'We have to trust some people, Adolin,' his father said in a normal voice. 'If there's one person in this army I can guarantee isn't working for Sadeas, it's that soldier.' He turned and glanced at Kaladin, once again studying him with those unfathomable eyes.

He didn't see me with the Stormlight, Kaladin told himself forcefully. *He was practically unconscious. He doesn't know.*

Does he?

Adolin threw up his hands but walked to the other side of the room, muttering something to his brother. Kaladin remained in position, standing comfortably at parade rest. *Yes, definitely spoiled.*

The general who arrived soon after was a limber, bald man with a straight back and pale yellow eyes. His wife, Teshav, had a pinched face and hair streaked blond. She took up position by the writing desk, which Navani had made no move to occupy.

'Reports,' Dalinar said from the window as the door clicked shut behind the two newcomers.

'I suspect you know what you'll hear, Brightlord,' said Teshav. 'They're irate. They sincerely hoped you would reconsider the command – and sending it out to the public has provoked them. Highprince Hatham was the only one to make a public announcement. He plans to – and I quote – "see that the king is dissuaded from this reckless and ill-advised course."'

The king sighed, settling into his seat. Renarin sat down immediately, as did the general. Adolin found his seat more reluctantly.

Dalinar remained standing, looking out the window.

'Uncle?' the king asked. 'Did you hear that reaction? It's a good thing you didn't go so far as you had considered: to proclaim that they *must* follow the Codes or face seizure of assets. We'd be in the middle of a rebellion.'

'That will come,' Dalinar said. 'I still wonder if I should have announced it all at once. When you've got an arrow stuck in you, it's sometimes best to just yank it out in one pull.'

Actually, when you had an arrow in you, the best thing to do was leave it there until you could find a surgeon. Often it would plug the blood flow and keep you alive. It was probably best not to speak up and undermine the highprince's metaphor, however.

'Storms, what a ghastly image,' the king said, wiping his face with a handkerchief. 'Do you have to say such things, Uncle? I *already* fear we'll be dead before the week is out.'

'Your father and I survived worse than this,' Dalinar said.

'You had allies, then! Three highprinces for you, only six against, and you never fought them all at the same time.'

'If the highprinces unite against us,' General Khal said, 'we will not be able to stand firm. We'll have no choice but to rescind this proclamation, which will weaken the Throne considerably.'

The king leaned back, hand to his forehead. 'Jezerezeh, this is going to be a disaster. . . .'

Kaladin raised an eyebrow.

'You disagree?' Syl asked, moving over toward him as a cluster of fluttering leaves. It was disconcerting to hear her voice coming from such shapes. The others in the room, of course, couldn't see or hear her.

'No,' Kaladin whispered. 'This proclamation sounds like a real tempest. I just expected the king to be less . . . well, whiny.'

'We need to secure allies,' Adolin said. 'Form a coalition. Sadeas will gather one, and so we counter him with our own.'

'Dividing the kingdom into two?' Teshav said, shaking her head. 'I don't see how a civil war would serve the Throne. Particularly one we're unlikely to win.'

'This could be the end of Alethkar as a kingdom,' the general agreed.

'Alethkar ended as a kingdom centuries ago,' Dalinar said softly, staring out that window. 'This thing we have created is not Alethkar. Alethkar was justice. We are children wearing our father's cloak.'

'But Uncle,' the king said, 'at least the kingdom is *something*. More than it has been in centuries! If we fail here, and fracture to ten warring princedoms, it will negate everything my father worked for!'

'This isn't what your father worked for, son,' Dalinar said. 'This game on the Shattered Plains, this nauseating political farce. This isn't what Gavilar envisioned. The Everstorm comes. . . .'

'What?' the king asked.

Dalinar turned from the window finally, walking to the others, and rested his hand on Navani's shoulder. 'We're going to find a way to do this, or we're going to destroy the kingdom in the process. I won't suffer this charade any longer.'

Kaladin, arms folded, tapped one finger against his elbow. 'Dalinar acts like he's the king,' he mouthed, whispering so softly only Syl could hear. 'And everyone else does as well.' Troubling. It was like what Amaram had done. Seizing the power he saw before him, even if it wasn't his.

Navani looked up at Dalinar, raising her hand to rest on his. She was in on whatever he was planning, judging by that expression.

The king wasn't. He sighed lightly. 'You've *obviously* got a plan, Uncle. Well? Out with it. This drama is tiring.'

'What I really want to do,' Dalinar said frankly, 'is beat the lot of them senseless. That's what I'd do to new recruits who weren't willing to obey orders.'

'I think you'll have a hard time *spanking* obedience into the high-princes, Uncle,' the king said dryly. For some reason, he absently rubbed at his chest.

'You need to disarm them,' Kaladin found himself saying.

All eyes in the room turned toward him. Brightness Teshav gave him a frown, as if speaking were not Kaladin's right. It probably wasn't.

Dalinar, however, nodded toward him. 'Soldier? You have a suggestion?'

'Your pardon, sir,' Kaladin said. 'And your pardon, Your Majesty. But if a squad is giving you trouble, the first thing you do is separate its members. Split them up, stick them in better squads. I don't think you can do that here.'

'I don't know how we'd break apart the highprinces,' Dalinar said. 'I doubt I could stop them from associating with one another. Perhaps if this war were won, I could assign different highprinces different duties, send them off, then work on them individually. But for the time being, we are trapped here.'

'Well, the second thing you do to troublemakers,' Kaladin said, 'is you disarm them. They're easier to control if you make them turn in their spears. It's embarrassing, makes them feel like recruits again. So . . . can you take their troops away from them, maybe?'

'We can't, I'm afraid,' Dalinar said. 'The soldiers swore allegiance to their lighteyes, not to the Crown specifically – it's only the highprinces who have sworn to the Crown. However, you are thinking along the right lines.'

He squeezed Navani's shoulder. 'For the last two weeks,' he said, 'I've been trying to decide how to approach this problem. My gut tells me that I need to treat the highprinces – the entire lighteyed population of Alethkar – like new recruits, in need of discipline.'

'He came to me, and we talked,' Navani said. 'We can't *actually* bust the highprinces down to a manageable rank, as much as Dalinar would like to do just that. Instead, we need to lead them to believe that we're *going* to take it all from them, if they don't shape up.'

'This proclamation will make them mad,' Dalinar said. 'I *want* them mad. I want them to think about the war, their place here, and I want to remind them of Gavilar's assassination. If I can push them to act more like soldiers, even if it starts with them taking up arms against me, then I might be able to persuade them. I can reason with soldiers. Regardless, a big part of this will involve the threat that I'm going to take away their authority and power if they don't use it correctly. And that begins, as Captain Kaladin suggested, with disarming them.'

'Disarm the *highprinces*?' the king asked. 'What foolishness is this?'

'It's not foolishness,' Dalinar said, smiling. 'We can't take their armies from them, but we *can* do something else. Adolin, I intend to take the lock off your scabbard.'

Adolin frowned, considering that for a moment. Then a wide grin split his face. 'You mean, letting me duel again? For real?'

'Yes,' Dalinar said. He turned to the king. 'For the longest time, I've forbidden him from important bouts, as the Codes prohibit duels of honor between officers at war. More and more, however, I've come to realize that the others don't see themselves as being at war. They're playing a game. It's time to allow Adolin to duel the camp's other Shardbearers in official bouts.'

'So he can humiliate them?' the king asked.

'It wouldn't be about humiliation; it would be about depriving them of their Shards.' Dalinar stepped into the middle of the group of chairs. 'The highprinces would have a hard time fighting against us if we controlled all of the Shardblades and Shardplate in the army. Adolin, I want you to challenge the Shardbearers of other highprinces in duels of honor, the prizes being the Shards themselves.'

'They won't agree to it,' General Khal said. 'They'll refuse the bouts.'

'We'll have to make sure they agree,' Dalinar said. 'Find a way to force them, or shame them, into the fights. I've considered that this would probably be easier if we could ever track down where Wit ran off to.'

'What happens if the lad loses?' General Khal asked. 'This plan seems too unpredictable.'

'We'll see,' Dalinar said. 'This is only one part of what we will do, the smaller part – but also the most visible part. Adolin, everyone tells me how good you are at dueling, and you have pestered me incessantly to relax my prohibition. There are thirty Shardbearers in the army, not counting our own. Can you defeat that many men?'

'Can I?' Adolin said, grinning. 'I'll do it without breaking a sweat, so long as I can start with Sadeas himself.'

So he's spoiled and *cocky*, Kaladin thought.

'No,' Dalinar said. 'Sadeas won't accept a personal challenge, though eventually bringing him down is our goal. We start with some of the lesser Shardbearers and work up to him.'

The others in the room seemed troubled. That included Brightness Navani, who drew her lips to a line and glanced at Adolin. She might be in on Dalinar's plan, but she didn't love the idea of her nephew dueling.

She didn't say so. 'As Dalinar indicated,' Navani said, 'this won't be our entire plan. Hopefully, Adolin's duels won't need to go far. They are meant mostly to inspire worry and fear, to apply pressure to some factions who are working against us. The greater part of what we must do will entail a complex and determined political effort to connect with those who can be swayed to our side.'

'Navani and I will work to persuade the highprinces of the advantages of a truly unified Alethkar,' Dalinar said, nodding. 'Though the Storm-father knows, I'm less certain of my political acumen than Adolin is of his dueling. It is what must be. If Adolin is to be the stick, I must be the feather.'

'There will be assassins, Uncle,' Elhokar said, sounding tired. 'I don't think Khal is right; I don't think Alethkar will shatter immediately. The highprinces have come to like the idea of being one kingdom. But they also like their sport, their fun, their gemhearts. So they will send assassins. Quietly, at first, and probably not directly at you or me. Our families. Sadeas and the others will try to hurt us, make us back down. Are you willing to risk your sons on this? How about my mother?'

'Yes, you are right,' Dalinar said. 'I hadn't . . . but yes. That is how they think.' He sounded regretful to Kaladin.

'And you're still willing to go through with this plan?' the king asked.

'I have no choice,' Dalinar said, turning away, walking back toward the window. Looking out westward, in toward the continent.

'Then at least tell me this,' Elhokar said. 'What is your endgame, Uncle? What is it you want out of all of this? In a year, if we survive this fiasco, what do you want us to be?'

Dalinar put his hands on the thick stone windowsill. He stared out, as if at something he could see and the rest of them could not. 'I'll have us be what we were before, son. A kingdom that can stand through storms, a kingdom that is a light and not a darkness. I will have a truly unified Alethkar, with highprinces who are loyal and just. I'll have more than that.' He tapped the windowsill. 'I'm going to refound the Knights Radiant.'

Kaladin nearly dropped his spear in shock. Fortunately, nobody was watching him – they were leaping to their feet, staring at Dalinar.

'The Radiants?' Brightness Teshav demanded. 'Are you mad? You're going to try to rebuild a sect of traitors who gave us over to the Voidbringers?'

'The rest of this sounds good, Father,' Adolin said, stepping forward. 'I know you think about the Radiants a lot, but you see them . . . differently than everyone else. It won't go well if you announce that you want to emulate them.'

The king just groaned, burying his face in his hands.

'People are wrong about them,' Dalinar said. 'And even if they are not, the original Radiants – the ones instituted by the Heralds – are something even the Vorin church admits were once moral and just. We'll need to remind people that the Knights Radiant, as an order, stood for something grand. If they hadn't, then they wouldn't have been able to 'fall' as the stories claim they did.'

'But *why*?' Elhokar asked. 'What is the point?'

'It is what I must do.' Dalinar hesitated. 'I'm not completely certain why, yet. Only that I've been instructed to do it. As a protection, and a preparation, for what is coming. A storm of some sort. Perhaps it is as simple as the other highprinces turning against us. I doubt that, but perhaps.'

'Father,' Adolin said, hand on Dalinar's arm. 'This is all well and good, and maybe you can change people's perception of the Radiants, but ... Ishar's soul, Father! They could do things we cannot. Simply naming someone a Radiant won't give them fanciful powers, like in the stories.'

'The Radiants were about more than what they could do,' Dalinar said. 'They were about an ideal. The kind of ideal we're lacking, these days. We may not be able to reach for the ancient Surgebindings – the powers they had – but we can seek to emulate the Radiants in other ways. I am set on this. Do not try to dissuade me.'

The others did not seem convinced.

Kaladin narrowed his eyes. So did Dalinar know about Kaladin's powers, or didn't he? The meeting moved on to more mundane topics, such as how to maneuver Shardbearers into facing Adolin and how to step up patrols of the surrounding area. Dalinar considered making the warcamps safe to be a prerequisite for what he was attempting.

When the meeting finally ended, most people inside departing to carry out orders, Kaladin was still considering what Dalinar had said about the Radiants. The man hadn't realized it, but he'd been very accurate. The Knights Radiant did have ideals – and they'd called them that very thing. The Five Ideals, the Immortal Words.

Life before death, Kaladin thought, playing with a sphere he'd pulled from his pocket, *strength before weakness, journey before destination.* Those Words made up the First Ideal in its entirety. He had only an inkling of what it meant, but his ignorance hadn't stopped him from figuring out the Second Ideal of the Windrunners, the oath to protect those who could not protect themselves.

Syl wouldn't tell him the other three. She said he would know them when he needed to. Or he wouldn't, and would not progress.

Did he want to progress? To become what? A member of the Knights

Radiant? Kaladin hadn't asked for someone else's ideals to rule his life. He'd just wanted to survive. Now, somehow, he was headed straight down a path that no man had trod in centuries. Potentially becoming something that people across Roshar would hate or revere. So much attention . . .

'Soldier?' Dalinar asked, stopping by the door.

'Sir.' Kaladin stood up straight again and saluted. It felt *good* to do that, to stand at attention, to find a place. He wasn't certain if it was the good feeling of remembering a life he'd once loved, or if it was the pathetic feeling of an axehound finding its leash again.

'My nephew was right,' Dalinar said, watching the king retreat down the hallway. 'The others might try to hurt my family. It's how they think. I'm going to need guard details on Navani and my sons at all times. Your best men.'

'I've got about two dozen of those, sir,' Kaladin said. 'That's not enough for full guard details running all day protecting all four of you. I should have more men trained before too long, but putting a spear in the hands of a bridgeman does not make him a soldier, let alone a good bodyguard.'

Dalinar nodded, looking troubled. He rubbed his chin.

'Sir?'

'Your force isn't the only one stretched thin in this warcamp, soldier,' Dalinar said. 'I lost a lot of men to Sadeas's betrayal. Very good men. Now I have a deadline. Just over sixty days . . .'

Kaladin felt a chill. The highprince was taking the number found scrawled on his wall very seriously.

'Captain,' Dalinar said softly, 'I need every able-bodied man I can get. I need to be training them, rebuilding my army, preparing for the storm. I need them assaulting plateaus, clashing with the Parshendi, to get battle experience.'

What did this have to do with him? 'You promised that my men wouldn't be required to fight on plateau runs.'

'I'll keep that promise,' Dalinar said. 'But there are two hundred and fifty soldiers in the King's Guard. They include some of my last remaining battle-ready officers, and I will need to put them in charge of new recruits.'

'I'm not just going to have to watch over your family, am I?' Kaladin asked, feeling a new weight settling in his shoulders. 'You're implying you want to turn over guarding the *king* to me as well.'

'Yes,' Dalinar said. 'Slowly, but yes. I need those soldiers. Beyond that, maintaining two separate guard forces seems like a mistake to me. I feel that your men, considering your background, are the least likely to include spies for my enemies. You should know that a while back, there may have been an attempt on the king's life. I still haven't figured out who was behind it, but I worry that some of his guards may have been involved.'

Kaladin took a deep breath. 'What happened?'

'Elhokar and I hunted a chasmfiend,' Dalinar said. 'During that hunt, at a time of stress, the king's Plate came close to failing. We found that many of the gemstones powering it had likely been replaced with ones that were flawed, making them crack under stress.'

'I don't know much of Plate, sir,' Kaladin said. 'Could they have just broken on their own, without sabotage?'

'Possible, but unlikely. I want your men to take shifts guarding the palace and the king, alternating with some of the King's Guard, to get you familiar with him and the palace. It might also help your men learn from the more experienced guards. At the same time, I'm going to start siphoning off the officers from his guard to train soldiers in my army.

'Over the next few weeks, we'll merge your group and the King's Guard into one. You'll be in charge. Once you've trained bridgemen from those other crews well enough, we'll replace soldiers in the guard with your men, and move the soldiers to my army.' He looked Kaladin in the eyes. 'Can you do this, soldier?'

'Yes, sir,' Kaladin said, though part of him was panicking. 'I can.'

'Good.'

'Sir, a suggestion. You've said you're going to expand patrols outside the warcamps, trying to police the hills around the Shattered Plains?'

'Yes. The number of bandits out there is embarrassing. This is Alethi land now. It needs to follow Alethi laws.'

'I have a thousand men I need to train,' Kaladin said. 'If I could patrol them out there, it might help them feel like soldiers. I could use a large enough force that it sends a message to the bandits, maybe making them withdraw – but my men won't need to see much combat.'

'Good. General Khal had been in command of patrol duty, but he's now my most senior commander, and will be needed for other things.

Train your men. Our goal will eventually be to have your thousand doing real roadway patrols between here, Alethkar, and the ports to the south and east. I'll want scouting teams, watching for signs of bandit camps and searching out caravans that have been attacked. I need numbers on how much activity is out there, and just how dangerous it is.'

'I'll see to it personally, sir.'

Storms. How was he going to do all of this?

'Good,' Dalinar said.

Dalinar walked from the chamber, clasping his hands behind him, as if lost in thought. Moash, Eth, and Mart fell in after him, as ordered by Kaladin. He'd have two men with Dalinar at all times, three if he could manage it. He'd once hoped to expand that to four or five, but storms, with so many to watch over now, that was going to be impossible.

Who is this man? Kaladin thought, watching Dalinar's retreating form. He ran a good camp. You could judge a man – and Kaladin did – by the men who followed him.

But a tyrant could have a good camp with disciplined soldiers. This man, Dalinar Kholin, had helped unite Alethkar – and had done so by wading through blood. Now . . . now he spoke like a king, even when the king himself was in the room.

He wants to rebuild the Knights Radiant, Kaladin thought. That wasn't something Dalinar Kholin could accomplish through simple force of will.

Unless he had help.

6

TERRIBLE DESTRUCTION

We had never considered that there might be Parshendi spies hiding among our slaves. This is something else I should have seen.

—From the journal of Navani Kholin, Jesesan 1174

Shallan sat again on her box on the ship's deck, though she now wore a hat on her head, a coat over her dress, and a glove on her freehand – her safehand was, of course, pinned inside its sleeve.

The chill out here on the open ocean was something unreal. The captain said that far to the south, the ocean itself actually froze. That sounded incredible; she'd like to see it. She'd occasionally seen snow and ice in Jah Keved, during the odd winter. But an entire ocean of it? Amazing.

She wrote with gloved fingers as she observed the spren she'd named Pattern. At the moment, he had lifted himself up off the surface of the deck, forming a ball of swirling blackness – infinite lines that twisted in ways she could never have captured on the flat page. Instead, she wrote descriptions supplemented with sketches.

'Food ...' Pattern said. The sound had a buzzing quality and he vibrated when he spoke.

'Yes,' Shallan said. 'We eat it.' She selected a small limafruit from the bowl beside her and placed it in her mouth, then chewed and swallowed.

'Eat,' Pattern said. 'You ... make it ... into you.'

'Yes! Exactly.'

He dropped down, the darkness vanishing as he entered the wooden deck of the ship. Once again, he became part of the material – making the wood ripple as if it were water. He slid across the floor, then moved up the box beside her to the bowl of small green fruits. Here, he moved *across* them, each fruit's rind puckering and rising with the shape of his pattern.

'Terrible!' he said, the sound vibrating up from the bowl.

'Terrible?'

'Destruction!'

'What? No, it's how we survive. Everything needs to eat.'

'Terrible destruction to eat!' He sounded aghast. He retreated from the bowl to the deck.

Pattern connects increasingly complex thoughts, Shallan wrote. *Abstractions come easily to him. Early, he asked me the questions 'Why? Why you? Why be?' I interpreted this as asking me my purpose. When I replied, 'To find truth,' he easily seemed to grasp my meaning. And yet, some simple realities – such as why people would need to eat – completely escape him. It—*

She stopped writing as the paper puckered and rose, Pattern appearing on the sheet itself, his tiny ridges lifting the letters she had just penned.

'Why this?' he asked.

'To remember.'

'Remember,' he said, trying the word.

'It means . . .' Stormfather. How did she explain memory? 'It means to be able to know what you did in the past. In other moments, ones that happened days ago.'

'Remember,' he said. 'I . . . cannot . . . remember . . .'

'What is the first thing you do remember?' Shallan asked. 'Where were you first?'

'First,' Pattern said. 'With you.'

'On the ship?' Shallan said, writing.

'No. Green. Food. Food not eaten.'

'Plants?' Shallan asked.

'Yes. Many plants.' He vibrated, and she thought she could hear in that vibration the blowing of wind through branches. Shallan breathed in. She could almost *see* it. The deck in front of her changing to a dirt path, her box becoming a stone bench. Faintly. Not really there, but *almost.* Her father's gardens. Pattern on the ground, drawn in the dust . . .

'Remember,' Pattern said, voice like a whisper.

No, Shallan thought, horrified. *NO!*

The image vanished. It hadn't really been there in the first place, had it? She raised her safehand to her breast, breathing in and out in sharp gasps. No.

'Hey, young miss!' Yalb said from behind. 'Tell the new kid here what happened in Kharbranth!'

Shallan turned, heart still racing, to see Yalb walking over with the 'new kid,' a six-foot-tall hulk of a man who was at least five years Yalb's senior. They'd picked him up at Amydlatn, the last port. Tozbek wanted to be sure they wouldn't be undermanned during the last leg to New Natanan.

Yalb squatted down beside her stool. In the face of the chill, he'd acquiesced to wearing a shirt with ragged sleeves and a kind of headband that wrapped over his ears.

'Brightness?' Yalb asked. 'You all right? You look like you swallowed a turtle. And not just the head, neither.'

'I'm well,' Shallan said. 'What . . . what was it you wanted of me, again?'

'In Kharbranth,' Yalb said, thumbing over his shoulder. 'Did we or did we not meet the king?'

'We?' Shallan asked. 'I met him.'

'And I was your retinue.'

'You were waiting outside.'

'Doesn't matter none,' Yalb said. 'I was your footman for that meeting, eh?'

Footman? He'd led her up to the palace as a favor. 'I . . . guess,' she said. 'You did have a nice bow, as I recall.'

'See,' Yalb said, standing and confronting the much larger man. 'I mentioned the bow, didn't I?'

The 'new kid' rumbled his agreement.

'So get to washing those dishes,' Yalb said. He got a scowl in response. 'Now, don't give me that,' Yalb said. 'I *told* you, galley duty is something the captain watches closely. If you want to fit in around here, you do it well, and do some extra. It will put you ahead with the captain *and* the rest of the men. I'm giving you quite the opportunity here, and I'll have you appreciate it.'

That seemed to placate the larger man, who turned around and went tromping toward the lower decks.

'Passions!' Yalb said. 'That fellow is as dun as two spheres made of mud. I worry about him. Somebody's going to take advantage of him, Brightness.'

'Yalb, have you been boasting again?' Shallan said.

' 'Tain't boasting if some of it's true.'

'Actually, that's *exactly* what boasting entails.'

'Hey,' Yalb said, turning toward her. 'What were you doing before? You know, with the colors?'

'Colors?' Shallan said, suddenly cold.

'Yeah, the deck turned green, eh?' Yalb said. 'I swear I saw it. Has to do with that strange spren, does it?'

'I . . . I'm trying to determine exactly what kind of spren it is,' Shallan said, keeping her voice even. 'It's a scholarly matter.'

'I thought so,' Yalb said, though she'd given him nothing in the way of an answer. He raised an affable hand to her, then jogged off.

She worried about letting them see Pattern. She'd tried staying in her cabin to keep him a secret from the men, but being cooped up had been too difficult for her, and he didn't respond to her suggestions that he stay out of their sight. So, during the last four days, she'd been forced to let them see what she was doing as she studied him.

They were understandably discomforted by him, but didn't say much. Today, they were getting the ship ready to sail all night. Thoughts of the open sea at night unsettled her, but that was the cost of sailing this far from civilization. Two days back, they'd even been forced to weather a storm in a cove along the coast. Jasnah and Shallan had gone ashore to stay in a fortress maintained for the purpose – paying a steep cost to get in – while the sailors had stayed on board.

That cove, though not a true port, had at least had a stormwall to help shelter the ship. Next highstorm, they wouldn't even have that. They'd find a cove and try to ride out the winds, though Tozbek said he'd send Shallan and Jasnah ashore to seek shelter in a cavern.

She turned back to Pattern, who had shifted into his hovering form. He looked something like the pattern of splintered light thrown on the wall by a crystal chandelier – except he was made of something black instead of light, and he was three-dimensional. So . . . Maybe not much like that at all.

'Lies,' Pattern said. 'Lies from the Yalb.'

'Yes,' Shallan said with a sigh. 'Yalb is far too skilled at persuasion for his own good, sometimes.'

Pattern hummed softly. He seemed pleased.

'You like lies?' Shallan asked.

'Good lies,' Pattern said. 'That lie. Good lie.'

'What makes a lie good?' Shallan asked, taking careful notes, recording Pattern's exact words.

'True lies.'

'Pattern, those two are opposites.'

'Hmmmm . . . Light makes shadow. Truth makes lies. Hmmmm.'

Liespren, Jasnah called them, Shallan wrote. *A moniker they don't like, apparently. When I Soulcast for the first time, a voice demanded a truth from me. I still don't know what that means, and Jasnah has not been forthcoming. She doesn't seem to know what to make of my experience either. I do not think that voice belonged to Pattern, but I cannot say, as he seems to have forgotten much about himself.*

She returned to making a few sketches of Pattern both in his floating and flattened forms. Drawing let her mind relax. By the time she was done, there were several half-remembered passages from her research that she wanted to quote in her notes.

She made her way down the steps belowdecks, Pattern following. He drew looks from the sailors. Sailors were a superstitious lot, and some took him as a bad sign.

In her quarters, Pattern moved up the wall beside her, watching without eyes as she searched for a passage she remembered, which mentioned spren that spoke. Not just windspren and riverspren, which would mimic people and make playful comments. Those were a step up from ordinary spren, but there was yet another level of spren, one rarely seen. Spren like Pattern, who had real conversations with people.

The Nightwatcher is obviously one of these, Alai wrote, Shallan copying the passage. *The records of conversations with her – and she is definitely female, despite what rural Alethi folktales would have one believe – are numerous and credible. Shubalai herself, intent on providing a firsthand scholarly report, visited the Nightwatcher and recorded her story word for word. . . .*

Shallan went to another reference, and before long got completely lost in her studies. A few hours later, she closed a book and set it on the table beside her bed. Her spheres were getting dim; they'd go out soon, and would need to be reinfused with Stormlight. Shallan released a contented sigh and leaned back against her bed, her notes from a dozen different sources laid out on the floor of her small chamber.

She felt . . . satisfied. Her brothers loved the plan of fixing the Soulcaster and returning it, and seemed energized by her suggestion that all was not lost. They thought they could last longer, now that a plan was in place.

Shallan's life was coming together. How long had it been since she'd just been able to sit and read? Without worried concern for her house, without dreading the need to find a way to steal from Jasnah? Even before the terrible sequence of events that had led to her father's death, she had always been anxious. That had been her life. She'd seen becoming a true scholar as something unreachable. Stormfather! She'd seen the *next town over* as being unreachable.

She stood up, gathering her sketchbook and flipping through her pictures of the santhid, including several drawn from the memory of her dip in the ocean. She smiled at that, recalling how she'd climbed back up on deck, dripping wet and grinning. The sailors had all obviously thought her mad.

Now she was sailing toward a city on the edge of the world, betrothed to a powerful Alethi prince, and was free to just learn. She was seeing incredible new sights, sketching them during the days, then reading through piles of books in the nights.

She had stumbled into the perfect life, and it was everything she'd wished for.

Shallan fished in the pocket inside her safehand sleeve, digging out some more spheres to replace those dimming in the goblet. The ones her hand emerged with, however, were completely dun. Not a glimmer of Light in them.

She frowned. These had been restored during the previous highstorm, held in a basket tied to the ship's mast. The ones in her goblet were two storms old now, which was why they were running out. How had the ones in her pocket gone dun faster? It defied reason.

'Mmmmm . . .' Pattern said from the wall near her head. 'Lies.'

Shallan replaced the spheres in her pocket, then opened the door into the ship's narrow companionway and moved to Jasnah's cabin. It was the cabin that Tozbek and his wife usually shared, but they had vacated it for the third – and smallest – of the cabins to give Jasnah the better quarters. People did things like that for her, even when she didn't ask.

Jasnah would have some spheres for Shallan to use. Indeed, Jasnah's door was cracked open, swaying slightly as the ship creaked and rocked along its evening path. Jasnah sat at the desk inside, and Shallan peeked in, suddenly uncertain if she wanted to bother the woman.

She could see Jasnah's face, hand against her temple, staring at the pages spread before her. Jasnah's eyes were haunted, her expression haggard.

This was *not* the Jasnah that Shallan was accustomed to seeing. The confidence had been overwhelmed by exhaustion, the poise replaced by worry. Jasnah started to write something, but stopped after just a few words. She set down the pen, closing her eyes and massaging her temples. A few dizzy-looking spren, like jets of dust rising into the air, appeared around Jasnah's head. Exhaustionspren.

Shallan pulled back, suddenly feeling as if she'd intruded upon an intimate moment. Jasnah with her defenses down. Shallan began to creep away, but a voice from the floor suddenly said, 'Truth!'

Startled, Jasnah looked up, eyes finding Shallan – who, of course, blushed furiously.

Jasnah turned her eyes down toward Pattern on the floor, then reset her mask, sitting up with proper posture. 'Yes, child?'

'I ... I needed spheres ...' Shallan said. 'Those in my pouch went dun.'

'Have you been Soulcasting?' Jasnah asked sharply.

'What? No, Brightness. I promised I would not.'

'Then it is the second ability,' Jasnah said. 'Come in and close that door. I should speak to Captain Tozbek; it won't latch properly.'

Shallan stepped in, pushing the door closed, though the latch didn't catch. She stepped forward, hands clasped, feeling embarrassed.

'What did you do?' Jasnah asked. 'It involved light, I assume?'

'I seemed to make plants appear,' Shallan said. 'Well, really just the color. One of the sailors saw the deck turn green, but it vanished when I stopped thinking about the plants.'

'Yes ...' Jasnah said. She flipped through one of her books, stopping at an illustration. Shallan had seen it before; it was as ancient as Vorinism. Ten spheres connected by lines forming a shape like an hourglass on its side. Two of the spheres at the center looked almost like pupils. The Double Eye of the Almighty.

'Ten Essences,' Jasnah said softly. She ran her fingers along the page. 'Ten Surges. Ten orders. But what does it mean that the spren have finally decided to return the oaths to us? And how much time remains to me? Not long. Not long . . .'

'Brightness?' Shallan asked.

'Before your arrival, I could assume I was an anomaly,' Jasnah said. 'I could hope that Surgebindings were not returning in large numbers. I no longer have that hope. The Cryptics sent you to me, of that I have no doubt, because they knew you would need training. That gives me hope that I was at least one of the first.'

'I don't understand.'

Jasnah looked up toward Shallan, meeting her eyes with an intense gaze. The woman's eyes were reddened with fatigue. How late was she working? Every night when Shallan turned in, there was still light coming from under Jasnah's door.

'To be honest,' Jasnah said, 'I don't understand either.'

'Are you all right?' Shallan asked. 'Before I entered, you seemed . . . distressed.'

Jasnah hesitated just briefly. 'I have merely been spending too long at my studies.' She turned to one of her trunks, digging out a dark cloth pouch filled with spheres. 'Take these. I would suggest that you keep spheres with you at all times, so that your Surgebinding has the opportunity to manifest.'

'Can you teach me?' Shallan asked, taking the pouch.

'I don't know,' Jasnah said. 'I will try. On this diagram, one of the Surges is known as Illumination, the mastery of light. For now, I would prefer you expend your efforts on learning this Surge, as opposed to Soulcasting. That is a dangerous art, more so now than it once was.'

Shallan nodded, rising. She hesitated before leaving, however. 'Are you sure you are well?'

'Of course.' She said it too quickly. The woman was poised, in control, but also obviously exhausted. The mask was cracked, and Shallan could see the truth.

She's trying to placate me, Shallan realized. *Pat me on the head and send me back to bed, like a child awakened by a nightmare.*

'You're worried,' Shallan said, meeting Jasnah's eyes.

The woman turned away. She pushed a book over something wiggling on her table – a small purple spren. Fearspren. Only one, true, but still.

'No ...' Shallan whispered. 'You're not worried. You're *terrified*.' Stormfather!

'It is all right, Shallan,' Jasnah said. 'I just need some sleep. Go back to your studies.'

Shallan sat down on the stool beside Jasnah's desk. The older woman looked back at her, and Shallan could see the mask cracking further. Annoyance as Jasnah drew her lips to a line. Tension in the way she held her pen, in a fist.

'You told me I could be part of this,' Shallan said. 'Jasnah, if you're worried about something ...'

'My worry is what it has always been,' Jasnah said, leaning back in her chair. 'That I will be too late. That I'm incapable of doing anything meaningful to stop what is coming – that I'm trying to stop a highstorm by blowing against it *really hard*.'

'The Voidbringers,' Shallan said. 'The parshmen.'

'In the past,' Jasnah said, 'the Desolation – the coming of the Voidbringers – was supposedly always marked by a return of the Heralds to prepare mankind. They would train the Knights Radiant, who would experience a rush of new members.'

'But we captured the Voidbringers,' Shallan said. 'And enslaved them.' That was what Jasnah postulated, and Shallan agreed, having seen the research. 'So you think a kind of revolution is coming. That the parshmen will turn against us as they did in the past.'

'Yes,' Jasnah said, rifling through her notes. 'And soon. Your proving to be a Surgebinder does not comfort me, as it smacks too much of what happened before. But back then, new knights had teachers to train them, generations of tradition. We have nothing.'

'The Voidbringers are captive,' Shallan said, glancing toward Pattern. He rested on the floor, almost invisible, saying nothing. 'The parshmen can barely communicate. How could they possibly stage a revolution?'

Jasnah found the sheet of paper she'd been seeking and handed it to Shallan. Written in Jasnah's own hand, it was an account by a captain's wife of a plateau assault on the Shattered Plains.

'Parshendi,' Jasnah said, 'can sing in time with one another no matter how far they are separated. They have some ability to communicate that we do not understand. I can only assume that their cousins the parshmen have the same. They may not need to *hear* a call to action in order to revolt.'

Shallan read the report, nodding slowly. 'We need to warn others, Jasnah.'

'You don't think I've tried?' Jasnah asked. 'I've written to scholars and kings all around the world. Most dismiss me as paranoid. The evidence you readily accept, others call flimsy.

'The ardents were my best hope, but their eyes are clouded by the interference of the Hierocracy. Besides, my personal beliefs make ardents skeptical of anything I say. My mother wants to see my research, which is something. My brother and uncle might believe, and that is why we are going to them.' She hesitated. 'There is another reason we seek the Shattered Plains. A way to find evidence that might convince everyone.'

'Urithiru,' Shallan said. 'The city you seek?'

Jasnah gave her another curt glance. The ancient city was something Shallan had first learned about by secretly reading Jasnah's notes.

'You still blush too easily when confronted,' Jasnah noted. 'I'm sorry.'

'And apologize too easily as well.'

'I'm . . . uh, indignant?'

Jasnah smiled, picking up the representation of the Double Eye. She stared at it. 'There is a secret hidden somewhere on the Shattered Plains. A secret about Urithiru.'

'You told me the city wasn't there!'

'It isn't. But the path to it may be.' Her lips tightened. 'According to legend, only a Knight Radiant could open the way.'

'Fortunately, we know two of those.'

'Again, you are not a Radiant, and neither am I. Being able to replicate some of the things they could do may not matter. We don't have their traditions or knowledge.'

'We're talking about the potential end of civilization itself, aren't we?' Shallan asked softly.

Jasnah hesitated.

'The Desolations,' Shallan said. 'I know very little, but the legends . . .'

'In the aftermath of each one, mankind was broken. Great cities in ashes, industry smashed. Each time, knowledge and growth were reduced to an almost prehistoric state – it took *centuries* of rebuilding to restore civilization to what it had been before.' She hesitated. 'I keep hoping that I'm wrong.'

'Urithiru,' Shallan said. She tried to refrain from just asking questions, trying instead to reason her way to the answer. 'You said the city was a kind of base or home to the Knights Radiant. I hadn't heard of it before speaking with you, and so can guess that it's not commonly referred to in the literature. Perhaps, then, it is one of the things that the Hierocracy suppressed knowledge of?'

'Very good,' Jasnah said. 'Although I think that it had begun to fade into legend even before then, the Hierocracy did not help.'

'So if it existed before the Hierocracy, and if the pathway to it was locked at the fall of the Radiants . . . then it might contain records that have not been touched by modern scholars. Unaltered, unchanged lore about the Voidbringers and Surgebinding.' Shallan shivered. '*That's* why we're really going to the Shattered Plains.'

Jasnah smiled through her fatigue. 'Very good indeed. My time in the Palanaeum was very useful, but also in some ways disappointing. While I confirmed my suspicions about the parshmen, I also found that many of the great library's records bore the same signs of tampering as others I'd read. This "cleansing" of history, removing direct references to Urithiru or the Radiants because they were embarrassments to Vorinism – it's infuriating. And people ask me why I am hostile to the church! I need primary sources. And then, there are stories – ones I dare to believe – claiming that Urithiru was holy and protected from the Voidbringers. Maybe that was wishful fancy, but I am not too much a scholar to hope that something like that might be true.'

'And the parshmen?'

'We will try to persuade the Alethi to rid themselves of those.'

'Not an easy task.'

'A nearly impossible one,' Jasnah said, standing. She began to pack her books away for the night, putting them in her waterproofed trunk. 'Parshmen are such perfect slaves. Docile, obedient. Our society has become far too reliant upon them. The parshmen wouldn't need to turn violent to throw us into chaos – though I'm certain that is what's coming – they could simply walk away. It would cause an economic crisis.'

She closed the trunk after removing one volume, then turned back to

Shallan. 'Convincing everyone of what I say is beyond us without more evidence. Even if my brother listens, he doesn't have the authority to force the highprinces to get rid of their parshmen. And, in all honesty, I fear my brother won't be brave enough to risk the collapse expelling the parshmen might cause.'

'But if they turn on us, the collapse will come anyway.'

'Yes,' Jasnah said. 'You know this, and I know it. My mother might believe it. But the risk of being wrong is so immense that . . . well, we will need evidence – overwhelming and irrefutable evidence. So we find the city. At all costs, we *find* that city.'

Shallan nodded.

'I did not want to lay all of this upon your shoulders, child,' Jasnah said, sitting back down. 'However, I will admit that it is a relief to speak of these things to someone who doesn't challenge me on every other point.'

'We'll do it, Jasnah,' Shallan said. 'We'll travel to the Shattered Plains and we'll find Urithiru. We'll get the evidence and convince everyone to listen.'

'Ah, the optimism of youth,' Jasnah said. 'That is nice to hear on occasion too.' She handed the book to Shallan. 'Among the Knights Radiant, there was an order known as the Lightweavers. I know precious little about them, but of all the sources I've read, this one has the most information.'

Shallan took the volume eagerly. *Words of Radiance*, the title read.

'Go,' Jasnah said. 'Read.'

Shallan glanced at her.

'I will sleep,' Jasnah promised, a smile creeping to her lips. 'And stop trying to mother me. I don't even let Navani do that.'

Shallan sighed, nodding, and left Jasnah's quarters. Pattern tagged along behind; he'd spent the entire conversation silent. As she entered her cabin, she found herself much heavier of heart than when she'd left it. She couldn't banish the image of terror in Jasnah's eyes. Jasnah Kholin shouldn't fear anything, should she?

Shallan crawled onto her cot with the book she'd been given and the pouch of spheres. Part of her was eager to begin, but she was exhausted, her eyelids drooping. It really had gotten late. If she started the book now . . .

Perhaps better to get a good night's sleep, then dig refreshed into a new day's studies. She set the book on the small table beside her bed, curled up, and let the rocking of the boat coax her to sleep.

She awoke to screams, shouts, and smoke.

I was unprepared for the grief my loss brought – like an unexpected rain – breaking from a clear sky and crashing down upon me. Gavilar's death years ago was overwhelming, but this... this nearly crushed me.

—From the journal of Navani Kholin, Jesesach 1174

S till half asleep, Shallan panicked. She scrambled off her cot, accidentally slapping the goblet of mostly drained spheres. Though she used wax to keep it in place, the swat knocked it free and sent spheres tumbling across her cabin.

The scent of smoke was powerful. She ran to her door, disheveled, heart thumping. At least she'd fallen asleep in her clothing. She threw open the door.

Three men crowded in the passageway outside, holding aloft torches, their backs to her.

Torches, sparking with flamespren dancing about the fires. Who brought open flame onto a ship? Shallan stopped in numb confusion.

The shouts came from the deck above, and it seemed that the ship wasn't on fire. But who were these men? They carried axes, and were focused on Jasnah's cabin, which was open.

Figures moved inside. In a frozen moment of horror, one threw something to the floor before the others, who stepped aside to make way.

A body in a thin nightgown, eyes staring sightlessly, blood blossoming from the breast. Jasnah.

'Be sure,' one of the men said.

The other one knelt and rammed a long, thin knife right into Jasnah's chest. Shallan heard it hit the wood of the floor beneath the body.

Shallan screamed.

One of the men spun toward her. 'Hey!' It was the blunt-faced, tall fellow that Yalb had called the 'new kid.' She didn't recognize the other men.

Somehow fighting through the terror and disbelief, Shallan slammed her door and threw the bolt with trembling fingers.

Stormfather! Stormfather! She backed away from the door as something heavy hit the other side. They wouldn't need the axes. A few determined smashes of shoulder to door would bring it down.

Shallan stumbled back against her cot, nearly slipping on the spheres rolling to and fro with the ship's motion. The narrow window near the ceiling – far too small to fit through – revealed only the dark of night outside. Shouts continued above, feet thumping on wood.

Shallan trembled, still numb. Jasnah. . . .

'Sword,' a voice said. Pattern, hanging on the wall beside her. 'Mmmm . . . The sword . . .'

'No!' Shallan screamed, hands to the sides of her head, fingers in her hair. Stormfather! She was trembling.

Nightmare. It was a nightmare! It couldn't be—

'Mmmm . . . Fight . . .'

'*No!*' Shallan found herself hyperventilating as the men outside continued to ram their shoulders against her door. She was not ready for this. She was not prepared.

'Mmmm . . .' Pattern said, sounding dissatisfied. 'Lies.'

'I don't know how to use the lies!' Shallan said. 'I haven't practiced.'

'Yes. Yes . . . remember . . . the time before . . .'

The door crunched. Dared she remember? *Could* she remember? A child, playing with a shimmering pattern of light . . .

'What do I do?' she asked.

'You need the Light,' Pattern said.

It sparked something deep within her memory, something prickled with barbs she dared not touch. She needed Stormlight to fuel the Surgebinding.

Shallan fell to her knees beside her cot and, without knowing exactly what she was doing, breathed in sharply. Stormlight left the spheres around her, pouring into her body, becoming a storm that raged in her veins. The cabin went dark, black as a cavern deep beneath the earth.

Then Light began to rise from her skin like vapors off boiling water. It lit the cabin with swimming shadows.

'Now what?' she demanded.

'Shape the lie.'

What did that mean? The door crunched again, cracking, a large split opening down the center.

Panicked, Shallan let out a breath. Stormlight streamed from her in a cloud; she almost felt as if she could touch it. She could *feel* its potential.

'How!' she demanded.

'Make the truth.'

'That makes no sense!'

Shallan screamed as the door broke open. New light entered the cabin, torchlight – red and yellow, hostile.

The cloud of Light *leaped* from Shallan, more Stormlight streaming from her body to join it. It formed a vague upright shape. An illuminated blur. It washed past the men through the doorway, waving appendages that could have been arms. Shallan herself, kneeling by the bed, fell into shadow.

The men's eyes were drawn to the glowing shape. Then, blessedly, they turned and gave chase.

Shallan huddled against the wall, shaking. The cabin was utterly dark. Above, men screamed.

'Shallan . . .' Pattern buzzed somewhere in the darkness.

'Go and look,' she said. 'Tell me what is happening up on deck.'

She didn't know if he obeyed, as he made no sound when he moved. After a few deep breaths, Shallan stood up. Her legs shook, but she stood.

She collected herself somewhat. This was terrible, this was awful, but nothing, *nothing*, could compare to what she'd had to do the night her father died. She had survived that. She could survive this.

These men, they would be of the same group Kabsal had been from – the assassins Jasnah feared. They had finally gotten her.

Oh, Jasnah . . . Jasnah was dead.

Grieve later. What was Shallan going to do about armed men taking over the ship? How would she find a way out?

She felt her way out into the passageway. There was a little light here, from torches above on the deck. The yells she heard there grew more panicked.

'Killing,' a voice suddenly said.

She jumped, though of course it was only Pattern.

'What?' Shallan hissed.

'Dark men killing,' Pattern said. 'Sailors tied in ropes. One dead, bleeding red. I . . . I do not understand. . . .'

Oh, Stormfather . . . Above, the shouting heightened, but there was no scramble of boots on the deck, no clanging of weapons. The sailors had been captured. At least one had been killed.

In the darkness, Shallan saw shaking, wiggling forms creep up from the wood around her. Fearspren.

'What of the men who chased after my image?' she asked.

'Looking in water,' Pattern said.

So they thought she'd jumped overboard. Heart thumping, Shallan felt her way to Jasnah's cabin, expecting at any moment to trip over the woman's corpse on the floor. She didn't. Had the men dragged it above?

Shallan entered Jasnah's cabin and closed the door. It wouldn't latch shut, so she pulled a box over to block it.

She had to do something. She felt her way to one of Jasnah's trunks, which had been thrown open by the men, its contents – clothing – scattered about. In the bottom, Shallan found the hidden drawer and pulled it open. Light suddenly bathed the cabin. The spheres were so bright they blinded Shallan for a moment, and she had to look away.

Pattern vibrated on the floor beside her, form shaking in worry. Shallan looked about. The small cabin was a shambles, clothing on the floor, papers strewn everywhere. The trunk with Jasnah's books was gone. Too fresh to have soaked in, blood was pooled on the bed. Shallan quickly looked away.

A shout suddenly sounded above, followed by a thump. The screaming grew louder. She heard Tozbek bellow for the men to spare his wife.

Almighty above . . . the assassins were executing the sailors one at a time. Shallan had to do something. Anything.

Shallan looked back at the spheres in their false bottom, lined with black cloth. 'Pattern,' she said, 'we're going to Soulcast the bottom of the ship and sink it.'

'What!' His vibrating increased, a buzz of sound. 'Humans . . . Humans . . . Eat water?'

'We drink it,' Shallan said, 'but we cannot breathe it.'

'Mmmm . . . Confused . . .' Pattern said.

'The captain and the others are captured and being executed. The best chance I can give them is chaos.' Shallan placed her hands on the spheres and drew in the Light with a sharp breath. She felt *afire* with it inside of her, as if she were going to burst. The Light was a living thing, trying to press out through the pores of her skin.

'Show me!' she shouted, far more loudly than she'd intended. That Stormlight urged her to action. 'I've Soulcast before. I must do it again!' Stormlight puffed from her mouth as she spoke, like breath on a cold day.

'Mmmmm . . .' Pattern said anxiously. 'I will intercede. See.'

'See what?'

'*See!*'

Shadesmar. The last time she'd gone to that place, she'd nearly gotten herself killed. Only, it wasn't a place. Or was it? Did it matter?

She reached back through recent memory to the time when she'd last Soulcast and accidentally turned a goblet into blood. 'I need a truth.'

'You have given enough,' Pattern said. 'Now. See.'

The ship vanished.

Everything . . . popped. The walls, the furniture, it all shattered into little globes of black glass. Shallan prepared herself to fall into the ocean of those glass beads, but instead she dropped onto solid ground.

She stood in a place with a black sky and a tiny, distant sun. The ground beneath her reflected light. Obsidian? Each way she turned, the ground was made of that same blackness. Nearby, the spheres – like those that would hold Stormlight, but dark and small – bounced to a rest on the ground.

Trees, like growing crystal, clustered here and there. The limbs were spiky and glassy, without leaves. Nearby, little lights hung in the air, flames without their candles. *People*, she realized. *Those are each a person's mind, reflected here in the Cognitive Realm.* Smaller ones were scattered about her feet, dozens upon dozens, but so small she almost couldn't make them out. *The minds of fish?*

She turned around and came face-to-face with a creature that had a symbol for a head. Startled, she screamed and jumped back. These things . . . they had haunted her . . . they . . .

It was Pattern. He stood tall and willowy, but slightly indistinct, translucent. The complex pattern of his head, with its sharp lines and impossible geometries, seemed to have no eyes. He stood with hands behind his back, wearing a robe that seemed too stiff to be cloth.

'Go,' he said. 'Choose.'

'Choose what?' she said, Stormlight escaping her lips.

'Your ship.'

He did not have eyes, but she thought she could follow his gaze toward one of the little spheres on the glassy ground. She snatched it, and suddenly was given the impression of a ship.

The *Wind's Pleasure*. A ship that had been cared for, loved. It had carried its passengers well for years and years, owned by Tozbek and his father before him. An old ship, but not ancient, still reliable. A proud ship. It manifested here as a sphere.

It could actually think. The ship could think. Or . . . well, it reflected the thoughts of the people who served on it, knew it, thought about it.

'I need you to change,' Shallan whispered to it, cradling the bead in her hands. It was too heavy for its size, as if the entire weight of the ship had been compressed to this singular bead.

'No,' the reply came, though it was Pattern who spoke. 'No, I cannot. I must serve. I am happy.'

Shallan looked to him.

'I will intercede,' Pattern repeated. '. . . Translate. You are not ready.'

Shallan looked back to the bead in her hands. 'I have Stormlight. Lots of it. I will give it to you.'

'No!' the reply seemed angry. 'I serve.'

It really wanted to stay a ship. She could feel it, the pride it took, the reinforcement of years of service.

'They are dying,' she whispered. 'No!'

'You can feel them dying. Their blood on your deck. One by one, the people you serve will be cut down.'

She could feel it herself, could see it in the ship. They were being executed. Nearby, one of the floating candle flames vanished. Three of the eight captives dead, though she did not know which ones.

'There is only one chance to save them,' Shallan said. 'And that is to change.'

'Change,' Pattern whispered for the ship.

'If you change, they might escape the evil men who kill,' Shallan whispered. 'It is uncertain, but they will have a chance to swim. To do something. You can do them a last service, *Wind's Pleasure*. Change for them.'

Silence.

'I . . .'

Another light vanished.

'I will change.'

It happened in a hectic second; the Stormlight *ripped* from Shallan. She heard distant cracks from the physical world as she withdrew so much Light from the nearby gemstones that they shattered.

Shadesmar vanished.

She was back in Jasnah's cabin.

The floor, walls, and ceiling melted into water.

Shallan was plunged into the icy black depths. She thrashed in the water, dress hampering her movements. All around her, objects sank, the common artifacts of human life.

Frantic, she searched for the surface. Originally, she'd had some vague idea of swimming out and helping untie the sailors, if they were bound. Now, however, she found herself desperately even trying to find the way up.

As if the darkness itself had come alive, something wrapped around her.

It pulled her farther into the deep.

KNIVES IN THE BACK · SOLDIERS ON THE FIELD

I seek not to use my grief as an excuse, but it is an explanation. People act strangely soon after encountering an unexpected loss. Though Jasnah had been away for some time, her loss was unexpected. I, like many, assumed her to be immortal.

—From the journal of Navani Kholin, Jesesach 1174

The familiar scraping of wood as a bridge slid into place. The stomping of feet in unison, first a flat sound on stone, then the ringing thump of boots on wood. The distant calls of scouts, shouting back the all-clear.

The sounds of a plateau run were familiar to Dalinar. Once, he had craved these sounds. He'd been impatient between runs, longing for the chance to strike down Parshendi with his Blade, to win wealth and recognition.

That Dalinar had been seeking to cover up his shame – the shame of lying slumped in a drunken stupor while his brother fought an assassin.

The setting of a plateau run was uniform: bare, jagged rocks, mostly the same dull color as the stone surface they sat on, broken only by the occasional cluster of closed rockbuds. Even those, as their name implied, could be mistaken for more rocks. There was nothing but more of the same from here where you stood, all the way out to the far horizon; and everything you'd brought with you, everything human, was dwarfed by the vastness of these endless, fractured plains and deadly chasms.

Over the years, this activity had become rote. Marching beneath that white sun like molten steel. Crossing gap after gap. Eventually, plateau runs had become less something to anticipate and more a dogged obligation. For Gavilar and glory, yes, but mainly because they – and the enemy – were here. This was what you did.

The scents of a plateau run were the scents of a great stillness: baked stone, dried crem, long-traveled winds.

Most recently, Dalinar was coming to detest plateau runs. They were a frivolity, a waste of life. They weren't about fulfilling the Vengeance Pact, but about greed. Many gemhearts appeared on the near plateaus, convenient to reach. Those didn't sate the Alethi. They had to reach farther, toward assaults that cost dearly.

Ahead, Highprince Aladar's men fought on a plateau. They had arrived before Dalinar's army, and the conflict told a familiar story. Men against Parshendi, fighting in a sinuous line, each army trying to shove the other back. The humans could field far more men than the Parshendi, but the Parshendi could reach plateaus faster and secure them quickly.

The scattered bodies of bridgemen on the staging plateau, leading up to the chasm, attested to the danger of charging an entrenched foe. Dalinar did not miss the dark expressions on his bodyguards' faces as they surveyed the dead. Aladar, like most of the other highprinces, used Sadeas's philosophy on bridge runs. Quick, brutal assaults that treated manpower as an expendable resource. It hadn't always been this way. In the past, bridges had been carried by armored troops, but success bred imitation.

The warcamps needed a constant influx of cheap slaves to feed the monster. That meant a growing plague of slavers and bandits roaming the Unclaimed Hills, trading in flesh. *Another thing I'll have to change,* Dalinar thought.

Aladar himself didn't fight, but had instead set up a command center on an adjacent plateau. Dalinar pointed toward the flapping banner, and one of his large mechanical bridges rolled into place. Pulled by chulls and full of gears, levers, and cams, the bridges protected the men who worked them. They were also very slow. Dalinar waited with self-disciplined patience as the workers ratcheted the bridge down, spanning the chasm between this plateau and the one where Aladar's banner flew.

Once the bridge was in position and locked, his bodyguard – led by one of Captain Kaladin's darkeyed officers – trotted onto it, spears to shoulders. Dalinar had promised Kaladin his men would not have to fight except to defend him. Once they were across, Dalinar kicked Gallant into motion to cross to Aladar's command plateau. Dalinar felt too light on the stallion's back – the lack of Shardplate. In the many years since he'd obtained his suit, he'd never gone out onto a battlefield without it.

Today, however, he didn't ride to battle – not truly. Behind him, Adolin's own personal banner flew, and he led the bulk of Dalinar's armies to assault the plateau where Aladar's men already fought. Dalinar didn't send any orders regarding how the assault should go. His son had been trained well, and he was ready to take battlefield command – with General Khal at his side, of course, for advice.

Yes, from now on, Adolin would lead the battles.

Dalinar would change the world.

He rode toward Aladar's command tent. This was the first plateau run following his proclamation requiring the armies to work together. The fact that Aladar had come as commanded, and Roion had not – even though the target plateau was closest to Roion's warcamp – was a victory unto itself. A small encouragement, but Dalinar would take what he could get.

He found Highprince Aladar watching from a small pavilion set up on a secure, raised part of this plateau overlooking the battlefield. A perfect location for a command post. Aladar was a Shardbearer, though he commonly lent his Plate and Blade to one of his officers during battles, preferring to lead tactically from behind the battle lines. A practiced Shardbearer could mentally command a Blade to not dissolve when he let go of it, though – in an emergency – Aladar could summon it to himself, making it vanish from the hands of his officer in an eyeblink, then appear in his own hands ten heartbeats later. Lending a Blade required a great deal of trust on both sides.

Dalinar dismounted. His horse, Gallant, glared at the groom who tried to take him, and Dalinar patted the horse on the neck. 'He'll be fine on his own, son,' he said to the groom. Most common grooms didn't know what to do with one of the Ryshadium anyway.

Trailed by his bridgeman guards, Dalinar joined Aladar, who stood at the edge of the plateau, overseeing the battlefield ahead and just below.

Slender and completely bald, the man had skin a darker tan than most Alethi. He stood with hands behind his back, and wore a sharp traditional uniform with a skirtlike takama, though he wore a modern jacket above it, cut to match the takama.

It was a style Dalinar had never seen before. Aladar also wore a thin mustache and a tuft of hair beneath his lip, again an unconventional choice. Aladar was powerful enough, and renowned enough, to make his own fashion – and he did so, often setting trends.

'Dalinar,' Aladar said, nodding to him. 'I thought you weren't going to fight on plateau runs any longer.'

'I'm not,' Dalinar said, nodding toward Adolin's banner. There, soldiers streamed across Dalinar's bridges to join the battle. The plateau was small enough that many of Aladar's men had to withdraw to make way, something they were obviously all too eager to do.

'You almost lost this day,' Dalinar noted. 'It is well that you had support.' Below, Dalinar's troops restored order to the battlefield and pushed against the Parshendi.

'Perhaps,' Aladar said. 'Yet in the past, I was victorious in one out of three assaults. Having support will mean I win a few more, certainly, but will also cost half my earnings. Assuming the king even assigns me any. I'm not convinced that I'll be better off in the long run.'

'But this way, you lose fewer men,' Dalinar said. 'And the total winnings for the entire army will rise. The honor of the—'

'Don't talk to me about honor, Dalinar. I can't pay my soldiers with honor, and I can't use it to keep the other highprinces from snapping at my neck. Your plan favors the weakest among us and undercuts the successful.'

'Fine,' Dalinar snapped, 'honor has no value to you. You will *still* obey, Aladar, because your king demands it. That is the only reason you need. You will do as told.'

'Or?' Aladar said.

'Ask Yenev.'

Aladar started as if slapped. Ten years back, Highprince Yenev had refused to accept the unification of Alethkar. At Gavilar's order, Sadeas had dueled the man. And killed him.

'Threats?' Aladar asked.

'Yes.' Dalinar turned to look the shorter man in the eyes. 'I'm done cajoling, Aladar. I'm done asking. When you disobey Elhokar, you mock my brother and what he stood for. I *will* have a unified kingdom.'

'Amusing,' Aladar said. 'Good of you to mention Gavilar, as he didn't bring the kingdom together with honor. He did it with knives in the back and soldiers on the field, cutting the heads off any who resisted. Are we back to that again, then? Such things don't sound much like the fine words of your precious book.'

Dalinar ground his teeth, turning away to watch the battlefield. His first instinct was to tell Aladar he was an officer under Dalinar's command, and take the man to task for his tone. Treat him like a recruit in need of correction.

But what if Aladar just ignored him? Would he *force* the man to obey? Dalinar didn't have the troops for it.

He found himself annoyed – more at himself than at Aladar. He'd come on this plateau run not to fight, but to talk. To persuade. Navani was right. Dalinar needed more than brusque words and military commands to save this kingdom. He needed loyalty, not fear.

But storms take him, *how*? What persuading he'd done in life, he'd accomplished with a sword in hand and a fist to the face. Gavilar had always been the one with the right words, the one who could make people listen.

Dalinar had no business trying to be a politician.

Half the lads on that battlefield probably didn't think they had any business being soldiers, at first, a part of him whispered. *You don't have the luxury of being bad at this. Don't complain. Change.*

'The Parshendi are pushing too hard,' Aladar said to his generals. 'They want to shove us off the plateau. Tell the men to give a little and let the Parshendi lose their advantage of footing; that will let us surround them.'

The generals nodded, one calling out orders.

Dalinar narrowed his eyes at the battlefield, reading it. 'No,' he said softly.

The general stopped giving orders. Aladar glanced at Dalinar.

'The Parshendi are preparing to pull back,' Dalinar said.

'They certainly don't act like it.'

'They want some room to breathe,' Dalinar said, reading the swirl of combat below. 'They nearly have the gemheart harvested. They will continue to push hard, but will break into a quick retreat around the chrysalis to buy time for the final harvesting. That's what you'll need to stop.'

The Parshendi surged forward.

'I took point on this run,' Aladar said. 'By your own rules, I get final say over our tactics.'

'I observe only,' Dalinar said. 'I'm not even commanding my own army today. You may choose your tactics, and I will not interfere.'

Aladar considered, then cursed softly. 'Assume Dalinar is correct. Prepare the men for a withdrawal by the Parshendi. Send a strike team forward to secure the chrysalis, which should be almost opened up.'

The generals set up the new details, and messengers raced off with the tactical orders. Aladar and Dalinar watched, side by side, as the Parshendi shoved forward. That singing of theirs hovered over the battlefield.

Then they pulled back, careful as always to respectfully step over the bodies of the dead. Ready for this, the human troops rushed after. Led by Adolin in gleaming Plate, a strike force of fresh troops broke through the Parshendi line and reached the chrysalis. Other human troops poured through the gap they opened, shoving the Parshendi to the flanks, turning the Parshendi withdrawal into a tactical disaster.

In minutes, the Parshendi had abandoned the plateau, jumping away and fleeing.

'Damnation,' Aladar said softly. 'I *hate* that you're so good at this.'

Dalinar narrowed his eyes, noticing that some of the fleeing Parshendi stopped on a plateau a short distance from the battlefield. They lingered there, though much of their force continued on away.

Dalinar waved for one of Aladar's servants to hand him a spyglass, then he raised it, focusing on that group. A figure stood at the edge of the plateau out there, a figure in glistening armor.

The Parshendi Shardbearer, he thought. *The one from the battle at the Tower. He almost killed me.*

Dalinar didn't remember much from that encounter. He'd been beaten near senseless toward the end of it. This Shardbearer hadn't participated in today's battle. Why? Surely with a Shardbearer, they could have opened the chrysalis sooner.

Dalinar felt a disturbing pit inside of him. This one fact, the watching Shardbearer, changed his understanding of the battle entirely. He thought he'd been able to read what was going on. Now it occurred to him that the enemy's tactics were more opaque than he'd assumed.

'Are some of them still out there?' Aladar asked. 'Watching?'

Dalinar nodded, lowering his spyglass.

'Have they done that before in any battle you've fought?'

Dalinar shook his head.

Aladar mulled for a moment, then gave orders for his men on the plateau to remain alert, with scouts posted to watch for a surprise return of the Parshendi.

'Thank you,' Aladar added, grudgingly, turning to Dalinar. 'Your advice proved helpful.'

'You trusted me when it came to tactics,' Dalinar said, turning to him. 'Why not try trusting me in what is best for this kingdom?'

Aladar studied him. Behind, soldiers cheered their victory and Adolin ripped the gemheart free from the chrysalis. Others fanned out to watch for a return attack, but none came.

'I wish I could, Dalinar,' Aladar finally said. 'But this isn't about you. It's about the other highprinces. Maybe I could trust you, but I'll never trust them. You're asking me to risk too much of myself. The others would do to me what Sadeas did to you on the Tower.'

'What if I can bring the others around? What if I can prove to you that they're worthy of trust? What if I can change the direction of this kingdom, and this war? Will you follow me then?'

'No,' Aladar said. 'I'm sorry.' He turned away, calling for his horse.

The trip back was miserable. They'd won the day, but Aladar kept his distance. How could Dalinar do so many things so right, yet still be unable to persuade men like Aladar? And what did it mean that the Parshendi were changing tactics on the battlefield, not committing their Shardbearer? Were they too afraid to lose their Shards?

When, at long last, Dalinar returned to his bunker in the warcamps – after seeing to his men and sending a report to the king – he found an unexpected letter waiting for him.

He sent for Navani to read him the words. Dalinar stood waiting in his private study, staring at the wall that had borne the strange glyphs. Those had been sanded away, the scratches hidden, but the pale patch of stone whispered.

Sixty-two days.

Sixty-two days to come up with an answer. Well, sixty now. Not much time to save a kingdom, to prepare for the worst. The ardents would condemn the prophecy as a prank at best, or blasphemous at worst. To foretell the future was forbidden. It was of the Voidbringers. Even games of chance were suspect, for they incited men to look for the secrets of what was to come.

He believed anyway. For he suspected his own hand had written those words.

Navani arrived and looked over the letter, then started reading aloud. It turned out to be from an old friend who was going to arrive soon on the Shattered Plains – and who might provide a solution to Dalinar's problems.

9

WALKING THE GRAVE

I wish to think that had I not been under sorrow's thumb, I would have seen earlier the approaching dangers. Yet in all honesty, I'm not certain anything could have been done.

—From the journal of Navani Kholin, Jesesach 1174

Kaladin led the way down into the chasms, as was his right.

They used a rope ladder, as they had in Sadeas's army. Those ladders had been unsavory things, the ropes frayed and stained with moss, the planks battered by far too many highstorms. Kaladin had never lost a man because of those storming ladders, but he'd always worried. This one was brand new. He knew that for a fact, as Rind the quartermaster had scratched his head at the request, and then had one built to Kaladin's specifications. It was sturdy and well made, like Dalinar's army itself.

Kaladin reached the bottom with a final hop. Syl floated down and landed on his shoulder as he held up a sphere to survey the chasm bottom. The single sapphire broam was worth more by itself than the entirety of his wages as a bridgeman.

In Sadeas's army, the chasms had been a frequent destination for bridgemen. Kaladin still didn't know if the purpose had been to scavenge every possible resource from the Shattered Plains, or if it had really been about finding something menial – and will-breaking – for bridgemen to do between runs.

The chasm bottom here, however, was untouched. There were no paths cut through the snarl of stormleavings on the ground, and there were no scratched messages or instructions in the lichen on the walls. Like the other chasms, this one opened up like a vase, wider at the bottom than at the cracked top – a result of waters rushing through during highstorms. The floor was relatively flat, smoothed by the hardened sediment of settling crem.

As he moved forward, Kaladin had to pick his way over all kinds of debris. Broken sticks and logs from trees blown in from across the Plains. Cracked rockbud shells. Countless tangles of dried vines, twisted through one another like discarded yarn.

And bodies, of course.

A lot of corpses ended up in the chasms. Whenever men lost their battle to seize a plateau, they had to retreat and leave their dead behind. Storms! Sadeas often left the corpses behind even if he won – and bridgemen he'd leave wounded, abandoned, even if they could have been saved.

After a highstorm, the dead ended up here, in the chasms. And since storms blew westward, toward the warcamps, the bodies washed in this direction. Kaladin found it hard to move without stepping on bones entwined in the accumulated foliage on the chasm floor.

He picked his way through as respectfully as he could as Rock reached the bottom behind him, uttering a quiet phrase in his native tongue. Kaladin couldn't tell if it was a curse or a prayer. Syl moved from Kaladin's shoulder, zipping into the air, then streaking in an arc to the ground. There, she formed into what he thought of as her true shape, that of a young woman with a simple dress that frayed to mist just below the knees. She perched on a branch and stared at a femur poking up through the moss.

She didn't like violence. He wasn't certain if, even now, she understood death. She spoke of it like a child trying to grasp something beyond her.

'What a mess,' Teft said as he reached the bottom. 'Bah! This place hasn't seen any kind of care at all.'

'It is a grave,' Rock said. 'We walk in a grave.'

'All of the chasms are graves,' Teft said, his voice echoing in the dank confines. 'This one's just a messy grave.'

'Hard to find death that isn't messy, Teft,' Kaladin said.

Teft grunted, then started to greet the new recruits as they reached the bottom. Moash and Skar were watching over Dalinar and his sons as they attended some lighteyed feast – something that Kaladin was glad to be able to avoid. Instead, he'd come with Teft down here.

They were joined by the forty bridgemen – two from each reorganized crew – that Teft was training with the hope that they'd make good sergeants for their own crews.

'Take a good look, lads,' Teft said to them. 'This is where we come from. This is why some call us the order of bone. We're not going to make you go through everything we did, and be glad! We could have been swept away by a highstorm at any moment. Now, with Dalinar Kholin's stormwardens to guide us, we won't have nearly as much risk – and we'll be staying close to the exit just in case . . .'

Kaladin folded his arms, watching Teft instruct as Rock handed practice spears to the men. Teft himself carried no spear, and though he was shorter than the bridgemen who gathered around him – wearing simple soldiers' uniforms – they seemed thoroughly intimidated.

What else did you expect? Kaladin thought. *They're bridgemen. A stiff breeze could quell them.*

Still, Teft looked completely in control. Comfortably so. This was right. Something about it was just . . . right.

A swarm of small glowing orbs materialized around Kaladin's head, spren the shape of golden spheres that darted this way and that. He started, looking at them. Gloryspren. Storms. He felt as if he hadn't seen the like in years.

Syl zipped up into the air and joined them, giggling and spinning around Kaladin's head. 'Feeling proud of yourself?'

'Teft,' Kaladin said. 'He's a leader.'

'Of course he is. You gave him a rank, didn't you?'

'No,' Kaladin said. 'I didn't give it to him. He claimed it. Come on. Let's walk.'

She nodded, alighting in the air and settling down, her legs crossed at the knees as if she were primly seating herself in an invisible chair. She continued to hover there, moving exactly in step with him.

'Giving up all pretense of obeying natural laws again, I see,' he said.

'*Natural* laws?' Syl said, finding the concept amusing. 'Laws are of men, Kaladin. Nature doesn't have them!'

'If I toss something upward, it comes back down.'

'Except when it doesn't.'

'It's a law.'

'No,' Syl said, looking upward. 'It's more like ... more like an agreement among friends.'

He looked at her, raising an eyebrow.

'We have to be consistent,' she said, leaning in conspiratorially. 'Or we'll break your brains.'

He snorted, walking around a clump of bones and sticks pierced by a spear. Cankered with rust, it looked like a monument.

'Oh, come on,' Syl said, tossing her hair. 'That was worth *at least* a chuckle.'

Kaladin kept walking.

'A snort is *not* a chuckle,' Syl said. 'I know this because I am intelligent and articulate. You should compliment me now.'

'Dalinar Kholin wants to refound the Knights Radiant.'

'Yes,' Syl said loftily, hanging in the corner of his vision. 'A brilliant idea. I wish I'd thought of it.' She grinned triumphantly, then scowled.

'What?' he said, turning back to her.

'Has it ever struck you as unfair,' she said, 'that spren cannot attract spren? I should *really* have had some gloryspren of my own there.'

'I have to protect Dalinar,' Kaladin said, ignoring her complaint. 'Not just him, but his family, maybe the king himself. Even though I failed to keep someone from sneaking into Dalinar's rooms.' He still couldn't figure out how someone had managed to get in. Unless it hadn't been a person. 'Could a spren have made those glyphs on the wall?' Syl had carried a leaf once. She had *some* physical form, just not much.

'I don't know,' she said, glancing to the side. 'I've seen ...'

'What?'

'Spren like red lightning,' Syl said softly. 'Dangerous spren. Spren I haven't seen before. I catch them in the distance, on occasion. Stormspren? Something dangerous *is* coming. About that, the glyphs are right.'

He chewed on that for a while, then finally stopped and looked at her. 'Syl, are there others like me?'

Her face grew solemn. 'Oh.'

'Oh?'

'Oh, *that* question.'

'You've been expecting it, then?'

'Yeah. Sort of.'

'So you've had plenty of time to think about a good answer,' Kaladin said, folding his arms and leaning back against a somewhat dry portion of the wall. 'That makes me wonder if you've come up with a solid explanation or a solid lie.'

'Lie?' Syl said, aghast. 'Kaladin! What do you think I am? A Cryptic?'

'And what is a Cryptic?'

Syl, still perched as if on a seat, sat up straight and cocked her head. 'I actually . . . I actually have no idea. Huh.'

'Syl . . .'

'I'm *serious*, Kaladin! I don't know. I don't remember.' She grabbed her hair, one clump of white translucence in each hand, and pulled sideways.

He frowned, then pointed. 'That . . .'

'I saw a woman do it in the market,' Syl said, yanking her hair to the sides again. 'It means I'm frustrated. I think it's supposed to hurt. So . . . ow? Anyway, it's not that I don't want to tell you what I know. I do! I just . . . I don't *know* what I know.'

'That doesn't make sense.'

'Well, imagine how frustrating it *feels*!'

Kaladin sighed, then continued along the chasm, passing pools of stagnant water clotted with debris. A scattering of enterprising rockbuds grew stunted along one chasm wall. They must not get much light down here.

He breathed in deeply the scents of overloaded life. Moss and mold. Most of the bodies here were mere bone, though he did steer clear of one patch of ground crawling with the red dots of rotspren. Just beside it, a group of frillblooms wafted their delicate fanlike fronds in the air, and those danced with green specks of lifespren. Life and death shook hands here in the chasms.

He explored several of the chasm's branching paths. It felt odd to not know this area; he'd learned the chasms closest to Sadeas's camp better than the camp itself. As he walked, the chasm grew deeper and the area opened up. He made a few marks on the wall.

Along one fork he found a round open area with little debris. He noted it, then walked back, marking the wall again before taking another branch. Eventually, they entered another place where the chasm opened up, widening into a roomy space.

'Coming here was dangerous,' Syl said.

'Into the chasms?' Kaladin asked. 'There aren't going to be any chasm-fiends this close to the warcamps.'

'No. I meant for me, coming into this realm before I found you. It was dangerous.'

'Where were you before?'

'Another place. With lots of spren. I can't remember well ... it had lights in the air. Living lights.'

'Like lifespren.'

'Yes. And no. Coming here risked death. Without you, without a mind born of this realm, I couldn't think. Alone, I was just another windspren.'

'But you're not windspren,' Kaladin said, kneeling beside a large pool of water. 'You're honorspren.'

'Yes,' Syl said.

Kaladin closed his hand around his sphere, bringing near-darkness to the cavernous space. It was day above, but that crack of sky was distant, unreachable.

Mounds of flood-borne refuse fell into shadows that seemed almost to give them flesh again. Heaps of bones took on the semblance of limp arms, of corpses piled high. In a moment, Kaladin remembered it. Charging with a yell toward lines of Parshendi archers. His friends dying on barren plateaus, thrashing in their own blood.

The thunder of hooves on stone. The incongruous chanting of alien tongues. The cries of men both lighteyed and dark. A world that cared nothing for bridgemen. They were refuse. Sacrifices to be cast into the chasms and carried away by the cleansing floods.

This was their true home, these rents in the earth, these places lower than any other. As his eyes adjusted to the dimness, the memories of death receded, though he would never be free of them. He would forever bear those scars upon his memory like the many upon his flesh. Like the ones on his forehead.

The pool in front of him glowed a deep violet. He'd noticed it earlier, but in the light of his sphere it had been harder to see. Now, in the dimness, the pool could reveal its eerie radiance.

Syl landed on the side of the pool, looking like a woman standing on an ocean's shore. Kaladin frowned, leaning down to inspect her more closely. She seemed . . . different. Had her face changed shape?

'There *are* others like you,' Syl whispered. 'I do not know them, but I know that other spren are trying, in their own way, to reclaim what was lost.'

She looked to him, and her face now had its familiar form. The fleeting change had been so subtle, Kaladin wasn't sure if he'd imagined it.

'I am the only honorspren who has come,' Syl said. 'I . . .' She seemed to be stretching to remember. 'I was forbidden. I came anyway. To find you.'

'You knew me?'

'No. But I knew I'd find you.' She smiled. 'I spent the time with my cousins, searching.'

'The windspren.'

'Without the bond, I am basically one of them,' she said. 'Though they don't have the capacity to do what we do. And what we do is important. So important that I left everything, defying the Stormfather, to come. You saw him. In the storm.'

The hair stood up on Kaladin's arms. He had indeed seen a being in the storm. A face as vast as the sky itself. Whatever the thing was – spren, Herald, or god – it had not tempered its storms for Kaladin during that day he'd spent strung up.

'We are needed, Kaladin,' Syl said softly. She waved for him, and he lowered his hand to the shore of the tiny violet ocean glowing softly in the chasm. She stepped onto his hand, and he stood up, lifting her.

She walked up his fingers and he could actually feel a little weight, which was unusual. He turned his hand as she stepped up until she was perched on one finger, her hands clasped behind her back, meeting his eyes as he held that finger up before his face.

'You,' Syl said. 'You're going to need to become what Dalinar Kholin is looking for. Don't let him search in vain.'

'They'll take it from me, Syl,' Kaladin whispered. 'They'll find a way to take *you* from me.'

'That's foolishness. You know that it is.'

'I know it is, but I *feel* it isn't. They broke me, Syl. I'm not what you think I am. I'm no Radiant.'

'That's not what I saw,' Syl said. 'On the battlefield after Sadeas's betrayal, when men were trapped, abandoned. That day I saw a hero.'

He looked into her eyes. She had pupils, though they were created only from the differing shades of white and blue, like the rest of her. She glowed more softly than the weakest of spheres, but it was enough to light his finger. She smiled, seeming utterly confident in him.

At least one of them was.

'I'll try,' Kaladin whispered. A promise.

'Kaladin?' The voice was Rock's, with his distinctive Horneater accent. He pronounced the name 'kal-ah-*deen*,' instead of the normal '*kal*-a-din.'

Syl zipped off Kaladin's finger, becoming a ribbon of light and flitting over to Rock. He showed respect to her in his Horneater way, touching his shoulders in turn with one hand, and then raising the hand to his forehead. She giggled; her profound solemnity had become girlish joy in moments. Syl might only be a cousin to windspren, but she obviously shared their impish nature.

'Hey,' Kaladin said, nodding to Rock, and fishing in the pool. He came out with an amethyst broam and held it up. Somewhere up there on the Plains, a lighteyes had died with this in his pocket. 'Riches, if we still were bridgemen.'

'We are still bridgemen,' Rock said, coming over. He plucked the sphere from Kaladin's fingers. 'And this is still riches. Ha! Spices they have for us to requisition are *tuma'alki*! I have promised I will not fix dung for the men, but it is hard, with soldiers being accustomed to food that is not much better.' He held up the sphere. 'I will use *him* to buy better, eh?'

'Sure,' Kaladin said. Syl landed on Rock's shoulder and became a young woman, then sat down.

Rock eyed her and tried to bow to his own shoulder.

'Stop tormenting him, Syl,' Kaladin said.

'It's so fun!'

'You are to be praised for your aid of us, *mafah'liki*,' Rock said to her. 'I will endure whatever you wish of me. And now that I am free, I can create a shrine fitting to you.'

'A *shrine*?' Syl said, eyes widening. 'Ooooh.'

'Syl!' Kaladin said. 'Stop it. Rock, I saw a good place for the men to practice. It's back a couple of branches. I marked it on the walls.'

'Yes, we saw this thing,' Rock said. 'Teft has led the men there. It is strange. This place is frightening; it is a place that nobody comes, and yet the new recruits . . .'

'They're opening up,' Kaladin guessed.

'Yes. How did you know this thing would happen?'

'They were there,' Kaladin said, 'in Sadeas's warcamp, when we were assigned to exclusive duty in the chasms. They saw what we did, and have heard stories of our training here. By bringing them down here, we're inviting them in, like an initiation.'

Teft had been having problems getting the former bridgemen to show interest in his training. The old soldier was always sputtering at them in annoyance. They'd insisted on remaining with Kaladin rather than going free, so why wouldn't they learn?

They had needed to be invited. Not just with words.

'Yes, well,' Rock said. 'Sigzil sent me. He wishes to know if you are ready to practice your abilities.'

Kaladin took a deep breath, glancing at Syl, then nodded. 'Yes. Bring him. We can do it here.'

'Ha! Finally. I will fetch him.'

RED CARPET ONCE WHITE

10

The world ended, and Shallan was to blame.

'Pretend it never happened,' her father whispered. He wiped something wet from her cheek. His thumb came back red. 'I'll protect you.'

Was the room shaking? No, that was Shallan. Trembling. She felt so small. Eleven had seemed old to her, once. But she was a child, still a child. So small.

She looked up at her father with a shudder. She couldn't blink; her eyes were frozen open.

Father started to whisper, blinking tears. 'Now go to sleep in chasms deep, with darkness all around you ...'

A familiar lullaby, one he always used to sing to her. In the room behind him, dark corpses stretched out on the floor. A red carpet once white.

'Though rock and dread may be your bed, so sleep my baby dear.'

Father gathered her into his arms, and she felt her skin squirming. No. No, this affection wasn't right. A monster should not be held in love. A monster who killed, who murdered. *No.*

She could not move.

'Now comes the storm, but you'll be warm, the wind will rock your basket ...'

Father carried Shallan over the body of a woman in blue and gold.

Little blood there. It was the man who bled. Mother lay facedown, so Shallan couldn't see the eyes. The horrible eyes.

Almost, Shallan could imagine that the lullaby was the end to a nightmare. That it was night, that she had awakened screaming, and her father was singing her to sleep . . .

'The crystals fine will glow sublime, so sleep my baby dear.'

They passed Father's strongbox set into the wall. It glowed brightly, light streaming from the cracks around the closed door. A monster was inside.

'And with a song, it won't be long, you'll sleep my baby dear.'

With Shallan in his arms, Father left the room and closed the door on the corpses.

Shallan made
landfall here.
—Nazh

11

AN ILLUSION OF PERCEPTION

But, understandably, we were focused on Sadeas. His betrayal was still fresh, and I saw its signs each day as I passed empty barracks and grieving widows. We knew that Sadeas would not simply rest upon his slaughters in pride. More was coming.

—From the journal of Navani Kholin, Jesesach 1174

Shallan awoke mostly dry, lying on an uneven rock that rose from the ocean. Waves lapped at her toes, though she could barely feel them through the numbness. She groaned, lifting her cheek from the wet granite. There was land nearby, and the surf sounded against it with a low roar. In the other direction stretched only the endless blue sea.

She was cold and her head throbbed as if she'd banged it repeatedly against a wall, but she was alive. Somehow. She raised her hand – rubbing at the itchy dried salt on her forehead – and hacked out a ragged cough. Her hair stuck to the sides of her face, and her dress was stained from the water and the seaweed on the rock.

How . . . ?

Then she saw it, a large brown shell in the water, almost invisible as it moved toward the horizon. The santhid.

She stumbled to her feet, clinging to the pointy tip of her rock perch. Woozy, she watched the creature until it was gone.

Something hummed beside her. Pattern formed his usual shape on the surface of the churning sea, translucent as if he were a small wave himself.

'Did . . .' She coughed, clearing her voice, then groaned and sat down on the rock. 'Did anyone else make it?'

'Make?' Pattern asked.

'Other people. The sailors. Did they escape?'

'Uncertain,' Pattern said, in his humming voice. 'Ship . . . Gone. Splashing. Nothing seen.'

'The santhid. It rescued me.' How had it known what to do? Were they intelligent? Could she have somehow communicated with it? Had she missed an opportunity to—

She almost started laughing as she realized the direction her thoughts were going. She'd nearly drowned, Jasnah was dead, the crew of the *Wind's Pleasure* likely murdered or swallowed by the sea! Instead of mourning them or marveling at her survival, Shallan was engaging in scholarly speculation?

That's what you do, a deeply buried part of herself accused her. *You distract yourself. You refuse to think about things that bother you.*

But that was how she survived.

Shallan wrapped her arms around herself for warmth on her stone perch and stared out over the ocean. She *had* to face the truth. Jasnah was dead.

Jasnah was dead.

Shallan felt like weeping. A woman so brilliant, so amazing, was just . . . gone. Jasnah had been trying to save everyone, protect the world itself. And they'd killed her for it. The suddenness of what had happened left Shallan stunned, and so she sat there, shivering and cold and just staring out at the ocean. Her mind felt as numb as her feet.

Shelter. She'd need shelter . . . something. Thoughts of the sailors, of Jasnah's research, those were of less immediate concern. Shallan was stranded on a stretch of coast that was almost completely uninhabited, in lands that froze at night. As she'd been sitting, the tide had slowly withdrawn, and the gap between herself and the shore was not nearly as wide as it had been. That was fortunate, as she couldn't really swim.

She forced herself to move, though lifting her limbs was like trying to budge fallen tree trunks. She gritted her teeth and slipped into the water. She could still feel its biting cold. Not completely numb, then.

'Shallan?' Pattern asked.

'We can't sit out here forever,' Shallan said, clinging to the rock and getting all the way down into the water. Her feet brushed rock beneath, and so she dared let go, half swimming in a splashing mess as she made her way toward the land.

She probably swallowed half the water in the bay as she fought through the frigid waves until she finally was able to walk. Dress and hair streaming, she coughed and stumbled up onto the sandy shore, then fell to her knees. The ground here was strewn with seaweed of a dozen different varieties that writhed beneath her feet, pulling away, slimy and slippery. Cremlings and larger crabs scuttled in every direction, some nearby making clicking sounds at her, as if to ward her off.

She dully thought it a testament to her exhaustion that she hadn't even considered – before leaving the rock – the sea predators she'd read about: a dozen different kinds of large crustaceans that were happy to have a leg to snip free and chew on. Fearspren suddenly began to wiggle out of the sand, purple and sluglike.

That was silly. Now she was frightened? *After* her swim? The spren soon vanished.

Shallan glanced back at her rock perch. The santhid probably hadn't been able to deposit her any closer, as the water grew too shallow. Stormfather. She was lucky to be alive.

Despite her mounting anxiety, Shallan knelt down and traced a glyphward into the sand in prayer. She didn't have a means of burning it. For now, she had to assume the Almighty would accept this. She bowed her head and sat reverently for ten heartbeats.

Then she stood and, hope against hope, began to search for other survivors. This stretch of coast was pocketed with numerous beaches and inlets. She put off seeking shelter, instead walking for a long time down the shoreline. The beach was composed of sand that was coarser than she'd expected. It certainly didn't match the idyllic stories she'd read, and it ground unpleasantly against her toes as she walked. Alongside her, it rose in a moving shape as Pattern kept pace with her, humming anxiously.

Shallan passed branches, even bits of wood that *might* have belonged to ships. She saw no people and found no footprints. As the day grew long, she gave up, sitting down on a weathered stone. She hadn't noticed that her feet were sliced and reddened from walking on the rocks. Her hair was a complete mess. Her safepouch had a few spheres in it, but none were infused. They'd be of no use unless she found civilization.

Firewood, she thought. She'd gather that and build a fire. In the night, that might signal other survivors.

Or it might signal pirates, bandits, or the shipboard assassins, if they had survived.

Shallan grimaced. What was she going to do?

Build a small fire to keep warm, she decided. *Shield it, then watch the night for other fires. If you see one, try to inspect it without getting too close.*

A fine plan, except for the fact that she'd lived her entire life in a stately manor, with servants to light fires for her. She'd never started one in a hearth, let alone in the wilderness.

Storms . . . she'd be lucky not to die of exposure out here. Or starvation. What would she do when a highstorm came? When was the next one? Tomorrow night? Or was it the night after.

'Come!' Pattern said.

He vibrated in the sand. Grains jumped and shook as he spoke, rising and falling around him. *I recognize that . . .* Shallan thought, frowning at him. *Sand on a plate. Kabsal . . .*

'Come!' Pattern repeated, more urgent.

'What?' Shallan said, standing up. Storms, but she was tired. She could barely move. 'Did you find someone?'

'Yes!'

That got her attention immediately. She didn't ask further questions, but instead followed Pattern, who moved excitedly down the coast. Would he know the difference between someone dangerous and someone friendly? For the moment, cold and exhausted, she almost didn't care.

He stopped beside something halfway submerged in the water and seaweed at the edge of the ocean. Shallan frowned.

A trunk. Not a person, but a large wooden trunk. Shallan's breath caught in her throat, and she dropped to her knees, working the clasps and pulling open the lid.

Inside, like a glowing treasure, were Jasnah's books and notes, carefully packed away, protected in their waterproof enclosure.

Jasnah might not have survived, but her life's work had.

Shallan knelt down by her improvised firepit. A grouping of rocks, filled with sticks she'd gathered from this little stand of trees. Night was almost upon her.

With it came the shocking cold, as bad as the worst winter back home. Here in the Frostlands, this would be common. Her clothing, which in this humidity hadn't completely dried despite the hours walking, felt like ice.

She did not know how to build a fire, but perhaps she could make one in another way. She fought through her weariness – storms, but she was exhausted – and took out a glowing sphere, one of many she'd found in Jasnah's trunk.

'All right,' she whispered. 'Let's do this.' Shadesmar.

'Mmm ...' Pattern said. She was learning to interpret his humming. This seemed anxious. 'Dangerous.'

'Why?'

'What is land here is sea there.'

Shallan nodded dully. *Wait. Think.*

That was growing hard, but she forced herself to go over Pattern's words again. When they'd sailed the ocean, and she'd visited Shadesmar, she'd found obsidian ground beneath her. But in Kharbranth, she'd dropped into that ocean of spheres.

'So what do we do?' Shallan asked.

'Go slowly.'

Shallan took a deep, cold breath, then nodded. She tried as she had before. Slowly, carefully. It was like ... like opening her eyes in the morning.

Awareness of another place consumed her. The nearby trees *popped* like bubbles, beads forming in their place and dropping toward a shifting sea of them below. Shallan felt herself falling.

She gasped, then blinked back that awareness, closing her metaphoric eyes. That place vanished, and in a moment, she was back in the stand of trees.

Pattern hummed nervously.

Shallan set her jaw and tried again. More slowly this time, slipping into that place with its strange sky and not-sun. For a moment, she hovered between the worlds, Shadesmar overlaying the world around her like a shadowy afterimage. Holding between the two was difficult.

Use the Light, Pattern said. *Bring them.*

Shallan hesitantly drew the Light into herself. The spheres in the ocean below moved like a school of fish, surging toward her, clinking together. In her exhaustion, Shallan could barely maintain her double state, and she grew woozy, looking down.

She held on, somehow.

Pattern stood beside her, in his form with the stiff clothing and a head made of impossible lines, arms clasped behind his back, and hovering as if in the air. He was tall and imposing on this side, and she absently noticed that he cast a shadow the wrong way, *toward* the distant, cold-seeming sun instead of away from it.

'Good,' he said, his voice a deeper hum here. 'Good.' He cocked his head, and though he had no eyes, turned around as if regarding the place. 'I am from here, yet I remember so little . . .'

Shallan had a sense that her time was limited. Kneeling, she reached down and felt at the sticks she'd piled to form the place for her fire. She could feel the sticks – but as she looked into this strange realm, her fingers also found one of the glass beads that had surged up beneath her.

As she touched it, she noticed something sweeping through the air above her. She cringed, looking up to find large, birdlike creatures circling around her in Shadesmar. They were a dark grey and seemed to have no specific shape, their forms blurry.

'What . . .'

'Spren,' Pattern said. 'Drawn by you. Your . . . tiredness?'

'Exhaustionspren?' she asked, shocked by their size here.

'Yes.'

She shivered, then looked down at the sphere beneath her hand. She was dangerously close to falling into Shadesmar completely, and could barely see the impressions of the physical realm around her. Only those beads. She felt as if she would tumble into their sea at any moment.

'Please,' Shallan said to the sphere. 'I need you to become fire.'

Pattern buzzed, speaking with a new voice, interpreting the sphere's words. 'I am a stick,' he said. He sounded satisfied.

'You could be fire,' Shallan said.

'I am a stick.'

The stick was not particularly eloquent. She supposed that she shouldn't be surprised.

'Why don't you become fire instead?'

'I am a stick.'

'How do I make it change?' Shallan asked of Pattern.

'Mm . . . I do not know. You must persuade it. Offer it truths, I think?' He sounded agitated. 'This place is dangerous for you. For us. Please. Speed.'

She looked back at the stick.

'You want to burn.'

'I am a stick.'

'Think how much fun it would be?'

'I am a stick.'

'Stormlight,' Shallan said. 'You could have it! All that I'm holding.'

A pause. Finally, 'I am a stick.'

'Sticks need Stormlight. For . . . things . . .' Shallan blinked away tears of fatigue.

'I am—'

'—a stick,' Shallan said. She gripped the sphere, feeling both it and the stick in the physical realm, trying to think through another argument. For a moment, she hadn't felt quite so tired, but it was returning – crashing back upon her. Why . . .

Her Stormlight was running out.

It was gone in a moment, drained from her, and she exhaled, slipping into Shadesmar with a sigh, feeling overwhelmed and exhausted.

She fell into the sea of spheres. That awful blackness, millions of moving bits, consuming her.

She threw herself from Shadesmar.

The spheres expanded outward, growing into sticks and rocks and trees, restoring the world as she knew it. She collapsed into her small stand of trees, heart pounding.

All grew normal around her. No more distant sun, no more sea of spheres. Just frigid cold, a night sky, and biting wind that blew between the trees. The single sphere she'd drained slipped from her fingers, clicking against the stone ground. She leaned back against Jasnah's trunk. Her arms still ached from dragging that up the beach to the trees.

She huddled there, frightened. 'Do you know how to make fire?' she asked Pattern. Her teeth chattered. Stormfather. She didn't feel cold anymore, but her teeth were chattering, and her breath was visible as vapor in the starlight.

She found herself growing drowsy. Maybe she should just sleep, then try to deal with it all in the morning.

'Change?' Pattern asked. 'Offer the change.'

'I tried.'

'I know.' His vibrations sounded depressed.

Shallan stared at that pile of sticks, feeling utterly useless. What was it Jasnah had said? Control is the basis of all true power? Authority and strength are matters of perception? Well, this was a direct refutation of *that*. Shallan could imagine herself as grand, could act like a queen, but that didn't change a thing out here in the wilderness.

Well, Shallan thought, *I'm not going to sit here and freeze to death. I'll at least freeze to death trying to find help.*

She didn't move, though. Moving was hard. At least here, huddled by the trunk, she didn't have to feel the wind so much. Just lying here until morning . . .

She curled into a ball.

No. This didn't seem right. She coughed, then somehow got to her feet. She stumbled away from her not-fire, dug a sphere from her safepouch, then started walking.

Pattern moved at her feet. Those were bloodier now. She left a red trail on the rock. She couldn't feel the cuts.

She walked and walked. And walked.

And . . .

Light.

She didn't move any more quickly. She couldn't. But she did keep going, shambling directly toward that pinprick in the darkness. A numb part of her worried that the light was really Nomon, the second moon. That she'd march toward it and fall off the edge of Roshar itself.

So she surprised herself by stumbling right into the middle of a small group of people sitting around a campfire. She blinked, looking from one face to another; then – ignoring the sounds they made, for words were meaningless to her in this state – she walked to the campfire and lay down, curled up, and fell asleep.

❖

147

'Brightness?'

Shallan grumbled, rolling over. Her face hurt. No, her *feet* hurt. Her face was nothing compared to that pain.

If she slept a little longer, maybe it would fade. At least for that time....

'B-Brightness?' the voice asked again. 'Are you feeling well, yes?'

That was a Thaylen accent. Dredged from deep within her, a light surfaced, bringing memories. The ship. Thaylens. The sailors?

Shallan forced her eyes open. The air smelled faintly of smoke from the still-smoldering fire. The sky was a deep violet, brightening as the sun broke the horizon. She'd slept on hard rock, and her body ached.

She didn't recognize the speaker, a portly Thaylen man with a white beard wearing a knit cap and an old suit and vest, patched in a few inconspicuous places. He wore his white Thaylen eyebrows tucked up over his ears. Not a sailor. A merchant.

Shallan stifled a groan, sitting up. Then, in a moment of panic, she checked her safehand. One of her fingers had slipped out of the sleeve, and she pulled it back in. The Thaylen's eyes flicked toward it, but he said nothing.

'You are well, then?' the man asked. He spoke in Alethi. 'We were going to pack to go, you see. Your arrival last night was ... unexpected. We did not wish to disturb you, but thought perhaps you would want to wake before we depart.'

Shallan ran her freehand through her hair, a mess of red locks stuck with twigs. Two other men – tall, hulking, and of Vorin descent – packed up blankets and bedrolls. She'd have killed for one of those during the night. She remembered tossing uncomfortably.

Stilling the needs of nature, she turned and was surprised to see three large chull wagons with cages on the back. Inside were a handful of dirty, shirtless men. It took just a moment for it all to click.

Slavers.

She shoved down an initial burst of panic. Slaving was a perfectly legal profession. Most of the time. Only this was the Frostlands, far from the rule of any group or nation. Who was to say what was legal here and what was not?

Be calm, she told herself forcefully. *They wouldn't have awakened you politely if they were planning something like that.*

Selling a Vorin woman of high dahn – which the dress marked her as being – would be a risky gambit for a slaver. Most owners in civilized lands would require documentation of the slave's past, and it was rare indeed that a lighteyes was made a slave, aside from ardents. Usually someone of higher breeding would simply be executed instead. Slavery was a mercy for the lower classes.

'Brightness?' the slaver asked nervously.

She was thinking like a scholar again, to distract herself. She'd need to get past that.

'What is your name?' Shallan asked. She hadn't intended to make her voice quite so emotionless, but the shock of what she'd seen left her in turmoil.

The man stepped back at her tone. 'I am Tvlakv, humble merchant.'

'Slaver,' Shallan said, standing up and pushing her hair back from her face.

'As I said. A merchant.'

His two guards watched her as they loaded equipment onto the lead wagon. She did not miss the cudgels they carried prominently at their waists. She'd had a sphere in her hand as she walked last night, hadn't she? Memories of that made her feet flare up again. She had to grit her teeth against the agony as painspren, like orange hands made of sinew, clawed out of the ground nearby. She'd need to clean her wounds, but bloodied and bruised as they were, she wasn't going to be walking anywhere anytime soon. Those wagons had seats. . . .

They likely stole the sphere from me, she thought. She felt around in her safepouch. The other spheres were still there, but the sleeve was unbuttoned. Had she done that? Had they peeked? She couldn't suppress a blush at the thought.

The two guards regarded her hungrily. Tvlakv acted humble, but his leering eyes were also very eager. These men were one step from robbing her.

But if she left them, she'd probably die out here, alone. Stormfather! What could she do? She felt like sitting down and sobbing. After everything that had happened, now this?

Control is the basis of all power.

How would Jasnah respond to this situation?

The answer was simple. She would be Jasnah.

'I will allow you to assist me,' Shallan said. She somehow kept her voice even, despite the anxious terror she felt inside.

'. . . Brightness?' Tvlakv asked.

'As you can see,' Shallan said, 'I am the victim of a shipwreck. My servants are lost to me. You and your men will do. I have a trunk. We will need to go fetch it.'

She felt like one of the ten fools. Surely he would see through the flimsy act. Pretending you had authority was not the same as having it, no matter what Jasnah said.

'It would . . . of course be our privilege to help,' Tvlakv said. 'Brightness . . . ?'

'Davar,' Shallan said, though she took care to soften her voice. Jasnah wasn't condescending. Where other lighteyes, like Shallan's father, went about with conceited egotism, Jasnah had simply expected people to do as she wished. And they had.

She could make this work. She had to.

'Tradesman Tvlakv,' Shallan said. 'I will need to go to the Shattered Plains. Do you know the way?'

'The Shattered Plains?' the man asked, glancing at his guards, one of whom had approached. 'We were there a few months ago, but are now heading to catch a barge over to Thaylenah. We have completed our trading in this area, with no need to return northward.'

'Ah, but you do have a need to return,' Shallan said, walking toward one of the wagons. Each step was agony. 'To take me.' She glanced around, and gratefully noticed Pattern on the side of a wagon, watching. She walked to the front of that wagon, then held out her hand to the other guard, who stood nearby.

He looked at the hand mutely, scratching his head. Then he looked at the wagon and climbed onto it, reaching down to help her up.

Tvlakv walked over to her. 'It will be an expensive trip for us to return without wares! I have only these slaves I purchased at the Shallow Crypts. Not enough to justify the trip back, not yet.'

'Expensive?' Shallan asked, seating herself, trying to project amusement. 'I assure you, tradesman Tvlakv, the expense is minuscule to me. You will be greatly compensated. Now, let us be moving. There are important people waiting for me at the Shattered Plains.'

'But Brightness,' Tvlakv said. 'You've obviously had a difficult time of events recently, yes, that I can see. Let me take you to the Shallow Crypts. It is much closer. You can find rest there and send word to those waiting for you.'

'Did I ask to be taken to the Shallow Crypts?'

'But . . .' He trailed off as she focused her gaze on him.

She softened her expression. 'I know what I am doing, and thank you for the advice. Now let us be moving.'

The three men exchanged befuddled looks, and the slaver took his knit cap off, wringing it in his hands. Nearby, a pair of parshmen with marbled skin walked into camp. Shallan nearly jumped as they trudged by, carrying dried rockbud shells they'd apparently been gathering for fires. Tvlakv gave them no heed.

Parshmen. Voidbringers. Her skin crawled, but she couldn't worry about them right now. She looked back at the slaver, expecting him to ignore her orders. However, he nodded. And then, he and his men simply . . . did as she said. They hitched up the chulls, the slaver got directions to her trunk, and they started moving without further objection.

They might just be going along for now, Shallan told herself, *because they want to know what's in my trunk. More to rob.* But when they reached it, they heaved it onto the wagon, lashed it in place, and then turned around and headed to the north.

Toward the Shattered Plains.

HERO

Unfortunately, we fixated upon Sadeas's plotting so much that we did not take note of the changed pattern of our enemies, the murderers of my husband, the true danger. I would like to know what wind brought about their sudden, inexplicable transformation.

– From the journal of Navani Kholin, Jesesach 1174

Kaladin pressed the stone against the wall of the chasm, and it stuck there. 'All right,' he said, stepping back.

Rock jumped up and grabbed it, then dangled from the wall, bending legs below. His deep, bellowing laugh echoed in the chasm. 'This time, he holds me!'

Sigzil made a notation on his ledger. 'Good. Keep hanging on, Rock.'

'For how long?' Rock asked.

'Until you fall.'

'Until I . . .' The large Horneater frowned, hanging from the stone with both hands. 'I do not like this experiment any longer.'

'Oh, don't whine,' Kaladin said, folding his arms and leaning on the wall beside Rock. Spheres lit the chasm floor around them, with its vines, debris, and blooming plants. 'You're not dropping far.'

'It is not the drop,' Rock complained. 'It is my arms. I am big man, you see.'

'So it's a good thing you have big arms to hold you.'

'It does not work that way, I think,' Rock said, grunting. 'And the handhold is not good. And I—'

The stone popped free and Rock fell downward. Kaladin grabbed his arm, steadying him as he caught himself.

'Twenty seconds,' Sigzil said. 'Not very long.'

'I warned you,' Kaladin said, picking up the fallen stone. 'It lasts longer if I use more Stormlight.'

'I think we need a baseline,' Sigzil said. He fished in his pocket and pulled out a glowing diamond chip, the smallest denomination of sphere. 'Take all of the Stormlight from this, put it into the stone, then we'll hang Rock from that and see how long he takes to fall.'

Rock groaned. 'My poor arms . . .'

'Hey, mancha,' Lopen called from farther down the chasm, 'at least you've got two of them, eh?' The Herdazian was watching to make sure none of the new recruits somehow wandered over and saw what Kaladin was doing. It shouldn't happen – they were practicing several chasms over – but Kaladin wanted someone on guard.

Eventually they'll all know anyway, Kaladin thought, taking the chip from Sigzil. *Isn't that what you just promised Syl? That you'd let yourself become a Radiant?*

Kaladin drew in the chip's Stormlight with a sharp intake of breath, then infused the Light into the stone. He was getting better at that, drawing the Stormlight into his hand, then using it like luminescent paint to coat the bottom of the rock. The Stormlight soaked into the stone, and when he pressed it against the wall, it stayed there.

Smoky tendrils of luminescence rose from the stone. 'We probably don't need to make Rock hang from it,' Kaladin said. 'If you need a baseline, why not just use how long the stone remains there on its own?'

'Well, that's less fun,' Sigzil said. 'But very well.' He continued to write numbers on his ledger. That would have made most of the other bridgemen uncomfortable. A man writing was seen as unmasculine, even blasphemous – though Sigzil was only writing glyphs.

Today, fortunately, Kaladin had with him Sigzil, Rock, and Lopen – all foreigners from places with different rules. Herdaz was Vorin, technically, but they had their own brand of it and Lopen didn't seem to mind a man writing.

'So,' Rock said as they waited, 'Stormblessed leader, you said there was something else you could do, did you not?'

'Fly!' Lopen said from down the passage.

'I can't fly,' Kaladin said dryly.

'Walk on walls!'

'I tried that,' Kaladin said. 'I nearly broke my head from the fall.'

'Ah, gancho,' Lopen said. 'No flying *or* walking on walls? I need to impress the women. I do not think sticking rocks to walls will be enough.'

'I think anyone would find that impressive,' Sigzil said. 'It defies the laws of nature.'

'You do not know many Herdazian women, do you?' Lopen asked, sighing. 'Really, I think we should try again on the flying. It would be the best.'

'There *is* something more,' Kaladin said. 'Not flying, but still useful. I'm not certain I can replicate it. I've never done it consciously.'

'The shield,' Rock said, standing by the wall, staring up at the rock. 'On the battlefield, when the Parshendi shot at us. The arrows hit your shield. *All* the arrows.'

'Yes,' Kaladin said.

'We should test that,' Sigzil said. 'We'll need a bow.'

'Spren,' Rock said, pointing. 'They pull the stone against the wall.'

'What?' Sigzil said, scrambling over, squinting at the rock Kaladin had pressed against the wall. 'I don't see them.'

'Ah,' Rock said. 'Then they do not wish to be seen.' He bowed his head toward them. 'Apologies, *mafah'liki.*'

Sigzil frowned, looking closer, holding up a sphere to light the area. Kaladin walked over and joined them. He could make out the tiny purple spren if he looked closely. 'They're there, Sig,' Kaladin said.

'Then why can't I see them?'

'It has to do with my abilities,' Kaladin said, glancing at Syl, who sat on a cleft in the rock nearby, one leg draping over and swinging.

'But Rock—'

'I am *alaii'iku,*' Rock said, raising a hand to his breast.

'Which means?' Sigzil asked impatiently.

'That I can see these spren, and you cannot.' Rock rested a hand on the smaller man's shoulder. 'It is all right, friend. I do not blame you for being blind. Most lowlanders are. It is the air, you see. Makes your brains stop working right.'

Sigzil frowned, but wrote down some notes while absently doing something with his fingers. Keeping track of the seconds? The rock finally popped off the wall, trailing a few final wisps of Stormlight as it hit the ground. 'Well over a minute,' Sigzil said. 'I counted eighty-seven seconds.' He looked to the rest of them.

'We were supposed to be counting?' Kaladin asked, glancing at Rock, who shrugged.

Sigzil sighed.

'Ninety-one seconds,' Lopen called. 'You're welcome.'

Sigzil sat down on a rock, ignoring a few finger bones peeking out of the moss beside him, and made some notations on his ledger. He scowled.

'Ha!' Rock said, squatting down beside him. 'You look like you have eaten bad eggs. What is problem?'

'I don't know what I'm doing, Rock,' Sigzil said. 'My master taught me to ask questions and find precise answers. But how can I be precise? I would need a clock for the timing, but they are too expensive. Even if we had one, I don't know how to measure Stormlight!'

'With chips,' Kaladin said. 'The gemstones are precisely weighed before being encased in glass.'

'And can they all hold the same amount?' Sigzil asked. 'We know that uncut gems hold less than cut ones. So is one that was cut better going to hold more? Plus, Stormlight fades from a sphere over time. How many days has it been since that chip was infused, and how much Light has it lost since then? Do they all lose the same amount at the same rate? We know too little. I think perhaps I am wasting your time, sir.'

'It's not a waste,' Lopen said, joining them. The one-armed Herdazian yawned, sitting down on the rock by Sigzil, forcing the other man over a little. 'We just need to be testing other things, eh?'

'Like what?' Kaladin said.

'Well, gancho,' Lopen said. 'Can you stick me to the wall?'

'I . . . I don't know,' Kaladin said.

'Seems like it would be good to know, eh?' Lopen stood up. 'Shall we try?'

Kaladin glanced at Sigzil, who shrugged.

Kaladin drew in more Stormlight. The raging tempest filled him, as if it were battering against his skin, a captive trying to find a way out. He drew the Stormlight into his hand and pressed it against the wall, painting the stones with luminescence.

Taking a deep breath, he picked up Lopen – the slender man was startlingly easy to lift, particularly with a measure of Stormlight still inside Kaladin's veins. He pressed Lopen against the wall.

When Kaladin dubiously stepped back, the Herdazian remained there, stuck to the stone by his uniform, which bunched up under his armpits.

Lopen grinned. 'It worked!'

'This thing could be useful,' Rock said, rubbing at his strangely cut Horneater beard. 'Yes, *this* is what we need to test. You are a soldier, Kaladin. Can you use this in combat?'

Kaladin nodded slowly, a dozen possibilities popping into his head. What if his enemies ran across a pool of Light he had put on the floor? Could he stop a wagon from rolling? Stick his spear to an enemy shield, then yank it from their hands?

'How does it feel, Lopen?' Rock asked. 'Does this thing hurt?'

'Nah,' Lopen said, wiggling. 'I'm worried my coat will rip, or the buttons will snap. Oh. Oh. Question for you! What did the one-armed Herdazian do to the man who stuck him to the wall?'

Kaladin frowned. 'I . . . I don't know.'

'Nothing,' Lopen said. 'The Herdazian was *'armless.'* The slender man burst into laughter.

Sigzil groaned, though Rock laughed. Syl had cocked her head, zipping over to Kaladin. 'Was that a joke?' she asked softly.

'Yes,' Kaladin said. 'A distinctly bad one.'

'Ah, don't say that!' Lopen said, still chuckling. 'It's the best one I know – and trust me, I'm an expert on one-armed Herdazian jokes. "Lopen," my mother always says, "you must learn these to laugh before others do. Then you steal the laughter from them, and have it all for yourself." She is a very wise woman. I once brought her the head of a chull.'

Kaladin blinked. 'You . . . What?'

'Chull head,' Lopen said. 'Very good to eat.'

'You are a strange man, Lopen,' Kaladin said.

'No,' Rock said. 'They really are good. The head, he is best part of chull.'

'I will trust you two on that,' Kaladin said. 'Marginally.' He reached up, taking Lopen by the arm as the Stormlight holding him in place began to fade. Rock grabbed the man's waist, and they helped him down.

'All right,' Kaladin said, instinctively checking the sky for the time, though he couldn't see the sun through the narrow chasm opening above. 'Let's experiment.'

❖

Tempest stoked within him, Kaladin dashed across the chasm floor. His movement startled a group of frillblooms, which pulled in frantically, like hands closing. Vines trembled on the walls and began to curl upward.

Kaladin's feet splashed in stagnant water. He leaped over a mound of debris, trailing Stormlight. He was filled with it, *pounding* with it. That made it easier to use; it *wanted* to flow. He pushed it into his spear.

Ahead, Lopen, Rock, and Sigzil waited with practice spears. Though Lopen wasn't very good – the missing arm was a huge disadvantage – Rock made up for it. The large Horneater would not fight Parshendi and would not kill, but had agreed to spar today, in the name of 'experimentation.'

He fought very well, and Sigzil was acceptable with the spear. Together on the battlefield, the three bridgemen might once have given Kaladin trouble.

Times changed.

Kaladin tossed his spear sideways at Rock, surprising the Horneater, who had raised his weapon to block. The Stormlight made Kaladin's spear stick to Rock's, forming a cross. Rock cursed, trying to turn his spear around to strike, but in doing so smacked himself on the side with Kaladin's spear.

As Lopen's spear struck, Kaladin pushed it down easily with one hand, filling the tip with Stormlight. The weapon hit the pile of refuse and stuck to the wood and bones.

Sigzil's weapon came in, missing Kaladin's chest by a wide margin as he stepped aside. Kaladin nudged and infused the weapon with the flat of his hand, shoving it into Lopen's, which he'd just pulled out of the refuse, plastered with moss and bone. The two spears stuck together.

Kaladin slipped between Rock and Sigzil, leaving the three of them in a jumbled mess, off balance and trying to disentangle their weapons. Kaladin smiled grimly, jogging down to the other end of the chasm. He picked up a spear, then turned, dancing from one foot to the other. The Stormlight encouraged him to move. Standing still was practically impossible while holding so much.

Come on, come on, he thought. The three others finally got their weapons apart as the Stormlight ran out. They formed up to face him again.

Kaladin dashed forward. In the dim light of the chasm, the glow of the smoke rising from him was strong enough to cast shadows that leaped and spun. He crashed through pools, the water cold on his unshod feet. He'd removed his boots; he wanted to feel the stone underneath him.

This time, the three bridgemen set the butts of their spears on the ground as if against a charge. Kaladin smiled, then grabbed the top of his spear – like theirs, it was a practice one, without a real spearhead – and infused it with Stormlight.

He slapped it against Rock's, intending to yank it out of the Horneater's hands. Rock had other plans, and *hauled* his spear back with a strength that took Kaladin by surprise. He nearly lost his grip.

Lopen and Sigzil quickly moved to come at him from either side. *Nice,* Kaladin thought, proud. He'd taught them formations like that, showing them how to work together on the battlefield.

As they drew close, Kaladin let go of his spear and stuck out his leg. The Stormlight flowed out of his bare foot as easily as it did his hands, and he was able to swipe a large glowing arc on the ground. Sigzil stepped in it and tripped, his foot sticking to the Light. He tried to stab as he fell, but there was no force behind the blow.

Kaladin slammed his weight against Lopen, whose strike was off-center. He shoved Lopen against the wall, then pulled back, leaving the Herdazian stuck to the stone, which Kaladin had infused in the heartbeat they'd been pressed together.

'Ah, not again,' Lopen said with a groan.

Sigzil had fallen face-first in the water. Kaladin barely had time to smile before he noticed Rock swinging a log at his head.

An entire log. How had Rock *lifted* that thing? Kaladin threw himself out of the way, rolling on the ground and scraping his hand as the log crashed against the floor of the chasm.

Kaladin growled, Stormlight passing between his teeth and rising into the air in front of him. He jumped onto Rock's log as the Horneater tried to lift it again.

Kaladin's landing slammed the wood back against the ground. He leaped toward Rock, and part of him wondered just what he was thinking, getting into a hand-to-hand fight with someone twice his weight. He slammed into the Horneater, hurling them both to the ground. They rolled in the moss, Rock twisting to pin Kaladin's arms. The Horneater obviously had training as a wrestler.

Kaladin poured Stormlight into the ground. It wouldn't affect or hamper him, he'd found. So, as they rolled, first Rock's arm stuck to the ground, then his side.

The Horneater kept fighting to get Kaladin into a hold. He almost had it, till Kaladin pushed with his legs, rolling both of them so Rock's other elbow touched the ground, where it stuck.

Kaladin tore away, gasping and puffing, losing most of his remaining Stormlight as he coughed. He leaned up against the wall, mopping sweat from his face.

'Ha!' Rock said, stuck to the ground, splayed with arms to the sides. 'I almost had you. Slippery as a fifth son, you are!'

'Storms, Rock,' Kaladin said. 'What I wouldn't do to get you on the battlefield. You are wasted as a cook.'

'You don't like the food?' Rock asked, laughing. 'I will have to try something with more grease. This thing will fit you! Grabbing you was like trying to keep my hands on a live lakefish! One that has been covered in butter! Ha!'

Kaladin stepped up to him, squatting down. 'You're a warrior, Rock. I saw it in Teft, and you can say whatever you want, but I see it in you.'

'I am wrong son to be soldier,' Rock said stubbornly. 'It is a thing of the *tuanalikina*, the fourth son or below. Third son cannot be wasted in battle.'

'Didn't stop you from throwing a tree at my head.'

'Was small tree,' Rock said. 'And very hard head.'

Kaladin smiled, then reached down, touching the Stormlight infused into the stone beneath Rock. He hadn't ever tried to take it back after using it in this way. Could he? He closed his eyes and breathed in, trying . . . yes.

Some of the tempest within him stoked again. When he opened his eyes, Rock was free. Kaladin hadn't been able to take it all back, but some. The rest was evaporating into the air.

He took Rock by the hand, helping the larger man to his feet. Rock dusted himself off.

'That was *embarrassing*,' Sigzil said as Kaladin walked over to free him too. 'It's like we're children. The Prime's own eyes have not seen such a shameful show.'

'I have a very unfair advantage,' Kaladin said, helping Sigzil to his feet. 'Years of training as a soldier, a larger build than you. Oh, and the ability to emit Stormlight from my fingers.' He patted Sigzil on the shoulder. 'You did well. This is just a test, like you wanted.'

A more useful type of test, Kaladin thought.

'Sure,' Lopen said from behind them. 'Just go ahead and leave the Herdazian stuck to the wall. The view here is wonderful. Oh, and is that slime running down my cheek? A fresh new look for the Lopen, who cannot brush it away, because – have I mentioned? – his hand is stuck to *the wall*.'

Kaladin smiled, walking over. 'You were the one who asked me to stick you to a wall in the first place, Lopen.'

'My other hand?' Lopen said. 'The one that was cut off long ago, eaten by a fearsome beast? It is making a rude gesture toward you right now. I thought you would wish to know, so that you can prepare to be insulted.' He said it with the same lightheartedness with which he seemed to approach everything. He had even joined the bridge crew with a certain crazy eagerness.

Kaladin let him down.

'This thing,' Rock said, 'it worked well.'

'Yes,' Kaladin said. Though honestly, he probably could have dispatched the three men more easily just by using a spear and the extra speed and strength the Stormlight lent. He didn't know yet whether that was because he was unfamiliar with these new powers, but he did think that forcing himself to use them had put him in some awkward positions.

Familiarity, he thought. *I need to know these abilities as well as I know my spear.*

That meant practice. Lots of practice. Unfortunately, the best way to practice was to find someone who matched or bested you in skill, strength, and capacity. Considering what he could now do, that was going to be a tall order.

The three others walked over to dig waterskins from their packs, and

Kaladin noticed a figure standing in the shadows a little ways down the chasm. Kaladin stood up, alarmed until Teft emerged into the light of their spheres.

'I thought you were going to be on watch,' Teft growled at Lopen.

'Too busy being stuck to walls,' Lopen said, raising his waterskin. 'I thought you had a bunch of greenvines to train?'

'Drehy has them in hand,' Teft said, picking his way around some debris, joining Kaladin beside the chasm wall. 'I don't know if the lads told you, Kaladin, but bringing that lot down here broke them out of their shells somehow.'

Kaladin nodded.

'How did you get to know people so well?' Teft asked.

'It involves a lot of cutting them apart,' Kaladin said, looking down at his hand, which he'd scraped while fighting Rock. The scrape was gone, Stormlight having healed the tears in his skin.

Teft grunted, glancing back at Rock and the other two, who had broken out rations. 'You ought to put Rock in charge of the new recruits.'

'He won't fight.'

'He just sparred with you,' Teft said. 'So maybe he will with them. People like him more than me. I'm just going to screw this up.'

'You'll do a fine job, Teft, I won't have you saying otherwise. We have resources now. No more scrimping for every last sphere. You'll train those lads, and you'll do it *right*.'

Teft sighed, but said no more.

'You saw what I did.'

'Aye,' Teft said. 'We'll need to bring down the entire group of twenty if we want to give you a proper challenge.'

'That or find another person like myself,' Kaladin said. 'Someone to spar with.'

'Aye,' Teft said again, nodding, as if he hadn't considered that.

'There were ten orders of knights, right?' Kaladin asked. 'Do you know much of the others?' Teft had been the first one to figure out what Kaladin could do. He'd known before Kaladin himself had.

'Not much,' Teft said with a grimace. 'I know the orders didn't always get along, despite what the official stories say. We'll need to see if we can find someone who knows more than I do. I . . . I kept away. And the people I knew who could tell us, they aren't around any longer.'

If Teft had been in a dour mood before, this drove him down even further. He looked at the ground. He spoke of his past infrequently, but Kaladin was more and more certain that whoever these people had been, they were dead because of something Teft himself had done.

'What would you think if you heard that somebody wanted to refound the Knights Radiant?' Kaladin said softly to Teft.

Teft looked up sharply. 'You—'

'Not me,' Kaladin said, speaking carefully. Dalinar Kholin had let him listen in on the conference, and while Kaladin trusted Teft, there were certain expectations of silence that an officer was required to uphold.

Dalinar is a lighteyes, part of him whispered. *He wouldn't think twice if he were revealing a secret you'd shared with him.*

'Not me,' Kaladin repeated. 'What if a king somewhere decided he wanted to gather a group of people and name them Knights Radiant?'

'I'd call him an idiot,' Teft said. 'Now, the Radiants weren't what people say. They weren't traitors. They just *weren't*. But everyone is sure they betrayed us, and you're not going to change minds quickly. Not unless you can Surgebind to quiet them.' Teft looked Kaladin up and down. 'Are you going to do it, lad?'

'They'd hate me, wouldn't they?' Kaladin said. He couldn't help noticing Syl, who walked through the air until she was close, studying him. 'For what the old Radiants did.' He held up a hand to stop Teft's objection. 'What people *think* they did.'

'Aye,' Teft said.

Syl folded her arms, giving Kaladin a look. *You promised,* that look said.

'We'll have to be careful about how we do it, then,' Kaladin said. 'Go gather the new recruits. They've had enough practice down here for one day.'

Teft nodded, then jogged off to do as ordered. Kaladin gathered his spear and the spheres he'd set out to light the sparring, then waved to the other three. They packed up their things and began the hike back out.

'So you're going to do it,' Syl said, landing on his shoulder.

'I want to practice more first,' Kaladin said. *And get used to the idea.*

'It will be fine, Kaladin.'

'No. It will be hard. People will hate me, and even if they don't, I'll be set apart from them. Separated. I've accepted that as my lot, though. I'll deal with it.' Even in Bridge Four, Moash was the only one who didn't treat Kaladin like some mythological savior Herald. Him and maybe Rock.

Still, the other bridgemen hadn't reacted with the fear he'd once worried about. They might idolize him, but they did not isolate him. It was good enough.

They reached the rope ladder before Teft and the greenvines, but there was no reason to wait. Kaladin climbed up out of the muggy chasm onto the plateau just east of the warcamps. It felt so strange to be able to carry his spear and money out of the chasm. Indeed, the soldiers guarding the approach to Dalinar's warcamp didn't pester him – instead, they saluted and stood up straight. It was as crisp a salute as he'd ever gotten, as crisp as the ones given to a general.

'They seem proud of you,' Syl said. 'They don't even know you, but they're proud of you.'

'They're darkeyes,' Kaladin said, saluting back. 'Probably men who were fighting on the Tower when Sadeas betrayed them.'

'Stormblessed,' one of them called. 'Have you heard the news?'

Curse the one who told them that nickname, Kaladin thought as Rock and the other two caught up to him.

'No,' Kaladin called. 'What news?'

'A hero has come to the Shattered Plains!' the soldier yelled back. 'He's going to meet with Brightlord Kholin, perhaps support him! It's a good sign. Might help calm things down around here.'

'What's this?' Rock called back. 'Who?' The soldier said a name.

Kaladin's heart became ice.

He nearly lost his spear from numb fingers. And then, he took off running. He didn't heed Rock's cry behind him, didn't stop to let the others catch up with him. He dashed through the camp, running toward Dalinar's command complex at its center.

He didn't want to believe when he saw the banner hanging in the air above a group of soldiers, probably matched by a much larger group outside the warcamp. Kaladin passed them, drawing cries and stares, questions if something was wrong.

He finally stumbled to a stop outside the short set of steps into Dalinar's bunkered complex of stone buildings. There, standing in front, the Blackthorn clasped hands with a tall man.

Square-faced and dignified, the newcomer wore a pristine uniform.

He laughed, then embraced Dalinar. 'Old friend,' he said. 'It's been too long.'

'Too long by far,' Dalinar agreed. 'I'm glad you finally made your way here, after years of promises. I heard you've even found yourself a Shardblade!'

'Yes,' the newcomer said, pulling back and holding his hand to the side. 'Taken from an assassin who dared try to kill me on the field of battle.'

The Blade appeared. Kaladin stared at the silvery weapon. Etched along its length, the Blade was shaped to look like flames in motion, and to Kaladin it seemed that the weapon was stained red. Names flooded his mind: Dallet, Coreb, Reesh . . . a squad before time, from another life. Men Kaladin had loved.

He looked up and forced himself to see the face of the newcomer. A man Kaladin hated, *hated* beyond any other. A man he had once worshipped.

Highlord Amaram. The man who had stolen Kaladin's Shardblade, branded his forehead, and sold him into slavery.

THE END OF

Part One

INTERLUDES

ESHONAI • YM • RYSN

The Rhythm of Resolve thrummed softly in the back of Eshonai's mind as she reached the plateau at the center of the Shattered Plains.

The central plateau. Narak. Exile.

Home.

She ripped the helm of the Shardplate from her head, taking a deep breath of cool air. Plate ventilated wonderfully, but even it grew stuffy after extended exertions. Other soldiers landed behind her – she had taken some fifteen hundred this run. Fortunately, this time they'd arrived well before the humans, and had harvested the gemheart with minimal fighting. Devi carried it; he had earned the privilege by being the one to spot the chrysalis from afar.

Almost she wished it had not been so easy a run. Almost.

Where are you, Blackthorn? she thought, looking westward. *Why have you not come to face me again?*

She thought she'd seen him on that run a week or so back, when they'd been forced off the plateau by his son. Eshonai had not participated in that fight; her wounded leg ached, and the jumping from plateau to plateau had stressed it, even in Shardplate. Perhaps she should not be going on these runs in the first place.

She'd wanted to be there in case her strike force grew surrounded, and needed a Shardbearer – even a wounded one – to break them free. Her leg still hurt, but Plate cushioned it enough. Soon she would have to return to the fighting. Perhaps if she participated directly, the Blackthorn would appear again.

She *needed* to speak with him. She felt an urgency to do so blowing upon the winds themselves.

Her soldiers raised hands in farewell as they went their separate ways. Many softly sang or hummed a song to the Rhythm of Mourning. These days, few sang to Excitement, or even to Resolve. Step by step, storm by storm, depression claimed her people – the listeners, as they called their race. 'Parshendi' was a human term.

Eshonai strode toward the ruins that dominated Narak. After so many years, there wasn't much left. Ruins of ruins, one might call them. The works of men and listeners alike did not last long before the might of the highstorms.

That stone spire ahead, that had probably once been a tower. Over the centuries, it had grown a thick coating of crem from the raging storms. The soft crem had seeped into cracks and filled windows, then slowly hardened. The tower now looked like an enormous stalagmite, rounded point toward the sky, side knobbed with rock that looked as if it had been melted.

The spire must have had a strong core to survive the winds so long. Other examples of ancient engineering had not fared so well. Eshonai passed lumps and mounds, remnants of fallen buildings that had slowly been consumed by the Shattered Plains. The storms were unpredictable. Sometimes huge sections of rock would break free from formations, leaving gouges and jagged edges. Other times, spires would stand for centuries, growing – not shrinking – as the winds both weathered and augmented them.

Eshonai had discovered similar ruins in her explorations, such as the one she'd been on when her people had first encountered humans. Only seven years ago, but also an eternity. She had loved those days, exploring a wide world that felt infinite. And now . . .

Now she spent her life trapped on this one plateau. The wilderness called to her, sang that she should gather up what things she could carry and strike out. Unfortunately, that was no longer her destiny.

She passed into the shadow of a big lump of rock that she always imagined might have been a city gate. From what little they'd learned from their spies over the years, she knew that the Alethi did not understand. They marched over the uneven surface of the plateaus and saw only natural rock, never knowing that they traversed the bones of a city long dead.

Eshonai shivered, and attuned the Rhythm of the Lost. It was a soft beat, yet still violent, with sharp, separated notes. She did not attune it for long. Remembering the fallen was important, but working to protect the living was more so.

She attuned Resolve again and entered Narak. Here, the listeners had built the best home they could during the years of war. Rocky shelves had become barracks, carapace from greatshells forming the walls and roofs. Mounds that had once been buildings now grew rockbuds for food on their leeward sides. Much of the Shattered Plains had once been populated, but the largest city had been here at the center. So now the ruins of her people made their home in the ruins of a dead city.

They had named it Narak – exile – for it was where they had come to be separated from their gods.

Listeners, both malen and femalen, raised hands to her as she passed. So few remained. The humans were relentless in their pursuit of vengeance.

She didn't blame them.

She turned toward the Hall of Art. It was nearby, and she hadn't put in an appearance there for days. Inside, soldiers did a laughable job of painting. Eshonai strode among them, still wearing her Shardplate, helm under her arm. The long building had no roof – allowing in plenty of light to paint by – and the walls were thick with long-hardened crem. Holding thick-bristled brushes, the soldiers tried their best to depict the arrangement of rockbud flowers on a pedestal at the center. Eshonai did a round of the artists, looking at their work. Paper was precious and canvas nonexistent, so they painted on shell.

The paintings were awful. Splotches of garish color, off-center petals … Eshonai paused beside Varanis, one of her lieutenants. He held the brush delicately between armored fingers, a hulking form before an easel. Plates of chitin armor grew from his arms, shoulders, chest, even head. They were matched by her own, under her Plate.

'You are getting better,' Eshonai said to him, speaking to the Rhythm of Praise.

He looked to her, and hummed softly to Skepticism.

Eshonai chuckled, resting a hand on his shoulder. 'It actually looks like flowers, Varanis. I mean it.'

'It looks like muddy water on a brown plateau,' he said. 'Maybe with some brown leaves floating in it. Why do colors turn brown when they mix? Three beautiful colors put together, and they become the *least* beautiful color. It makes no sense, General.'

General. At times, she felt as awkward in the position as these men did trying to paint pictures. She wore warform, as she needed the armor for battle, but she preferred workform. More limber, more rugged. It wasn't that she disliked leading these men, but doing the same thing every day – drills, plateau runs – numbed her mind. She wanted to be seeing new things, going new places. Instead, she joined her people in a long funeral vigil as, one by one, they died.

No. We will find a way out of it.

The art was part of that, she hoped. By her order, each man or woman took a turn in the Hall of Art at their appointed time. And they tried; they tried *hard*. So far, it had been about as successful as trying to leap a chasm with the other side out of sight. 'No spren?' she asked.

'Not a one.' He said it to the Rhythm of Mourning. She heard that rhythm far too often these days.

'Keep trying,' she said. 'We will not lose this battle for lack of effort.'

'But General,' Varanis said, 'what is the *point*? Having artists won't save us from the swords of humans.'

Nearby, other soldiers turned to hear her answer.

'Artists won't help,' she said to the Rhythm of Peace. 'But my sister is confident that she is close to discovering new forms. If we can discover how to create artists, then it might teach her more about the process of change – and that might help her with her research. Help her discover forms stronger, even, than warform. Artists won't get us out of this, but some other form might.'

Varanis nodded. He was a good soldier. Not all of them were – warform did not intrinsically make one more disciplined. Unfortunately, it did hamper one's artistic skill.

Eshonai had tried painting. She couldn't think the right way, couldn't grasp the abstraction needed to create art. Warform was a good form, versatile. It didn't impede thought, like mateform did. As with workform, you were yourself when you were warform. But each had its quirks. A worker had difficulty committing violence – there was a block in the mind somewhere. That was one of the reasons she liked the form. It forced her to think differently to get around problems.

Neither form could create art. Not well, at least. Mateform was better, but came with a whole host of other problems. Keeping those types focused on anything productive was almost impossible. There were two other forms, though the first – dullform – was one they rarely used. It was a relic of the past, before they'd rediscovered something better.

That left only nimbleform, a general form that was lithe and careful. They used it for nurturing young and doing the kind of work that required more dexterity than brawn. Few could be spared for that form, though it was more skilled at art.

The old songs spoke of hundreds of forms. Now they knew of only five. Well, six if one counted slaveform, the form with no spren, no soul, and no song. The form the humans were accustomed to, the ones they called parshmen. It wasn't really a form at all, however, but a lack of any form.

Eshonai left the Hall of Art, helm under her arm, leg aching. She passed through the watering square, where nimbles had crafted a large pool from sculpted crem. It caught rain during the riddens of a storm, thick with nourishment. Here, workers carried buckets to fetch water. Their forms were strong, almost like that of warform, though with thinner fingers and no armor. Many nodded to her, though as a general she had no authority over them. She was their last Shardbearer.

A group of three mateforms – two female, one male – played in the water, splashing at one another. Barely clothed, they dripped with what others would be *drinking*.

'You three,' Eshonai snapped at them. 'Shouldn't you be doing something?'

Plump and vapid, they grinned at Eshonai. 'Come in!' one called. 'It's fun!'

'Out,' Eshonai said, pointing.

The three muttered to the Rhythm of Irritation as they climbed from the water. Nearby, several workers shook their heads as they passed, one singing to Praise in appreciation of Eshonai. Workers did not like confrontation.

It was an excuse. Just as those who took on mateform used their form as an excuse for their inane activities. When a worker, Eshonai had trained herself to confront when necessary. She'd even been a mate once, and had proven to herself firsthand that one could indeed be productive as a mate, despite . . . distractions.

Of course, the rest of her experiences as a mate had been an utter disaster.

She spoke to Reprimand to the mateforms, her words so passionate that she actually attracted angerspren. She saw them coming from a ways off, drawn by her emotion, moving with an incredible speed – like lightning dancing toward her across the distant stone. The lightning pooled at her feet, turning the stones red.

That put the fear of the gods into the mateforms, and they ran off to report to the Hall of Art. Hopefully, they wouldn't end up in an alcove along the way, mating. Her stomach churned at the thought. She had never been able to fathom people who wanted to *remain* in mateform. Most couples, in order to have a child, would enter the form and sequester themselves away for a year – then would be out of the form as soon after the child's birth as possible. After all, who would want to go out in public like that?

The humans did it. That had baffled her during those early days, when she'd spent time learning their language, trading with them. Not only did humans not change forms, they were *always* ready to mate, always distracted by sexual urges.

What she wouldn't have given to be able to go among them unnoticed, to adopt their monochrome skin for a year and walk their highways, see their grand cities. Instead, she and the others had ordered the murder of the Alethi king in a desperate gambit to stop the listener gods from returning.

Well, that had worked – the Alethi king hadn't been able to put his plan into action. But now, her people were slowly being destroyed as a result.

She finally reached the rock formation she called home: a small, collapsed dome. It reminded her of the ones on the edge of the Shattered Plains, actually – the enormous ones that the humans called warcamps. Her people had lived in those, before abandoning them for the security of the Shattered Plains, with its chasms the humans couldn't jump.

Her home was much, much smaller, of course. During the early days of living here, Venli had crafted a roof of greatshell carapace and built walls to divide the space into chambers. She'd covered it all over with crem, which had hardened with time, creating something that actually felt like a home instead of a shanty.

Eshonai set her helm on a table just inside, but left the rest of her armor on. Shardplate just felt right to her. She liked the sensation of strength. It let her know that something was still reliable in the world. And with the power of Shardplate, she could mostly ignore the wound to her leg.

She ducked through a few rooms, nodding to the people she passed. Venli's associates were scholars, though no one knew the proper form for true scholarship. Nimbleform was their makeshift substitute for now. Eshonai found her sister beside the window of the farthest chamber. Demid, Venli's once-mate, sat next to her. Venli had held nimbleform for three years, as long as they'd known of the form, though in Eshonai's mind's eye she still saw her sister as a worker, with thicker arms and a stouter torso.

That was the past. Now, Venli was a slender woman with a thin face, her marblings delicate swirling patterns of red and white. Nimbleform grew long hairstrands, with no carapace helm to block them. Venli's, a deep red, flowed down to her waist, where they were tied in three places. She wore a robe, drawn tight at the waist and showing a hint of breasts at the chest. This was not mateform, so they were small.

Venli and her once-mate were close, though their time as mates had produced no children. If they'd gone to the battlefield, they'd have been a warpair. Instead, they were a researchpair, or something. The things they spent their days doing were very un-listener. That was the point. Eshonai's people could not afford to be what they had been in the past. The days of lounging isolated on these plateaus – singing songs to one another, only occasionally fighting – were over.

'So?' Venli asked to Curiosity.

'We won,' Eshonai said, leaning back against the wall and folding her arms with a clink of Shardplate. 'The gemheart is ours. We will continue to eat.'

'That is well,' Venli said. 'And your human?'

'Dalinar Kholin. He did not come to this battle.'

'He will not face you again,' Venli said. 'You nearly killed him last time.' She said it to the Rhythm of Amusement as she rose, picking up a piece of paper – they made it from dried rockbud pulp following a harvest – which she handed to her once-mate. Looking it over, he nodded and began making notes on his own sheet.

That paper required precious time and resources to make, but Venli insisted the reward would be worth the effort. She'd better be right.

Venli regarded Eshonai. She had keen eyes – glassy and dark, like those of all listeners. Venli's always seemed to have an extra depth of secret knowledge to them. In the right light, they had a violet cast.

'What would you do, Sister?' Venli asked. 'If you and this Kholin were actually able to stop trying to kill each other long enough to have a conversation?'

'I'd sue for peace.'

'We murdered his brother,' Venli said. 'We slaughtered King Gavilar on a night when he'd invited us into his home. That is not something the Alethi will forget, or forgive.'

Eshonai unfolded her arms and flexed a gauntleted hand. That night. A desperate plan, made between herself and five others. She had been part of it despite her youth, because of her knowledge of the humans. All had voted the same.

Kill the man. Kill him, and risk destruction. For if he had lived to do what he told them that night, all would have been lost. The others who had made that decision with her were dead now.

'I have discovered the secret of stormform,' Venli said.

'*What?*' Eshonai stood up straight. 'You were to be working on a form to help! A form for diplomats, or for scholars.'

'Those will not save us,' Venli said to Amusement. 'If we wish to deal with the humans, we will need the ancient powers.'

'Venli,' Eshonai said, grabbing her sister by the arm. 'Our gods!'

Venli didn't flinch. 'The humans have Surgebinders.'

'Perhaps not. It could have been an Honorblade.'

'You fought him. Was it an Honorblade that struck you, wounded your leg, sent you limping?'

'I . . .' Her leg ached.

'We don't know which of the songs are true,' Venli said. Though she said it to Resolve, she sounded tired, and she drew exhaustionspren. They came with a sound like wind, blowing in through the windows and doors like jets of translucent vapor before becoming stronger, more visible, and spinning around her head like swirls of steam.

My poor sister. She works herself as hard as the soldiers do.

'If the Surgebinders have returned,' Venli continued, 'we must strive for something meaningful, something that can ensure our freedom. The forms of *power*, Eshonai . . .' She glanced at Eshonai's hand, still on her arm. 'At least sit and listen. And stop looming like a mountain.'

Eshonai removed her fingers, but did not sit. Her Shardplate's weight would break a chair. Instead, she leaned forward, inspecting the table full of papers.

Venli had invented the script herself. They'd learned that concept from the humans – memorizing songs was good, but not perfect, even when you had the rhythms to guide you. Information stored on pages was more practical, especially for research.

Eshonai had taught herself the script, but reading was still difficult for her. She did not have much time to practice.

'So . . . stormform?' Eshonai said.

'Enough people of that form,' Venli said, 'could control a highstorm, or even summon one.'

'I remember the song that speaks of this form,' Eshonai said. 'It was a thing of the gods.'

'Most of the forms are related to them in some way,' Venli said. 'Can we really trust the accuracy of words first sung so long ago? When those songs were memorized, our people were mostly dullform.'

It was a form of low intelligence, low capacity. They used it now to spy on the humans. Once, it and mateform had been the only forms her people had known.

Demid shuffled some of the pages, moving a stack. 'Venli is right, Eshonai. This is a risk we must take.'

'We *could* negotiate with the Alethi,' Eshonai said.

'To what end?' Venli said, again to Skepticism, her exhaustionspren finally fading, the spren spinning away to search out more fresh sources of emotion. 'Eshonai, you keep saying you want to negotiate. I think it is because you are fascinated by humans. You think they'll let you go freely among them? A person they see as having the form of a rebellious slave?'

'Centuries ago,' Demid said, 'we escaped both our gods and the humans. Our ancestors left behind civilization, power, and might in order to secure freedom. I would not give that up, Eshonai. Stormform. With it, we can destroy the Alethi army.'

'With them gone,' Venli said, 'you can return to exploration. No responsibility – you could travel, make your maps, discover places no person has ever seen.'

'What I want for myself is meaningless,' Eshonai said to Reprimand, 'so long as we are all in danger of destruction.' She scanned the specks on the page, scribbles of songs. Songs without music, written out as they were. Their souls stripped away.

Could the listeners' salvation really be in something so terrible? Venli and her team had spent five years recording all of the songs, learning the nuances from the elderly, capturing them in these pages. Through collaboration, research, and deep thought, they had discovered nimbleform.

'It is the only way,' Venli said to Peace. 'We will bring this to the Five, Eshonai. I would have you on our side.'

'I . . . I will consider.'

YM

Ym carefully trimmed the wood from the side of the small block. He held it up to the spherelight beside his bench, pinching his spectacles by the rim and holding them closer to his eyes.

Such delightful inventions, spectacles. To live was to be a fragment of the cosmere that was experiencing itself. How could he properly experience if he couldn't see? The Azish man who had first created these devices was long deceased, and Ym had submitted a proposal that he be considered one of the Honored Dead.

Ym lowered the piece of wood and continued to carve it, carefully whittling off the front to form a curve. Some of his colleagues bought their lasts – the wooden forms around which a cobbler built his shoes – from carpenters, but Ym had been taught to make his own. That was the old way, the way it had been done for centuries. If something had been done one way for such a long time, he figured there was probably a good reason.

Behind him stood the shadowed cubbies of a cobbler's shop, the toes of dozens of shoes peeking out like the noses of eels in their holes. These were test shoes, used to judge size, choose materials, and decide styles so he could construct the perfect shoe to fit the foot and character of the individual. A fitting could take quite a while, assuming you did it properly.

Something moved in the dimness to his right. Ym glanced in that direction, but didn't change his posture. The spren had been coming more often lately – specks of light, like those from a piece of crystal suspended in a sunbeam. He did not know its type, as he had never seen one like it before.

It moved across the surface of the workbench, slinking closer. When it stopped, light crept upward from it, like small plants growing or climbing from their burrows. When it moved again, those withdrew.

Ym returned to his sculpting. 'It will be for making a shoe.'

The evening shop was quiet save for the scraping of his knife on wood.

'Sh-shoe . . . ?' a voice asked. Like that of a young woman, soft, with a kind of chiming musicality to it.

'Yes, my friend,' he said. 'A shoe for young children. I find myself in need of those more and more these days.'

'Shoe,' the spren said. 'For ch-children. Little people.'

Ym brushed wooden scraps off the bench for later sweeping, then set the last on the bench near the spren. It shied away, like a reflection off a mirror – translucent, really just a shimmer of light.

He withdrew his hand and waited. The spren inched forward – tentative, like a cremling creeping out of its crack after a storm. It stopped, and light grew upward from it in the shape of tiny sprouts. Such an odd sight.

'You are an interesting experience, my friend,' Ym said as the shimmer of light moved onto the last itself. 'One in which I am honored to participate.'

'I . . .' the spren said. 'I . . .' The spren's form shook suddenly, then grew more intense, like light being focused. '*He comes.*'

Ym stood up, suddenly anxious. Something moved on the street outside. Was it that one? That watcher, in the military coat?

But no, it was just a child, peering in through the open door. Ym smiled, opening his drawer of spheres and letting more light into the room. The child shied back, just as the spren had.

The spren had vanished somewhere. It did that when others drew near.

'No need to fear,' Ym said, settling back down on his stool. 'Come in. Let me get a look at you.'

The dirty young urchin peered back in. He wore only a ragged pair of trousers, no shirt, though that was common here in Iri, where both days and nights were usually warm.

The poor child's feet were dirty and scraped.

'Now,' Ym said, 'that won't do. Come, young one, settle down. Let's 'get something on those feet.' He moved out one of his smaller stools.

'They say you don't charge nothin',' the boy said, not moving.

'They are quite wrong,' Ym said. 'But I think you will find my cost bearable.'

'Don't have no spheres.'

'No spheres are needed. Your payment will be your story. Your experiences. I would hear them.'

'They said you was strange,' the boy said, finally walking into the shop.

'They were right,' Ym said, patting the stool.

The urchin stepped timidly up to the stool, walking with a limp he tried to hide. He was Iriali, though the grime darkened his skin and hair, both of which were golden. The skin less so – you needed the light to see it right – but the hair certainly. It was the mark of their people.

Ym motioned for the child to raise his good foot, then got out a washcloth, wetted it, and cleaned away the grime. He wasn't about to do a fitting on feet so dirty. Noticeably, the boy tucked back the foot he'd limped on, as if trying to hide that it had a rag wrapped around it.

'So,' Ym said, 'your story?'

'You're old,' the boy said. 'Older than anyone I know. Grandpa old. You must know everythin' already. Why do you want to hear from me?'

'It is one of my quirks,' Ym said. 'Come now. Let's hear it.'

The boy huffed, but talked. Briefly. That wasn't uncommon. He wanted to hold his story to himself. Slowly, with careful questions, Ym pried the story free. The boy was the son of a whore, and had been kicked out as soon as he could fend for himself. That had been three years ago, the boy thought. He was probably eight now.

As he listened, Ym cleaned the first foot, then clipped and filed the nails. Once done, he motioned for the other foot.

The boy reluctantly lifted it up. Ym undid the rag, and found a nasty cut on the bottom of that foot. It was already infected, crawling with rotspren, tiny motes of red.

Ym hesitated.

'Needed to get some shoes,' the urchin said, looking the other way. 'Can't keep on without 'em.'

The rip in the skin was jagged. *Done climbing over a fence, perhaps?* Ym thought.

The boy looked at him, feigning nonchalance. A wound like this would slow an urchin down terribly, which on the streets could easily mean death. Ym knew that all too well.

He looked up at the boy, noting the shadow of worry in those little eyes. The infection had spread up the leg.

'My friend,' Ym whispered, 'I believe I am going to need your help.'

'What?' the urchin said.

'Nothing,' Ym replied, reaching into the drawer of his table. The light spilling out was just from five diamond chips. Every urchin who had come to him had seen those. So far, Ym had been robbed of them only twice.

He dug more deeply, unfolding a hidden compartment in the drawer and taking a more powerful sphere – a broam – from there, covering its light quickly in his hand while reaching for some antiseptic with the other hand.

The medicine wasn't going to be enough, not with the boy unable to stay off his feet. Lying in bed for weeks to heal, constantly applying expensive medication? Impossible for an urchin fighting for food each day.

Ym brought his hands back, sphere tucked inside of one. Poor child. It must hurt something fierce. The boy probably ought to have been laid out in bed, feverish, but every urchin knew to chew ridgebark to stay alert and awake longer than they should.

Nearby, the sparkling light spren peeked out from underneath a stack of leather squares. Ym applied the medication, then set it aside and lifted the boy's foot, humming softly.

The glow in Ym's other hand vanished.

The rotspren fled from the wound.

When Ym removed his hand, the cut had scabbed over, the color returning to normal, the signs of infection gone. So far, Ym had used this ability only a handful of times, and had always disguised it as medicine. It was unlike anything he had ever heard of. Perhaps that was why he had been given it – so the cosmere could experience it.

'Hey,' the boy said, 'that feels *a lot* better.'

'I'm glad,' Ym said, returning the sphere and the medicine to his drawer. The spren had retreated. 'Let us see if I have something that fits you.'

He began fitting shoes. Normally, after fitting, he'd send the patron away and craft a perfect set of shoes just for them. For this child, unfortunately, he'd have to use shoes he'd already made. He'd had too many urchins never return for their pair of shoes, leaving him to fret and wonder. Had something happened to them? Had they simply forgotten? Or had their natural suspicion gotten the better of them?

Fortunately, he had several good, sturdy pairs that might fit this boy. *I need more treated hogshide,* he thought, making a note. Children would not properly care for shoes. He needed leather that would age well even if unattended.

'You're really gonna give me a pair of shoes,' the urchin said. 'For *nothin*?'

'Nothing but your story,' Ym said, slipping another testing shoe onto the boy's foot. He'd given up on trying to train urchins to wear socks.

'Why?'

'Because,' Ym said, 'you and I are One.'

'One what?'

'One being,' Ym said. He set aside that shoe and got out another. 'Long ago, there was only One. One knew everything, but had experienced nothing. And so, One became many – us, people. The One, who is both male and female, did so to experience all things.'

'One. You mean God?'

'If you wish to say it that way,' Ym said. 'But it is not completely true. I accept no god. You should accept no god. We are Iriali, and part of the Long Trail, of which this is the Fourth Land.'

'You sound like a priest.'

'Accept no priests either,' Ym said. 'Those are from other lands, come to preach to us. Iriali need no preaching, only experience. As each experience is different, it brings completeness. Eventually, all will be gathered back in – when the Seventh Land is attained – and we will once again become One.'

'So you an' me . . .' the urchin said. 'Are the same?'

'Yes. Two minds of a single being experiencing different lives.'

'That's stupid.'

'It is simply a matter of perspective,' Ym said, dusting the boy's feet with powder and slipping back on a pair of the test shoes. 'Please walk on those for a moment.'

The boy gave him a strange look, but obeyed, trying a few steps. He didn't limp any longer.

'Perspective,' Ym said, holding up his hand and wiggling his fingers. 'From very close up, the fingers on a hand might seem individual and alone. Indeed, the thumb might think it has very little in common with the pinky. But with proper perspective, it is realized that the fingers are part of something much larger. That, indeed, they are One.'

The urchin frowned. Some of that had probably been beyond him. *I need to speak more simply, and—*

'Why do you get to be the finger with the expensive ring,' the boy said, pacing back the other direction, 'while I gotta be the pinky with the broken fingernail?'

Ym smiled. 'I know it sounds unfair, but there can *be* no unfairness, as we are all the same in the end. Besides, I didn't always have this shop.'

'You didn't?'

'No. I think you'd be surprised at where I came from. Please sit back down.'

The boy settled down. 'That medicine works real well. Real, real well.'

Ym slipped off the shoes, using the powder – which had rubbed off in places – to judge how the shoe fit. He fished out a pair of premade shoes, then worked at them for a moment, flexing them in his hands. He'd want a cushion on the bottom for the wounded foot, but something that would tear off after a few weeks, once the wound was healed. . . .

'The things you're talking about,' the boy said. 'They sound dumb to me. I mean, if we're all the same person, shouldn't everyone know this already?'

'As One, we knew truth,' Ym said, 'but as many, we need ignorance. We exist in variety to experience all kinds of thought. That means some of us must know and others must not – just like some must be rich, and others must be poor.' He worked the shoe a moment longer. 'More people *did* know this, once. It's not talked about as much as it should be. Here, let's see if these fit right.'

He handed the boy the shoes, who put them on and tied the laces.

'Your life might be unpleasant – ' Ym began.

'Unpleasant?'

'All right. Downright awful. But it will get better, young one. I promise it.'

'I thought,' the boy said, stamping his good foot to test the shoes, 'that you were gonna tell me that life is awful, but it all don't matter in the end, 'cuz we're going the same place.'

'That's true,' Ym said, 'but isn't very comforting right now, is it?'

'Nope.'

Ym turned back to his worktable. 'Try not to walk on that wounded foot too much, if you can help it.'

The urchin strode to the door with a sudden urgency, as if eager to get away before Ym changed his mind and took back the shoes. He did stop at the doorway, though.

'If we're all just the same person trying out different lives,' the boy said, 'you don't need to give away shoes. 'Cuz it don't matter.'

'You wouldn't hit yourself in the face, would you? If I make your life better, I make my own better.'

'That's crazy talk,' the boy said. '*I* think you're just a nice person.' He ducked out, not speaking another word.

Ym smiled, shaking his head. Eventually, he went back to work on his last. The spren peeked out again.

'Thank you,' Ym said. 'For your help.' He didn't know why he could do what he did, but he knew the spren was involved.

'He's *still here*,' the spren whispered.

Ym looked up toward the doorway out onto the night street. The urchin was there?

Something rustled behind Ym.

He jumped, spinning. The workroom was a place of dark corners and cubbies. Had he perhaps heard a rat?

Why was the door into the back room – where Ym slept – open? He usually left that closed.

A shadow moved in the blackness back there.

'If you've come for the spheres,' Ym said, trembling, 'I have only the five chips here.'

More rustling. The shadow separated itself from the darkness, resolving into a man with dark, Makabaki skin – all save for a pale crescent on his cheek. He wore black and silver, a uniform, but not one from any military that Ym recognized. Thick gloves, with stiff cuffs at the back.

'I had to look very hard,' the man said, 'to discover your indiscretion.'

'I . . .' Ym stammered. 'Just . . . five chips . . .'

'You have lived a clean life, since your youth as a carouser,' the man said, his voice even. 'A young man of means who drank and partied away what his parents left him. That is not illegal. Murder, however, is.'

Ym sank down onto his stool. 'I didn't know. I didn't *know* it would kill her.'

'Poison delivered,' the man said, stepping into the room, 'in the form of a bottle of wine.'

'They told me the vintage itself was the sign!' Ym said. 'That she'd know the message was from them, and that it meant she would need to pay! I was desperate for money. To eat, you see. Those on the streets are not kind . . .'

'You were an accomplice to murder,' the man said, pulling his gloves on more tightly, first one hand, then the other. He spoke with such a stark lack of emotion, he could have been conversing about the weather.

'I didn't know . . .' Ym pled.

'You are guilty nonetheless.' The man reached his hand to the side, and a weapon formed from mist there, then fell into his hand.

A *Shardblade*? What kind of constable of the law was this? Ym stared at that wondrous, silvery Blade.

Then he ran.

It appeared that he still had useful instincts from his time on the streets. He managed to fling a stack of leather toward the man and duck the Blade as it swung for him. Ym scrambled out onto the dark street and charged away, shouting. Perhaps someone would hear. Perhaps someone would help.

Nobody heard.

Nobody helped.

Ym was an old man now. By the time he reached the first cross street, he was gasping for air. He stopped beside the old barber shop, dark inside, door locked. The little spren moved along beside him, a shimmering light that sprayed outward in a circle. Beautiful.

'I guess,' Ym said, panting, 'it is . . . my time. May One . . . find this memory . . . pleasing.'

Footsteps slapped on the street behind, getting closer.

'No,' the spren whispered. 'Light!'

Ym dug in his pocket and pulled out a sphere. Could he use it, somehow, to—

The constable's shoulder slammed Ym against the wall of the barber shop. Ym groaned, dropping the sphere.

The man in silver spun him around. He looked like a shade in the night, a silhouette against the black sky.

'It was *forty* years ago,' Ym whispered.

'Justice does not expire.'

The man shoved the Shardblade through Ym's chest.

Experience ended.

Rysn liked to pretend that her pot of Shin grass was not stupid, but merely contemplative. She sat near the prow of her catamaran, holding the pot in her lap. The otherwise still surface of the Reshi Sea rippled from the paddling of the guide behind her. The warm, damp air made beads of sweat form on Rysn's brow and neck.

It was probably going to rain again. Precipitation here on the sea was the worst kind – not mighty or impressive like a highstorm, not even insistent like an ordinary shower. Here, it was just a misting haze, more than a fog but less than a drizzle. Enough to ruin hair, makeup, clothing – indeed, every element of a careful young woman's efforts to present a suitable face for trading.

Rysn shifted the pot in her lap. She'd named the grass Tyvnk. Sullen. Her babsk had laughed at the name. He understood. In naming the grass, she acknowledged that he was right and she had been wrong; his trade with the Shin people last year had been exceptionally profitable.

Rysn chose not to be sullen at being proven so clearly wrong. She'd let her plant be sullen instead.

They'd traversed these waters for two days now, and then only after waiting at port for weeks until the right time between highstorms for a trip onto the nearly enclosed sea. Today, the waters were shockingly still. Almost as serene as those of the Purelake.

Vstim himself rode two boats over in their irregular flotilla. Paddled by new parshmen, the sixteen sleek catamarans were laden with goods that had been purchased with the profits of their last expedition. Vstim was still resting in the back of his boat. He looked like little more than another bundle of cloth, almost indistinguishable from the sacks of goods.

He would be fine. People got sick. It happened, but he would become well again.

And the blood you saw on his handkerchief?

She suppressed the thought and pointedly turned around in her seat, shifting Tyvnk to the crook of her left arm. She kept the pot *very* clean. That soil stuff the grass needed in order to live was even worse than crem, and it had a proclivity for ruining clothing.

Gu, the flotilla's guide, rode in her own boat, just behind her. He looked a lot like a Purelaker with those long limbs, the leathery skin, and dark hair. Every Purelaker she'd met, however, had cared deeply about those gods of theirs. She doubted Gu had ever cared about *anything*.

That included getting them to their destination in a timely manner.

'You said we were near,' she said to him.

'Oh, we are,' he said, lifting his oar and then slipping it back down into the water. 'Soon, now.' He spoke Thaylen rather well, which was why he'd been hired. It *certainly* wasn't for his punctuality.

'Define "soon,"' Rysn said.

'Define . . .'

'What do you mean by "soon"?'

'Soon. Today, maybe.'

Maybe. Delightful.

Gu continued to paddle, only doing so on one side of the boat, yet somehow keeping them from going in circles. At the rear of Rysn's boat, Kylrm – head of their guards – played with her parasol, opening it and closing it again. He seemed to consider it a wondrous invention, though they'd been popular in Thaylenah for *ages* now.

Shows how rarely Vstim's workers get back to civilization. Another cheerful thought. Well, she'd apprenticed under Vstim wanting to travel to exotic places, and exotic this was. True, she'd expected cosmopolitan and exotic to go hand in hand. If she'd had half a wit – which she wasn't sure she did, these days – she'd have realized that the *really* successful traders weren't the ones who went where everyone else wanted to go.

'Hard,' Gu said, still paddling with his lethargic pace. 'Patterns are off, these days. The gods do not walk where they always should. We shall find her. Yes, we shall.'

Rysn stifled a sigh and turned forward. With Vstim incapacitated again, she was in charge of leading the flotilla. She wished she knew where she was leading it – or even knew how to find their destination.

That was the trouble with islands that moved.

The boats glided past a shoal of branches breaking the sea's surface. Encouraged by the wind, gentle waves lapped against the stiff branches, which reached out of the waters like the fingers of drowning men. The sea was deeper than the Purelake, with its bafflingly shallow waters. Those trees would be dozens of feet tall at the very least, with bark of stone. Gu called them *i-nah*, which apparently meant bad. They could slice up a boat's hull.

Sometimes they'd pass branches hiding just beneath the glassy surface, almost invisible. She didn't know how Gu knew to steer clear of them. In this, as in so much else, they just had to trust him. What would they do if he led them into an ambush out here on these silent waters? Suddenly, she felt very glad that Vstim had ordered their guards to monitor his fabrial that showed if people were drawing near. It—

Land.

Rysn stood up in the catamaran, making it rock precariously. There *was* something ahead, a distant dark line.

'Ah,' Gu said. 'See? Soon.'

Rysn remained standing, waving for her parasol when a sprinkle of rain started to fall. The parasol barely helped, though it was waxed to double as an umbrella. In her excitement, she hardly gave it – or her increasingly frizzy hair – a thought. *Finally.*

The island was much bigger than she'd expected. She'd imagined it to be like a very large boat, not this towering rock formation jutting from the waters like a boulder in a field. It was different from other islands she'd seen; there didn't seem to be any beach, and it wasn't flat and low, but mountainous. Shouldn't the sides and top have eroded over time?

'It's so green,' Rysn said as they drew closer.

'The Tai-na is a good place to grow,' Gu said. 'Good place to live. Except when it's at war.'

'When two islands get too close,' Rysn said. She'd read of this in preparation, though there were not many scholars who cared enough about the Reshi to write of them. Dozens, perhaps hundreds, of these moving islands floated in the sea. The people on them lived simple lives, interpreting the movements of the islands as divine will.

'Not always,' Gu said, chuckling. 'Sometimes close Tai-na is good. Sometimes bad.'

'What determines?' Rysn asked.

'Why, the Tai-na itself.'

'The island decides,' Rysn said flatly, humoring him. Primitives. What *was* her babsk expecting to gain by trading here? 'How can an island—'

Then the island ahead of them moved.

Not in the drifting way she'd imagined. The island's very shape changed, stones twisting and undulating, a huge section of rock rising in a motion that seemed lethargic until one appreciated the grand scale.

Rysn sat down with a plop, her eyes wide. The rock – the *leg* – lifted, streaming water like rainfall. It lurched forward, then crashed back down into the sea with incredible force.

The Tai-na, the gods of the Reshi Isles, were greatshells.

This was the largest beast she'd ever seen, or ever heard of. Big enough to make mythological monsters like the chasmfiends of distant Natanatan seem like pebbles in comparison!

'Why didn't anyone tell me?' she demanded, looking back at the boat's other two occupants. Surely Kylrm at least should have said something.

'Is better to see,' Gu said, paddling with his usual relaxed posture. She did not much care for his smirk.

'And take away that moment of discovery?' Kylrm said. 'I remember when I first saw one move. It's worth not spoiling. We never tell the new guards when they first come.'

Rysn contained her annoyance and looked back at the 'island.' Curse those inaccurate accounts from her readings. Too much hearsay, not enough experience. She found it hard to believe that no one had ever recorded the truth. Likely, she simply had the wrong sources.

A falling haze of rain shrouded the enormous beast in mist and enigma. What did a thing so big eat? Did it notice the people living upon its back; did it care? Kelek . . . What was *mating* like for these monsters?

It had to be ancient. The boat drew into its shadow, and she could see the greenery growing across its stony skin. Shalebark mounds made vast fields of vibrant colors. Moss coated nearly everything. Vines and rockbuds wound around trunks of small trees that had gained a foothold in cracks between plates of the animal's shell.

Gu led the convoy around the hind leg – giving it a very wide berth, to her relief – and came up along the creature's flank. Here, the shell dipped down into the water, forming a platform. She heard the people before she saw them, their laughter rising amid splashes. The rain stopped, so Rysn lowered her parasol and shook it over the water. She finally spotted the people, a group of youths both male and female climbing up onto a ridge of shell and leaping from it into the sea.

That was not so surprising. The water of the Reshi Sea, like that of the Purelake, was remarkably warm. She had once ventured into the water near her homeland. It was a frigid experience, and not one to be engaged in while of sound mind. Frequently, alcohol and bravado were involved in any ocean dip.

Out here, though, she expected that swimmers were commonplace. She had not expected them to be unclothed.

Rysn blushed furiously as a group of people ran past on the docklike shell outcropping, as bare as the day they were born. Young men and women alike, uncaring of who saw. She was no Alethi prude, but ... Kelek! Shouldn't they wear *something*?

Shamespren fell around her, shaped like white and red flower petals that drifted on a wind. Behind her, Gu chuckled.

Kylrm joined him. 'That's another thing we don't warn the newcomers about.'

Primitives, Rysn thought. She shouldn't blush so. She was an adult. Well, almost.

The flotilla continued toward a section of shell that formed a kind of dock – a low plate that hung mostly above water. They settled in to wait, though for what, she didn't know.

After a few moments, the plate lurched – water streaming off it – as the beast took another lethargic step. Waves lapped against the boats from the splashdown ahead. Once things were settled, Gu guided the boat to the dock. 'Up you go,' he said.

'Shall we tie the boats to anything?' Rysn said.

'No. Not safe, with movement. We will pull back.'

'And at night? How do you dock the boats?'

'When we sleep, we move boats away, tie together. Sleep out there. Find island again in the morning.'

'Oh,' Rysn said, taking a calming breath and checking to make sure her pot of grass was carefully stored in the bottom of the catamaran.

She stood up. This was not going to be kind to her shoes, which had been *quite* expensive. She had a feeling the Reshi wouldn't care. She could probably meet their king barefooted. Passions! From what she'd seen, she could probably meet him bare-*chested*.

She climbed up carefully, and was pleased to find that despite being an inch or so underwater, the shell was not slippery. Kylrm climbed up with her and she handed him the folded-up parasol, stepping back and waiting as Gu maneuvered his boat away. Another oarsman brought up his boat instead, a longer catamaran with parshmen to help row.

Her babsk huddled inside, wrapped in his blanket despite the heat, head propped up against the back of the boat. His pale skin had a waxy cast.

'Babsk ...' Rysn said, heart wrenching. 'We should have turned around.'

'Nonsense,' he said, his voice frail. He smiled anyway. 'I've suffered worse. The trade must happen. We've leveraged too much.'

'I will go to the island's king and traders,' Rysn said. 'And ask for them to come here to negotiate with you on the docks.'

Vstim coughed into his hand. 'No. These people aren't like the Shin. My weakness will ruin the deal. Boldness. You must be bold with the Reshi.'

'Bold?' Rysn said, glancing at the boat guide, who lounged with fingers in the water. 'Babsk ... the Reshi are a relaxed people. I do not think much matters to them.'

'You will be surprised, then,' Vstim said. He followed her gaze toward the nearby swimmers, who giggled and laughed as they leaped into the waters. 'Life can be simple here, yes. It attracts such people like war attracts painspren.'

Attracts ... One of the women scampered past, and Rysn noticed with shock that she had *Thaylen* eyebrows. Her skin had been tanned in the sun, so the difference in tones hadn't been immediately obvious. Picking through those swimming, Rysn saw others. Two that were probably Herdazians, even ... an *Alethi*? Impossible.

'People seek out this place,' Vstim said. 'They like the life of the Reshi. Here, they can simply go with the island. Fight when it fights another island. Relax otherwise. There will be people like this in any culture, for every society is made of individuals. You must learn this. Do not let your assumptions about a culture block your ability to perceive the individual, or you will fail.'

She nodded. He seemed so frail, but his words were firm. She tried not to think about the swimming people. The fact that at least one of them was of her own kind made her even *more* embarrassed.

'If you cannot trade with them . . .' Rysn said.

'You must do it.'

Rysn felt cold, despite the heat. This was what she'd joined with Vstim to do, wasn't it? How many times had she wished he would let her lead? Why feel so timid now?

She glanced toward her own boat, moving off, carrying her pot of grass. She looked back at her babsk. 'Tell me what to do.'

'They know much of foreigners,' Vstim said. 'More than we know of them. This is because so many of us come to live among them. Many of the Reshi are as carefree as you say, but there are also many who are not. Those prefer to fight. And a trade . . . it is like a fight to them.'

'To me too,' Rysn said.

'I know these people,' Vstim said. 'We must have Passion that Talik is not here. He is their best, and often goes to trade with other islands. Whichever you do meet for trade, he or she will judge you as they would judge a rival in battle. And to them, battle is about posturing.

'I once had the misfortune to be on an isle during war.' He paused, coughing, but spurned the drink Kylrm tried to give him. 'As the two islands raged, the people climbed down into boats to exchange insults and boasts. They would each start with their weakest, who would yell out boasts, then progress in a kind of verbal duel up to their greatest. After that, arrows and spears, struggling on ships and in the water. Fortunately, there was more yelling than actual cutting.'

Rysn swallowed, nodding.

'You are not ready for this, child,' Vstim said.

'I know.'

'Good. Finally you realize it. Go now. They will not suffer us long on their island unless we agree to join them permanently.'

'Which would require . . . ?' Rysn said.

'Well, for one, it requires giving all you own to their king.'

'Lovely,' Rysn said, rising. 'I wonder how he'd look wearing my shoes.' She took a deep breath. 'You still haven't told me what we're trading for.'

'They know,' her babsk said, then coughed. 'Your conversation will not be a negotiation. The terms were set years ago.'

She turned to him, frowning. 'What?'

'This is not about what you can get,' Vstim said, 'but about whether or not they think you are worthy of it. Convince them.' He hesitated. 'Passions guide you, child. Do well.'

It seemed a plea. If their flotilla was turned away . . . The cost of this trade was not in the goods – woods, cloth, simple supplies purchased cheaply – but in the outfitting of a convoy. It was in traveling so far, paying guides, wasting time waiting for a break between storms, then more time searching for the right island. If she was turned away, they could still sell what they had – but at a stiff devastating loss, considering the high overhead of the trip.

Two of the guards, Kylrm and Nlent, joined her as she left Vstim and walked along the docklike protrusion of shell. Now that they were so close, it was difficult to see a creature and not an island. Just ahead of her, the patina of lichen made the shell nearly indistinguishable from rock. Trees clustered here, their roots draping into the water, their branches reaching high and creating a forest.

She hesitantly stepped onto the only path leading up from the waters. Here, the 'ground' formed steps that seemed far too square and regular to be natural.

'They cut into its shell?' Rysn said, climbing.

Kylrm grunted. 'Chulls can't feel their shells. This monster probably can't either.'

As they walked, he kept his hand on his gtet, a type of traditional Thaylen sword. The thing had a large triangular wedge of a blade with a grip directly at the base; you'd hold the grip like a fist, and the long blade would extend out down past the knuckles, with parts of the hilt resting around the wrist for support. Right now, he wore it in a sheath at his side, along with a bow on his back.

Why was he was so anxious? The Reshi were not supposed to be dangerous. Perhaps when you were a paid guard, it was better to assume *everyone* was dangerous.

The pathway wound upward through thick jungle. The trees here were limber and hale, their branches almost constantly moving. And when the beast stepped, everything shook.

Vines trembled and twisted on the pathway or drooped from branches, and these pulled out of the way at her approach, but crept back quickly after her passing. Soon, she couldn't see the sea, or even smell its brine. The jungle enveloped everything. Its thick green and brown were broken occasionally by pink and yellow mounds of shalebark that seemed to have been growing for generations.

She'd found the humidity oppressive before, but here it was over-whelming. She felt as if she were swimming, and even her thin linen skirt, blouse, and vest seemed as thick as old Thaylen highland winter gear.

After an interminable climb, she heard voices. To her right, the forest opened up to a view of the ocean beyond. Rysn caught her breath. End-less blue waters, clouds dropping a haze of rain in patches that seemed so distinct. And in the distance . . .

'Another one?' she asked, pointing toward a shadow on the horizon.

'Yeah,' Kylrm said. 'Hopefully going the other way. I'd rather not be here when they decide to war.' His grip tightened on the handle of his sword.

The voices came from farther up the way, so Rysn resigned herself to more climbing. Her legs ached from the effort.

Though the jungle remained impenetrable to her left, it remained open to her right, where the massive flank of the greatshell formed ridges and shelves. She caught sight of some people sitting around tents, lean-ing back and staring out over the sea. They hardly gave her and the two guards more than a glance. Up farther, she found more Reshi.

These were jumping.

Men and women alike – and in various states of undress – were taking turns leaping off the shell's outcroppings with whoops and shouts, plum-meting toward the waters far below. Rysn grew nauseated just watching them. How high up *were* they?

'They do it to shock you. They always jump from greater heights when a foreigner is here.'

Rysn nodded, then – with a sudden start – realized that the comment hadn't come from one of her guards. She turned and discovered that to her left, the forest had moved back around a large outcrop of shell like a rock mound.

There, hanging upside down and tied by his feet to a point at the top of the shell, was a lanky man with pale white skin verging on blue. He wore only a loincloth, and his skin was covered with hundreds upon hundreds of small, intricate tattoos.

Rysn took a step toward him, but Kylrm grabbed her shoulder and pulled her back. 'Aimian,' he hissed. 'Keep your distance.'

The blue fingernails and deep blue eyes should have been a clue. Rysn stepped back, though she couldn't see his Voidbringer shadow.

'Keep your distance indeed,' the man said. 'Always a wise idea.' His accent was unlike any she'd heard, though he spoke Thaylen well. He hung there with a pleasant smile on his face, as if completely indifferent to the fact that he was upside down.

'Are you . . . well?' Rysn asked the man.

'Hmmm?' he said. 'Oh, between blackouts, yes. Quite well. I think I'm growing numb to the pain of my ankles, which is just delightful.'

Rysn brought her hands up to her chest, not daring to get any closer. Aimian. Very bad luck. She wasn't particularly superstitious – she was even skeptical of the Passions sometimes – but . . . well, this was an *Aimian*.

'What fell curses did you bring on this people, beast?' Kylrm demanded.

'Improper puns,' the man said lazily. 'And a stench from something I ate that did *not* sit well with me. Are you off to speak with the king, then?'

'I . . .' Rysn said. Behind her, another Reshi whooped and leaped from the shelf. 'Yes.'

'Well,' the creature said, 'don't ask about the soul of their god. They don't like to speak of that, it turns out. Must be spectacular, to let the beasts grow this large. Beyond even the spren who inhabit the bodies of ordinary greatshells. Hmmm . . .' He seemed very pleased by something.

'Do not feel for him, trademaster,' Kylrm said softly to her, steering her away from the dangling prisoner. 'He could escape if he wished.'

Nlent, the other guard, nodded. 'They can take off their limbs. Take off their skin too. No real body to them. Just something evil, taking human form.' The squat guard wore a charm on his wrist, a charm of courage, which he took off and held tightly in one hand. The charm hadn't any properties itself, of course. It was a reminder. Courage. Passion. Want what you need, embrace it, *desire* it and bring it to you.

Well, what *she* needed was her babsk to be here with her. She turned her steps upward again, the confrontation with the Aimian leaving her unnerved. More people ran and leaped from the shelves to her right. Crazy.

Trademaster, she thought. *Kylrm called me 'trademaster.'* She wasn't, not yet. She was property owned by Vstim; for now just an apprentice who provided occasional slave labor.

She didn't deserve the title, but hearing it strengthened her. She led the way up the steps, which twisted farther around the beast's shell. They passed a place where the ground split, the shell showing skin far beneath. The rift was like a chasm; she couldn't have leaped from one side to the other without falling in.

Reshi she passed on the path refused to respond to her questions. Fortunately, Kylrm knew the way, and when the path split, he pointed to the right fork. At times, the path leveled out for significant distances, but then there were always more steps.

Her legs burning, her clothing damp with sweat, they reached the top of this flight and – at long last – found no more steps. Here, the jungle fell away completely, though rockbuds clutched the shell in the open field – beyond which was only the empty sky.

The head, Rysn thought. *We've climbed all the way to the beast's head.*

Soldiers lined the path, armed with spears bearing colorful tassels. Their breastplates and armguards were of carapace carved wickedly with points, and though they wore only wraps for clothing, they stood as stiff-backed as any Alethi soldier, with stern expressions to match. So her babsk was right. Not every Reshi was the 'lounge and swim' type.

Boldness, she thought to herself, remembering Vstim's words. She could not show these people a timid face. The king stood at the end of the pathway of guards and rockbuds, a diminutive figure on the edge of a carapace shelf, looking toward the sun.

Rysn strode forward, passing through a double row of spears. She would have expected the same kind of clothing on the king, but instead the man wore full, voluminous robes of vibrant green and yellow. They looked terribly hot.

As she drew nearer, Rysn got a sense for just how high she had climbed. The waters below shimmered in the sunlight, so far down that Rysn wouldn't have heard a rock hit if she'd dropped one. Far enough that looking over the side made her stomach twist upon itself and her legs tremble.

Getting close to the king would require stepping out onto that shelf where he stood. It would place her within a breath of plummeting down hundreds and hundreds of feet.

Steady, Rysn told herself. She *would* show her babsk that she was capable. She was not the ignorant girl who had misjudged the Shin or who had offended the Iriali. She had learned.

Still, perhaps she should have asked Nlent to lend her his charm of courage.

She stepped out onto the shelf. The king seemed young, at least from behind. Built like a youth, or . . .

No, Rysn thought with a start as the king turned. It was a woman, old enough that her hair was greying, but not so old that she was bent with age.

Someone stepped out onto the shelf behind Rysn. Younger, he wore the standard wrap and tassels. His hair was in two braids that fell over tan, bare shoulders. When he spoke, there wasn't even a *hint* of an accent to his voice. 'The king wishes to know why his old trading partner, Vstim, has not come in person, and has instead sent a child in his place.'

'And are you the king?' Rysn asked the newcomer.

The man laughed. 'You stand beside him, yet ask that of me?'

Rysn looked toward the robed figure. The robes were tied with the front open enough to show that the 'king' definitely had breasts.

'We are led by a king,' the newcomer said. 'Gender is irrelevant.'

It seemed to Rysn that gender was part of the definition, but it wasn't worth arguing over. 'My master is indisposed,' she said, addressing the newcomer – he'd be the island's trademaster. 'I am authorized to speak for him, and to accomplish the trade.'

The newcomer snorted, sitting down on the edge of the shelf, legs hanging out over the edge. Rysn's stomach did a somersault. 'He should have known better. The trade is off, then.'

'You are Talik, I assume?' Rysn said, folding her arms. The man was no longer facing her. It seemed an intentional slight.

'Yes.'

'My master warned me about you.'

'Then he isn't a complete fool,' Talik said. 'Just mostly.'

His pronunciation was astonishing. She found herself checking him for Thaylen eyebrows, but he was obviously Reshi.

Rysn clenched her teeth, then forced herself to sit down beside him on the edge. She tried to do it as nonchalantly as he had, but she just couldn't. Instead, she settled down – not easy in a fashionable skirt – and scooted out beside him.

Oh, Passions! I'm going to fall off of this and die. Don't look down! Do not look down!

She couldn't help it. She glanced downward, and felt immediately woozy. She could see the side of the head down there, the massive line of a jaw. Nearby, standing on a ridge above the eye to Rysn's right, people pushed large bundles of fruit off the side. Tied with vine rope, the bundles swung down beside the maw below.

Mandibles moved slowly, pulling the fruit in, jerking the ropes. The Reshi pulled those back up to affix more fruit, all under the eyes of the king, who was supervising the feeding from the very tip of the nose to Rysn's left.

'A treat,' Talik said, noticing where she watched. 'An offering. These small bundles of fruit, of course, do not sustain our god.'

'What does?'

He smiled. 'Why are you still here, young one? Did I not dismiss you?'

'The trade does not have to be off,' Rysn said. 'My master told me the terms were already set. We have brought everything you require in payment.' *Though for what, I don't know.* 'Turning me aside would be pointless.'

The king, she noticed, had stepped closer to listen.

'It would serve the same purpose as everything in life,' Talik said. 'To please Relu-na.'

That would be the name of their god, the greatshell. 'And your island would approve of such waste? Inviting traders all this way, only to send them off empty-handed?'

'Relu-na approves of boldness,' Talik said. 'And, more importantly, *respect*. If we do not respect the one with whom we trade, then we should not do it.'

What ridiculous logic. If a merchant followed that line of reasoning, he'd never be able to trade. Except . . . in her months with Vstim, it seemed that he'd often sought out people who liked trading with him. People he respected. Those kinds of people certainly would be less likely to cheat you.

Perhaps it wasn't bad logic . . . simply incomplete.

Think like the other trader, she recalled. One of Vstim's lessons – which were so different from the ones she'd learned at home. *What do they want? Why do they want it? Why are you the best one to provide it?*

'It must be hard to live out here, in the waters,' Rysn said. 'Your god is impressive, but you cannot make everything you need for yourselves.'

'Our ancestors did it just fine.'

'Without medicines,' Rysn said, 'that could have saved lives. Without cloth from fibers that grow only on the mainland. Your ancestors survived without these things because they had to. You do not.'

The trademaster hunched forward.

Don't do that! You'll fall!

'We are not idiots,' Talik said.

Rysn frowned. Why—

'I'm so tired of explaining this,' the man continued. 'We live simply. That does not make us stupid. For years the outsiders came, trying to exploit us because of our ignorance. We are tired of it, woman. Everything you say is true. Not true – *obvious.* Yet you say it as if we'd never stopped to consider. "Oh! Medicine! Of course we need medicine! Thank you for pointing that out. I was just going to sit here and *die.*"'

Rysn blushed. 'I didn't—'

'Yes, you *did* mean that,' Talik said. 'The condescension dripped from your lips, young lady. We're tired of being taken advantage of. We're tired of foreigners who try to trade us trash for riches. We don't have knowledge of the current economic situation on the mainland, so we can't know for certain if we are being cheated or not. Therefore, we trade *only* with people we know and trust. That is that.'

Current economic situation on the mainland . . . ? Rysn thought. 'You've trained in Thaylenah,' she guessed.

'Of course I have,' Talik said. 'You have to know a predator's tricks before you can catch him.' He settled back, which let her relax a little. 'My parents sent me to train as a child. I had one of your babsks. I made trademaster on my own before returning here.'

'Your parents being the king and queen?' Rysn guessed again.

He eyed her. 'The king and king's consort.'

'You could just call her a queen.'

'This trade is not happening,' Talik said, standing. 'Go and tell your master we are sorry for his illness and hope that he recovers. If he does, he may return next year during the trading season and we will meet with him.'

'You imply you respect him,' Rysn said, scrambling to her feet – and away from that drop. 'So just trade with him!'

'He is sickly,' Talik said, not looking at her. 'It would not do him justice. We'd be taking advantage of him.'

Taking advantage of . . . Passions, these people were *strange*. It seemed even odder to hear such things coming from the mouth of a man who spoke such perfect Thaylen.

'You'd trade with me if you respected me,' Rysn said. 'If you thought I was worthy of it.'

'That will take years,' Talik said, joining his mother at the front of the shelf. 'Go away, and—'

He cut off as the king spoke to him softly in Reshi.

Talik drew his lips into a line.

'What?' Rysn asked, stepping forward.

Talik turned toward her. 'You have apparently impressed the king. You argue fiercely. Though you dismiss us as primitives, you're not as bad as some.' He ground his teeth for a moment. 'The king will hear your argument for a trade.'

Rysn blinked, looked from one to the other. Hadn't she just made her argument for a trade, with the king listening?

The woman regarded Rysn with dark eyes and a calm expression. *I've won the first fight*, Rysn realized, *like the warriors on the battlefield. I've dueled and been judged worthy to spar with the one of greater authority.*

The king spoke, and Talik interpreted. 'The king says that you are talented, but that the trade cannot – of course – continue. You should return with your babsk when he comes again. In a decade or so, perhaps we will trade with you.'

Rysn searched for an argument. 'And is that how Vstim gained respect, Your Majesty?' She would *not* fail in this. She couldn't! 'Over years, with his own babsk?'

'Yes,' Talik said.

'You didn't interpret that,' Rysn said.

'I . . .' Talik sighed, then interpreted her question.

The king smiled with apparent fondness. She spoke a few words in their language, and Talik turned to his mother, looking shocked. 'I . . . Wow.'

'What?' Rysn demanded.

'Your babsk slew a coracot with some of our hunters,' Talik said. 'On his own? A foreigner? I had not heard of such a thing.'

Vstim. Slaying something? With *hunters*? Impossible.

Though he obviously hadn't always been the wizened old ledgerworm that he was now, she'd imagined he'd been a wizened *young* ledgerworm in the past.

The king spoke again.

'I doubt you'll be slaying any beasts, child,' Talik interpreted. 'Go. Your babsk will recover from this. He is wise.'

No. He is dying, Rysn thought. It came to her mind unbidden, but the truth of it terrified her. More than the height, more than anything else she'd known. Vstim was dying. This might be his final trade.

And she was ruining it.

'My babsk trusts me,' Rysn said, stepping closer to the king, moving along the greatshell's nose. 'And you said you trust him. Can you not trust his judgment that I am worthy?'

'One cannot substitute for personal experience,' Talik translated.

The beast stepped, ground trembling, and Rysn clenched her teeth, imagining them all toppling off. Fortunately, up this high, the motion was more like a gentle sway. Trees rustled, and her stomach lurched, but it wasn't any more dangerous than a ship surging on a wave.

Rysn stepped closer to where the king stood beside the beast's nose. 'You are king – you know the importance of trusting those beneath you. You cannot be everywhere, know everything. At times, you must accept the judgment of those you know. My babsk is such a man.'

'You make a valid point,' Talik translated, sounding surprised. 'But what you do not realize is that I have already paid your babsk this respect. That is why I agreed to speak with you myself. I would not have done this for another.'

'But—'

'Return below,' the king said through Talik, her voice growing harder. She seemed to think this was the end. 'Tell your babsk that you proceeded far enough to speak with me personally. Doubtless, this is more than he expected. You may leave the island, and return when he is well.'

'I . . .' Rysn felt as if a fist were crushing her throat, making it hard for her to speak. She couldn't fail him, not now.

'Give him my best wishes for his recovery,' the king said, turning away.

Talik smiled in what seemed to be satisfaction. Rysn glanced at her two guards, who bore grim expressions.

Rysn stepped away. She felt numb. Turned away, like a child demanding sweets. She felt a furious blush consume her as she walked past the men and women preparing more bundles of fruit.

Rysn stopped. She looked to her left, out at the endless expanse of blue. She turned back toward the king. 'I believe,' Rysn said loudly, 'that I need to speak with someone with more authority.'

Talik turned toward her. 'You have spoken to the king. There *is* nobody with more authority.'

'I beg your pardon,' Rysn said. 'But I do think there is.'

One of the ropes shook from having its fruit gift consumed. *This is stupid, this is stupid, this is—*

Don't think.

Rysn scrambled to the rope, causing her guards to cry out. She grabbed the length of rope and let herself over the side, climbing down beside the greatshell's head. The *god's* head.

Passions! This was hard in a skirt. The rope bit into the skin of her arms, and it vibrated as the creature below crunched on the fruit upon its end.

Talik's head appeared above. 'What in Kelek's name are you doing, idiot woman?' he screamed. She found it amusing that he'd learned their curses while studying with them.

Rysn clung to the rope, heart rushing in a mad panic. What *was* she doing? 'Relu-na,' she yelled back at Talik, 'approves of boldness!'

'There is a difference between boldness and stupidity!'

Rysn continued to climb down. It was more of a slide. *Oh, Craving, Passion of need . . .*

'Pull her back up!' Talik ordered. 'You soldiers, help.' He gave further orders in Reshi.

Rysn looked up as workers grabbed the rope to haul her back upward. A new face appeared above, however, looking down. The king. She raised a hand, halting them as she studied Rysn.

Rysn continued on down. She didn't go terribly far, maybe fifty feet or so. Not even down to the creature's eye. She stopped herself, with effort, her fingers burning. 'O great Relu-na,' Rysn said loudly, 'your people refuse to trade with me, and so I come to you to beg. Your people need what I have brought, but I need a trade even more. I cannot afford to return.'

The creature, of course, did not reply. Rysn hung in place beside its shell, which was crusted with lichen and small rockbuds.

'Please,' Rysn said. 'Please.'

What am I expecting to happen? Rysn wondered. She didn't expect the thing to make any sort of reply. But maybe she could persuade those above that she was bold enough to be worthy. It couldn't hurt, at least.

The rope quivered in her hands, and she made the mistake of glancing down.

Actually, what she was doing could hurt. Very much.

'The king,' Talik said above, 'has commanded that you return.'

'Will our negotiation continue?' Rysn asked, glancing up. The king actually looked concerned.

'That's not important,' Talik said. 'You have been issued a command.'

Rysn gritted her teeth, clinging to the rope, looking at the plates of chitin before her. 'And what do *you* think?' she asked softly.

Down below, the thing bit down, and the rope suddenly became very tight, slapping Rysn against the side of the enormous head. Above, workers shouted. The king yelled at them in a sudden, sharp voice.

Oh no . . .

The rope pulled even tighter.

Then snapped.

The shouts grew frantic above, though Rysn barely noticed them as panic struck. She did not fall gracefully, but as a flurry of screaming cloth and legs, her skirt flapping, her stomach lurching. What had she done? She—

She saw an eye. The god's eye. Only a glimpse as she passed; it was as large as a house, glassy and black, and it reflected her falling form.

She seemed to hang before it for a fraction of a second, and her scream died in her throat.

It was gone in a moment. Then rushing wind, another scream, and a crash into water hard as stone.

Blackness.

Rysn found herself floating when she awoke. She didn't open her eyes, but she could sense that she was floating. Drifting, bobbing up and down . . .

'She is an idiot.' She knew that voice. Talik, the one she'd been trading with.

'Then she fits well with me,' Vstim said. He coughed. 'I have to say, old friend, you were supposed to help train her, *not* drop her off a cliff.'

Floating . . . Drifting . . .

Wait.

Rysn forced her eyes open. She was in a bed inside a hut. It was hot. Her vision swam, and she drifted . . . drifted because her mind was cloudy. What had they given her? She tried to sit up. Her legs wouldn't move. Her *legs wouldn't move*.

She gasped, then began breathing quickly.

Vstim's face appeared above her, followed by a concerned Reshi woman with ribbons in her hair. Not the queen . . . king . . . whatever. This woman spoke quickly in the barking language of the Reshi.

'Calm now,' Vstim said to Rysn, kneeling beside her. 'Calm . . . They'll get you something to drink, child.'

'I lived,' Rysn said. Her voice rasped as she spoke.

'Barely,' Vstim said, though with fondness. 'The spren cushioned your fall. From that height . . . Child, what were you thinking, climbing over the side like that?'

'I needed to do something,' Rysn said. 'To prove courage. I thought . . . I needed to be bold . . .'

'Oh, child. This is my fault.'

'You were his babsk,' Rysn said. 'Talik, their trader. You set this up with him, so I could have a chance to trade on my own, but in a controlled setting. The trade was never in danger, and you are not as sick as you appear.' The words boiled out, tumbling over one another like a hundred men trying to leave through the same doorway at once.

'When did you figure that out?' Vstim asked, then coughed.

'I . . .' She didn't know. It just all kind of fell together for her. 'Right now.'

'Well, you must know that I feel a true fool,' Vstim said. 'I thought this would be a perfect chance for you. A practice with real stakes. And then . . . Then you went and fell off the island's head!'

Rysn squeezed her eyes shut as the Reshi woman arrived with a cup of something. 'Will I walk again?' Rysn asked softly.

'Here, drink this,' Vstim said.

'Will I walk again?' She didn't take the cup, and kept her eyes closed.

'I don't know,' Vstim said. 'But you *will* trade again. Passions! Daring to go above the king's authority? Being saved by the island's soul itself?' He chuckled. It sounded forced. 'The other islands will be clamoring to trade with us.'

'Then I accomplished *something*,' she said, feeling a complete and utter idiot.

'Oh, you accomplished something indeed,' Vstim said.

She felt a prickling pressure on her arm and opened her eyes with a snap. Something crawled there, about as big as the palm of her hand – a creature that looked like a cremling, but with wings that folded along the back.

'What is it?' Rysn demanded.

'Why we came here,' Vstim said. 'The thing we trade for, a treasure that very few know still exists. They were supposed to have died with Aimia, you see. I came here with all of these goods in tow because Talik sent to me to say they had the corpse of one to trade. Kings pay fortunes for them.'

He leaned down. 'I have never seen one alive before. I was given the corpse I wanted in trade. This one has been given to you.'

'By the Reshi?' Rysn asked, mind still clouded. She didn't know what to make of any of this.

'The Reshi could not command one of the larkin,' Vstim said, standing. 'This was given you by the island itself. Now drink your medicine and sleep. You shattered both of your legs. We will be staying on this island for a long while as you recover, and as I seek forgiveness for being a foolish, foolish man.'

She accepted the drink. As she drank, the small creature flew up toward the rafters of the hut and perched there, looking down at her with eyes of solid silver.

'So what kind of spren *is* it?' Thude asked to the slow Rhythm of Curiosity. He held up the gemstone, peering in at the smoky creature moving about inside.

'Stormspren, my sister says,' Eshonai replied as she leaned against the wall, arms folded.

The strands of Thude's beard were tied with bits of raw gemstone that shook and twinkled as he rubbed his chin. He held the large cut gemstone up to Bila, who took it and tapped it with her finger.

They were a warpair of Eshonai's own personal division. They dressed in simple garments that were tailored around the chitinous armor plates on their arms, legs, and chests. Thude also wore a long coat, but he wouldn't take that to battle.

Eshonai, by contrast, wore her uniform – tight red cloth that stretched over her natural armor – and a cap on her skullplate. She never spoke of how that uniform imprisoned her, felt like manacles that tied her in place.

'A stormspren,' Bila said to the Rhythm of Skepticism as she turned the stone over in her fingers. 'Will it help me kill humans? Otherwise, I don't see why I should care.'

'This could change the world, Bila,' Eshonai said. 'If Venli is right, and she can bond with this spren and come out with anything other than dullform ... well, at the very least we will have an entirely new form to choose. At the greatest we will have power to control the storms and tap their energy.'

'So she will try this personally?' Thude asked to the Rhythm of Winds, the rhythm that they used to judge when a highstorm was near.

'If the Five give her permission.' They were to discuss it, and make their decision, today.

'That's great,' Bila said, 'but will it help me *kill humans*?'

Eshonai attuned Mourning. 'If stormform is truly one of the ancient powers, Bila, then yes. It will help you kill humans. Many of them.'

'Good enough for me, then,' Bila said. 'Why are you so worried?'

'The ancient powers are said to have come from our gods.'

'Who cares? If the gods would help us kill those armies out there, then I'd swear to them right now.'

'Don't say that, Bila,' Eshonai said to Reprimand. '*Never* say anything like that.'

The woman quieted, tossing the stone onto the table. She hummed softly to Skepticism. That walked the line of insubordination. Eshonai met Bila's eyes and found herself softly humming to Resolve.

Thude glanced from Bila to Eshonai. 'Food?' he asked.

'Is that your answer to every disagreement?' Eshonai asked, breaking her song.

'It's hard to argue with your mouth full,' Thude said.

'I'm sure I've seen you do just that,' Bila said. 'Many times.'

'The arguments end happy, though,' Thude said. 'Because everyone is full. So . . . food?'

'Fine,' Bila said, glancing at Eshonai.

The two withdrew. Eshonai sat down at the table, feeling drained. When had she started worrying if her friends were insubordinate? It was this horrid uniform.

She picked up the gemstone, staring into its depths. It was a large one, about a third the size of her fist, though gemstones didn't have to be large to trap a spren inside.

She hated trapping them. The right way was to go into the highstorm with the proper attitude, singing the proper song to attract the proper spren. You bonded it in the fury of the raging storm and were reborn with a new body. People had been doing this from the arrival of the first winds.

The listeners had learned that capturing spren was possible from the humans, then had figured out the process on their own. A captive spren made the transformation much more reliable. Before, there had always been an element of chance. You could go into the storm wanting to become a soldier, and come out a mate instead.

This is progress, Eshonai thought, staring at the little smoky spren inside the stone. *Progress is learning to control your world. Put up walls to stop the storms, choose when to become a mate.* Progress was taking nature and putting a box around it.

Eshonai pocketed the gemstone, and checked the time. Her meeting with the rest of the Five wasn't scheduled until the third movement of the Rhythm of Peace, and she had a good half a movement until then.

It was time to speak with her mother.

Eshonai stepped out into Narak and walked along the path, nodding to those who saluted. She passed mostly soldiers. So much of their population wore warform these days. Their small population. Once, there had been hundreds of thousands of listeners scattered across these plains. Now a fraction remained.

Even then, the listeners had been a united people. Oh, there had been divisions, conflicts, even wars among their factions. But they had been a single people – those who had rejected their gods and sought freedom in obscurity.

Bila no longer cared about their origins. There would be others like her, people who ignored the danger of the gods and focused only on the fight with the humans.

Eshonai passed dwellings – ramshackle things constructed of hardened crem over frames of shell, huddled in the leeward shadow of lumps of stone. Most of those were empty now. They'd lost thousands to war over the years.

We do *have to do something,* she thought, attuning the Rhythm of Peace in the back of her mind. She sought comfort in its calm, soothing beats, soft and blended. Like a caress.

Then she saw the dullforms.

They looked much like what the humans called 'parshmen,' though they were a little taller and not nearly as stupid. Still, dullform was a limiting form, without the capacities and advantages of newer forms. There shouldn't have been any here. Had these people bonded the wrong spren by mistake? It happened sometimes.

Eshonai strode up to the group of three, two femalen and one malen. They were hauling rockbuds harvested on one of the nearby plateaus, plants which had been encouraged to grow quickly by use of Stormlight-infused gems.

'What is this?' Eshonai asked. 'Did you choose this form in error? Or are you new spies?'

They looked at her with insipid eyes. Eshonai attuned Anxiety. She had once tried dullform – she had wanted to know what their spies would suffer. Trying to force concepts through her brain had been like trying to think rationally while in a dream.

'Did someone ask you to adopt this form?' Eshonai said, speaking slowly and clearly.

'Nobody asked it,' the malen said to no rhythm at all. His voice sounded dead. 'We did it.'

'Why?' Eshonai said. '*Why* would you do this?'

'Humans won't kill us when they come,' the malen said, hefting his rockbud and continuing on his way. The others joined him without a word.

Eshonai gaped, the Rhythm of Anxiety strong in her mind. A few fearspren, like long purple worms, dove in and out of the rock nearby, collecting toward her until they crawled up out of the ground around her.

Forms could not be commanded; every person was free to choose for themselves. Transformations could be cajoled and requested, but they could not be forced. Their gods had not allowed this freedom, so the listeners *would* have it, no matter what. These people could choose dullform if they wished. Eshonai could do nothing about it. Not directly.

She hastened her pace. Her leg still ached from her wound, but was healing quickly. One of the benefits of warform. She could almost ignore the damage at this point.

A city full of empty buildings, and Eshonai's mother chose a shack on the very edge of the city, almost fully exposed to the storms. Mother worked her shalebark rows outside, humming softly to herself to the Rhythm of Peace. She wore workform; she'd always preferred it. Even after nimbleform had been discovered, Mother had not changed. She had said she didn't want to encourage people to see one form as more valuable than another, that such stratification could destroy them.

Wise words. The type Eshonai hadn't heard out of her mother in years.

'Child!' Mother said as Eshonai approached. Solid despite her years, Mother had a neat round face and wore her hairstrands in a braid, tied with a ribbon. Eshonai had brought her that ribbon from a meeting with the Alethi years ago. 'Child, have you seen your sister? It is her day of first transformation! We need to prepare her.'

'It is attended to, Mother,' Eshonai said to the Rhythm of Peace, kneeling down beside the woman. 'How goes the pruning?'

'I should be finishing soon,' Mother said. 'I need to leave before the people who own this house return.'

'You own it, Mother.'

'No, no. It belongs to two others. They were in the house last night, and told me I needed to leave. I'll just finish with this shalebark before I go.' She got out her file, smoothing one side of a ridge, then painting it with sap to encourage growth in that direction.

Eshonai sat back, attuning Mourning, and Peace left her. Perhaps she should have chosen the Rhythm of the Lost instead. It changed in her head.

She forced it back. No. No, her mother was *not* dead.

She wasn't fully alive, either.

'Here, take this,' Mother said to Peace, handing Eshonai a file. At least Mother recognized her today. 'Work on that outcropping there. I don't want it to keep growing downward. We need to send it up, up toward the light.'

'The storms are too strong on this side of the city.'

'Storms? Nonsense. No storms here.' Mother paused. 'I wonder *where* we'll be taking your sister. She'll need a storm for her transformation.'

'Don't worry about that, Mother,' Eshonai said, forcing herself to speak to Peace. 'I will care for it.'

'You are so good, Venli,' Mother said. 'So helpful. Staying home, not running off, like your sister. That girl . . . She's never where she should be.'

'She is now,' Eshonai whispered. 'She's trying to be.'

Mother hummed to herself, continuing working. Once, this woman had one of the best memories in the city. She still did, in a way.

'Mother,' Eshonai said, 'I need help. I think something terrible is going to happen. I can't decide if it is *less* terrible than what is already happening.'

Mother filed at a section of shalebark, then blew off the dust.

'Our people are crumbling,' Eshonai said. 'We're being weathered away. We moved to Narak and chose a war of attrition. That has meant six years with steady losses. People are giving up.'

'That's not good,' Mother said.

'But the alternative? Dabbling in things we shouldn't, things that might bring the eyes of the Unmade upon us.'

'You're not working,' Mother said, pointing. 'Don't be like your sister.'

Eshonai placed her hands in her lap. This wasn't helping. Seeing Mother like this . . .

'Mother,' Eshonai said to Supplication, 'why did we leave the dark home?'

'Ah, now that's an old song, Eshonai,' Mother said. 'A dark song, not for a child like you. Why, it's not even your day of first transformation.'

'I'm old enough, Mother. Please?'

Mother blew on her shalebark. Had she forgotten, finally, this last part of what she had been? Eshonai's heart sank.

'Long are the days since we knew the dark home,' Mother sang softly to one of the Rhythms of Remembrance. 'The Last Legion, that was our name then. Warriors who had been set to fight in the farthest plains, this place that had once been a nation and was now rubble. Dead was the freedom of most people. The forms, unknown, were forced upon us. Forms of power, yes, but also forms of obedience. The gods commanded, and we did obey, always. Always.'

'Except for that day,' Eshonai said along with her mother, in rhythm. 'The day of the storm when the Last Legion fled,' Mother continued in song. 'Difficult was the path chosen. Warriors, touched by the gods, our only choice to seek dullness of mind. A crippling that brought freedom.'

Mother's calm, sonorous song danced with the wind. As frail as she seemed other times, when she sang the old songs, she seemed herself again. A parent who had at times conflicted with Eshonai, but a parent whom Eshonai had always respected.

'Daring was the challenge made,' Mother sang, 'when the Last Legion abandoned thought and power in exchange for freedom. They risked forgetting all. And so songs they composed, a hundred stories to tell, to remember. I tell them to you, and you will tell them to your children, until the forms are again discovered.'

From there, Mother launched into one of the early songs, about how the people would make their home in the ruins of an abandoned kingdom. How they would spread out, act as simple tribes and refugees. It was their plan to remain hidden, or at least ignored.

The songs left out so much. The Last Legion hadn't known how to transform into anything other than dullform and mateform, at least not without the help of the gods. How had they known the other forms were possible? Had these facts originally been recorded in the songs, and then lost over the years as words changed here and there?

Eshonai listened, and though her mother's voice did help her attune Peace again, she found herself deeply troubled anyway. She had come here for answers. Once, that would have worked.

No longer.

Eshonai stood to leave her mother singing.

'I found some of your things,' Mother said, breaking the song, 'when cleaning today. You should take them. They clutter the home, and I will be moving out soon.'

Eshonai hummed Mourning to herself, but went to see just what her mother had 'discovered.' Another pile of rocks, in which she saw child's playthings? Strips of cloth she imagined were clothing?

Eshonai found a small sack in front of the building. She opened it to find paper.

Paper made from local plants, not human paper. Rough paper, with varied color, made after the old listener way. Textured and full, not neat and sterile. The ink on it was beginning to fade, but Eshonai recognized the drawings.

My maps, she thought. *From those early days.*

Without meaning to, she attuned Remembrance. Days spent hiking across the wilderness of what the humans called Natanatan, passing through forests and jungles, drawing her own maps and expanding the world. She'd started alone, but her discoveries had excited an entire people. Soon, though still in her teenage years, she'd been leading entire expeditions to find new rivers, new ruins, new spren, new plants.

And humans. In a way, this was all her fault.

Her mother started singing again.

Looking through her old maps, Eshonai found a powerful longing within her. Once, she'd seen the world as something fresh and exciting.

New, like a blossoming forest after a storm. She was dying slowly, as surely as her people were.

She packed up the maps and left her mother's house, walking toward the center of town. Her mother's song, still beautiful, echoed behind her. Eshonai attuned Peace. That let her know that she was nearly late for the meeting with the rest of the Five.

She did not hasten her pace. She let the steady, sweeping beats of the Rhythm of Peace carry her forward. Unless you concentrated on attuning a certain rhythm, your body would naturally choose the one that fit your mood. Therefore, it was always a conscious decision to listen to a rhythm that did not match how you felt. She did this now with Peace.

The listeners had made a decision centuries ago, a decision that set them back to primitive levels. Choosing to murder Gavilar Kholin had been an act to affirm that decision of their ancestors. Eshonai had not then been one of their leaders, but they had listened to her counsel and given her the right to vote among them.

The choice, horrible though it seemed, had been one of courage. They'd hoped that a long war would bore the Alethi.

Eshonai and the others had underestimated Alethi greed. The gemhearts had changed everything.

In the center of town, near the pool, was a tall tower that remained proudly erect in defiance of centuries' worth of storms. Once, there had been steps within, but crem leaking in windows had filled the building up with rock. So workers had carved steps running around its outside.

Eshonai started up the steps, holding to the chain for safety. It was a long but familiar climb. Though her leg ached, warform had great endurance – though it required more food than any other form to keep it strong. She made it to the top with ease.

She found the other members of the Five waiting for her, one member wearing each known form. Eshonai for warform, Davim for workform, Abronai for mateform, Chivi for nimbleform, and the quiet Zuln for dullform. Venli waited as well, with her once-mate, though he was flushed from the difficult climb. Nimbleform, though good for many delicate activities, did not have great endurance.

Eshonai stepped up onto the flat top of the once-tower, wind blowing against her from the east. There were no chairs up here, and the Five sat on the bare rock itself.

Davim hummed to Annoyance. With the rhythms in one's head, it was difficult to be late by accident. They rightly suspected that Eshonai had dallied.

She sat on the rock and took the spren-filled gemstone from her pocket, setting it on the ground in front of her. The violet stone glowed with Stormlight.

'I am worried about this test,' Eshonai said. 'I do not think we should allow it to proceed.'

'What?' Venli said to Anxiety. 'Sister, don't be ridiculous. Our people need this.'

Davim leaned forward, arms on his knees. He was broad faced, his workform skin marbled mostly of black with tiny swirls of red here and there. 'If this works, it will be an amazing advance. The first of the forms of ancient power, rediscovered.'

'Those forms are tied to the gods,' Eshonai said. 'What if, in choosing this form, we invite them to return?'

Venli hummed Irritation. 'In the old day, *all* forms came from the gods. We have found that nimbleform does not harm us. Why would stormform?'

'It is different,' Eshonai said. 'Sing the song; hum it to yourself. "Its coming brings the gods their night." The ancient powers are dangerous.'

'Men have them,' Abronai said. He wore mateform, lush and plump, though he controlled its passions. Eshonai had never envied him the position; she knew, from private conversations, that he would have preferred to have another form. Unfortunately, others who held mateform either did so transiently – or did not possess the proper solemnity to join the Five.

'You yourself brought us the report, Eshonai,' Abronai continued. 'You saw a warrior among the Alethi using ancient powers, and many others confirmed it to us. Surgebindings have returned to men. The spren again betray us.'

'If Surgebindings are back,' Davim said to Consideration, 'then it might indicate that the gods are returning anyway. If so, we'd best be prepared to deal with them. Forms of power will help with that.'

'We don't know they will come,' Eshonai said to Resolve. 'We don't know *any* of this. Who knows if men even have Surgebindings – it might be one of the Honorblades. We left one in Alethkar that night.'

Chivi hummed to Skepticism. Her nimbleform face had elongated features, her hairstrands tied back in a long tail. 'We are fading as a people. I passed some today who had taken dullform, and not to remember our past. They did so because they worried that men would kill them otherwise! They prepare themselves to become slaves!'

'I saw them too,' Davim said to Resolve. 'We must do something, Eshonai. Your soldiers are losing this war, beat by beat.'

'The next storm,' Venli said. She used the Rhythm of Pleading. 'I can test this at the next storm.'

Eshonai closed her eyes. Pleading. It was a rhythm not often attuned. It was hard to deny her sister in this.

'We must be unified in this decision,' Davim said. 'I will accept nothing else. Eshonai, do you insist on objecting? Will we need to spend hours here making this decision?'

She took a deep breath, coming to a decision that had been working its way through the back of her mind. The decision of an explorer. She glanced at the sack of maps she'd set on the floor beside her.

'I will agree to this test,' Eshonai said.

Nearby, Venli hummed to Appreciation.

'However,' Eshonai continued to Resolve, 'I must be the one who tries the new form first.'

All humming stopped. The others of the Five gaped at her.

'What?' Venli said. 'Sister, no! It is my right.'

'You are too valuable,' Eshonai said. 'You know too much about the forms, and much of your research is held only in your head. I am simply a soldier. I can be spared if this goes wrong.'

'You are a Shardbearer,' Davim said. 'Our last.'

'Thude has trained with my Blade and Plate,' Eshonai said. 'I will leave both with him, just in case.'

The others of the Five hummed to Consideration.

'This is a good suggestion,' Abronai said. 'Eshonai has both strength and experience.'

'It was *my* discovery!' Venli said to Irritation.

'And you are appreciated for it,' Davim said. 'But Eshonai is right; you and your scholars are too important to our future.'

'More than that,' Abronai added. 'You are too close to the project, Venli. The way you speak makes that clear. If Eshonai enters the storms and discovers that something is off about this form, she can halt the experiment and return to us.'

'This is a good compromise,' Chivi said, nodding. 'Are we in agreement?'

'I believe so,' Abronai said, turning toward Zuln.

The representative of the dullforms rarely spoke. She wore the smock of a parshman, and had indicated that she considered it her duty to represent them – those with no songs – along with any dullforms among them.

Hers was as noble a sacrifice as Abronai holding to mateform. More so. Dullform was a difficult form to suffer, one that only a few ever experienced for longer than a stormpause or so.

'I agree to this,' Zuln said.

The others hummed to Appreciation. Only Venli did not join in the song. If this stormform turned out to be real, would they add another person to the Five? At first, the Five had all been dullforms, then all workers. It was only at the discovery of nimbleform that it had been decided that they would have one of each form.

A question for later. The others of the Five stood up, then began to make their way down the long flight of steps spiraling around the tower. Wind blew from the east, and Eshonai turned toward it, looking out over the broken Plains – toward the Origin of Storms.

During a coming highstorm, she would step into the winds and become something new. Something powerful. Something that would change the destiny of the listeners, and perhaps the humans, forever.

'I nearly had cause to hate you, Sister,' Venli said to Reprimand, idling beside where Eshonai sat.

'I did not forbid this test,' Eshonai said.

'Instead you take its glory.'

'If there is glory to be had,' Eshonai said to Reprimand, 'it will be yours for discovering the form. That should not be a consideration. Only our future should matter.'

Venli hummed to Irritation. 'They called you wise, experienced. It makes one wonder if they've forgotten who you were – that you went off recklessly into the wilds, *ignoring* your people, while I stayed home and memorized songs. When did everyone start believing you were the responsible one?'

It's this cursed uniform, Eshonai thought, rising. 'Why didn't you tell us what you were researching? You let me believe your studies were to find artform or mediationform. Instead, you were looking for one of the forms of ancient power.'

'Does that matter?'

'Yes. It makes all the difference, Venli. I love you, but your ambition frightens me.'

'You don't trust me,' Venli said to Betrayal.

Betrayal. That was a song rarely sung. It stung enough to make Eshonai wince.

'We'll see what this form does,' Eshonai said, picking up her maps and the gemstone with the trapped spren. 'Then we will talk further. I just want to be careful.'

'You want to do it yourself,' Venli said to Irritation. 'You always want to be first. But enough. It is done. Come with me; I will need to train you in the proper mindset to help the form work. Then we will pick a highstorm for the transformation.'

Eshonai nodded. She would go through this training. In the meantime, she would consider. Perhaps there was another way. If she could get the Alethi to listen to her, find Dalinar Kholin, sue for peace . . .

Perhaps then, this would not be needed.

PART
TWO

Winds' Approach

SHALLAN • KALADIN • ADOLIN • SADEAS

Warform is worn for battle and reign.
Claimed by the gods, given to kill.
Unknown, unseen, but vital to gain.
It comes to those with the will.

—From the Listener Song of Listing, 15th stanza

The wagon rattled and shook its way across the stone ground, Shallan perched on the hard seat next to Bluth, one of the slab-faced mercenaries Tvlakv employed. He guided the chull pulling the wagon, and didn't speak much, though when he thought she wasn't looking, he would inspect her with eyes like beads of dark glass.

It was chilly. She wished the weather would turn, and spring – or even summer – would come for a time. That wasn't likely in a place notorious for its permanent chill. Having improvised a blanket from the lining of Jasnah's trunk, Shallan draped it over her knees and down to her feet, as much to obscure how tattered her skirt had become as against the cold.

She tried to distract herself by studying the surroundings; the flora out here in the southern Frostlands was completely unfamiliar to her. If there was grass, it grew in patches along the leeward sides of rocks, with short spiky blades rather than long, waving ones. The rockbuds never grew larger than a fist, and they didn't open all the way, even when she'd tried pouring water on one. Their vines were lazy and slow, as if numbed by the cold. There were also spindly little shrubs that grew in cracks and along hillsides. Their brittle branches scraped the sides of the wagon, their tiny green leaves the size of raindrops folding and pulling into the stalks.

The shrubs grew prolifically, spreading wherever they could find purchase. As the wagon rolled past a particularly tall clump, Shallan reached out and snapped off a branch. It was tubular, with an open center, and felt rough like sand.

'These are too fragile for highstorms,' Shallan said, holding it up. 'How does this plant survive?'

Bluth grunted.

'It is common, Bluth,' Shallan said, 'to engage one's traveling companion in mutually diverting dialogue.'

'I'd do that,' he said darkly, 'if I knew what in Damnation half those words meant.'

Shallan started. She honestly hadn't expected a response. 'Then we are even,' she said, 'as you use plenty of words *I* don't know. Admittedly, I think most of them are curses. . . .'

She'd meant it lightheartedly, but his expression only darkened further. 'You think I'm as dumb as that stick.'

Stop insulting my stick. The words came to her mind, and almost to her lips, unbidden. She should have been better at holding her tongue, considering her upbringing. But freedom – without the fear that her father was looming behind every closed door – had severely diminished her selfcontrol.

She suppressed the taunt this time. 'Stupidity is a function of one's surroundings,' she said instead.

'You're saying I'm dumb because I was raised that way?'

'No. I'm saying that everyone is stupid in some situations. After my ship was lost, I found myself ashore but unable to make a fire to warm myself. Would you say that I'm stupid?'

He shot her a glance, but did not speak. Perhaps to a darkeyes, that question sounded like a trap.

'Well I am,' Shallan said. 'In many areas, I'm stupid. Perhaps when it comes to large words, you're stupid. That's why we need both scholars and caravan workers, guardsman Bluth. Our stupidities complement one another.'

'I can see why we need fellows who know how to light fires,' Bluth said. 'But I don't see why we need people to use fancy words.'

'Shhhh,' Shallan said. 'Don't say that so loudly. If the lighteyes hear, they might stop wasting their time making up new words, and instead start interfering with the business of honest men.'

He glanced at her again. Not even a glimmer of humor in the eyes beneath that thick brow. Shallan sighed, but turned her attention back to the plants. How *did* they survive highstorms? She should get out her sketchpad and—

No.

She blanked her mind and let it go. A short time later, Tvlakv called the midday halt. Shallan's wagon slowed, and one of the others pulled up beside it.

Tag drove this one, with the two parshmen sitting in the cage behind, working quietly at weaving hats from reeds they'd gathered in the morning. People often ordered parshmen to do such menial work – something to make sure all of their time was spent earning money for those who owned them. Tvlakv would sell the hats for a few chips at his destination.

They kept working as the wagon stopped. They would have to be told to do something else, and had to be trained specifically for each job they did. But once they were trained, they would work without complaint.

Shallan had difficulty not seeing their quiet obedience as something pernicious. She shook her head, then held out her hand to Bluth, who helped her from the wagon without further prodding. On the ground, she rested her hand on the side of the vehicle and breathed in sharply through her teeth. *Stormfather*, what had she done to her feet? Painspren wiggled out of the wall beside her, little orange bits of sinew – like hands with the flesh removed.

'Brightness?' Tvlakv said, waddling her direction. 'I'm afraid we haven't much to offer you in the way of meals. We are poor for merchants, you see, and cannot afford delicacies.'

'Whatever you have will suffice,' Shallan said, trying to keep the pain from showing in her face, though the spren had already given her away. 'Please have one of your men get down my trunk.'

Tvlakv did so without complaint, though he watched hungrily as Bluth lowered it to the ground. It seemed a particularly bad idea to let him see what was inside; the less information he had, the better off she would be.

'These cages,' Shallan said, looking over the back of her wagon, 'from those clasps at top, it looks like the wooden sides can be affixed over the bars.'

'Yes, Brightness,' Tvlakv said. 'For highstorms, you see.'

'You only have enough slaves to fill one of the three wagons,' Shallan said. 'And the parshmen ride in another. This one is empty, and will make an excellent traveling wagon for me. Put the sides on.'

'Brightness?' he said with surprise. 'You want to be put into the *cage*?'

'Why not?' Shallan asked, meeting his eyes. 'Certainly I'm safe in your custody, tradesman Tvlakv.'

'Er . . . yes . . .'

'You and your men must be well acquainted with rough travel,' Shallan said calmly, 'but I am not. Sitting day in and out in the sun on a hard bench will not suit me. A proper carriage, however, would be a welcome amelioration of this wilderness journey.'

'Carriage?' Tvlakv said. 'It's a slave wagon!'

'Mere words, tradesman Tvlakv,' Shallan said. 'If you please?'

He sighed, but gave the order, and the men pulled the sides out from beneath the wagon and hooked them up on the outside. They left off the back one, where the cage door was. The result did not look especially comfortable, but it *would* offer some privacy. Shallan had Bluth haul her chest up and inside, to Tvlakv's dismay. Then, she climbed in and pulled the cage door shut. She held her hand out through the bars toward Tvlakv.

'Brightness?'

'The key,' she said.

'Oh.' He pulled it out of a pocket, regarding it for a moment – too long a moment – before handing it to her.

'Thank you,' she replied. 'You may send Bluth with my meal when it is ready, but I shall require a bucket of clean water immediately. You have been most accommodating. I will not forget your service.'

'Er . . . Thank you.' It almost sounded like a question, and as he walked away, he seemed confused. Good.

She waited for Bluth to bring the water, then crawled – to stay off her feet – through the enclosed wagon. It stank of dirt and sweat, and she grew nauseated thinking of the slaves who had been held here. She would ask Bluth to have the parshmen scrub it later.

She stopped before Jasnah's trunk, then knelt and gingerly raised the lid. Light spilled out from the infused spheres inside. Pattern waited there as well – she had instructed him not to be seen – his shape raising the cover of a book.

Shallan had survived, so far. She certainly wasn't safe, but at least she wasn't going to freeze or starve immediately. That meant she finally had to face greater questions and problems. She rested her hand on the books, ignoring her throbbing feet for the moment. 'These have to reach the Shattered Plains.'

Pattern vibrated with a confused sound – a questioning pitch that implied curiosity.

'Someone needs to continue Jasnah's work,' Shallan said. 'Urithiru must be found, and the Alethi must be convinced that the return of the Voidbringers is imminent.' She shivered, thinking of the marbled parshmen working just one wagon over.

'You . . . mmm . . . continue?' Pattern asked.

'Yes.' She'd made that decision the moment she'd insisted that Tvlakv head for the Shattered Plains. 'That night before the sinking, when I saw Jasnah with her guard down . . . I know what I must do.'

Pattern hummed, again sounding confused.

'It's hard to explain,' Shallan said. 'It's a human thing.'

'Excellent,' Pattern said, eager.

She raised an eyebrow toward him. He'd quickly come a long way from spending hours spinning in the center of a room or climbing up and down walls.

Shallan took out some spheres for better light, then removed one of the cloths Jasnah had wrapped around her books. It was immaculately clean. Shallan dipped the cloth into the bucket of water and began to wash her feet.

'Before I saw Jasnah's expression that night,' she explained, 'before I talked to her through her fatigue and got a sense of just how worried she was, I had fallen into a trap. The trap of a scholar. Despite my initial horror at what Jasnah had described about the parshmen, I had come to see it all as an intellectual puzzle. Jasnah was so outwardly dispassionate that I assumed she did the same.'

Shallan winced as she dug a bit of rock from a crack in her foot. *More* painspren wiggled out of the floor of the wagon. She wouldn't be walking great distances anytime soon, but at least she didn't see any rotspren yet. She had better find some antiseptic.

'Our danger isn't just theoretical, Pattern. It is real and it is terrible.'

'Yes,' Pattern said, voice sounding grave.

She looked up from her feet. He had moved up onto the inside of the chest's lid, lit by the varied light of the differently colored spheres. 'You know something about the danger? The parshmen, the Voidbringers?' Perhaps she was reading too much into his tones. He wasn't human, and often spoke with strange inflections.

'My return . . .' Pattern said. 'Because of this.'

'What? Why haven't you said something!'

'Say . . . speaking . . . Thinking . . . All hard. Getting better.'

'You came to me because of the Voidbringers,' Shallan said, moving closer to the trunk, bloodied rag forgotten in her hand.

'Yes. Patterns . . . we . . . us . . . Worry. One was sent. Me.'

'Why to me?'

'Because of lies.'

She shook her head. 'I don't understand.'

He buzzed in dissatisfaction. 'You. Your family.'

'You watched me with my family? That long ago?'

'Shallan. Remember . . .'

Again those memories. This time, not a garden seat, but a sterile white room. Her father's lullaby. Blood on the floor.

No.

She turned away and began cleaning her feet again.

'I know . . . little of humans,' Pattern said. 'They break. Their minds break. You did not break. Only cracked.'

She continued her washing.

'It is the lies that save you,' Pattern said. 'The lies that drew me.'

She dipped her rag in the bucket. 'Do you have a name? I've called you Pattern, but it's more of a description.'

'Name is numbers,' Pattern said. 'Many numbers. Hard to say. Pattern . . . Pattern is fine.'

'As long as you don't start calling me Erratic as a contrast,' Shallan said.

'Mmmmmm . . .'

'What does that mean?' she asked.

'I am thinking,' Pattern said. 'Considering the lie.'

'The joke?'

'Yes.'

'Please don't think too hard,' Shallan said. 'It wasn't a particularly good joke. If you want to ponder a real one, consider that stopping the return of the Voidbringers might depend on *me*, of all people.'

'Mmmmm . . .'

She finished with her feet as best she could, then wrapped them with several other cloths from the trunk. She had no slippers or shoes. Perhaps she could buy an extra pair of boots from one of the slavers? The mere thought made her stomach churn, but she didn't have a choice.

Next, she sorted through the contents of the trunk. This was only one of Jasnah's trunks, but Shallan recognized it as the one the woman kept in her own cabin – the one the assassins had taken. It contained Jasnah's notes: books and books full of them. The trunk contained few primary sources, but that didn't matter, as Jasnah had meticulously transcribed all relevant passages.

As Shallan set aside the last book, she noticed something on the bottom of the trunk. A loose piece of paper? She picked it up, curious – then nearly dropped it in surprise.

It was a picture of Jasnah, drawn by Shallan herself. Shallan had given it to the woman after being accepted as her ward. She'd assumed Jasnah had thrown it away – the woman had little fondness for visual arts, which she considered a frivolity.

Instead, she'd kept it here with her most precious things. No. Shallan didn't want to think about that, didn't want to face it.

'Mmm . . .' Pattern said. 'You cannot keep all lies. Only the most important.'

Shallan reached up and found tears in her eyes. For Jasnah. She'd been avoiding the grief, had stuffed it into a little box and set it away.

As soon as she let that grief come, another piled on top of it. A grief that seemed frivolous in comparison to Jasnah's death, but one that threatened to tow Shallan down as much, or even more.

'My sketchpads . . .' she whispered. 'All gone.'

'Yes,' Pattern said, sounding sorrowful.

'Every drawing I've ever kept. My brothers, my father, Mother . . .' All sunk into the depths, along with her sketches of creatures and her musings on their connections, biology, and nature. Gone. Every bit of it gone.

The world didn't depend upon Shallan's silly pictures of skyeels. She felt as if everything was broken anyway.

'You will draw more,' Pattern whispered.

'I don't want to.' Shallan blinked free more tears.

'I will not stop vibrating. The wind will not stop blowing. You will not stop drawing.'

Shallan brushed her fingers across the picture of Jasnah. The woman's eyes were alight, almost alive again – it was the first picture Shallan had drawn of Jasnah, done on the day they'd met. 'The broken Soulcaster was with my things. It's now on the bottom of the ocean, lost. I won't be able to repair it and send it to my brothers.'

Pattern buzzed in what sounded like a morose tone to her.

'Who are they?' Shallan asked. 'The ones who did this, who killed her and took my art from me. Why would they do such horrible things?'

'I do not know.'

'But you are certain that Jasnah was right?' Shallan said. 'The Void-bringers are going to return?'

'Yes. Spren . . . spren of *him*. They come.'

'These people,' Shallan said, 'they killed Jasnah. They were probably of the same group as Kabsal, and . . . and as my father. Why would they kill the person closest to understanding how, and why, the Voidbringers are coming back?'

'I . . .' He faltered.

'I shouldn't have asked,' Shallan said. 'I already know the answer, and it is a very human one. These people seek to control the knowledge so that they can profit from it. Profit from the apocalypse itself. We're going to see that doesn't happen.'

She lowered the sketch of Jasnah, setting it between the pages of a book to keep it safe.

Excerpt from a longer scroll. The bottom half was eaten by an axehound as I fled the place where I'd stolen this.

Mateform meek, for love to share,
Given to life. it brings us joy.
To find this form, one must care.
True empathy one must employ.

—From the Listener Song of Listing, 5th stanza

'It's been a while,' Adolin said, kneeling and holding his Shardblade before him, point sunken a few inches into the stone ground. He was alone. Just him and the sword in one of the new preparation rooms, built alongside the dueling arena.

'I remember when I won you,' Adolin whispered, looking at his reflection in the blade. 'Nobody took me seriously then, either. The fop with the nice clothing. Tinalar thought to duel me just to embarrass my father. Instead I got his Blade.' If he'd lost, he would have had to give Tinalar his Plate, which he'd inherited from his mother's side of the family.

Adolin had never named his Shardblade. Some did, some didn't. He'd never thought it appropriate – not because he didn't think the Blade deserved a name, but because he figured he didn't know the right one. This weapon had belonged to one of the Knights Radiant, long ago. That man had named the weapon, undoubtedly. To call it something else seemed presumptuous. Adolin had felt that way even before he'd

228

started thinking of the Radiants in a good light, as his father did.

This Blade would continue after Adolin died. He didn't own it. He was borrowing it for a time.

Its surface was austerely smooth, long, sinuous like an eel, with ridges at the back like growing crystals. Shaped like a larger version of a standard longsword, it bore some resemblance to the enormous, two-handed broadswords he'd seen Horneaters wield.

'A real duel,' Adolin whispered to the Blade. 'For real stakes. Finally. No more tiptoeing around it, no more limiting myself.'

The Shardblade didn't respond, but Adolin imagined that it listened to him. You couldn't use a weapon like this, a weapon that seemed like an extension of the soul itself, and not feel at times that it was alive.

'I speak so confidently to everyone else,' Adolin said, 'since I know they rely on me. But if I lose today, that's it. No more duels, and a severe knot in Father's grand plan.'

He could hear people outside. Stomping feet, a buzz of chatter. Scraping on the stone. They'd come. Come to see Adolin win or be humiliated. 'This might be our last fight together,' Adolin said softly. 'I appreciate what you've done for me. I know you'd do it for anyone who held you, but I still appreciate it. I . . . I want you to know: I believe in Father. I believe he's right, that the things he sees are real. That the world needs a united Alethkar. Fights like this one are my way to make it happen.'

Adolin and his father weren't politicians. They were soldiers – Dalinar by choice, Adolin more by circumstance. They wouldn't be able to just talk their way into a unified kingdom. They'd have to fight their way into one.

Adolin stood up, patting his pocket, then dismissing his Blade to mist and crossing the small chamber. The stone walls of the narrow hallway he entered were etched with reliefs depicting the ten basic stances of swordsmanship. Those had been carved elsewhere, then placed here when this room was built – a recent addition, to replace the tents that dueling preparation had once happened in.

Windstance, Stonestance, Flamestance . . . There was a relief, with depicted stance, for each of the Ten Essences. Adolin counted them off to himself as he passed. This small tunnel had been cut into the stone of the arena itself, and ended in a small room cut into the rock. The bright sunlight of the dueling grounds glared around the edges of the final pair of doors between him and his opponent.

With a proper preparation room for meditation, then this staging room to put on armor or retreat between bouts, the dueling arena at the warcamps was transforming into one as proper as those back in Alethkar. A welcome addition.

Adolin stepped into the staging room, where his brother and aunt were waiting. Stormfather, his hands were sweating. He hadn't felt this nervous when riding into battle, when his life was actually in danger.

Aunt Navani had just finished a glyphward. She stepped away from the pedestal, setting aside her brushpen, and held up the ward for him to see. It was painted in bright red on a white cloth.

'Victory?' Adolin guessed.

Navani lowered it, raising an eyebrow at him.

'What?' Adolin said as his armorers entered, carrying the pieces of his Shardplate.

'It says "safety and glory,"' Navani said. 'It wouldn't kill you to learn some glyphs, Adolin.'

He shrugged. 'Never seemed that important.'

'Yes, well,' Navani said, reverently folding the prayer and setting it in the brazier to burn. 'Hopefully, you will eventually have a wife to do this for you. Both the reading of glyphs and the making of them.'

Adolin bowed his head, as was proper while the prayer burned. Pailiah knew, this wasn't the time to offend the Almighty. Once it was done, however, he glanced at Navani. 'And what of the news of the ship?'

They had expected word from Jasnah when she reached the Shallow Crypts, but none had been forthcoming. Navani had checked in with the harbormaster's office in that distant city. They said the *Wind's Pleasure* had not yet arrived. That put it a week overdue.

Navani waved a dismissive hand. 'Jasnah was on that ship.'

'I know, Aunt,' Adolin said, shuffling uncomfortably. What had happened? Had the ship been caught in a highstorm? What of this woman Adolin might be marrying, if Jasnah had her way?

'If the ship is delayed, it's because Jasnah is up to something,' Navani said. 'Watch. We'll get a communication from her in a few weeks, demanding some task or piece of information. I'll have to pry from her why she vanished. Battah send that girl some sense to go with her intelligence.'

Adolin didn't press the issue. Navani knew Jasnah better than anyone else. But ... he was certainly concerned for Jasnah, and felt a sudden worry that he might not get to meet the girl, Shallan, when expected. Of course, the causal betrothal wasn't likely to work out – but a piece of him wished that it would. Letting someone else choose for him had a strange appeal, considering how loudly Danlan had cursed at him when he'd broken off that particular relationship.

Danlan was still one of his father's scribes, so he saw her on occasion. More glares. But storm it, that one was *not* his fault. The things she'd said to her friends …

An armorer set out his boots, and Adolin stepped into them, feeling them click into place. The armorers quickly affixed the greaves, then moved upward, covering him in too-light metal. Soon, all that remained were the gauntlets and the helm. He knelt down, placing his hands into the gauntlets at his side, fingers in their positions. In the strange manner of Shardplate, the armor constricted on its own, like a skyeel curling around its rat, pulling to comfortable tightness around his wrists.

He turned and reached for his helm from the last armorer. It was Renarin.

'You ate chicken?' Renarin asked as Adolin took the helm.

'For breakfast.'

'And you talked to the sword?'

'Had an entire conversation.'

'Mother's chain in your pocket?'

'Checked three times.'

Navani folded her arms. 'You still hold to those foolish superstitions?' Both brothers looked at her sharply.

'They're not superstitions,' Adolin said at the same time Renarin said, 'It's just good luck, Aunt.'

She rolled her eyes.

'I haven't done a formal duel in a long time,' Adolin said, pulling on the helm, faceplate open. 'I don't want anything to go wrong.'

'Foolishness,' Navani repeated. 'Trust in the Almighty and the Heralds, not whether or not you had the right *meal* before you duel. Storms. Next thing I know, you'll be believing in the Passions.'

Adolin shared a look with Renarin. His little traditions probably didn't help him win, but, well, why risk it? Every duelist had his own quirks. His hadn't let him down yet.

'Our guards aren't happy about this,' Renarin said softly. 'They keep talking about how hard it's going to be to protect you when someone else is swinging a Shardblade at you.'

Adolin slammed down his faceplate. It misted at the sides, locking into place, becoming translucent and giving him a full view of the room. Adolin grinned, knowing full well Renarin couldn't see the expression. 'I'm so sad to be denying them the chance to babysit me.'

'Why do you enjoy tormenting them?'

'I don't like minders.'

'You've had guards before.'

'On the battlefield,' Adolin said. It felt different to be followed about everywhere he went.

'There's more. Don't lie to me, Brother. I know you too well.'

Adolin inspected his brother, whose eyes were so earnest behind his spectacles. The boy was too solemn all the time.

'I don't like their captain,' Adolin admitted.

'Why? He saved Father's life.'

'He just bothers me.' Adolin shrugged. 'There's something about him that is off, Renarin. That makes me suspicious.'

'I think you don't like that he ordered you around, on the battlefield.'

'I barely even remember that,' Adolin said lightly, stepping toward the door out.

'Well, all right then. Off with you. And Brother?'

'Yes?'

'Try not to lose.'

Adolin pushed open the doors and stepped out onto the sand. He'd been in this arena before, using the argument that though the Alethi Codes of War proscribed duels between officers, he still needed to maintain his skills.

To placate his father, Adolin had stayed away from important bouts – bouts for championships or for Shards. He hadn't dared risk his Blade and Plate. Now everything was different.

The air was still chill with winter, but the sun was bright overhead. His breath sounded against the plate of his helm, and his feet crunched in sand. He checked to see that his father was watching. He was. As was the king.

Sadeas hadn't come. Just as well. That might have distracted Adolin with memories of one of the last times that Sadeas and Dalinar had been amiable, sitting together up on those stone steps, watching Adolin duel. Had Sadeas been planning a betrayal even then, while laughing with his father and chatting like an old friend?

Focus. His foe today wasn't Sadeas, though someday . . . Someday soon he'd get that man in the arena. It was the goal of everything he was doing here.

For now, he'd have to settle for Salinor, one of Thanadal's Shardbearers. The man had only the Blade, though he'd been able to borrow a set of the King's Plate for a bout with a full Shardbearer.

Salinor stood on the other side of the arena, wearing the unornamented slate-grey Plate and waiting for the highjudge – Brightlady Istow – to signal the start of the bout. This fight was, in a way, an insult to Adolin. In order to get Salinor to agree to the duel, Adolin had been forced to bet *both* his Plate and his Blade against just Salinor's Blade. As if Adolin weren't worthy, and had to offer more potential spoils to justify bothering Salinor.

As expected, the arena was overflowing with lighteyes. Even if it was speculated that Adolin had lost his former edge, bouts for Shards were very, very rare. This would be the first in over a year's time.

'Summon Blades!' Istow ordered.

Adolin thrust his hand to the side. The Blade fell into his waiting hand ten heartbeats later – a moment before his opponent's appeared. Adolin's heart was beating more quickly than Salinor's. Perhaps that meant his opponent wasn't frightened, and underestimated him.

Adolin fell into Windstance, elbows bent, turned to the side, sword's tip pointing up and backward. His opponent fell into Flamestance, sword held one-handed, other hand touching the blade, standing with a square posture of the feet. The stances were more a philosophy than a predefined set of moves. Windstance: flowing, sweeping, majestic. Flamestance: quick and flexible, better for shorter Shardblades.

Windstance was familiar to Adolin. It had served him well throughout his career.

But it didn't feel right today.

We're at war, Adolin thought as Salinor edged forward, looking to test him. *And every lighteyes in this army is a raw recruit.*

It wasn't time for a show.

It was time for a beating.

As Salinor drew close for a cautious strike to feel out his opponent, Adolin twisted and fell into Ironstance, with his sword held two-handed up beside his head. He slapped away Salinor's first strike, then stepped in and slammed his Blade down into the man's helm. Once, twice, three times. Salinor tried to parry, but he was obviously surprised by Adolin's attack, and two of the blows landed.

Cracks crawled across Salinor's helm. Adolin heard grunts accompanying curses as Salinor tried to bring his weapon back to strike. This wasn't the way it was supposed to go. Where were the test blows, the art, the dance?

Adolin growled, feeling the old Thrill of battle as he shoved aside Salinor's attack – careless of the hit it scored on his side – then brought his Blade in two-handed and *crashed* it into his opponent's breastplate, like he was chopping wood. Salinor grunted again and Adolin raised his foot and *kicked* the man backward, throwing him to the ground.

Salinor dropped his Blade – a weakness of Flamestance's one-handed posture – and it vanished to mist. Adolin stepped over the man and dismissed his own Blade, then kicked down with a booted heel into Salinor's helm. The piece of Plate exploded into molten bits, exposing a dazed, panicked face.

Adolin slammed the heel of his foot against the breastplate next. Though Salinor tried to grab his foot, Adolin kicked relentlessly until the breastplate, too, shattered.

'Stop! *Stop!*'

Adolin halted, lowering his foot beside Salinor's head, looking up at the highjudge. The woman stood in her box, face red, voice furious.

'Adolin Kholin!' she shouted. 'This is a duel, not a *wrestling match!*'

'Did I break any rules?' he shouted back.

Silence. It struck him, through the rush in his ears, that the entire crowd had gone quiet. He could hear their breathing.

'Did I break any *rules?*' Adolin demanded again.

'This is not how a duel—'

'So I win,' Adolin said.

The woman sputtered. 'This duel was to three broken pieces of Plate. You broke only two.'

Adolin looked down at the dazed Salinor. Then he reached down, ripped off the man's pauldron, and smashed it between two fists. 'Done.'

Stunned silence.

Adolin knelt beside his opponent. 'Your Blade.'

Salinor tried to stand, but with the breastplate missing, doing so was more difficult. His armor wouldn't work properly, and he'd need to roll onto his side and work his way to his feet. Doable, but he obviously didn't have the experience with Plate to perform the maneuver. Adolin slammed him back down to the sand by his shoulder.

'You've lost,' Adolin growled.

'You cheated!' Salinor sputtered.

'How?'

'I don't know how! It just – It's not supposed to . . .'

He trailed off as Adolin carefully placed a gauntleted hand against his neck. Salinor's eyes widened. 'You wouldn't.'

Fearspren crawled out of the sand around him.

'My prize,' Adolin said, suddenly feeling drained. The Thrill faded from him. Storms, he'd never before felt like this in a duel.

Salinor's Blade appeared in his hand.

'Judgment,' the highjudge said, sounding reluctant, 'goes to Adolin Kholin, the victor. Salinor Eved forfeits his Shard.'

Salinor let the Blade slip from his fingers. Adolin took it and knelt beside Salinor, holding the weapon with pommel toward the man. 'Break the bond.'

Salinor hesitated, then touched the ruby at the weapon's pommel. The gemstone flashed with light. The bond had been broken.

Adolin stood, ripping the ruby free, then crushing it in a gauntleted hand. That wouldn't be needed, but it was a nice symbol. Sound finally rose in the crowd, frantic chattering. They'd come for a spectacle and had instead been given brutality. Well, that was how things often went in war. Good for them to see it, he supposed, though as he ducked back into the waiting room he was uncertain of himself. What he'd done was reckless. Dismissing his Blade? Putting himself in a position where the enemy could have gotten at his feet?

Adolin entered the staging room, where Renarin looked at him wide-eyed. 'That,' his younger brother said, 'was *incredible*. It has to be the shortest Shard bout on record! You were amazing, Adolin!'

'I . . . Thanks.' He handed Salinor's Shardblade toward Renarin. 'A present.'

'Adolin, are you sure? I mean, I'm not exactly the best with the Plate I already have.'

'Might as well have the full set,' Adolin said. 'Take it.'

Renarin seemed hesitant.

'Take it,' Adolin said again.

Reluctantly, Renarin did so. He grimaced as he took it. Adolin shook his head, sitting down on one of the reinforced benches intended to hold a Shardbearer. Navani stepped into the room, having come down from the seats above.

'What you did,' she noted, 'would not have worked on a more skillful opponent.'

'I know,' Adolin said.

'It was wise, then,' Navani said. 'You mask your true skill. People can assume this was won by trickery, pit-fighting instead of proper dueling. They might continue to underestimate you. I can work with this to get you more duels.'

Adolin nodded, pretending that was why he'd done it.

15

A HAND WITH THE TOWER

Workform worn for strength and care.
Whispering spren breathe at your ear.
Seek first this form, its mysteries to bear.
Found here is freedom from fear.

—From the Listener Song of Listing, 19th stanza

'Tradesman Tvlakv,' Shallan said, 'I believe that you are wearing a different pair of shoes today than you were on the first day of our trip.'

Tvlakv stopped on his way to the evening fire, but adapted smoothly to her challenge. He turned toward her with a smile, shaking his head. 'I fear you must be mistaken, Brightness! Just after leaving on this trip, I lost one of my clothing trunks to a storm. I have but this one pair of shoes to my name.'

It was a flat-out lie. However, after six days of traveling together, she had discovered that Tvlakv didn't much mind being caught in a lie.

Shallan perched on her wagon's front seat in the dim light, feet bandaged, staring Tvlakv down. She'd spent most of the day milking knobweed stems for their sap, then rubbing it on her feet to keep away the rotspren. She felt extremely satisfied to have noticed the plants – it showed that though she lacked much practical knowledge, some of her studies could be useful in the wild.

Did she confront him about his lie? What would it accomplish? He didn't seem to get embarrassed by such things. He watched her in the darkness, eyes beady, shadowed.

'Well,' Shallan said to him, 'that is unfortunate. Perhaps in our travels we will meet another merchant group with whom I can trade for proper footwear.'

'I will be certain to look for such an opportunity, Brightness.' Tvlakv gave her a bow and a fake smile, then continued toward the evening cook fire, which was burning fitfully – they were out of wood, and the parshmen had gone out into the evening to search for more.

'Lies,' Pattern said softly, his shape nearly invisible on the seat beside her.

'He knows if I can't walk, I'm more dependent upon him.'

Tvlakv settled down beside the struggling fire. Nearby, the chulls – unhooked from their wagons – lumbered around, crunching tiny rockbuds beneath their gargantuan feet. They never strayed far.

Tvlakv started whispering quietly with Tag, the mercenary. He kept a smile on his face, but she didn't trust those dark eyes of his, glittering in the firelight.

'Go see what he's saying,' Shallan told Pattern.

'See . . . ?'

'Listen to his words, then come back and repeat them to me. Don't get too close to the light.'

Pattern moved down the side of the wagon. Shallan leaned back against the hard seat, then took a small mirror she'd found in Jasnah's trunk out of her safepouch along with a single sapphire sphere for light. Just a mark, nothing too bright, and it was failing at that. *When is that next highstorm due? Tomorrow?*

It was nearing the start of a new year – and that meant the Weeping was coming, though not for a number of weeks. It was a Light Year, wasn't it? Well, she could endure highstorms out here. She'd already been forced to suffer that indignity once, locked within her wagon.

In the mirror, she could see that she looked awful. Red eyes with bags under them, her hair a frazzled mess, her dress frayed and soiled. She looked like a beggar who had found a once-nice dress in a trash heap.

It didn't bother her overly much. Was she worried about looking pretty for slavers? Hardly. However, Jasnah hadn't cared what people thought of her, yet had always kept her appearance immaculate. Not that Jasnah had acted alluringly – never for a moment. In fact, she'd disparaged such behavior in no uncertain terms. *Using a fetching face to make a man buy you something is no different from a man using muscle to force someone to do the same,* she'd said. *Both methods are base, and both will fail a person as they age.*

No, Jasnah had not approved of seduction as a tool. However, people responded differently to those who looked in control of themselves.

But what can I do? Shallan thought. *I have no makeup; I don't even have shoes to wear.*

'. . . she could be someone important,' Tvlakv's voice said abruptly nearby. Shallan jumped, then looked to the side, where Pattern now rested on the seat beside her. The voice came from there.

'She is trouble,' Tag's voice said. Pattern's vibrations produced a perfect imitation. 'I still think we should just leave her and go.'

'It is fortunate for us,' Tvlakv's voice said, 'that the decision is not yours. You worry about making dinner. I shall worry about our little lighteyed companion. Someone is missing her, someone rich. If we can sell her back to them, Tag, it could be what finally digs us out.'

Pattern imitated the sounds of a crackling fire for a short time, then fell silent.

The precise reproduction of the conversation was marvelous. *This,* Shallan thought, *could be very useful.*

Unfortunately, something needed to be done about Tvlakv. She couldn't have him regarding her as something to be sold back to those missing her – that was discomfortingly close to viewing her as a slave. If she let him continue in such a mindset, she'd spend the entire trip worrying about him and his thugs.

So what would Jasnah do, in this situation?

Gritting her teeth, Shallan slipped down off the wagon, stepping gingerly on her wounded feet. She could walk, barely. She waited for the painspren to retreat, then – covering up her agony – she approached the meager fire and sat down. 'Tag, you are excused.'

He looked to Tvlakv, who nodded. Tag retreated to check on the parshmen. Bluth had gone to scout the area, as he often did at night, checking for signs of others passing this way.

'It is time to discuss your payment,' Shallan said.

'Service to one so illustrious is payment in itself, of course.'

'Of course,' she said, meeting his eyes. *Don't back down. You can do this.* 'But a merchant must make a living. I am not blind, Tvlakv. Your men do not agree with your decision to help me. They think it a waste.'

Tvlakv glanced at Tag, looking unsettled. Hopefully, he wondered what else she had guessed.

'Upon arriving at the Shattered Plains,' Shallan said, 'I will acquire a grand fortune. I do not have it yet.'

'That is . . . unfortunate.'

'Not in the slightest,' Shallan said. 'It is an opportunity, tradesman Tvlakv. The fortune I will acquire is the result of a betrothal. If I arrive safely, those who rescued me – saved me from pirates, sacrificed greatly to see me brought to my new family – will undoubtedly be well rewarded.'

'I am but a humble servant,' Tvlakv said with a broad, false smile. 'Rewards are the farthest thing from my mind.'

He thinks I'm lying about the fortune. Shallan ground her teeth in frustration, anger beginning to burn inside of her. This was just what Kabsal had done! Treating her like a plaything, a means to an end, not a real person.

She leaned closer to Tvlakv into the firelight. 'Do not toy with me, slaver.'

'I wouldn't dare—'

'You have no idea the storm you have wandered into,' Shallan hissed, holding his eyes. 'You have no idea what stakes have been wagered upon my arrival. Take your petty schemes and stuff them in a crevice. Do as I say, and I will see your debts canceled. You will be a free man again.'

'What? How . . . how did you—'

Shallan stood up, cutting him off. She felt somehow stronger than she had before. More determined. Her insecurities fluttered in the pit of her stomach, but she paid them no heed.

Tvlakv didn't know she was timid. He didn't know she had been raised in rural isolation. To him, she was a woman of the court, accomplished at argument and accustomed to being obeyed.

Standing before him, feeling radiant in the glow of the flames – towering above him and his grubby machinations – she *saw*. Expectation wasn't just about what people expected of you.

It was about what you expected of yourself.

Tvlakv leaned away from her like a man before a raging bonfire. He shrank back, eyes wide, raising an arm. Shallan realized that she *was* glowing faintly with the light of spheres. Her dress no longer bore the tears and smudges it had before. It was majestic.

Instinctively, she let the glow from her skin fade, hoping Tvlakv would think it a trick of the firelight. She spun and left him shaking beside the fire as she walked back to the wagon. Darkness was fully upon them, the first moon having yet to rise. As she walked, her feet didn't hurt nearly as much as they had. Was the knobweed sap doing that much good?

She reached the wagon and began climbing back into the seat, but Bluth chose that moment to crash into camp.

'Put out the fire!' he cried.

Tvlakv looked at him dumbfounded.

Bluth dashed ahead, passing Shallan and reaching the fire, where he grabbed the pot of steaming broth. He turned it over onto the flames, splashing out ashes and steam with a hiss, scattering flamespren, which faded away.

Tvlakv jumped up, looking down as filthy broth – faintly lit by the dying embers – ran past his feet. Shallan, gritting her teeth against the pain, got off the wagon and approached. Tag ran up from the other direction.

'. . . seem to be several dozen of them,' Bluth was saying in a low voice. 'They are well armed, but have no horses or chulls, so they are not rich.'

'What is this?' Shallan demanded.

'Bandits,' Bluth said. 'Or mercenaries. Or whatever you want to call them.'

'Nobody polices this area, Brightness,' Tvlakv said. He glanced at her, then looked away quickly, obviously still shaken. 'It is truly a wilderness, you see. The presence of the Alethi on the Shattered Plains means many like to come and go. Trading caravans like ours, craftsmen seeking work, lowborn lighteyed sellswords with an eye toward enlisting. Those two conditions – no laws, but plenty of travelers – attract a certain kind of ruffian.'

'Dangerous,' Tag agreed. 'These types take what they want. Leave only corpses.'

'Did they see our fire?' Tvlakv asked, wringing his cap in his hands.

'Don't know,' Bluth said, glancing over his shoulder. Shallan could barely make out his expression in the darkness. 'Didn't want to get close. I snuck up to get a count, then ran back here fast.'

'How can you be sure they're bandits?' Shallan asked. 'They might just be soldiers on their way to the Shattered Plains, as Tvlakv said.'

'They fly no banners, display no sigils,' Bluth said. 'But they have good equipment and keep a tight guard. They're deserters. I'd bet the chulls on it.'

'Bah,' Tvlakv said. 'You'd bet my chulls on a hand with the tower, Bluth. But Brightness, for all his terrible gambling sense, I believe the fool is right. We must harness the chulls and depart immediately. The night's darkness is our ally, and we must make the most of it.'

She nodded. The men moved quickly, even the portly Tvlakv, breaking down camp and hooking up the chulls. The slaves grumbled at not getting their food for the night. Shallan stopped beside their cage, feeling ashamed. Her family had owned slaves – and not just parshmen and ardents. Ordinary slaves. In most cases, they were nothing worse than darkeyes without the right of travel.

These poor souls, however, were sickly and half-starved.

You're only one step from being in one of those pens yourself, Shallan, she thought with a shiver as Tvlakv passed, hissing curses at the captives. *No. He wouldn't dare put you in there. He'd just kill you.*

Bluth had to be reminded again to give her a hand up into the wagon. Tag ushered the parshmen into their wagon, cursing at them for moving so slowly, then climbed into his seat and took up the tail position.

The first moon began to rise, making it lighter than Shallan would have liked. It seemed to her that each crunching footstep of the chulls was as loud as a highstorm's thunder. They brushed the plants she'd named crustspines, with their branches like tubes of sandstone. Those cracked and shook.

Progress was not quick – chulls never were. As they moved, she picked out lights on a hillside, frighteningly close. Campfires not a ten-minute walk away. A shifting of winds brought the sound of distant voices, of metal on metal, perhaps men sparring.

Tvlakv turned the wagons eastward. Shallan frowned in the night. 'Why this way?' she whispered.

'Remember that gully we saw?' Bluth whispered. 'Putting it between us and them, in case they hear and come looking.'

Shallan nodded. 'What can we do if they catch us?'

'It won't be good.'

'Couldn't we bribe our way past them?'

'Deserters ain't like common bandits,' Bluth said. 'These men, they've given up everything. Oaths. Families. When you desert, it breaks you. It leaves you willing to do anything, because you've already given away everything you could have cared about losing.'

'Wow,' Shallan said, looking over her shoulder.

'I . . . Yeah, you spend your whole life with a decision like that, you do. You wish any honor were left for you, but know you've already given it away.'

He fell silent, and Shallan was too nervous to prod him further. She continued watching those lights on the hillside as the wagons – blessedly – rolled farther and farther into the night, eventually escaping into the darkness.

Nimbleform has a delicate touch.
Gave the gods this form to many.
Tho' once defied, by the gods they were crushed.
This form craves precision and plenty.

—From the Listener Song of Listing, 27th stanza

'You know,' Moash said from Kaladin's side, 'I always thought this place would be . . .'

'Bigger?' Drehy offered in his lightly accented voice.

'*Better*,' Moash said, looking around the practice grounds. 'It looks just like where darkeyed soldiers practice.'

These sparring grounds were reserved for Dalinar's lighteyes. In the center, the large open courtyard was filled with a thick layer of sand. A raised wooden walkway ran around the perimeter, stretching between the sand and the narrow surrounding building, which was just one room deep. That narrow building wrapped around the courtyard except at the front, which had a wall with an archway for the entrance, and had a wide roof that extended, giving shade to the wooden walkway. Lighteyed officers stood chatting in the shade or watching men sparring in the sunlight of the yard, and ardents moved this way and that, delivering weapons or drinks.

It was a common layout for training grounds. Kaladin had been in several buildings like this. Mostly back when he'd first been training in Amaram's army.

Kaladin set his jaw, resting his fingers on the archway leading into the training grounds. It had been seven days since Amaram's arrival in the warcamps. Seven days of dealing with the fact that Amaram and Dalinar were friends.

He'd decided to be storming happy about Amaram's arrival. After all, it meant that Kaladin would be able to find a chance to finally stick a spear in that man.

No, he thought, entering the training grounds, *not a spear. A knife. I want to be up close to him, face-to-face, so I can watch him panic as he dies. I want to* feel *that knife going in.*

Kaladin waved to his men and entered through the archway, forcing himself to focus on his surroundings instead of Amaram. That archway was good stone, quarried nearby, built into a structure with the traditional eastward reinforcement. Judging by the modest crem deposits, these walls hadn't been here long. It was another sign that Dalinar was starting to think of the warcamps as permanent – he was taking down simple, temporary buildings and replacing them with sturdy structures.

'I don't know what you expected,' Drehy said to Moash as he inspected the grounds. 'How would you make *sparring grounds* different for the lighteyes? Use diamond dust instead of sand?'

'Ouch,' Kaladin said.

'I don't know how,' Moash said. 'It's just that they make such a big deal of it. No darkeyes on the "special" sparring grounds. I don't see what makes them special.'

'That's because you don't think like lighteyes,' Kaladin said. 'This place is special for one simple reason.'

'Why's that?' Moash asked.

'Because *we're* not here,' Kaladin said, leading the way in. 'Not normally, at least.'

He had with him Drehy and Moash, along with five other men, a mix of Bridge Four members and a few survivors of the old Cobalt Guard. Dalinar had assigned those to Kaladin, and to Kaladin's surprise and pleasure, they had accepted him as their leader without a word of complaint. To a man, he'd been impressed with them. The old Guard had deserved its reputation.

A few, all darkeyed, had started eating with Bridge Four. They'd asked for Bridge Four patches, and Kaladin had gotten them some – but ordered them to put their Cobalt Guard patches on the other shoulder, and continue to wear them as a mark of pride.

Spear in hand, Kaladin led his team toward a group of ardents who bustled in their direction. The ardents wore Vorin religious garb – loose trousers and tunics, tied at the waist with simple ropes. Pauper's clothing. They were slaves, and then they also weren't. Kaladin had never given much thought to them. His mother would probably lament how little Kaladin cared for religious observance. The way Kaladin figured it, the Almighty didn't show much concern for him, so why care back?

'This is the *lighteyes'* training ground,' said the lead ardent sternly. She was a willowy woman, though you weren't supposed to think of ardents as male or female. She had her head shaven, like all ardents. Her male companions wore square beards with clean upper lips.

'Captain Kaladin, Bridge Four,' Kaladin said, scanning the practice grounds and shouldering his spear. It would be very easy for an accident to happen here, during sparring. He'd have to watch for that. 'Here to guard the Kholin boys while they practice today.'

'Captain?' one of the ardents scoffed. 'You—'

Another ardent silenced him by whispering something. News about Kaladin had traveled quickly through camp, but ardents could be an isolated lot, sometimes.

'Drehy,' Kaladin said, pointing. 'See those rockbuds growing up on the top of the wall there?'

'Yup.'

'They're cultivated. That means there's a way up.'

'Of course there is,' the lead ardent said. 'The stairwell is at the northwestern corner. I have the key.'

'Good, you can let him in,' Kaladin said. 'Drehy, keep an eye on things from up there.'

'On it,' Drehy said, trotting in the direction of the stairwell.

'And what kinds of danger do you expect them to be in here?' the ardent said, folding her arms.

'I see lots of weapons,' Kaladin said, 'lots of people moving in and out, and . . . are those Shardblades I see? I wonder what could *possibly* go wrong.' He gave her a pointed look. The woman sighed, then handed her key to an assistant, who jogged off after Drehy.

Kaladin pointed to positions for his other men to watch from. They moved off, leaving only him and Moash. The lean man had turned immediately at the mention of Shardblades, and now watched them hungrily. A pair of lighteyed men bearing them had moved out into the center of the sands. One Blade was long and thin, with a large crossguard, while the other was wide and enormous, with wicked spikes – slightly flamelike – jutting out of both sides along the lower third. Both weapons had protective strips on the edges, like a partial sheath.

'Huh,' Moash said, 'I don't recognize either of those men. I thought I knew all the Shardbearers in camp.'

'They aren't Shardbearers,' the ardent said. 'They're using the King's Blades.'

'Elhokar lets people use his Shardblade?' Kaladin asked.

'It is a grand tradition,' the ardent said, seeming annoyed that she had to explain. 'The highprinces used to do it in their own princedoms, before the reunification, and now it is the king's obligation and honor. Men may use the King's Blade and Plate to practice. The lighteyes of our armies must be trained with Shards, for the good of all. Blade and Plate are difficult to master, and if a Shardbearer falls in battle, it is important that others be capable of their immediate use.'

That made sense, Kaladin supposed, though he found it hard to imagine any lighteyes letting someone else touch his Blade. 'The king has two Shardblades?'

'One is that of his father, kept for the tradition of training Shardbearers.' The ardent glanced at the sparring men. 'Alethkar has always had the finest Shardbearers in the world. This tradition is part of it. The king has hinted that someday, he might bestow his father's Blade upon a worthy warrior.'

Kaladin nodded in appreciation. 'Not bad,' he said. 'I'll bet that a lot of men come to practice with them, each hoping to prove he's the most skilled and most deserving. A good way for Elhokar to trick a bunch of men into training.'

The ardent huffed and walked away. Kaladin watched the Shardblades flash in the air. The men using them barely knew what they were doing.

The real Shardbearers he'd seen, the real Shardbearers he'd *fought*, hadn't lurched about swinging the oversized swords like polearms. Even Adolin's duel the other day had—

'Storms, Kaladin,' Moash said, watching the ardent stalk away. 'And you were telling *me* to be respectful?'

'Hmm?'

'You didn't use an honorific for the king,' Moash said. 'Then you implied that the lighteyes coming to practice were lazy and needed to be tricked into it. I thought we were supposed to avoid antagonizing the lighteyes?'

Kaladin looked away from the Shardbearers. Distracted, he'd spoken thoughtlessly. 'You're right,' he said. 'Thanks for the reminder.'

Moash nodded.

'I want you by the gate,' Kaladin said, pointing. A group of parshmen came in, bearing boxes, probably foodstuffs. Those wouldn't be dangerous. Would they? 'Pay particularly close attention to servants, sword runners, or anyone else seemingly innocuous who approaches Highprince Dalinar's sons. A knife to the side from someone like that would be one of the best ways to pull off an assassination.'

'Fine. But tell me something, Kal. Who is this Amaram fellow?'

Kaladin turned sharply toward Moash.

'I see how you look at him,' Moash said. 'I see how your face gets when the other bridgemen mention him. What did he do to you?'

'I was in his army,' Kaladin said. 'The last place I fought, before . . .'

Moash gestured to Kaladin's forehead. 'That's his work, then?'

'Yeah.'

'So he's not the hero people say he is,' Moash said. He seemed pleased by that fact.

'His soul is as dark as any I've ever known.'

Moash took Kaladin by the arm. 'We *are* going to get back at them somehow. Sadeas, Amaram. The ones who have done these things to us?' Angerspren boiled up around him, like pools of blood in the sand.

Kaladin met Moash's eyes, then nodded.

'Good enough for me,' Moash said, shouldering his spear and jogging off toward the position Kaladin had indicated, the spren vanishing.

'He's another who needs to learn to smile more,' Syl whispered.

Kaladin hadn't noticed her flitting nearby, and now she settled down on his shoulder.

Kaladin turned to walk around the perimeter of the practice grounds, noting each entrance. Perhaps he was being overly cautious. He just liked doing jobs well, and it had been a lifetime since he'd had a job other than saving Bridge Four.

Sometimes, though, it seemed like his job was impossible to do well. During the highstorm last week, someone had *again* sneaked into Dalinar's rooms, scrawling a second number on the wall. Counting it down, it pointed at the same date a little over a month away.

The highprince didn't seem worried, and wanted the event kept quiet. Storms . . . was he writing the glyphs himself while he had fits? Or was it some kind of spren? Kaladin was *sure* nobody could have gotten past him this time to get in.

'Do you want to talk about the thing that is bothering you?' Syl asked from her perch.

'I'm worried about what's happening during the highstorms with Dalinar,' Kaladin said. 'Those numbers . . . something is wrong. You still seeing those spren about?'

'Red lightning?' she asked. 'I think so. They're hard to spot. You haven't seen them?'

Kaladin shook his head, hefting his spear and walking over onto the walkway around the sands. Here, he peeked into a storage room. Wooden practice swords, some the size of Shardblades, and sparring leathers lined the wall.

'Is that all that's bothering you?' Syl asked.

'What else would be?'

'Amaram and Dalinar.'

'It's not a big deal. Dalinar Kholin is friends with one of the worst murderers I've ever met. So? Dalinar is lighteyed. He's probably friends with a lot of murderers.'

'Kaladin . . .' Syl said.

'Amaram's worse than Sadeas, you know,' Kaladin said, walking around the storage room, checking for doorways. 'Everyone knows that Sadeas is a rat. He's straight with you. "You're a bridgeman," he told me, "and I'm going to use you up until you die." Amaram, though . . . He promised to be more, a brightlord like those in the stories. He told me he'd protect

Tien. He feigned honor. That's worse than any depth Sadeas could ever reach.'

'Dalinar's not like Amaram,' Syl said. 'You know he's not.'

'People say the same things about him that they did of Amaram. That they *still do* of Amaram.' Kaladin stepped back out into the sunlight and continued his circuit of the grounds, passing dueling lighteyes who kicked up sand as they grunted, sweated, and clacked wooden swords against one another.

Each pair was attended by a half-dozen darkeyed servants carrying towels and canteens – and many had a parshman or two bring them chairs to sit on when they rested. Stormfather. Even in something routine like this, the lighteyes had to be pampered.

Syl zipped out into the air in front of Kaladin, coming down like a storm. *Literally* like a storm. She stopped in the air right in front of him, a cloud boiling from beneath her feet, flashing with lightning. 'You can honestly say,' she demanded, 'that you think Dalinar Kholin is only *pretending* to be honorable?'

'I—'

'Don't you lie to me, Kaladin,' she said, stepping forward, pointing. Diminutive though she was, in that moment, she seemed as vast as a highstorm. 'No lies. Ever.'

He took a deep breath. 'No,' he finally said. 'No, Dalinar gave up his Blade for us. He's a good man. I accept that. Amaram has him fooled. He had me fooled too, so I suppose I can't blame Kholin too much.'

Syl nodded curtly, the cloud dissipating. 'You should talk to him about Amaram,' she said, walking in the air beside Kaladin's head as he continued scouting the structure. Her steps were small, and she should have fallen behind, but she didn't.

'And what should I say?' Kaladin asked. 'Should I go to him and accuse a lighteyes of the third dahn of murdering his own troops? Of stealing my Shardblade? I'll sound like either a fool or a madman.'

'But—'

'He won't listen, Syl,' Kaladin said. 'Dalinar Kholin might be a good man, but he won't let me speak ill of a powerful lighteyes. It's the way of the world. And that *is* truth.'

He continued his inspection, wanting to know what was in the rooms where people could watch people spar. Some were for storage, others for bathing and resting. Several of those were locked, with lighteyes inside recovering from their daily sparring. Lighteyes liked baths.

The back side of the structure, opposite the entrance gate, held the living quarters for the ardents. Kaladin had never seen so many shaved heads and robed bodies scurrying about. Back in Hearthstone, the city-lord had kept only a few wizened old ardents for tutoring his son. Those had also come down to the town periodically to burn prayers and elevate darkeyes' Callings.

These ardents didn't seem to be the same type. They had the physiques of warriors, and would often step in to practice with lighteyes who needed a sparring partner. Some of the ardents had dark eyes, but still used the sword – they weren't considered lighteyed or darkeyed. They were just ardents.

And what do I do if one of them *decides to try killing the princelings?* Storms, but he hated some aspects of bodyguard duty. If nothing happened, then you were never sure if it was because nothing was wrong, or because you had deterred potential assassins.

Adolin and his brother finally arrived, both fully armored in their Shardplate, helms under their arms. They were accompanied by Skar and a handful of former members of the Cobalt Guard. Those saluted Kaladin as he walked up and gestured that they were dismissed, the shift officially changed. Skar would be off to join Teft and the group protecting Dalinar and Navani.

'The area is as secure as I can make it without disrupting training, Brightlord,' Kaladin said, walking up to Adolin. 'My men and I will keep an eye out while you spar, but don't hesitate to give a holler if something seems amiss.'

Adolin grunted, surveying the place, barely paying Kaladin any heed. He was a tall man, his few black Alethi hairs overwhelmed by quite a bit of golden blond. His father didn't have that. Adolin's mother had been from Rira, perhaps?

Kaladin turned to walk toward the northern side of the courtyard, where he'd have a different view from Moash.

'Bridgeman,' Adolin called. 'You've decided to start using proper titles for people? Didn't you call my father "sir"?'

'He's in my chain of command,' Kaladin said, turning back. The simple answer seemed the best.

'And I'm not?' Adolin asked, frowning.

'No.'

'And if I give you an order?'

'I'll comply with any reasonable requests, Brightlord. But if you wish for someone to fetch you tea between bouts, you'll have to send someone else. There should be plenty here willing to lick your heels.'

Adolin stepped up to him. Though the deep blue Shardplate added only a few inches to his height, he seemed to tower because of it. Perhaps that line about licking heels had been brash.

Adolin represented something, though. The privilege of the lighteyes. He wasn't like Amaram or Sadeas, who brought out Kaladin's hatred. Men like Adolin just annoyed him, reminding him that in this world, some sipped wine and wore fancy clothing while others were made slaves almost on a whim.

'I owe you my life,' Adolin growled, as if it hurt to say the words. 'That's the only reason I haven't yet thrown you through a window.' He reached up with a gauntleted finger and tapped at Kaladin's chest. 'But my patience with you won't extend as far as my father's, little bridgeman. There's something off about you, something I can't put my finger on. I'm watching you. Remember your place.'

'Great. I'll keep you alive, Brightlord,' Kaladin said, pushing aside the finger. '*That's* my place.'

'I can keep myself alive,' Adolin said, turning away and tromping across the sand with a clink of Plate. 'Your job is to watch over my brother.'

Kaladin was more than happy to let him leave. 'Spoiled child,' he muttered. Kaladin supposed that Adolin was a few years older than him. Just recently, Kaladin had realized that he'd passed his twentieth birthday while a bridgeman, and never known it. Adolin was in his early twenties. But being a child had little to do with age.

Renarin still stood awkwardly near the front gate, wearing Dalinar's former Shardplate, carrying his newly won Shardblade. Adolin's quick duel from yesterday was the talk of the warcamps, and it would take Renarin five days to fully bond his Blade before he could dismiss it.

The young man's Shardplate was the color of dark steel, unpainted. That was how Dalinar had preferred it. By giving his Plate away, Dalinar suggested that he felt he needed to win his next victories as a politician. It was a laudable move; you couldn't always have men following you because they feared you could beat them up – or even because you were the best soldier among them. You needed more, far more, to be a true leader.

Yet Kaladin did wish Dalinar had kept the Plate. Anything that helped the man stay alive would have been a boon for Bridge Four.

Kaladin leaned back against a column, folding his arms, spear in the crook of his arm, watching the area for trouble and inspecting everyone that got too close to the princelings. Adolin walked over and grabbed his brother by the shoulder, towing him across the courtyard. Various people sparring in the square stopped and bowed – if not in uniform – or saluted the princelings as they passed. A group of grey-clothed ardents had gathered at the back of the courtyard, and the woman from earlier stepped forward to chat with the brothers. Adolin and Renarin both bowed formally to her.

It had been three weeks now since Renarin had been given his Plate. Why had Adolin waited so long to bring him here for training? Had he been waiting until the duel, so he could win the lad a Blade too?

Syl landed on Kaladin's shoulder. 'Adolin and Renarin are both bowing to her.'

'Yeah,' Kaladin said.

'But isn't the ardent a slave? One their father owns?'

Kaladin nodded.

'Humans don't make sense.'

'If you're only now learning that,' Kaladin said, 'then you haven't been paying attention.'

Syl tossed her hair, which moved realistically. The gesture itself was very human. Perhaps she'd been paying attention after all. 'I don't like them,' she said airily. 'Either one. Adolin or Renarin.'

'You don't like anyone who carries Shards.'

'Exactly.'

'You called the Blades abominations before,' Kaladin said. 'But the Radiants carried them. So were the Radiants wrong to do so?'

'Of course not,' she said, sounding like he was saying something completely stupid. 'The Shards weren't abominations back then.'

'What changed?'

'The knights,' Syl said, growing quiet. 'The knights changed.'

'So it's not that the weapons are abominations specifically,' Kaladin said. 'It's that the wrong people are carrying them.'

'There are no right people anymore,' Syl whispered. 'Maybe there never were. . . .'

'And where did they come from in the first place?' Kaladin asked. 'Shardblades. Shardplate. Even modern fabrials are nowhere near as good. So where did the ancients get weapons so amazing?'

Syl fell silent. She had a frustrating habit of doing that when his questions got too specific.

'Well?' he prompted.

'I wish I could tell you.'

'Then do.'

'I wish it worked that way. It doesn't.'

Kaladin sighed, turning his attention back to Adolin and Renarin, where it was supposed to be. The senior ardent had led them to the very back of the courtyard, where another group of people sat on the ground. They were ardents too, but something was different about them. Teachers of some sort?

As Adolin spoke to them, Kaladin did another quick scan around the courtyard, then frowned.

'Kaladin?' Syl asked.

'Man in the shadows over there,' Kaladin said, gesturing with his spear toward a place under the eaves. A man stood there, leaning cross-armed against a waist-high wooden railing. 'He's watching the princelings.'

'Um, so is everyone else.'

'He's different,' Kaladin said. 'Come on.'

Kaladin wandered over casually, unthreatening. The man was probably just a servant. Long-haired, with a short but scruffy black beard, he wore loose tan clothing tied with ropes. He looked out of place in the sparring yard, and that itself was probably enough to indicate he wasn't an assassin. The best assassins never stood out.

Still, the man had a robust build and a scar on his cheek. So he'd seen fighting. Best to check on him. The man watched Renarin and Adolin intently and, from this angle, Kaladin couldn't see if his eyes were light or dark.

As Kaladin got close, his foot audibly scraped the sand. The man spun immediately, and Kaladin leveled his spear by instinct. He could see the man's eyes now – they were brown – but Kaladin had trouble placing his age. Those eyes seemed old somehow, but the man's skin didn't seem wrinkled enough to match them. He could have been thirty-five. Or he could have been seventy.

Too young, Kaladin thought, though he couldn't say why.

Kaladin lowered his spear. 'Sorry, I'm a little jumpy. First few weeks on the job.' He tried to say it disarmingly.

It didn't work. The man looked him up and down, still showing the chained menace of a warrior deciding whether or not to strike. Finally, he turned away from Kaladin and relaxed, watching Adolin and Renarin.

'Who are you?' Kaladin asked, stepping up beside the man. 'I'm new, as I said. I'm trying to learn everyone's names.'

'You're the bridgeman. The one who saved the highprince.'

'I am,' Kaladin said.

'You don't need to keep prying,' the man said. 'I'm not going to hurt your Damnation prince.' He had a low, grinding voice. Scratchy. Strange accent too.

'He's not my prince,' Kaladin said. 'Just my responsibility.' He looked the man over again, noticing something. The light clothing, tied with ropes, was very similar to what some of the ardents were wearing. The full head of hair had thrown Kaladin off.

'You're a soldier,' Kaladin guessed. 'Ex-soldier, I mean.'

'Yeah,' the man said. 'They call me Zahel.'

Kaladin nodded, the irregularities clicking into place. Occasionally, a soldier retired to the ardentia, if he had no other life to return to. Kaladin would have expected them to require the man to at least shave his head.

I wonder if Hav is in one of these monasteries somewhere, Kaladin thought idly. *What would he think of me now?* He'd probably be proud. He always had seen guard duty as the most respectable of a soldier's assignments.

'What are they doing?' Kaladin asked Zahel, nodding toward Renarin and Adolin – who, despite the encumbrance of their Shardplate, had seated themselves on the ground before the elder ardents.

Zahel grunted. 'The younger Kholin has to be chosen by a master. For training.'

'Can't they just pick whichever one they want?'

'Doesn't work that way. It's kind of an awkward situation, though. Prince Renarin, he's never practiced much with a sword.' Zahel paused. 'Being chosen by a master is a step that most lighteyed boys of suitable rank take by the time they're ten.'

Kaladin frowned. 'Why didn't he ever train?'

'Health problems of some sort.'

'And they'd really turn him down?' Kaladin asked. 'The highprince's own son?'

'They could, but they probably won't. Not brave enough.' The man narrowed his eyes as Adolin stood up and gestured. 'Damnation. I knew it was suspicious that he waited for this until I got back.'

'Swordmaster Zahel!' Adolin called. 'You aren't sitting with the others!'

Zahel sighed, then gave Kaladin a resigned glance. 'I'm probably not brave enough either. I'll try not to hurt him too much.' He walked around the railing and jogged over. Adolin clasped Zahel's hand eagerly, then pointed to Renarin. Zahel looked distinctly out of place among the other ardents with their bald heads, neatly trimmed beards, and cleaner clothing.

'Huh,' Kaladin said. 'Did he seem odd to you?'

'You all seem odd to me,' Syl said lightly. 'Everyone but Rock, who is a complete gentleman.'

'He thinks you're a god. You shouldn't encourage him.'

'Why not? I *am* a god.'

He turned his head, looking at her flatly as she sat on his shoulder. 'Syl . . .'

'What? I am!' She grinned and held up her fingers, as if pinching something very small. 'A little piece of one. Very, very little. You have permission to bow to me now.'

'Kind of hard to do when you're sitting on my shoulder,' he mumbled. He noticed Lopen and Shen arriving at the gate, likely bearing the daily reports from Teft. 'Come on. Let's see if Teft has anything he needs from me, then we'll do a circuit and check on Drehy and Moash.'

The Pattern is changing shape almost constantly!

It shifts pace often, changing slowly at some times and very quickly at others.

- cannot yet tell that might cause these changes in timing.

It appears to be made up of lines. They're not exactly tendrils or tentacles, they don't grasp or reach. They keep dividing and combining into d

The lines be connected the central Pattern or from a root shapes mix reduce by

It almost in and out three-dim it prefers with, through

It ce of dep appear to dimensions

It seems to have an infinite variety of permutations!

The lines that make up the Pattern sweep and curl and straighten and twist, smoothly dividing and combining together and moving apart again in a constant tangle of lines. It never looks chaotic, there is always a pattern to the shapes.

The divisions of the Pattern vary, but appear to be consistently even.

I am almost cer have seen this somewhere be

It shares some resemblance I observed in

You have no idea what I went through to recover this from the bottom of the Roshavan ocean. You owe me a new coat. —Nav

Dullform dread, with the mind most lost.
The lowest, and one not bright.
To find this form, one need banish the cost.
It finds you and brings you to blight.

—From the Listener Song of Listing, final stanza

Riding on her wagon, Shallan covered her anxiety with scholarship. There was no way to tell if the deserters had spotted the trails of crushed rockbuds made by the caravan. They might be following. They might not be.

No use dwelling on it, she told herself. And so she found a distraction. 'The leaves can start their own shoots,' she said, holding up one of the small, round leaves on the tip of her finger. She turned it toward the sunlight.

Bluth sat beside her, hulking like a boulder. Today, he wore a hat that was entirely too stylish for him — dusty white, with a brim that folded upward at the sides. He would occasionally flick his guiding reed — it was at least as long as Shallan was tall — on the shell of the chull ahead.

Shallan had made a small list of the beats he used in the back of her book. Bluth hit twice, paused, and hit again. That made the animal slow as the wagon in front of them — driven by Tvlakv — began moving up a hillside covered in tiny rockbuds.

'You see?' Shallan said, showing him the leaf. 'That's why the plant's limbs are so fragile. When the storm comes, it will shatter these branches and break off the leaves. They will blow away and start new shoots, building their own shell. They grow so quickly. Faster than I'd have expected out here, in these infertile lands.'

Bluth grunted.

Shallan sighed, lowering her finger and putting the tiny plant back in the cup she'd been using to nurture it. She glanced over her shoulder.

No sign of pursuit. She really should just stop worrying.

She turned back to her new sketchbook – one of Jasnah's notebooks that didn't have many pages filled – then began a quick sketch of the small leaf. She didn't have very good materials, only a single charcoal pencil, some pens, and a little ink, but Pattern had been right. She could not stop.

She had begun with a replacement sketch of the santhid as she remembered it from her dip in the sea. The picture wasn't equal to the one she'd crafted right after the event, but having it again – in any form – had started healing the wounds inside.

She finished the leaf, then turned the page and began a sketch of Bluth. She didn't particularly want to restart her collection of people with him, but her options were limited. Unfortunately, that hat really did look silly – it was far too small for his head. The image of him huddled forward like a crab, back to the sky and hat on his head . . . well, at least it would be an interesting composition.

'Where did you get the hat?' she asked as she sketched.

'Traded for it,' Bluth mumbled, not looking at her.

'Did it cost much?'

He shrugged. Shallan had lost her own hats in the sinking, but had persuaded Tvlakv to give her one of the ones woven by the parshmen. It wasn't particularly attractive, but it kept the sun off her face.

Despite the bumping wagon, Shallan eventually managed to finish her sketch of Bluth. She inspected it, dissatisfied. It *was* a poor way to start her collection, particularly as she felt she'd caricatured him somewhat. She pursed her lips. What would Bluth look like if he weren't always scowling at her? If his clothing were neater, if he carried a proper weapon instead of that old cudgel?

She flipped the page and started again. A different composition

– idealized, perhaps, but somehow also *right*. He could actually look dashing, once you dressed him up properly. A uniform. A spear, planted to his side. Eyes toward the horizon. By the time she'd finished, she was feeling much better about the day. She smiled at the product, then held it up to Bluth as Tvlakv called the midday halt.

Bluth glanced at the picture, but said nothing. He gave the chull a few whacks to stop it alongside the one pulling Tvlakv's wagon. Tag rolled up his wagon – he carried the slaves, this time.

'Knobweed!' Shallan said, lowering her sketch and pointing at a patch of thin reeds growing behind a nearby rock.

Bluth groaned. 'More of that plant?'

'Yes. Would you kindly fetch them for me?'

'Can't the parshmen do it? I'm supposed to feed the chulls. . . .'

'Which would you rather make wait, guardsman Bluth? The chulls, or the lighteyed woman?'

Bluth scratched his head underneath the hat, then sullenly climbed down from the wagon and walked toward the reeds. Nearby, Tvlakv stood on his wagon, watching the horizon to the south.

A thin trail of smoke rose in that direction.

Shallan felt an immediate chill. She scrambled from the wagon and hurried to Tvlakv. 'Storms!' Shallan said. 'Is it the deserters? They *are* following us?'

'Yes. They have stopped to cook for midday, it seems,' Tvlakv said from his perch atop his wagon. 'They do not care about us seeing their fire.' He forced out a laugh. 'That is a good sign. They probably know we are only three wagons, and are barely worth chasing. So long as we keep moving and don't stop often, they will give up the chase. Yes. I'm certain.'

He hopped down from his wagon, then hurriedly began to water the slaves. He didn't bother to make the parshmen do it – he did the work himself. That, more than anything, testified to his nervousness. He wanted to be moving again quickly.

That left the parshmen to continue weaving in their cage behind Tvlakv's wagon. Anxious, Shallan stood there watching. The deserters had spotted the wagons' trail of broken rockbuds.

She found herself sweating, but what could she do? She couldn't hurry the caravan. She had to simply hope, as Tvlakv said, that they could stay ahead of pursuit.

That didn't seem likely. The chull wagons couldn't be faster than marching men.

Distract yourself, Shallan thought as she started to panic. *Find something to take your mind off the pursuit.*

What about Tvlakv's parshmen? Shallan eyed them. Perhaps a drawing of the two of them in their cage?

No. She was too nervous for drawing, but perhaps she could find something out. She walked to the parshmen. Her feet complained, but the pain was manageable. In fact, in contrast to how she'd covered it up on previous days, now she exaggerated her winces. Better to make Tvlakv think she was less well than she was.

She stopped at the cage's bars. The back was unlocked – parshmen never ran. Buying these two must have been quite an investment for Tvlakv. Parshmen weren't cheap, and many monarchs and powerful lighteyes hoarded them.

One of the two glanced at Shallan, then turned back to his work. Her work? It was difficult to tell the males from the females without undressing them. Both of these two had red on white marbled skin. They had squat bodies, perhaps five feet tall, and were bald.

It was so difficult to see these two humble workers as a threat. 'What are your names?' Shallan asked.

One looked up. The other kept working.

'Your name,' Shallan prodded.

'One,' the parshman said. He pointed at his companion. 'Two.' He put his head down and kept working.

'Are you happy with your life?' Shallan asked. 'Would you rather be free, given the chance?'

The parshman looked up at her and frowned. He scrunched up his brow, mouthing a few of the words, then shook his head. He didn't understand.

'Freedom?' Shallan prodded.

He hunched down to work.

He actually looks uncomfortable, Shallan thought. *Embarrassed for not understanding.* His posture seemed to say, 'Please stop asking me questions.' Shallan tucked her sketchbook under her arm and took a Memory of the two of them working there.

These are evil monsters, she told herself forcefully, *creatures of legend who will soon be bent on destroying everyone and everything around them.* Standing here, looking in at them, she found it difficult to believe, even though she had accepted the evidence.

Storms. Jasnah was right. Persuading the lighteyes to rid themselves of their parshmen was going to be nearly impossible. She would need very, very solid proof. Troubled, she walked back to her seat and climbed up, making sure to wince. Bluth had left her a bundle of knobweed, and was now caring for the chulls. Tvlakv was digging out some food for a quick lunch, which they'd probably eat while moving.

She quieted her nerves and forced herself to do some sketches of nearby plants. She soon moved on to a sketch of the horizon and the rock formations nearby. The air didn't feel as cold as it had during her first days with the slavers, though her breath still steamed before her in the mornings.

As Tvlakv passed by, he gave her an uncomfortable glance. He had treated her differently since their confrontation at the fire last night.

Shallan continued sketching. It was certainly a lot flatter out here than back home. And there were far fewer plants, though they were more robust. And . . .

. . . And was that *another* column of smoke up ahead? She stood up and raised a hand to shade her eyes. Yes. More smoke. She looked southward, toward the pursuing mercenaries.

Nearby, Tag stopped, noticing what she had. He hustled over to Tvlakv, and the two started arguing softly.

'Tradesman Tvlakv' – Shallan refused to call him 'Trademaster,' as would be his proper title as a full merchant – 'I would hear your discussion.'

'Of course, Brightness, of course.' He waddled over, wringing his hands. 'You have seen the smoke ahead. We have entered a corridor running between the Shattered Plains and the Shallow Crypts and its sister villages. There is more traffic here than in other parts of the Frostlands, you see. So it is not unexpected that we should encounter others . . .'

'Those ahead?'

'Another caravan, if we are lucky.'

And if we're unlucky . . . She didn't need to ask. It would mean more deserters or bandits.

'We can avoid them,' Tvlakv said. 'Only a large group would dare make smoke for midday meals, as it is an invitation – or a warning. The small caravans, like ourselves, do not risk it.'

'If it's a large caravan,' Tag said, rubbing his brow with a thick finger, 'they'll have guards. Good protection.' He looked southward.

'Yes,' Tvlakv said. 'But we could also be placing ourselves between two enemies. Danger on all sides . . .'

'Those behind *will* catch us, Tvlakv,' Shallan said.

'I—'

'A man hunting game will return with a mink if there are no telm to be found,' she said. 'Those deserters have to kill to survive out here. Didn't you say there was probably going to be a highstorm tonight?'

'Yes,' Tvlakv said, reluctant. 'Two hours after sunset, if the list I bought is correct.'

'I don't know how bandits normally weather the storms,' Shallan said, 'but they've obviously committed to chasing us down. I'd bet they plan to use the wagons as shelter after killing us. They're not going to let us go.'

'Perhaps,' Tvlakv said. 'Yes, perhaps. But Brightness, if we see that second column of smoke ahead, so might the deserters. . . .'

'Yeah,' Tag said, nodding, as if he'd only just realized it. 'We cut east. The killers might go after the group ahead.'

'We let them attack someone else instead of us?' Shallan said, folding her arms.

'What else would you expect us to do, Brightness?' Tvlakv said, exasperated. 'We are small cremlings, you see. Our only choice is to keep away from larger creatures and hope for them to hunt one another.'

Shallan narrowed her eyes, inspecting that small column of smoke ahead. Was it her eyes, or was it growing thicker? She looked backward. Actually, the columns looked to be about the same size.

They won't hunt prey their own size, Shallan thought. *They left the army, ran away. They're cowards.*

Nearby, she could see Bluth looking backward as well, watching that smoke with an expression she couldn't read. Disgust? Longing? Fear? No spren to give her a clue.

Cowards, she thought again, *or just men disillusioned? Rocks who started rolling down a hillside, only to start going so quickly they don't know how to stop?*

It didn't matter. Those rocks would crush Shallan and the others, if given the chance. Cutting eastward wouldn't work. The deserters would take the easy kill – slow-moving wagons – instead of the potentially harder kill straight ahead.

'We make for the second column of smoke,' Shallan said, sitting down.

Tvlakv looked at her. 'You don't get to –' He broke off as she met his eyes.

'You . . .' Tvlakv said, licking his lips. 'You won't get . . . to the Shattered Plains as quickly, Brightness, if we get tied up with a larger caravan, you see. It could be bad.'

'I will deal with that if the problem arises, tradesman Tvlakv.'

'Those ahead will keep moving,' Tvlakv warned. 'We may arrive at that camp and find them gone.'

'In which case,' Shallan said, 'they will either be moving toward the Shattered Plains or coming this way, along the corridor toward the port cities. We will intersect them eventually one way or another.'

Tvlakv sighed, then nodded, calling to Tag to hurry.

Shallan sat down, feeling a thrill. Bluth returned and took his seat, then shoved a few wizened roots in her direction. Lunch, apparently. Shortly, the wagons began rolling northward, Shallan's wagon falling into place third in line this time.

Shallan settled into her seat for the trip – they were hours away from that second group, even if they did manage to catch up to it. To keep from worrying, she finished her sketches of the landscape. She then turned to idle sketches, simply letting her pencil go where it willed.

She drew skyeels dancing in the air. She drew the docks of Kharbranth. She did a sketch of Yalb, though the face felt off to her, and she didn't quite capture the mischievous spark in his eyes. Perhaps the errors related to how sad she became, thinking of what had probably happened to him.

She flipped the page and started a random sketch, whatever came into her mind. Her pencil moved into a depiction of an elegant woman in a stately gown. Loose but sleek below the waist, tight across the chest and stomach. Long, open sleeves, one hiding the safehand, the other cut at the elbow exposing the forearm and draping down below.

A bold, poised woman. In control. Still drawing unconsciously, Shallan added her own face to the elegant woman's head.

She hesitated, pencil hovering above the image. That wasn't her. Was it? Could it be?

She stared at that image as the wagon bumped over rocks and plants. She flipped to the next page and started another drawing. A ball gown, a woman at court, surrounded by the elite of Alethkar as she imagined them. Tall, strong. The woman belonged among them.

Shallan added her face to the figure.

She flipped the page and did another one. And then another.

The last one was a sketch of her standing at the edge of the Shattered Plains as she imagined them. Looking eastward, toward the secrets that Jasnah had sought.

Shallan flipped the page and drew again. A picture of Jasnah on the ship, seated at her desk, papers and books sprawled around her. It wasn't the setting that mattered, but the face. That worried, terrified face. Exhausted, pushed to her limits.

Shallan got this one right. The first drawing since the disaster that captured perfectly what she'd seen. Jasnah's burden.

'Stop the wagon,' Shallan said, not looking up.

Bluth glanced at her. She resisted the urge to say it again. He didn't, unfortunately, obey immediately.

'Why?' he demanded.

Shallan looked up. The smoke column was still distant, but she'd been right, it was growing thicker. The group ahead had stopped and built a sizable fire for the midday meal. Judging by that smoke, they were a much larger group than the one behind.

'I'm going to get into the back,' Shallan said. 'I need to look something up. You can continue when I'm settled, but please stop and call to me once we're near to the group ahead.'

He sighed, but stopped the chull with a few whacks on the shell. Shallan climbed down, then took the knobweed and notebook, moved to the back of the wagon. Once she was in, Bluth started up again immediately, shouting back to Tvlakv, who had demanded to know the meaning of the delay.

With the walls up her wagon was shaded and private, particularly with it being last in line so nobody could look in the back door at her. Unfortunately, riding in the back wasn't as comfortable as riding in the front. Those tiny rockbuds caused a surprising amount of jarring and jolting.

Jasnah's trunk was tied in place near the front wall. She opened the lid – letting the spheres inside provide dusky illumination – then settled back on her improvised cushion, a pile of the cloths Jasnah had used to wrap her books. The blanket she used at night – as Tvlakv had been unable to produce one for her – was the velvet lining she had ripped out of the trunk.

Settling back, she unwrapped her feet to apply the new knobweed. They were scabbed over and much improved from their condition just a day before. 'Pattern?'

He vibrated from somewhere nearby. She'd asked him to remain in the back so as to not alarm Tvlakv and the guards.

'My feet are healing,' she said. 'Did you do this?'

'Mmmm ... I know almost nothing of why people break. I know less of why they ... unbreak.'

'Your kind don't get wounded?' she asked, snapping off a knobweed stem and squeezing the drops onto her left foot.

'We break. We just do it ... differently than men do. And we do not unbreak without aid. I do not know why you unbreak. Why?'

'It is a natural function of our bodies,' she said. 'Living things repair themselves automatically.' She held one of her spheres close, searching for signs of little red rotspren. Where she found a few of them along one cut, she was quick to apply sap and chase them off.

'I would like to know why things work,' Pattern said.

'So would many of us,' Shallan said, bent over. She grimaced as the wagon hit a particularly large rock. 'I made myself glow last night, by the fire with Tvlakv.'

'Yes.'

'Do you know why?'

'Lies.'

'My dress changed,' Shallan said. 'I swear the scuffs and rips were gone last night. They've returned now, though.'

'Mmm. Yes.'

'I have to be able to control this thing we can do. Jasnah called it Lightweaving. She implied it was far safer to practice than Soulcasting.'

'The book?'

Shallan frowned, sitting back against the bars on the side of the wagon. Beside her, a long line of scratches on the floor looked like they'd been made by fingernails. As if one of the slaves had tried, in a fit of madness, to claw his way to freedom.

The book Jasnah had given her, *Words of Radiance*, had been swallowed by the ocean. It seemed a greater loss than the other one Jasnah had given her, the *Book of Endless Pages*, which had strangely been blank. She didn't understand the full significance of that yet.

'I never got a chance to actually read that book,' Shallan said. 'We'll need to see if we can find another copy once we reach the Shattered Plains.' Their destination being a warcamp, though, she doubted that many books would be for sale.

Shallan held one of her spheres up before herself. It was growing dim, and needed to be reinfused. What would happen if the highstorm came, and they hadn't caught up to the group ahead? Would the deserters push through the storm itself to reach them? And, potentially, the safety of their wagons?

Storms, what a mess. She needed an edge. 'The Knights Radiant formed a bond with spren,' Shallan said, more to herself than to Pattern. 'It was a symbiotic relationship, like a little cremling who lives in the shalebark. The cremling cleans off the lichen, getting food, but also keeping the shalebark clean.'

Pattern buzzed in confusion. 'Am I . . . the shalebark or the cremling?'

'Either,' Shallan said, turning the diamond sphere in her fingers – the tiny gemstone trapped inside glowed with a vigilant light, suspended in glass. 'The Surges – the forces that run the world – are more pliable to spren. Or . . . well . . . since spren are *pieces* of those Surges, maybe it's that the spren are better at influencing one another. Our bond gives me the ability to manipulate one of the Surges. In this case, light, the power of Illumination.'

'Lies,' Pattern whispered. 'And truths.'

Shallan gripped the sphere in her fist, the light shining through her skin making her hand glow red. She willed the Light to enter her, but nothing happened. 'So, how do I make it work?'

'Perhaps eat it?' Pattern said, moving over onto the wall beside her head.

'Eat it?' Shallan asked, skeptical. 'I didn't need to eat it before to get the Stormlight.'

'Might work, though. Try?'

'I doubt I could swallow an entire sphere,' Shallan said. 'Even if I wanted to, which I distinctly do *not*.'

'Mmmm,' Pattern said, his vibrations making the wood shake. 'This . . . is not one of the things humans like to eat, then?'

'Storms, no. Haven't you been paying attention?'

'I have,' he said with an annoyed zip of a vibration. 'But it is difficult to tell! You consume some things, and turn them into other things . . . Very curious things that you hide. They have value? But you leave them. Why?'

'We are done with that conversation,' Shallan said, opening her fist and holding up the sphere again. Though, admittedly, something about what he said felt *right*. She hadn't eaten any spheres before, but she had somehow . . . consumed the Light. Like drinking it.

She'd breathed it in, right? She stared at the sphere for a moment, then sucked in a sharp breath.

It worked. The Light left the sphere, quick as a heartbeat, a bright line streaming into her chest. From there it spread, filling her. The unusual sensation made her feel anxious, alert, ready. Eager to be about . . . something. Her muscles tensed.

'It worked,' she said, though when she spoke, Stormlight – glowing faintly – puffed out in front of her. It rose from her skin, too. She had to practice before it all left. Lightweaving . . . She needed to create something. She decided to go with what she'd done before, improving the look of her dress.

Again, nothing happened. She didn't know what to do, what muscles to use, or even if muscles mattered. Frustrated, she sat there trying to find a way to make the Stormlight work, feeling inept as it escaped through her skin.

It took several minutes for it to dissipate completely. 'Well, that was distinctly unimpressive,' she said, moving to get more stalks of knobweed. 'Maybe I should practice Soulcasting instead.'

Pattern buzzed. 'Dangerous.'

'So Jasnah told me,' Shallan said. 'But I don't have her to teach me anymore, and so far as I know, she's the only one who could have done so. It's either practice on my own or never learn to use the ability.' She squeezed out another few drops of knobweed sap, moved to massage it into a cut on her foot, then stopped. The wound was noticeably smaller than it had been just moments ago.

'The Stormlight is healing me,' Shallan said.

'It makes you unbreak?'

'Yes. Stormfather! I'm doing things almost by accident.'

'Can something be "almost" an accident?' Pattern asked, genuinely curious. 'This phrase, I do not know what it means.'

'I . . . Well, it's mostly a figure of speech.' Then, before he could ask further, she continued, 'And by that I mean something we say to convey an idea or a feeling, but not a literal fact.'

Pattern buzzed.

'What does *that* mean?' Shallan asked, massaging the knobweed in anyway. 'When you buzz like that. What are you feeling?'

'Hmmm . . . Excited. Yes. It has been so long since anyone has learned of you and your kind.'

Shallan squeezed some more sap onto her toes. 'You came to learn? Wait . . . you're a *scholar*?'

'Of course. Hmmm. Why else would I come? I will learn so much before—'

He stopped abruptly.

'Pattern?' she asked. 'Before what?'

'A figure of speech.' He said it perfectly flatly, absent of tone. He was growing better and better at speaking like a person, and at times he sounded just like one. But now all of the color had gone from his voice.

'You're lying,' she accused him, glancing at his pattern on the wall. He had shrunk, growing as small as a fist, half his usual size.

'Yes,' he said reluctantly.

'You're a terrible liar,' Shallan said, surprised at the realization.

'Yes.'

'But you love lies!'

'So fascinating,' he said. 'You are all so *fascinating*.'

'Tell me what you were going to say,' Shallan ordered. 'Before you stopped yourself. I'll know if you lie.'

'Hmmmm. You sound like her. More and more like her.'

'Tell me.'

He buzzed with an annoyed sound, quick and high pitched. 'I will learn what I can of you before you kill me.'

'You think . . . You think I'm going to *kill* you?'

'It happened to the others,' Pattern said, his voice softer now. 'It will happen to me. It is . . . a pattern.'

'This has to do with the Knights Radiant,' Shallan said, raising her hands to start braiding her hair. That would be better than leaving it wild – though without a comb and brush, even braiding it was hard. *Storms,* she thought, *I need a bath. And soap. And a dozen other things.*

'Yes,' Pattern said. 'The knights killed their spren.'

'How? Why?'

'Their oaths,' Pattern said. 'It is all I know. My kind, those who were unbonded, we retreated, and many kept our minds. Even still, it is hard to think apart from my kind, unless . . .'

'Unless?'

'Unless we have a person.'

'So that's what you get out of it,' Shallan said, untangling her hair with her fingers. 'Symbiosis. I get access to Surgebinding, you get thought.'

'Sapience,' Pattern said. 'Thought. Life. These are of humans. We are ideas. Ideas that wish to live.'

Shallan continued working on her hair. 'I'm not going to kill you,' she said firmly. 'I *won't* do it.'

'I don't suppose the others intended to either,' he said. 'But it is no matter.'

'It is an *important* matter,' Shallan said. 'I won't do it. I'm not one of the Knights Radiant. Jasnah made that clear. A man who can use a sword isn't necessarily a soldier. Just because I can do what I do doesn't make me one of them.'

'You spoke oaths.'

Shallan froze.

Life before death . . . The words drifted toward her from the shadows of her past. A past she would not think of.

'You live lies,' Pattern said. 'It gives you strength. But the truth . . . Without speaking truths you will not be able to grow, Shallan. I know this somehow.'

She finished with her hair and moved to rewrap her feet. Pattern had moved to the other side of the rattling wagon chamber, settling onto the wall, only faintly visible in the dim light. She had a handful of infused spheres left. Not much Stormlight, considering how quickly that other had left her. Should she use what she had to further heal her feet? Could she even do that intentionally, or would the ability elude her, as Light-weaving had?

She tucked the spheres into her safepouch. She would save them, just in case. For now, these spheres and their Light might be the only weapon available to her.

Bandages redone, she stood up in the rattling wagon and found that her foot pain was nearly gone. She could walk almost normally, though she still wouldn't want to go far without shoes. Pleased, she knocked on the wood nearest to Bluth. 'Stop the wagon!'

This time, she didn't have to repeat herself. She rounded the wagon and, taking her seat beside Bluth, immediately noticed the smoke column ahead. It had grown darker, larger, roiling violently.

'That's no cook fire,' Shallan said.

'Aye,' Bluth said, expression dark. 'Something big is burning. Probably wagons.' He glanced at her. 'Whoever is up there, it doesn't look like things went well for them.'

Scholarform shown for patience and thought.
Beware its ambitions innate.
Though study and diligence bring the reward,
Loss of innocence may be one's fate.

—From the Listener Song of Listing, 69th stanza

'New guys are coming along, gancho,' Lopen said, taking a bite of the paper-wrapped something he was eating. 'Wearing their uniforms, talking like real men. Funny. It only took them a fewdays. Took us weeks.'

'It took the rest of the men weeks, but not you,' Kaladin said, shading his eyes from the sun and leaning on his spear. He was still on the lighteyes' practice grounds, watching over Adolin and Renarin – the latter of whom was receiving his first instructions from Zahel the swordmaster. 'You had a good attitude from the first day we found you, Lopen.'

'Well, life was pretty good, you know?'

'Pretty good? You'd just been assigned to carry siege bridges until you died on the plateaus.'

'Eh,' Lopen said, taking a bite of his food. It looked like a thick piece of flatbread wrapped around something goopy. He licked his lips, then handed it to Kaladin to free his single hand so he could dig in his pocket for a moment. 'You have bad days. You have good days. Evens out eventually.'

'You're a strange man, Lopen,' Kaladin said, inspecting the 'food' Lopen had been eating. 'What *is* this?'

'Chouta.'

'Chowder?'

'Cha-ou-ta. Herdazian food, gon. Good stuff. You can have a bite, if you want.'

It seemed to be chunks of undefinable meat slathered in some dark liquid, all wrapped in overly thick bread. 'Disgusting,' Kaladin said, handing it back as Lopen gave him the thing he'd dug out of his pocket, a shell with glyphs written on both sides.

'Your loss,' Lopen said, taking another bite.

'You shouldn't be walking around eating like that,' Kaladin noted. 'It's rude.'

'Nah, it's *convenient*. See, it's wrapped up good. You can walk about, get stuff done, eat at the same time . . .'

'Slovenly,' Kaladin said, inspecting the shell. It listed Sigzil's tallies of how many troops they had, how much food Rock thought they'd need, and Teft's assessments of how many of the former bridgemen were fit for training.

That last number was pretty high. If bridgemen lived, they got strong carrying bridges. As Kaladin had proven firsthand, that translated to their making fine soldiers, assuming they could be motivated.

On the reverse side of the shell, Sigzil had outlined a path for Kaladin to take on patrol outside the warcamps. He'd soon have enough of the greenvines ready to begin patrolling the region outside of the warcamps, as he'd told Dalinar he would do. Teft thought it would be good for Kaladin to go himself, as it would let the new men spend time with Kaladin.

'Highstorm tonight,' Lopen noted. 'Sig says it will come two hours after sunset. He thought you'd want to make preparations.'

Kaladin nodded. Another chance for those mysterious numbers to appear – both times before, they'd come during storms. He'd make extra certain Dalinar and his family were being watched.

'Thanks for the report,' Kaladin said, tucking the shell into his pocket. 'Send back and tell Sigzil his proposed route takes me too far from the warcamps. Have him draw up another one. Also, tell Teft I need a few more men to come here today and relieve Moash and Drehy. They've both been pulling too many hours lately. I'll guard Dalinar tonight myself – suggest to the highprince it would be convenient if his entire family would be together for the highstorm.'

'If the winds will, gon,' Lopen said, finishing his last bite of chouta. He whistled then, looking in at the practice grounds. 'That *is* something, isn't it?'

Kaladin followed Lopen's gaze. Adolin, having left his brother with Zahel, was now executing a training sequence with his Shardblade. Gracefully, he spun and twisted on the sands, sweeping his sword in broad, flowing patterns.

On a practiced Shardbearer, Plate never looked clumsy. Imposing, resplendent, it fit to the form of the wearer. Adolin's reflected sunlight like a mirror as he made sweeps of the sword, moving from one posture to the next. Kaladin knew it was just a warm-up sequence, more impressive than functional. You'd never do something like this on the battlefield, though many of the individual postures and cuts represented practical movements.

Even knowing that, Kaladin had to shake off a feeling of awe. Shardbearers in Plate looked inhuman when they fought, more like Heralds than men.

He caught Syl sitting on the edge of the roof overhang near Adolin, watching the young man. She was too distant for Kaladin to make out her expression.

Adolin finished his warm-up in a move where he fell to one knee and slammed his Shardblade into the ground. It sank up to mid-blade, then vanished when he released it.

'I've seen him summon that weapon before,' Kaladin said.

'Yeah, gancho, on the battlefield, when we saved his sorry ass from Sadeas.'

'No, before that,' Kaladin said, remembering an incident with a whore in Sadeas's camp. 'He saved someone who was being bullied.'

'Huh,' Lopen said. 'He can't be too bad then, you know?'

'I suppose. Anyway, off with you. Make sure to send that replacement team.'

Lopen saluted, collecting Shen, who had been poking at practice swords along the side of the courtyard. Together, they jogged off on the errand.

Kaladin did his rounds, checking on Moash and the others before walking over to where Renarin sat – still armored – on the ground before his new master.

Zahel, the ardent with the ancient eyes, sat in a solemn posture that belied his ragged beard. 'You will need to relearn how to fight, wearing that Plate. It changes the way a man steps, grips, moves.'

'I . . .' Renarin looked down. It was very odd to see a man wearing spectacles in the magnificent armor. 'I will not need to relearn how to fight, master. I never learned in the first place.'

Zahel grunted. 'That's good. It means I don't have to break down any old, bad habits.'

'Yes, master.'

'We'll start you off easily, then,' Zahel said. 'There are some steps at the corner over there. Climb up onto the roof of the dueling grounds. Then jump off.'

Renarin looked up sharply. '. . . Jump?'

'I'm old, son,' Zahel said. 'Repeating myself makes me eat the wrong flower.'

Kaladin frowned, and Renarin cocked his head, then looked at Kaladin questioningly. Kaladin shrugged.

'Eat . . . what . . . ?' Renarin asked.

'It means I get angry,' Zahel snapped. 'You people don't have proper idioms for anything. Go!'

Renarin sprang to his feet, kicking up sand, and hustled away.

'Your helmet, son!' Zahel called.

Renarin stopped, then scrambled back and snatched his helmet off the ground, nearly slipping onto his face as he did so. He spun, off balance, and ran awkwardly toward the stairs. He nearly plowed into a pillar on the way.

Kaladin snorted softly.

'Oh,' Zahel said, 'and you assume *you'd* do better your first time wearing Shardplate, bodyguard?'

'I doubt I'd forget my helmet,' Kaladin said, shouldering his spear and stretching. 'If Dalinar Kholin intends to force the other highprinces into line, I think he's going to need better Shardbearers than this. He should have picked someone else for that Plate.'

'Like you?'

'Storms no,' Kaladin said, perhaps too vehemently. 'I'm a soldier, Zahel. I want nothing to do with Shards. The boy is likable enough, but I wouldn't trust men to his command – let alone armor that could keep a much better soldier alive on the field – and that's it.'

'He'll surprise you,' Zahel replied. 'I gave him the whole "I'm your master and you do what I say" talk, and he actually listened.'

'Every soldier hears that on their first day,' Kaladin said. 'Sometimes they listen. That the boy did is hardly noteworthy.'

'If you knew how many spoiled ten-year-old lighteyed brats came through here,' Zahel said, 'you'd think it worth noting. I thought a nineteen-year-old like him would be insufferable. And don't call him a boy, boy. He's probably close to your own age, and is the son of the most powerful human on this—'

He cut off as scraping from atop the building announced Renarin Kholin charging and throwing himself off into the air, boots grinding against the stone coping of the roof. He sailed a good ten or twelve feet out over the courtyard – practiced Shardbearers could do far better – before floundering like a dying skyeel and crashing down into the sand.

Zahel looked toward Kaladin, raising an eyebrow.

'What?' Kaladin asked.

'Enthusiasm, obedience, no fear of looking foolish,' Zahel said. 'I can teach him how to fight, but those qualities are innate. This lad is going to do just fine.'

'Assuming he doesn't fall on anyone,' Kaladin said.

Renarin climbed to his feet. He looked down, as if surprised that he hadn't broken anything.

'Go up and do it again!' Zahel called to Renarin. 'This time, fall headfirst!'

Renarin nodded, then turned and trotted off toward the stairwell.

'You want him to be confident in how the Plate protects him,' Kaladin said.

'Part of using Plate is knowing its limits,' Zahel said, turning back to Kaladin. 'Plus, I just want him moving in it. Either way he's listening, and that's good. Teaching him is going to be a real pleasure. You, on the other hand, are another story.'

Kaladin raised his hand. 'Thanks, but no.'

'You'd turn down an offer to train with a full weapons master?' Zahel asked. 'I can count on one hand the number of darkeyes I've seen given that chance.'

'Yes, well, I've already done the "new recruit" thing. Yelled at by sergeants, worked to the bone, marched for hours on end. Really, I'm fine.'

'This isn't the same at all,' Zahel said, waving down one of the ardents walking past. The man was carrying a Shardblade with metal guards over the sharp edges, one of the ones the king provided for training use.

Zahel took the Shardblade from the ardent, holding it up.

Kaladin nodded his chin at it. 'What's that on the Blade?'

'Nobody's sure,' Zahel said, swiping with the Blade. 'Fit it to the edges of a Blade, and it will adapt to the shape of the weapon and make it safely blunt. Off the weapons, they break surprisingly easily. Useless in a fight on their own. Perfect for training, though.'

Kaladin grunted. Something created long ago, for use in training? Zahel inspected the Shardblade for a moment, then pointed it directly toward Kaladin.

Even with it blunted – even knowing the man wasn't going to really attack him – Kaladin felt an immediate moment of panic. A Shardblade. This one had a slender, sleek form with a large crossguard. The flat sides of the blade were etched with the ten fundamental glyphs. It was a handspan wide and easily six feet long, yet Zahel held it with one hand and didn't seem off balance.

'Niter,' Zahel said.

'What?' Kaladin asked, frowning.

'He was head of the Cobalt Guard before you,' Zahel said. 'He was a good man, and a friend. He died keeping the men of the Kholin house alive. Now you've got the same Damnation job, and you're going to have a tough time doing it half as well as he did.'

'I don't see what that has to do with you waving a Shardblade at me.'

'Anyone who sends assassins after Dalinar or his sons is going to be powerful,' Zahel said. 'They'll have access to Shardbearers. That's what you're up against, son. You're going to need far more training than a battlefield gives a spearman. Have you ever fought a man holding one of these?'

'Once or twice,' Kaladin said, relaxing against the nearby pillar.

'Don't lie to me.'

'I'm not lying,' Kaladin said, meeting Zahel's eyes. 'Ask Adolin what I pulled his father out of a few weeks back.'

Zahel lowered the sword. Behind him, Renarin dove face-first off the roof and crashed into the ground. He groaned inside his helm, rolling over. His helm leaked Light but he seemed otherwise unharmed.

'Well done, Prince Renarin,' Zahel called without looking. 'Now do a few more jumps and see if you can land on your feet.'

Renarin rose and clinked off.

'All right then,' Zahel said, sweeping the Shardblade in the air. 'Let's see what you can do, kid. Convince me to leave you alone.'

Kaladin didn't respond other than to heft his spear and settle into a defensive posture, one foot behind, one out front. He held his weapon with the butt forward instead of the point. Nearby, Adolin sparred with another one of the masters, who had the second King's Blade and a suit of Plate.

How would this work? If Zahel scored a hit on Kaladin's spear, would they pretend it had cut through?

The ardent approached in a rush, raising the Blade in a two-handed grip. The familiar calmness and focus of battle enveloped Kaladin. He did not draw in Stormlight. He needed to be certain not to come to rely on it too much.

Watch that Shardblade, Kaladin thought, stepping forward, trying to get inside the weapon's reach. In fighting a Shardbearer, everything became about that Blade. The Blade that nothing could stop, the Blade that didn't just kill the body – but severed the soul itself. The Blade—

Zahel dropped the Blade.

It hit the ground as Zahel got inside Kaladin's reach. Kaladin had been too focused on the weapon, and though he tried to get his spear in position to strike, Zahel twisted and buried his fist into Kaladin's stomach. The next punch – to the face – slammed Kaladin to the floor of the practice grounds.

Kaladin immediately rolled, ignoring the painspren wiggling in the sand. He found his feet as his vision swam. He grinned. 'Nice move, that.'

Zahel was already turning back to Kaladin, Blade recovered. Kaladin scuttled backward on the sand, spear still forward, staying away. Zahel knew his way around a Blade. He didn't fight like Adolin; fewer sweeping blows, more overhand chops. Quick and furious. He backed Kaladin around the side of the practice ground.

He'll get tired keeping this up, Kaladin's instincts said. *Keep him moving.*

After an almost complete circuit of the grounds, Zahel slowed his offense and instead rounded on Kaladin, watching for an opening. 'You'd be in trouble if I had Plate,' Zahel said. 'I'd be faster, wouldn't tire.'

'You don't have Plate.'

'And if someone comes for the king wearing it?'

'I'll use a different tactic.'

Zahel grunted as Renarin crashed to the ground nearby. The prince almost kept his footing, but stumbled and fell to the side, skidding in the sand.

'Well, if this were a real assassination attempt,' Zahel said, 'I'd be using different tactics too.'

He dashed toward Renarin.

Kaladin cursed, taking off after Zahel.

Immediately, the man reversed, skidding to a stop in the sand and spinning to swing at Kaladin with a powerful two-handed blow. The strike connected with Kaladin's spear, sending a sharp *crack* echoing across the practice grounds. If the Blade hadn't been guarded, it would have split the spear in two and perhaps grazed Kaladin's chest.

A watching ardent tossed Kaladin half a spear. They'd been waiting for his spear to be 'cut,' and wanted to replicate a real fight as much as possible. Nearby, Moash had arrived, looking concerned, but several ardents intercepted him and explained.

Kaladin looked back to Zahel.

'In a real fight,' the man said, 'I might have chased down the prince by now.'

'In a real fight,' Kaladin said, 'I might have stabbed you with half a spear when you thought me disarmed.'

'I wouldn't have made that mistake.'

'Then we'll have to assume I wouldn't have made the mistake of letting you get to Renarin.'

Zahel grinned. It looked a dangerous expression on him. He stepped forward, and Kaladin understood. There would be no backing away and leading him off this time. Kaladin wouldn't have that option if he were protecting a member of Dalinar's family. Instead, he had to try his best to pretend to kill this man.

That meant an attack.

A prolonged, close-quarters fight would favor Zahel, as Kaladin couldn't parry a Shardblade. Kaladin's best bet was to strike fast and hope to score an early hit. Kaladin barreled forward, then threw himself to his knees, skidding on the sands underneath Zahel's strike. That would get him close, and—

Zahel kicked Kaladin in the face.

Vision swimming, Kaladin rammed his fake spear into Zahel's leg. The man's Shardblade came down a second later, stopping where Kaladin's shoulder met his neck.

'You're dead, son,' Zahel said.

'You've got a spear through the leg,' Kaladin said, puffing. 'You aren't chasing down Renarin like that. I win.'

'You're still dead,' Zahel said with a grunt.

'My job is to stop you from killing Renarin. With what I just did, he escapes. Doesn't matter if the bodyguard is dead.'

'And what if the assassin had a friend?' another voice asked from behind.

Kaladin twisted to see Adolin, in full Plate and standing with his Shardblade point stuck into the ground before him. He'd removed his helm, and held it in one hand, the other hand resting on the Blade's crossguard.

'If there were two of them, bridgeboy?' Adolin asked with a smirk. 'Could you fight two Shardbearers at once? If I wanted to kill Father or the king, I'd never send just one.'

Kaladin stood, rolling his shoulder in its socket. He met Adolin's gaze. So condescending. So sure of himself. Arrogant bastard.

'All right,' Zahel said. 'I'm sure he sees the point, Adolin. No need—'

Kaladin charged the princeling, and he thought he heard Adolin chuckling as he put on his helm.

Something boiled inside of Kaladin.

The nameless Shardbearer who had killed so many of his friends.

Sadeas, sitting regally in red armor.

Amaram, hands on a sword stained with blood.

Kaladin screamed as Adolin's unguarded Shardblade came for him in one of the careful, sweeping strokes from Adolin's practice session. Kaladin pulled himself up short, raising his half-spear and letting the Blade pass right before him. Then he *slapped* the back edge of the Shardblade with his spear, knocking Adolin's grip to the side and fouling up the followthrough.

Kaladin barreled forward and threw his shoulder against the prince. It was like slamming into a wall. Kaladin's shoulder flared with pain, but the momentum – along with the surprise of his cudgel blow – knocked Adolin off balance. Kaladin forced both of them backward, the Shardbearer toppling to the ground with a crash and a surprised grunt.

Renarin made a twin crash, falling to the ground nearby. Kaladin raised his half-spear like a dagger to plunge it toward Adolin's faceplate. Unfortunately, Adolin had dismissed his Blade as they fell. The princeling got a gauntleted hand up underneath Kaladin.

Kaladin slammed his weapon downward.

Adolin heaved upward with one hand.

Kaladin's blow didn't connect; instead he found himself airborne, thrown with all the Plate-augmented strength of a Shardbearer. He floundered in the air before slamming down eight feet away, the sand grinding into his side, the shoulder he'd hit against Adolin flaring in pain again. Kaladin gasped.

'Idiot!' Zahel yelled.

Kaladin groaned, rolling over. His vision swam.

'You could have killed the boy!' He was talking to Adolin somewhere far away.

'He attacked me!' Adolin's voice was muffled by the helm.

'You challenged him, fool child.' Zahel's voice was closer.

'Then he asked for it,' Adolin said.

Pain. Someone at Kaladin's side. Zahel?

'You're wearing *Plate*, Adolin.' Yes, that was Zahel kneeling above Kaladin, whose vision refused to focus. 'You don't throw an unarmored sparring partner like he's a bundle of sticks. Your father taught you better than that!'

Kaladin sucked in sharply and forced his eyes open. Stormlight from the pouch at his belt filled him. *Not too much. Don't let them see. Don't let them take it away from you!*

Pain vanished. His shoulder reknit – he didn't know if he'd broken it or just dislocated it. Zahel cried out in surprise as Kaladin pitched himself up to his feet and dashed back toward Adolin.

The prince stumbled away, hand out to his side, obviously summoning his Blade. Kaladin kicked his fallen half-spear up in a spray of sand, then grabbed it in midair as he got near.

In that moment, the strength drained from him. The tempest inside of him fled without warning, and he stumbled, gasping at the returning pain of his shoulder.

Adolin caught him by the arm with a gauntleted fist. The prince's Shardblade formed in his other hand, but in that moment, a second Blade stopped at Kaladin's neck.

'You're dead,' Zahel said from behind, holding the Blade against Kaladin's skin. 'Again.'

Kaladin sank down in the middle of the practice grounds, dropping his half-spear. He felt completely drained. What had happened?

'Go give your brother some help with his jumping,' Zahel ordered Adolin. Why did he get to order around princes?

Adolin left and Zahel knelt beside Kaladin. 'You don't flinch when someone swings a Blade at you. You actually *have* fought Shardbearers before, haven't you?'

'Yeah.'

'You're lucky to be alive, then,' Zahel said, probing at Kaladin's shoulder. 'You've got tenacity. A stupid amount of it. You have good form, and you think well in a fight. But you hardly know what you're doing against Shardbearers.'

'I ...' What should he say? Zahel was right. It was arrogant to say otherwise. Two fights – three, if he counted today – did not make one an expert. He winced as Zahel prodded a sore tendon. More painspren on the ground. He was giving them a workout today.

'Nothing broken here,' Zahel said with a grunt. 'How are your ribs?'

'They're fine,' Kaladin said, lying back in the sand, staring up at the sky.

'Well, I won't force you to learn,' Zahel said, standing up. 'I don't think I *could* force you, actually.'

Kaladin squeezed his eyes shut. He felt humiliated, but why should he? He'd lost sparring matches before. It happened all the time.

'You remind me a lot of him,' Zahel said. 'Adolin wouldn't let me teach him either. Not at first.'

Kaladin opened his eyes. 'I'm nothing like him.'

Zahel barked a laugh at that, then stood and walked away, chuckling, as if he'd heard the finest joke in all the world. Kaladin continued to lie on the sand, staring upward at the deep blue sky, listening to the sounds of men sparring. Eventually, Syl flitted over and landed on his chest.

'What happened?' Kaladin asked. 'The Stormlight drained from me. I *felt* it go.'

'Who were you protecting?' Syl asked.

'I . . . I was practicing how to fight, like when I practiced with Skar and Rock down in the chasms.'

'Is that *really* what you were doing?' Syl asked.

He didn't know. He lay there, staring at the sky, until he finally caught his breath and forced himself to his feet with a groan. He dusted himself off, then went to check on Moash and the other guards. As he went, he drew in a little Stormlight, and it worked, slowly healing his shoulder and soothing away his bruises.

The physical ones, at least.

19

SAFE THINGS

FIVE AND A HALF YEARS AGO

The silk of Shallan's new dress was softer than any she had owned before. It touched her skin like a comforting breeze. The left cuff clipped closed over the hand; she was old enough now to cover her safehand. She had once dreamed of wearing a woman's dress. Her mother and she . . .

Her mother . . .

Shallan's mind went still. Like a candle suddenly snuffed, she stopped thinking. She leaned back in her chair, legs tucked up underneath her, hands in her lap. The dreary stone dining chamber bustled with activity as Davar Manor prepared for guests. Shallan did not know which guests, only that her father wanted the place immaculate.

Not that she could do anything to help.

Two maids bustled past. 'She saw,' one whispered softly to the other, a new woman. 'Poor thing was in the room when it happened. Hasn't spoken a word in five months. The master killed his own wife and her lover, but don't let it . . .'

They continued talking, but Shallan didn't hear.

She kept her hands in her lap. Her dress's vibrant blue was the only real color in the room. She sat on the dais, beside the high table. A half-dozen maids in brown, wearing gloves on their safehands, scrubbed the floor and polished the furniture. Parshmen carted in a few more tables. A maid threw open the windows, letting in damp fresh air from the recent highstorm.

Shallan caught mention of her name again. The maids apparently thought that because she didn't speak, she didn't hear either. At times, she wondered if she was invisible. Perhaps she wasn't real. That would be nice. . . .

The door to the hall slammed open, and Nan Helaran entered. Tall, muscular, square-chinned. Her oldest brother was a man. The rest of them . . . they were children. Even Tet Balat, who had reached the age of adulthood. Helaran scanned the chamber, perhaps looking for their father. Then he approached Shallan, a small bundle under his arm. The maids made way with alacrity.

'Hello, Shallan,' Helaran said, squatting down beside her chair. 'Here to supervise?'

It was a place to be. Father did not like her being where she could not be watched. He worried.

'I brought you something,' Helaran said, unwrapping his bundle. 'I ordered it for you in Northgrip, and the merchant only just passed by.' He took out a leather satchel.

Shallan took it hesitantly. Helaran's grin was so wide, it practically glowed. It was hard to frown in a room where he was smiling. When he was around, she could almost pretend . . . Almost pretend . . .

Her mind went blank.

'Shallan?' he asked, nudging her.

She undid the satchel. Inside was a sheaf of drawing paper, the thick kind – the expensive kind – and a set of charcoal pencils. She raised her covered safehand to her lips.

'I've missed your drawings,' Helaran said. 'I think you could be very good, Shallan. You should practice more.'

She ran the fingers of her right hand across the paper, then picked up a pencil. She started to sketch. It had been too long.

'I need you to come back, Shallan,' Helaran said softly.

She hunched over, pencil scratching on paper.

'Shallan?'

No words. Just drawing.

'I'm going to be away a lot in the next few years,' Helaran said. 'I need you to watch the others for me. I'm worried about Balat. I gave him a new axehound pup, and he . . . wasn't kind to it. You need to be strong, Shallan. For them.'

The maids had grown quiet since Helaran's arrival. Lethargic vines curled down outside the window nearby. Shallan's pencil continued to move. As if she weren't doing the drawing; as if it were coming up out of the page, the charcoal seeping out of the texture. Like blood.

Helaran sighed, standing. Then he saw what she was drawing. Bodies, facedown, on the floor with—

He grabbed the paper and crumpled it. Shallan started, pulling back, fingers shaking as she clutched the pencil.

'Draw plants,' Helaran said, 'and animals. Safe things, Shallan. Don't dwell on what happened.'

Tears trickled down her cheeks.

'We can't have vengeance yet,' Helaran said softly. 'Balat can't lead the house, and I must be away. Soon, though.'

The door slammed open. Father was a big man, bearded in careless defiance of fashion. His Veden clothing eschewed the modern designs. Instead, Father wore a skirtlike garment of silk called an ulatu and a tight shirt with a robe over the top. No mink pelts, as his grandfathers might have worn, but otherwise very, very traditional.

He towered taller than Helaran, taller than anyone else on the estate. More parshmen entered after him, carrying bundles of food for the kitchens. All three had marbled skin, two red on black and one red on white. Father liked parshmen. They did not talk back.

'I got word that you told the stable to prepare one of my carriages, Helaran!' Father bellowed. 'I'll not have you gallivanting off again!'

'There are more important things in this world,' Helaran said. 'More important even than you and your crimes.'

'Do not speak that way to me,' Father said, stalking forward, finger pointed at Helaran. 'I am your father.' Maids scurried to the side of the room, trying to stay out of the way. Shallan pulled the satchel up against her chest, trying to hide in her chair.

'You are a murderer,' Helaran said calmly.

Father stopped in place, face gone red beneath his beard. He then continued forward. 'How *dare* you! You think I can't have you imprisoned? Because you're my heir, you think I—'

Something formed in Helaran's hand, a line of mist that coalesced into silvery steel. A Blade some six feet long, curved and thick, with the side that wasn't sharp rising into a shape like burning flames or perhaps ripples of water. It had a gemstone set at the pommel, and as light reflected off the metal, the ridges seemed to move.

Helaran was a Shardbearer. Stormfather! How? When?

Father cut off, pulling up short. Helaran hopped down from the low dais, then leveled the Shardblade at his father. The point touched Father's chest.

Father raised his hands to the sides, palms forward.

'You are a vile corruption upon this house,' Helaran said. 'I should shove this through your chest. To do so would be a mercy.'

'Helaran . . .' The passion seemed to have bled from Father, like the color from his face, which had gone stark white. 'You don't know what you think you know. Your mother—'

'I will *not* listen to your lies,' Helaran said, rotating his wrist, twisting the sword in his hand, point still against Father's chest. 'So easy.'

'No,' Shallan whispered.

Helaran cocked his head, then turned, not moving the sword.

'No,' Shallan said, 'please.'

'You speak now?' Helaran said. 'To defend *him*?' He laughed. A wild bark of a noise. He whipped the sword away from Father's chest.

Father sat down in a dining chair, face still pale. 'How? A *Shardblade*. Where?' He glanced suddenly upward. 'But no. It's different. Your new friends? They trust you with this wealth?'

'We have an important work to do,' Helaran said, turning and striding to Shallan. He laid a hand fondly on her shoulder. He continued more softly. 'I will tell you of it someday, Sister. It is good to hear your voice again before I leave.'

'Don't go,' she whispered. The words felt like gauze in her mouth. It had been months since she'd last spoken.

'I must. Please do some drawings for me while I'm gone. Of fanciful things. Of brighter days. Can you do that?'

She nodded.

'Farewell, Father,' Helaran said, turning and striding from the room. 'Try not to ruin too much while I'm gone. I *will* come back periodically to check.' His voice echoed in the hallway outside as he left.

Brightlord Davar stood, roaring. The few maids left in the room fled out the side door into the gardens. Shallan shrank back, horrified, as her father picked up his chair and slammed it into the wall. He kicked over a small dining table, then took the chairs one at a time and smashed them into the floor with repeated, brutal blows.

Breathing deeply, he turned his eyes on her.

Shallan whimpered at the rage, the lack of humanity, in his eyes. As they focused on her, the life returned to them. Father dropped a broken chair and turned his back toward her, as if ashamed, before fleeing the room.

Artform applied for beauty and hue.
One yearns for the songs it creates.
Most misunderstood by the artist it's true.
Come the spren to foundation's fates.

—From the Listener Song of Listing, 90th stanza

The sun was a smoldering ember on the horizon, sinking toward oblivion, as Shallan and her little caravan neared the source of the smoke in front of them. Though the column had dwindled, she could now make out that it had three different sources, rising into the air and twisting into one.

She climbed to her feet on the rocking wagon as they rolled up one last hill, then stopped on the side, mere feet away from letting her see what was out there. Of course; cresting the hill would be a very bad idea if bandits waited below.

Bluth climbed down from his wagon and jogged forward. He wasn't terribly nimble, but he was the best scout they had. He crouched and removed his too-fine hat, then made his way up the hillside to peek over. A moment later, he stood up straight, no longer attempting stealth.

Shallan hopped down from her seat and hurried over, skirts catching on the twisted branches of crustspines here and there. She reached the top of the hill just before Tvlakv did.

Three caravan wagons smoldered quietly below, and the signs of a battle littered the ground. Fallen arrows, a group of corpses in a pile. Shallan's heart leaped as she saw the living among the dead. A scattering of tired figures combed through the rubble or moved bodies. They weren't dressed like bandits, but like honest caravan workers. Five more wagons were clustered on the far side of the camp. Some were scorched, but they all looked functional and still laden with goods.

Armed men and women tended their wounds. Guards. A group of frightened parshmen cared for the chulls. These people had been attacked, but they had survived. 'Kelek's breath . . .' Tvlakv said. He turned and shooed Bluth and Shallan backward. 'Back, before they see.'

'What?' Bluth said, though he obeyed. 'But it's another caravan, as we'd hoped.'

'Yes, and they needn't know we are here. They might want to speak to us, and that could slow us. Look!' He pointed backward.

In the waning light, Shallan could make out a shadow cresting a hill not far behind them. The deserters. She waved for Tvlakv to surrender his spyglass, and he did so reluctantly. The lens was cracked, but Shallan still got a good look at the force. The thirty or so men *were* soldiers, as Bluth had reported. They flew no banner, and did not march in formation or wear one uniform, but they looked well equipped.

'We need to go down and ask the other caravan for help,' Shallan said.

'No!' Tvlakv said, snatching the spyglass back. 'We need to flee! The bandits will see this richer but weakened group and will fall upon them instead of us!'

'And you think they won't chase us after that?' Shallan said. 'With our tracks so easily visible? You think they won't run us down in the following days?'

'There should be a highstorm tonight,' Tvlakv said. 'It might cover our tracks, blowing away the shells of the plants we crush.'

'Unlikely,' Shallan said. 'If we stand with this new caravan, we can add our little strength to theirs. We can hold. It—'

Bluth held up a hand suddenly, turning. 'A noise.' He spun around, reaching for his cudgel.

A figure stood up nearby, hidden by shadows. Apparently, the caravan below had a scout of its own. 'You led them right toward us, did you?' asked a woman's voice. 'What are they? More bandits?'

Tvlakv held up his sphere, which revealed the scout to be a lighteyed woman of medium height and wiry build. She wore trousers and a long coat that almost looked like a dress, buckled at the waist. She wore a tan glove over her safehand, and spoke Alethi without an accent.

'I . . .' Tvlakv said. 'I am just a humble merchant, and—'

'The ones chasing us are certainly bandits,' Shallan cut in. 'They have chased us all day.'

The woman cursed, raising a spyglass of her own. 'Good equipment,' she mumbled. 'Deserters, I'd guess. As if this weren't bad enough. Yix!'

A second figure stood up nearby, wearing tan clothing the color of stone. Shallan jumped. How had she missed spotting him? He was so close! He had a sword at his waist. A lighteyes? No, a foreigner, judging by that golden hair. She never was sure what eye color meant for their social standing. There weren't people with light eyes in the Makabaki region, though they had kings, and practically everyone in Iri had light yellow eyes.

He jogged over, hand on his weapon, watching Bluth and Tag with overt hostility. The woman said something to him in a tongue Shallan didn't know, and he nodded, then jogged off toward the caravan below. The woman followed.

'Wait,' Shallan called to her.

'I don't have time to talk,' the woman snapped. 'We've got two bandit groups to fight.'

'Two?' Shallan said. 'You didn't defeat the one that attacked you earlier?'

'We fought them off, but they'll be back soon.' The woman hesitated on the side of the hill. 'The fire was an accident, I think. They were using flaming brands to scare us. They pulled back to let us fight the fires, as they didn't want to lose any more goods.'

Two forces, then. Bandits ahead and behind. Shallan found herself sweating in the cold air as the sun finally vanished beneath the western horizon.

The woman was looking northward, toward where her group of bandits must have retreated. 'Yeah, they'll be back,' the woman said. 'They'll want to be done with us before the storm comes tonight.'

'I offer you my protection,' Shallan found herself saying.

'Your protection?' the woman said, turning back to Shallan, sounding baffled.

'You may accept me and mine into your camp,' Shallan said. 'I will see to your safety tonight. I will need your service after that to convey me to the Shattered Plains.'

The woman laughed. 'You are gutsy, whoever you are. You can join our camp, but you'll die there with the rest of us!'

Cries rose from the caravan. A second later, a flight of arrows fell through the night from that direction, pelting wagons and caravan workers.

Screams.

Bandits followed, emerging from the blackness. They weren't nearly as well equipped as the deserters, but they didn't need to be. The caravan had fewer than a dozen guards left. The woman cursed and started running down the hillside.

Shallan shivered, eyes wide at the sudden slaughter below. Then she turned and walked to Tvlakv's wagons. This sudden chill was familiar to her. The coldness of clarity. She knew what she had to do. She didn't know if it would work, but she saw the solution – like lines in a drawing, coming together to transform random scribbles into a full picture.

'Tvlakv,' she said, 'take Tag below and try to help those people fight.'

'What!' he said. 'No. No, I will not throw my life away for your foolishness.'

She met his eyes in the near darkness, and he stopped. She knew that she was glowing softly; she could feel the storm within. 'Do it.' She left him and walked to her wagon. 'Bluth, turn this wagon around.'

He stood with a sphere beside the wagon, looking down at something in his hand. A sheet of paper? Surely *Bluth* of all people didn't know glyphs.

'Bluth!' Shallan snapped, climbing into the wagon. 'We need to be moving. *Now!*'

He shook himself, then tucked the paper away and scrambled into the seat beside her. He whipped at the chull, turning it. 'What are we doing?' he asked.

'Heading south.'

'Into the bandits?'

'Yes.'

For once, he did as she told him without complaint, whipping the chull faster – as if he were eager to just get this all over with. The wagon rattled and shook as they went down one hillside, then climbed another.

They reached the top and looked down at the force climbing toward them. The men carried torches and sphere lanterns, so she could see their faces. Dark expressions on grim men with weapons drawn. Their breast-plates or leather jerkins might once have held symbols of allegiance, but she could see where those had been cut or scratched away.

The deserters looked at her with obvious shock. They had not expected their prey to come to them. Her arrival stunned them for a moment. An important moment.

There will be an officer, Shallan thought, standing up on her seat. *They are soldiers, or once were. They'll have a command structure.*

She took a deep breath. Bluth raised his sphere, looking at her, and grunted as if surprised.

'Bless the Stormfather that you're here!' Shallan cried to the men. 'I need your help desperately.'

The group of deserters just stared at her.

'Bandits,' Shallan said. 'They're attacking our friends in the caravan just two hills over. It's a slaughter! I said I'd seen soldiers back here, moving toward the Shattered Plains. Nobody believed me. Please. You must help.'

Again, they just stared at her. *A little like the mink wandering into the whitespine's den and asking when dinner is . . .* she thought. Finally, the men shuffled uneasily and turned toward a man near the center. Tall, bearded, he had arms that looked too long for his body.

'Bandits, you say,' the man replied, voice empty of emotion.

Shallan leaped down from the wagon and walked toward the man, leaving Bluth sitting as a silent lump. Deserters stepped away from her, wearing ripped and dirty clothing, with grizzled, unkempt hair and faces that hadn't seen a razor – or a washcloth – in ages. And yet, by torchlight, their weapons gleamed without a spot of rust and their breastplates were polished to the point where they reflected her features.

The woman she glimpsed in one breastplate looked too tall, too stately, to be Shallan herself. Instead of tangled hair, she had flowing red locks. Instead of refugee rags, she wore a gown woven with golden embroidery.

She had not been wearing a necklace before, and when she raised her hand toward the leader of the band, her chipped fingernails appeared perfectly manicured.

'Brightness,' the man said as she stepped up to him, 'we aren't what you think we are.'

'No,' Shallan replied. 'You aren't what *you* think yourselves to be.'

Those around her in the firelight regarded her with eager stares, and she felt the hair rising in a shiver across her body. Into the predator's den indeed. Yet the tempest within her spurred her to action, and urged her to greater confidence.

The leader opened his mouth as if to give some order. Shallan cut him off. 'What is your name?'

'I'm called Vathah,' the man said, turning toward his allies. It was a Vorin name, like Shallan's own. 'And I'll decide what to do with you later. Gaz, take this one and—'

'What would you do, Vathah,' Shallan said in a loud voice, 'to erase the past?'

He looked back toward her, face lit on one side by primal torchlight.

'Would you protect instead of kill, if you had the choice?' Shallan asked. 'Would you rescue instead of rob if you could do it over again? Good people are dying as we speak here. You can stop it.'

Those dark eyes of his seemed dead. 'We can't change the past.'

'I can change your future.'

'We are wanted men.'

'Yes, I came here wanting men. Hoping to find *men*. You are offered the chance to be soldiers again. Come with me. I will see to it you have new lives. Those lives start by saving instead of killing.'

Vathah snorted in derision. His face looked unfinished in the night, rough, like a sketch. 'Brightlords have failed us in the past.'

'Listen,' Shallan said. 'Listen to the screams.'

The piteous sounds reached them from behind her. Shouts for help. Workers, both men and women, from the caravan. Dying. Haunting sounds. Shallan was surprised, despite having pointed them out, how well the sounds carried. How much they sounded like pleas for help.

'Give yourself another chance,' Shallan said softly. 'If you return with me, I will see that your crimes are erased. I promise it to you, by all that I have, by the Almighty himself. You *can* start over. Start over as heroes.'

Vathah held her eyes. This man was stone. She could see, with a sinking feeling, that he wasn't swayed. The tempest inside of her began to fade away, and her fears boiled higher. What was she *doing*? This was crazy!

Vathah looked away from her again, and she knew she'd lost him. He barked the order to take her captive.

Nobody moved. Shallan had focused only on him, not the other two dozen or so men, who had drawn in close, torches raised high. They looked at her with open faces, and she saw very little of the lust she'd noticed before. Instead, they bore wide eyes, longing, reacting to the distant yells. Men fingered their uniforms, where the insignias had been. Others looked down at spears and axes, weapons of their service perhaps not so long ago.

'You fools are *considering* this?' Vathah said.

One man, a short fellow with a scarred face and an eye patch, nodded his head. 'I wouldn't mind starting over,' he muttered. 'Storms, but it would be nice.'

'I saved a woman's life once,' another said, a tall, balding man who was easily into his forties. 'I felt a hero for weeks. Toasts in the tavern. Warmth. Damnation! We're dying out here.'

'We left to get away from their oppression!' Vathah bellowed.

'And what have we done with our freedom, Vathah?' a man asked from the back of the group.

In the silence that followed, Shallan could hear only the screams for help.

'Storm it, I'm going,' said the short man with the eye patch, jogging up the hill. Others broke off and followed him. Shallan turned – hands clasped in front of her – as nearly the *entire group* took off in a charge. Bluth stood up on his wagon, his shocked face showing in the torchlight that passed. Then he actually *whooped*, jumping down from the wagon and raising his cudgel high as he joined the deserters charging toward the battle.

Shallan was left with Vathah and two other men. Those seemed dumbfounded by what had just happened. Vathah folded his arms, letting out an audible sigh. 'Idiots, every one.'

'They are not idiots for wanting to be better than they are,' Shallan said.

He snorted, looking her over. She had an immediate flash of fear.

Moments ago, this man was ready to rob her and probably worse. He didn't make any moves toward her, though his face looked even more threatening now that most of the torches had gone.

'Who are you?' he asked.

'Shallan Davar.'

'Well, Brightness Shallan,' he said, 'I hope for your sake you can keep your word. Come on, boys. Let's see if we can keep those fools alive.' He left with the others who had remained behind, marching up over the hill toward the fighting.

Shallan stood alone in the night, exhaling softly. No Light came out; she'd used it all. Her feet were no longer so much as sore, but she felt *exhausted*, drained like a punctured wineskin. She walked to the wagon and slumped against it, then finally settled down on the ground. Head back, she looked up at the sky. A few exhaustionspren rose around her, little swirls of dust spinning into the air.

Salas, the first moon, made a violet disc in the center of a cluster of bright white stars. The screams and yells of fighting continued. Would the deserters be enough? She didn't know how many bandits there were.

She'd be useless there, only getting in the way. She squeezed her eyes shut, then climbed up into the seat and took out her sketchbook. To the sounds of the fighting and dying, she sketched the glyphs for a prayer of hope.

'They listened,' Pattern said, buzzing from beside her. 'You changed them.'

'I can't believe it worked,' Shallan said.

'Ah . . . You are good with lies.'

'No, I mean, that was a figure of speech. It seems impossible that they'd actually listen to me. Hardened criminals.'

'You are lies and truth,' Pattern said softly. 'They transform.'

'What does that mean?' It was hard to sketch with only the light of Salas to see by, but she did her best.

'You spoke of one Surge, earlier,' Pattern said. 'Lightweaving, the power of light. But you have something else. The power of transformation.'

'Soulcasting?' Shallan said. 'I didn't Soulcast anyone.'

'Mmmm. And yet, you transformed them. And yet. Mmmm.'

Shallan finished her prayer, then held it up, noticing that a previous page had been ripped out of the notebook. Who had done that?

She couldn't burn the prayer, but she didn't think the Almighty would mind. She pressed it close to her breast and closed her eyes, waiting until the shouts from below quieted.

Mediationform made for peace, it's said.
Form of teaching and consolation.
When used by the gods, it became instead
Form of lies and desolation.

—From the Listener Song of Listing, 33rd stanza

S hallan closed Bluth's eyes, not looking at the ripped-out hole in his torso, the bloody entrails. Around her, workers salvaged what they could from the camp. People groaned, though some of those groans cut off as Vathah executed the bandits one by one.

Shallan didn't stop him. He did the duty grimly, and as he walked past he didn't look at her. *He's thinking these bandits could have easily been him and his men,* Shallan thought, looking back down at Bluth, his dead face lit by fires. *What separates the heroes from the villains? One speech in the night?*

Bluth wasn't the only casualty of the assault; Vathah had lost seven soldiers. They had killed over twice that many bandits. Exhausted, Shallan rose, but hesitated as she saw something poking out of Bluth's jacket. She leaned down and pushed the jacket open.

There, stuffed in his pocket, was her picture of him. The one that depicted him not as he was, but as she imagined he might once have been.

A soldier in an army, in a crisp uniform. Eyes forward, rather than looking down all the time. A hero.

When had he taken it from her sketchbook? She slipped it free and folded it, flattening the wrinkles.

'I was wrong,' she whispered. 'You were a fine way to restart my collection, Bluth. Fight well for the Almighty in your sleep, bold one.'

She rose and looked over the camp. Several of the caravan's parshmen pulled corpses to the fires for burning. Shallan's intervention had rescued the merchants, but not without heavy losses. She hadn't counted, but the toll looked high. Dozens dead, including most of the caravan's guards – among them the Iriali man from earlier in the night.

In her fatigue, Shallan wanted to crawl into her wagon and curl up for sleep. Instead, she went looking for the caravan leaders.

The haggard, bloodstained scout from before stood beside a travel table, where she was talking to an older, bearded man in a felt cap. His eyes were blue, and he moved his fingers through his beard as he looked over a list the woman had brought him.

Both looked up as Shallan approached. The woman rested a hand on her sword; the man continued to stroke his beard. Nearby, caravan workers sorted through the contents of a wagon that had toppled over, spilling bales of cloth.

'And here is our savior,' the older man said. 'Brightness, the winds themselves cannot speak of your majesty or the wonder of your timely arrival.'

Shallan didn't feel majestic. She felt tired, sore, and grungy. Her bare feet – hidden by the bottom of her skirts – had started to ache again, and her ability to Lightweave was expended. Her dress looked almost as bad as a pauper's, and her hair – though braided – was an absolute mess.

'You are the caravan owner?' Shallan asked.

'Macob is my name,' he said. She couldn't place his accent. Not Thaylen or Alethi. 'You have met my associate Tyn.' He nodded toward the woman. 'She is head of our guards. Both her soldiers and my goods have . . . dwindled from tonight's encounters.'

Tyn folded her arms. She still wore her tan coat, and in the light of Macob's spheres, Shallan could see that it was of fine leather. What to make of a woman who dressed like a soldier and wore a sword at her waist?

'I've been telling Macob of your offer,' Tyn said. 'Earlier, on the hill.'
Macob chuckled, an incongruous sound considering their surroundings.
'Offer, she calls it. My associate is under the impression that it was really
a threat! These mercenaries obviously work for you. We are wondering
what your intention is for this caravan.'

'The mercenaries didn't work for me before,' Shallan said, 'but they do
now. It took a little persuasion.'

Tyn raised an eyebrow. 'That must have been some mighty fine persuasion, Brightness. . .'

'Shallan Davar. All I ask of you is what I said to Tyn before. Accompany me to the Shattered Plains.'

'Surely your soldiers can do that,' Macob said. 'You don't need our
assistance.'

I want you here to remind the 'soldiers' what they've done, Shallan thought.
Her instincts said that the more reminders of civilization the deserters
had, the better off she would be.

'They are soldiers,' Shallan said. 'They have no idea how to properly
convey a lighteyed woman in comfort. You, however, have nice wagons
and goods aplenty. If you can't tell from my humble aspect, I am in dreadful need of a little luxury. I'd rather not arrive at the Shattered Plains
looking like a vagabond.'

'We *could* use her soldiers,' Tyn said. 'My own force is reduced to a
handful.' She inspected Shallan again, this time with curiosity. It wasn't
an unfriendly look.

'Then we shall make an accord,' Macob said, smiling broadly and
reaching across the table toward Shallan. 'In my gratitude for my life, I
shall see you cared for with new apparel and fine foodstuffs for the dura-
tion of our travels together. You and your men will ensure our safety the
rest of the way, and then we will part, nothing more owed to one another.'

'Agreed,' Shallan said, taking his hand. 'I shall allow you to join me,
your caravan unto mine.'

He hesitated. 'Your caravan.'

'Yes.'

'And your authority, then, I assume?'

'You expected otherwise?'

He sighed, but shook on the deal. 'No, I suppose not. I suppose
not.' He released her hand, then waved toward a pair of people off at the

side of the wagons. Tvlakv and Tag. 'And what of those?'

'They are mine,' Shallan said. 'I will deal with them.'

'Just keep them at the *back* of the caravan, if you will,' Macob said, wrinkling his nose. 'Grimy business. I'd rather not our caravan stink of those wares. Either way, you'd best be about gathering your people. There will be a highstorm soon. With our lost wagons, we have no extra shelter.'

Shallan left them and made her way across the valley, trying to ignore the mingled stench of blood and char. A shape split from the darkness, moving in beside her. Vathah didn't look any less intimidating in the better light here.

'Well?' Shallan asked him.

'Some of my men are dead,' he said, his voice a monotone.

'They died doing a very good work,' Shallan said, 'and the families of these who lived will bless them for their sacrifice.'

Vathah took her arm, pulling her to a stop. His grip was firm, even painful. 'You don't look like you did before,' he said. She hadn't realized how much he towered over her. 'Did my eyes mistake me? I saw a queen in the darkness. Now I see a child.'

'Perhaps you saw what your conscience needed you to see,' Shallan said, tugging – unsuccessfully – on her arm. She blushed.

Vathah leaned in. His breath wasn't particularly sweet. 'My men have done worse things than this,' he whispered, waving his other hand at the burning dead. 'Out in the wilderness, we took. We killed. You think one night absolves us? You think one night will stop the nightmares?'

Shallan felt a hollowness in her stomach.

'If we go with you to the Shattered Plains, we're dead men,' Vathah said. 'We'll be hanged the moment we return.'

'My word—'

'Your word means nothing, woman!' he shouted, grip tensing.

'You should let her go,' Pattern said calmly from behind him.

Vathah spun, looking about, but they weren't near anyone in particular. Shallan spotted Pattern on the back of Vathah's uniform as he turned.

'Who said that?' Vathah demanded.

'I heard nothing,' Shallan said, somehow managing to sound calm.

'You should let her go,' Pattern repeated.

Vathah looked around again, then back at Shallan, who met his gaze with a level stare. She even forced out a smile.

He let go of her and wiped his hand on his trousers, then retreated. Pattern slipped down his back and leg onto the ground, then skimmed toward Shallan.

'That one will be trouble,' Shallan said, rubbing the place where he'd gripped her.

'Is this a figure of speech?' Pattern asked.

'No. I mean what I said.'

'Curious,' Pattern said, watching Vathah retreat, 'because I think he already *is* trouble.'

'True.' She continued her way toward Tvlakv, who sat on the seat of his wagon with hands clasped before him. He smiled toward Shallan as she arrived, though the expression seemed particularly thin on him today.

'So,' he asked conversationally, 'were you in on it from the start?'

'In on what?' Shallan asked wearily, shooing Tag away so she could talk to Tvlakv in private.

'Bluth's plan.'

'Please, do tell.'

'Obviously,' Tvlakv said, 'he was in league with the deserters. That first night, when he came running back to the camp, he'd met with them and promised to let them take us if he could share in the wealth. That was why they did not immediately kill you two when you went to speak with them.'

'Oh?' Shallan asked. 'And if that were the case, why did Bluth come back and warn us that night? Why did he flee with us, instead of just letting his "friends" kill us right then?'

'Perhaps he only met with a few of them,' Tvlakv said. 'Yes, *they* lit fires on that hillside in the night to make us think there were more, and then his friends went to gather a larger crowd ... And ...' He deflated. 'Storms. That doesn't make any sense. But how, why? We should be dead.'

'The Almighty preserved us,' Shallan said.

'Your Almighty is a farce.'

'You should hope he is,' Shallan said, walking to the back of Tag's wagon nearby. 'For if he is not, then Damnation itself awaits men like you.' She inspected the cage. Five slaves in grimy clothing huddled inside, each one looking alone, though they were crammed in close.

'These are mine now,' Shallan told Tvlakv.

'What!' he stood up on his seat. 'You—'

'I saved your life, you oily little man,' Shallan said. 'You will give me these slaves in payment. Dues in recompense for my soldiers protecting you and your worthless life.'

'This is robbery.'

'This is justice. If it bothers you, submit a grievance with the king in the Shattered Plains, once we arrive.'

'I'm not going to the Shattered Plains,' Tvlakv spat. 'You have some-one else to convey you now, *Brightness*. I'm heading south, as I originally intended.'

'Then you'll do so without these,' Shallan said, using her key – the one he had given her to get into her wagon – to open the cage. 'You will give me their writs of slavery. And the Stormfather help you if not everything is in order, Tvlakv. I'm very good at spotting a forgery.'

She hadn't ever even seen a writ of slavery, and wouldn't know how to tell if one was faked. She didn't care. She was tired, frustrated, and eager to be done with this night.

One by one, five hesitant slaves stepped from the wagon, shaggy bearded and shirtless. Her trip with Tvlakv had not been pleasant, but it had been luxurious compared to what these men had been through. Several glanced at the darkness nearby, as if eager.

'You may run if you wish,' Shallan said, softening her tone. 'I will not hunt you. I need servants, however, and I will pay you well. Six firemarks a week if you agree to put five of them toward paying down your slave debt. One if you don't.'

One of the men cocked his head. 'So . . . we take away the same amount either way? What kind of sense does that make?'

'The best kind,' Shallan said, turning to Tvlakv, who sat stewing on the side of his seat. 'You have three wagons but only two drivers. Will you sell me the third wagon?' She wouldn't need the chull – Macob would have an extra she could use, since several of his wagons had burned.

'Sell the wagon? Bah! Why not just steal it from me?'

'Stop being a child, Tvlakv. Do you want my money or not?'

'Five sapphire broams,' he snapped. 'And it's a steal at that price; don't you argue otherwise.'

She didn't know if it was or not, but she could afford it, with the spheres she had, even if most of them were dun.

'You can't have my parshmen,' Tvlakv snapped.

'You can keep them,' Shallan said. She would need to talk to the caravan master about shoes and clothing for her servants.

As she walked off to see if she could use an extra chull of Macob's, she passed a group of the caravan workers waiting to the side of one of the bonfires. The deserters threw the last body – one of their own – into the flames, then stepped back, wiping brows.

One of the darkeyed caravan women stepped up, holding out a sheet of paper to a former deserter. He took it, scratching at his beard. He was the shorter, one-eyed man who'd spoken during her speech. He held up the sheet to the others. It was a prayer made from familiar runes, but not one of mourning, as Shallan would have expected to see. It was a prayer of thanks.

The former deserters gathered in front of the flames and looked at the prayer. Then they turned and looked outward, seeing – as if for the first time – the two dozen people standing there and watching. Silent in the night. Some had tears on their cheeks; some held the hands of children. Shallan had not noticed the children before, but was not surprised to see them. Caravan workers would spend their lives traveling, and their families would travel with them.

Shallan stopped just beyond the caravaneers, mostly hidden in the darkness. The deserters didn't seem to know how to react, surrounded by that constellation of thankful eyes and tearful appreciation. Finally, they burned the prayer. Shallan bowed her head as they did, as did most of those watching.

She left them standing taller, watching the ashes of that prayer rise toward the Almighty.

A page from a folio of fashion pages out of
Liafor. The model, it should be noted, is Alethi,
as this folio was intended for sale in the Alethi
and Veden markets.

Stormform is said to cause
A tempest of winds and showers.
Beware its powers, beware its powers.
Though its coming brings the gods their night.
It obliges a bloodred spren.
Beware its end, beware its end.

—From the Listener Song of Winds, 4th stanza

Kaladin watched the window shutters. Motion came in bursts.

First stillness. Yes, he could hear a distant howling, the wind passing through some hollow, but nothing nearby.

A tremble. Then wood rattling wickedly in its frame. Violent shaking, with water seeping in at the joints. Something was out there, in the dark chaos of the highstorm. It thrashed and pounded at the window, wanting in.

Light flashed out there, glistening through the drops of water. Another flash.

Then the light stayed. Steady, like glowing spheres, just outside. Faintly red. For some reason he couldn't explain, Kaladin had the impression of eyes.

Transfixed, he raised his hand toward the latch, to open it and see.

'Someone really needs to fix that loose shutter,' King Elhokar said, annoyed.

The light faded. The rattling stopped. Kaladin blinked, lowering his hand.

'Someone remind me to ask Nakal to see to it,' Elhokar said, pacing behind his couch. 'The shutter shouldn't leak. This is my palace, not a village tavern!'

'We'll make sure it's seen to,' Adolin said. He sat in a chair beside the hearth, flipping through a book filled with sketches. His brother sat in a chair next to him, hands clasped in his lap. He was probably sore from his training, but he didn't show it. Instead, he had gotten a small box out of his pocket and was repeatedly opening it, turning it in his hand, rubbing one side, then shutting it with a click. He did it over and over and over.

He stared at nothing as he did it. He seemed to do that a lot.

Elhokar continued pacing. Idrin – head of the King's Guard – stood near the king, straight-backed, green eyes forward. He was dark-skinned for an Alethi, perhaps with some Azish blood in him, and wore a full beard.

Men from Bridge Four had been taking shifts with his men, as Dalinar suggested, and so far Kaladin had been impressed by the man and the team he had run. However, when the horns for a plateau run sounded, Idrin would turn toward them and his expression would grow longing. He wanted to be out there fighting. Sadeas's betrayal had made a lot of the soldiers in camp similarly eager – as if they wanted the chance to prove how strong Dalinar's army was.

More rumbling came from the storm outside. It was odd not to be cold during a highstorm – the barrack always felt chilly. This room was well heated, though not by a fire. Instead, the hearth held a ruby the size of Kaladin's fist, one that could have paid to feed everyone in his hometown for weeks.

Kaladin left the window and sauntered toward the fireplace under the pretext of inspecting the gemstone. He really wanted a glimpse of whatever it was Adolin was looking through. Many men refused to even look at books, considering it unmasculine. Adolin didn't seem to be bothered by that. Curious.

As he approached the hearth, Kaladin passed the door to a side room where Dalinar and Navani had retired at the advent of the storm. Kaladin had wanted to post a guard inside. They'd refused.

Well, this is the only way into that room, he thought. *There's not even a window.* This time, if words appeared on the wall, he would know for certain nobody was sneaking in.

Kaladin stooped down, inspecting the ruby in the hearth, which was held in place by a wire enclosure. Its strong heat made his face prickle with sweat; storms, that ruby was so large that the Light infusing it should have blinded him. Instead, he could stare into its depths and see the Light moving inside.

People thought that the illumination from gemstones was steady and calm, but that was just in contrast to flickering candlelight. If you looked deeply into a stone, you could see the Light shifting with the chaotic pattern of a blowing storm. It was not calm inside. Not by a wind or a whisper.

'Never seen a heating fabrial before, I assume?' Renarin asked.

Kaladin glanced at the bespectacled prince. He wore an Alethi highlord's uniform, like that of Adolin. In fact, Kaladin had never seen them wearing anything else – other than Shardplate, of course.

'No, I haven't,' Kaladin said.

'New technology,' Renarin said, still playing with his little metal box. 'My aunt built that one herself. Every time I turn around, it seems the world has changed somehow.'

Kaladin grunted. *I know how that feels.* Part of him yearned to suck in the Light of that gemstone. A foolish move. There'd be enough in there to make him glow like a bonfire. He lowered his hands and strolled past Adolin's chair.

The sketches in Adolin's book were of men in fine clothing. The drawings were quite good, their faces done in as much detail as their garments.

'Fashion?' Kaladin asked. He hadn't intended to speak, but it came out anyway. 'You're spending the highstorm looking for new clothing?'

Adolin snapped the book closed.

'But you only wear uniforms,' Kaladin said, confused.

'Do you *need* to be here, bridgeboy?' Adolin demanded. 'Surely nobody is going to come for us during a highstorm, of all things.'

'The fact that you assume that,' Kaladin said, 'is why I need to be here. What better time would there be for an assassination attempt? The winds would cover shouts, and help would be slow in coming when everyone has taken cover to wait out the storm. Seems to me this is one of the times when His Majesty most needs guards.'

The king stopped pacing and pointed. 'That makes sense. Why hasn't anyone else ever explained that to me?' He looked at Idrin, who remained stoic.

Adolin sighed. 'You could at least leave Renarin and me out of it,' he said softly to Kaladin.

'It's easier to protect you when you're all together, Brightlord,' Kaladin said, walking away. 'Plus, you can defend each other.'

Dalinar had been intending to stay with Navani during the storm anyway. Kaladin approached the window again, listening to the storm pass outside. Had he really seen the things he thought he had during his time out in the storm? A face as vast as the sky? The Stormfather himself?

I am a god, Syl had said. *A little piece of one.*

Eventually, the storm passed, and Kaladin opened the window to a black sky, a few phantom clouds shining with Nomon's light. The storm had started a few hours into the night, but nobody could sleep during a storm. He hated when a highstorm came so late; he often felt exhausted the next day.

The side room door opened and Dalinar stepped out, trailed by Navani. The statuesque woman carried a large notebook. Kaladin had heard, of course, about the highprince's fits during storms. His men were divided on the topic. Some thought Dalinar was frightened of highstorms, and his terror sent him into convulsions. Others whispered that with age, the Blackthorn was losing his mind.

Kaladin badly wanted to know which it was. His fate, and that of his men, was tied to this man's health.

'Numbers, sir?' Kaladin asked, peeking into the room, looking at the walls.

'No,' Dalinar said.

'Sometimes they come just after the storm,' Kaladin said. 'I have men in the hall outside. I would prefer if everyone remained here for a short time.'

Dalinar nodded. 'As you wish, soldier.'

Kaladin walked to the exit. Beyond, some men of Bridge Four and of the King's Guard stood on watch. Kaladin nodded to Leyten, then pointed for them to watch out on the balcony. Kaladin *would* catch the phantom scratching those numbers. If, indeed, such a person existed.

Behind, Renarin and Adolin approached their father. 'Anything new?' Renarin asked softly.

'No,' Dalinar said. 'The vision was a repeat. But they're not coming in the same order as last time, and some are new, so perhaps there is something to learn we have not yet discovered . . .' Noticing Kaladin, he trailed off, then changed the topic. 'Well, as long as we're waiting here, perhaps I can get an update. Adolin, when can we expect more duels?'

'I'm trying,' Adolin said with a grimace. 'I thought beating Salinor would drive others to want to try me, but they're stalling instead.'

'Problematic,' Navani said. 'Weren't you always saying that everyone wanted to duel you?'

'They did!' Adolin said. 'When I couldn't duel, at least. Now, every time I make an offer, people start shuffling their feet and looking away.'

'Have you tried anyone in Sadeas's camp?' the king asked eagerly.

'No,' Adolin said. 'But he's only got one Shardbearer other than himself. Amaram.'

Kaladin felt a shiver.

'Well, you won't be dueling *him*,' Dalinar said, chuckling. He sat down on the couch, Brightness Navani settling in beside him, hand fondly on his knee. 'We might have him on our side. I've been speaking to Highlord Amaram . . .'

'You think you can get him to secede?' the king asked.

'Is that possible?' Kaladin asked, surprised.

The lighteyes turned to him. Navani blinked, as if noticing him for the first time.

'Yes, it is possible,' Dalinar said. 'Most of the territory that Amaram oversees would remain with Sadeas, but he could bring his personal land to my princedom – along with his Shards. Usually it requires a land trade with a princedom bordering the one a highlord wishes to join.'

'It hasn't happened in over a decade,' Adolin said, shaking his head.

'I'm working on him,' Dalinar said. 'But Amaram . . . he wants to bring Sadeas and me together instead. He thinks we can get along again.'

Adolin snorted. '*That* possibility blew away the day Sadeas betrayed us.'

'Probably long before that day,' Dalinar said, 'even if I didn't see it. Is there anyone else you could challenge, Adolin?'

'I'm going to try Talanor,' Adolin said, 'and then Kalishor.'

'Neither full Shardbearers,' Navani said with a frown. 'The first has only the Blade, the second only the Plate.'

'All of the full Shardbearers have refused me,' Adolin said with a shrug. 'Those two are eager, thirsty for notoriety. One of them might agree where others haven't.'

Kaladin folded his arms, leaning back against the wall. 'And if you defeat them, won't it scare off others from fighting you?'

'*When* I beat them,' Adolin said, glancing at Kaladin's relaxed posture and frowning, 'Father will maneuver others into agreeing to duels.'

'But it will have to stop sometime, right?' Kaladin asked. 'Eventually the other highprinces will realize what's happening. They'll refuse to be goaded into further duels. It might be happening already. That's why they don't accept.'

'Someone will,' Adolin said, standing. 'And once I start winning, others will begin to see me as a real challenge. They'll want to test themselves.'

That seemed optimistic to Kaladin.

'Captain Kaladin is right,' Dalinar said.

Adolin turned toward his father.

'There's no need to fight every Shardbearer in camp,' Dalinar said softly. 'We need to narrow our attack, choose duels for you that point us toward the ultimate goal.'

'Which is?' Adolin asked.

'Undermining Sadeas.' Dalinar almost sounded regretful. 'Killing him in a duel, if we have to. Everyone in camp knows the sides in this power struggle. This won't work if we punish everyone equally. We need to show those in the middle, those deciding whom to follow, the advantages of trust. Cooperation on plateau runs. Help from one another's Shardbearers. We show them what it's like to be part of a *real* kingdom.'

The others grew quiet. The king turned away with a shake of his head. He didn't believe, at least not fully, in what Dalinar wished to achieve.

Kaladin found himself annoyed. Why should he be? Dalinar had agreed with him. He stewed for a moment, and realized that he was probably still upset because someone had mentioned Amaram.

Even hearing the man's name put Kaladin out of sorts. He kept thinking something should happen, something should change, now that such a murderer was in camp. Yet everything just kept on going. It was frustrating. Made him want to lash out.

He needed to do something about it.

'I assume we've waited long enough?' Adolin said to his father. 'I can go?'

Dalinar sighed, nodding. Adolin pulled open the door and strode away; Renarin followed at a slower pace, hauling that Shardblade he was still bonding, sheathed in its protective strips. As they passed the group of guards Kaladin had put outside, Skar and three others broke off to follow them.

Kaladin walked to the door, doing a quick count of who was left. Four men total. 'Moash,' Kaladin said, noticing the man yawning. 'How long have you been on duty today?'

Moash shrugged. 'One shift guarding Brightness Navani. One shift with the King's Guard.'

I'm working them too hard, Kaladin thought. *Stormfather. I don't have enough men. Even with the leftover Cobalt Guard that Dalinar is sending to me.* 'Head back and get some sleep,' Kaladin said. 'You too, Bisig. I saw you on shift this morning.'

'And you?' Moash asked Kaladin.

'I'm fine.' He had Stormlight to keep him alert. True, using Stormlight that way could be dangerous – it provoked him to act, to be more impulsive. He wasn't sure he liked what it did to him when he used it outside of battle.

Moash raised an eyebrow. 'You've *got* to be at least as tired as I am, Kal.'

'I'll go back in a bit,' Kaladin said. 'You need some time off, Moash. You'll get sloppy if you don't take it.'

'I have to pull two shifts,' Moash said, shrugging. 'At least, if you want me to train with the King's Guard as well as doing my regular guard duty.'

Kaladin drew his lips to a line. That *was* important. Moash needed to think like a bodyguard, and there was no better way than serving on an already-established crew.

'My shift here with the King's Guard is almost over,' Moash noted. 'I'll head back after.'

'Fine,' Kaladin said. 'Keep Leyten with you. Natam, you and Mart guard Brightness Navani. I'll see Dalinar back to camp and post guards at his door.'

'Then you'll get some sleep?' Moash asked. The others glanced at Kaladin. They were worried as well.

'Yes, fine.' Kaladin turned back to the room, where Dalinar was helping Navani to her feet. He'd walk her to her door, as he did most evenings.

Kaladin debated for a moment, then stepped up to the highprince. 'Sir, there's something I need to talk to you about.'

'Can it wait until I'm done here?' Dalinar said.

'Yes, sir,' Kaladin said. 'I'll wait at the palace's front doors, then will be your guard on the way back to camp.'

Dalinar led Navani away, joined by two bridgeman guards. Kaladin made his own way down the corridor, thinking. Servants had already come by to open the corridor windows, and Syl floated in through one as a spinning swirl of mist. Giggling, she spun around him a few times before going out another window. She always got more sprenlike during a highstorm.

The air smelled wet and fresh. The whole world felt clean after a highstorm, scrubbed by nature's abrasive.

He reached the front of the palace, where a pair of the King's Guard stood on watch. Kaladin nodded to them and got crisp salutes in return, then he fetched a sphere lantern from the guard post and filled it with his own spheres.

From the front of the palace, Kaladin could look out over all ten warcamps. As always after a storm, the Light of refreshed spheres sparkled everywhere, their gemstones ablaze with captured fragments of the tempest that had passed.

Standing there, Kaladin confronted what he needed to say to Dalinar. He rehearsed it silently more than once, but still wasn't ready when the highprince emerged at last from the palace doors. Natam saluted from behind them, handing Dalinar off to Kaladin, then jogged back to join Mart outside Brightness Navani's door.

The highprince started down the switchbacks of the side route down from the Pinnacle to the stables below. Kaladin fell in beside him. Dalinar appeared deeply distracted by something.

He hasn't ever announced anything about his fits during highstorms, Kaladin thought. *Shouldn't he say something?*

They'd talked about visions, earlier. What was it Dalinar saw, or thought he saw?

'So, soldier,' Dalinar said as they walked. 'What is it you wanted to discuss?'

Kaladin took a deep breath. 'A year ago, I was a soldier in Amaram's army.'

'So that's where you learned,' Dalinar said. 'I should have guessed. Amaram is the only general in Sadeas's princedom with any real leadership ability.'

'Sir,' Kaladin said, stopping on the steps. 'He betrayed me and my men.'

Dalinar stopped and turned to look at him. 'A poor battle decision, then? Nobody is perfect, soldier. If he sent your men into a bad situation, I doubt he intended to do so.'

Just push through it, Kaladin told himself, noticing Syl sitting on a shalebark ridge just to the right. She nodded at him. *He has to know.* It was just . . .

He'd never spoken of this, not in full. Not even to Rock, Teft, and the others.

'It wasn't that, sir,' Kaladin said, meeting Dalinar's eyes by spherelight. 'I know where Amaram got his Shardblade. I was there. I killed the Shardbearer carrying it.'

'That can't be the case,' Dalinar said slowly. 'If you had, you'd hold the Plate and Blade.'

'Amaram took it for himself, then slaughtered everyone who knew the truth,' Kaladin said. 'Everyone but a lone soldier who, in his guilt, Amaram branded a slave and sold rather than murdering.'

Dalinar stood in silence. From this angle, the hillside behind him was completely dark, lit only by stars. A few spheres glowed in Dalinar's pocket, shining through the fabric of his uniform.

'Amaram is one of the best men I know,' Dalinar said. 'His honor is spotless. I've never even known him to take undue advantage of an opponent in a duel, despite cases when it would have been acceptable.'

Kaladin didn't respond. He'd believed that too, at one point.

'Do you have any proof?' Dalinar asked. 'You understand that I can't take one man's word on something of this nature.'

'One darkeyed man's word, you mean,' Kaladin said, gritting his teeth.

'It's not the color of your eyes that is the problem,' Dalinar said, 'but the severity of your accusation. The words you speak are dangerous. Do you have any *proof*, soldier?'

'There were others there when he took the Shards. Men of his personal guard did the actual killing at his command. And there was a storm-warden there. Middle-aged, with a peaked face. He wore a beard like an ardent.' He paused. 'They were all complicit in the act, but maybe . . .'

Dalinar sighed softly in the night. 'Have you spoken this accusation to anyone else?'

'No,' Kaladin said.

'Continue to hold your tongue. I'll talk to Amaram. Thank you for telling me of this.'

'Sir,' Kaladin said, taking a step closer to Dalinar. 'If you really believe in justice, you—'

'That's enough for the moment, son,' Dalinar cut in, voice calm but cool. 'You've had your say, unless you can offer me anything else by way of evidence.'

Kaladin forced down his immediate burst of anger. It was difficult.

'I appreciated your input when we were talking about my son's duels earlier,' Dalinar said. 'This is the second time you've added something important to one of our conferences, I believe.'

'Thank you, sir.'

'But soldier,' Dalinar said, 'you're walking quite a line between help-fulness and insubordination in the way you treat me and mine. You have a chip on your shoulder the size of a boulder. I ignore it, because I know what was done to you, and I can see the soldier beneath. That's the man I hired for this job.'

Kaladin ground his teeth, and nodded. 'Yes, sir.'

'Good. Now run along.'

'Sir, but I must escort—'

'I think I'll return to the palace,' Dalinar said. 'I don't think I'll get much sleep tonight, so I might want to pester the dowager with my thoughts. Her guards can watch over me. I'll take one with me when I return to my camp.'

Kaladin let out a long breath. Then saluted. *Fine*, he thought, continu-ing down the dark, damp path. When he reached the bottom, Dalinar was still standing up above, now just a shadow. He seemed lost in thought.

Kaladin turned and walked back toward Dalinar's warcamp. Syl flitted up and landed on his shoulder. 'See,' she said. 'He listened.'

'No he didn't, Syl.'

'What? He replied and said—'

'I told him something he didn't want to hear,' Kaladin said. 'Even if he does look into it, he'll find plenty of reasons to dismiss what I said. In the end, it will be my word against Amaram's. Stormfather! I shouldn't have said anything.'

'You'd let it go, then?'

'Storms, no,' Kaladin said. 'I'd find my own justice.'

'Oh . . .' Syl settled on his shoulder.

They walked for a long while, eventually approaching the warcamp.

'You're not a Skybreaker, Kaladin,' Syl finally said. 'You're not supposed to be like this.'

'A what?' he asked, stepping over scuttling cremlings in the dark. They came out in force after a storm, when plants unfolded to lap up the water. 'That was one of the orders, wasn't it?' He did know some little of them. Everyone did, from the legends.

'Yes,' Syl said, voice soft. 'I'm worried about you, Kaladin. I thought things would be better, once you were free from the bridges.'

'Things *are* better,' he said. 'None of my men have been killed since we were freed.'

'But you . . .' She didn't seem to know what else to say. 'I thought you might be like the person you were before. I can remember a man on a field of battle . . . A man who fought . . .'

'That man is dead, Syl,' Kaladin said, waving to the guards as he entered the warcamp. Once again, light and motion surrounded him, people running quick errands, parshmen repairing buildings damaged by the storm. 'During my time as a bridgeman, all I had to worry about was my men. Now things are different. I have to become someone. I just don't know who yet.'

When he reached Bridge Four's barrack, Rock was dishing out the evening stew. Far later than usual, but some of the men were on odd shifts. The men weren't limited to stew any longer, but they still insisted on it for the evening meal. Kaladin took a bowl gratefully, nodding to Bisig, who was relaxing with several of the others and chatting about how they actually *missed* carrying their bridge. Kaladin had instilled in them a respect for it, much as a soldier respected his spear.

Stew. Bridges. They spoke so fondly of things that had once been emblems of their captivity. Kaladin took a bite, then stopped, noticing a new man leaning against a rock beside the fire.

'Do I know you?' he asked, pointing at the bald, muscular man. He had tan skin, like an Alethi, but he didn't seem to have the right face shape. Herdazian?

'Oh, don't mind Punio,' Lopen called from nearby. 'He's my cousin.'

'You had a cousin on the bridge crews?' Kaladin asked.

'Nah,' Lopen said. 'He just heard my mother say we needed more guards, so he came to help. I got him a uniform and things.'

The newcomer, Punio, smiled and raised his spoon. 'Bridge Four,' he said with a thick Herdazian accent.

'Are you a soldier?' Kaladin asked him.

'Yes,' the man said. 'Brightlord Roion army. Not worry. I swore to Kholin instead, now. For my cousin.' He smiled affably.

'You can't just leave your army, Punio,' Kaladin said, rubbing his forehead. 'It's called desertion.'

'Not for us,' Lopen called. 'We're Herdazian – nobody can tell us apart anyway.'

'Yes,' Punio said. 'I leave for the homeland once a year. When I come back, nobody remembers me.' He shrugged. 'This time, I come here.'

Kaladin sighed, but the man looked like he knew his way around a spear, and Kaladin *did* need more men. 'Fine. Just pretend you were one of the bridgemen from the start, all right?'

'Bridge Four!' the man said enthusiastically.

Kaladin passed him and found his customary place by the fire to relax and think. He didn't get that chance, however, as someone stepped up and squatted down before him. A man with marbled skin and a Bridge Four uniform.

'Shen?' Kaladin asked.

'Sir.'

Shen continued to stare at him.

'Is there something you wanted?' Kaladin asked.

'Am I really Bridge Four?' Shen asked.

'Of course you are.'

'Where is my spear?'

Kaladin looked Shen in the eyes. 'What do you think?'

'I think that I am not Bridge Four,' Shen said, taking time to think with each word. 'I am Bridge Four's slave.'

It was like a punch to Kaladin's gut. He'd hardly heard a dozen words out of the man during their time together, and now this?

The words smarted either way. Here was a man who, unlike the others, wasn't welcome to leave and make his way in the world. Dalinar had freed the rest of Bridge Four – but a parshman . . . he'd be a slave no matter where he went or what he did.

What could Kaladin say? Storms.

'I appreciate your help when we were scavenging. I know it was difficult for you to see what we did down there sometimes.'

Shen waited, still squatting, listening. He regarded Kaladin with those impenetrable, solid black parshman eyes of his.

'I *can't* start arming parshmen, Shen,' Kaladin said. 'The lighteyes barely accept us as it is. If I gave *you* a spear, think of the storm it would cause.'

Shen nodded, face displaying no hint of his emotions. He stood up straight. 'A slave I am, then.'

He withdrew.

Kaladin knocked his head back against the stone behind him, staring up at the sky. Storming man. He had a good life, for a parshman. Certainly more freedom than any other of his kind.

And were you satisfied with that? a voice inside him asked. *Were you happy to be a well-treated slave? Or did you try to run, fight your way to freedom?*

What a mess. He mulled over those thoughts, digging into his stew. He got two bites down before Natam – one of the men who'd been guarding at the palace – came stumbling into their camp, sweating, frantic, and red-cheeked from running.

'The king!' Natam said, puffing. 'An assassin.'

ASSASSIN

Nightform predicting what will be,
The form of shadows, mind to foresee.
As the gods did leave, the nightform whispered.
A new storm will come, someday to break.
A new storm a new world to make.
A new storm a new path to take, the nightform listens.

—From the Listener Song of Secrets, 17th stanza

T he king was fine.

One hand on the doorframe, Kaladin stood gasping from his run back to the palace. Inside, Elhokar, Dalinar, Navani, and both of Dalinar's sons spoke together. Nobody was dead. Nobody was dead.

Stormfather, he thought, stepping into the room. *For a moment, I felt like I did on the plateaus, watching my men charge the Parshendi.* He hardly knew these people, but they were his duty. He hadn't thought that his protectiveness could apply to lighteyes.

'Well, at least *he* ran here,' the king said, waving off the attentions of a woman who was trying to bandage a gash on his forehead. 'You see, Idrin. This is what a *good* bodyguard looks like. I bet he wouldn't have let this happen.'

The captain of the King's Guard stood near the door, red-faced. He looked away, then stalked out into the hallway. Kaladin raised a hand to his head, bewildered. Comments like that one from the king were *not* going to help his men get along with Dalinar's soldiers.

Inside the room, a mess of guards, servants, and members of Bridge Four stood around, looking confused or embarrassed. Natam was there – he'd been on duty with the King's Guard – as was Moash.

'Moash,' Kaladin called. 'You're supposed to be back in the camp asleep.'

'So are you,' Moash said.

Kaladin grunted, trotting over, speaking more softly. 'Were you here when it happened?'

'I'd just left,' Moash said. 'Finishing my shift with the King's Guard. I heard yelling, and came back as quickly as I could.' He nodded toward the open balcony door. 'Come have a look.'

They walked out onto the balcony, which was a circular stone pathway that ran around the peak rooms of the palace – a terrace cut into the stone itself. From such a height, the balcony offered an unparalleled view overlooking the warcamps and the Plains beyond. Some members of the King's Guard stood here, inspecting the balcony railing with sphere lamps. A section of the ironwork structure had twisted outward and hung precariously over the drop.

'From what we've figured,' Moash said, pointing, 'the king came out here to think, as he likes to do.'

Kaladin nodded, walking with Moash. The stone floor beneath was still wet from highstorm rain. They reached the place where the railing was ripped, several guards making way for them. Kaladin looked down over the side. The drop was a good hundred feet onto the rocks below. Syl drifted through the air down there, making lazy glowing circles.

'Damnation, Kaladin!' Moash said, taking his arm. 'Are you trying to make me panic?'

I wonder if I could survive that fall.... He'd dropped half that once before, filled with Stormlight, and had landed without trouble. He stepped back for Moash's sake, though even before gaining his special abilities, heights had fascinated him. It felt liberating to be up so high. Just you and the air itself.

He knelt down, looking at the places where the footings of the iron railing had been mortared into holes in the stone. 'The railing pulled free of its mountings?' he asked, poking his finger into a hole, then pulling it out with mortar dust on his fingers.

'Yeah,' Moash said, several of the men of the king's guard nodding.

'Could just be a flaw in the design,' Kaladin said.

'Captain,' said one of the guardsmen. 'I was here when it happened, watching him on the balcony. It fell right out. Barely a sound. I was standing here, looking out at the Plains and thinking to myself, and next I knew His Majesty was hanging right there, holding on for his life and cursing like a caravan worker.' The guard blushed. 'Sir.'

Kaladin stood, inspecting the metalwork. So the king had leaned against this section of the railing, and it had bent forward – the mountings at the bottom giving way. It had almost come free completely, but fortunately one bar had held tight. The king had grabbed hold and clung to it long enough to be rescued.

This should never have been possible. The thing looked as if it had been constructed of wood and rope first, then Soulcast into iron. Shaking another section, he found it incredibly secure. Even a few footings giving out shouldn't have let the whole thing fall off – the metal pieces would have had to come apart.

He moved to the right, inspecting some of those that had ripped free of one another. The two pieces of metal had been sheared at a joint. Smoothly, cleanly.

The doorway into the king's chamber darkened as Dalinar Kholin stepped out onto the balcony. 'In,' he said to Moash and the other guards. 'Close the door. I'd like to speak to Captain Kaladin.'

They obeyed, though Moash went reluctantly. Dalinar walked up to Kaladin as the windows closed, giving them privacy. Despite his age, the highprince's figure was an intimidating one, wide shouldered, built like a brick wall.

'Sir,' Kaladin said. 'I should have—'

'This wasn't your fault,' Dalinar said. 'The king wasn't under your care. Even if he was, I wouldn't reprimand you – just as I won't reprimand Idrin. I wouldn't expect bodyguards to inspect architecture.'

'Yes, sir,' Kaladin said.

Dalinar knelt down to inspect the mountings. 'You like to take responsibility for things, don't you? A commendable attribute in an officer.'

Dalinar rose and looked at the place where the rail had been cut. 'What is your assessment?'

'Someone definitely chipped at the mortar,' Kaladin said, 'and sabotaged the railing.'

Dalinar nodded. 'I agree. This was a deliberate attempt on the king's life.'

'However . . . sir . . .'

'Yes?'

'Whoever tried this is an idiot.'

Dalinar looked to him, raising an eyebrow in the lantern light.

'How could they know where the king would lean?' Kaladin said. 'Or even that he would? This trap could easily have caught someone else, and then the would-be assassins would have exposed themselves for nothing. In fact, that *is* what happened. The king survived, and now we're aware of them.'

'We've been expecting assassins,' Dalinar said. 'And not just because of the incident with the king's armor. Half the powerful men in this camp are probably contemplating some kind of assassination attempt, so an attempt on Elhokar's life doesn't tell us as much as you'd think. As to how they knew to catch him here, he has a favorite spot for standing, leaning against the rail and looking out over the Shattered Plains. Anyone who watches his patterns would have known where to apply their sabotage.'

'But sir,' Kaladin said, 'it's just so *convoluted*. If they have access to the king's private chambers, then why not hide an assassin inside? Or use poison?'

'Poison is as unlikely to work as this was,' Dalinar said, waving toward the railing. 'The king's food and drink is tasted. As for a hidden assassin, one might run into guards.' He stood up. 'But I agree that such methods would probably have had a greater chance at success. The fact that they didn't try it that way tells us something. Assuming these are the same people who planted those flawed gemstones in the king's armor, they prefer nonconfrontational methods. It's not that they're idiots, they're . . .'

'They're cowards,' Kaladin realized. 'They want to make the assassination look like an accident. They're timid. They may have waited this long so that suspicion would die down.'

'Yes,' Dalinar said, rising, looking troubled.

'This time, though, they made a big mistake.'

'How?'

Kaladin walked to the cut section he had inspected earlier and knelt down to rub the smooth section. 'What cuts iron so cleanly?'

Dalinar leaned down, inspecting the cut, then took out a sphere for more light. He grunted. 'It's supposed to look like the joint came apart, I'd guess.'

'And does it?' Kaladin asked.

'No. That was a Shardblade.'

'Narrows down our suspects a tad, I'd think.'

Dalinar nodded. 'Don't tell anyone else. We'll hide that we noticed the Shardblade cut, maybe gain an edge. It's too late to pretend that we think this was an accident, but we don't have to reveal everything.'

'Yes, sir.'

'The king is insisting that I put you in charge of guarding him,' Dalinar said. 'We might have to move up our timetable for that.'

'I'm not ready,' Kaladin said. 'My men are stretched thin with the duties they already have.'

'I know,' Dalinar said softly. He seemed hesitant. 'This was done by someone on the inside, you realize.'

Kaladin felt cold.

'The king's own chambers? That means a servant. Or one of his guards. Men in the King's Guard might have had access to his armor, too.' Dalinar looked at Kaladin, face lit by the sphere in his hand. A strong face, with a nose that had once been broken. Blunt. *Real*. 'I don't know whom I can trust these days. Can I trust you, Kaladin Stormblessed?'

'Yes. I swear it.'

Dalinar nodded. 'I'm going to relieve Idrin of this post and assign him to a command in my army. It will sate the king, but I'll make certain Idrin knows he isn't being punished. I suspect he'll enjoy the new command more anyway.'

'Yes, sir.'

'I'll ask him for his best men,' Dalinar said, 'and those will be under your command for now. Use them as little as possible. I eventually want the king being guarded only by men from the bridge crews – men you trust, men who have no part in warcamp politics. Choose carefully. I don't want to replace potential traitors with former thieves who can be easily bought.'

'Yes, sir,' Kaladin said, feeling a large weight settle on his shoulders.

Dalinar stood up. 'I don't know what else to do. A man needs to be able to trust his own guards.' He walked back toward the door into the room. The tone of his voice sounded deeply troubled.

'Sir?' Kaladin asked. 'This wasn't the assassination attempt you were expecting, was it?'

'No,' Dalinar said, hand on the doorknob. 'I agree with your assessment. This wasn't the work of someone who knows what they're doing. Considering how contrived it was, I'm actually surprised at how close it came to working.' He leveled his gaze at Kaladin. 'If Sadeas decides to strike – or, worse, the assassin who claimed my brother's life – it will not go so well for us. The storm is yet to come.'

He pulled open the door, letting out the complaints of the king, which had been muffled behind it. Elhokar was ranting that nobody took his safety seriously, that nobody listened, that they should be looking for the things he saw over his shoulder in the mirror, whatever that meant. The tirade sounded like the whining of a spoiled child.

Kaladin looked at the twisted rail, imagining the king dangling from it. He had good reason to be out of sorts. But then, wasn't a king supposed to be better than that? Didn't his Calling demand that he be able to keep his composure under pressure? Kaladin found it difficult to imagine Dalinar reacting with such ranting, regardless of the situation.

Your job isn't to judge, he told himself, waving to Syl and walking away from the balcony. *Your job is to protect these people.*

Somehow.

24

TYN

Decayform destroys the souls of dreams.
A form of gods to avoid, it seems.
Seek not its touch, nor beckon its screams, deny it.
Watch where you walk, your toes to tread,
O'er hill or rocky riverbed
Hold dear the fears that fill your head, defy it.

—From the Listener Song of Secrets, 27th stanza

'Well, you see,' Gaz said as he sanded the wood on Shallan's wagon. She sat nearby, listening as she worked. 'Most of us, we joined the fight at the Shattered Plains for revenge, you know? Those marbles killed the king. It was gonna be this grand thing and such. A fight for vengeance, a way to show the world that the Alethi don't stand for betrayal.'

'Yeah,' Red agreed. The lanky, bearded soldier pulled free a bar from her wagon. With this one removed, it left only three at each corner to hold up the roof. He dropped the bar with satisfaction, then dusted off his work gloves. This would help transform the vehicle from a rolling cage into a conveyance more suitable for a lighteyed lady.

'I remember it,' Red continued, sitting down on the wagon's bed, legs dangling. 'The call to arms came to us from Highprince Vamah himself, and it moved through Farcoast like a bad stench. Every second man of age joined the cause. People wondered if you were a coward if you went to the pub for a drink but didn't wear a recruit's patch. I joined up with five of my buddies. They're all dead now, rotting in those storm-cursed chasms.'

'So you just ... got tired of fighting?' Shallan asked. She had a desk now. Well, a table – a small piece of travel furniture that could be taken apart easily. They'd moved it out of the wagon, and she was using it to review some of Jasnah's notes.

The caravan was making camp as the day waned; they'd traveled well today, but Shallan wasn't pushing them hard, after what they'd all been through. After four days of travel, they were approaching the section of the corridor where bandit strikes were much less likely. They were getting close to the Shattered Plains, and the safety they offered.

'Tired of fighting?' Gaz said, chuckling as he took a hinge and began nailing it in place. Occasionally, he would glance to the side, a kind of nervous tic. 'Damnation, no. It wasn't us, it was the storming lighteyes! No offense intended, Brightness. But storm them, and storm them good!'

'They stopped fighting to win,' Red softly added. 'And they started fighting for spheres.'

'Every day,' Gaz said. 'Every storming day, we'd get up and fight on those plateaus. And we wouldn't make any progress. Who cared if we made progress? It was the gemhearts the highprinces were after. And there we were, locked into virtual slavery by our military oaths. No right of travel as good citizens should have, since we'd enlisted. We were dying, bleeding, and suffering so they could get rich! That was all. So we left. A bunch of us who drank together, though we served different highprinces. We left them and their war behind.'

'Now, Gaz,' Red said. 'That isn't everything. Be honest with the lady. Didn't you owe some spheres to the debtmongers too? What was that you told us about being one step from being turned into a bridgeman—'

'Here now,' Gaz said. 'That's my old life. Ain't nothing in that old life that matters anymore.' He finished with the hammer. 'Besides. Brightness Shallan said our debts would be taken care of.'

'Everything will be forgiven,' Shallan said.

'See?'

'Except your breath,' she added.

Gaz looked up, a blush rising on his scarred face, but Red just laughed. After a moment, Gaz gave in to chuckling. There was something desperately affable about these soldiers. They had seized the chance to live a normal life again and were determined to hold to it. There hadn't been a single problem with discipline in the days they'd been together, and they were quick, even eager, to be of service to her.

Evidence of that came as Gaz folded the side of her wagon back up – then opened a latch and lowered a small window to let the light in. He gestured with a smile at his new window. 'Maybe not nice enough to befit a lighteyed lady, but at least you'll be able to see out now.'

'Not bad,' Red said, clapping slowly. 'Why didn't you tell us you'd trained as a carpenter?'

'I haven't trained as one,' Gaz said, expression turning oddly solemn. 'I spent some time around a lumberyard, that's all. You pick up a few things.'

'It's very nice, Gaz,' Shallan said. 'I appreciate it deeply.'

'It's nothing. You should probably have one on the other side too. I'll see if I can scrounge another hinge off the merchants.'

'Already kissing the feet of our new master, Gaz?' Vathah stepped up to the group. Shallan hadn't noticed him approaching.

The leader of the former deserters held a small bowl of steaming curry from the dinner cauldron. Shallan could smell the pungent peppers. While it would have made a nice change from the stew she'd eaten with the slavers, the caravan had proper women's food, which she was obliged to eat. Maybe she could sneak a bite of the curry when nobody was looking.

'You didn't ever offer to make things like this for me, Gaz,' Vathah said, dipping his bread and tearing off a chunk with his teeth. He spoke while chewing. 'You seem happy to have been made a servant to the lighteyes again. It's a wonder your shirt isn't torn up from all the crawling and scraping you've been doing.'

Gaz blushed again.

'So far as I know, Vathah,' Shallan said, 'you didn't have a wagon. So what is it you'd have wanted Gaz to make a window in? Your head, perhaps? I'm certain we can arrange that.'

Vathah smiled as he ate, though it wasn't a particularly pleasant smile. 'Did he tell you about the money he owes?'

'We will handle that problem when the time comes.'

'This lot is going to be more trouble than you think, little lighteyes,' Vathah said, shaking his head as he dipped his bread again. 'Going right back to where they were before.'

'This time they'll be heroes for rescuing me.'

He snorted. 'This lot will *never* be heroes. They're crem, Brightness. Pure and simple.'

Nearby Gaz looked down and Red turned away, but neither disagreed with the assessment.

'You're trying very hard to beat them down, Vathah,' Shallan said, standing. 'Are you *that* afraid of being wrong? One would assume you'd be accustomed to it by now.'

He grunted. 'Be careful, girl. You wouldn't want to accidentally insult a man.'

'The last thing I'd want to do is accidentally insult you, Vathah,' Shallan said. 'To think that I couldn't manage it on purpose if I wanted!'

He looked at her, then flushed and took a moment, trying to come up with a response.

Shallan cut in before he could do so. 'I'm not surprised you're at a loss for words, as it's *also* an experience I'm sure you're accustomed to. You must feel it every time someone asks you a challenging question – such as the color of your shirt.'

'Cute,' he said. 'But words aren't going to change these men or the troubles they are in.'

'On the contrary,' Shallan said, meeting his eyes, 'in my experience, words are where most change begins. I have promised them a second chance. I *will* keep my promise.'

Vathah grunted, but wandered away without further comment. Shallan sighed, sitting down and returning to her work. 'That one always walks around acting like a chasmfiend ate his mother,' she said with a grimace. 'Or perhaps the chasmfiend *was* his mother.'

Red laughed. 'If you don't mind me saying, Brightness. You have quite the clever tongue on you!'

'I've never actually had someone's tongue *on* me,' Shallan said, turning a page and not looking up, 'clever or not. I'd hazard to consider it an unpleasant experience.'

'It ain't so bad,' Gaz said.

They both looked at him.

He shrugged. 'Just saying. It ain't . . .'

Red laughed, slapping Gaz on the shoulder. 'I'm going to get some food. I'll help you hunt down that hinge afterward.'

Gaz nodded, though he glanced to the side again – that same nervous tic – and didn't join Red as the taller man walked toward the dinner cauldron. Instead, he settled down to begin sanding the floor of her wagon where the wood had begun to splinter.

She set aside the notebook in front of her, in which she had been attempting to devise ways to help her brothers. Those included everything from trying to buy one of the Soulcasters owned by the Alethi king to trying to track down the Ghostbloods and somehow deflect their attention. She couldn't do anything, however, until she reached the Shattered Plains – and then, most of her plans would require her to have powerful allies.

Shallan needed to make the betrothal to Adolin Kholin go forward. Not just for her family, but for the good of the world. Shallan would need the allies and resources that would give her. But what if she couldn't maintain the betrothal? What if she couldn't bring Brightness Navani to her side? She might need to proceed in finding Urithiru and preparing for the Voidbringers on her own. That terrified her, but she wanted to be ready.

She dug out a different book – one of the few from Jasnah's stash that didn't describe the Voidbringers or legendary Urithiru. Instead, it listed the current Alethi highprinces and discussed their political maneuvers and goals.

Shallan had to be ready. She had to know the political landscape of the Alethi court. She couldn't afford ignorance. She had to know who among these people might be potential allies, if all else failed her.

What of this Sadeas? she thought, flipping to a page in the notebook. It listed him as conniving and dangerous, but noted that both he and his wife were sharp of wit. A man of intelligence might listen to Shallan's arguments and understand them.

Aladar was listed as another highprince that Jasnah respected. Powerful, known for his brilliant political maneuvers. He was also fond of games of chance. Perhaps he would risk an expedition to find Urithiru, if Shallan highlighted the potential riches to be found.

Hatham was listed as a man of delicate politics and careful planning. Another potential ally. Jasnah didn't think much of Thanadal, Bethab, or Sebarial. The first she called oily, the second a dullard, and the third outrageously rude.

She studied them and their motivations for some time. Eventually, Gaz stood up and dusted sawdust from his trousers. He nodded in respect to her and moved to get himself some food.

'A moment, Master Gaz,' she said.

'I'm no master,' he said, walking up to her. 'Sixth nahn only, Brightness. Never could buy myself anything better.'

'How bad, exactly, are these debts of yours?' she asked, digging some spheres out of her safepouch to put in the goblet on her desk.

'Well, one of the fellows I owed was executed,' Gaz said, rubbing his chin. 'But there is more.' He hesitated. 'Eighty ruby broams, Brightness. Though they might not take them anymore. It's my head they may want, these days.'

'Quite a debt for a man such as yourself. Are you a gambler, then?'

'Ain't no difference,' he said. 'Sure.'

'And that's a lie,' Shallan said, cocking her head. 'I would know the truth from you, Gaz.'

'Just turn me over to them,' he said, turning and walking toward the soup. 'Ain't no matter. I'd rather that than be out here, wondering when they'll find me, anyways.'

Shallan watched him go, then shook her head, turning back to her studies. *She says that Urithiru is not on the Shattered Plains*, Shallan thought, turning a few pages. *But how is she certain? The Plains were never fully explored, because of the chasms. Who knows what is out there?*

Fortunately, Jasnah was very complete in her notes. It appeared that most of the old records spoke of Urithiru as being in the mountains. The Shattered Plains filled a basin.

Nohadon could walk there, Shallan thought, flipping to a quote from *The Way of Kings*. Jasnah questioned the validity of that statement, though Jasnah questioned pretty much everything. After an hour of study as the sun sank down through the sky, Shallan found herself rubbing her temples.

'Are you well?' Pattern's voice asked softly. He liked to come out when it was darker, and she did not forbid him. She searched and found him on the table, a complex formation of ridges in the wood.

'Historians,' Shallan said, 'are a bunch of liars.'

'Mmmmm,' Pattern said, sounding satisfied.

'That wasn't a compliment.'

'Oh.'

Shallan slammed her current book closed. 'These women were supposed to be scholars! Instead of recording facts, they wrote opinions and presented them as truth. They seem to take great pains to contradict one another, and they dance around topics of import like spren around a fire – never providing heat themselves, just making a show of it.'

Pattern hummed. 'Truth is individual.'

'What? No it's not. Truth is . . . it's *Truth*. Reality.'

'Your truth is what you see,' Pattern said, sounding confused. 'What else could it be? That is the truth that you spoke to me, the truth that brings power.'

She looked at him, his ridges casting shadows in the light of her spheres. She'd renewed those in the highstorm last night, while she was cooped up in her box of a wagon. Pattern had started buzzing in the middle of the storm – a strange, angry sound. After that, he'd ranted in a language she didn't understand, panicking Gaz and the other soldiers she'd invited into the shelter. Luckily, they took it for granted that terrible things happened during highstorms, and none had spoken of it since.

Fool, she told herself, flipping to an empty page in the notes. *Start acting like a scholar. Jasnah would be disappointed.* She wrote down what Pattern had said just now.

'Pattern,' she said, tapping her pencil – one she'd gotten from the merchants, along with paper. 'This table has four legs. Would you not say that is a truth, independent of my perspective?'

Pattern buzzed uncertainly. 'What is a leg? Only as it is defined by you. Without a perspective, there is no such thing as a leg, or a table. There is only wood.'

'You've told me the table perceives itself this way.'

'Because people have considered it, long enough, as being a table,' Pattern said. 'It becomes truth to the table because of the truth the people create for it.'

Interesting, Shallan thought, scribbling away at her notebook. She wasn't so interested in the nature of truth at the moment, but in how

Pattern perceived it. *Is this because he's from the Cognitive Realm? The books say that the Spiritual Realm is a place of pure truth, while the Cognitive is more fluid.*

'Spren,' Shallan said. 'If people weren't here, would spren have thought?'

'Not here, in this realm,' Pattern said. 'I do not know about the other realm.'

'You don't sound concerned,' Shallan said. 'Your entire existence might be dependent on people.'

'It is,' Pattern said, again unconcerned. 'But children are dependent upon parents.' He hesitated. 'Besides, there are others who think.'

'Voidbringers,' Shallan said, cold.

'Yes. I do not think that my kind would live in a world with only them. They have their own spren.'

Shallan sat up sharply. 'Their *own* spren?'

Pattern shrank on her table, scrunching up, his ridges growing less distinct as they mashed together.

'Well?' Shallan asked.

'We do not speak of this.'

'You might want to start,' Shallan said. 'It's important.'

Pattern buzzed. She thought he was going to insist on the point, but after a moment, he continued in a very small voice. 'Spren are . . . power . . . shattered power. Power given thought by the perceptions of men. Honor, Cultivation, and . . . and another. Fragments broken off.'

'Another?' Shallan prodded.

Pattern's buzz became a whine, going so high pitched she almost couldn't hear it. 'Odium.' He spoke the word as if needing to force it out.

Shallan wrote furiously. Odium. Hatred. A type of spren? Perhaps a large unique one, like Cusicesh from Iri or the Nightwatcher. Hatred-spren. She'd never heard of such a thing.

As she wrote, one of her slaves approached in the darkening night. The timid man wore a simple tunic and trousers, one of the sets given to Shallan by the merchants. The gift was welcome, as the last of Shallan's spheres were in the goblet before her, and wouldn't be enough to buy a meal at some of the finer restaurants in Kharbranth.

'Brightness?' the man asked.

'Yes, Suna?'

'I . . . um . . .' He pointed. 'The other lady, she asked me to tell you . . .'

He was pointing toward the tent used by Tyn, the tall woman who was leader of the few remaining caravan guards.

'She wants me to visit her?' Shallan asked.

'Yes,' Suna said, looking down. 'For food, I guess?'

'Thank you, Suna,' Shallan said, freeing him to go back toward the fire where he and the other slaves were helping with the cooking while parshmen gathered wood.

Shallan's slaves were a quiet group. They had tattoos on their foreheads, rather than brands. It was the kinder way to do it, and usually marked a person who had entered servitude willingly, as opposed to being forced into it as a punishment for a violent or terrible crime. They were men with debts or the children of slaves who still bore the debt of their parents.

These were accustomed to labor, and seemed frightened by the idea of what she was paying them. Pittance though it was, it would see most of them freed in under two years. They were obviously uncomfortable with that idea.

Shallan shook her head, packing away her things. As she walked toward Tyn's tent, Shallan paused at the fire and asked Red to lift her table back into the wagon and secure it there.

She did worry about her things, but she no longer kept any spheres in there, and had left it open so Red and Gaz could glimpse inside and see only books. Hopefully there would be no incentive for people to go rooting through them.

You dance around the truth too, she thought to herself as she walked away from the fire. *Just like those historians you were ranting about.* She pretended these men were heroes, but had no illusions about how quickly they could change coats in the wrong circumstances.

Tyn's tent was large and well lit. The woman didn't travel like a simple guard. In many ways, she was the most intriguing person here. One of the few lighteyes aside from the merchants themselves. A woman who wore a sword.

Shallan peeked in through the open flaps and found several parshmen setting up a meal on a low travel table, meant for people to eat at while sitting on the floor. The parshmen hurried out, and Shallan watched them suspiciously.

Tyn herself stood by a window cut into the cloth. She wore her long, tan coat, buckled at the waist and almost closed. It had a dresslike feel to it, though it was far stiffer than any dress Shallan had worn, matched by the stiff trousers the woman wore underneath.

'I asked your men,' Tyn said without turning, 'and they said you hadn't dined yet. I had the parshmen bring enough for two.'

'Thank you,' Shallan said, entering and trying to keep the hesitation from her voice. Among these people, she wasn't a timid girl but a powerful woman. Theoretically.

'I've ordered my people to keep the perimeter clear,' Tyn said. 'We can speak freely.'

'That is well,' Shallan said.

'It means,' Tyn said, turning around, 'that you can tell me who you really are.'

Stormfather! What did *that* mean? 'I'm Shallan Davar, as I have said.'

'Yes,' Tyn said, walking over and sitting down at the table. 'Please,' she said, gesturing.

Shallan seated herself carefully, using a ladylike posture, with legs bent to the side.

Tyn sat cross-legged after flipping her coat out behind her. She dug into her meal, dipping flatbread in a curry that seemed too dark – and smelled too peppery – to be feminine.

'Men's food?' Shallan asked.

'I've always hated those definitions,' Tyn said. 'I was raised in Tu Bayla by parents who worked as interpreters. I didn't realize certain foods were supposed to be for women or men until I visited my parents' homeland for the first time. Still seems stupid to me. I'll eat what I want, thank you very much.'

Shallan's own meal was more proper, smelling sweet rather than savory. She ate, only now realizing how hungry she was.

'I have a spanreed,' Tyn said.

Shallan looked up, tip of her bread in her dipping bowl.

'It's connected to one over in Tashikk,' Tyn continued, 'at one of their new information houses. You hire an intermediary there, and they can perform services for you. Research, make inquiries – even relay messages for you via spanreed to any major city in the world. Quite spectacular.'

'That sounds useful,' Shallan said carefully.

'Indeed. You can find out all kinds of things. For example, I had my contact find what they could on House Davar. It's apparently a small, out-of-the-way house with large debts and an erratic house leader who may or may not still be alive. He has a daughter, Shallan, whom nobody seems to have met.'

'I am that daughter,' Shallan said. 'So I'd say that "nobody" is a stretch.'

'And why,' Tyn said, 'would an unknown scion of a minor Veden family be traveling the Frostlands with a group of slavers? All the while claiming she's expected at the Shattered Plains, and that her rescue will be celebrated? That she has powerful connections, enough to pay the salaries of a full mercenary troop?'

'Truth is sometimes more surprising than a lie.'

Tyn smiled, then leaned forward. 'It's all right; you don't need to keep up the front with me. You're actually doing a good job here. I've discarded my annoyance with you and have decided to be impressed instead. You're new to this, but talented.'

'This?' Shallan asked.

'The art of the con, of course,' Tyn said. 'The grand act of pretending to be someone you aren't, then running off with the goods. I like what you pulled with those deserters. It was a big gamble, and it paid off.

'But now you're in a predicament. You're pretending to be someone several steps above your station, and are promising a grand payoff. I've run that scam before, and the trickiest part is the end. If you don't handle this well, these "heroes" you've recruited will have no qualms stringing you up by the neck. I've noticed that you're dragging your feet moving us toward the Plains. You're uncertain, aren't you? In over your head?'

'Most definitely,' Shallan said softly.

'Well,' Tyn said, digging into her food, 'I'm here to help.'

'At what cost?' This woman certainly did like to talk. Shallan was inclined to let her continue.

'I want in on whatever you're planning,' Tyn said, stabbing her bread down into the bowl like a sword into a greatshell. 'You came all the way here to the Frostlands for *something*. Your plot is likely no small con, but I can't help but assume you don't have the experience to pull it off.'

Shallan tapped her finger against the table. Who would she be for this woman? Who did she *need* to be?

She seems like a master con artist, Shallan thought, sweating. *I can't fool someone like this.*

Except that she already had. Accidentally.

335

'How did you end up here?' Shallan asked. 'Leading guards on a caravan? Is that part of a con?'

Tyn laughed. 'This? No, it wouldn't be worth the trouble. I may have exaggerated my experience in talking to the caravan leaders, but I needed to get to the Shattered Plains and didn't have the resources to do it on my own. Not safely.'

'How does a woman like you end up without resources, though?' Shallan asked, frowning. 'I'd think you would never be without.'

'I'm not,' Tyn said, gesturing. 'As you can plainly see. You're going to have to get used to rebuilding, if you want to join the profession. It comes, it goes. I got stuck down south without any spheres, and am finding my way to more civilized countries.'

'To the Shattered Plains,' Shallan said. 'You have a job there of some sort as well? A . . . con you're intending to pull?'

Tyn smiled. 'This isn't about me, kid. It's about you, and what I can do for you. I know people in the warcamps. It's practically the new capital of Alethkar; everything interesting in the country is happening there. Money is flowing like rivers after a storm, but everyone considers it a frontier, and so laws are lax. A woman can get ahead if she knows the right people.'

Tyn leaned forward, and her expression darkened. 'But if she doesn't, she can make enemies really quickly. Trust me, you want to know who I know, and you want to work with them. Without their approval, nothing big happens at the Shattered Plains. So I ask you again. What are you hoping to accomplish there?'

'I . . . know something about Dalinar Kholin.'

'Old Blackthorn himself?' Tyn said, surprised. 'He's been living a boring life lately, all superior, like he's some hero from the legends.'

'Yes, well, what I know is going to be very important to him. Very.'

'Well, what is this secret?'

Shallan didn't answer.

'Not willing to divulge the goods yet,' Tyn said. 'Well, that's understandable. Blackmail is a tricky one. You'll be glad you brought me on. You *are* bringing me on, aren't you?'

'Yes,' Shallan said. 'I do believe I could learn some things from you.'

Smokeform for hiding and slipping between men.
A form of power, like human Surges.
Bring it 'round again.
Though crafted of gods,
It was by Unmade hand.
Leaves its force to be but one of foe or friend.

—From the Listener Song of Histories, 127th stanza

Kaladin figured that it took a lot to put him in a situation he'd never before seen. He'd been a slave and a surgeon, served on a battlefield and in a lighteyes' dining room. He'd seen a lot for his twenty years. Too much, it felt at times. He had many memories he'd rather be without.

Regardless, he had not expected this day to present him with something so utterly and disconcertingly unfamiliar. 'Sir?' he asked, taking a step backward. 'You want me to do *what?*'

'Get on that horse,' Dalinar Kholin said, pointing toward an animal grazing nearby. The beast would stand perfectly still, waiting for grass to creep up out of its holes. Then it would pounce, taking a quick bite, which would cause the grass to shoot back down into its burrows. It got a mouthful each time, often pulling the grass out by its roots.

It was one of many such animals dawdling and prancing through the area. It never ceased to stun Kaladin just how rich people like Dalinar were; each horse was worth spheres in profusion. And Dalinar wanted him to climb on one of them.

'Soldier,' Dalinar said, 'you need to know how to ride. The time might come when you need to guard my sons on the battlefield. Besides, how long did it take you to reach the palace the other night, when coming to hear about the king's accident?'

'Almost three-quarters of an hour,' Kaladin admitted. It had been four days since that night, and Kaladin had frequently found himself on edge since then.

'I have stables near the barracks,' Dalinar said. 'You could have made that trip in a fraction of the time if you could ride. Perhaps you won't spend much of your time in the saddle, but this is going to be an important skill for you and your men to know.'

Kaladin looked back at the other members of Bridge Four. Shrugs all around – a few timid ones – except for Moash, who nodded eagerly. 'I suppose,' Kaladin said, looking back at Dalinar. 'If you think it's important, sir, we'll give it a try.'

'Good man,' Dalinar said. 'I'll send over Jenet, the stablemaster.'

'We'll await him with eagerness, sir,' Kaladin said, trying to sound like he meant it.

Two of Kaladin's men escorted Dalinar as he walked toward the stables, a set of large, sturdy stone buildings. From what Kaladin saw, when the horses weren't inside, they were allowed to roam freely inside this open area west of the warcamp. A low stone wall enclosed it, but surely the horses could jump that at will.

They didn't. The brutes wandered about, stalking grass or lying down, snorting and whinnying. The entire place smelled strange to Kaladin. Not of dung, just ... of horse. Kaladin eyed one eating nearby, just inside the wall. He didn't trust it; there was something too *smart* about horses. Proper beasts of burden like chulls were slow and docile. He'd ride a chull. A creature like this, though ... who knew what it was thinking?

Moash stepped up beside him, watching Dalinar go. 'You like him, don't you?' he asked softly.

'He's a good commander,' Kaladin said, as he instinctively sought out Adolin and Renarin, who were riding their horses nearby. Apparently, the things needed to be exercised periodically to keep them functioning properly. Devilish creatures.

'Don't get too close to him, Kal,' Moash said, still watching Dalinar. 'And don't trust him too far. He's lighteyed, remember.'

'I'm not likely to forget,' Kaladin said dryly. 'Besides, you're the one who looked like you'd faint from joy the moment he offered to let us ride these monsters.'

'Have you ever faced a lighteyes riding one of these things?' Moash asked. 'On the battlefield, I mean?'

Kaladin remembered thundering hooves, a man in silvery armor. Dead friends. 'Yes.'

'Then you know the advantage it offers,' Moash said. 'I'll take Dalinar's offer gladly.'

The stablemaster turned out to be a she. Kaladin raised an eyebrow as the pretty, young lighteyed woman walked up to them, a pair of grooms in tow. She wore a traditional Vorin gown, though it wasn't silk but something coarser, and was slit up the front and back, ankle to thigh. Underneath, she wore a feminine pair of trousers.

The woman wore her dark hair in a tail, no ornaments, and had a tautness to her face that he didn't expect in a lighteyed woman. 'The highprince says I'm to let you ruffians touch my horses,' Jenet said, folding her arms. 'I'm not pleased about it.'

'Fortunately,' Kaladin said, 'neither are we.'

She looked him up and down. 'You're that one, aren't you? The one everyone is talking about?'

'Maybe.'

She sniffed. 'You need a haircut. All right, listen up, soldier boys! We're going to do this properly. I won't have you hurting my horses, all right? You listen, and you listen well.'

What proceeded was one of the dullest, most protracted lectures of Kaladin's life. The woman went on and on about posture – straight-backed, but not too tense. About getting the horses to move – nudges with the heels, nothing too sharp. About how to ride, how to respect the animal, how to hold the reins properly and how to balance. All before being allowed to even *touch* one of the creatures.

Eventually, the boredom was interrupted by the arrival of a man on horseback. Unfortunately, it was Adolin Kholin, riding that white monster of a horse of his. It was several hands taller than the one Jenet was showing them. Adolin's almost looked a completely different species, with those massive hooves, glistening white coat, and unfathomable eyes.

Adolin looked the bridgemen over with a smirk, then caught the stablemaster's eye and smiled in a less condescending way. 'Jenet,' he said. 'Looking fetching today, as always. Is that a new riding dress?'

The woman bent down without looking – she was now talking about how to guide the horses – and selected a stone from the ground. Then she turned and threw it at Adolin.

The princeling flinched, raising an arm protectively over his face, though Jenet's aim was off.

'Oh, come on now,' Adolin said. 'You're not still sore that – '

Another rock. This one clipped him on the arm.

'Right, then,' Adolin said, jogging his horse away, hunched down to present a smaller target for rocks.

Eventually, after demonstrating saddling and bridling on her horse, Jenet finished the lecture and deemed them worthy of touching some horses. A flock of her grooms, both male and female, scurried out onto the field to select proper mounts for the six bridgemen.

'Lots of women on your staff,' Kaladin noted to Jenet as the grooms worked.

'Horseback riding isn't mentioned in *Arts and Majesty*,' she replied. 'Horses weren't terribly well known back then. Radiants had Ryshadium, but even kings had little access to ordinary horses.' She wore her safehand in a sleeve, unlike most of the darkeyed groom women, who wore gloves.

'Which matters because . . . ?' Kaladin said.

Frowning, she looked at him, baffled. '*Arts and Majesty* . . .' she prompted. 'Foundation of masculine and feminine arts . . . Of course. I keep looking at those captain's knots on your shoulder, but—'

'But I'm just an ignorant darkeyes?'

'Sure, if that's how you want to put it. Whatever. Look, I'm not going to give you a lecture on the arts – I'm tired of talking to you people already. Let's just say that anyone who wants can be a groom, all right?'

She lacked a polished refinement that Kaladin had come to expect in lighteyed women, and he found it refreshing. Better a woman who was *overtly* condescending than the alternative. The grooms walked the horses out of their enclosure and to a riding ground, shaped like a ring. A group of parshmen with eyes downcast brought the saddles, saddle pads, and bridles – equipment that, following Jenet's lecture, Kaladin could name.

Kaladin selected a beast that didn't look too evil, a shorter horse with a shaggy mane and a brown coat. He saddled it with help from a groom. Nearby, Moash finished and threw himself up into his saddle. Once the groom let go, Moash's horse wandered off without him asking it to do so.

'Hey!' Moash said. 'Stop. Whoa. How do I get it to stop walking?'

'You dropped the reins,' Jenet called after him. 'Storming fool! Were you even listening?'

'Reins,' Moash said, scrambling for them. 'Can't I just slap it over the head with a reed, like you do a chull?'

Jenet rubbed her forehead.

Kaladin looked into the eye of his own chosen beast. 'Look,' he said softly, 'you don't want to do this. I don't want to do this. Let's just be pleasant to one another and get it over with as quickly as possible.'

The horse snorted softly. Kaladin took a deep breath, then grabbed the saddle as instructed, lifting one foot into the stirrup. He rocked a few times, then threw himself up into the saddle. He grabbed the saddle horn in a death grip and held on tight, ready to be thrown about as the beast went charging away.

His horse bent her head and began licking some rocks.

'Hey, now,' Kaladin said, raising the reins. 'Come on. Let's move.'

The horse ignored him.

Kaladin tried cuing it in the flanks as he'd been told. The horse didn't budge.

'You're supposed to be some kind of wagon with legs,' Kaladin said to the thing. 'You're worth more than a village. Prove it to me. Get going! Forward! Onward!'

The horse licked the rocks.

What is *the thing doing?* Kaladin thought, leaning to the side. With surprise, he noticed grass poking out of its holes. *Licking fools the grass into thinking rain has come.* Often after a storm, plants would unfold to glut themselves on the water even if insects decided to chew them. *Clever beast. Lazy. But clever.*

'You need to show her you're in charge,' Jenet said, wandering past.

'Tighten the reins, sit up straight, pull her head up, and don't let her eat. She'll walk all over you if you aren't firm.'

Kaladin tried to obey, and did manage – finally – to pull the horse away from her meal. The horse did smell odd, but it wasn't a bad smell really. He got her walking, and once that happened, steering wasn't *that* difficult. It felt strange to have some other thing in control of where he was going, however. Yes, he had the reins, but at any time this horse could just up and take off running and he'd be unable to do anything about it. Half of Jenet's training had been about not spooking the horses – about remaining still if one started to gallop, and about never surprising one from behind.

It looked higher from atop the horse than he'd assumed it would. That was a long fall to the ground. He guided the horse about, and after a short time, he managed to pull up beside Natam on purpose. The long-faced bridgeman held his reins as if they were precious gemstones, afraid to yank them or direct his horse.

'Can't believe people ride these things on storming purpose,' Natam said. He had a rural Alethi accent, his words bluntly clipped, like he was biting them off before he'd quite finished them. 'I mean, we ain't moving any faster than walking, right?'

Again, Kaladin remembered the image of that charging mounted Shardbearer from long ago. Yes, Kaladin could see the reason for horses. Sitting up higher made it easier to strike with power, and the size of the horse – its bulk and momentum – frightened soldiers on foot and sent them scattering.

'I think most go faster than these,' Kaladin said. 'I'd bet they gave us the old horses to practice on.'

'Yeah, I suppose,' Natam said. 'It's warm. Didn't expect that. I've ridden chulls before. This thing shouldn't be so . . . warm. Hard to feel like this thing is worth as much as it is. It's like I'm riding about on a pile of emerald broams.' He hesitated, glancing backward. 'Only, emeralds' backsides ain't nearly so busy . . .'

'Natam,' Kaladin asked. 'Do you remember much about the day when someone tried to kill the king?'

'Oh, sure,' Natam said. 'I was with the guys who ran out there and found him flapping in the wind, like the Stormfather's own ears.'

Kaladin smiled. Once, this man would barely say two sentences together, instead always staring at the ground, somber. Used up by his time as a bridgeman. These last few weeks had been good for Natam. Good for them all.

'Before the storm that night,' Kaladin said. 'Was anyone out on the balcony? Any servants you didn't recognize? Any soldiers who weren't from the King's Guard?'

'No servants that I recall,' Natam said, squinting. The once-farmer got a pensive look on his face. 'I guarded the king all day, sir, with the King's Guard. Ain't nothing standing out to me. I – Whoa!' His horse had suddenly picked up speed, outpacing Kaladin's.

'Think about it!' Kaladin called to him. 'See what you can remember!'

Natam nodded, still holding his reins like they were glass, refusing to pull them tight or steer the horse. Kaladin shook his head.

A small horse galloped past him. In the air. Made of light. Syl giggled, changing shape and spinning around as a ribbon of light before settling on the neck of Kaladin's horse, just in front of him.

She lounged back, grinning, then frowned at his expression. 'You're not enjoying yourself,' Syl said.

'You're starting to sound a lot like my mother.'

'Captivating?' Syl said. 'Amazing, witty, meaningful?'

'Repetitive.'

'Captivating?' Syl said. 'Amazing, witty, meaningful?'

'Very funny.'

'Says the man not laughing,' she replied, folding her arms. 'All right, so what is drearifying you today?'

'Drearifying?' Kaladin frowned. 'Is that a word?'

'You don't know?'

He shook his head.

'Yes,' Syl said solemnly. 'Yes, it absolutely is.'

'Something's off,' he said. 'About the conversation I just had with Natam.' He tugged on the reins, stopping the horse from trying to bend down and nibble at grass again. The thing was *very* focused.

'What did you talk about?'

'The assassination attempt,' Kaladin said, narrowing his eyes. 'And if he'd seen anyone before the . . .' He paused. 'Before the storm.'

He looked down and met Syl's eyes.

'The storm itself would have blown down the railing,' Kaladin said.

'Bending it!' Syl said, standing up and grinning. 'Ooohhh . . .'

'It was cut clean through, the mortar on the bottom chipped away,' Kaladin continued. 'I'll bet the force of the winds was easily equal to the weight the king put on it.'

'So the sabotage must have happened *after* the storm,' Syl said.

A much narrower time frame. Kaladin turned his horse toward where Natam was riding. Unfortunately, catching up wasn't easy. Natam was moving at a trot, much to his obvious dismay, and Kaladin couldn't get his mount to go faster.

'Having trouble, bridgeboy?' Adolin asked, trotting up.

Kaladin glanced at the princeling. Stormfather, but it was difficult not to feel tiny when riding beside that monster of Adolin's. Kaladin tried to kick his horse faster. She kept clopping along at her one speed, walking around the circle here that was a kind of running track for horses.

'Spray might have been fast during her youth,' Adolin said, nodding at Kaladin's mount, 'but that was fifteen years ago. I'm surprised she's still around, honestly, but she seems perfectly suited for training children. And bridgemen.'

Kaladin ignored him, eyes forward, still trying to get the horse to pick up her pace and catch Natam.

'Now, if you want something with more spunk,' Adolin said, pointing toward the side, 'Dreamstorm over there might be more to your liking.'

He indicated a larger, leaner animal in its own enclosure, saddled and roped to a pole firmly mortared into a hole in the ground. The long rope let it run in short bursts, though only around in a circle. It tossed its head, snorting.

Adolin heeled his own animal forward and past Natam.

Dreamstorm, eh? Kaladin thought, inspecting the creature. It certainly did seem to have more spunk than Spray. It also looked like it wanted to take a bite out of anyone who drew too close.

Kaladin turned Spray in that direction. Once near, he slowed – Spray was all too happy to do *that* – and climbed off. Doing so proved more difficult than he'd expected, but he managed to avoid tripping onto his face.

Once down, he put his hands on his hips and inspected the running horse inside its fence.

'Weren't you just complaining,' Syl said, walking up onto Spray's head, 'that you'd rather walk than let a horse carry you about?'

'Yeah,' Kaladin said. He hadn't realized it, but he had been holding some Stormlight. Just a tad. It escaped when he spoke, invisible unless he looked closely and detected a slight warping of the air.

'So what are you doing thinking about riding *that*?'

'This horse,' he said, nodding to Spray, 'is only for walking. I can walk just fine on my own. That other one, that's an animal for war.' Moash was right. Horses were an advantage on the battlefield, so Kaladin should be at least familiar with them.

The same argument Zahel made to me about learning to fight against a Shardblade, Kaladin thought with discomfort. *And I turned him down.*

'What do you think you're doing?' Jenet asked, riding up to him.

'I'm going to get on *that*,' Kaladin said, pointing at Dreamstorm.

Jenet snorted. 'She'll throw you in a heartbeat and you'll break your crown, bridgeman. She's not good with riders.'

'She has a saddle on.'

'So she can get used to wearing one.'

The horse finished a round of cantering and slowed.

'I don't like that look in your eyes,' Jenet told him, turning her own animal to the side. It stomped impatiently, as if eager to be running.

'I'm going to give it a try,' Kaladin said, walking forward.

'You won't even be able to get on,' Jenet said. She watched him carefully, as if curious what he'd do – though it seemed to him she might be more worried for the horse's safety than his.

Syl alighted on Kaladin's shoulder as he walked.

'This is going to be like back at the lighteyes practice grounds, isn't it?' Kaladin asked. 'I'm going to end up on my back, staring at the sky, feeling like a fool.'

'Probably,' Syl said lightly. 'So why are you doing this? Because of Adolin?'

'Nah,' Kaladin said. 'The princeling can storm away.'

'Then why?'

'Because I'm scared of these things.'

Syl looked at him, seeming baffled, but it made perfect sense to Kaladin. Ahead, Dreamstorm – huffing out huge breaths from her run – looked at him. She met his eyes.

'Storms!' Adolin's voice called from behind. 'Bridgeboy, don't actually *do* it! Are you mad?'

Kaladin stepped up to the horse. She danced a few steps back, but let him touch the saddle. So he breathed in a little more Stormlight and threw himself at the saddle.

'Damnation! What –' Adolin shouted.

That was all Kaladin heard. His Stormlight-aided leap let him get higher than an ordinary man could probably have managed, but his aim was off. He got hold of the pommel and threw one leg over, but the horse started thrashing.

The beast was incredibly strong, a distinct and powerful contrast to Spray. Kaladin was quite nearly hurled from the seat on the first buck.

With a wild swipe of the hand, Kaladin poured Stormlight onto the saddle and stuck himself in place. That only meant that instead of being tossed from horseback like a limp cloth, he got whipped back and forth like a limp cloth. He somehow managed to get hold of the horse's mane and, with teeth gritted, did his best to keep from being bounced senseless.

The stable grounds were a blur. The only sounds he could hear were his beating heart and the smashing hooves. The Voidbringer beast moved like a storm itself, but Kaladin was stuck to the saddle as surely as if he'd been nailed there. After what seemed an eternity, the horse – blowing out big, frothy breaths – stilled.

Kaladin's swimming vision cleared to show a group of bridgemen – keeping their distance – cheering him on. Adolin and Jenet, both mounted, stared at him with what seemed to be a mixture of horror and awe. Kaladin grinned.

Then, in one last, powerful motion, Dreamstorm bucked him free.

He hadn't realized that the Stormlight in the saddle was exhausted. In a fitting fulfillment of his earlier prediction, Kaladin found himself dazed, lying on his back staring at the sky, having trouble remembering the last few seconds of his life. A number of painspren wiggled out of the ground beside him, little orange hands that grabbed this way and that.

An equine head with unfathomably dark eyes leaned down over Kaladin. The horse snorted at him. The smell was moist and grassy.

'You monster,' Kaladin said. 'You waited until I was relaxed, *then* threw me.'

The horse snorted again, and Kaladin found himself laughing. Storms, but that had felt good! He couldn't explain why, but the act of clinging for dear life to the thrashing animal had been truly exhilarating.

As Kaladin stood and dusted himself off, Dalinar himself broke through the crowd, brow furrowed. Kaladin hadn't realized the highprince had still been nearby. He looked from Dreamstorm to Kaladin, then raised an eyebrow.

'You don't chase down assassins on a placid mount, sir,' Kaladin said, saluting.

'Yes,' Dalinar said, 'but it is customary to start training men by using weapons *without* edges, soldier. Are you all right?'

'Fine, sir,' Kaladin said.

'Well, it seems your men are taking to the training,' Dalinar said. 'I'm going to put in a requisition release. You and five others you select are to come here and practice every day for the next few weeks.'

'Yes, sir.' He'd find the time. Somehow.

'Good,' Dalinar said. 'I received your proposal for initial patrols outside of the warcamps, and thought it looked good. Why don't you start in two weeks, and bring some horses with you to practice out in the field.'

Jenet made a strangled sound. 'Outside the city, Brightlord? But ... bandits ...'

'The horses are here to be used, Jenet,' Dalinar said. 'Captain, you'll be sure to bring enough troops to protect the horses, won't you?'

'Yes, sir,' Kaladin said.

'Good. But *do* leave that one behind,' Dalinar said, waving toward Dreamstorm.

'Er, yes, sir.'

Dalinar nodded, moving off and raising his hand toward someone Kaladin couldn't see. Kaladin rubbed his elbow, which he'd smacked. The remaining Stormlight in his body had healed his head first, then run out before getting to his arm.

Bridge Four moved to their horses as Jenet called out for them to remount and start a second phase of training. Kaladin found himself standing near Adolin, who remained mounted.

'Thanks,' Adolin said, grudgingly.

'For?' Kaladin asked, walking past him toward Spray, who continued to chew at grass, uncaring of the fuss.

'Not telling Father I put you up to that.'

'I'm not an idiot, Adolin,' Kaladin said, swinging into his saddle. 'I could see what I was getting myself into.' He turned his horse away

347

from her meal with some difficulty, and got some more pointers from a groom. Eventually, Kaladin trotted over toward Natam again. The gait was bouncy, but he mostly got the hang of moving with the horse – they called it posting – to keep from slapping around too much.

Natam watched him as he moved up. 'That's unfair, sir.'

'What I did with Dreamstorm?'

'No. The way you just ride like that. Seems so natural for you.'

Didn't feel that way. 'I want to talk some more about that night.'

'Sir?' the long-faced man asked. 'I haven't thought of anything yet. Been a little distracted.'

'I have another question,' Kaladin said, bringing their horses up beside one another. 'I asked you about your shift during the day, but what about right after I left? Did anyone other than the king go out onto the balcony?'

'Just guards, sir,' Natam said.

'Tell me which ones,' Kaladin said. 'Maybe they saw something.'

Natam shrugged. 'I mainly watched the door. The king remained in the sitting room for a time. I guess Moash went out.'

'Moash,' Kaladin said, frowning. 'Wasn't his shift supposed to be done soon?'

'Yeah,' Natam said. 'He stayed around a little extra time; said he wanted to see the king settled. While waiting, Moash went out to watch the balcony. You usually want one of us out there.'

'Thanks,' Kaladin said. 'I'll ask him.'

Kaladin found Moash diligently listening to Jenet explain something. Moash seemed to have picked up riding quickly – he seemed to pick up everything quickly. Certainly, he'd been the best student among the bridgemen when it came to fighting.

Kaladin watched him for a few moments, frowning. Then it struck him. *What are you thinking? That Moash might have had something to do with the assassination attempt? Don't be stupid.* That was ridiculous. Besides, the man didn't have a Shardblade.

Kaladin turned his horse away. As he did, however, he saw the person Dalinar had gone to meet. Brightlord Amaram. The two were too far away for Kaladin to hear them, but he could see the amusement on Dalinar's face. Adolin and Renarin rode up to them, smiling broadly as Amaram waved to them.

The anger that surged within Kaladin – sudden, passionate, almost *chokingly* strong – made him clench his fists. His breath hissed out. That surprised him. He'd thought the hatred buried deeper than that.

He turned his horse pointedly the other direction, suddenly looking forward to the chance to go on patrol with the new recruits.

Getting away from the warcamps sounded very good to him.

They blame our people
For the loss of that land.
The city that once covered it
Did range the eastern strand.
The power made known in the tomes of our clan
Our gods were not who shattered these plains.

—From the Listener Song of Wars, 55th stanza

Adolin crashed into the Parshendi line, ignoring weapons, throwing his shoulder against the enemy at the front. The Parshendi man grunted, his song faltering, as Adolin spun about himself and swept with his Shardblade. Tugs on the weapon marked when it passed through flesh.

Adolin came out of his spin, ignoring the glow of Stormlight coming from a crack at his shoulder. Around him, bodies dropped, eyes burning in their skulls. Adolin's breath, hot and humid, filled his helm as he puffed in and out.

There, he thought, raising his Blade and charging, his men filling in around him. Not those bridgemen, for once, but real soldiers. He'd left the bridgemen back on the assault plateau. He didn't want men around him who didn't want to fight Parshendi.

Adolin and his soldiers pushed through the Parshendi, joining up with a frantic set of soldiers in green uniforms with gold accents, led by a Shardbearer in matching colors. The man fought with a large Shardbearer's hammer – he had no Blade of his own.

Adolin pushed through to him. 'Jakamav?' he asked. 'You all right?'

'All right?' Jakamav asked, voice muffled by his helm. He slammed the faceplate up, revealing a grin. 'I'm wonderful.' He laughed, pale green eyes alight with the Thrill of the fight. Adolin recognized that feeling well.

'You were almost surrounded!' Adolin said, turning to face a group of Parshendi running up in pairs. Adolin respected them for coming at Shardbearers, rather than fleeing. It meant almost certain death, but if you won, you could turn the tide of a battle.

Jakamav laughed, sounding as pleased now as when enjoying a wine-house singer, and that laughter was infectious. Adolin found himself grinning as he engaged the Parshendi, sweeping them down with blow after blow. He never enjoyed simple warfare as much as a good duel, but for the moment, despite its crassness, he found challenge and joy in the fight.

Moments later, the dead lying at his feet, he spun about and searched for another challenge. This plateau was shaped very strangely; it had been a tall hill before the Plains were shattered, but half of it had ended up on the adjacent plateau. He couldn't imagine what kind of force would have split the hill down the center, as opposed to cracking it at the base.

Well, it wasn't an ordinary-shaped hill, so maybe that had something to do with the split. It was shaped more like a wide, flat pyramid with only three steps. A large base, a second plateau atop it that was perhaps a hundred feet across, then a third, smaller peak atop the other two, placed right in the center. Almost like a cake with three tiers that had been cut with a large knife right down the center.

Adolin and Jakamav fought on the second tier of the battlefield. Technically, Adolin wasn't required to be on this run. It wasn't his army's turn in the rotation. However, the time had come to implement another part of Dalinar's plan. Adolin had arrived with only a small strike force, but it was a good thing he had. Jakamav had been surrounded up here, on the second tier, and the regular army hadn't been able to break through.

Now, the Parshendi had been pushed back to the sides of this tier.

They still held the top tier completely; it was where the chrysalis had appeared. That put them in a bad position. Yes, they had the high ground, but they also had to hold the slopes between tiers to secure their withdrawal. They'd obviously hoped to get the harvesting done before the humans arrived.

Adolin kicked a Parshendi soldier over the edge, toppling him down thirty feet or so onto those fighting on the bottom tier, then looked to his right. The slope upward was there, but the Parshendi had the approach clogged. He'd really like to reach the top. . . .

He looked at the sheer cliff face between his tier and the one above. 'Jakamav,' he called, pointing.

Jakamav followed Adolin's gesture, looking upward. Then stepped back from the fighting.

'That's crazy!' Jakamav said as Adolin jogged up.

'Sure is.'

'Let's be at it, then!' He handed his hammer to Adolin, who slipped it into the sheath on his friend's back. Then the two of them ran to the rock wall and started to climb.

Adolin's Plated fingers ground against rock as he pulled himself straight up. Soldiers below cheered them on. There were handholds aplenty, though he would never have wanted to do this without Plate to propel his climb and protect him if he fell.

It was still crazy; they'd end up surrounded. However, two Shardbearers could do amazing things when supporting one another. Besides, if they got overwhelmed, they could always jump off the cliff, assuming their Plate was healthy enough to survive the fall.

It was the sort of risky move that Adolin would never dare when his father was on the battlefield.

He paused halfway up the cliff. Parshendi gathered on the edge of the tier above, preparing for them.

'You have a plan for getting a foothold up there?' Jakamav asked, clinging to the rocks beside Adolin.

Adolin nodded. 'Just be ready to support me.'

'Sure.' Jakamav scanned the heights, face hidden behind his helm. 'What are you doing here, by the way?'

'I figured no army would turn away some Shardbearers who wanted to help.'

'Shardbearers? Plural?'

'Renarin is down below.'

'Hopefully not fighting.'

'He's surrounded by a large squad of soldiers with careful instructions *not* to let him get into the fighting. Father wanted him to see a few of these, though.'

'I know what Dalinar is doing,' Jakamav said. 'He's trying to show a spirit of cooperation, trying to get the highprinces to stop being rivals. So he sends his Shardbearers to help, even when the run isn't his.'

'Are you complaining?'

'Nope. Let's see you make an opening up there. I'll need a moment to get the hammer out.'

Adolin grinned inside his helmet, then continued climbing. Jakamav was a landlord and Shardbearer under Highprince Roion, and a fairly good friend. It was important that lighteyes like Jakamav saw Dalinar and Adolin actively working toward a better Alethkar. Perhaps a few episodes like this would show the value of a trustworthy alliance, instead of the backstabbing, temporary coalition Sadeas represented.

Adolin climbed farther, Jakamav close behind, until he was a dozen feet from the top. The Parshendi clustered there, hammers and maces at the ready – weapons for fighting a man in Shardplate. A few farther down launched arrows, which bounced ineffectively off the Plate.

All right, Adolin thought, holding his hand to the side – clinging to the rocks with the other – and summoned his Blade. He slammed it directly into the rock wall with the flat of the blade facing upward. He climbed up beside the sword.

Then he stepped onto the flat of the blade.

Shardblades couldn't break – they could barely bend – so it held him. He suddenly had leverage and good footing, and so when he crouched down and leaped, the Plate hurled him upward. As he passed the edge of the top tier, he grabbed the rock there – just beneath the feet of the Parshendi – and pulled on it to throw himself into the waiting foe.

They broke off their singing as he smashed into them with the force of a boulder. He got his feet underneath him, mentally sending a summons to his Blade, then slammed his shoulder into one group. He began to lay about himself with punches, smashing the chest of one Parshendi, then the head of another. The soldiers' carapace armor cracked with sickening sounds, and the punches flung them backward, knocking some off the cliff.

Adolin took a few hits on his forearms before his Blade finally re-formed in his hands. He swung about, so focused on holding his ground that he didn't notice Jakamav until the Shardbearer in green fell in beside him, crushing Parshendi with his hammer.

'Thanks for tossing a platoon's worth of Parshendi down on my head,' Jakamav called as he swung. 'That was a wonderful surprise.'

Adolin grinned, pointing. 'Chrysalis.'

The top tier wasn't well populated – though more Parshendi were flooding up the incline. He and Jakamav had a direct path to the chrysalis, a hulking, oblong boulder of brown and faint green. It was matted to the rocks with the same stuff that made up its shell.

Adolin leaped over the twitching form of a Parshendi with dead legs and charged the chrysalis, Jakamav following at a clanking jog. Getting to a gemheart was tough – the chrysalises had skin like rock – but with a Shardblade, it could be easy. They just had to kill the thing, then cut a hole so they could rip out the heart and—

The chrysalis was already open.

'No!' Adolin said, scrambling up to it, grabbing the sides of the hole and peering into the slushy violet interior. Chunks of carapace floated within the goop, and a conspicuous gap lay where the gemheart normally connected to veins and sinew.

Adolin spun, searching across the top of the plateau. Jakamav clanked up and cursed. 'How did they get it out so quickly?'

There. Nearby, Parshendi soldiers scattered, yelling in their impenetrable, rhythmic language. Standing behind them was a tall figure in silvery Shardplate, a red cloak billowing out behind. The armor had peaked joints, ridges rising like the points on a crab's shell. The figure was easily seven feet tall, the armor making him look massive, perhaps because it covered a Parshendi who had that carapace armor growing from his skin.

'It's him!' Adolin said, running forward. This was the one his father had fought on the Tower, the only Shardbearer they'd seen among the Parshendi for weeks, maybe months.

Perhaps the last one they had.

The Shardbearer turned toward Adolin, gripping a large uncut gemstone in his hand. It dripped ichor and plasma.

'Fight me!' Adolin said.

A group of Parshendi soldiers charged past the Shardbearer, running toward the long drop-off at the back of the formation, where the hill had been split down the center. The Shardbearer handed his gemheart to one of these charging men, then turned and watched them jump.

They soared across the gap to land on the top of the other half of the hill, the one on the adjacent plateau. It still amazed Adolin that these Parshendi soldiers could leap chasms. He felt a fool as he realized that these heights were not a trap for them as they would be for humans. To them, a mountain split in half was just another chasm to leap.

More and more of the Parshendi made the leap, flowing away from the humans below and jumping to safety. Adolin did spot one who stumbled as he leapt. The poor fellow screamed as he plummeted into the chasm. This was dangerous for them, but it was obviously less so than trying to fight off the humans.

The Shardbearer remained. Adolin ignored the fleeing Parshendi – ignored Jakamav, who called for him to fall back – and ran up to that Shardbearer, swinging his Blade full force. The Parshendi raised his own Blade, slapping aside Adolin's blow.

'You are the son, Adolin Kholin,' the Parshendi said. 'Your father? Where is?'

Adolin froze in place. The words were in Alethi – heavily accented, yes, but understandable.

The Shardbearer slammed up his faceplate. And, to Adolin's shock, there was no beard on that face. Didn't that make this a woman? Telling the difference with Parshendi was difficult for him. The vocal timbre was rough and low-pitched, though he supposed it could be feminine.

'I must need speak to Dalinar,' the woman said, stepping forward. 'I met him one time, much long ago.'

'You refused our every messenger,' Adolin said, backing away, sword out. 'Now you wish to speak with us?'

'That was long ago. Time does change.'

Stormfather. Something inside of Adolin urged him to go in swinging, to batter this Shardbearer down and get some answers, win some Shards. Fight! He was here to *fight*!

His father's voice, in the back of his mind, held him at bay. Dalinar would want this chance. It could change the course of the entire war.

'He will want to contact you,' Adolin said, taking a deep breath, shoving down the Thrill of battle. 'How?'

'Will send messenger,' the Shardbearer said. 'Do not kill one who comes.' She raised her Shardblade toward him in salute, then let it drop and dematerialize. She turned to charge toward the chasm and hurled herself across in a prodigious leap.

···

Adolin pulled off his helm as he strode across the plateau. Surgeons saw to the wounded while the hale sat around in groups, drinking water and grousing about their failure.

A rare mood hovered over the armies of Roion and Ruthar this day. Usually when the Alethi lost a plateau run it was because the Parshendi pushed them back in a wild scrambling retreat across bridges. It wasn't often that a run ended with the Alethi controlling the plateau, but with no gemheart to show for it.

He released one gauntlet, the straps undoing themselves automatically at his will, then hooked it at his waist. He used a sweaty hand to push back sweatier hair. Now where had Renarin gotten to?

There, on the staging plateau, sitting on a rock surrounded by guards. Adolin tromped across one of the bridges, raising a hand to Jakamav, who was removing his Plate nearby. He'd want to ride back in comfort.

Adolin jogged up to his brother, who sat on a boulder with his helm off, staring at the ground in front of him.

'Hey,' Adolin said. 'Ready to head back?'

Renarin nodded.

'What happened?' Adolin asked.

Renarin continued staring at the ground. Finally, one of the bridgeman guards – a compact man with silvering hair – nodded his head to the side. Adolin walked with him a short distance away.

'A group of shellheads tried to seize one of the bridges, Brightlord,' the bridgeman said softly. 'Brightlord Renarin insisted on going to help. Sir, we tried hard to dissuade him. Then, when he got near and summoned his Blade, he just kind of . . . stood there. We got him away, sir, but he's been sitting on that rock ever since.'

One of Renarin's fits. 'Thank you, soldier,' Adolin said. He walked back over and laid his ungauntleted hand on Renarin's shoulder. 'It's all right, Renarin. It happens.'

Renarin shrugged again. Well, if he was in one of his moods, there was nothing to do but let him stew. The younger man would talk about it when he was ready.

Adolin organized his two hundred troops, then paid his respects to the highprinces. Neither seemed very grateful. In fact, Ruthar seemed convinced that Adolin and Jakamav's stunt had driven the Parshendi off with the gemheart. As if they wouldn't have withdrawn the moment they had it anyway. Idiot.

Adolin smiled affably, regardless. Hopefully Father was right, and the extended hand of fellowship would help. Personally, Adolin just wanted a chance at each of them in the dueling ring, where he could teach them a little respect.

On his way back to his army, he searched out Jakamav, who sat under a small pavilion, having a cup of wine as he watched the rest of his army trudge back across the bridges. There were a lot of slumped shoulders and long faces.

Jakamav gestured for his steward to get Adolin a cup of sparkling yellow wine. Adolin took it in his unarmored hand, though he didn't drink.

'That was quite nearly awesome,' Jakamav said, staring out at the battle plateau. From this lower vantage, it looked truly imposing, with those three tiers.

Almost looks man-made, Adolin thought idly, considering the shape. 'Nearly,' Adolin agreed. 'Can you imagine what an assault would look like if we had twenty or thirty Shardbearers on the battlefield at once? What chance would the Parshendi have?'

Jakamav grunted. 'Your father and the king are seriously committed to this course, aren't they?'

'As am I.'

'I can see what you and your father are doing here, Adolin. But if you keep dueling, you're going to lose your Shards. Even you can't *always* win. Eventually you'll hit an off day. Then it will all be gone.'

'I might lose at some point,' Adolin agreed. 'Of course by then I'll have won half the Shards in the kingdom, so I should be able to arrange a replacement.'

Jakamav sipped his wine, smiling. 'You are a cocky bastard, I'll give you that.'

Adolin smiled, then settled down in a squat beside Jakamav's chair – he couldn't sit in one himself, not in Shardplate – so he could meet his friend's eyes. 'The truth is, Jakamav, I'm not really worried about losing my Shards – I'm more worried about finding duels in the *first* place. I can't seem to get any Shardbearers to agree to a bout, at least not for Shards.'

'There have been certain . . . inducements going around,' Jakamav admitted. 'Promises made to Shardbearers if they refused you.'

'Sadeas.'

Jakamav inspected his wine. 'Try Eranniv. He's been boasting that he's better than the standings give him credit for. Knowing him, he'll see everyone else refusing, and see it as an opportunity for him to do something spectacular. He's pretty good, though.'

'So am I,' Adolin said. 'Thanks, Jak. I owe you.'

'What's this I hear about you being betrothed?'

Storms. How had that gotten out? 'It's just a causal,' Adolin said. 'And it might not even get that far. The woman's ship seems to have been severely delayed.'

Two weeks now, with no word. Even Aunt Navani was getting worried. Jasnah should have sent word.

'I never thought you were the type to let yourself be nailed into an arranged marriage, Adolin,' Jakamav said. 'There are lots of winds to ride out there, you know?'

'Like I said,' Adolin replied, 'it's far from official.'

He still didn't know how he felt about all this. Part of him had wanted to push back simply because he resisted being subject to Jasnah's manipulation. But then, his recent track record wasn't anything to boast of. After what had happened with Danlan . . . It wasn't his fault, was it, that he was a friendly man? Why did every woman have to be so jealous?

The idea of letting someone else just take care of it all for him was more tempting than he'd ever publicly admit.

'I can tell you the details,' Adolin said. 'Maybe at the winehouse later tonight? Bring Inkima? You can tell me how stupid I'm being, give me some perspective.'

Jakamav stared at his wine.

'What?' Adolin asked.

'Being seen with you isn't good for one's reputation these days, Adolin,' Jakamav said. 'Your father and the king aren't particularly popular.'

'It will all blow over.'

'I'm sure it will,' Jakamav said. 'So let's . . . wait until then, shall we?'

Adolin blinked, the words hitting him harder than any blow on the battlefield. 'Sure,' Adolin forced himself to say.

'Good man.' Jakamav actually had the audacity to smile at him and lift his cup of wine.

Adolin set aside his own cup untouched and stalked off.

Sureblood was ready and waiting for him when he reached his men. Adolin moved to swing into the saddle, stewing, but the white Ryshadium nudged him with a butt of the head. Adolin sighed, scratching at the horse's ears. 'Sorry,' he said. 'Haven't been paying much attention to you lately, have I?'

He gave the horse a good scratch, and felt somewhat better after climbing into the saddle. Adolin patted Sureblood's neck, and the horse pranced a bit as they started moving. He often did that when Adolin was feeling annoyed, as if trying to improve his master's mood.

His four guards for the day followed behind him. They'd obligingly brought their old bridge from Sadeas's army to get Adolin's team where they needed to go. They seemed to find it very amusing that Adolin had his soldiers take shifts carrying the thing.

Storming Jakamav. *This has been coming,* Adolin admitted to himself. *The more you defend Father, the more they'll pull away.* They were like children. Father really *was* right.

Did Adolin have *any* true friends? Anyone who would actually stand by him when things were difficult? He knew practically everyone of note in the warcamps. Everyone knew him.

How many of them actually cared?

'I didn't have a fit,' Renarin said softly.

Adolin shook out of his brooding. They rode side by side, though Adolin's mount was several hands taller. With Adolin astride a Ryshadium, Renarin looked like a child on a pony by comparison, even in his Plate.

Clouds had rolled across the sun, giving some relief from the glare, though the air had turned cold lately and it looked like winter was here for a season. The empty plateaus stretched ahead, barren and broken.

'I just stood there,' Renarin said. 'I wasn't frozen because of my ...
ailment. I'm just a coward.'

'You're no coward,' Adolin said. 'I've seen you act as brave as any man.
Remember the chasmfiend hunt?'

Renarin shrugged.

'You don't know how to fight, Renarin,' Adolin said. 'It's a good thing
you froze. You're too new at this to go into battle right now.'

'I shouldn't be. You started training when you were six.'

'That's different.'

'You're different, you mean,' Renarin said, eyes forward. He wasn't
wearing his spectacles. Why was that? Didn't he need them?

Trying to act like he doesn't, Adolin thought. Renarin so desperately
wanted to be useful on a battlefield. He'd resisted all suggestions that he
should become an ardent and pursue scholarship, as might have better
suited him.

'You just need more training,' Adolin said. 'Zahel will whip you into
shape. Just give it time. You'll see.'

'I need to be ready,' Renarin said. 'Something is coming.'

The way he said it gave Adolin a shiver. 'You're talking about the numbers on the walls.'

Renarin nodded. They'd found another scratched set of them, after the
recent highstorm, outside Father's room. *Forty-nine days. A new storm
comes.*

According to the guards, nobody had gone in or out – different men
from last time, which made it unlikely it had been one of them. Storms.
That had been scratched on the wall while Adolin had been sleeping just
one room away. Who, or what, had done it?

'Need to be ready,' Renarin said. 'For the coming storm. So little
time ...'

27

FABRICATIONS TO DISTRACT

FIVE YEARS AGO

Shallan longed to stay outside. Here in the gardens, people didn't scream at each other. Here there was peace.

Unfortunately, it was a fake peace – a peace of carefully planted shalebark and cultivated vines. A fabrication, designed to amuse and distract. More and more she longed to escape and visit places where the plants weren't carefully trimmed into shapes, where people didn't step lightly, as if afraid of causing a rockslide. A place away from the shouting.

A cool mountain breeze came down from the heights and swept through the gardens, making vines shy backward. She sat away from the flowerbeds, and the sneezing they would bring her, instead studying a section of sturdy shalebark. The cremling she sketched turned at the wind, its enormous feelers twitching, before leaning back down to chew on the shalebark. There were so *many* kinds of cremlings. Had anyone tried to count them all?

By luck, her father had owned a drawing book – one of the works of Dandos the Oilsworn – and she used that for instruction, letting it rest open beside her.

A yell sounded from inside the nearby manor house. Shallan's hand stiffened, making an errant streak across her sketch. She took a deep breath and tried to return to her drawing, but another series of shouts put her on edge. She set her pencil down.

She was nearly out of sheets from the latest stack her brother had brought her. He returned unpredictably but never for long, and when he came, he and Father avoided one another.

Nobody in the manor knew where Helaran went when he left.

She lost track of time, staring at a blank sheet of paper. That happened to her sometimes. When she raised her eyes, the sky was darkening. Almost time for Father's feast. He had those regularly now.

Shallan packed up her things in the satchel, then took off her sun hat and walked toward the manor house. Tall and imposing, the building was an exemplar of the Veden ideal. Solitary, strong, towering. A work of square blocks and small windows, dappled by dark lichen. Some books called manors like this the soul of Jah Keved – isolated estates, each brightlord ruling independently. It seemed to her that those writers romanticized rural life. Had they ever actually visited one of the manors, experienced the true dullness of country life in person, or did they merely fantasize about it from the comfort of their cosmopolitan cities?

Inside the house, Shallan turned up the stairs toward her quarters. Father would want her looking nice for the feast. There would be a new dress for her to wear as she sat quietly, not interrupting the discussion. Father had never said so, but she suspected he thought it a pity she had begun speaking again.

Perhaps he did not wish her to be able to speak of things she'd seen. She stopped in the hallway, her mind going blank.

'Shallan?'

She shook herself to find Van Jushu, her fourth brother, on the steps behind her. How long had she been standing and staring at the wall? The feast would start soon!

Jushu's jacket was undone and hung askew, his hair mussed, his cheeks flushed with wine. No cufflinks or belt; they had been fine pieces, each with a glowing gemstone. He'd have gambled those away.

'What was Father yelling about earlier?' she asked. 'Were you here?'

'No,' Jushu said, running his hand through his hair. 'But I heard. Balat has been starting fires again. Nearly burned down the storming servants' building.' Jushu pushed past her, then stumbled, grabbing the bannister to keep from falling.

Father was not going to like Jushu coming to the feast like this. More yelling.

'Storms-cursed idiot,' Jushu said as Shallan helped him right himself. 'Balat is going straight crazy. I'm the only one left in this family with any sense. You were staring at the wall again, weren't you?'

She didn't reply.

'He'll have a new dress for you,' Jushu said as she helped him toward his room. 'And nothing for me but curses. Bastard. He loved Helaran, and none of us are him, so we don't matter. Helaran is never here! He betrayed Father, almost killed him. And still, he's the only one who matters. . . .'

They passed Father's chambers. The heavy stumpweight door was open a crack as a maid tidied the room, allowing Shallan to see the far wall.

And the glowing strongbox.

It was hidden behind a painting of a storm at sea that did nothing to dim the powerful white glow. Right through the canvas, she saw the outline of the strongbox blazing like a fire. She stumbled, pulling to a stop.

'What are you staring at?' Jushu demanded, holding to the bannister.

'The light.'

'What light?'

'Behind the painting.'

He squinted, lurching forward. 'What in the Halls are you talking about, girl? It really did ruin your mind, didn't it? Watching him kill Mother?' Jushu pulled away from her, cursing softly to himself. 'I'm the only one in this family who hasn't gone crazy. The only storming one . . .'

Shallan stared into that light. There hid a monster.

There hid Mother's soul.

28

BOOTS

The betrayal of spren has brought us here.
They gave their Surges to human heirs,
But not to those who know them most dear, before us.
'Tis no surprise we turned away
Unto the gods we spent our days
And to become their molding clay, they changed us.

—From the Listener Song of Secrets, 40th stanza

'Th'information'll cost ya twelve broams,' Shallan said. 'Ruby, you see. I'll check each one.'

Tyn laughed, tossing her head back, jet-black hair falling free around her shoulders. She sat in the driver's seat of the wagon. Where Bluth used to sit.

'You call *that* a Bav accent?' Tyn demanded.

'I've only heard them three or four times.'

'You sounded like you have rocks in your mouth!'

'That's how they sound!'

'Nah, it's more like they have pebbles in their mouths. But they talk really slow, with overemphasized sounds. Like this. "Oi looked over the paintings that ya gave me, and they're roit nice. Roit nice indeed. Ain't never had a cloth for my backside that was so pleasant."'

'You're exaggerating that!' Shallan said, though she couldn't help laughing.

'A tad,' Tyn said, leaning back and sweeping her long, chull-guiding reed in front of her like a Shardblade.

'I don't see why knowing a Bav accent would be useful,' Shallan said. 'They're not a very important people.'

'Kid, that's *why* they're important.'

'They're important because they're unimportant,' Shallan said. 'All right, I know I'm bad at logic sometimes, but something about that statement seems off.'

Tyn smiled. She was so relaxed, so . . . free. Not at all what Shallan had expected after their first encounter.

But then the woman had been playing a part. Leader of the guard. This woman Shallan was talking to now, this seemed real.

'Look,' Tyn said, 'if you're going to fool people, you'll need to learn how to act beneath them as well as above them. You're getting the whole "important lighteyes" thing down. I assume you've had good examples.'

'You could say that,' Shallan replied, thinking of Jasnah.

'Thing is, in a lot of situations, being an important lighteyes is useless.'

'Being unimportant is important. Being important is useless. Got it.'

Tyn eyed her, chewing on some jerky. Her sword belt hung from a peg on the side of the seat, swaying to the rhythm of the chull's gait. 'You know, kid, you get kind of mouthy when you let your mask down.'

Shallan blushed.

'I like it. I prefer people who can laugh at life.'

'I can guess what you're trying to teach me,' Shallan said. 'You're saying that a person with a Bav accent, someone who looks lowly and simple, can go places a lighteyes never could.'

'And can hear or do things a lighteyes never could. Accent is important. Elocute with distinction, and it often won't matter how little money you have. Wipe your nose on your arm and speak like a Bav, and sometimes people won't even glance to see if you're wearing a sword.'

'But my eyes are light blue,' Shallan said. 'I'll never pass for lowly, no matter what my voice sounds like!'

Tyn fished in her trouser pocket. She had slung her coat over another peg, and so wore only the pale tan trousers – tight, with high boots – and a buttoned shirt. Almost a worker's shirt, though of nicer material.

'Here,' Tyn said, tossing something to her.

Shallan barely caught it. She blushed at her clumsiness, then held it up toward the sun: a small vial with some dark liquid inside.

'Eyedrops,' Tyn said. 'They'll darken your eyes for a few hours.'

'*Really?*'

'Not hard to find, if you have the right connections. Useful stuff.'

Shallan lowered the vial, suddenly feeling a chill. 'Is there—'

'The reverse?' Tyn cut in. 'Something to turn a darkeyes into a lighteyes? Not that I know of. Unless you believe the stories about Shardblades.'

'Makes sense,' Shallan said, relaxing. 'You can darken glass by painting it, but I don't think you can lighten it without melting down the whole thing.'

'Anyway,' Tyn said, 'you'll need a good backwater accent or two. Herdazian, Bavlander, something like that.'

'I probably *have* a rural Veden accent,' Shallan admitted.

'That won't work out here. Jah Keved is a cultured country, and your internal accents are too similar to one another for outsiders to recognize. Alethi won't hear rural from you, like a fellow Veden would. They'll just hear exotic.'

'You've been to a lot of places, haven't you?' Shallan asked.

'I go wherever the winds take me. It's a good life, so long as you're not attached to stuff.'

'Stuff?' Shallan asked. 'But you're – pardon – you're a *thief*. That's all about getting more stuff!'

'I take what I can get, but that just proves how transient *stuff* is. You'll take some things, but then you'll lose them. Just like the job I pulled down south. My team never returned from their mission; I'm half convinced they ran off without seeing me paid.' She shrugged. 'It happens. No need to get worked up.'

'What kind of job was it?' Shallan asked, blinking pointedly to take a Memory of Tyn lounging there, sweeping her reed as if conducting musicians, not a care in the world. They'd nearly died a couple of weeks back, but Tyn took it in stride.

'It was a big job,' Tyn said. 'Important, for the kinds of people who make things change in the world. I still haven't heard back from the ones who hired us. Maybe my men didn't run off; maybe they just failed. I don't know for certain.' Here, Shallan caught tension in Tyn's face. A tightening of the skin around the eyes, a distance to her gaze. She was worried about what her employers might do to her. Then it was gone, smoothed away. 'Have a look,' Tyn said, nodding up ahead.

Shallan followed the gesture and noticed moving figures a few hills over. The landscape had slowly changed as they approached the Plains. The hills grew steeper, but the air a little warmer, and plant life was more prevalent. Stands of trees clustered in some of the valleys, where waters would flow after highstorms. The trees were squat, different from the flowing majesty of the ones she'd known in Jah Keved, but it was still nice to see something other than scrub.

The grass here was fuller. It pulled smartly away from the wagons, sinking into its burrows. The rockbuds here grew large, and shalebark cropped up in patches, often with lifespren bouncing about like tiny green motes. During their days traveling they'd passed other caravans, more plentiful now that they were closer to the Shattered Plains. So Shallan wasn't surprised to see someone up ahead. The figures, however, rode *horses*. Who could afford animals like that? And why didn't they have an escort? There seemed to be only four of them.

The caravan rolled to a stop as Macob yelled an order from the first wagon. Shallan had learned, through awful experience, just how dangerous *any* encounter out here could be. None were taken lightly by caravan masters. She was the authority here, but she allowed those with more experience to call stops and choose their path.

'Come on,' Tyn said, stopping the chull with a whack of the stick, then hopping down from the wagon and grabbing her coat and sword off their pegs.

Shallan scrambled down, putting on her Jasnah face. She let herself be herself with Tyn. With the others, she needed to be a leader. Stiff, stern, but hopefully inspiring. To that end, she was pleased with the blue dress that Macob had given her. Embroidered with silver, made of the finest silk, it was a wonderful upgrade from her tattered one.

They walked past where Vathah and his men marched just behind the lead wagon. The leader of the deserters shot Tyn a glare. His dislike of the woman was only more reason to respect her, despite her criminal proclivities.

'Brightness Davar and I will handle this,' Tyn said to Macob as they passed.

'Brightness?' Macob said, standing and looking toward Shallan. 'What if they are bandits?'

'There are only four of them, Master Macob,' Shallan said lightly. 'The day I can't handle four bandits on my own is a day I deserve to be robbed.'

They passed the wagon, Tyn tying on her belt.

'What if they *are* bandits?' Shallan hissed once they were out of earshot.

'I thought you said you could handle four.'

'I was just going along with your attitude!'

'That's dangerous, kid,' Tyn said with a grin. 'Look, bandits wouldn't let us see them, and they *certainly* wouldn't just sit there.'

The group of four men waited on the top of the hill. As Shallan drew closer, she could see that they were wearing crisp blue uniforms that looked quite genuine. At the bottom of the ravine between hills, Shallan stubbed her toe on a rockbud. She grimaced – Macob had given her lighteyed shoes to match her dress. They were luxurious, and probably worth a fortune, but they were little more than slippers.

'We'll wait here,' Shallan said. 'They can come to us.'

'Sounds good to me,' Tyn said. Indeed, up above, the men started moving down the hillside when they noticed Shallan and Tyn were waiting for them. Two more came and followed after them on foot, men not in uniforms, but workers' clothing. Grooms?

'Who are you going to be?' Tyn asked softly.

'. . . Myself?' Shallan replied.

'What's the fun in that?' Tyn said. 'How's your Horneater?'

'Horneater! I—'

'Too late,' Tyn said as the men rode up.

Shallan found horses intimidating. The large brutish things weren't docile like chulls. Horses were always stomping about, snorting.

The lead rider reined in his horse with some obvious annoyance. He didn't seem in complete control of the beast. 'Brightness,' he said, nodding to her as he saw her eyes. Shockingly, he was darkeyed, a tall man with black Alethi hair he wore down to his shoulders. He looked over Tyn, noting the sword and the soldier's uniform, but let slip no reaction. A hard man, this one.

'Her Highness,' Tyn announced in a loud voice, gesturing toward

Shallan, 'Princess Unulukuak'kina'autu'atai! You are in the presence of royalty, darkeyes!'

'A Horneater?' the man said, leaning down, inspecting Shallan's red hair. 'Wearing a Vorin dress. Rock would have a fit.'

Tyn looked to Shallan and raised an eyebrow.

I'm going to strangle you, woman, Shallan thought, then took a deep breath. 'This thing,' Shallan said, gesturing at her dress. 'He is not what you have a princess wear? He is good for me. You will be respect!' Fortunately, her red face would fit for a Horneater. They were a passionate people.

Tyn nodded to her, looking appreciative.

'I'm sorry,' the man said, though he didn't seem very apologetic. What was a darkeyes doing riding an animal of such value? One of the man's companions was inspecting the caravan through a spyglass. He was dark-eyed too, but looked more comfortable on his mount.

'Seven wagons, Kal,' the man said. 'Well guarded.'

The man, Kal, nodded. 'I've been sent out to look for signs of bandits,' he said to Tyn. 'Has all been well with your caravan?'

'We ran into some bandits three weeks ago,' Tyn said, thumbing over her shoulder. 'Why do you care?'

'We represent the king,' the man said. 'And are from the personal guard of Dalinar Kholin.'

Oh, *storms*. Well, that was going to be inconvenient.

'Brightlord Kholin,' Kal continued, 'is investigating the possibility of a wider range of control around the Shattered Plains. If you really were attacked, I would like to know the details.'

'*If* we were attacked?' Shallan asked. 'You doubt our word?'

'No—'

'I am offend!' Shallan declared, folding her arms.

'You'd better watch yourself,' Tyn told the men. 'Her Highness does not like to be offended.'

'How surprising,' Kal said. 'Where did the attack take place? You fought it off? How many bandits were there?'

Tyn filled him in on the details, which gave Shallan a chance to think. Dalinar Kholin was her future father-in-law, if the causal matured into a marriage. Hopefully, she wouldn't run into these particular soldiers again.

I really am going to strangle you, Tyn. . . .

Their leader listened to the details of the attack with a stoic air. He didn't seem like a very pleasant man.

'I am sorry to hear of your losses,' Kal said. 'But you're only a day and a half by caravan from the Shattered Plains now. You should be safe the rest of the way.'

'I am curiosity,' Shallan said. 'These animals, they are horses? Yet you are darkeyed. This . . . Kholin trusts you well.'

'I do my duty,' Kal said, studying her. 'Where are the rest of your people? That caravan looks as if it's all Vorin. Also, you look a little spindly for a Horneater.'

'Did you just insult the princess's weight?' Tyn asked, aghast.

Storms! She was good. She actually managed to produce angerspren with the remark.

Well, nothing to do but soldier on.

'I am offend!' Shallan yelled.

'You have offended Her Highness again!'

'*Very* offend!'

'You'd better apologize.'

'No apologize!' Shallan declared. 'Boots!'

Kal leaned back, looking between the two of them, trying to parse what had just been said. 'Boots?' he asked.

'Yes,' Shallan said. 'I am liking your boots. You will apology with boots.'

'You . . . want my boots?'

'Did you not hear Her Highness?' Tyn asked, arms folded. 'Are soldiers of this Dalinar Kholin's army so disrespectful?'

'I'm not disrespectful,' Kal said. 'But I'm not giving her my boots.'

'You insult!' Shallan declared, stepping forward, pointing at him. Stormfather, those horses were enormous! 'I will tell all who are to listen! When arriving, I will say, "Kholin is stealer of boots and taker of women's virtue!"'

Kal sputtered. 'Virtue!'

'Yes,' Shallan said; then she glanced over to Tyn. 'Virtue? No, wrong word. Virture . . . No . . . Vesture. Vesture! Taker of woman's vesture! That is word I wanted.'

The soldier glanced to his companions, looking confused. *Drat,* Shallan thought. *Good puns are lost on men with poor vocabulary.*

'Is no matter,' Shallan said, throwing up her hand. 'All will know what you have done in wronging me. You have laid me bare, here in this wilderness. Stripping me! Is an insult to my house and my clan. All will know that Kholin—'

'Oh, stop, stop,' Kal said, reaching down and awkwardly pulling his boot from his foot while on horseback. His sock had a hole in the heel. 'Storming woman,' he muttered. He tossed the first boot down to her, then removed the other.

'Your apology is accepted,' Tyn said, fetching the boots.

'By Damnation, it had better be,' Kal said. 'I'll pass along your story. Maybe we can get this storming place patrolled. Come on, men.' He turned and left them without another word, perhaps fearing another Horneater diatribe.

Once they were out of earshot, Shallan looked at the boots, then started laughing uncontrollably. Joyspren rose around her, like blue leaves that started at her feet then moved up in a swirl before flaring out above her as if in a blast of wind. Shallan watched them with a big smile. Those were very rare.

'Ah,' Tyn said with a smile. 'No use denying. That was fun.'

'I'm *still* going to strangle you,' Shallan said. 'He knew we were playing with him. That has to be the worst Horneater impression a woman has ever done.'

'It was actually pretty good,' Tyn said. 'You overdid the words, but the accent itself was spot on. That wasn't the point, though.' She handed back the boots.

'What *was* the point?' Shallan asked as they hiked back toward the caravan. 'Making a fool out of me?'

'Partially,' Tyn said.

'That was sarcasm.'

'If you're going to learn to do this,' Tyn said, 'you have to be comfortable in situations like that. You can't be embarrassed when you pose as someone else. The more outrageous the attempt, the straighter you have to play it. The only way to get better is to practice – and in front of people who very well might catch you.'

'I suppose,' Shallan said.

'Those boots are too big for you,' Tyn noted. 'Though I *did* love the look on his face when you asked for them. 'No apologize. Boots!''

'I *really* need some boots,' Shallan said. 'I'm tired of walking around on rock barefoot or in slippers. A little padding, and these will fit.' She held them up. They *were* rather large. 'Er, maybe.' She looked backward. 'I hope he'll be all right without them. What if he has to fight bandits on his way back?'

Tyn rolled her eyes. 'We're going to have to talk about that kindheartedness of yours sometime, kid.'

'It's not a bad thing to be nice.'

'You're training to be a con artist,' Tyn said. 'For now, let's get back to the caravan. I want to talk you through the finer points of a Horneater accent. With that red hair of yours, you'll probably find more chances to use it than you would others.'

Artform for colors beyond our ken;
For its grand songs we yearn.
We must attract creationspren;
These songs suffice 'til we learn.

—From the Listener Song of Revision, 279th stanza

Torol Sadeas closed his eyes and rested Oathbringer on his shoulder, breathing in the sweet, moldy scent of Parshendi blood. The Thrill of battle surged within him, a blessed and beautiful strength.

His own blood pumped so loudly in his ears he almost couldn't hear the battlefield shouts and groans of pain. For a moment, he reveled only in the delicious glow of the Thrill, the heady euphoria at having spent an hour engaged in the only thing that brought true joy anymore: contending for his life, and taking those of enemies lesser than himself.

It faded. As always, the Thrill was fleeting once battle itself ended. It had grown less and less sweet during these raids on the Parshendi, likely because he knew deep inside that this contest was pointless. It did not stretch him, did not carry him further toward his ultimate goals of conquest. Slaughtering crem-covered savages in a Heralds-forsaken land had truly lost its savor.

He sighed, lowering his Blade, opening his eyes. Amaram approached across the battlefield, stepping over corpses of men and Parshendi. His Shardplate was bloodied purple up to the elbows, and he carried a glimmering gemheart in one gauntleted hand. He kicked aside a Parshendi corpse and joined Sadeas, his own honor guard fanning out to join those of his highprince. Sadeas spared a moment of annoyance for how efficiently they moved, particularly when compared to his own men.

Amaram pulled off his helm and hefted the gemheart, tossing it up and catching it. 'Your maneuver here today failed, you realize?'

'Failed?' Sadeas said, lifting his faceplate. Nearby, his soldiers slaughtered a pocket of fifty Parshendi who hadn't managed to get off the plateau when the rest retreated. 'I think this went quite nicely.'

Amaram pointed. A stain had appeared on the plateaus to the west, toward the warcamps. The banners indicated that Hatham and Roion, the two highprinces who were *supposed* to have gone on this plateau run, had arrived together – they used bridges like Dalinar's, slow plodding things it had been easy to outrun. One of the advantages of the bridge crews Sadeas preferred was that they needed very little training to function. If Dalinar had thought to slow him down with his stunt of trading Oathbringer for Sadeas's bridgemen, he had been proven a fool.

'We needed to get out here,' Amaram said, 'seize the gemheart, and return before the others arrived. Then you could have claimed that you didn't realize you weren't in the rotation today. The arrival of both other armies removes that shred of deniability.'

'You mistake me,' Sadeas said. 'You assume I still care about deniability.' The last Parshendi died with enraged screams; Sadeas felt proud of that. Others said Parshendi warriors on the field never surrendered, but he'd seen them try it once, long ago, in the first year of the war. They'd laid down their weapons. He'd slaughtered them all personally, with Shardhammer and Plate, beneath the eyes of their retreating companions watching from a nearby plateau.

Never again had any Parshendi denied him or his men their right to finish a battle the proper way. Sadeas waved for the vanguard to gather and escort him back to the warcamps while the rest of the army licked its wounds. Amaram joined him, crossing a bridge and passing idling bridgemen who lay on the ground and slept while better men died.

'I am duty-bound to join you on the battlefield, Your Highness,'

Amaram said as they walked, 'but I want you to know that I do not approve of our actions here. We should be seeking to bridge our differences with the king and Dalinar, not trying to agitate them further.'

Sadeas snorted. 'Don't give me that noble talk. It works fine for others, but I know you for the ruthless bastard you really are.'

Amaram set his jaw, eyes forward. When they reached their horses, he reached out, hand on Sadeas's arm. 'Torol,' he said softly, 'there is so much more to the world than your squabbles. You're right about me, of course. Take that admission with the understanding that to you, above all others, I can speak the truth. Alethkar needs to be strong for what is coming.'

Sadeas climbed the mounting block the groom had set out. Getting onto a horse in Shardplate could be dangerous to the animal if not done correctly. Besides, he'd once had a stirrup snap on him when he stepped into it to haul himself into the saddle. He'd ended up on his backside.

'Alethkar does need to be strong,' Sadeas said, holding out a gauntleted hand. 'So I'll make it so by force of fist and the rule of blood.'

Amaram reluctantly placed the gemheart there, and Sadeas gripped it, holding his reins in the other hand.

'Do you ever worry?' Amaram asked. 'About what you do? About what *we* must do?' He nodded toward a group of surgeons, carrying wounded men across the bridges.

'Worry?' Sadeas said. 'Why should I? It gives the wretches a chance to die in battle for something worthwhile.'

'You say things like that a lot these days, I've noticed,' Amaram said. 'You weren't like that before.'

'I've learned to accept the world as it is, Amaram,' Sadeas said, turning his horse. 'That's something very few people are willing to do. They stumble along, hoping, dreaming, pretending. That doesn't change a single storming thing in life. You have to stare the world in the eyes, in all its grimy brutality. You have to acknowledge its depravities. Live with them. It's the only way to accomplish anything meaningful.'

With a squeeze of the knees, Sadeas started his horse forward, leaving Amaram behind for the moment.

The man would remain loyal. Sadeas and Amaram had an understanding. Even Amaram now being a Shardbearer would not change that.

As Sadeas and his vanguard approached Hatham's army, he noticed a group of Parshendi on a nearby plateau, watching. Those scouts of theirs were getting bold. He sent a team of archers to go chase them off, then rode toward a figure in resplendent Shardplate at the front of Hatham's army: the highprince himself, seated upon a Ryshadium. Damnation. Those animals were far superior to any other horseflesh. How to get one?

'Sadeas?' Hatham called out to him. 'What have you *done* here?'

After a quick moment of decision, Sadeas lifted his arm back and hurled the gemheart across the plateau separating them. It hit the rock near Hatham and bounced along in a roll, glowing faintly.

'I was bored,' Sadeas shouted back. 'I thought I'd save you some trouble.'

Then, ignoring further questions, Sadeas continued on his way. Adolin Kholin had a duel today, and he'd decided not to miss it, just in case the youth embarrassed himself again.

※

A few hours later, Sadeas settled down into his place in the dueling arena, tugging at the stock on his neck. Insufferable things – fashionable, but insufferable. He would never tell a soul, not even Ialai, that he secretly wished he could just go about in a simple uniform like Dalinar.

He couldn't ever do that, of course. Not just because he wouldn't be seen bowing to the Codes and the king's authority, but because a military uniform was actually the *wrong* uniform for these days. The battles they fought for Alethkar at the moment weren't battles with sword and shield.

It was important to dress the part when you had a role to play. Dalinar's military outfits proved he was lost, that he didn't understand the game he was playing.

Sadeas leaned back to wait as whispers filled the arena like water in a bowl. A large attendance today. Adolin's stunt in his previous duel had drawn attention, and anything novel was of interest to the court. Sadeas's seat had a space cleared around it to give him extra room and privacy, though it was really just a simple chair built onto the stone bleachers of this pit of an arena.

He hated how his body felt outside of Shardplate, and he hated more how he looked. Once, he'd turned heads as he walked. His power had filled a room; everyone had looked to him, and many had *lusted* when seeing him. Lusted for his power, for who he was.

He was losing that. Oh, he was still powerful – perhaps more so. But the look in their eyes was different. And every way of responding to his loss of youthfulness made him look petulant.

He was dying, step by step. Like every man, true, but he *felt* that death looming. Decades away, hopefully, but it cast a long, long shadow. The only path to immortality was through conquest.

Rustling cloth announced Ialai slipping into the seat beside his. Sadeas reached out absently, resting his hand on the small of her back and scratching at that place she liked. Her name was symmetrical. A tiny bit of blasphemy from her parents – some people dared imply such holiness of their children. Sadeas liked those types. Indeed, the name was what had first intrigued him about her.

'Mmmm,' his wife said with a sigh. 'Very nice. The duel hasn't started yet, I see.'

'Mere moments away, I believe.'

'Good. I can't stand waiting. I hear you gave away the gemheart you captured today.'

'Threw it at Hatham's feet and rode away, as if I didn't have a care.'

'Clever. I should have seen that as an option. You'll undermine Dalinar's claim that we only resist him because of our greed.'

Below, Adolin finally stepped out onto the field, wearing his blue Shardplate. Some of the lighteyes clapped politely. Across the way, Eranniv left his own preparatory room, his polished Plate its natural color except across the breastplate, which he'd painted a deep black.

Sadeas narrowed his eyes, still scratching Ialai's back. 'This duel should not even be happening,' he said. 'Everyone was supposed to be too afraid, or too dismissive, to accept his challenges.'

'Idiots,' Ialai said softly. 'They know, Torol, what they're supposed to do – I've dropped the right hints and promises. And yet every one of them secretly wants to be the man who brings down Adolin. Duelists are not a particularly dependable lot. They are brash, hotheaded, and care too much about showing off and gaining renown.'

'His father's plan cannot be allowed to work,' Sadeas said.

'It won't.'

Sadeas glanced at where Dalinar had set up. Sadeas's own position was not too far away – within shouting distance. Dalinar didn't look at him.

'I built this kingdom,' Sadeas said softly. 'I know how fragile it is, Ialai.

It should not be so difficult to knock the thing down.' That would be the only way to properly build it anew. Like reforging a weapon. You melted down the remnants of the old before you created the replacement.

The duel began down below, Adolin striding across the sands toward Eranniv, who wielded old Gavilar's Blade, with its wicked design. Adolin engaged too quickly. Was the boy that eager?

In the crowd, lighteyes grew quiet and darkeyes shouted, eager for another display like last time. However, this didn't devolve into a wrestling match. The two exchanged testing blows and Adolin backed away, having taken a hit on his shoulder.

Sloppy, Sadeas thought.

'I finally discovered the nature of that disturbance at the king's chambers two weeks ago,' Ialai noted.

Sadeas smiled, eyes still on the bout. 'Of course you did.'

'Assassination attempt,' she said. 'Someone sabotaged the king's balcony in a crude attempt at dropping him a hundred feet to the rocks. From what I hear, it nearly worked.'

'Not so crude then, if it almost killed him.'

'Pardon, Torol, but *almost* is a big distinction in assassinations.'

True.

Sadeas searched within himself, seeking some sign of emotion at hearing that Elhokar had almost died. He found none beside a faint sense of pity. He was fond of the boy, but to rebuild Alethkar, all vestiges of former rule would need to be removed. Elhokar would need to die. Preferably in a quiet manner, after Dalinar had been dealt with. Sadeas expected he'd have to cut the boy's throat himself, out of respect for old Gavilar.

'Who commissioned the assassins, do you suppose?' Sadeas asked, speaking softly enough that – with the buffer his guards kept around their seats – he didn't have to worry about being overheard.

'Hard to tell,' Ialai replied, scooting to the side and twisting to get him to scratch a different part of her back. 'It wouldn't be Ruthar or Aladar.'

Both were solidly in Sadeas's palm. Aladar with some resignation, Ruthar eagerly. Roion was too much a coward, others too careful. Who else could have done it?

'Thanadal,' Sadeas guessed.

'He's the most likely. But I will see what I can discover.'

'It might be the same ones as with the king's armor,' Sadeas said.

'Perhaps we could find out more if I exercise my authority.'

Sadeas was Highprince of Information – one of the old designations, from previous centuries, which split duties in the kingdom among high-princes. It technically gave Sadeas authority over investigations and policing.

'Perhaps,' Ialai said hesitantly.

'But?'

She shook her head, watching another exchange of the duelists down below. This bout of fighting left Adolin with Stormlight streaming from one gauntlet, to the booing of some of the darkeyes. Why were those people even allowed in? There were lighteyes who were unable to attend because Elhokar reserved seating for their inferiors.

'Dalinar,' Ialai said, 'has responded to our ploy of making you High-prince of Information. He used it as precedent for making himself Highprince of War. And so now, every step you take invoking your rights as Highprince of Information cements *his* authority over this conflict.'

Sadeas nodded. 'You have a plan, then?'

'Not quite yet,' Ialai said. 'But I'm forming one. You've noticed how he started up patrols outside of the camps? And in the Outer Market. Should that be your duty?'

'No, that's the job of a Highprince of Commerce, which the king hasn't appointed. However, I *should* have authority over policing all ten camps, and appointing judges and magistrates. He should have involved me the moment an attempt was made on the king's life. But he didn't.' Sadeas chewed on the thought for a moment, removing his hand from Ialai's back, letting her sit up straight.

'There is a weakness here we can exploit,' Sadeas said. 'Dalinar has always had a problem giving up authority. He never *really* trusts anyone to do their job. He didn't come to me when he should have. This weakens his claims that all parts of the kingdom should work together. It's a chink in his armor. Can you ram a dagger in it?'

Ialai nodded. She'd use her informants to start questions in court: Why, if Dalinar was trying to forge a better Alethkar, was he unwilling to give up any power? Why hadn't he involved Sadeas in the king's protection? Why wouldn't he open his doors to Sadeas's judges?

What authority did the Throne have, really, if it made assignments like the one to Sadeas, only to pretend they hadn't been given?

'You should renounce your appointment as Highprince of Information in protest,' Ialai said.

'No. Not yet. We wait until the rumors have nipped at old Dalinar, made him decide he needs to let me do my job. Then, the moment before he tries to involve me, I renounce.'

It would widen the cracks that way, both in Dalinar, and in the kingdom itself.

Adolin's bout continued below. He certainly didn't look like his heart was in it. He kept leaving himself open, taking hits. This was the youth who had bragged about his skill so often? He was good, of course, but not nearly *that* good. Not as good as Sadeas had himself seen when the boy had been on the battlefield fighting the . . .

He was faking.

Sadeas found himself grinning. 'Now that's almost *clever*,' he said softly.

'What?' Ialai asked.

'Adolin is fighting beneath his capacity,' Sadeas explained as the youth got a hit – barely – on Eranniv's helm. 'He's reluctant to display his real skill, as he fears it will scare others away from dueling him. If he looks *barely* capable enough to win this fight, others might decide to pounce.'

Ialai narrowed her eyes, watching the fight. 'Are you sure? Couldn't he just be having an off day?'

'I'm sure,' Sadeas said. Now that he knew what to watch for, he could easily read it in Adolin's specific moves, the way he teased Eranniv to attack him, then barely fended off the blows. Adolin Kholin was cleverer than Sadeas had given him credit for.

Better at dueling as well. It took skill to win a bout – but it took *true mastery* to win while making it look the whole time that you were behind. As the fight progressed, the crowd got into it, and Adolin made it a close contest. Sadeas doubted many others would see what he did.

When Adolin, moving lethargically and leaking Light from a dozen hits – all carefully allowed on different sections of Plate, so none shattered and exposed him to real danger – managed to bring down Eranniv with a 'lucky' blow at the end, the crowd roared in appreciation. Even the lighteyes seemed drawn in.

Eranniv stormed off, shouting about Adolin's luck, but Sadeas found himself quite impressed. *There might be a future for this boy,* he thought. *More so than his father, at least.*

'Another Shard won,' Ialai said with dissatisfaction as Adolin raised a hand and walked off the field. 'I'll redouble my efforts to make certain this doesn't happen again.'

Sadeas tapped his finger against the side of his seat. 'What was it you said about duelists? That they're brash? Hotheaded?'

'Yes. And?'

'Adolin is both of those things and more,' Sadeas said softly, considering. 'He can be goaded, pushed around, brought to anger. He has passion like his father, but he controls it less securely.'

Can I get him right up to the cliff's edge, Sadeas thought, *then shove him off?*

'Stop discouraging people from fighting him,' Sadeas said. 'Don't encourage them *to* fight him, either. Step back. I want to see how this develops.'

'That sounds dangerous,' Ialai said. 'That boy is a weapon, Torol.'

'True,' Sadeas said, standing, 'but you are rarely cut by a weapon if you are the one holding its hilt.' He helped his wife to her feet. 'I also want you to tell Ruthar's wife that he can ride with me next time I decide to strike out on my own for a gemheart. Ruthar is eager. He can be of use to us.'

She nodded, walking toward the exit. Sadeas followed, but hesitated, casting a glance toward Dalinar. How would this be if the man weren't trapped in the past? If he'd been willing to see the real world, rather than imagining it?

You'd probably have ended up killing him then too, Sadeas admitted to himself. *Don't try to pretend otherwise.*

Best to be honest, at the very least, with oneself.

The upper lip of the formation which shapes the left shows distinct signs of crem buildup, resulting in large spikes that rim the edge the predominant direction of the winds.

Many of these species are new to me. The plant life here isn't nearly as lush as it was on Father's estates, or even Kharbranth, but there is a frantic determination to the way it grows.

'Tis said it was warm in the land far away
When Voidbringers entered our songs.
We brought them home to stay
And then those homes became their own.
It happened gradually.
And years ahead 'twil still be said 'tis how it has to be.

—From the Listener Song of Histories, 12th stanza

Shallan gasped at the sudden flare of color.

It disrupted the landscape like breaking lightning in an otherwise clear sky. Shallan set down her spheres – Tyn was having her practice palming them – and stood up in the wagon, steadying herself with her freehand on the back of her seat. Yes, it was unmistakable. Brilliant red and yellow on an otherwise dull canvas of brown and green.

'Tyn,' Shallan said. 'What's that?'

The other woman lounged with feet out, a wide-brimmed white hat tipped over her eyes despite the fact that she was supposed to be driving. Shallan wore Bluth's hat, which she'd recovered from his things, to keep the sun off.

Tyn turned to the side, lifting her hat. 'Huh?'

'Right there!' Shallan said. 'The color.'

Tyn squinted. 'I don't see anything.'

How could she miss that color, so vibrant when compared to the rolling hills full of rockbuds, reeds, and patches of grass? Shallan took the woman's spyglass and raised it to look more closely. 'Plants,' Shallan said. 'There's a rock overhang there, sheltering them from the east.'

'Oh, is that all?' Tyn settled back, closing her eyes. 'Thought it might be a caravan tent or something.'

'Tyn, it's *plants*.'

'So?'

'Divergent flora in an otherwise uniform ecosystem!' Shallan exclaimed. 'We're going! I'll go tell Macob to steer the caravan that way.'

'Kid, you're kind of strange,' Tyn said as Shallan yelled at the other wagons to stop.

Macob was reluctant to agree to the detour, but fortunately he accepted her authority. The caravan was about a day out from the Shattered Plains. They'd been taking it easy. Shallan struggled to contain her excitement. So much out here in the Frostlands was uniformly dull; something new to draw was exciting beyond normal reason.

They approached the ridge, which had caused a high shelf of rock at exactly the right angle to form a windbreak. Larger versions of these formations were called laits. Sheltered valleys where a town could flourish. Well, this wasn't nearly so large, but life had still found it. A grove of short, bone-white trees grew here. They had vivid red leaves. Vines of numerous varieties draped the rock wall itself, and the ground teemed with rockbuds, a variety that remained open even when there wasn't rain, blossoms drooping with heavy petals from the inside, along with tongue-like tendrils that moved like worms, seeking water.

A small pond reflected the blue sky, feeding the rockbuds and trees. The leafy shade in turn gave shelter to a bright green moss. The beauty was like veins of ruby and emerald in a drab stone.

Shallan hopped down the moment the wagons pulled up. She frightened something in the underbrush, and a few very small, feral axehounds burst away. She wasn't sure of the breed – she honestly wasn't even sure they were axehounds, they moved so quickly.

Well, she thought, walking into the tiny lait, *that probably means I don't have to worry about anything larger*. A predator like a whitespine would have frightened away smaller life.

Shallan walked forward with a smile. It was almost like a garden, though the plants were obviously wild rather than cultivated. They moved quickly to retract blooms, feelers, and leaves, opening a patch around her. She stifled a sneeze and pushed through to find a dark green pond.

Here, she set down a blanket on a boulder, then settled herself to sketch. Others from the caravan went scouting through the lait or around the top of the rock wall.

Shallan breathed in the wonderful humidity as the plants relaxed. Rockbud petals stretching out, timid leaves unfolding. Color swelled around her like nature blushing. Stormfather! She hadn't realized how much she'd missed the variety of beautiful plants. She opened her sketch-book and drew out a quick prayer in the name of Shalash, Herald of Beauty, Shallan's namesake.

The plants retracted again as someone moved through them. Gaz stumbled past a group of rockbuds, cursing as he tried not to step on their vines. He came up to her, then hesitated, looking down at the pool. 'Storms!' he said. 'Are those fish?'

'Eels,' Shallan guessed as something rippled the green surface of the pool. 'Bright orange ones, it appears. We had some like them back in my father's ornamental garden.'

Gaz leaned down, trying to get a good look, until one of the eels broke the surface with a flipping tail, spraying him with water. Shallan laughed, taking a Memory of the one-eyed man peering into those verdant depths, lips pursed, wiping his forehead.

'What do you want, Gaz?'

'Well,' he said, shuffling. 'I was wondering ...' He glanced at the sketchpad.

Shallan flipped to a new page in the pad. 'Of course. Like the one I did for Glurv, I assume?'

Gaz coughed into his hand. 'Yeah. That one looked right nice.'

Shallan smiled, then started sketching.

'Do you need me to pose or something?' Gaz asked.

'Sure,' she said, mostly to keep him busy while she drew. She tidied up his uniform, smoothing out his paunch, taking liberties with his chin. Most of the difference, however, had to do with the expression. Looking up, into the distance. With the right expression, that eye patch became noble, that scarred face became wise, that uniform became a mark of pride. She filled it in with some light background details reminiscent of that night beside the fires, when the people of the caravan had thanked Gaz and the others for their rescue.

She removed the sheet from the pad, then turned it toward him. Gaz took it reverently, running his hand through his hair. 'Storms,' he whispered. 'Is that really what I looked like?'

'Yes,' Shallan said. She could faintly feel Pattern as he vibrated softly nearby. A lie . . . but also a truth. That was certainly how the people Gaz saved had viewed him.

'Thank you, Brightness,' Gaz said. 'I . . . Thank you.' Ash's eyes! He actually seemed to be tearing up.

'Keep it safe,' Shallan said, 'and don't fold it until tonight. I'll lacquer it so it won't smudge.'

He nodded and walked, frightening the plants again as he retreated. He was the sixth of the men to ask her for a likeness. She encouraged the requests. Anything to remind them of what they could, and should, be.

And you, Shallan? she thought. *Everyone seems to want you to be something. Jasnah, Tyn, your father . . . What do you want to be?*

She flipped back through her sketchbook, finding the pages where she'd drawn herself in a half-dozen different situations. A scholar, a woman of the court, an artist. Which did she want to be?

Could she be them all?

Pattern hummed. Shallan glanced to the side, noticing Vathah lurking in the trees nearby. The tall mercenary leader hadn't said anything of the sketches, but she saw his sneers.

'Stop frightening my plants, Vathah,' Shallan said.

'Macob says we'll stop for the night,' Vathah replied, then moved away.

'Trouble . . .' Pattern buzzed. 'Yes, trouble.'

'I know,' Shallan said, waiting as the foliage returned, then sketching it. Unfortunately, though she'd been able to get charcoal and lacquer from the merchants, she didn't have any colored chalks, or she might have tried something more ambitious. Still, this would be a nice series of studies. Quite a change from the rest in this sketchbook.

She pointedly did not think about what she had lost.

She drew and drew, enjoying the simple peace of the small thicket. Lifespren joined her, the little green motes bobbing between leaves and blossoms. Pattern moved out onto the water and, amusingly, began quietly counting the leaves on a nearby tree. Shallan got a good half-dozen drawings of the pond and trees, hoping she'd be able to identify those from a book later on. She made sure to do some close-up views showing the leaves in detail, then moved on to drawing whatever struck her.

It was so *nice* to not be moving on a wagon while sketching. The environment here was just perfect – sufficient light for drawing, still and serene, surrounded by life . . .

She paused, noticing what she'd drawn: a rocky shore near the ocean, with distinctive cliffs rising behind. The perspective was distant; on the rocky shore, several shadowy figures helped one another out of the water. She *swore* one of them was Yalb.

A hopeful fancy. She wished so much for them to be alive. She would probably never know.

She turned the page and drew what came to her. A sketch of a woman kneeling over a body, raising a hammer and chisel, as if to slam it down into the person's face. The one beneath her was stiff, wooden . . . maybe even stone?

Shallan shook her head as she lowered her pencil and studied this drawing. Why had she drawn it? The first one made sense – she was worried about Yalb and the other sailors. But what did it say about her subconscious that she'd drawn this strange depiction?

She looked up, realizing that shadows had grown long, the sun easing down to rest on the horizon. Shallan smiled at it, then jumped as she saw someone standing not ten paces away.

'Tyn!' Shallan said, raising her safehand to her breast. 'Stormfather! You gave me a fright.'

The woman picked her way through the foliage, which shied away from her. 'Those drawings are nice, but I think you should spend more time practicing to forge signatures. You're a natural at that, and it's a kind of work you could do without having to worry about getting into trouble.'

'I do practice it,' Shallan said. 'But I need to practice my art too.'

'You get really into those drawings, don't you?'

'I don't get into them,' Shallan said, 'I put others into them.'

Tyn grinned, reaching Shallan's stone. 'Always fast with a quip. I like that. I need to introduce you to some friends of mine once we reach the Shattered Plains. They'll spoil you right quick.'

'That doesn't sound very pleasant.'

'Nonsense,' Tyn said, hopping up onto a dry part of the next rock over. 'You'd still be yourself. Your jokes would merely be dirtier.'

'Lovely,' Shallan said, blushing.

She thought the blush might make Tyn laugh, but instead the woman became thoughtful. 'We *are* going to have to figure out a way to give you a taste of realism, Shallan.'

'Oh? Does it come in the form of a tonic these days?'

'No,' Tyn said, 'it comes in the form of a punch to the face. It leaves nice girls crying, assuming they're lucky enough to survive.'

'I think you'll find,' Shallan said, 'that my life hasn't been one of non-stop blossoms and cake.'

'I'm sure you think that,' Tyn said. 'Everyone does. Shallan, I like you, I really do. I think you've got heaps of potential. But what you're training for ... it will require you to do very difficult things. Things that wrench the soul, rip it apart. You're going to be in situations that you've never been in before.'

'You barely know me,' Shallan said. 'How can you be so certain I've never done things like this?'

'Because you aren't broken,' Tyn said, expression distant.

'Perhaps I'm faking.'

'Kid,' Tyn said, 'you draw pictures of criminals to turn them into heroes. You dance around in flower patches with a sketchpad, and you blush at the mere *hint* of something racy. However bad you think you've had it, brace yourself. It's going to get worse. And I honestly don't know that you'll be able to handle it.'

'Why are you telling me this?' Shallan asked.

'Because in a little over a day's time, we're going to reach the Shattered Plains. This is the last chance for you to back out.'

'I . . .'

What *was* she going to do about Tyn when she arrived? Admit that she had only gone along with Tyn's assumptions in order to learn from her? *She knows people,* Shallan thought. *People in the warcamps who might be very useful to know.*

Should Shallan continue with the subterfuge? She wanted to, though part of her knew it was because she liked Tyn, and didn't want to give the woman a reason to stop teaching her. 'I am committed,' Shallan found herself saying. 'I want to go through with my plan.'

A lie.

Tyn sighed, then nodded. 'All right. Are you ready to tell me what this grand scam is?'

'Dalinar Kholin,' Shallan said. 'His son is betrothed to a woman from Jah Keved.'

Tyn raised an eyebrow. 'Now that's curious. And the woman isn't going to arrive?'

'Not when he expects,' Shallan said.

'And you look like her?'

'You could say that.'

Tyn smiled. 'Nice. You had me thinking it would be blackmail, which is very tough. This, though, this is a scam you might actually be able to do. I'm impressed. It's bold, but attainable.'

'Thank you.'

'So what's your plan?' Tyn said.

'Well, I'll go introduce myself to Kholin, indicate I'm the woman his son is to marry, and let him set me up in his household.'

'No good.'

'No?'

Tyn shook her head sharply. 'It puts you too much in Kholin's debt. It will make you seem needy, and that will undermine your ability to be respected. What you're doing here is called a pretty face con, an attempt to relieve a rich man of his spheres. That kind of job is all about presentation and image. You want to set up in an inn somewhere in a different warcamp and act like you're completely self-sufficient. Maintain an air of mystery. Don't be too easy for the son to capture. Which one is it, by the way? The older one or the younger one?'

'Adolin,' Shallan said.

'Hmmm ... Not sure if that's better or worse than Renarin. Adolin Kholin is a flirt by reputation, so I can see why his father wants him married off. It will be tough to keep his attention, though.'

'Really?' Shallan asked, feeling a spike of real concern.

'Yeah. He's been almost engaged a dozen times. I think he *has* been engaged before, actually. It's good you met me. I'll have to work on this one awhile to determine the right approach, but you are certainly *not* going to accept Kholin hospitality. Adolin will never express interest if you're not in some way unobtainable.'

'Hard to be unobtainable when we're already in a causal.'

'Still important,' Tyn said, raising a finger. 'You're the one who wants to do a love scam. They're tricky, but relatively safe. We'll figure this out.'

Shallan nodded, though inside, her worries had spiked. What *would* happen with the betrothal? Jasnah wasn't around to push for it any longer. The woman had wanted Shallan tied to her family, presumably because of the Surgebinding potential. Shallan doubted the rest of the Kholin house would be so determined to have a nobody Veden girl marry into the family.

As Tyn rose, Shallan stuffed away her anxiety. If the betrothal ended, so be it. She had far more important concerns in Urithiru and the Voidbringers. She *would* have to figure out a way to deal with Tyn, though – a way that didn't involve actually scamming the Kholin family. Just one more thing to juggle.

Oddly, she found herself excited by the prospect as she decided to do one more drawing before finding some food.

Smokeform for hiding and slipping 'tween men.
A form of power – like Surges of spren.
Do we dare to wear this form again? It spies.
Crafted of gods, this form we fear.
By Unmade touch its curse to bear.
Formed from shadow – and death is near. It lies.

—From the Listener Song of Secrets, 51st stanza

Kaladin led his troop of sore, tired men up to Bridge Four's barrack, and – as he'd secretly requested – the men got a round of cheers and welcoming calls. It was early evening, and the familiar scent of stew was one of the most inviting things Kaladin could imagine.

He stepped aside and let the forty men tromp past him. They weren't members of Bridge Four, but for tonight, they'd be considered such. They held their heads higher, smiles breaking out as men passed them bowls of stew. Rock asked one how the patrolling had gone, and though Kaladin couldn't hear the soldier's reply, he could definitely hear the bellowing laughter it prompted from Rock.

Kaladin smiled, leaning back against the barrack wall, folding his arms. Then he found himself checking the sky. The sun hadn't quite set, but in the darkening sky, stars had begun to appear around Taln's Scar. The Tear hung just above the horizon, a star much brighter than the others, named for the single tear that Reya was said to have shed. Some of the stars moved – starspren, nothing to be surprised by – but something felt odd about the evening. He breathed in deeply. Was the air stale?

'Sir?'

Kaladin turned. One of the bridgemen, an earnest man with short dark hair and strong features, had not joined the others at the stew cauldron. Kaladin searched for his name . . .

'Pitt, isn't it?' Kaladin said.

'Yes, sir,' the man replied. 'Bridge Seventeen.'

'What did you need?'

'I just . . .' The man glanced at the inviting fire, with members of Bridge Four laughing and chatting with the patrol group. Nearby, someone had hung a few distinctive suits of armor on the barrack walls. They were carapace helms and breastplates, attached to the leathers of common bridgemen. Those had now been replaced with fine steel caps and breastplates. Kaladin wondered who had hung the old suits up. He hadn't even known that some of the men had fetched them; they were the extra suits that Leyten had crafted for the men and stashed down in the chasms before being freed.

'Sir,' Pitt said, 'I just want to say that I'm sorry.'

'For?'

'Back when we were bridgemen.' Pitt raised a hand to his head. 'Storms, that seems like a different life. I couldn't think rightly during those times. It's all hazy. But I remember being *glad* when your crew was sent out instead of mine. I remember hoping you'd fail, since you dared to walk with your chin up . . . I—'

'It's all right, Pitt,' Kaladin said. 'It wasn't your fault. You can blame Sadeas.'

'I suppose.' Pitt got a distant look on his face. 'He broke us right good, didn't he, sir?'

'Yes.'

'Turns out, though, men can be reforged. I wouldn't have thought that.' Pitt looked over his shoulder. 'I'm going to have to go do this for the other lads of Bridge Seventeen, aren't I?'

'With Teft's help, yes, but that's the hope,' Kaladin said. 'Do you think you can do it?'

'I'll just have to pretend to be you, sir,' Pitt said. He smiled, then moved on, taking a bowl of stew and joining the others.

These forty would be ready soon, ready to become sergeants to their own teams of bridgemen. The transformation had happened more quickly than Kaladin had hoped. *Teft, you marvelous man,* he thought. *You did it.*

Where was Teft, anyway? He'd gone on the patrol with them, and now he'd vanished. Kaladin glanced over his shoulder but didn't see him; perhaps he'd gone to check on some of the other bridge crews. He did catch Rock shooing away a lanky man in an ardent's robe.

'What was that?' Kaladin asked, catching the Horneater as he passed.

'That one,' Rock said. 'Keeps loitering here with sketchbook. Wants to draw bridgemen. Ha! Because we are famous, you see.'

Kaladin frowned. Strange actions for an ardent – but, then, all ardents were strange, to an extent. He let Rock return to his stew and stepped away from the fire, enjoying the peace.

Everything was so quiet out there, in the camp. Like it was holding its breath.

'The patrol seems to have worked out,' Sigzil said, strolling up to Kaladin. 'Those men are changed.'

'Funny what a couple of days spent marching as a unit can do to soldiers,' Kaladin said. 'Have you seen Teft?'

'No, sir,' Sigzil said. He nodded toward the fire. 'You'll want to get some stew. We won't have much time for chatting tonight.'

'Highstorm,' Kaladin realized. It seemed like too soon since the last one, but they weren't always regular – not in the way he thought of it. The stormwardens had to do complex mathematics to predict them; Kaladin's father had made a hobby of it.

Perhaps that was what he was noticing. Was he suddenly predicting highstorms because the night seemed too . . . something?

You're imagining things, Kaladin thought. Shrugging off his fatigue from the extended ride and march, he went over to get some stew. He'd have to eat quickly – he'd want to go join the men guarding Dalinar and the king during the storm.

The men from the patrol cheered him as he filled his bowl.

Shallan sat on the rattling wagon and moved her hand over the sphere on the seat beside her, palming it and dropping another.

Tyn raised an eyebrow. 'I heard the replacement hit.'

'Drynets!' Shallan said. 'I thought I had it.'

'Drynets?'

'It's a curse,' Shallan said, blushing. 'I heard it from the sailors.'

'Shallan, do you have any idea at *all* what that means?'

'Like . . . for fishing?' Shallan said. 'The nets are dry, maybe? They haven't been catching any fish, so it's bad?'

Tyn grinned. 'Dear, I'm going to do my *very* best to corrupt you. Until then, I think you should avoid using sailor curses. Please.'

'All right.' Shallan passed her hand over the sphere again, swapping the spheres. 'No clink! Did you hear that? Or, um, did you *not* hear that? It didn't make a noise!'

'Nice,' Tyn said, getting out a pinch of some kind of mossy substance. She began rubbing it between her fingers, and Shallan thought she saw *smoke* rising from the moss. 'You *are* getting better. I also feel like we should figure out some way to use that drawing talent of yours.'

Shallan already had an inkling of how it would come in handy. More of the former deserters had asked her for pictures.

'You've been working on your accents?' Tyn asked, eyes glazing as she rubbed the moss.

'I have indeed, my good woman,' Shallan said with a Thaylen accent.

'Good. We'll get around to costuming once we have more resources. I, for one, am going to be very amused to watch your face when you have to go out in public with that hand of yours uncovered.'

Shallan immediately pulled her safehand up to her breast. 'What!'

'I warned you about difficult things,' Tyn said, smiling in a devious way. 'West of Marat, almost all women go out with both hands uncovered. If you're going to go to those places and not stand out, you'll have to be able to do as they do.'

'It's immodest!' Shallan said, blushing furiously.

'It's just a hand, Shallan,' Tyn said. 'Storms, you Vorins are so prim. That hand looks *exactly* like your other hand.'

'A lot of women have breasts that aren't much more pronounced than male ones,' Shallan snapped. 'That doesn't make it right for them to go out wearing no shirt, like a man would!'

'Actually, in parts of the Reshi Isles and Iri, it's not uncommon for women to walk about topless. It gets hot up there. Nobody minds. I rather like it, myself.'

Shallan raised both hands to her face – one clothed, one not – hiding her blush. 'You're doing this just to provoke me.'

'Yeah,' Tyn said, chuckling. 'I am. This is the girl that scammed an entire troop of deserters and took over our caravan?'

'I didn't have to go naked to do *that*.'

'Good thing you didn't,' Tyn said. 'You still think you're experienced and worldly? You blush at the mere mention of exposing your safehand. Can't you see how it's going to be hard for you to run any kind of pro- ductive scam?'

Shallan took a deep breath. 'I guess.'

'Showing your hand off isn't going to be the toughest thing you need to do,' Tyn said, looking distant. 'Not the toughest by a breeze or a storm- wind. I . . .'

'What?' Shallan asked.

Tyn shook her head. 'We'll talk about it later. Can you see those war- camps yet?'

Shallan stood up on her seat, shading her eyes against the setting sun in the west. To the north, she saw a haze. Hundreds of fires – no, thou- sands – seeping darkness into the sky. Her breath caught in her throat. 'We're there.'

'Call camp for the night,' Tyn said, not moving from her relaxed position.

'It looks like it's only a few hours away,' Shallan said. 'We could push on—'

'And arrive after nightfall, then be forced to camp anyway,' Tyn said. 'Better to arrive fresh in the morning. Trust me.'

Shallan settled down, calling for one of the caravan workers, a youth who walked barefoot – his calluses must be frightening – alongside the caravan. Only those senior among them rode.

'Ask Trademaster Macob what he thinks of stopping here for the night,' Shallan said to the young man.

He nodded, then jogged up the line, passing lumbering chulls.

'You don't trust my assessment?' Tyn asked, sounding amused.

'Trademaster Macob doesn't like being told what to do,' Shallan said.

'If stopping is a good move, perhaps he'll suggest it. It seems like a better way to lead.'

Tyn closed her eyes, face toward the sky. She still held one hand up, absently rubbing moss between her fingers. 'I might have some information for you tonight.'

'About?'

'Your homeland.' Tyn cracked an eye. Though her posture was lazy, that eye was curious.

'That's nice,' Shallan said, noncommittal. She tried not to say much about her home or her life there – she also hadn't told Tyn about her trip, or about the sinking of the ship. The less Shallan said about her background, the less likely that Tyn would realize the truth about her new student.

It's her own fault for jumping to conclusions about me, Shallan thought. *Besides, she's the one teaching me about pretending. I shouldn't feel bad about lying to her. She lies to everyone.*

Thinking that made her wince. Tyn was right; Shallan *was* naive. She couldn't help feeling guilty about lying, even to a professed con woman!

'I'd have expected more from you,' Tyn said, closing her eye. 'Considering.'

That provoked Shallan, and she found herself wiggling on her seat. 'Considering what?' she finally asked.

'So you *don't* know,' Tyn said. 'I thought as much.'

'There are many things I don't know, Tyn,' Shallan said, exasperated. 'I don't know how to build a wagon, I don't know how to speak Iriali, and I *certainly* don't know how to prevent you from being annoying. Not that I haven't tried to figure out all three.'

Tyn smiled, eyes closed. 'Your Veden king is dead.'

'Hanavanar? Dead?' She'd never met the highprince, let alone the king. The monarchy was a far-off thing. She found that it didn't particularly matter to her. 'His son will inherit, then?'

'He would. If he weren't dead too. Along with six of Jah Keved's highprinces.'

Shallan gasped.

'They say it was the Assassin in White,' Tyn said softly, eyes still closed. 'The Shin man who killed the Alethi king six years back.'

Shallan pushed through her confusion. Her brothers. Were they all right? 'Six highprinces. Which ones?' If she knew that, it might tell her how her own princedom was faring.

'I don't know for certain,' Tyn said. 'Jal Mala and Evinor for sure, and probably Abrial. Some died in the attack, others before that, though the information is vague. Getting any kind of reliable information out of Vedenar these days is tough.'

'Valam. He still lives?' Her own highprince.

'He was fighting for the succession, reports say. I have my informants sending me word tonight via spanreed. Might have something for you then.'

Shallan settled back. The king, dead? A succession war? Stormfather! How could she find out about her family and their estate? They were nowhere near the capital, but if the entire country was consumed by war, it could reach even to the backwater areas. There was no easy way to reach her brothers. She'd lost her own spanreed in the sinking of the *Wind's Pleasure*.

'Any information would be appreciated,' Shallan said. 'Any at all.'

'We'll see. I'll let you come by for the report.'

Shallan settled back to digest this information. *She suspected I didn't know, but didn't tell me until now.* Shallan liked Tyn, but had to remember that the woman made a profession of hiding information. What else did Tyn know that she wasn't sharing?

Ahead, the caravan youth walked back down the line of moving wagons. As he reached Shallan, he turned and walked beside her vehicle. 'Macob says you are wise to ask, and says we should probably camp here. The warcamps each have secure borders, and aren't likely to let us in during the night. Beyond that, he is uncertain if we could reach the camps before tonight's storm.'

To the side, eyes still closed, Tyn grinned.

'We camp, then,' Shallan said.

The spren betrayed us, it's often felt.
Our minds are too close to their realm
That gives us our forms, but more is then
Demanded by the smartest spren.
We can't provide what the humans lend,
Though broth are we, their meat is men.

—From the Listener Song of Spren, 9th stanza

I n his dream, Kaladin was the storm.

He claimed the land, surging across it, a cleansing fury. All washed before him, broke before him. In his darkness, the land was reborn.

He soared, alive with lightning, his flashes of inspiration. The wind's howling was his voice, the thunder his heartbeat. He overwhelmed, overcame, overshadowed, and—

And he had done this before.

An awareness came to Kaladin, like water seeping under a door. Yes. He'd dreamed this dream before.

With effort, he turned around. A face as large as eternity stretched behind him, the force behind the tempest, the Stormfather himself.

SON OF HONOR, said a voice like roaring wind.

'This is real!' Kaladin yelled into the storm. He was wind itself. Spren. He found voice somehow. 'You are real!'

SHE TRUSTS YOU.

'Syl?' Kaladin called. 'Yes, she does.'

SHE SHOULD NOT.

'Are you the one who forbade her to come to me? Are you the one who keeps the spren back?'

YOU WILL KILL HER. The voice, so deep, so *powerful*, sounded regretful. Mournful. YOU WILL MURDER MY CHILD AND LEAVE HER CORPSE TO WICKED MEN.

'I will *not*!' Kaladin shouted.

YOU BEGIN IT ALREADY.

The storm continued. Kaladin saw the world from above. Ships in sheltered harbors rocking on violent swells. Armies huddled in valleys, preparing for war in a place of many hills and mountains. A vast lake going dry ahead of his arrival, the water retreating into holes in the rock beneath.

'How can I prevent it?' Kaladin demanded. 'How can I protect her?'

YOU ARE HUMAN. YOU WILL BE A TRAITOR.

'No I won't!'

YOU WILL CHANGE. MEN CHANGE. ALL MEN.

The continent was so vast. So many people speaking languages he could not comprehend, everyone hiding in their rooms, their caverns, their valleys.

AH, the Stormfather said. SO IT WILL END.

'What?' Kaladin shouted into the winds. 'What changed? I feel –'

HE COMES FOR YOU, LITTLE TRAITOR. I AM SORRY.

Something rose before Kaladin. A second storm, one of red lightning, so enormous as to make the continent – the *world itself* – into nothing by comparison. Everything fell into its shadow.

I AM SORRY, the Stormfather said. HE COMES.

Kaladin awoke, heart thundering in his chest.

He almost fell from his chair. Where was he? The Pinnacle, the king's conference chamber. Kaladin had sat down for a moment and . . .

He blushed. He'd dozed off.

Adolin stood nearby, talking to Renarin. 'I'm not sure if anything will come from the meeting, but I'm glad Father agreed to it. I'd almost given up hope of it happening, with how long the Parshendi messenger took to arrive.'

'You're sure the one you met out there was a woman?' Renarin asked. He seemed more at ease since he had finished bonding his Blade a couple weeks back, and no longer needed to carry it around. 'A woman Shardbearer?'

'The Parshendi are pretty odd,' Adolin said with a shrug. He glanced toward Kaladin, and his lips rose in a smirk. 'Sleeping on the job, bridgeboy?'

The leaking shutter shook nearby, water dribbling in under the wood. Navani and Dalinar would be in the room next door.

The king wasn't there.

'His Majesty!' Kaladin cried, scrambling to his feet.

'In the privy, bridgeboy,' Adolin said, nodding to another door. 'You can sleep during a highstorm. That's impressive. Almost as impressive as how much you drool when you're dozing.'

No time for gibes. That dream . . . Kaladin turned toward the balcony door, breathing quickly.

He comes. . . .

Kaladin pulled open the balcony door. Adolin shouted and Renarin called out, but Kaladin ignored them, facing the tempest.

The wind still howled and rain pelted the stone balcony with a sound like sticks breaking. There was no lightning, however, and the wind – while violent – was not nearly strong enough to fling boulders or topple walls. The bulk of the highstorm had passed.

Darkness. Wind from the depths of nothingness, battering him. He felt as if he were standing above the void itself, Damnation, known as Braize in the old songs. Home to demons and monsters. He stepped out hesitantly, light from the still-open door spilling onto the wet balcony. He found the railing – a part that was still secure – and clenched it in cold fingers. Rain bit him on the cheek, seeping through his uniform, burrowing through the cloth and seeking warm skin.

'Are you *mad?*' Adolin demanded from the doorway. Kaladin could barely hear his voice over the wind and distant rumbles of thunder.

Pattern hummed softly as rain fell on the wagon.

Shallan's slaves huddled together and whimpered. She wished she could quiet the blasted spren, but Pattern wasn't responding to her promptings. At least the highstorm was nearly over. She wanted to get away and read what Tyn's correspondents had to say about Shallan's homeland.

Pattern's hums sounded almost like a whimper. Shallan frowned and leaned down close to him. Were those words?

'Bad . . . bad . . . so bad . . .'

∴

Syl shot out of the highstorm's dense darkness, a sudden flash of light in the black. She spun about Kaladin before coming to rest on the iron railing before him. Her dress seemed longer and more flowing than usual. The rain passed through her without disturbing her shape.

Syl looked into the sky, then turned her head sharply over her shoulder. 'Kaladin. Something is wrong.'

'I know.'

Syl spun about, twisting this way, then that. Her small eyes opened wide. 'He's coming.'

'Who? The storm?'

'The one who hates,' she whispered. 'The darkness inside. Kaladin, he's watching. Something's going to happen. Something bad.'

Kaladin hesitated only a moment, then scrambled back into the room, pushing past Adolin and entering the light. 'Get the king. We're leaving. *Now*.'

'What?' Adolin demanded.

Kaladin threw open the door into the small room where Dalinar and Navani waited. The highprince sat on a sofa, expression distant, Navani holding his hand. That wasn't what Kaladin had expected. The highprince didn't seem frightened or mad, just thoughtful. He was speaking softly.

Kaladin froze. *He sees things during the storms.*

'What are you doing?' Navani demanded. 'How *dare* you?'

'Can you wake him?' Kaladin asked, stepping into the room. 'We need to leave this room, leave this palace.'

'Nonsense.' It was the king's voice. Elhokar stepped into the room behind him. 'What are you babbling about?'

'You're not safe here, Your Majesty,' Kaladin said. 'We need to get you out of the palace and take you to the warcamp.' Storms. Would that be safe? Should he go somewhere nobody would expect?

Thunder rumbled outside, but the sound of rainfall slackened. The storm was dying.

'This is ridiculous,' Adolin said from behind the king, throwing his hands into the air. 'This is the safest place in the warcamps. You want us to leave? Drag the king out into the storm?'

'We need to wake the highprince,' Kaladin said, reaching for Dalinar.

Dalinar caught his arm as he did so. 'The highprince is awake,' Dalinar said, his gaze clearing, returning from the distant place where it had been. 'What is going on here?'

'The bridgeboy wants us to evacuate the palace,' Adolin said.

'Soldier?' Dalinar asked.

'It's not safe here, sir.'

'What makes you say that?'

'Instinct, sir.'

The room grew still. Outside, the rainfall slackened to a gentle patter. The riddens had arrived.

'We go, then,' Dalinar said, rising.

'What?' the king demanded.

'You put this man in charge of your guard, Elhokar,' Dalinar said. 'If he thinks our position is not safe, we should do as he says.'

There was an implied *for now* after that sentence, but Kaladin didn't care. He shoved past the king and Adolin, rushing back through the main chamber to the doorway out. His heart hammered inside of him, his muscles tense. Syl, visible only to his eyes, flitted through the room, frantic.

Kaladin threw open the doors. Six men stood on watch in the hallway beyond, mostly bridgemen with one member of the King's Guard, a man named Ralinor. 'We're leaving,' Kaladin said, pointing. 'Beld and Hobber, you're an advance squad. Scout the way out of the building – the back way, down through the kitchens – and give a shout if you see anything unusual. Moash, you and Ralinor are the rear guard – watch this room until I've got the king and the highprince out of sight, then follow. Mart and Eth, you stay at the king's side, no matter what.'

The guards scrambled into action without question. As the scouts ran ahead, Kaladin moved back to the king and grabbed him by the arm, then hauled him toward the door. Elhokar allowed it, a stunned expression on his face.

The other lighteyes followed. The bridgeman brothers Mart and Eth fell in, flanking the king, Moash holding the doorway. He gripped his spear nervously, pointing it in one direction, then another.

Kaladin rushed the king and his family down the corridor along the chosen path. Instead of heading left and down the incline toward the palace's formal entrance, they would head right, farther into its bowels. Down to the right, through the kitchens, then out into the night.

The hallways were silent. Everyone was sheltering in their rooms during the highstorm.

Dalinar joined Kaladin at the front of the group. 'I will be curious to hear exactly what prompted this, soldier,' he said. 'Once we are safely evacuated.'

My spren is having a fit, Kaladin thought, watching her zip back and forth in the corridor. *That's what prompted it.* How was he going to explain that? That he'd listened to a *windspren*?

Deeper they went. Storms, these empty corridors were disturbing. Much of the palace was really just a burrow cut through the rock of the peak, with windows carved out of the sides.

Kaladin froze in place.

The lights ahead were out, the corridor dimming into the distance until it was dark as a mine.

'Wait,' Adolin said, stopping in place. 'Why is it dark? What happened to the spheres?'

They've been drained of Light.

Damnation. And what was that on the wall of the hallway up ahead? A large patch of blackness. Kaladin frantically fished a sphere from his pocket and raised it. It was a hole! A doorway had been cut into this corridor from the outside, sliced directly through the rock. A cold breeze blew inward.

Kaladin's light also illuminated something on the floor just ahead. A body lying where corridors crossed. It wore a blue uniform. Beld, one of the men Kaladin had sent on ahead.

The huddle of people stared at the body in horror. The corridor's eerie silence, the lack of lights, had stilled even the king's protests.

'He's here,' Syl whispered.

A solemn figure stepped out of the side corridor, holding a long, silvery Blade that cut a trail in the stone floor. The figure had flowing white clothing: filmy trousers and an overshirt that rippled with each step. Bald head, pale skin. Shin.

Kaladin recognized the figure. Every person in Alethkar had heard of this man. The Assassin in White. Kaladin had seen him once in a dream, like the one earlier, though he hadn't recognized him at that point.

Stormlight streamed from the assassin's body.

He was a Surgebinder.

'Adolin, with me!' Dalinar shouted. 'Renarin, protect the king! Take him back the way we came!' With that, Dalinar – the Blackthorn – seized a spear from one of Kaladin's men and charged the assassin.

He's going to get himself killed, Kaladin thought, running after him. 'Go with Prince Renarin!' he yelled at his men. 'Do as he tells you! Protect the king!'

The men – including Moash and Ralinor, who had caught up to them – began a frantic retreat, towing away Navani and the king.

'Father!' Renarin cried. Moash grabbed him by the shoulder and hauled him back. 'I can fight!'

'Go!' Dalinar bellowed. 'Protect the king!'

As Kaladin charged with Dalinar and Adolin, the last thing he heard of the group was King Elhokar's whimpering voice. 'He's come for me. I always knew he would. Like he came for Father . . .'

Kaladin drew in as much Stormlight as he dared. The Assassin in White stood calmly in the corridor, streaming with his own Light. How could he be a Surgebinder? What spren had chosen this man?

Adolin's Shardblade formed in his hands.

'Trident,' Dalinar said softly, slowing as the three of them approached the assassin. 'I'm the middle. You familiar with that, Kaladin?'

'Yes, sir.' It was a simple, small-squad battlefield formation.

'Let me handle this, Father,' Adolin said. 'He has a Shardblade, and I don't like the look of that glow—'

'No,' Dalinar said, 'we hit him together.' His eyes narrowed as he regarded the assassin, still standing calmly above the body of poor Beld. 'I'm not asleep at the table this time, you bastard. You're not taking another one from me!'

The three charged together. Dalinar, as the middle tine of the trident, would try to hold the assassin's attention while Kaladin and Adolin attacked from either side. He'd wisely taken the spear for reach, rather than using his side sword. They charged in a rush to confuse and overwhelm.

The assassin waited until they were close, then jumped, trailing Light. He twisted in the air as Dalinar bellowed and thrust with his spear.

The assassin did not come down. Instead, he landed on the *ceiling* of the corridor some twelve feet above.

'It's true,' Adolin said, sounding haunted. He bent back, raising his Shardblade to attack at the awkward angle. The assassin, however, *ran down the wall* in a rustle of white cloth, battering aside Adolin's Shardblade with his own, then slammed his hand into Adolin's chest.

Adolin flipped upward as if he'd been tossed. His body streamed Stormlight and he crashed into the ceiling above. He groaned, rolling over, but remained on the ceiling.

Stormfather! Kaladin thought, pulse pounding, tempest within raging. He thrust his spear alongside that of the Blackthorn in an attempt to hit the assassin.

The man didn't dodge.

Both spears struck flesh, Dalinar's in the shoulder, Kaladin's in the side. The assassin spun, sweeping his Shardblade through the spears and cutting them in half, as if he didn't even care about the wounds. He lunged forward, slapping Dalinar across the face, sending him sprawling to the ground, then swept his Blade toward Kaladin.

Kaladin barely ducked the blow, then scrambled backward, the top of his spear clattering to the ground beside Dalinar, who rolled with a groan, holding a hand to his cheek where the assassin had struck him. Blood seeped from torn skin. The blow of a Surgebinder bearing Stormlight could not just be shaken off.

The assassin stood poised and confident in the center of the corridor. Stormlight swirled in the slashes in his now-reddened clothing, healing his flesh.

Kaladin backed away, holding a spear missing its head. The things this man did . . . He couldn't be a *Windrunner*, could he?

Impossible.

'Father!' Adolin shouted from above. The youth had climbed to his feet, but the Stormlight streaming from him had nearly run out. He tried to attack the assassin, but slipped from the ceiling and crashed to the ground, landing on his shoulder. His Shardblade vanished as it fell from his fingers.

The assassin stepped over Adolin, who stirred but did not rise. 'I am sorry,' the assassin said, Stormlight streaming from his mouth. 'I don't want to do this.'

'I won't give you the chance,' Kaladin growled, dashing forward. Syl spun around him, and he felt the wind stirring. He felt the tempest raging, urging him onward. He came at the assassin with the remnant of his spear wielded like a quarterstaff, and *felt* the wind guiding him.

Strikes made with precision, a moment of oneness with the weapon. He forgot his worries, forgot his failures, forgot even his rage. Just Kaladin and a spear.

As the world was meant to be.

The assassin took a blow to the shoulder, then the side. He couldn't ignore them all – his Stormlight would run out as it healed him. The assassin cursed, letting out another mouthful of Light, and backed away, his Shin eyes – slightly too large, colored like pale sapphires – widening at the continued flurry of strikes.

Kaladin sucked in the rest of his Stormlight. So little. He hadn't picked up new spheres before coming to guard duty. Stupid. Sloppy.

The assassin turned his shoulder, lifting his Shardblade, preparing to thrust. *There*, Kaladin thought. He could *feel* what would happen. He would twist around the strike, bringing up the butt of his spear. It would hit the assassin on the side of the head, a powerful blow that even Stormlight would not easily compensate for. He'd be left dazed. An opening.

I have him.

Somehow, the assassin twisted out of the way.

He moved too quickly, faster than Kaladin anticipated. As quickly . . . as Kaladin himself. Kaladin's blow found only open air, and he narrowly avoided being run through by the Shardblade.

Kaladin's next moves came by instinct. Years of training gave his muscles minds of their own. If he'd been fighting an ordinary foe, the way he automatically shifted his weapon to block the next swing would have been perfect. But the assassin had a Shardblade. Kaladin's instincts – instilled so diligently – betrayed him.

The silvery weapon sheared through the remnant of Kaladin's spear, then through Kaladin's right arm, just below the elbow. A shock of incredible pain washed through Kaladin, and he gasped, falling to his knees.

Then ... nothing. He couldn't feel the arm. It turned grey and dull, lifeless, the palm opening, fingers spreading as half of his spear shaft dropped from his fingers and thumped to the ground.

The assassin kicked Kaladin out of the way, slamming him against the wall. Kaladin groaned, slumping there.

The man in the white clothing turned up the corridor in the direction the king had gone. He again stepped over Adolin.

'Kaladin!' Syl said, her form a ribbon of light.

'I can't beat him,' Kaladin whispered, tears in his eyes. Tears of pain. Tears of frustration. 'He's one of us. A Radiant.'

'No!' Syl said forcefully. 'No. He's something far more terrible. No spren guides him, Kaladin. Please. Get up.'

Dalinar had regained his feet in the corridor between the assassin and the path to the king. The Blackthorn's cheek was a bloody mess, but his eyes were lucid. 'I won't let you have him!' Dalinar bellowed. 'Not Elhokar. You took my brother! You won't take the only thing I have left of him!'

The assassin stopped in the corridor just in front of Dalinar. 'But I'm not here for him, Highprince,' he whispered, Stormlight puffing from his lips. 'I'm here for you.' The assassin lunged forward, slapping away Dalinar's strike, and kicked the Blackthorn in the leg.

Dalinar went down on one knee, his grunt echoing in the hallway as he dropped his spear. A frigid wind blew into the corridor through the opening in the wall just beside him.

Kaladin growled, forcing himself to stand and charge down the corridor, one hand useless and dead. He'd never wield a spear again. He couldn't think about that. He *had* to reach Dalinar.

Too slow.

I'm going to fail.

The assassin swung his terrible Blade down in a final overhead sweep. Dalinar did not dodge.

Instead, he caught the Blade.

Dalinar brought the heels of his palms together as the Blade fell, and he *caught* it just before it hit.

The assassin grunted in surprise.

At that moment, Kaladin plowed into him, using his weight and momentum to throw the assassin against the wall. Except there wasn't a wall here. They hit the place where the assassin had cut his entrance into the corridor.

Both tumbled out into the open air.

But it is not impossible to blend
Their Surges to ours in the end.
It has been promised and it can come.
Or do we understand the sum?
We question not if they can have us then,
But if we dare to have them again.

—From the Listener Song of Spren, 10th stanza

Kaladin fell with the rain.

He clung to the assassin's bone-white clothing with his one working hand. The assassin's dropped Shardblade exploded into mist beside them, and together they plummeted toward the ground a hundred feet below.

The tempest within Kaladin was almost still. *Too little Stormlight!* The assassin suddenly started glowing more powerfully.

He has spheres.

Kaladin breathed in sharply, and Light streamed from spheres in pouches at the assassin's waist. As the Light streamed into Kaladin, the assassin kicked at him. One handhold was not enough, and Kaladin was thrown free.

Then he hit.

He hit hard. No preparation, no getting his feet beneath him. He smacked against cold, wet stone, and his vision flashed like lightning.

It cleared a moment later, and he found himself lying on the rocks at the base of the rise that led to the king's palace, a gentle rain sprinkling him. He looked up at the distant light of the hole in the wall above. He'd survived.

One question answered, he thought, struggling to his knees on the wet rock. The Stormlight was already working on his skin, which was shredded along his right side. He'd broken something in his shoulder; he could feel its healing as a burning pain that slowly retreated.

But his right forearm and hand, faintly lit by the Stormlight rising from the rest of him, were still a dull grey. Like a dead candle in a row, this part of him did not glow. He couldn't feel it; he couldn't even move the fingers. They drooped, limp, as he cradled the hand.

Nearby, the Assassin in White stood up straight in the rain. He'd somehow gotten his feet beneath him and landed, in control, with poise. This man had a level of experience with his powers that made Kaladin look like a new recruit.

The assassin turned on Kaladin, then stopped short. He spoke softly in a language Kaladin didn't understand, the words breathy and sibilant, bearing lots of 'sh' sounds.

Got to move, Kaladin thought. *Before he summons that Blade again.* Unfortunately, he failed to shove down the horror at having lost the hand. No more spear fighting. No more surgery. Both men he had learned to be were now lost to him.

Except . . . he could *almost* feel . . .

'Did I Lash you?' the assassin asked in accented Alethi. His eyes had darkened, losing their sapphire blue quality. 'To the ground? But why did you not die falling? No. I must have Lashed you upward. Impossible.' He stepped back.

A moment of surprise. A moment to live. Perhaps . . . Kaladin felt the Light working, the tempest within straining and pushing. He gritted his teeth and *heaved* somehow.

The color returned to his hand, and feeling – cold pain – suddenly flooded his arm, hand, fingers. Light began to stream from his hand.

'No . . .' the assassin said. 'No!'

Whatever Kaladin had done to his hand had consumed much of

his Light and his overall glow faded, leaving him barely alight. Still on his knees, gritting his teeth, Kaladin grabbed the knife from his belt, but found his grip weak. He almost fumbled the weapon as he got it free.

He swapped the knife to his off hand. It would have to do.

He threw himself to his feet and charged the assassin. *Have to hit him quickly to have a chance.*

The assassin jumped backward, soaring a good ten feet, his white clothing rippling in the night air. He landed with a lithe grace, Shardblade appearing in his hand. 'What are you?' he demanded.

'Same thing you are,' Kaladin said. He felt a wave of nausea, but forced himself to appear firm. 'Windrunner.'

'You can't be.'

Kaladin held up the knife, the few wisps of remaining Light steaming from his skin. Rain sprinkled him.

The assassin scrambled backward, eyes as wide as if Kaladin had turned into a chasmfiend. 'They told me I was a liar!' the assassin screamed. 'They told me I was wrong! Szeth-son-son-Vallano . . . Truthless. They named me *Truthless*!'

Kaladin stepped forward as threateningly as he could manage, hoping his Stormlight would last long enough to be imposing. He breathed out, letting it puff before him, faintly luminescent in the darkness.

The assassin scrambled back through a puddle. 'Are they back?' he demanded. 'Are they *all* back?'

'Yes,' Kaladin said. It seemed like the right answer. The answer that would keep him alive, at least.

The assassin stared at him a moment longer, then turned and fled. Kaladin watched the glowing form run, then lurch into the sky. He zipped eastward as a streak of light.

'Storms,' Kaladin said, then breathed out the last of his Light and collapsed in a heap.

⁘

When he regained consciousness, Syl stood beside him on the rocky ground, hands on her hips. 'Sleeping when you're supposed to be on guard duty?'

Kaladin groaned and sat up. He felt horribly weak, but he was alive.

Good enough. He held up his hand, but couldn't see much in the darkness now that his Stormlight had faded.

He could move his fingers. His entire hand and forearm ached, but it was the most wonderful ache he'd ever felt.

'I healed,' he whispered, then coughed. 'I healed from a *Shardblade* wound. Why didn't you tell me I could do that?'

'Because I didn't know you could do it until you did it, silly.' She said it as if it were the most obvious fact in the world. Her voice grew softer. 'There are dead. Up above.'

Kaladin nodded. Could he walk? He managed to get to his feet, and slowly made his way around the base of the Pinnacle, toward the steps on the other side. Syl flitted around him anxiously. His strength began to return a little as he found the steps and began to climb. He had to stop several times to catch his breath, and at one point he ripped off the sleeve of his coat to hide that it had been cut through with a Shardblade.

He reached the top. Part of him feared that he'd find everyone dead. The hallways were silent. No shouts, no guards. Nothing. He continued on, feeling alone, until he saw light ahead.

'Stop!' called a trembling voice. Mart, of Bridge Four. 'You in the dark! Identify yourself!'

Kaladin continued forward into the light, too exhausted to reply. Mart and Moash stood guard at the door to the king's chambers, along with some of the men from the King's Guard. They let out whoops of surprise as they recognized Kaladin. They ushered him into the warmth and light of Elhokar's quarters.

Here, he found Dalinar and Adolin – alive – sitting on the couches. Eth tended their wounds; Kaladin had trained a number of the men in Bridge Four in basic field medicine. Renarin slumped in a chair near the corner, his Shardblade discarded at his feet like a piece of refuse. The king paced at the back of the room, speaking softly with his mother.

Dalinar stood up, shaking off Eth's attention, as Kaladin entered. 'By the Almighty's tenth name,' Dalinar said, voice hushed. 'You're *alive*?'

Kaladin nodded, then slumped down in one of the plush royal chairs, uncaring if he got water or blood on it. He let out a soft groan – half relief at seeing them all well, half exhaustion.

'How?' Adolin demanded. 'You fell. I was barely awake, but I *know* I saw you fall.'

I am a Surgebinder, Kaladin thought as Dalinar looked over at him. *I used Stormlight.* He wanted to say the words, but they wouldn't come out. Not in front of Elhokar and Adolin.

Storms. I'm a coward.

'I had a good grip on him,' Kaladin said. 'I don't know. We tumbled in the air, and when we hit, I wasn't dead.'

The king nodded. 'Didn't you say he stuck *you* to the ceiling?' he said to Adolin. 'They probably floated all the way down.'

'Yeah,' Adolin said. 'I suppose.'

'After you landed,' the king said, hopefully, 'did you kill him?'

'No,' Kaladin said, 'He ran off, though. I think he was surprised we fought back as capably as we did.'

'Capably?' Adolin asked. 'We were like three children attacking a chasmfiend with sticks. Stormfather! I've never been routed so soundly in my life.'

'At least we were alerted,' the king said, sounding shaken. 'This bridgeman . . . he makes a good bodyguard. You will be commended, young man.'

Dalinar stood and crossed the room. Eth had cleaned up his face and plugged his bleeding nose. His skin was split along the left cheekbone, his nose broken, though surely not for the first time in Dalinar's long military career. Both were wounds that looked worse than they really were.

'How did you know?' Dalinar asked.

Kaladin met his eyes. Behind him, Adolin glanced over, narrowing his eyes. He looked down at Kaladin's arm and frowned.

That one saw something, Kaladin thought. As if he didn't have enough trouble with Adolin as it was.

'I saw a light moving in the air outside,' Kaladin said. 'I moved by instinct.'

Nearby, Syl zipped into the room and looked pointedly at him, frowning. But it wasn't a lie. He *had* seen a light in the night. Hers.

'All those years ago,' Dalinar said, 'I dismissed the stories the witnesses told of my brother's assassination. Men walking on walls, others falling up instead of down . . . Almighty above. What *is* he?'

'Death,' Kaladin whispered.

Dalinar nodded.

'Why has he come back now?' Navani asked, moving up to Dalinar's side. 'After all these years?'

'He wants to claim me,' Elhokar said. His back was to them, and Kaladin could make out a cup in his hand. He downed the contents, then immediately refilled it from a jug. Deep violet wine. Elhokar's hand was trembling as he poured.

Kaladin met Dalinar's eyes. The highprince had heard. This Szeth had not come for the king, but Dalinar.

Dalinar didn't say anything to correct the king, so Kaladin didn't either.

'What do we do if he comes back?' Adolin asked.

'I don't know,' Dalinar said, sitting back down on the couch beside his son. 'I don't know . . .'

Tend his wounds. It was the voice of Kaladin's father, whispering inside him. The surgeon. *Stitch that cheek. Reset the nose.*

He had a more important duty. Kaladin forced himself to his feet, though he felt like he was carrying lead weights, and took a spear from one of the men at the door. 'Why are the hallways silent?' he asked Moash. 'Do you know where the servants are?'

'The highprince,' Moash said, nodding to Dalinar. 'Brightlord Dalinar sent a couple of the men to the servants' quarters to move everyone out. He thought that if the assassin came back, he might start killing indiscriminately. Figured the more people who left the palace, the fewer casualties there would be.'

Kaladin nodded, taking a sphere lamp and moving out into the hallway. 'Hold here. I need to do something.'

⁘

Adolin slumped in his seat as the bridgeboy left. Kaladin gave no explanation, of course, and didn't ask the king for permission to withdraw. Storming man seemed to consider himself above lighteyes. No, the storming man seemed to consider himself above the *king*.

He did fight alongside you, part of him said. How many men, lighteyes or dark, would stand so firm against a Shardbearer?

Troubled, Adolin stared up at the ceiling. He couldn't have seen what he thought he had. He'd been dazed from his fall from the ceiling. Surely the assassin hadn't *actually* cut Kaladin through the arm with his Shardblade. The arm seemed perfectly fine now, after all.

But why was the sleeve missing?

He fell with the assassin, Adolin thought. *He fought, and looked like he was wounded, but it turns out he wasn't.* Could this all be part of some ruse?

Stop it, Adolin thought at himself. *You'll get as paranoid as Elhokar.* He glanced at the king, who was staring – face pale – at his empty wine cup. Had he really gone through everything in the pitcher? Elhokar walked toward his bedroom, where there would be more waiting for him, and pulled open the door.

Navani gasped, causing the king to freeze in place. He turned toward the door. The back side of the wood had been scratched with a knife, jagged lines forming a series of glyphs.

Adolin stood up. Several of those were numbers, weren't they?

'Thirty-eight days,' Renarin read. 'The end of all nations.'

※

Kaladin moved tiredly through the palace hallways, retracing the route he'd led them along only a short time before. Down toward the kitchens, into the hallway with the hole cut out into the air. Past the place where Dalinar's blood spotted the floor, to the intersection.

Where Beld's corpse lay. Kaladin knelt down, rolling the body over. The eyes were burned out. Above those dead eyes remained the tattoos of freedom that Kaladin had designed.

Kaladin closed his own eyes. *I've failed you*, he thought. The balding, square-faced man had survived Bridge Four and the rescue of Dalinar's armies. He'd survived Damnation itself, only to fall here, to an assassin with powers he should not have.

Kaladin groaned.

'He died protecting.' Syl's voice.

'I should be able to keep them alive,' Kaladin said. 'Why didn't I just let them go free? Why did I bring them to this duty, and more death?'

'Someone has to fight. Someone has to protect.'

'They've done enough! They've bled their share. I should banish them all. Dalinar can find different bodyguards.'

'They made the choice,' Syl said. 'You can't take that from them.'

Kaladin knelt, struggling with his grief.

You have to learn when to care, son. His father's voice. *And when to let go. You'll grow calluses.*

He never had. Storm him, he never had. It was why he'd never made a good surgeon. He couldn't lose patients.

And now, now he killed? Now he was a soldier? How did that make any sense? He hated how good he was at killing.

He took a deep breath, regaining control, with effort. 'He can do things I can't,' he finally said, opening his eyes and looking toward Syl, who stood in the air near him. 'The assassin. Is it because I have more Words to speak?'

'There are more,' Syl said. 'You're not ready for them yet, I don't think. Regardless, I think you could already do what he does. With practice.'

'But how is he Surgebinding? You said that the assassin had no spren.'

'No honorspren would give that creature the means to slaughter as he does.'

'Perspectives can be different among humans,' Kaladin said, trying to keep the emotion from his voice as he turned Beld facedown so he wouldn't have to see those shriveled, burned-out eyes. 'What if the honorspren thought this assassin was doing the right thing? You gave me the means to slaughter Parshendi.'

'To protect.'

'In their eyes, the Parshendi are protecting their kind,' Kaladin said. 'To them, I'm the aggressor.'

Syl sat down, wrapping her arms around her knees. 'I don't know. Maybe. But no other honorspren are doing what I do. I am the only one who disobeyed. But his Shardblade . . .'

'What of it?' Kaladin asked.

'It was different. Very different.'

'It looked ordinary to me. Well, as ordinary as a Shardblade can.'

'It was *different*,' she repeated. 'I feel I should know why. Something about the amount of Light he was consuming . . .'

Kaladin rose, then walked down the side corridor, holding up his lamp. It bore sapphires, turning the walls blue. The assassin had cut that hole with his Blade, entered the corridor, and killed Beld. But Kaladin had sent *two* men on ahead.

Yes, another body. Hobber, one of the first men Kaladin had saved in Bridge Four. Storms take that assassin! Kaladin remembered saving this man after he had been left by everyone else to die on the plateau.

Kaladin knelt beside the corpse, rolled it over.

And found it weeping.

'I ... I'm ... sorry,' Hobber said, overcome with emotion and barely able to speak. 'I'm sorry, Kaladin.'

'Hobber!' Kaladin said. 'You're alive!' Then he noticed that the legs of Hobber's uniform had been sliced through at midthigh. Beneath the fabric, Hobber's legs were darkened and grey, dead, as Kaladin's arm had been.

'I didn't even see him,' Hobber said. 'He cut me down, then stabbed Beld straight through. I listened to you fighting. I thought you'd all died.'

'It's all right,' Kaladin said. 'You're all right.'

'I can't feel my legs,' Hobber said. 'They're gone. I'm no soldier anymore, sir. I'm useless now. I—'

'No,' Kaladin said firmly. 'You're still Bridge Four. You're *always* Bridge Four.' He forced himself to smile. 'We'll just have Rock teach you how to cook. How are you with stew?'

'Awful, sir,' Hobber said. 'I can burn broth.'

'Then you'll fit right in with most military cooks. Come on, let's get you back to the others.' Kaladin strained, getting his arms under Hobber, trying to lift him.

His body would have none of it. He let out an involuntary groan, putting Hobber back down.

'It's all right, sir,' Hobber said.

'No,' Kaladin said, sucking in the Light of one of the spheres in the lamp. 'It's not.' He heaved again, lifting Hobber, then carried him back toward the others.

Our gods were born splinters of a soul,
Of one who seeks to take control,
Destroys all lands that he beholds, with spite.
They are his spren, his gift, his price.
But the nightforms speak of future life,
A challenged champion. A strife even he must requite.

—From the Listener Song of Secrets, final stanza

Highprince Valam might be dead, Brightness Tyn, the spanreed wrote. *Our informants are uncertain. He was never in the best of health, and now there are rumors that his illness finally overcame him. His forces are gearing up to seize Vedenar, however, so if he's dead, his bastard son is likely pretending he is not.*

Shallan sat back, though the reed continued writing. It moved seemingly of its own volition, paired to an identical reed used by Tyn's associate somewhere in Tashikk. They'd set up regular camp following the highstorm, Shallan joining Tyn in her magnificent tent. The air still smelled of rain, and the floor of the tent let some water leak through, wetting Tyn's rug. Shallan wished she'd worn her oversized boots instead of slippers.

What would it mean for her family if the highprince *was* dead? He had been one of her father's main problems in the latter days of his life, and her house had gone into debt securing allies to win the highprince's ear or perhaps – instead – to try to unseat him. A succession war could pressure the people who held her family's debts, and that might make them come to her brothers demanding payments. Or, instead, the chaos could cause the creditors to forget about Shallan's brothers and their insignificant house. And what of the Ghostbloods? Would the succession war make them more or less likely to come, demanding their Soulcaster?

Stormfather! She needed more information.

The reed continued to move, listing the names of those who were making a play for the throne of Jah Keved. 'Do you know any of these people personally?' Tyn asked, arms crossed contemplatively as she stood beside the writing table. 'What's happening might offer us some opportunities.'

'I wasn't important enough for those types,' Shallan said with a grimace. It was true.

'We might want to make our way to Jah Keved, regardless,' Tyn said. 'You know the culture, the people. That'll be useful.'

'It's a war zone!'

'War means desperation, and desperation is our mother's milk, kid. Once we follow your lead at the Shattered Plains – maybe pick up another member or two for our team – we probably will want to go visit your homeland.'

Shallan felt an immediate stab of guilt. From what Tyn said, the stories she told, it had become clear that she often chose to have someone like Shallan under her wing. An acolyte, someone to nurture. Shallan suspected that was at least partly because Tyn liked having someone around to impress.

Her life must be so lonely, Shallan thought. *Always moving, always taking whatever she can get, but never giving. Except once in a while, to a young thief she can foster . . .*

A strange shadow moved across the wall of the tent. Pattern, though Shallan only noticed him because she knew what to look for. He could be practically invisible when he wanted to be, though unlike some spren he could not vanish completely.

The spanreed continued to write, giving Tyn a longer rundown of conditions in various countries. After that, it produced a curious statement.

I have checked with informants at the Shattered Plains, the pen wrote. *The ones you asked after are, indeed, wanted men. Most are former members of the army of Highprince Sadeas. He is not forgiving of deserters.*

'What's this?' Shallan asked, rising from her stool and going to look more closely at what the pen wrote.

'I implied earlier we'd have to discuss this,' Tyn said, changing the paper for the spanreed. 'As I keep explaining, the life we lead requires doing some harsh things.'

The leader, whom you call Vathah, is worth a bounty of four emerald broams, the pen wrote. *The rest, two broams each.*

'Bounty?' Shallan demanded. 'I gave promises to these men!'

'Hush!' Tyn said. 'We're not alone in this camp, fool child. If you want us dead, all you need to do is let them overhear this conversation.'

'We're *not* turning them in for money,' Shallan said more softly. 'Tyn, I gave my word.'

'Your word?' Tyn said, laughing. 'Kid, what do you think we are? Your *word*?'

Shallan blushed. On the table, the spanreed continued to write, oblivious to the fact they weren't paying attention. It was saying something about a job Tyn had done before.

'Tyn,' Shallan said, 'Vathah and his men can be useful.'

Tyn shook her head, walking over to the side of the tent, pouring herself a cup of wine. 'You should be proud of what you did here. You have barely any experience, yet you took over three *separate* groups, convincing them to put you – practically sphereless and completely without authority – in charge. Brilliant!

'But here's the thing. The lies we tell, the dreams we create, they're not real. We can't let them be real. This might be the hardest lesson you have to learn.' She turned to Shallan, her expression having gone hard, all sense of relaxed playfulness gone. 'When a good con woman dies, it's usually because she starts believing her own lies. She finds something good and wants it to continue. She keeps it going, thinking she can juggle it. One day more, she tells herself. One day more, and then ...'

Tyn dropped the cup. It hit the ground, the wine splashing bloodred across the tent floor and Tyn's rug.

Red carpet ... once it was white ...

'Your rug,' Shallan said, feeling numb.

'You think I can afford to haul a *rug* with me when I leave the Shattered Plains?' Tyn asked softly, stepping across the spilled wine, taking Shallan by the arm. 'You think we can take *any* of this? It's meaningless. You've lied to these men. You've built yourself up, and tomorrow – when we enter that warcamp – the truth will hit you like a slap in the face.

'You think you can *actually* get clemency for these men? From a man like Highprince Sadeas? Don't be an idiot. Even if you get the con going with Dalinar, you want to spend what little credibility we can fake in order to free murderers from Dalinar's political enemy? How long did you think you could keep this lie going?'

Shallan sat back down on the stool, agitated – both at Tyn and at herself. She shouldn't be surprised that Tyn wanted to betray Vathah and his men – she knew what Tyn was, and had eagerly let the woman teach her. In truth, Vathah and his men probably *did* deserve their punishments.

That didn't mean Shallan was going to betray them. She had told them they could change. She had given her word.

Lies . . .

Just because you learned how to lie didn't mean you had to let the lie rule you. But how could she protect Vathah without alienating Tyn? Did she even have that option?

What would Tyn do when Shallan proved to *actually* be the woman betrothed to Dalinar Kholin's son?

How long did you think you could keep this lie going . . .

'Here now,' Tyn said, smiling broadly. '*That's* some good news.' Shallan shook herself from her ruminations, glancing at what the spanreed had been writing.

In regards to your mission in Amydlatn, it read, *our benefactors have written to say that they are pleased. They do want to know if you recovered the information, but I think this is secondary to them. They let slip that they've found the information they need elsewhere, something about a city they've been researching.*

For your part, there is no news of the target surviving. It seems that your worry about the mission's failure is unfounded. Whatever happened aboard the ship, it worked to our favor. The Wind's Pleasure *is reported lost with all hands. Jasnah Kholin is dead.*

Jasnah Kholin is dead.

Shallan gaped, jaw dropping. *That . . . it isn't . . .*

'Maybe those idiots *did* manage to complete the job,' Tyn said, satisfied. 'It looks like I'll be paid after all.'

'Your mission in Amydlatn,' Shallan whispered. 'It was to assassinate Jasnah Kholin.'

'Run the operation, at least,' Tyn said, distracted. 'Would have gone myself, but can't stand ships. Those churning seas turn my stomach inside out. . . .'

Shallan couldn't speak. Tyn was an assassin. Tyn had been behind the hit on Jasnah Kholin.

The spanreed was still writing.

. . . some interesting news. You asked after House Davar in Jah Keved. It looks like Jasnah, before leaving Kharbranth, took a new ward . . .

Shallan reached for the spanreed.

Tyn caught her hand, the woman's eyes widening as the reed wrote a few last sentences.

. . . a girl named Shallan. Red hair. Pale skin. Nobody knows much about her. Didn't seem important news to our informants until I pried.

Shallan looked up just as Tyn did, meeting the woman's eyes.

'Ah, *Damnation*,' Tyn said.

Shallan tried to pull free. Instead, she found herself being hauled off the chair.

She couldn't follow Tyn's quick motions as the woman slammed her to the ground, face-first. The woman's boot followed to Shallan's back, knocking the air from her and throwing a shock through her body. Shallan's vision fuzzed as she gasped for air.

'Damnation, *Damnation*!' Tyn said. 'You're Kholin's ward? Where's Jasnah? Did she live?'

'Help!' Shallan croaked, barely able to speak as she tried to crawl toward the tent wall.

Tyn knelt on Shallan's back, pressing the air from her lungs again. 'I had my men clear the area around this tent. I was worried about you alerting the deserters that we would turn them in. Stormfather!' She knelt down, head closer to Shallan's ear. As Shallan struggled, Tyn grabbed her on the shoulder and squeezed hard. '*Did. Jasnah. Live?*'

'No,' Shallan whispered, tears of pain coming to her eyes.

'The ship, you may have noticed,' Jasnah's voice said from behind them, 'has two very fine cabins which I hired out for us at no small expense.'

Tyn cursed, leaping up and spinning to see who had spoken. It was, of course, Pattern. Shallan didn't give him a glance, but scrambled toward the tent wall. Vathah and the others were out there, somewhere. If she could just—

Tyn caught her leg, yanking her backward.

I can't escape, a primal part of her thought. Panic surged within Shallan, bringing with it memories of days spent completely impotent. Her father's increasingly destructive violence. A family falling apart.

Powerless.

Can't run, can't run, can't run . . .

Fight.

Shallan pulled her leg free of Tyn and spun, launching herself at the woman. She would not be powerless again. She would *not*!

Tyn gasped as Shallan attacked with everything she had. A clawing, angry, frantic mess. It wasn't effective. Shallan knew next to nothing about how to fight, and in moments she found herself croaking in pain a second time, Tyn's fist buried in her stomach.

Shallan sank to her knees, tears on her cheeks. She tried, ineffectively, to inhale. Tyn cracked her on the side of the head, making her vision go all white.

'Where did *that* come from?' Tyn said.

Shallan blinked, looking up, vision swimming. She was on the ground again. Her fingernails had left a set of bloody rips across Tyn's cheek. Tyn reached up, hand coming away red. Her expression darkened, and she reached to the table, where her sword rested in its sheath.

'What a mess,' Tyn growled. 'Storm it! I'm going to have to invite that Vathah here, then find a way to blame this on him.' Tyn pulled the sword from its sheath.

Shallan struggled to her knees, then tried to climb to her feet, but her legs were unsteady and the room lurched around her, as if she were still on the ship.

'Pattern?' she croaked. 'Pattern?'

She heard something outside. Shouts?

'I'm sorry,' Tyn said, voice cold. 'I'm going to have to tie this up tight.

In a way, I'm proud of you. You fooled me. You'd have been good at this.'

Calm, Shallan told herself. *Be calm!*

Ten heartbeats.

But for her, it didn't have to be ten, did it?

No. It must be. Time, I need time!

She had spheres in her sleeve. As Tyn approached, Shallan breathed in sharply. Stormlight became a raging tempest inside of her and she raised her hand, thrusting out a pulse of Light. She couldn't form it into anything – she still didn't know how – but it seemed for a moment to show a rippling image of Shallan, standing proudly like a woman of the court.

Tyn stopped short at the sight of the projection of light and color, then waved her sword out in front of her. The Light rippled, dissipating into smoky trails.

'So I'm going mad,' Tyn said. 'Hearing voices. Seeing things. I guess part of me doesn't want to do this.' She advanced, raising her blade. 'I'm sorry that you have to learn the lesson this way. Sometimes, we must do things we don't like, kid. Difficult things.'

Shallan growled, thrusting her hands forward. Mist twisted and writhed in her hands as a brilliantly silver Blade formed there, spearing Tyn through the chest. The woman barely had time to gasp in surprise as her eyes burned in her skull.

Tyn's corpse slid back off the weapon, collapsing in a heap.

'Difficult things,' Shallan growled. 'Yes. I believe I *told* you. I've learned that lesson already. Thank you.' She crawled to her feet, wobbling.

The tent flap ripped open and Shallan turned, holding up the Shardblade point-first toward the opening. Vathah, Gaz, and a few other soldiers stopped there in a jumble, weapons bloodied. They looked from Shallan to the corpse on the floor with its burned-out eyes, then back to Shallan.

She felt numb. She wanted to dismiss the Blade, hide it. It was *terrible*.

She did not. She crushed those emotions and hid them deep within. At the moment, she needed something strong to hold to, and the weapon served that purpose. Even if she hated it.

'Tyn's soldiers?' Was that *her* voice, completely cold, purged of emotion?

'Stormfather!' Vathah said, stepping into the tent, hand to his chest as he stared at the Shardblade. 'That night, when you pled with us, you could have killed us every one, and the bandits too. You could have done it on your own—'

'Tyn's men!' Shallan shouted.

'Dead, Brightness,' Red said. 'We heard . . . heard a voice. Telling us to come get you, and they wouldn't let us pass. Then we heard you screaming, and—'

'Was it the voice of the Almighty?' Vathah asked in a whisper.

'It was my spren,' Shallan said. 'That is all you need know. Search this tent. This woman was hired to assassinate me.' It was true, after a fashion. 'There might be records of who hired her. Bring me anything you find with writing on it.'

As they swarmed in and set to work, Shallan sat down on the stool beside the table. The spanreed still waited there, hovering, paused at the bottom of the page. It needed a new sheet.

Shallan dismissed the Shardblade. 'Do not speak of what you saw here to the others,' she told Vathah and his men. Though they promised quickly, she doubted that would hold for long. Shardblades were near-mythical objects, and a *woman* holding one? Rumors would spread. Just what she needed.

You're alive because of that cursed thing, she thought to herself. *Again. Stop complaining.*

She took the spanreed up and changed the paper, then set it with its point at the corner. After a moment, Tyn's distant accomplice started writing again.

Your benefactors on the Amydlatn job wish to meet with you, the pen wrote. *It seems that the Ghostbloods have something else for you to do. Would you like me to arrange a meeting with them in the warcamps?*

The pen stopped in place, waiting for a response. What had the spanreed said above? That these people – Tyn's benefactors, the Ghostbloods – had found the information they sought . . . information about a city.

Urithiru. The people who had killed Jasnah, the people who threatened her family, were searching for the city too. Shallan stared at the paper and its words for an extended moment as Vathah and his men began pulling clothing out of Tyn's trunk, knocking on its sides to find anything hidden.

Would you like me to arrange a meeting with them . . .

Shallan took the spanreed, switched the fabrial's setting, then wrote a single word.

Yes.

THE END OF

Part Two

İNTERLUDES

ESHONAI • ZAHEL • TALN

I-5

THE RIDER OF STORMS

I n the city of Narak, people closed up windows tightly as night approached and the storm loomed. They stuffed rags under doors, shoved bracing boards into position, pounded large, square blocks of wood into windows.

Eshonai did not join in the preparations, but stood outside Thude's dwelling, listening to his report – he'd just returned from meeting with the Alethi, arranging a parley to discuss peace. She had wanted to send someone earlier, but the Five had deliberated and complained until Eshonai wanted to throttle the lot of them. At least they'd finally agreed to let her send a messenger.

'Seven days,' Thude said. 'The meeting will happen on a neutral plateau.'

'Did you see him?' Eshonai asked, eager. 'The Blackthorn?'

Thude shook his head.

'What of the other one?' Eshonai asked. 'The Surgebinder?'

'No sign of him either.' Thude looked troubled. He looked eastward. 'You'd better go. I can give you more details after the storm is done.'

Eshonai nodded, resting her hand on her friend's shoulder. 'Thank you.'

'Good luck,' Thude said to Resolve.

'To all of us,' she replied as he shut the door, leaving her alone in a dark, seemingly empty city. Eshonai checked the stormshield on her back, then took the sphere with Venli's captive spren from her pocket and attuned the Rhythm of Resolve.

The time had come. She ran toward the storm.

Resolve was a stately beat with a steady, rising sense of import and power. She left Narak, and reaching the first chasm, she jumped. Only warform had the strength for such leaps; for the workers to reach outer plateaus and grow food, they used rope bridges that were pulled back and stowed before each storm.

She landed in full stride, her footsteps falling to the beat of Resolve. The stormwall appeared in the distance, barely visible in the darkness. Winds rose, pushing against her, as if to hold her back. Above, windspren zipped and danced in the air. They were heralds of what was to come.

Eshonai jumped two more chasms, then slowed, striding up to the top of a low hill. The stormwall now dominated the night sky, advancing at a terrible pace. The enormous sheet of darkness mingled debris with rain, a banner of water, rock, dust, and fallen plants. Eshonai unhooked the large shield on her back.

For the listeners, there was a certain romanticism to going out in the storm. Yes, the storms were terrible – but every listener would have to spend a number of nights out in them, alone. The songs said that someone seeking a new form would be protected. She wasn't certain if this was fancy or fact, but the songs didn't prevent most listeners from hiding in a cleft of rock to avoid the stormwall, then coming out once it had passed.

Eshonai preferred a shield. It felt more like facing the Rider straight on. This one, the soul of the storm, was the one the humans called Stormfather – and he was not one of her people's gods. In fact, the songs named him a traitor – a spren who had chosen to protect humans instead of the listeners.

Still, her people respected him. He would kill any who did not respect him.

She placed the base of the shield against a ridge of rock on the ground, then turned her shoulder against it, lowered her head, and braced herself with one foot back. Her other hand held the stone with the spren in it. She'd have preferred to wear her Plate, but for some reason having it on interfered with the transformation process.

She felt and heard the storm approach. The ground shook, the air roared. Bits of leaves swept across her in a chill gust, like scouts before an oncoming army that charged behind, the howling wind its battle cry.

She squeezed her eyes shut.

It slammed against her.

Despite her posture and her braced muscles, something *cracked* against the shield and flipped it away. The wind caught it and ripped it from her fingers. She stumbled backward, then threw herself to the ground, shoulder to the wind, head ducked.

Thunder beat against her as the raging wind tried to pull her off the plateau and toss her into the air. She kept her eyes closed, as all was black within the storm save for the flashes of lightning. It did not seem to her she was being protected. Her shoulder against the wind, huddling down behind a hillock, it seemed that the wind was doing its best to destroy her. Rocks crunched against the dark plateau nearby, shaking the ground. All she could hear was the roar of wind in her ears, punctuated occasionally by thunder. A terrible song without rhythm.

She kept Resolve attuned inside of her. She could feel that, at least, even if she couldn't hear.

Rain that fell like arrowheads beat into her body, bouncing off her skullplate and her armor. She set her jaw against the deep, bone-chilling cold and stayed in place. She had done this many times before, either when transforming or when on the occasional surprise raid against the Alethi. She could survive. She *would* survive.

She focused on the rhythm in her head, clinging to some rocks as the wind tried to push her back off the plateau. Demid, Venli's once-mate, had started a movement where people who wanted to transform waited inside buildings until the storm had been going for a while. They only stepped out once the initial burst of fury was past. That was risky, as you never knew when the point of transformation would come.

Eshonai had never tried it. The storms were violent, they were dangerous, but they were also things of discovery. Within them, the familiar became something grand, majestic, and terrible. She did not look forward to entering them, but when she had to, she always found the experience thrilling.

She lifted her head, eyes closed, and put her face to the winds – feeling them blast her, shake her. She felt the rain on her skin. The Rider of Storms was a traitor, yes – but you could not have a traitor who had not originally been a friend. These storms belonged to her people. The listeners were *of* the storms.

The rhythms changed in her mind. In a moment, they all aligned and became the same. No matter which one she attuned, she heard the same rhythm – single, steady beats. Like that of a heart. The moment had arrived.

The storm vanished. Wind, rain, sound ... gone. Eshonai stood up, dripping wet, her muscles cold, her skin numb. She shook her head, spraying water, and looked up into the sky.

The face was there. Infinite, expansive. The humans spoke of their Stormfather, yet they never knew him as a listener did. As wide as the sky itself, with eyes full of countless stars. The gemstone in Eshonai's hand burst alight.

Power, energy. She imagined it coursing through her, energizing her, *enlivening* her. Eshonai threw the gemstone against the ground, smashing it and releasing the spren. She worked hard to get the proper *feel* down, as Venli had trained her.

IS THIS REALLY WHAT YOU WANT? The voice reverberated through her like crashing thunder.

The Rider had *spoken* to her! That happened in songs, but not ... never ... She attuned Appreciation, but of course it was the same rhythm now. *Beat. Beat. Beat.*

The spren escaped from its prison and spun around her, giving off a strange red light. Splinters of lightning sprang from it. Angerspren?

This was wrong.

I SUPPOSE THIS MUST BE, the Rider of Storms said. IT WAS GOING TO HAPPEN.

'No,' Eshonai said, stepping back from that spren. In a moment of panic, she cast from her mind the preparations that Venli had given her. 'No!'

The spren became a streak of red light and hit her in the chest. Tendrils of red spread outward.

I CANNOT STOP THIS, the Rider of Storms said. I WOULD SHELTER YOU, LITTLE ONE, IF I WERE GIVEN THAT POWER. I AM SORRY.

Eshonai gasped, the rhythms fleeing her mind, and fell to her knees. She felt it wash through her, the transformation.

I AM SORRY.

The rains came again, and her body began to change.

Someone was near.

Zahel awoke, snapping his eyes open, knowing instantly that someone was approaching his room.

Blast! It was the middle of the night. If this was another lighteyed brat he'd turned away, come to beg ... He grumbled to himself, climbing off his cot. *I am far, far too old for this.*

He pulled open his door, revealing the courtyard of the practice grounds at night. The air was wet. Oh, right. One of those storms had come, Invested to the hilt and looking for a place to stick it all. Cursed things.

A young man, hand poised to knock, jumped back in surprise from the opening door. Kaladin. The bridgeman-turned-bodyguard. The one with that spren Zahel could sense always spinning about.

'You look like death itself,' Zahel snapped at the boy. Kaladin's clothing was bloodied, his uniform ripped up on one side. The right sleeve was missing. 'What happened?'

'Attempt on the king's life,' the boy said softly. 'Not two hours ago.'

'Huh.'

'Is your offer to learn how to fight a Shardblade still good?'

'No.' Zahel slammed the door. He turned to walk back toward his cot.

The boy pushed the door open, of course. Blasted monks. Saw

themselves as property and couldn't own anything, so they figured they didn't need locks on the doors.

'Please,' the boy said. 'I—'

'Kid,' Zahel said, turning back toward him. 'Two people live in this room.'

The boy frowned, looking at the single cot.

'The first,' Zahel said, 'is a grouchy swordsman who has a soft spot for kids who are in over their heads. He comes out by day. The other is a very, *very* grouchy swordsman who finds everything and everyone utterly contemptible. He comes out when some fool wakes him at a horrid hour of the night. I suggest you ask the first man and *not* the second. All right?'

'All right,' the boy said. 'I'll be back.'

'Good,' Zahel said, settling down on the bed. 'And don't be green from the ground.'

The boy paused by the door. 'Don't be . . . Huh?'

Stupid language, Zahel thought, climbing into his cot. *No proper metaphors at all.* 'Just leave your attitude and come to learn. I hate beating up people younger than me. It makes me feel like a bully.'

The kid grunted, sliding the door shut. Zahel pulled up his blanket – damn monks only got one – and turned over on his cot. He expected a voice to speak in his mind as he drifted off. Of course, there wasn't one.

Hadn't been one in years.

Of fires that burned and yet they were gone. Of heat he could feel when others felt not. Of screams his own that nobody heard. Of torture sublime, for life it meant.

'He just stares like that, Your Majesty.'

Words.

'He doesn't seem to see anything. Sometimes he mumbles. Sometimes he shouts. But always, he just *stares*.'

The Gift and words. Not his. Never his. Now his.

'Storms, it's haunting, isn't it? I had to ride all this way with that, Your Majesty. Listening to him ranting in the back of the wagon half the time. Then feeling him stare at the back of my head the rest.'

'And Wit? You mentioned him.'

'Started on the trip with me, Your Majesty. But on the second day, he declared that he needed a rock.'

'A . . . rock.'

'Yes, Your Majesty. He hopped out of the wagon and found one, then, er, he hit himself on the head with it, Your Majesty. Did it three or four times. Came right back to the wagon with an odd grin, and said . . . um . . .'

'Yes?'

'Well, he said that he'd needed, uh, I had this remembered for you. He said, "I needed an objective frame of reference by which to judge the

434

experience of your company. Somewhere between four and five blows, I place it." I don't rightly understand what he meant, sir. I think he was mocking me.'

'Safe bet.'

Why didn't they scream? That *heat*! Of death. Of death and the dead and the dead and their talking and not screaming of death except of the death that did not come.

'After that, Your Majesty, Wit just kind of, well, ran off. Into the hills. Like some storming Horneater.'

'Don't try to understand Wit, Bordin. You'll only cause yourself pain.'

'Yes, Brightlord.'

'I *like* this Wit.'

'We're quite aware, Elhokar.'

'Honestly, Your Majesty, I preferred the madman for company.'

'Well of course you did. If people *liked* to be around Wit, he wouldn't be much of a Wit, would he?'

They were on fire. The walls were on fire. The floor was on fire. Burning and the inside of a cannot where to be and then at all. Where?

A trip. Water? Wheels?

Fire. Yes, fire.

'Can you hear me, madman?'

'Elhokar, look at him. I doubt he understands.'

'I am Talenel'Elin, Herald of War.' Voice. He spoke it. He didn't think it. The words came, like they always came.

'What was that? Speak louder, man.'

'The time of the Return, the Desolation, is near at hand. We must prepare. You will have forgotten much, following the destruction of the times past.'

'I can make out some of it, Elhokar. It's Alethi. Northern accent. Not what I'd have expected from one with such dark skin.'

'Where did you get the Shardblade, madman? Tell me. Most Blades are accounted for through the generations, their lineage and history recorded. This one is completely unknown. From whom did you take it?'

'Kalak will teach you to cast bronze, if you have forgotten this. We will Soulcast blocks of metal directly for you. I wish we could teach you steel, but casting is so much easier than forging, and you must have something

435

we can produce quickly. Your stone tools will not serve against what is to come.'

'He said something about bronze. And stone?'

'Vedel can train your surgeons, and Jezrien . . . he will teach you leadership. So much is lost between Returns . . .'

'The Shardblade! Where did you get it?'

'How did you separate it from him, Bordin?'

'We didn't, Brightlord. He just dropped it.'

'And it didn't vanish away? Not bonded, then. He couldn't have had it for long. Were his eyes this color when you found him?'

'Yes, sir. A darkeyed man with a Shardblade. Odd sight, that.'

'I will train your soldiers. We should have time. Ishar keeps talking about a way to keep information from being lost following Desolations. And you have discovered something unexpected. We will use that. Surgebinders to act as guardians . . . Knights . . .'

'He's said this all before, Your Majesty. When he mumbles, uh, he just keeps at it. Over and over. I don't think he even knows what he's saying. Eerie, how his expression doesn't change as he talks.'

'That *is* an Alethi accent.'

'He looks like he's been living in the wild for some time, with that long hair and those broken nails. Perhaps a villager lost their mad father.'

'And the Blade, Elhokar?'

'Surely you don't think it's *his*, Uncle.'

'The coming days will be difficult, but with training, humanity *will* survive. You must bring me to your leaders. The other Heralds should join us soon.'

'I am willing to consider anything, these days. Your Majesty, I suggest you send him to the ardents. Perhaps they can help his mind to recover.'

'What will you do with the Shardblade?'

'I'm certain we can find a good use for it. In fact, something occurs to me right now. I might have need of you, Bordin.'

'Whatever you need, Brightlord.'

'I think . . . I think I am late . . . this time . . .'

How long had it been?

How long had it been?

How long had it been?

How long had it been?

How long had it been?
How long had it been?
How long had it been?

Too long.

A FORM OF POWER

They were waiting for Eshonai when she returned.

A gathering of thousands crowded the edge of the plateau just outside of Narak. Workers, nimbles, soldiers, and even some mates who had been drawn away from their hedonism by the prospect of something novel. A new form, a form of *power*?

Eshonai strode toward them, marveling at the energy. Tiny, almost invisible lines of red lightning flared from her hand if she made a fist quickly. Her marbled skin tone – mostly black, with a slight grain of red streaks – had not changed, but she'd lost the bulky armor of warform. Instead, small ridges peeked out through the skin of her arms, which was stretched tightly in places. She'd tested the new armor against stones and found it very durable.

She had hairstrands again. How long had it been since she'd felt those? More wondrous, she felt *focused*. No more worries about the fate of her people. She knew what to do.

Venli pushed to the front of the crowd as Eshonai reached the edge of the chasm. They looked across the void at one another, and Eshonai could see the question on her sister's lips. *It worked?*

Eshonai leapt the chasm. She didn't require the running start that warform used; she crouched down, then threw herself up and into the air. The wind seemed to writhe around her. She shot over the chasm and landed among her people, red lines of power running up her legs as she crouched, absorbing the impact of the landing.

People backed away. So clear. Everything was *so clear*.

'I have returned from the storms,' she said to Praise, which could also be used for true satisfaction. 'I bring with me the future of two peoples. Our time of loss is at an end.'

'Eshonai?' It was Thude, wearing his long coat. 'Eshonai, your *eyes*.'

'Yes?'

'They're red.'

'They are a representation of what I've become.'

'But, in the songs—'

'Sister!' Eshonai called to Resolve. 'Come look upon what you have wrought!'

Venli approached, timid at first. 'Stormform,' she whispered to Awe. 'It works, then? You can move in the storms without danger?'

'More than that,' Eshonai said. 'The winds obey me. And Venli, I can feel something . . . something *building*. A storm.'

'You feel a storm right now? In the rhythms?'

'Beyond the rhythms,' Eshonai said. How could she explain it? How could she describe taste to one with no mouth, sight to one who had never seen? 'I feel a tempest brewing just beyond our experience. A powerful, angry tempest. A highstorm. With enough of us bearing this form together, we could bring it. We could *bend* the storms to our will, and could bring them down upon our enemies.'

Humming to the Rhythm of Awe spread through those who watched. As they were listeners, they could feel the rhythm, hear it. All were in tune, all were in rhythm with one another. Perfection.

Eshonai held out her arms to the sides and spoke in a loud voice. 'Cast aside despair and sing to the Rhythm of Joy! I have looked into the depths of the Storm Rider's eyes, and I have seen his betrayal. I know his mind, and have seen his intent to help the humans against us. But my sister has discovered salvation! With this form we can stand on our own, independent, and we can sweep our enemies from this land like leaves before the tempest!'

The humming to Awe grew louder, and some began to sing. Eshonai gloried in it.

She pointedly ignored the voice deep within her that was screaming in horror.

PART

THREE

Deadly

SHALLAN • KALADIN • ADOLIN • NAVANI

They also, when they had settled their rulings in the nature of each bond's placement, called the name of it the Nahel bond, with regard to its effect upon the souls of those caught in its grip: in this description, each was related to the bonds that drive Roshar itself, ten Surges, named in turn and two for each order: in this light, it can be seen that each order would by necessity share one Surge with each of its neighbors.

—From *Words of Radiance*, chapter 8, page 6

A dolin threw his Shardblade.

Wielding the weapons was about more than just practicing stances and growing accustomed to the too-light swordplay. A master of the Blade learned to do more with the bond. He learned to command it to remain in place after being dropped, and learned to summon it back from the hands of those who might have picked it up. He learned that man and sword were, in some ways, one. The weapon became a piece of your soul.

Adolin had learned to control his Blade in this way. Usually. Today, the weapon disintegrated almost immediately after leaving his fingers.

The long, silvery Blade transmuted to white vapor – holding its shape for just a brief moment, like a smoke ring – before exploding in a puff of writhing white streams. Adolin growled in frustration, pacing back and forth on the plateau, hand held out to the side as he resummoned the weapon. Ten heartbeats. At times, it felt like an eternity.

He wore his Plate without the helm, which sat atop a nearby rock, and so his hair blew free in the early morning breeze. He needed the Plate; his left shoulder and side were a mass of purple bruises. His head still ached from slamming into the ground during the assassin's attack last night. Without the Plate, he wouldn't be nearly so nimble today.

Besides, he *needed* its strength. He kept looking over his shoulder, expecting the assassin to be there. He'd stayed up all night last night, sitting on the floor outside his father's room, wearing Plate, arms crossed on his knees, chewing ridgebark to stay awake.

He'd been caught without his Plate once. Not again.

And what will you do? he thought to himself as his Blade reappeared. *Wear it all the time?*

The part of him that asked such questions was rational. He didn't want to be rational right now.

He shook the condensation from his Blade, then twisted and hurled it, transmitting the mental commands that would tell it to hold together. Once again, the weapon shattered to mist moments after it left his fingers. It didn't even cross half the distance to the rock formation he was aiming for.

What was wrong with him? He'd mastered Blade commands years ago. True, he hadn't often practiced *throwing* his sword – such things were forbidden in duels, and he hadn't ever thought he'd need to use the maneuver. That was before he'd been trapped on the *ceiling* of a hallway, unable to properly engage an assassin.

Adolin walked to the edge of the plateau, staring out over the uneven expanse of the Shattered Plains. A huddle of three guards watched him nearby. Laughable. What would three *bridgemen* do if the Assassin in White returned?

Kaladin was worth something in the attack, Adolin thought. *More than you were.* That man had been suspiciously effective.

Renarin said that Adolin was unfair toward the bridgeman captain, but there *was* something strange about that man. More than his attitude – the way he always acted like by talking to you, he was doing you a favor. The way he seemed so decidedly gloomy at everything, angry at the world itself. He was unlikable, plain and simple, but Adolin had known plenty of unlikable people.

Kaladin was also strange. In ways Adolin couldn't explain.

Well, for all that, Kaladin's men were just doing their duty. No use in snapping at them, so he gave them a smile.

Adolin's Shardblade dropped into his fingers again, too light for its size. He had always felt a certain strength when holding it. Never before had Adolin felt powerless when bearing his Shards. Even surrounded by the Parshendi, even certain he was going to die, he'd still felt *power*.

Where was that feeling now?

He spun and threw the weapon, focusing as Zahel had taught him years before, sending a direct *instruction* to the Blade – picturing what he needed it to do. It held together, spinning end over end, flashing in the air. It sank up to its hilt into the stone of the rock formation. Adolin let out the breath he had been holding. Finally. He released the Blade, and it burst into mist, which streamed like a tiny river from the hole left behind.

'Come,' he said to his bodyguards, snatching his helm from the rock and walking toward the nearby warcamp. As one might expect, the crater edge that formed the warcamp wall was most weathered here, in the east. The camp had spilled out like the contents of a broken turtle egg, and – over the years – had even started to creep down onto the near plateaus.

Emerging from that creep of civilization was a distinctly odd procession. The congregation of robed ardents chanted in unison, surrounding parshmen who carried large poles upright like lances. Silk cloth shimmered between these poles, a good forty feet wide, rippling in the breeze and cutting off the view of something in the center.

Soulcasters? They didn't normally come out during the day. 'Wait here,' he told his bodyguards, then jogged over toward the ardents.

The three bridgemen obeyed. If Kaladin had been with them, he would have insisted on following. Maybe the way the fellow acted was a result of his strange position. Why had father put a darkeyed soldier *outside* the command structure? Adolin was all for treating men with respect and honor regardless of eye shade, but the Almighty had put some men in command and others beneath them. It was simply the natural order of things.

The parshmen carrying the poles watched him come, then looked down at the ground. Nearby ardents let Adolin pass, though they looked uncomfortable. Adolin was allowed to see Soulcasters, but having him visit them was irregular.

Inside the temporary silk room, Adolin found Kadash – one of the foremost of Dalinar's ardents. The tall man had once been a soldier, as the scars on his head testified. He spoke with ardents in bloodred robes.

Soulcasters. It was the word for both the people who performed the art and the fabrials they used. Kadash was not one himself; he wore the standard grey robes instead of red, his head shaven, face accented by a square beard. He noticed Adolin, hesitated briefly, then bowed his head in respect. Like all of the ardents, Kadash was technically a slave.

That included the five Soulcasters. Each stood with right hand to breast, displaying a sparkling fabrial across the back of the palm. One of the ardents glanced at Adolin. Stormfather – that gaze wasn't completely human, not any longer. Prolonged use of the Soulcaster had transformed the eyes so that they sparkled like gemstones themselves. The woman's skin had hardened to something like stone, smooth, with fine cracks. It was as if the person were a living statue.

Kadash hustled over toward Adolin. 'Brightlord,' he said. 'I had not realized you were coming to supervise.'

'I'm not here to supervise,' Adolin said, glancing with discomfort at the Soulcasters. 'I'm just surprised. Don't you usually do this at night?'

'We can't afford to any longer, bright one,' Kadash said. 'There are too many demands upon the Soulcasters. Buildings, food, removal of waste ... To fit it all in, we are going to need to start training multiple ardents on each fabrial, then working them in shifts. Your father approved this earlier in the week.'

This drew glances from several of the red-robed ardents. What did they think about others training on their fabrials? Their almost-alien expressions were unreadable.

'I see,' Adolin said. *Storms, we rely on these things a lot.* Everyone talked about Shardblades and Shardplate, and their advantages in war. But in truth, it was these strange fabrials – and the grain they created – that had allowed this war to proceed as it had.

'May we proceed, bright one?' Kadash asked.

Adolin nodded, and Kadash walked back to the five and gave a few brief commands. He spoke quickly, nervous. It was odd to see that in

Kadash, who was normally so placid and unflappable. Soulcasters had that effect on everyone.

The five started softly chanting, a harmony to the singing of the ardents outside. The five stepped forward and raised their hands in a line, and Adolin found his face breaking out in a sweat, blown cold by the wind that managed to sneak past the silken walls.

At first there was nothing. And then *stone*.

Adolin thought he caught a brief glimpse of mist coalescing – like the moment a Shardblade appeared – as a massive wall sprang into existence. Wind blew inward, as if sucked by that materializing rock, making the cloth flap violently, snapping and writhing in the air. Why should the wind pull inward? Shouldn't it have been blown outward by rock displacing it?

The large barrier abutted the cloth on either side, causing the silk screens to bulge outward, and rose high into the air.

'We'll need taller poles,' Kadash muttered to himself.

The stone wall had the same utilitarian look as the barracks, but this was a new shape. Flat on the side facing the warcamps, it was sloped on the other side, like a wedge. Adolin recognized it as something his father had been deliberating building for months now.

'A windbreak!' Adolin said. 'That's wonderful, Kadash.'

'Yes, well, your father seemed to like the proposal. A few dozen of these out here, and the construction yards will be able to expand onto the entire plateau without fear of highstorms.'

That wasn't *completely* true. You always had to worry about highstorms, since they could hurl boulders and blow hard enough to rip buildings from their foundations. But a good solid windbreak would be a blessing of the Almighty out here in the stormlands.

The Soulcasters retreated, not speaking with the other ardents. The parshmen scrambled to keep up, those on one side of the barrier running along behind it with their silk and opening the back of the room to let the new windbreak slip out of the enclosure. They passed by Adolin and Kadash, leaving them exposed on the plateau and standing in the shade of the large new stone structure.

The silk wall went back up, blocking sight of the Soulcasters. Just before it did, Adolin noticed one of the Soulcasters' hands. The fabrial's glow was gone. Likely one or more of the gemstones in it had shattered.

'I still find it incredible,' Kadash said, looking up at the stone barrier. 'Even after all these years. If we needed proof of the Almighty's hand in our lives, this is certainly it.' A few gloryspren appeared around him, spinning and golden.

'The Radiants could Soulcast,' Adolin said, 'couldn't they?'

'It is written that they could,' Kadash said carefully. The Recreance – the term for the Radiants' betrayal of mankind – was often seen as a failure of Vorinism as a religion. The way the Church sought to seize power in the centuries that followed was even more embarrassing.

'What else could the Radiants do?' Adolin asked. 'They had strange powers, right?'

'I have not read on it extensively, bright one,' Kadash said. 'Perhaps I should have spent more time learning about them, if only to remember the evils of pride. I will be certain to do this, bright one, in order to remain faithful and remember the proper place of all ardents.'

'Kadash,' Adolin said, watching the shimmering silken procession re-treat, 'I need information right now, not humility. The Assassin in White has returned.'

Kadash gasped. 'The disturbance at the palace last night? The rumors are *true*?'

'Yes.'

There was no use hiding it. His father and the king had told the high-princes, and were planning on how to release the information to everyone else.

Adolin met the ardent's eyes. 'That assassin walked on the walls, as if the pull of the earth were nothing to him. He fell a hundred feet without injury. He was like a Voidbringer, death given form. So I ask you again. What could the Radiants do? Were abilities like these ascribed to them?'

'Those and more, bright one,' Kadash whispered, face drained of color. 'I spoke with some of the soldiers who survived that first terrible night when the old king was killed. I thought the things they claimed to have seen the result of trauma—'

'I need to know,' Adolin said. 'Look into it. Read. Tell me what this creature might be capable of doing. We have to know how to fight him. He *will* return.'

'Yes,' Kadash said, visibly shaken. 'But . . . Adolin? If what you say is true . . . Storms! It could mean the Radiants are not dead.'

'I know.'

'Almighty preserve us,' Kadash whispered.

⁘

Navani Kholin loved warcamps. In ordinary cities, everything was so *messy*. Shops where they hardly belonged, streets that refused to run in straight lines.

Military men and women, however, valued order and rationality – at least, the better ones did. Their camps reflected that. Barracks in neat rows, shops confined to marketplaces, as opposed to popping up on every corner. From her vantage atop her observation tower, she could see much of Dalinar's camp. So *neat*, so *intentional*.

This was the mark of humankind: to take the wild, unorganized world and make something logical of it. You could get so much more done when everything was in its place, when you could easily find what or whom you needed. Creativity required such things.

Careful planning was, indeed, the water that nourished innovation.

She took in a deep breath and turned back toward the engineering grounds, which dominated the eastern section of Dalinar's warcamp. 'All right, everyone!' she called. 'Let's give it a try!' This test had been planned long before the assassin's attack, and she'd decided to proceed. What else was she going to do? Sit around and worry?

The grounds below became a buzz of activity. Her elevated observation platform was perhaps twenty-five feet high, and gave her a good view of the engineering grounds. She was flanked by a dozen different ardents and scholars – and even Matain and a few other stormwardens. She still wasn't sure what she thought of those fellows – they spent too much time talking about numerology and reading the winds. They called it a science in an attempt to dodge Vorin prohibitions of predicting the future.

They *had* offered some useful wisdom from time to time. She'd invited them for that reason – and because she wanted to keep an eye on them.

The object of her attention, and the subject of today's test, was a large circular platform at the center of the engineering yards. The wooden structure looked like the top of a siege tower that had been cut off and laid on the ground. Crenellations ringed it, and they'd set up dummies at those, the kinds that the soldiers used for archery practice. Next to that grounded platform was a tall wooden tower with a latticework of scaffolding up the sides. Workers scuttled over it, checking that everything was operational.

'You really should read this, Navani,' Rushu said, looking over a report. The young woman was an ardent, and had no right whatsoever to have such lush eyelashes or delicate features. Rushu had joined the ardentia to escape the advances of men. A silly choice, judging by the way male ardents always wanted to work with her. Fortunately, she was also brilliant. And Navani could always find a use for someone brilliant.

'I'll read it later,' Navani said in a gently chiding voice. 'We have work to do now, Rushu.'

'... changed even when he was in the other room,' Rushu mumbled, flipping to another page. 'Repeatable and measurable. Only flamespren so far, but so many potential other applications ...'

'Rushu,' Navani said, a little more firmly this time. 'The test?'

'Oh! Sorry, Brightness.' The woman tucked the folded pages into a pocket of her robes. Then she ran her hand across her shaved head, frowning. 'Navani, have you ever wondered why the Almighty gave beards to men, but not women? For that matter, why do we consider it feminine for a woman to have long hair? Should not more hair be a *masculine* trait? Many of them have quite a lot of it, you see.'

'Focus, child,' Navani said. 'I want you watching when the test happens.' She turned to the others. 'That goes for all of you. If this thing crashes to the ground again, I don't want to lose another week attempting to figure out what went wrong!'

The others nodded, and Navani found herself growing excited, some of the tension from the night's attack finally bleeding away. She went over the protocols for the test in her head. People moved out of danger ... Ardents on various platforms nearby, watching intently with quills and paper to record ... Stones infused ...

Everything had been done and checked three times over. She stepped up to the front of her platform – holding the railing tightly with freehand and gloved safehand – and blessed the Almighty for the distracting power of a good fabrial project. She'd used this one at first to divert herself from worrying about Jasnah, though she'd eventually realized that Jasnah would be fine. True, reports now said the ship had been lost with all hands, but this wasn't the first time that supposed disaster had struck Navani's daughter. Jasnah played with danger as a child played with a captive cremling, and she always came through.

The assassin's return, though ... Oh, *Stormfather*. If he took Dalinar as he had Gavilar ...

'Give the signal,' she said to the ardents. 'We've checked everything more times than is useful.'

The ardents nodded and wrote, via spanreed, to the workers below. Navani noticed with annoyance that a figure in blue Shardplate had wandered onto the engineering grounds, helm under arm, exposing a messy mop of blond hair speckled black. The guards were supposed to have kept people out, but such prohibitions would not apply to the highprince's heir. Well, Adolin would know to keep his distance. She hoped.

She turned back to the wooden tower. Ardents at the top had activated the fabrials there, and now climbed down the ladders at the sides, unhooking latches as they went. Once they were down, workers carefully pulled the sides away on their rollers. Those were the only things that had been holding the top of the tower in place. Without them, it should fall.

The top of the platform, however, remained in place – hanging impossibly in the air. Navani's breath caught. The only thing connecting it to the ground was a set of two pulleys and ropes, but those offered no support. That square, thick section of wood now hung in the air completely unsupported.

The ardents around her murmured in excitement. Now for the real test. Navani waved, and the men below worked the cranks on the pulleys, pulling down the floating section of wood. The archer parapet nearby shook, wobbled, then began to rise into the air in a motion exactly opposite to the square's.

'It's working!' Rushu exclaimed.

'I don't like that wobble,' said Falilar. The ancient engineer scratched at his ardent's beard. 'That ascent should be smoother.'

'It's not falling,' Navani said. 'I'll settle for that.'

'Winds willing, I'd have been up there,' Rushu said, raising a spyglass. 'I can't see even a sparkle from the gemstones. What if they're cracking?'

'Then we'll find out eventually,' Navani said, though in truth she wouldn't have minded being on top of the rising parapet herself. Dalinar would have had a heart attack if he'd learned of her doing such a thing. The man was a dear, but he was a touch overprotective. In the way a highstorm was a touch windy.

The parapet wobbled its way upward. It acted as if it were being hoisted, though it had no support at all. Finally, it peaked. The square of wood that had been hanging in the air before was now down against the ground and tied in place. The round parapet hung in the air instead, slightly off-kilter.

It did not fall.

Adolin clomped up the steps to her viewing platform, rattling and shaking the entire thing with that Shardplate of his. By the time he reached her, the other scholars were chattering among themselves and furiously making notes. Logicspren, in the shape of tiny stormclouds, rose around them.

It had worked. *Finally*.

'Hey,' Adolin said. 'Is that platform *flying*?'

'And you only just now noticed this, dear?' Navani asked.

He scratched his head. 'I've been distracted, Aunt. Huh. That . . . That's really odd.' He seemed troubled.

'What?' Navani asked him.

'It's, it's like . . .'

Him. The assassin, who had – according to both Adolin and Dalinar – somehow manipulated gravityspren.

Navani looked to the scholars. 'Why don't you all go down and have them lower the platform? You can inspect the gemstones and see if any broke.'

The others heard it as a dismissal and went down the steps in an ex-cited bunch, though Rushu – dear Rushu – remained. 'Oh!' the woman said. 'It would be better to watch from up here, in case—'

'I will speak with my nephew. Alone, please.' Sometimes, working with scholars, you had to be a touch blunt.

Rushu finally blushed, then bobbed a bow and hastened away. Adolin stepped up to the railing. It was difficult to not feel dwarfed by a man wearing Plate, and when he reached out to hold the railing, she thought she could hear the wood groan from the strength of that grip. He could have snapped that rail without a second thought.

I will figure out how to make more of that, she thought. While she was no warrior, there might be things she could do to protect her family. The more she understood the secrets of technology and the power of spren locked within gemstones, the closer she grew to finding what she sought.

Adolin was staring at her hand. Oh, so he'd finally noticed that, had he?

'Aunt?' he said, voice strained. 'A *glove?*'

'Far more practical,' she said, holding up her safehand and wiggling the fingers. 'Oh, don't look like that. Darkeyed women do it all the time.'

'You're not darkeyed.'

'I'm the dowager queen,' Navani said. 'Nobody cares what in Damnation I do. I could prance around completely nude, and they'd all just shake their heads and talk about how eccentric I am.'

Adolin sighed, but let the matter drop, instead nodding toward the platform. 'How did you do it?'

'Conjoined fabrials,' Navani said. 'The trick was finding a way to overcome the structural weaknesses of the gemstones, which succumb easily to the multiplied strain of simultaneous infusion drain and physical stress. We . . .'

She trailed off as she caught Adolin's eyes glazing over. He was a bright young man when it came to most social interactions, but he didn't have a single scholarly breath in him. Navani smiled, switching to layman's terms. 'If you split a fabrial gemstone in a certain way,' Navani said, 'you can link the two pieces together so they mimic each other's motions. Like a spanreed?'

'Ah, right,' Adolin said.

'Well,' Navani said, 'we can also make two halves that move *opposite* one another. We filled the floor of that parapet with such gemstones and put their other halves in the wooden square. Once we engage them all – so they are mimicking one another in reverse – we can pull one platform down and make the other go up.'

'Huh,' Adolin said. 'Can you make this work on a battlefield?'

That was, of course, the exact thing Dalinar had asked when she'd shown him the concepts. 'Proximity is a problem right now,' she said. 'The farther the pairs grow from one another, the weaker their interaction, and that causes them to crack more easily. You don't see it with something light like a spanreed, but when working with heavy weights . . . Well, we can probably get them working on the Shattered Plains. That's our goal right now. You could roll one of these out there, then engage it and write back to us via reed. We pull the platform here down, and your archers get raised up fifty feet to gain a perfect archery position.'

This, finally, seemed to get Adolin excited. 'The enemy wouldn't be able to topple it or climb it! Stormfather. The tactical advantage!'

'Exactly.'

'You don't sound enthusiastic.'

'I am, dear,' Navani said. 'But this isn't the most ambitious idea we've had for this technique. Not by a faint breeze or a stormwind.'

He frowned at her.

'It's all very technical and theoretical right now,' Navani said, smiling. 'But just wait. When you see the things the ardents are imagining—'

'Not you?' Adolin asked.

'I'm their patron, dear,' Navani said, patting him on the arm. 'I don't have time to make all of the diagrams and figures, even were I up to the task.' She looked down at the gathered ardents and women scientists who were inspecting the floor of the parapet platform. 'They suffer me.'

'Surely it's more than that.'

Perhaps in another life it could have been. She was sure some of them saw her as a colleague. Many, however, just saw her as the woman who sponsored them so she'd have new fabrials to show off at parties. Perhaps she was just that. A lighteyed lady of rank had to have some hobbies, didn't she?

'I assume you're here to escort me to the meeting?' The highprinces, abuzz about the assassin's attack, had demanded that Elhokar meet with them today.

Adolin nodded, twitching and glancing over his shoulder as he heard a noise, instinctively stepping protectively to put himself between Navani and whatever it was. The noise, however, was just some workers taking the side off one of Dalinar's massive rolling bridges. Those were the main purpose of these grounds; she'd merely appropriated the area for her test.

She held her arm out to him. 'You're as bad as your father.'

'Perhaps I am,' he said, taking her arm. That Plated hand of his might have made some women uncomfortable, but she'd been around Plate far, far more often than most.

They started down the wide steps together. 'Aunt,' he said. 'Have you been, uh, doing anything to encourage my father's advances? Between you two, I mean.' For a boy who spent half his life flirting with anything in a dress, he certainly did blush a lot when he said that.

'Encourage him?' Navani said. 'I did more than that, child. I practically had to *seduce* the man. Your father is certainly stubborn.'

'I hadn't noticed,' Adolin said dryly. 'You realize how much more difficult you've made his position? He's trying to force the other highprinces to follow the Codes using the social constraints of honor, yet he's pointedly ignoring something similar.'

'A bothersome tradition.'

'You seem content to ignore only the ones you find bothersome, while expecting us to follow all the others.'

'Of course,' Navani said, smiling. 'You haven't figured that out before now?'

Adolin's expression grew grim.

'Don't sulk,' Navani said. 'You're free from the causal for now, as Jasnah has apparently decided to gallivant off someplace. I won't have the chance to marry you off quite yet, at least not until she reappears.' Knowing her, that could be tomorrow – or it could be months from now.

'I'm not sulking,' Adolin said.

'Of course you aren't,' she said, patting his armored arm as they reached the bottom of the steps. 'Let's get to the palace. I don't know if your father will be able to delay the meeting for us if we're tardy.'

And when they were spoken of by the common folk, the Releasers claimed
to be misjudged because of the dreadful nature of their power; and when
they dealt with others, always were they firm in their claim that other
epithets, notably 'Dustbringers,' often heard in the common speech, were
unacceptable substitutions, in particular for their similarity to the word
'Voidbringers.' They did also exercise anger in great prejudice regarding
it, though to many who speak, there was little difference between these
two assemblies.

—From *Words of Radiance,* chapter 17, page 11

S hallan awoke as a new woman.

She wasn't yet completely certain who that woman was, but she knew who that woman was not. She was not the same frightened girl who had suffered the storms of a broken home. She was not the same naive woman who had tried to steal from Jasnah Kholin. She was not the same woman who had been deceived by Kabsal and then Tyn.

That did not mean she was not still frightened or naive. She was both. But she was also tired. Tired of being shoved around, tired of being misled, tired of being dismissed. During the trip with Tvlakv, she'd pretended she could lead and take charge. She no longer felt the need to pretend.

She knelt beside one of Tyn's trunks. She'd resisted letting the men break it open – she wanted a few trunks for keeping clothing – but her search of the tent hadn't found the proper key.

'Pattern,' she said. 'Can you look inside of this? Squeeze in through the keyhole?'

'Mmm ...' Pattern moved onto the side of the trunk, then shrank down to be the size of her thumbnail. He moved in easily. She heard his voice from inside. 'Dark.'

'Drat,' she said, fishing out a sphere and holding it up to the keyhole. 'Does that help?'

'I see a pattern,' he said.

'A pattern? What kind of—'

Click.

Shallan started, then reached to lift the lid of the trunk. Pattern buzzed happily inside.

'You unlocked it.'

'A pattern,' he said happily.

'You can move things?'

'Push a little here and there,' he said. 'Very little strength on this side. Mmm ...'

The trunk was filled with clothing and had a pouch of spheres in a black cloth bag. Both would be very useful. Shallan searched through and found a dress with fine embroidery and a modern cut. Tyn needed it, of course, for times when she pretended to be of a higher status. Shallan put it on, found it loose through the bust but otherwise acceptable, then did her face and hair at the mirror using the dead woman's makeup and brushes.

When she left the tent that morning, she felt – for the first time in what seemed ages – like a true lighteyed woman. That was well, for today she would finally reach the Shattered Plains. And, hopefully, destiny.

She strode out into the morning light. Her men worked alongside the caravan's parshmen to break down camp. With Tyn's guards dead, the only armed force in the camp belonged to Shallan.

Vathah fell into step beside her. 'We burned the bodies last night as you instructed, Brightness. And another guard patrol stopped by this morning while you were getting ready. They obviously wanted us to know that they intend to keep the peace. If someone camps in this spot and finds the bones of Tyn and her soldiers in the ashes, it could lead to questions. I don't know that the caravan workers will keep your secret if asked.'

'Thank you,' Shallan said. 'Have one of the men gather the bones into a sack. I'll deal with them.'

Had she really just said that?

Vathah nodded curtly, as if this were the expected answer. 'Some of the men are uncomfortable, now that we're so close to the warcamps.'

'Do you still think I'm incapable of keeping my promises to them?'

He actually smiled. 'No. I think I've been right convinced, Brightness.'

'Well then?'

'I'll reassure them,' he said.

'Excellent.' They parted ways as Shallan sought out Macob. When she found him, the bearded, aging caravan trademaster bowed to her with far more respect than he'd ever shown her before. He'd already heard about the Shardblade.

'I will need one of your men to run down to the warcamps and find me a palanquin,' Shallan said. 'Sending one of my soldiers is currently impossible.' She wouldn't risk them being recognized and imprisoned.

'Certainly,' Macob said, voice stiff. 'The price will be . . .'

She gave him a pointed stare.

'. . . paid out of my own purse, as thanks to you for a safe arrival.' He put an odd emphasis on the word *safe*, as if it were of questionable merit in the sentence.

'And the price for your discretion?' Shallan asked.

'My discretion can always be assured, Brightness,' the man said. 'And my lips are not the ones that should trouble you.'

True enough.

He climbed up into his wagon. 'One of my men will run on ahead, and we will send a palanquin back for you. With that, I bid you farewell. I hope it is not insulting for me to say, Brightness, that I hope we never meet again.'

'Then our views in that regard are in agreement.'

He nodded to her and tapped his chull. The wagon rolled away.

'I listened to them last night,' Pattern said with a buzzing, excited voice from the back of her dress. 'Is nonexistence really such a fascinating concept to humans?'

'They spoke of death, did they?' Shallan asked.

'They kept wondering if you would "come for them." I realize that nonexistence is not something to look forward to, but they talked on, and on, and *on* about it. Fascinating indeed.'

'Well, keep your ears open, Pattern. I suspect this day is going to only get *more* interesting.' She walked back toward the tent.

'But, I don't have ears,' he said. 'Ah yes. A metaphor? Such delicious lies. I will remember that idiom.'

·:·

The Alethi warcamps were so much *more* than Shallan had expected them to be. Ten compact cities in a row, each casting up smoke from thousands of fires. Lines of caravans streamed in and out, passing the crater rims that made up their walls. Each camp flew hundreds of banners proclaiming the presence of high-ranked lighteyes.

As the palanquin carried her down a slope, she was truly *stunned* at the magnitude of the population. Stormfather! She'd once considered the regional fair on her father's lands to be a huge gathering. How many mouths were there to feed down below? How much water did they require from each highstorm?

Her palanquin lurched. She'd left the wagon behind; the chulls belonged to Macob. She'd try to sell the wagon, if it remained when she sent her men for it later. For now, she rode the palanquin, which was carried by parshmen under the watchful eyes of a lighteyed man who owned them and rented out the vehicle. He strolled along ahead. The irony of being carried on the backs of Voidbringers as she entered the warcamps was not lost on her.

Behind the vehicle marched Vathah and her eighteen guards, then her five slaves, who carried her trunks. She'd dressed them in shoes and clothing from the merchants, but you couldn't cover up months of slavery with a new outfit – and the soldiers weren't much better. Their uniforms had only been washed when a highstorm hit, and that was more of a *douse* than a *wash*. The occasional whiff she got of them was why she had them marching *behind* her palanquin.

She hoped she wasn't as bad. She had Tyn's perfume, but the Alethi elite preferred frequent bathing and a clean scent – part of the wisdom of the Heralds. *Wash with the coming highstorm, both servant and brightlord, to ward away rotspren and purify the body.*

She'd done what she could with some pails of water, but did not have the luxury of stopping to prepare more properly. She needed the protection of a highprince, and quickly. Now that she had arrived, the immensity of her tasks struck her afresh: Discover what Jasnah had been looking for on the Shattered Plains. Use the information there to persuade the Alethi leadership to take measures against the parshmen. Investigate the people Tyn had been meeting with and . . . do what? Scam them somehow? Find out what they knew about Urithiru, deflect their attention away from her brothers, and perhaps find a way to repay them for what they'd done to Jasnah?

So *much* to do. She would need resources. Dalinar Kholin was her best hope for that.

'But will he take me in?' she whispered.

'Mmmm?' Pattern said from the seat nearby.

'I will need him as a patron. If Tyn's sources know that Jasnah is dead, then Dalinar probably knows as well. How will he react to my unexpected arrival? Will he take her books, pat me on the head, and send me back to Jah Keved? The Kholin house has no need of a bond to a minor Veden like me. And I . . . I'm just rambling out loud, aren't I?'

'Mmmm,' Pattern said. He sounded drowsy, though she didn't know if spren could get tired.

Her anxiety grew as her procession approached the warcamps. Tyn had been adamant that Shallan *not* ask for Dalinar's protection, as that would make her beholden to him. Shallan had killed the woman, but she still respected Tyn's opinion. Was there merit to what she'd said about Dalinar?

A knock came at her palanquin window. 'We're going to have the parshmen put you down for a bit,' Vathah said. 'Need to ask around and see where the highprince is.'

'Fine.'

She waited impatiently. They must have sent the palanquin owner on the errand – Vathah was as nervous as she was at the idea of sending one of his men into the warcamps alone. She eventually heard a muffled conversation outside, and Vathah returned, his boots scraping rock. She drew back the curtain, looking up at him.

'Dalinar Kholin is with the king,' Vathah said. 'The whole lot of the highprinces are there.' He looked disturbed as he turned toward the warcamps. 'Something's on the winds, Brightness.' He squinted. 'Too many patrols. Lots of soldiers out. The palanquin owner won't say, but from the sound of it, something happened recently. Something deadly.'

'Take me to the king, then,' Shallan said.

Vathah raised an eyebrow at her. The king of Alethkar was arguably the most powerful man in the world. 'You aren't going to kill him, are you?' Vathah asked softly, leaning down.

'*What?*'

'I figure it's one reason a woman would have ... you know.' He didn't meet her eyes. 'Get close, summon the thing, have it through a man's chest before anyone knows what happened.'

'I'm not going to kill your king,' she said, amused.

'Wouldn't care if you did,' Vathah said softly. 'Almost hope you would. He's a child wearing his father's clothes, that one is. Everything's gotten worse for Alethkar since he took the throne. But my men, we'd have a hard time getting away if you did something like that. Hard time indeed.'

'I will keep my promise.'

He nodded, and she let the drapes fall back down over the palanquin window. Stormfather. Give a woman a Shardblade, get her close ... Had anyone ever tried that? They must have, though thinking about it made her sick.

The palanquin turned northward. Passing the warcamps took a long time; they were enormous. Eventually, she peeked out and saw a tall hill to the left with a building sculpted from – and onto – the stone of the top. A palace?

What if she did convince Brightlord Dalinar to take her in and trust her with Jasnah's research? What would she be in Dalinar's household? A lesser scribe, to be tucked aside and ignored? That was how she'd spent most of her life. She found herself suddenly, passionately determined *not* to let it happen again. She needed the freedom and the funding to investigate Urithiru and Jasnah's murder. Shallan would accept nothing else. She *could* accept nothing else.

So make it happen, she thought.

Would that it were so easy as wishing. As the palanquin turned up the switchbacks leading to the palace, her new satchel – from Tyn's things – shook and hit her foot. She picked it up and flipped through the pages inside, finding the crinkled sketch of Bluth as she'd imagined him. A hero instead of a slaver.

'Mmmmm . . .' Pattern said from the seat beside her.

'This picture is a lie,' Shallan said.

'Yes.'

'And yet it isn't. This is what he became, at the end. To a small degree.'

'Yes.'

'So what is the lie, and what is the truth?'

Pattern hummed softly to himself, like a contented axehound before the hearth. Shallan fingered the picture, smoothing it. Then she pulled out a sketchpad and a pencil, and started drawing. It was a difficult task in the lurching palanquin; this would not be her finest drawing. Still, her fingers moved across the sketch with an intensity she hadn't felt in weeks.

Broad lines at first, to fix the image in her head. She wasn't copying a Memory this time. She was searching for something nebulous: a lie that could be real if she could just imagine it correctly.

She scratched frantically at the paper, hunkering down, and soon stopped feeling the rhythm of the porters' steps. She saw only the drawing, knew only the emotions she bled onto that page. Jasnah's determination. Tyn's confidence. A sense of *rightness* that she could not describe, but which she drew from her brother Helaran, the best person she'd ever known.

It all *poured* from her into the pencil and onto the page. Streaks and lines that became shadows and patterns that became figures and faces. A quick sketch, hurried, yet one alive. It depicted Shallan as a confident young woman standing before Dalinar Kholin, as she imagined him. She'd put him in Shardplate as he, and those around him, studied Shallan with penetrating consternation. She stood strong, hand raised toward them as she spoke with confidence and power. No trembling here. No fear of confrontation.

This is what I would have been, Shallan thought, *if I had not been raised in a household of fear. So this is what I will be today.*

It wasn't a lie. It was a different truth.

A knock came at the palanquin's door. It had stopped moving; she'd barely noticed. With a nod to herself, she folded the sketch and slipped it into the pocket of her safehand sleeve. Then she stepped out of the vehicle and onto cold rock. She felt invigorated, and realized she had sucked in a tiny amount of Stormlight without meaning to.

The palace was both finer and more mundane than she might have expected. Certainly, this was a warcamp, and so the king's seat wouldn't match the majesty of the royal dwellings of Kharbranth. At the same time, it was amazing that such a structure could have been crafted here, away from the culture and resources of Alethkar proper. The towering stone fortress of sculpted rock, several stories high, perched at the pinnacle of the hill.

'Vathah, Gaz,' she said. 'Attend me. The rest of you, take up position here. I will send word.'

They saluted her; she wasn't certain if that was appropriate or not. She strode forward, and noticed with amusement that she'd chosen one of the tallest of the deserters and one of the shortest to accompany her, and so when they flanked her, it created an even slope of height: Vathah, herself, Gaz. Had she really just chosen her guards based on aesthetic appeal?

The front gates of the palace complex faced west, and here Shallan found a large group of guards standing before open doors that led to a deep tunnel of a corridor into the hill itself. Sixteen guards at the door? She had read that King Elhokar was paranoid, but this seemed excessive.

'You'll need to announce me, Vathah,' she said softly as they walked up.

'As?'

'Brightness Shallan Davar, ward of Jasnah Kholin and causal betrothed of Adolin Kholin. Wait to say it until I indicate.'

The grizzled man nodded, hand on his axe. Shallan didn't share his discomfort. If anything, she was *excited*. She strode by the guards with head held high, acting as if she belonged.

They let her pass.

Shallan almost stumbled. Over a dozen guards at the door, and they didn't challenge her. Several raised hands as if to do so – she saw this from the corner of her eye – but they backed down into silence. Vathah snorted softly from beside her as they entered the tunnel-like corridor beyond the gates.

The acoustics caught echoing whispers as the guards at the door conversed. Finally, one of them did call out after her. '. . . Brightness?'

She stopped, turning toward them and raising an eyebrow.

'I'm sorry, Brightness,' the guard called. 'But you are . . . ?'

She nodded to Vathah.

'You don't recognize Brightness Davar?' he barked. 'The causal *betrothed* of Brightlord Adolin Kholin?'

The guards hushed, and Shallan turned around to continue on her way. The conversation behind started up again almost immediately, loud enough this time that she could catch a few words. '. . . never can keep track of that man's women . . .'

They reached an intersection. Shallan looked one way, then the other. 'Upward, I'd guess,' she said.

'Kings do like to be at the top of everything,' Vathah said. 'Attitude might get you past the outer door, Brightness, but it's not going to get you in to see Kholin.'

'Are you *really* his betrothed?' Gaz asked nervously, scratching at his eye patch.

'Last I checked,' Shallan said, leading the way. 'Which, granted, was before my ship sank.' She wasn't worried about getting in to see Kholin. She'd at least get an audience.

They continued upward, asking servants for directions. Those scuttled about in clusters, jumping when spoken to. Shallan recognized that kind of timidity. Was the king as terrible a master as her father had been?

As they went higher, the structure seemed less like a fortress and more like a palace. There were reliefs on the walls, mosaics on the floor, carved shutters, an increasing number of windows. By the time they approached the king's conference chamber near the top, wood trim framed the stone walls, with silver and gold leaf worked into the carvings. Lamps held massive sapphires, beyond the size of ordinary denominations, radiating bright blue light. At least she wouldn't lack for Stormlight, should she need it.

The passage into the king's conference room was *clogged* with men. Soldiers in a dozen different uniforms.

'Damnation,' Gaz said. 'Those are Sadeas's colors there.'

'And Thanadal, and Aladar, and Ruthar . . .' Vathah said. 'He's meeting with all the highprinces, as I said.'

Shallan could pick out factions easily, dredging from her studies of Jasnah's book the names – and heraldry – of all ten highprinces. Sadeas's soldiers chatted with those of Highprince Ruthar and Highprince Aladar. Dalinar's stood alone, and Shallan could sense hostility between them and the others in the hallway.

Dalinar's guards had very few lighteyes among them. That was odd. And did that one man at the door look familiar? The tall darkeyed man with the blue coat that went down to his knees. The man with the shoulderlength hair, curling slightly ... He was speaking in a low voice with another soldier, who was one of the men from the gates below.

'Looks like they beat us up here,' Vathah said softly.

The man turned and looked her right in the eyes, then glanced down toward her feet.

Oh no.

The man – an officer, by the uniform – strode directly toward her. He ignored the hostile stares of the other highprinces' soldiers as he walked right up to Shallan. 'Prince Adolin,' he said flatly, 'is engaged to a Horneater?'

She'd almost forgotten the encounter two days outside of the warcamps. *I'm going to strangle that* – She cut off, feeling a stab of depression. She *had* ended up killing Tyn.

'Obviously not,' Shallan said, raising her chin and not using the Horneater accent. 'I was traveling alone through the wilderness. Revealing my true identity did not seem prudent.'

The man grunted. 'Where are my boots?'

'Is this how you address a lighteyed lady of rank?'

'It's how I address a thief,' the man said. 'I'd just gotten those boots.'

'I'll have a dozen new pairs sent to you,' Shallan said. 'After I have spoken with Highprince Dalinar.'

'You think I'm going to let you see him?'

'You think you get to choose?'

'I'm captain of his guard, woman.'

Blast, she thought. That was going to be inconvenient. At least she wasn't trembling from the confrontation. She really *was* past that. Finally.

'Well tell me, *Captain*,' she said. 'What is your name?'

'Kaladin.' Odd. That sounded like a lighteyes's name.

'Excellent. Now I have a name to use when I tell the highprince about you. He's not going to like his son's betrothed being treated this way.'

Kaladin waved to several of his soldiers. The men in blue surrounded her and Vathah and ...

Where had Gaz gotten off to?

She turned and found him backing down the corridor. Kaladin spotted him, and started visibly.

'Gaz?' Kaladin demanded. 'What is this?'

'Uh ...' The one-eyed man stammered. 'Lordsh ... Um, Kaladin. You're, ah, an officer? So things have been going well for you ...'

'You know this man?' Shallan asked Kaladin.

'He tried to get me killed,' Kaladin said, voice even. 'On multiple occasions. He's one of the most hateful little rats I've ever known.'

Great.

'You're not Adolin's betrothed,' Kaladin said, meeting her gaze as several of his men gleefully seized Gaz, who had backed into other guards coming up from below. 'Adolin's betrothed has drowned. *You* are an opportunist with a very bad sense of timing. I doubt that Dalinar Kholin will be pleased to find a swindler trying to capitalize on the death of his niece.'

She finally started to feel nervous. Vathah glanced at her, obviously worried that this Kaladin's guesses were correct. Shallan steadied herself and reached into her safepouch, pulling out a piece of paper she'd found in Jasnah's notes. 'Is Highlady Navani in that room?'

Kaladin didn't reply.

'Show her this, please,' Shallan said.

Kaladin hesitated, then took the sheet. He looked it over, but obviously couldn't tell that he was holding it upside down. It was one of the written communications between Jasnah and her mother, arranging for the causal. Communicated via spanreed, there would be two copies – the one that had been written on Jasnah's side, and the one on Brightness Navani's side.

'We'll see,' Kaladin said.

'We'll ...' Shallan found herself sputtering. If she couldn't get in to see Dalinar, then ... Then ... Storm this man! She took his arm in her freehand as he turned to give orders to his men. 'Is this really all because I lied to you?' she demanded more softly.

He looked back at her. 'It's about doing my job.'

'Your job is to be offensive and asinine?'

'No, I'm offensive and asinine on my own time too. My *job* is to keep people like you away from Dalinar Kholin.'

'I guarantee he will want to see me.'

'Well, forgive me for not trusting the word of a Horneater princess.

Would you like some shells to chew on while my men tow you away to the dungeons?'

All right, that's enough.

'The dungeons sound wonderful!' she said. 'At least there, I'd be away from *you*, idiot man!'

'Only for a short time. I'd be by to interrogate you.'

'What? I couldn't pick a more pleasant option? Like being executed?'

'You're assuming I could find a hangman willing to put up with your blathering long enough to fit the rope.'

'Well, if you want to kill me, you could always let your breath do the job.'

He reddened, and several guards nearby started snickering. They tried to stifle their reaction as Captain Kaladin looked at them.

'I should envy you,' he said, turning back to her. 'My *breath* needs to be up close to kill, while that face of yours can kill any man from a distance.'

'Any man?' she asked. 'Why, it's not working on you. I guess that's proof that you're not much of a man.'

'I misspoke. I didn't mean *any* man, just males of your own species – but don't worry, I'll take care not to let our chulls get close.'

'Oh? Your parents are in the area, then?'

His eyes widened, and for the first time she seemed to have really gotten under his skin. 'My parents have nothing to do with this.'

'Yes, that makes sense. I'd *expect* that they want nothing to do with you.'

'At least my ancestors had the sense not to breed with a sponge!' he snapped, probably a reference to her red hair.

'At least I *know* my parentage!' she snapped back.

They glared at each other. Part of Shallan felt satisfaction at being able to make him lose his temper, though from the heat she felt in her face, she'd let go of hers as well. Jasnah would have been disappointed. How often had she tried to get Shallan to control her tongue? True wit was controlled wit. It shouldn't be allowed to run free, any more than an arrow should be loosed in a random direction.

For the first time, Shallan realized that the large hallway had grown silent. A great number of the soldiers and attendants were staring at her and the officer.

'Bah!' Kaladin shook her arm free of his – she hadn't let go after getting his attention earlier. 'I revise my opinion of you. You're obviously a high-born lighteyes. Only they are capable of being *this* infuriating.' He stalked away from her toward the doors to the king's chamber.

Nearby, Vathah relaxed visibly. 'Getting into a shouting match with the head of Highprince Dalinar's guard?' he whispered to her. 'Was that wise?'

'We created an incident,' she said, calming herself. 'Now Dalinar Kholin will hear of this one way or another. That guardsman won't be able to keep my arrival secret from him.'

Vathah hesitated. 'So it was part of the *plan*.'

'Hardly,' Shallan said. 'I'm not nearly that clever. But it should work anyway.' She looked to Gaz, who was released by Kaladin's guards so he could join the two of them, though all were still under careful watch.

'Even for a deserter,' Vathah said under his breath, 'you're a coward, Gaz.'

Gaz just stared at the ground.

'How do you know him?' Shallan asked.

'He was a slave,' Gaz said, 'at the lumberyards where I used to work. Storming man. He's dangerous, Brightness. Violent, a troublemaker. I don't know how he got to such a high position in such a short time.'

Kaladin hadn't entered the conference chamber. However, the doors cracked a moment later. The meeting appeared to be over, or at least on break. Several aides rushed in to see if their highprinces needed anything, and chatter started up among the guards. Captain Kaladin shot her a glance, then reluctantly entered, carrying her sheet of paper.

Shallan forced herself to stand with hands clasped before her – one sleeved, the other not – to keep herself from looking nervous. Eventually, Kaladin stepped back out, a look of annoyed resignation on his face. He pointed at her, then thumbed over his shoulder, indicating she could enter. His guards let her pass, though they restrained Vathah when he tried to follow her.

She waved him back, took a deep breath, then strode through the moving crowd of soldiers and aides, entering the king's conference chamber.

Now, as each order was thus matched to the nature and temperament of the Herald it named patron, there was none more archetypal of this than the Stonewards, who followed after Talenelat'Elin, Stonesinew, Herald of War: they thought it a point of virtue to exemplify resolve, strength, and dependability. Alas, they took less care for imprudent practice of their stubbornness, even in the face of proven error.

—From *Words of Radiance*, chapter 13, page 1

The meeting finally reached a break. They weren't done – Stormfather, it didn't seem like they'd *ever* be done – but the arguing was over for the moment. Adolin stood, wounds along his legand side protesting, and left his father and aunt to speak in hushed tones as the large chamber filled with a buzz of conversation.

How did Father stand it? A full two hours had passed, according to Navani's fabrial clock on the wall. Two hours of highprinces and their wives complaining about the Assassin in White. Nobody could agree on what should be done.

They all ignored the truth stabbing them in the face. Nothing *could* be done. Nothing other than Adolin staying alert and practicing, training to face the monster when he returned.

And you think you can beat him? When he can walk on walls and make the very spren of nature obey him?

It was a discomforting question. At his father's suggestion, Adolin had reluctantly changed out of his Plate and into something more appropriate. *We need to project confidence at this meeting,* Dalinar had said, *not fear.*

General Khal wore the armor instead, hiding in a room to the side with a strike force. Father seemed to think it unlikely the assassin would strike during the meeting. If the assassin wanted to kill the highprinces, he could take them much more easily alone, in the night. Attacking them all together, in the company of their guards and dozens of Shardbearers, seemed like it would be an imprudent decision. Indeed, there were Shards aplenty at this meeting. Three of the highprinces wore their Plate, and the others had Shardbearers in attendance. Abrobadar, Jakamav, Resi, Relis . . . Adolin had rarely seen so many collected together at once.

Would any of it matter? Accounts had been flooding in from around the world for weeks. Kings slaughtered. Ruling bodies decapitated all across Roshar. In Jah Keved, the assassin had reportedly killed dozens of soldiers bearing half-shard shields that could block his Blade, as well as *three* Shardbearers, including the king. It was a crisis that spanned the entire world, and one man was behind it. Assuming he was even a man.

Adolin found himself a cup of sweet wine at the edge of the room, poured by an eager servant in blue and gold. Orange wine, basically just juice. Adolin downed an entire cup anyway, then went looking for Relis. He needed to be doing *something* other than sitting and listening to people complain.

Fortunately, he'd concocted something while sitting there.

Relis, Ruthar's son and star Shardbearer, was a man with a face like a shovel – flat and wide, with a nose that seemed like it had been smashed. He wore a frilly outfit of green and yellow. It wasn't even interesting. He had the choice to wear anything, and he chose this?

He was a full Shardbearer, one of the few in the camps. He was also the current dueling champion – which, along with his parentage, made him of particular interest to Adolin. He stood speaking with his cousin Elit and a group of three of Sadeas's attendants: women in the traditional Vorin havah. One of those women, Melali, gave Adolin a pointed glare.

She was as pretty as she'd ever been, her hair up in complex braids and stuck with hairspikes. What had he done to annoy her, again? It had been forever since they'd courted.

'Relis,' Adolin said, raising his cup, 'I just wanted you to know that I found it very brave of you to offer to fight the assassin yourself, when you spoke earlier. It is inspiring that you'd be willing to die for the Crown.'

Relis scowled at Adolin. How *did* someone get a face so flat? Had he been dropped as a child? 'You're assuming I'd lose.'

'Well, of course you would,' Adolin said, chuckling. 'I mean, let's be honest, Relis. You've been sitting on your title for almost half a year. You haven't won a duel of any importance since you defeated Epinar.'

'This from a man who spent years refusing almost all challenges,' Melali said, looking Adolin up and down. 'I'm surprised your daddy let you free to come talk. Isn't he afraid you might hurt yourself?'

'Nice to see you too, Melali,' Adolin said. 'How's your sister?'

'Off limits.'

Oh, right. That was what he'd done. Honest mistake. 'Relis,' Adolin said. 'You claim you'd face this assassin, yet you're frightened of dueling *me*?'

Relis spread his hands, one holding a shimmering goblet of red wine. 'It's protocol, Adolin! I'll duel you once you fight up through the brackets for a year or two. I can't just take on any old challenger, particularly not in a bout with our Shards on the line!'

'Any old challenger?' Adolin said. 'Relis, I'm one of the best there is.'

'Are you?' Relis asked, smiling. 'After that display with Eranniv?'

'Yes, Adolin,' said Elit, Relis's short, balding cousin. 'You've only had a handful of duels of any consequence in recent memory – in one of those you basically cheated, and in the second you won by sheer luck!'

Relis nodded. 'If I bend the rules and accept your challenge, then it will break the stormwall. I'll have dozens of inferior swordsmen nipping at me.'

'No you won't,' Adolin said. 'Because you won't be a Shardbearer any longer. You'll have lost to me.'

'So confident,' Relis said, chuckling, turning to Elit and the women. 'Listen to him. He ignores the rankings for months, then leaps back in and assumes he can beat me.'

'I'll wager both my Plate and Blade,' Adolin said. 'And my brother's

Plate and Blade, along with the Shard I won from Eranniv. Five Shards to your two.'

Elit started. The man was a Shardbearer with only the Plate – given to him by his cousin. He turned to Relis, looking hungry.

Relis paused. Then he closed his mouth and cocked his head lazily to the side as he met Adolin's eyes. 'You're a fool, Kholin.'

'I'm offering it here, before witnesses,' Adolin said. 'You win this bout, you take every Shard my family owns. What's stronger? Your fear or your greed?'

'My *pride*,' Relis said. 'No contest, Adolin.'

Adolin ground his teeth. He'd hoped the duel with Eranniv would make others underestimate him, make them more likely to duel him. It wasn't working. Relis barked out a laugh. He held out his arm to Melali, and tugged her away, his attendants following.

Elit hesitated.

Well, it's better than nothing, Adolin thought, a plan forming. 'What about you?' Adolin asked the cousin.

Elit looked him up and down. Adolin didn't know the man well. He was said to be a passable duelist, though he was often in his cousin's shadow.

But that *hunger* – Elit wanted to be a full Shardbearer.

'Elit?' Relis said.

'Same offer?' Elit said, meeting Adolin's gaze. 'Your five to my one?'

What a terrible deal.

'Same offer,' Adolin said.

'I'm in,' Elit said.

Behind him, Ruthar's son groaned. He grabbed Elit by the shoulder, towing him to the side with a growl.

'You told me to fight up through the brackets,' Adolin said to Relis. 'I'm doing that.'

'*Not* my cousin.'

'Too late,' Adolin said. 'You heard it. The ladies heard it. When do we fight, Elit?'

'Seven days,' Elit said. 'On Chachel.'

Seven days – a long wait, considering a challenge like this. So, he wanted time to train, did he? 'How about tomorrow instead?'

Relis snarled at Adolin, a very un-Alethi display, and shoved his cousin farther away. 'I can't see why you're so eager, Adolin. Shouldn't you focus on protecting that father of yours? It's always sad when a soldier lives long enough to see his wits go. Has he started wetting himself in public yet?'

Steady, Adolin told himself. Relis was trying to goad him, maybe get Adolin to take a hasty swing. That would let him petition to the king for redress and a voiding of all contracts with his house – including the dueling agreement with Elit. But the insult went too far. His companions gasped slightly, pulling away at the very un-Alethi bluntness.

Adolin didn't give in to the desperate goading. He had what he wanted. He wasn't certain what he could do about the assassin – but this, this was a way to help. Elit wasn't ranked highly, but he served Ruthar, who was – more and more – acting as Sadeas's right-hand man. Beating him would take Adolin one step closer to the real goal. A duel with Sadeas himself.

He turned to leave, and stopped short. Someone stood behind him – a stout man with a bulbous face and black curly hair. His complexion was ruddy, the nose too red, fine veins visible in his cheeks. The man had the arms of a soldier, despite his frivolous outfit – which was, Adolin admitted grudgingly, quite fashionable. Dark slacks that were trimmed with forest green silk, a short open coat over a stiff matching shirt. Scarf at the neck.

Torol Sadeas, highprince, Shardbearer, and the very man Adolin had been thinking of – the single person he hated most in the world.

'Another duel, young Adolin,' Sadeas said, taking a sip of wine. 'You really are determined to embarrass yourself out there. I still find it strange your father abandoned his prohibition of you dueling – indeed, I thought it a matter of honor to him.'

Adolin pushed past Sadeas, not trusting himself to speak so much as a single word to this eel of a man. Sight of the man brought memories of stark panic as he watched Sadeas retreat from the field of battle to leave Adolin and his father alone and surrounded.

Havar, Perethom, and Ilamar – good soldiers, good friends – had died that day. They and six thousand more.

Sadeas grabbed Adolin's shoulder as he passed. 'Think what you will, son,' the man whispered, 'but what I did was intended as a kindness to your father. A tip of the sword to an old ally.'

'*Let. Go.*'

'If you lose your mind as you age, pray to the Almighty there are people like myself willing to give you a good death. People who care enough not to snicker, but instead hold the sword for you as you fall on it.'

'I'll have your throat in my hands, Sadeas,' Adolin hissed. 'I'll squeeze and squeeze, then I'll sink my dagger into your gut and *twist*. A quick death is too good for you.'

'Tsk,' Sadeas said, smiling. 'Careful. It's a full room. What if someone heard you threatening a highprince?'

The Alethi way. You could abandon an ally on the battlefield, and everyone could know it – but an offense in person, well, that just wouldn't do. *Society* would *frown* on that. Nalan's hand! His father was right about them all.

Adolin turned in a quick motion, reversing out of Sadeas's grip. His next moves were by instinct, his fingers balling, stepping in preparation to plant a fist in that smiling, self-satisfied face.

A hand fell on Adolin's shoulder, causing him to hesitate.

'I don't think that would be wise, Brightlord Adolin,' said a soft but stern voice. It reminded Adolin of his father, though the timbre was off. He glanced at Amaram, who had stepped up beside him.

Tall, with a face like chipped stone, Brightlord Meridas Amaram was one of the only lighteyed men in the room who wore a proper uniform. As much as Adolin wished he himself could wear something more fashionable, he had come to realize the importance of the uniform as a symbol.

Adolin took a deep breath, lowering his fist. Amaram nodded to Sadeas, then turned Adolin by his shoulder and walked him away from the highprince.

'You mustn't let him provoke you, Your Highness,' Amaram said softly. 'He'll use you to embarrass your father, if he can.'

They moved through the room full of chattering attendants. Drinks and finger food had been distributed. It had turned from a short break during the meeting into a full-blown party. Not surprising. With all the important lighteyes here, people would want to mingle and connive.

'Why do you remain with him, Amaram?' Adolin asked.

'He is my liege lord.'

'You're of a rank that you could choose a new liege. Stormfather! You're a Shardbearer now. Nobody would even question you. Come to our camp. Join with Father.'

'In doing that, I would create a divide,' Amaram said softly. 'So long as I remain with Sadeas, I can help bridge gaps. He trusts me. So does your father. My friendship with both is a step toward keeping this kingdom together.'

'Sadeas will betray you.'

'No. Highprince Sadeas and I have an understanding.'

'We thought *we* had one. Then he set us up.'

Amaram's expression grew distant. Even the way he walked was so full of decorum, straight back, nodding with respect to many they passed. The perfect lighteyed general – brilliantly capable, yet not lofty. A sword for his highprince to employ. He'd spent the majority of the war diligently training new troops and sending the best of them to Sadeas while guarding sections of Alethkar. Amaram was half the reason that Sadeas had been so effective out here on the Shattered Plains.

'Your father is a man who cannot bend,' Amaram said. 'I wouldn't have it any other way, Adolin – but it does mean that the man he has become is not someone who can work with Highprince Sadeas.'

'And you're different?'

'Yes.'

Adolin snorted. Amaram was one of the finest the kingdom had, a man with a sterling reputation. 'I doubt that.'

'Sadeas and I agree that the means we choose to reach an honorable goal are allowed to be distasteful. Your father and I agree on what that goal should be – a better Alethkar, a place without all of this squabbling. It is a matter of perspective. . . .'

He continued talking, but Adolin found his mind drifting. He'd heard enough of this speech from his father. If Amaram started quoting *The Way of Kings* at him, he'd probably scream. At least—

Who was *that*?

Gorgeous red hair. There wasn't a *single* lock of black in it. A slender build, so different from the curvaceous Alethi. A silken blue dress, simple yet elegant. Pale skin – it almost had a Shin look to it – matched by light blue eyes. A slight dusting of freckles under the eyes, giving her an exotic cast.

The young woman seemed to glide through the room. Adolin twisted about, watching her pass. She was so *different*.

'Ash's eyes!' Amaram said, chuckling. 'You're still doing that, are you?'

Adolin pried his eyes away from the girl. 'Doing what?'

'Letting your eyes be drawn by every flitting little thing that swishes by. You need to settle down, son. Pick one. Your mother would be mortified to find you still unwed.'

'Jasnah's unwed too. She's a decade older than me.' Assuming she was still alive, as Aunt Navani was convinced.

'Your cousin is hardly a role model in that regard.' His tone implied more. *Or any regard.*

'*Look* at her, Amaram,' Adolin said, craning to the side and watching the young woman approach his father. 'That hair. Have you ever seen anything such a deep shade of red?'

'Veden, I'd warrant,' Amaram said. 'Horneater blood. There are family lines that pride themselves on it.'

Veden. It couldn't be . . . Could it?

'Excuse me,' Adolin said, breaking away from Amaram and shoving – politely – his way over to where the young woman was speaking to his father and his aunt.

'Brightlady Jasnah did go down with the ship, I'm afraid,' the woman was saying. 'I'm sorry for your loss . . .'

THE SILENT STORM

Now, as the Windrunners were thus engaged, arose the event which has hitherto been referenced: namely, that discovery of some wicked thing of eminence, though whether it be some rogueries among the Radiants' adherents or of some external origin, Avena would not suggest.

—From *Words of Radiance*, chapter 38, page 6

'. . . sorry for your loss,' Shallan said. 'I have brought with me what things of Jasnah's I was able to recover. My men have them outside.'

She found it surprisingly difficult to say the words with an even tone. She'd grieved for Jasnah during her weeks traveling, yet speaking of the death – remembering that terrible night – returned the emotions like surging waves, threatening to overwhelm again.

The image she'd drawn of herself came to her rescue. She could be that woman today – and that woman, while not emotionless, could push through the loss. She focused her attention on the moment, and the task at hand – specifically the two people in front of her. Dalinar and Navani Kholin.

The highprince was exactly what she'd expected him to be: a man with blunted features, short black hair silvering at the sides. His stiff uniform made him seem the only one in the room who knew anything about combat. She wondered if those bruises on his face were the result of the campaign against the Parshendi. Navani looked like a version of Jasnah twenty years older, still pretty, though with a motherly air. Shallan could never imagine Jasnah being motherly.

Navani had been smiling as Shallan approached, but now that levity was gone. *She still had hope for her daughter*, Shallan thought as the woman sat down in a nearby seat. *I just crushed it.*

'I thank you for bringing us this news,' Brightlord Dalinar said. 'It is . . . good to have confirmation.'

It felt terrible. Not just to be reminded of the death, but to weigh others down with it as well. 'I have information for you,' Shallan said, trying to be delicate. 'About the things Jasnah was working on.'

'More about those parshmen?' Navani snapped. 'Storms, that woman was too fascinated by them. Ever since she got it into her head that she was to blame for Gavilar's death.'

What was this? That wasn't a side of all this that Shallan had ever heard.

'Her research can wait,' Navani said, eyes fierce. 'I want to know exactly what happened when you think you saw her die. Precisely as you remember it, girl. No details passed over.'

'Perhaps after the meeting . . .' Dalinar said, resting a hand on Navani's shoulder. The touch was surprisingly tender. Was this not his brother's wife? That look in his eyes; was that familial affection for his sister, or was it something more?

'No, Dalinar,' Navani said. 'Now. I would hear it now.'

Shallan took a deep breath, preparing to begin, steeling herself against the emotions – and finding herself surprisingly in control. As she gathered her thoughts, she noticed a blond-haired young man watching her. That would likely be Adolin. He was handsome, as rumors indicated, and wore a blue uniform like his father. And yet Adolin's was somehow more . . . stylish? Was that the right word? She liked how his somewhat unruly hair contrasted with the crisp uniform. It made him seem more real, less picturesque.

She turned back to Navani. 'I woke in the middle of the night to shouting and the smell of smoke. I opened my door to unfamiliar men crowded around the doorway to Jasnah's cabin, across the companionway from my own. They had her body on the floor, and . . . Brightness, I watched them stab her through the heart. I'm sorry.'

Navani tensed, head flinching, as if she'd been slapped.

Shallan continued. She tried to give Navani as much truth as she could, but obviously the things Shallan had done – weaving light, Soulcasting the ship – weren't wise to share, at least for now. Instead, she indicated that she'd barricaded herself in her cabin, a lie she'd already prepared.

'I heard the men yelling up above as they were being executed, one by one,' Shallan said. 'I realized that the only hope I could give them was a crisis for the brigands, so I used the torch I'd taken and set the ship on fire.'

'On *fire*?' Navani asked, horrified. 'With my daughter unconscious?'

'Navani—' Dalinar said, squeezing her shoulder.

'You doomed her,' Navani said, locking eyes with Shallan. 'Jasnah wouldn't have been able to swim, like the others. She—'

'Navani,' Dalinar repeated, more firmly. 'This child's choice was a good one. You can hardly expect her to have taken on a band of men single-handed. And what she saw ... Jasnah was not unconscious, Navani. It was too late to do anything for her at that point.'

The woman took a deep breath, obviously struggling to keep her emotions in check. 'I ... apologize,' she said to Shallan. 'I am not myself at the moment, and I stray toward the irrational. Thank ... thank you for bringing word to us.' She stood. 'Excuse me.'

Dalinar nodded, letting her make a reasonably graceful exit. Shallan stepped back, hands clasped before herself, feeling impotent and strangely ashamed as she watched Navani leave. She hadn't expected that to go particularly well. And it hadn't.

She took the moment to check on Pattern, who was on her skirt, practically invisible. Even if he was noticed, he'd be thought an odd part of the fabric design – assuming, that was, he did as she'd ordered and didn't move or speak.

'I assume your trip here was an ordeal,' Dalinar said, turning to Shallan. 'Shipwrecked in the Frostlands?'

'Yes. Fortunately, I met with a caravan and traveled with them this way. We did encounter bandits, I regret to say, but were rescued by the timely arrival of some soldiers.'

'Soldiers?' Dalinar said, surprised. 'From what banner?'

'They did not say,' Shallan replied. 'I take it they were formerly of the Shattered Plains.'

'Deserters?'

'I have not asked for specifics, Brightlord,' Shallan said. 'But I *did* promise them clemency for previous crimes, in recognition of their act of nobility. They saved dozens of lives. Everyone in the caravan I joined can vouch for the bravery of these men. I suspect they sought atonement and a chance to start over.'

'I will see that the king seals pardons for them,' Dalinar said. 'Prepare a list for me. Hanging soldiers always feels like a waste.'

Shallan relaxed. One item dealt with.

'There is another matter of some delicacy we must discuss, Brightlord,' Shallan said. They both turned toward Adolin, loitering nearby. He smiled.

And he *did* have a very nice smile.

When Jasnah had first explained the causal to her, Shallan's interest had been completely abstract. Marriage into a powerful Alethi house? Allies for her brothers? Legitimacy, and a way to continue working with Jasnah for the salvation of the world? These had seemed like wonderful things.

Looking at Adolin's grin, however, she didn't consider *any* of those advantages. Her pains of speaking of Jasnah didn't fade completely, but she found it much easier to ignore them when looking at him. She found herself blushing.

This, she thought, *could be dangerous.*

Adolin stepped up to join them, the hum of conversation all around giving them some privacy within the crowd. He had found a cup of orange wine for her somewhere, which he held out. 'Shallan Davar?' he asked.

'Um . . .' Was she? Oh, right. She took the wine. 'Yes?'

'Adolin Kholin,' he said. 'I am sorry to hear of your hardships. We will need to speak to the king of his sister. I can spare you that task, if I might go in your place.'

'Thank you,' Shallan said. 'But I would prefer to see him myself.'

'Of course,' Adolin said. 'As for our . . . involvement. It *did* make a lot more sense when you were Jasnah's ward, didn't it?'

'Probably.'

'Though, now that you're here, perhaps we should go for a walk and just see how things feel.'

'I like to walk,' Shallan said. *Stupid! Quick, say something witty.* 'Um. Your hair is nice.'

A part of her – the part trained by Tyn – groaned.

'My hair?' Adolin said, touching it.

'Yes,' Shallan said, trying to get her sluggish brain working again. 'Blond hair isn't often seen in Jah Keved.'

'Some people see it as a mark of my bloodline being impure.'

'Funny. They say the same about me because of my hair.' She smiled at him. That seemed the right move, since he smiled back. Her verbal recovery hadn't been the deftest of her career, but she couldn't be doing too poorly, so long as he was smiling.

Dalinar cleared his throat. Shallan blinked. She'd completely forgotten that the highprince was there.

'Adolin,' he said, 'fetch me some wine.'

'Father?' Adolin turned to him. 'Oh. All right, then.' He walked off. Ash's *eyes*, that man was handsome. She turned to Dalinar who, well, wasn't. Oh, he was distinguished, but his nose had been broken at some point, and his face was a tad unfortunate. The bruises didn't help either.

In fact, he was downright intimidating.

'I would know more of you,' he said softly, 'the precise status of your family, and why you are so eager to be involved with my son.'

'My family is destitute,' Shallan said. Frankness seemed the right approach with this man. 'My father is dead, though the people to whom we owe money do not yet know it. I had not considered a union with Adolin until Jasnah suggested it, but I would seize it eagerly, if allowed. Marriage into your house would provide my family with a great deal of protection.'

She still didn't know what to do about the Soulcaster her brothers owed. One step at a time.

Dalinar grunted. He wouldn't have expected her to be so direct. 'So you have nothing to offer,' he said.

'From what Jasnah said to me of your opinions,' Shallan said, 'I did not assume that my monetary or political offerings would be your first consideration. If such a union was your goal, you'd have had Prince Adolin married off years ago.' She winced at her forwardness. 'With all due respect, Brightlord.'

'No offense taken,' Dalinar said. 'I like it when people are direct. Just because I want to let my son have a say in the matter doesn't mean I don't want him to marry well. A woman from a minor foreign house who professes her family is destitute and who brings nothing to the union?'

'I did not say I could offer nothing,' Shallan replied. 'Brightlord, how many wards has Jasnah Kholin taken in the last ten years?'

'None that I know of,' he admitted.

'Do you know how many she has turned away?'

'I've an inkling.'

'Yet she took me. Might that not constitute an endorsement of what I can offer?'

Dalinar nodded slowly. 'We will maintain the causal for now,' he said. 'The reason I agreed to it in the first place still stands – I want Adolin to be seen as unavailable to those who would manipulate him for political gain. If you can somehow persuade me, Brightness Navani, and of course the lad himself, we can progress the causal to a full betrothal. In the meantime, I'll give you a position among my lesser clerks. You can prove yourself there.'

The offer, though generous, felt like ropes tightening about her. The stipend of a lesser clerk would be enough to live on, but nothing to brag about. And she had no doubt that Dalinar would be watching her. Those eyes of his were scarily discerning. She wouldn't be able to move without her actions being reported to him.

His charity would be her prison.

'That is generous of you, Brightlord,' she found herself saying, 'but I actually have—'

'Dalinar!' one of the others in the room called. 'Are we going to start this meeting again sometime today, or am I going to have to order in a proper dinner!'

Dalinar turned toward a plump, bearded man in traditional clothing – an open-fronted robe over a loose shirt and warrior's skirt, called a takama. *Highprince Sebarial*, Shallan thought. Jasnah's notes dismissed him as obnoxious and useless. She'd had kinder words even for Highprince Sadeas, whom she had noted was not to be trusted.

'Fine, fine, Sebarial,' Dalinar said, breaking away from Shallan and walking to a group of seats in the center of the room. He settled down in one beside the desk there. A proud man with a prominent nose settled down next to him. That would be the king, Elhokar. He was younger than

Shallan had pictured. Why had Sebarial called on Dalinar to reconvene the meeting, and not the king?

The next few moments were a test of Shallan's preparation as highborn men and women settled themselves in the lavish chairs. Beside each one was a small table and behind that, a master-servant for important needs. A number of parshmen kept the tables filled with wine, nuts, and fresh and dried fruit. Shallan shivered each time one of those passed her.

She counted the highprinces off in her head. Sadeas was easy to pick out, red-faced from visible veins under the skin, like her father had displayed after drinking. Others nodded to him and let him seat himself first. He seemed to command as much respect as Dalinar. His wife, Ialai, was a slender-necked woman with thick lips, large bust, and a wide mouth. Jasnah had noted that she was as shrewd as her husband.

Two highprinces sat to either side of the couple. One was Aladar, a renowned duelist. The short man was listed in Jasnah's notes as a powerful highprince, fond of taking risks, known to gamble in the type of games of random chance that the devotaries forbade. He and Sadeas seemed to be on very friendly terms. Weren't they enemies? She'd read that they often squabbled over lands. Well, that was obviously a broken stone, for they seemed united as they regarded Dalinar.

Joining them were Highprince Ruthar and his wife. Jasnah considered them to be little more than thieves, but warned that the pair were dangerous and opportunistic.

The room seemed oriented so that all eyes were on those two factions. The king and Dalinar against Sadeas, Ruthar, and Aladar. Obviously, the political alignments had changed since Jasnah made her notes.

The room hushed, and nobody seemed to care that Shallan was watching. Adolin took a seat behind his father, next to a younger man in spectacles and an empty seat probably vacated by Navani. Shallan carefully rounded the room – the peripheries were clogged with guards, attendants, and even some men in Shardplate – getting out of Dalinar's direct line of sight, just in case he noticed her and decided to eject her.

Brightlady Jayla Ruthar spoke first, leaning forward over clasped hands. 'Your Majesty,' she said, 'I fear that our conversation this day has run in circles, and that nothing is being accomplished. Your safety is, of course, our greatest concern.'

Across the circle of highprinces, Sebarial snorted loudly as he chewed on slices of melon. Everyone else seemed to pointedly ignore the obnoxious, bearded man.

'Yes,' Aladar said. 'The Assassin in White. We *must* do something. I will not wait in my palace to be assassinated.'

'He is murdering princes and kings all across the world!' Roion added. The man looked like a turtle to Shallan, with those hunched shoulders and that balding head. What had Jasnah said about him . . . ?

That he's a coward, Shallan thought. *He always chooses the safe option.*

'We must present a unified Alethkar,' Hatham said – she recognized him immediately, with that long neck and refined way of speaking. 'We must not allow ourselves to be attacked one at a time, and we must not squabble.'

'That's precisely why you should follow my commands,' the king said, frowning at the highprinces.

'No,' Ruthar said, 'it is why we must abandon these ludicrous restrictions you have placed upon us, Your Majesty! This is not a time to look foolish before the world.'

'Listen to Ruthar,' Sebarial said dryly, leaning back in his chair. 'He's an expert at looking like a fool.'

The arguing continued, and Shallan got a better feel for the room. There were actually three factions. Dalinar and the king, the team with Sadeas, and what she dubbed the peacemakers. Led by Hatham – who seemed, when he spoke, the most natural politician in the room – this third group sought to mediate.

So that's what it's really about, she thought, listening as Ruthar argued with the king and Adolin Kholin. *They're each trying to persuade these neutral highprinces to join their faction.*

Dalinar said little. The same for Sadeas, who seemed content to let Highprince Ruthar and his wife speak for him. The two watched each other, Dalinar with a neutral expression, Sadeas with a faint smile. It seemed innocent enough until you saw their eyes. Locked on to one another, rarely blinking.

There was a storm in this room. A silent one.

Everyone seemed to fall into one of the three factions except for Sebarial, who kept rolling his eyes, occasionally throwing out commentary that bordered on the obscene. He obviously made the other Alethi, with their haughty airs, uncomfortable.

Shallan slowly picked apart the conversation's subtext. This talk of prohibitions and rules placed by the king ... it wasn't the rules *themselves* that seemed to matter, but the authority behind them. How much would the highprinces submit to the king, and how much autonomy could they demand? It was fascinating.

Right up to the moment when one of them mentioned her.

'Wait,' said Vamah – one of the neutral highprinces. 'Who is that girl over there? Does someone have a Veden in their retinue?'

'She was speaking with Dalinar,' Roion said. 'Is there news of Jah Keved that you're keeping from us, Dalinar?'

'You, girl,' said Ialai Sadeas. 'What can you tell us of your homeland's succession war? Do you have information on this assassin? Why would someone in the employ of the Parshendi seek to undermine *your* throne?'

All eyes in the room turned toward Shallan. She felt a moment of sheer panic. The most important people in the world, interrogating her, their eyes drilling into her—

And then she remembered the drawing. *That* was who she was.

'Alas,' Shallan said, 'I will be of little use to you, Brightlords and Brightladies. I was away from my homeland when that tragic assassination occurred, and I have no insight into its cause.'

'Then what are you doing here?' Hatham asked, polite, but insistent.

'She's watching the zoo, obviously,' Sebarial said. 'The lot of you making fools of yourselves is the best free entertainment to be found in this frozen wasteland.'

It probably *was* wise to ignore that one. 'I am the ward of Jasnah Kholin,' Shallan said, meeting Hatham's eyes. 'My purpose here is of a personal nature.'

'Ah,' Aladar said. 'The phantom betrothal I've heard rumors of.'

'That's right,' Ruthar said. He had a decidedly oily look about him, with dark slicked hair, burly arms, and a beard around the mouth. Most disturbing, however, was that smile of his – a smile that seemed far too predatory. 'Child, what would it take for you to visit my warcamp and speak to my scribes? I need to know what is happening in Jah Keved.'

'I will do better than that,' Roion said. 'Where are you staying, girl? I offer an invitation to visit my palace. I too would hear of your homeland.'

But ... she'd just said she didn't know anything ...

Shallan dredged up Jasnah's training. They didn't care about Jah Keved. They wanted to get information about her betrothal – they suspected that there was more to the story.

The two who had just invited her were among those Jasnah rated the least politically savvy. The others – like Aladar and Hatham – would wait until a private time to make the invitation, so they didn't reveal their interest in public.

'Your concern is unwarranted, Roion,' Dalinar said. 'She is, of course, staying in my warcamp and has a position among my clerks.'

'Actually,' Shallan said, 'I didn't get a chance to respond to your offer, Brightlord Kholin. I would love the opportunity to be in your service, but alas, I have already taken a position in another warcamp.'

Stunned silence.

She knew what she *wanted* to say next. A huge gamble, one of which Jasnah would never have approved. She found herself speaking anyway, trusting her instincts. It worked in art, after all.

'Brightlord Sebarial,' Shallan said, looking toward the bearded man that Jasnah so thoroughly detested, 'was the first to offer me a position and invite me to stay with him.'

The man almost choked on his wine. He looked up over the cup toward her, narrowing his eyes.

She shrugged with what she hoped was an innocent gesture, and smiled. *Please . . .*

'Uh, that's right,' Sebarial said, leaning back. 'She's a distant family relation. Couldn't possibly live with myself if I didn't give her a place to stay.'

'His offer was quite generous,' Shallan said. 'Three full broams a week support.'

Sebarial's eyes bugged out.

'I wasn't aware of this,' Dalinar said, looking from Sebarial to her.

'I'm sorry, Brightlord,' Shallan said. 'I should have told you. I didn't find it appropriate to be staying in the house of someone who was courting me. Surely you understand.'

He frowned. 'What I'm having trouble understanding is why anyone would want to be closer to Sebarial than they need to be.'

'Oh, Uncle Sebarial is quite tolerable, once you get used to him,' Shallan said. 'Like a very annoying noise that you eventually learn to ignore.'

Most seemed horrified at her comment, though Aladar smiled. Sebarial – as she'd hoped – laughed out loud.

'I guess that is settled,' Ruthar said, dissatisfied. 'I do hope you'll at least be willing to come brief me.'

'Give it up, Ruthar,' Sebarial said. 'She's too young for you. Though with you involved, I'm sure it *would* be brief.'

Ruthar sputtered. 'I wasn't implying . . . You moldy old . . . Bah!'

Shallan was glad that attention then turned from her back to the topics at hand, because that last comment had her blushing. Sebarial *was* inappropriate. Still, he seemed to be making an effort to leave himself out of these political discussions, and that seemed like the place where Shallan wanted to be. The position with the most freedom. She *would* still work with Dalinar and Navani on Jasnah's notes, but she didn't want to be beholden to them.

Who is to say being beholden to this man is any different? Shallan thought, rounding the room to approach where Sebarial sat, without wife or family members to attend him. He was unmarried.

'Almost threw you out on your ear, girl,' Sebarial said quietly, sipping his wine and not looking at her. 'Stupid move, putting yourself in my hands. Everyone knows I like to set things on fire and watch them burn.'

'And yet you *didn't* throw me out,' she said. 'So it wasn't a stupid move. Merely a risk that paid rewards.'

'Still might drop you. I'm certainly not paying that three broams. That's almost as much as my mistress costs, and at least I get something from that arrangement.'

'You'll pay,' Shallan said. 'It's a matter of public record now. But don't worry. I will earn my keep.'

'You have information about Kholin?' Sebarial asked, studying his wine.

So he *did* care.

'Information, yes,' Shallan said. 'Less about Kholin, and more about the world itself. Trust me, Sebarial. You've just entered into a very profitable arrangement.'

She'd have to figure out why that was.

The others continued arguing about the Assassin in White, and she gathered that he had attacked here but had been fought off. As Aladar steered the conversation to a complaint that his gemstones were being taken by the Crown – Shallan didn't know the reason they'd been seized – Dalinar Kholin slowly stood up. He moved like a rolling boulder. Inevitable, implacable.

Aladar trailed off.

'I passed a curious pile of stones along my path,' Dalinar said. 'Of a type I found remarkable. The fractured shale had been weathered by highstorms, blown up against stone of a more durable nature. This pile of thin wafers lay as if stacked by some mortal hand.'

The others looked at Dalinar as if he were mad. Something about the words tugged at Shallan's memory. They were a quotation from something she'd once read.

Dalinar turned, walking toward the open windows on the leeward side of the room. 'But no man had stacked these stones. Precarious though they looked, they were actually quite solid, a formation from once-buried strata now exposed to open air. I wondered how it was possible they remained in such a neat stack, with the fury of the tempests blowing against them.

'I soon ascertained their true nature. I found that force from one direction pushed them back against one another and the rock behind. No amount of pressure I could produce in that manner caused them to shift. And yet, when I removed one stone from the bottom – pulling it out instead of pushing it in – the entire formation collapsed in a miniature avalanche.'

The room's occupants stared at him until Sebarial finally spoke for all of them. 'Dalinar,' the plump man said, 'what in *Damnation's* eleventh name are you on about?'

'Our methods aren't working,' Dalinar said, looking back at the lot of them. 'Years at war, and we find ourselves in the same position as before. We can no more fight this assassin now than on the night he killed my brother. The king of Jah Keved put three Shardbearers and half an army up against the creature, then died with a Blade through the chest, his Shards left to be scavenged by opportunists.

'If we cannot defeat the assassin, then we must remove his reason for attacking. If we can capture or eliminate his employers, then perhaps we can invalidate whatever contract binds him. Last we knew, he was employed by the Parshendi.'

'Great,' Ruthar said dryly. 'All we have to do is win the war, which we've only been trying to do for five years.'

'We *haven't* been trying,' Dalinar said. 'Not hard enough. I intend to make peace with the Parshendi. If they will not have it on our terms, then I will set out into the Shattered Plains with my army and any who will join me. No more games on plateaus, fighting over gemhearts. I will strike toward the Parshendi camp, find it, and defeat them once and for all.'

The king sighed softly, leaning back behind his desk. Shallan guessed he'd been expecting this.

'Out onto the Shattered Plains,' Sadeas said. 'That sounds like a marvelous thing for you to try.'

'Dalinar,' Hatham said, speaking with obvious care, 'I don't see that our situation has changed. The Shattered Plains are still largely unexplored, and the Parshendi camp could be literally *anywhere* out there, hidden among miles and miles of terrain that our army cannot traverse without great difficulty. We agreed that attacking their camp was imprudent, so long as they were willing to come to us.'

'Their willingness to come to us, Hatham,' Dalinar said, 'has proved to be a problem, because it puts the battle on their terms. No, our situation hasn't changed. Merely our resolve. This war has persisted far too long already. I will finish it, one way or another.'

'Sounds wonderful,' Sadeas repeated. 'Will you be off tomorrow or wait until the next day?'

Dalinar gave him a disdainful look.

'Just trying to estimate when there will be an open warcamp,' Sadeas said innocently. 'I've almost outgrown mine, and wouldn't mind spilling into a second once the Parshendi slaughter you and yours. To think, after all the trouble you got yourself into by getting surrounded out there, that you're going to go do it again.'

Adolin stood up behind his father, face red, angerspren bubbling at his feet like pools of blood. His brother coaxed him back down into his seat. There was something here, obviously, that Shallan was missing.

I wandered into the middle of all this without nearly enough context, she thought. *Storms, I'm lucky I haven't been chewed up already.* Suddenly, she wasn't quite so proud of her accomplishments this day.

'Before the highstorm last night,' Dalinar said, 'we had a messenger from the Parshendi – the first willing to speak with us in ages. He said that his leaders wished to discuss the possibility of peace.'

The highprinces looked stunned. *Peace?* Shallan thought, heart leaping. That would certainly make it easier to get out and search for Urithiru.

'That very night,' Dalinar said softly, 'the assassin struck. Again. Last time he came was just after we had signed a peace treaty with the Parshendi. Now, he comes again the day of another peace offer.'

'Those bastards,' Aladar said softly. 'Is this some kind of twisted ritual of theirs?'

'It might be a coincidence,' Dalinar said. 'The assassin has been striking all over the world. Surely the Parshendi haven't contacted all of these people. However, the events make me wary. Almost, I wonder if the Parshendi are being framed – if someone is using this assassin to make certain that Alethkar never knows peace. But then, the Parshendi *did* claim to have hired him to kill my brother. . . .'

'Maybe they're desperate,' Roion said, hunkering down in his chair. 'One faction among them sues for peace while the other does whatever it can to destroy us.'

'Either way, I intend to plan for the worst,' Dalinar said, looking to Sadeas. 'I *will* be making my way to the center of the Shattered Plains – either to defeat the Parshendi for good, or to accept their surrender and disarmament – but such an expedition will take time to arrange. I'll need to train my men for an extended operation and send scouts to map farther into the middle of the Plains. Beyond that, I need to choose some new Shardbearers.'

'. . . new Shardbearers?' Roion asked, turtle-like head rising in curiosity.

'I will soon come into the possession of more Shards,' Dalinar said.

'And are we allowed to know the source of this amazing trove?' Aladar asked.

'Why, Adolin is going to win them from all of you,' Dalinar said.

Some of the others chuckled, as if it were a joke. Dalinar did not seem to intend it as one. He sat back down, and the others took this as marking an end to the meeting – once again, it seemed that Dalinar, and not the king, truly led.

The entire balance of power has shifted here, Shallan thought. *As has the nature of the war.* Jasnah's notes about the court were *definitely* outdated.

'Well, I suppose you're going to accompany me back to my camp now,'

Sebarial said to her, rising. 'Which means this meeting wasn't just the usual waste of time listening to blowhards make veiled threats to one another – it actually cost me money as well.'

'It could be worse,' Shallan said, helping the older man rise, as he seemed somewhat unsteady on his feet. That passed once he was standing, and he pulled his arm free.

'Worse? How?'

'I could be boring as well as expensive.'

He looked at her, then laughed. 'I suppose that's true. Well, come on then.'

'Just a moment,' Shallan said, 'you go on ahead, and I'll catch up at your carriage.'

She walked off, seeking the king, to whom she personally delivered news of Jasnah's death. He took it well, with regal dignity. Dalinar had probably already informed him.

That task done, she sought out the king's scribes. A short time later, she left the conference chamber and found Vathah and Gaz waiting nervously outside. She handed a sheet of paper to Vathah.

'What's this?' he asked, twisting it about.

'Writ of pardon,' she said. 'Sealed by the king. It's for you and your men. We'll soon receive specific ones with their names on them, but meanwhile this will keep you from being arrested.'

'You actually did it?' Vathah asked, looking it over, though he obviously couldn't make sense of the writing. 'Storms, you actually kept your word?'

'Of course I did,' Shallan said. 'Note that it only covers *past* crimes, so tell the men to be on their best behavior. Now, let's be going. I have arranged a place for us to stay.'

FOUR YEARS AGO

Father held feasts because he wanted to pretend that everything was all right. He invited local brightlords from nearby hamlets, he fed them and gave them wine, he displayed his daughter.

Then, the next day after everyone was gone, he sat at his table and listened to his scribes tell him how impoverished he had grown. Shallan saw him afterward sometimes, holding his forehead, staring straight ahead at nothing.

For tonight, however, they feasted and pretended.

'You've met my daughter, of course,' Father said, gesturing to Shallan as his guests were seated. 'The jewel of House Davar, our pride above all others.'

The visitors – lighteyes from two valleys over – nodded politely as Father's parshmen brought wine. Both the drink and the slaves were a way to display riches Father didn't actually possess. Shallan had begun helping with the accounts, her duty as daughter. She knew the truth of their finances.

The evening's chill was offset by the crackling hearth; this room might have felt homey somewhere else. Not here.

The servants poured her wine. Yellow, mildly intoxicating. Father drank violet, prepared in its strength. He settled himself down at the high table, which ran the width of the room – the same room where Helaran had threatened to kill him a year and a half ago. They'd received a brief letter from Helaran six months back, along with a book by the famous Jasnah Kholin for Shallan to read.

Shallan had read his note to her father in a trembling whisper. It hadn't said much. Mostly veiled threats. That night, Father had beaten one of the maids near to death. Isan still walked with a limp. The servants no longer gossiped about Father having killed his wife.

Nobody does anything at all to resist him, Shallan thought, glancing toward her father. *We're all too scared.*

Shallan's three other brothers sat in a huddled knot at their own table. They avoided looking at their father or interacting with the guests. Several small sphere goblets glowed on the tables, but the room as a whole could have used more light. Neither spheres nor hearthlight were enough to drive out the gloom. She thought that her father liked it that way.

The visiting lighteyes – Brightlord Tavinar – was a slender, well-dressed man with a deep red silk coat. He and his wife sat close together at the high table, their teenaged daughter between them. Shallan had not caught her name.

As the evening progressed, Father tried to speak to them a few times, but they gave only terse responses. For all that it was supposed to be a feast, nobody seemed to be enjoying themselves. The visitors looked as if they wished they'd never accepted the invitation, but Father was more politically important than they, and good relations with him would be valuable.

Shallan picked at her own food, listening to her father boast about his new axehound breeding stud. He spoke of their prosperity. Lies.

She did not want to contradict him. He had been good to her. He was always good to her. Yet, shouldn't someone do something?

Helaran might have. He'd left them.

It's growing worse and worse. Someone needs to do something, say something, to change Father. He shouldn't be doing the things that he did, growing drunk, beating the darkeyes ...

The first course passed. Then Shallan noticed something. Balat – whom Father had started calling Nan Balat, as if he were the oldest – kept glancing at the guests. That was surprising. He usually ignored them.

Tavinar's daughter caught his eye, smiled, then looked back at her food. Shallan blinked. Balat ... and a girl? How odd to consider.

Father didn't seem to notice. He eventually stood and raised his cup to the room. 'Tonight, we celebrate. Good neighbors, strong wine.'

Tavinar and his wife hesitantly raised their cups. Shallan had only just begun to study propriety – it was hard to do, as her tutors kept leaving – but she knew that a good Vorin brightlord was not supposed to celebrate drunkenness. Not that they *wouldn't* get drunk, but it was the Vorin way not to talk about it. Such niceties were not her father's strong point.

'It is an important night,' Father said after taking a sip of his wine. 'I have just received word from Brightlord Gevelmar, whom I believe you know, Tavinar. I have been without a wife for too long. Brightlord Gevelmar is sending his youngest daughter along with writs of marriage. My ardents will perform the service at the end of the month, and I will have a wife.'

Shallan felt cold. She pulled her shawl closer. The aforementioned ardents sat at their own table, dining silently. The three men were greying in equal measure, and had served long enough to know Shallan's grandfather as a youth. They treated her with kindness, however, and studying with them brought her pleasure when all other things seemed to be collapsing.

'Why does nobody speak?' Father demanded, turning around the room. 'I have just become betrothed! You look like a bunch of storming Alethi. We're Veden! Make some noise, you idiots.'

The visitors clapped politely, though they looked even more uncomfortable than they had before. Balat and the twins shared looks, and then lightly thumped the table.

'To the void with all of you.' Father slumped back into his chair as his parshmen approached the low table, each bearing a box. 'Gifts for my children to mark the occasion,' Father said with a wave of the hand. 'Don't know why I bother. Bah!' He drank the rest of his wine.

The boys got daggers, very fine pieces engraved like Shardblades. Shallan's gift was a necklace of fat silvery links. She held it silently. Father didn't like her speaking much at feasts, though he always placed her table close to the high table.

He never shouted at her. Not directly. Sometimes, she wished he would. Maybe then Jushu wouldn't resent her so. It—

The door to the feast hall slammed open. The poor light revealed a tall man in dark clothing standing at the threshold.

'What is this!' Father demanded, rising, slamming his hands on the table. 'Who interrupts my feast?'

The man strode in. His face was so long and slender, it looked as if it had been pinched. He wore ruffles at the cuffs of his soft maroon coat, and the way he pursed his lips made him look as if he'd just found a latrine that had overflowed in the rain.

One of his eyes was intense blue. The other dark brown. Both lighteyed and dark. Shallan felt a chill.

A Davar house servant dashed up to the high table, then whispered to Father. Shallan did not catch what was said, but whatever it was, it drained the thunder right out of Father's expression. He remained standing, but his jaw dropped.

A handful of servants in maroon livery filed in around the newcomer. He stepped forward with a precise air, as if choosing his steps with some care to avoid stepping in anything. 'I have been sent by His Highness, Highprince Valam, ruler of these lands. It has come to his attention that dark rumors persist in these lands. Rumors regarding the death of a lighteyed woman.' He met Father's eyes.

'My wife was killed by her lover,' Father said. 'Who then killed himself.'

'Others tell a different story, Brightlord Lin Davar,' the newcomer said. 'Such rumors are . . . troublesome. They provoke dissatisfaction with His Highness. If a brightlord under his rule *were* to have murdered a lighteyed woman of rank, it is not something he can ignore.'

Father did not respond with the outrage Shallan would have predicted. Instead he waved his hands toward Shallan and the visitors. 'Away,' he said. 'Give me space. You there, messenger, let us speak alone. No need to drag mud into the hallway.'

The Tavinars rose, looking all too eager to be going. The girl did glance back at Balat as they left, whispering softly.

Father looked toward Shallan, and she realized she'd frozen in place again at the mention of her mother, sitting at her table just before the high table.

'Child,' Father said softly, 'go sit with your brothers.'

She withdrew, passing the messenger as he stepped up to the high table. Those eyes . . . It was Redin, the highprince's bastard son. His father used him as an executioner and assassin, it was said.

495

Since her brothers hadn't been explicitly banished from the room, they took chairs around the hearth, far enough away to give father privacy. They left a spot for Shallan, and she settled down, the fine silk of her dress rumpling. The voluminous way it enveloped her made her feel as if she weren't really there and only the dress mattered.

The highprince's bastard settled down at the table with Father. At least someone was confronting him. But what if the highprince's bastard decided Father was guilty? What then? Inquest? She didn't want Father to fall; she wanted to stop the darkness that was slowly strangling them all. It seemed like their light had gone out when Mother died.

When Mother . . .

'Shallan?' Balat asked. 'Are you well?'

She shook herself. 'Can I see the daggers? They looked quite fine from my table.'

Wikim just stared at the fire, but Balat tossed his to her. She caught it clumsily, then pulled it from its sheath, admiring the way the metal folds reflected the hearthlight.

The boys watched the flamespren dance on the fire. The three brothers never talked anymore.

Balat glanced over his shoulder, toward the high table. 'I wish I could hear what was being said,' he whispered. 'Maybe they'll drag him away. That would be fitting, for what he's done.'

'He didn't kill Mother,' Shallan said softly.

'Oh?' Balat snorted. 'Then what did happen?'

'I . . .'

She didn't know. She couldn't think. Not of that time, that day. Had Father actually done it? She felt cold again, despite the fire's warmth.

The silence returned.

Someone . . . someone needed to *do* something.

'They're talking about plants,' Shallan said.

Balat and Jushu looked at her. Wikim continued staring at the fire.

'Plants,' Balat said flatly.

'Yes. I can hear them faintly.'

'I can't hear a thing.'

Shallan shrugged from within her too-enveloping dress. 'My ears are better than yours. Yes, plants. Father is complaining that the trees in his gardens never listen when he tells them to obey. "They have been dropping their leaves because of a sickness," he says, "and they refuse to grow new ones."

' "Have you tried beating them for their disobedience?" the messenger asks.

' "All the time," Father replies. "I even break off their limbs, yet they still do not obey! It is untidy. At the very least, they should clean up after themselves."

' "A problem," the messenger says, "as trees without foliage are hardly worth keeping. Fortunately, I have the solution. My cousin once had trees that acted this way, and he found that all he needed to do was sing to them and their leaves popped right back out."

' "Ah, of course," Father says. "I will try that immediately."

' "I hope that it works for you."

' "Well, if it does, I will certainly be relieved."'

Her brothers stared at her, baffled.

Finally, Jushu cocked his head. He was the youngest of the brothers, just above Shallan herself. 'Re . . . leaf . . . ed . . .'

Balat burst into laughter – loud enough that their father glared at them. 'Oh, that is *awful*,' Balat said. 'That is purely awful, Shallan. You should be ashamed.'

She huddled down in her dress, grinning. Even Wikim, the older twin, cracked a smile. She hadn't seen him smile in . . . how long?

Balat wiped his eyes. 'I actually thought, for a moment, you could really hear them. You little Voidbringer.' He let out a deep breath. 'Storms, but that felt good.'

'We should laugh more,' Shallan said.

'This hasn't been a place for laughter,' Jushu said, sipping his wine.

'Because of Father?' Shallan asked. 'There's one of him and four of us. We just need to be more optimistic.'

'Being optimistic does not change facts,' Balat said. 'I wish Helaran hadn't left.' He thumped his fist down on the side of his chair.

'Do not begrudge him his travels, Tet Balat,' Shallan said softly. 'There are so many places to see, places we will probably never visit. Let one of us go to them. Think of the stories he will bring back to us. The colors.'

Balat looked across the drab blackrock room, with its muted hearths glowing red-orange. 'Colors. I wouldn't mind a little more color around here.'

Jushu smiled. 'Anything would be a nice change from Father's face.'

'Now, don't be down on Father's face,' Shallan said. 'It's quite adept at doing its duty.'

'Which is?'

'Reminding us all that there are worse things than his odor. It's really quite a noble Calling.'

'Shallan!' Wikim said. He looked dramatically unlike Jushu. Spindly and sunken-eyed, Wikim had hair cut so short he almost looked like an ardent. 'Don't say such things where Father could hear.'

'He's engrossed in conversation,' Shallan said. 'But you are right. I probably shouldn't mock our family. House Davar is distinctive and enduring.'

Jushu raised his cup. Wikim nodded sharply.

'Of course,' she added, 'the same could be said for a wart.'

Jushu just about spat out his wine. Balat let out another roaring laugh.

'Stop that racket!' Father shouted at them.

'It's a feast!' Balat called back. 'Did you not ask us to be more Veden!'

Father glared at him, then returned to his conversation with the messenger. The two huddled together at the high table, Father's posture supplicating, the highprince's bastard sitting back with an arched eyebrow and a still face.

'Storms, Shallan,' Balat said. 'When did you become so clever?'

Clever? She didn't feel clever. Suddenly, the forwardness of what she'd said caused her to shrink back into her chair. These things, they'd simply slid out of her mouth. 'Those are just things . . . just things I read in a book.'

'Well, you should read more of those books, small one,' Balat said. 'It seems brighter in here for it.'

Father slammed his hand down on the table, shaking cups, rattling plates. Shallan glanced at him, worried as he pointed his finger at the messenger and said something. It was too soft and far away for Shallan to make it out, but she knew that look in her father's eyes. She had seen it many times before he took his cane – or even once the fireplace poker – to one of the servants.

The messenger stood up in a smooth motion. His refinement seemed a shield that rebuffed Father's temper.

Shallan envied him.

'It appears I will get nowhere with this conversation,' the messenger said loudly. He looked at Father, but his tone seemed to imply that his words were for them all. 'I came prepared for that inevitability. The high-prince has given me authority, and I would very much like to know the *truth* of what happened in this household. Any lighteyes of birth who can provide witness will be welcomed.'

'They need the testimony of a lighteyes,' Jushu said softly to his siblings. 'Father is important enough that they can't just remove him.'

'There was one,' the messenger said loudly, 'who was willing to speak to us of the truth. He has since made himself unavailable. Do any of you have his courage? Will you come with me and testify to the highprince of the crimes committed on these lands?'

He looked toward the four of them. Shallan huddled in her chair, trying to look small. Wikim didn't look away from the flames. Jushu looked like he might stand, but then turned to his wine, cursing, his face growing red.

Balat. Balat grabbed the sides of his chair as if to stand, but then glanced at Father. That intensity in Father's eyes remained. When his rage was redhot, he yelled, he threw things at the servants.

It was now, when his rage became cold, that he grew truly dangerous. This was when Father got quiet. This was when the yelling stopped.

Father's yelling, at least.

'He'll kill me,' Balat whispered. 'If I say a word, he'll kill me.' His earlier bravado melted away. He seemed not a man any longer, but a youth – a terrified teenager.

'You could do it, Shallan,' Wikim hissed at her. 'Father won't dare hurt you. Besides, you actually *saw* what happened.'

'I didn't,' she whispered.

'You were there!'

'I don't know what happened. I don't remember it.'

It didn't happen. It didn't.

A log shifted in the hearth. Balat stared at the floor, and did not stand. None of them would. A whirling group of translucent flower petals stirred among them, fading into view. Shamespren.

'I see,' the messenger said. 'If any of you . . . *remember* the truth at some point in the future, you will find willing ears in Vedenar.'

'You will not tear this house apart, bastard,' Father said, standing. 'We stand by one another.'

'Save for those who can no longer stand, I assume.'

'Leave this house!'

The messenger gave Father a look of disgust, a demeaning sneer. It said, *I am a bastard, but even I am not as low as you.* He then left, sweeping from the room and gathering his men outside, his terse orders indicating that he wished to be back on the road despite the late hour, on another errand beyond Father's estates.

Once he was gone, Father placed both of his hands on the table and breathed out deeply. 'Go,' he said to the four of them, lowering his head.

They hesitated.

'Go!' Father roared.

They fled the room, Shallan scrambling after her brothers. She was left with the sight of her father sinking down into his seat, holding his head. The gift he'd given her, the fine necklace, sat forgotten in the opened box on the table just before him.

40

PALONA

That they responded immediately and with great consternation is un-
deniable, as these were primary among those who would forswear and
abandon their oaths. The term Recreance was not then applied, but has
since become a popular title by which this event is named.

—From *Words of Radiance,* chapter 38, page 6

S ebarial shared his carriage with Shallan as they left the king's palace
and rode toward his warcamp. Pattern kept vibrating softly on the
folds of her skirt, and she had to shush him.

The highprince sat across from her, head tilted back against the cushioned wall, snoring softly as the carriage rattled. The ground here had
been scraped clean of rockbuds and set with a line of flagstones down the
center, to divide left from right.

Her soldiers were safe, and would catch up later. She had a base of op-
erations and an income. In the tension of the meeting, and then Navani's
withdrawal, the Kholin house hadn't yet demanded that Shallan turn over
Jasnah's things. She still needed to approach Navani about helping with
the research, but so far, the day had actually worked out quite well.

Now Shallan just needed to save the world.

Sebarial snorted and shook awake from his short nap. He settled into
his seat, wiping his cheek. 'You've changed.'

'Excuse me?'

'You look younger. In there, I would have guessed you were twenty, maybe twenty-five. But now I see that you can't be older than *fourteen*.'

'I am seventeen,' Shallan said dryly.

'Same difference.' Sebarial grunted. 'I could have sworn your dress was more vibrant before, your features sharper, prettier . . . Must have been the light.'

'Do you always make a habit of insulting the looks of young ladies?' Shallan asked. 'Or is it only after you drool in front of them?'

He grinned. 'You weren't trained in the court, obviously. I like that. But be careful – insult the wrong people in this place, and retribution can be swift.'

Through the carriage window Shallan saw that they were finally approaching a warcamp flying Sebarial's banner. It bore the glyphs *sebes* and *laial* stylized into a skyeel, deep gold on a black field.

The soldiers at the gates saluted, and Sebarial gave orders for one to conduct Shallan's men to his manor when they arrived. The carriage continued, and Sebarial settled back to watch her, as if anticipating something.

She couldn't fathom what. Perhaps she was reading him wrong. She turned her attention out the window, and soon decided that this place was a warcamp in name only. The streets were straighter than you might have in a city that had grown naturally, but Shallan saw far more civilians than she did soldiers.

They passed taverns, open markets, shops, and tall buildings that surely could hold a dozen different families. People crowded many of the streets. The place wasn't as varied and vibrant as Kharbranth had been, but the buildings were of solid wood and stone, constructed up against one another to share support.

'Rounded roofs,' Shallan said.

'My engineers say they repel the winds better,' Sebarial said proudly. 'Also, buildings with rounded corners and sides.'

'So many people!'

'Almost all permanent residents. I have the most complete force of tailors, artisans, and cooks in the camps. Already, I've set up twelve manufactories – textiles, shoes, ceramics, several mills. I control the glass-blowers as well.'

Shallan turned back toward him. That pride in his voice didn't *at all* match what Jasnah had written of the man. Of course, most of her notes and knowledge of the highprinces came from infrequent visits to the Shattered Plains, and none had been recent.

'From what I've heard,' Shallan said, 'your forces are among the least successful in the war against the Parshendi.'

Sebarial got a twinkle in his eyes. 'The others hunt quick income from gemhearts, but what will they spend their money on? My textile mills will soon produce uniforms at a much cheaper price than they can be shipped in for, and my farmers will provide food far more varied than what is supplied through Soulcasting. I'm growing both lavis and tallew, not to mention my hog farms.'

'You sly eel,' Shallan said. 'While the others fight a war, you've been building an economy.'

'I've had to be careful,' he confided, leaning in. 'I didn't want them to notice what I was doing at first.'

'Clever,' Shallan said. 'But why are you telling me?'

'You'll see it anyway, if you're to act as one of my clerks. Besides, the secrecy doesn't matter anymore. The manufactories are now producing, and my armies barely go on a single plateau run a month. I have to pay Dalinar's fines for avoiding them and forcing him to send someone else, but it's worth the cost. Anyway, the smarter highprinces have figured out what I'm up to. The others just think I'm a lazy fool.'

'And so you're not a lazy fool?'

'Of course I am!' he exclaimed. 'Fighting is too much work. Besides, soldiers die, and that makes me pay out to their families. It's just useless all around.' He looked out the window. 'I saw the secret three years back. Everyone was moving here, but nobody thought of the place as permanent – despite the value of those gemhearts, which ensured that Alethkar would always have a presence here. . . .' He smiled.

The carriage eventually pulled up to a modest manor-style home amid the taller tenement buildings. The manor had grounds filled with ornamental shalebark, a flagstone drive, and even some trees. The stately home, while not enormous, had a refined classical design, with pillars along the front. It used the row of taller stone buildings behind it as a perfect windbreak.

'We probably have a room for you,' Sebarial said. 'Maybe in the cellars.

Never do seem to have enough space for all of the stuff I'm expected to have. Three full sets of dining furniture. Bah! As if I'm ever going to have anyone over.'

'You really don't think highly of the others, do you?' Shallan asked.

'I hate them,' Sebarial said. 'But I try to hate everyone. That way, I don't risk leaving out anyone who is particularly deserving. Anyway, here we are. Don't expect me to help you out of the carriage.'

She didn't need his help, as a footman quickly arrived and assisted her as she stepped out onto the stone steps built in beside the driveway. Another footman went to Sebarial, who cursed at him, but accepted the aid.

A short woman in a fine dress stood on the manor's steps, hands on her hips. She had curly dark hair. From northern Alethkar, then?

'Ah,' Sebarial said as he and Shallan walked up toward the woman. 'The bane of my existence. Please try to hold your laughter until we separate. My frail, aging ego can no longer handle the mockery.'

Shallan gave him a confused look.

Then the woman spoke. '*Please* tell me you didn't kidnap her, Turi.'

No, not Alethi at all, Shallan thought, trying to judge the woman's accent. *Herdazian.* The fingernails, with a rocklike cast to them, proved that. She was darkeyed, but her fine dress indicated she was not a servant.

Of course. The mistress.

'She insisted on coming with me, Palona,' Sebarial said, climbing the steps. 'I couldn't dissuade her. We'll have to give her a room or something.'

'And who *is* she?'

'Some foreigner,' Sebarial said. 'When she said she wanted to come with me, it seemed to annoy old Dalinar, so I allowed it.' He hesitated. 'What was your name?' he asked, turning to Shallan.

'Shallan Davar,' Shallan said, bowing to Palona. She might be darkeyed, but she was apparently head of this household.

The Herdazian woman cocked an eyebrow. 'Well, she is polite, which means she probably won't fit in here. I honestly can't believe you brought home a random girl because you thought it would annoy one of the other highprinces.'

'Bah!' Sebarial said. 'Woman, you make me the most henpecked man in all of Alethkar—'

'We aren't *in* Alethkar.'

'—and I'm not even storming married!'

'I'm not marrying you, so stop asking,' Palona said, folding her arms, looking Shallan up and down speculatively. 'She's far too young for you.'

Sebarial grinned. 'I used that line already. On Ruthar. It was delightful – he sputtered so much, you could have mistaken him for a storm.'

Palona smiled, then waved him inside. 'There's mulled wine in your study.'

He sauntered toward the door. 'Food?'

'You ran the cook off. Remember?'

'Oh, right. Well, you could have made the food.'

'As could you.'

'Bah. You're useless, woman! All you do is spend my money. Why do I put up with you, again?'

'Because you love me.'

'Can't be that,' Sebarial said, pausing beside the front doors. 'I'm not capable of love. Too much a curmudgeon. Well, do something with the girl.' He walked inside.

Palona beckoned Shallan up to join her. 'What *really* happened, child?'

'He didn't say anything untrue,' Shallan said, realizing that she was blushing. 'But he did leave out a few facts. I have come for the purpose of an arranged marriage to Adolin Kholin. I thought staying in the Kholin household might leave me too restricted, so I sought other options.'

'Huh. That actually makes it sound like Turi—'

'Don't call me that!' a voice called from inside.

' – that the idiot did something politically savvy.'

'Well,' Shallan said, 'I *did* kind of bully him into taking me in. And I implied publicly that he was going to give me a very generous stipend.'

'Too large a one!' the voice said from inside.

'Is he . . . standing in there listening?' Shallan asked.

'He's good at skulking,' Palona said. 'Well, come along. Let's get you settled. Make sure you tell *me* how much he's promised – even by implication – for your stipend. I'll make sure it happens.'

Several footmen unloaded Shallan's trunks from the coach. Her soldiers hadn't arrived yet. Hopefully, they hadn't run into trouble. She followed Palona into the building, which proved to have as classic a decor as the exterior implied. Lots of marble and crystal. Statues trimmed in gold. A sweeping, broad staircase leading to a second-floor balcony overlooking the entrance hall. Shallan didn't notice the highprince around, skulking or otherwise.

Palona led Shallan to a very nice set of rooms in the eastern wing. They were all white, and richly furnished, the hard stone walls and floors softened with silk hangings and thick rugs. She hardly deserved such rich decor.

I suppose I shouldn't feel that way, Shallan thought as Palona checked the closet for towels and linen. *I'm betrothed to a prince.*

Still, so much finery reminded her of her father. The lace, jewelry, and silk he'd given her in attempts to make her forget about . . . other times . . .

Shallan blinked, turning to Palona, who was speaking about something. 'Excuse me?' Shallan asked.

'Servants,' Palona said. 'You have your own lady's maid?'

'I don't,' Shallan said. 'I've got eighteen soldiers, though, and five slaves.'

'And they'll be helping you change clothes?'

Shallan blushed. 'I mean that I'd like them to be housed, if you can manage it.'

'I can,' Palona said lightly. 'I can probably even find something productive for them to do. You'll want them paid out of your stipend, I assume – your maid as well, which I'll get for you. Food is served at second bell, noon, and tenth bell. If you want something at other times, ask at the kitchens. Cook might swear at you, assuming I can get him to come back this time. We've a storm cistern, so there's usually running water. If you want it warm for a bath, the boys will need an hour or so to heat it.'

'Running water?' Shallan said, eager. She'd seen this for the first time in Kharbranth.

'As I said, storm cistern.' Palona pointed upward. 'Each highstorm fills it, and the shape of the cistern sifts out the crem. Don't use the system until midday after a highstorm, or the water will be brown. And you look entirely too eager about this.'

'Sorry,' Shallan said. 'We didn't have this sort of thing in Jah Keved.'

'Welcome to civilization. I trust you left your club and loincloth at the door. Let me set to finding you a maid.' The short woman started to leave.

'Palona?' Shallan asked. 'Yes, child?'

'Thank you.'

Palona smiled. 'Winds know, you're not the first stray he's brought home. Some of us even end up staying.' She left.

Shallan sat down on the plush, white bed, and sank almost down to her neck. What had they made the thing out of? Air and wishes? It felt luxurious.

In her sitting room – her *sitting room* – thumps announced the footmen arriving with her trunks. They left a moment later, closing the door. For the first time in quite a long while, Shallan found herself not fighting for her survival or worrying about being murdered by one of her traveling companions.

So she fell asleep.

41

SCARS

This act of great villainy went beyond the impudence which had hitherto been ascribed to the orders; as the fighting was particularly intense at this time, many attributed this act to a sense of inherent betrayal; and after they withdrew, about two thousand made assault upon them, destroying much of the membership; but this was only nine of the ten, as one said they would not abandon their arms and flee, but instead entertained great subterfuge at the expense of the other nine.

—From *Words of Radiance*, chapter 38, page 20

K aladin rested his fingers on the chasm wall as Bridge Seventeen formed up behind him.

He remembered being frightened of these chasms when he first descended into them. He had feared that heavy rains would cause a flash flood while his men were scavenging. He was a little surprised Gaz hadn't found a way to 'accidentally' get Bridge Four assigned to chasm duty on the day of a highstorm.

Bridge Four had embraced its punishment, claiming these pits. Kaladin was startled to realize that coming down here felt more like coming home than returning to Hearthstone and his parents would have. The chasms were *his*.

'The lads are ready, sir,' Teft said, stepping up beside him.

'Where were you the other night?' Kaladin asked, looking up toward the crack of open sky above.

'I was off duty, sir,' Teft said. 'Went to see what I could find in the market. Do I need to report every little thing I do?'

'You went to the market,' Kaladin said, 'in a highstorm?'

'Time may have gotten away from me for a breath or two . . .' Teft said, looking away.

Kaladin wanted to press further, but Teft was entitled to his privacy. *They're not bridgemen anymore. They don't have to spend all of their time together. They'll start having lives again.*

He wanted to encourage that. Still, it was disturbing. If he didn't know where they all were, how could he make sure they were all safe?

He turned around to regard Bridge Seventeen – a motley crew. Some had been slaves, purchased for the bridges. Others had been criminals, though the crimes punishable by bridge duty in Sadeas's army could be practically anything. Falling into debt, insulting an officer, fighting.

'You,' Kaladin said to the men, 'are Bridge Seventeen, under the command of Sergeant Pitt. You are not soldiers. You may wear the uniforms, but they don't fit you yet. You're playing dress-up. We're going to change that.'

The men shuffled and looked about. Though Teft had been working with them and the other crews for weeks now, these didn't yet *see* themselves as soldiers. As long as that was true, they'd hold those spears at awkward angles, look around lazily when being addressed, and shuffle in line.

'The chasms are mine,' Kaladin said. 'I give you leave to practice here. Sergeant Pitt!'

'Yes, sir!' Pitt said, standing at attention.

'This is a sloppy mess of stormleavings you've got to work with, but I've seen worse.'

'I find that hard to believe, sir!'

'Believe it,' Kaladin said, looking over the men. 'I was in Bridge Four. Lieutenant Teft, they're yours. Make them sweat.'

'Aye, sir,' Teft said. He began to call out orders as Kaladin picked up his spear and made his way farther down the chasms. It would be slow going, getting all twenty crews into shape, but at least Teft had successfully trained the sergeants. Heralds send that the same training worked on the common men.

Kaladin wished he could explain, even to himself, why he felt so anxious about getting these men ready. He felt he was racing toward something. Though what, he didn't know. That writing on the wall . . . Storms, it had him on edge. Thirty-seven days.

He passed Syl sitting on the frond of a frillbloom growing from the wall. It pulled closed at Kaladin's approach. She didn't notice, but remained sitting in the air.

'What is it that you want, Kaladin?' she asked.

'To keep my men alive,' he said immediately.

'No,' Syl said, 'that was what you *wanted*.'

'You're saying I don't want them to be safe?'

She slid down onto his shoulder, moving like a stiff breeze had blown her. She crossed her legs, sitting ladylike, skirt rippling as he walked.

'In Bridge Four, you dedicated everything you had to saving them,' Syl said. 'Well, they're saved. You can't go about protecting every one like a . . . um . . . Like a . . .'

'Father kurl watches over his eggs?'

'Exactly!' She paused. 'What's a kurl?'

'A crustacean,' Kaladin said, 'about the size of a small axehound. Looks kind of like a cross between a crab and a tortoise.'

'Ooooo . . .' Syl said. 'I wanna see one!'

'They don't live out here.'

Kaladin walked with his eyes forward, so she poked him in the neck until he looked at her. Then she rolled her eyes exaggeratedly. 'So you admit that your men are relatively safe,' she said. 'That means you haven't really answered my question. What do you want?'

He passed piles of bones and wood, overgrown with moss. On one pile, rotspren and lifespren spun about one another, little motes of red and green glowing around the vines that sprouted incongruously from the mass of death.

'I want to beat that assassin,' Kaladin said, surprised by how vehemently he felt it.

'Why?'

'Because it's my job to protect Dalinar.'

Syl shook her head. 'That's not it.'

'What? You think you've gotten that good at reading human intentions?'

'Not all humans. Just you.'

Kaladin grunted, stepping carefully around the edge of a dark pool. He'd rather not spend the rest of the day with soaked boots. These new ones didn't hold out the water as well as they should.

'Maybe,' he said, 'I want to beat that assassin because this is all his fault. If he hadn't killed Gavilar, Tien wouldn't have been drafted, and I wouldn't have followed him. Tien wouldn't have died.'

'And you don't think Roshone would have found another way of getting back at your father?'

Roshone was the citylord of Kaladin's hometown back in Alethkar. Sending Tien into the army had been an act of petty vengeance on his part, a way to get back at Kaladin's father for not being a good enough surgeon to save Roshone's son.

'He probably would have done something else,' Kaladin admitted. 'Still, that assassin deserves to die.'

He heard the others before he reached them, their voices echoing down the cavernous chasm bottom.

'What I'm trying to explain,' one said, 'is that nobody seems to be asking the right questions.' Sigzil's voice, with his elevated Azish accent. 'We call the Parshendi savages, and everyone says they hadn't ever met people until that day they encountered the Alethi expedition. If those things are true, then what storm brought them a *Shin* assassin? A Shin assassin who can Surgebind, no less.'

Kaladin stepped into the light of their spheres sprinkled about on the floor of the chasm, which had been cleared of debris since the last time Kaladin had been here. Sigzil, Rock, and Lopen sat on boulders, waiting for him.

'Are you implying that the Assassin in White never really worked for the Parshendi?' Kaladin asked. 'Or are you implying that the Parshendi lied about being as isolated as they claimed?'

'I'm not implying anything,' Sigzil said, turning toward Kaladin. 'My master trained me to ask questions, so I'm asking them. Something doesn't make sense about this whole matter. The Shin are extremely xenophobic. They rarely leave their lands, and you never find them working as mercenaries. Now this one goes about assassinating kings? With a Shardblade? Is he still working for the Parshendi? If so, why did they wait so long to unleash him against us again?'

'Does it matter who he's working for?' Kaladin asked, sucking in Stormlight.

'Of course it does,' Sigzil said.

'Why?'

'Because it's a *question*,' he said, as if offended. 'Besides, discovering his true employer might give us a clue to their goal, and knowing that might help us defeat him.'

Kaladin smiled, then tried to run up the wall.

After falling to the ground, ending up flat on his back, he sighed.

Rock's head leaned in over him. 'Is fun to watch,' he said. 'But this thing, you are certain she can work?'

'The assassin walked on the ceiling,' Kaladin said.

'Are you sure he wasn't just doing what we did?' Sigzil asked skeptically. 'Using the Stormlight to stick one object to another? He could have sprayed the ceiling with Stormlight, then jumped up into it to stick there.'

'No,' Kaladin said, Stormlight escaping his lips. 'He jumped up and landed on the ceiling. Then he ran down the wall and sent *Adolin* to the ceiling somehow. The prince didn't stick there, he *fell* that way.' Kaladin watched his Stormlight rise and evaporate. 'At the end of it all, the assassin . . . he flew away.'

'Ha!' Lopen said from his rock perch. 'I knew it. When we have this figured out, the king of all Herdaz, he will say to me, "Lopen, you are glowing, and this is impressive. But you can also fly. For this, you may marry my daughter."'

'The king of Herdaz doesn't have a daughter,' Sigzil said.

'He doesn't? I have been lied to all this time!'

'You don't know your royal family?' Kaladin asked, sitting up.

'Gon, I haven't been to Herdaz since I was a baby. There are as many Herdazians in Alethkar and Jah Keved these days as there are in our homeland. Flick my sparks, I'm practically an Alethi! Only not so tall and not so grouchy.'

Rock gave Kaladin a hand and pulled him to his feet. Syl had taken a perch on the wall.

'Do you know how this works?' Kaladin asked her.

She shook her head.

'But the assassin *is* a Windrunner,' Kaladin said.

'I think?' Syl said. 'Something like you? Maybe?' She shrugged.

Sigzil followed the direction that Kaladin was looking. 'I wish I could see it,' he mumbled. 'It would be a – Gah!' He jumped backward, pointing. 'It looks like a little person!'

Kaladin raised an eyebrow toward Syl.

'I like him,' she said. 'Also, Sigzil, I'm a "she" and not an "it," thank you very much.'

'Spren have genders?' Sigzil asked, amazed.

'Of course,' she said. 'Though, technically, it probably has something to do with the way people view us. Personification of the forces of nature or some similar gobbletyblarthy.'

'Doesn't that bother you?' Kaladin asked. 'That you might be a creation of human perception?'

'You're a creation of your parents. Who cares how we were born? I can think. That's good enough.' She grinned in a mischievous way, then zipped down as a ribbon of light toward Sigzil, who had settled down on a rock with a stunned expression. She stopped right in front of him, returned to the form of a young woman, then leaned in and made her face look exactly like his.

'Gah!' Sigzil cried again, scrambling away, making her giggle and change her face back.

Sigzil looked toward Kaladin. 'She talks . . . She talks like a real person.' He raised a hand to his head. 'The stories say the Nightwatcher might be capable of that. . . . Powerful spren. Vast spren.'

'Is he calling me vast?' Syl said, cocking her head to the side. 'Not sure what I think of that.'

'Sigzil,' Kaladin said, 'could the Windrunners fly?'

The man gingerly sat back down, still staring at Syl. 'Stories and lore aren't my specialty,' he said. 'I tell of different places, to make the world smaller and to help men understand each other. I've heard legends speak of people dancing on the clouds, but who is to say what is fancy and what is truth, from stories so old?'

'We've got to figure this out,' Kaladin said. 'The assassin will return.'

'So,' Rock said, 'jump at wall some more. I will not laugh much.' He settled down on a boulder and plucked a small crab off the ground beside him. He inspected it, then popped it into his mouth and began chewing.

'Ew,' Sigzil said.

'Tastes good,' Rock said, speaking with his mouth full. 'But better with salt and oil.'

Kaladin regarded the wall, then closed his eyes and drew in more Stormlight. He felt it inside of him, beating against the walls of his veins and arteries, trying to escape. Daring him forward. To jump, to move, to *do*.

'So,' Sigzil said to the others, 'are we assuming that the Assassin in White was the one who sabotaged the king's railing?'

'Bah,' Rock said. 'Why would he do this thing? He could kill more easily.'

'Yeah,' Lopen agreed. 'Maybe the railing was done by one of the other highprinces.'

Kaladin opened his eyes and looked at his arm, palm against the slick wall of the chasm, elbow straight. Stormlight rose from his skin. Curling wisps of Light that vaporized in the air.

Rock nodded. 'All highprinces want the king dead, though they will not speak of this. One of them sent saboteur.'

'So how did this saboteur get to the balcony?' Sigzil asked. 'It must have taken some time to cut through the railing. It was metal. Unless . . . How smooth was that cut, Kaladin?'

Kaladin narrowed his eyes, watching that Stormlight rise. It was raw power. No. 'Power' was the wrong term. It was a force, like the Surges that ruled the universe. They made fire burn, made rocks fall, made light glow. These wisps, they were the Surges reduced to some primal form.

He could use it. Use it to . . .

'Kal?' Sigzil's voice asked, though it seemed distant. Like an unimportant buzzing. 'How smooth was the cut to the railing? Could it have been a Shardblade?'

The voice faded. For a moment, Kaladin thought he saw shadows of a world that was not, shadows of another place. And in that place, a distant sky with a sun enclosed, almost as if by a corridor of clouds.

There.

He made the direction of the wall become down.

Suddenly, his arm was all that was supporting him. He fell forward into the wall, grunting. His awareness of his surroundings returned in a crash – only, his perspective was bizarre. He scrambled to his feet, and found himself standing *on* the wall.

He backed up a few paces – walking up the side of the chasm. To him, that wall was the floor, and the other three bridgemen stood on the actual floor, which looked like the wall. . . .

This, Kaladin thought, *is going to get confusing.*

'Wow,' Lopen said, standing up excitedly. 'Yeah, this is *really* going to be fun. Run up the wall, gancho!'

Kaladin hesitated, then turned and started running. It was like he was in a cave, the two walls of the chasm the top and bottom. Those slowly squeezed together as he moved toward the sky.

Feeling the rush of the Stormlight within him, Kaladin grinned. Syl streaked along beside him, laughing. The closer they got to the top, the narrower the chasm became. Kaladin slowed, then stopped.

Syl streaked out in front of him, zipping out of the chasm as if leaping from the mouth of the cave. She turned about, a ribbon of light.

'Come on!' she called to him. 'Out onto the plateau! Into the sunlight!'

'There are scouts out there,' he said, 'watching for gemhearts.'

'Come out anyway. Stop hiding, Kaladin. *Be.*'

Lopen and Rock whooped below in excitement. Kaladin stared outward at the blue sky. 'I have to know,' he whispered.

'Know?'

'You ask me why I protect Dalinar. I have to know if he really is what he seems, Syl. I *have* to know if one of them lives up to his reputation. That will tell me—'

'Tell you?' she asked, becoming the image of a full-size young woman standing on the wall before him. She was nearly as tall as he was, her dress fading to mist. 'Tell you what?'

'If honor is dead,' Kaladin whispered.

'He is,' Syl said. 'But he lives on in men. And in me.'

Kaladin frowned.

'Dalinar Kholin is a good man,' Syl said.

'He is friends with Amaram. He could be the same, inside.'

'You don't believe that.'

'I have to *know*, Syl,' he said, stepping forward. He tried to take her arm as he would a human's, but she was too insubstantial. His hand passed through. 'I can't just believe it. I need to know it. You asked what I want. Well, that's it. I want to know if I can trust Dalinar. And if I can . . .'

He nodded toward the light of the day outside the chasm.

'If I can, I'll tell him what I can do. I will believe that at least one lighteyes won't try to take everything from me. Like Roshone did. Like Amaram did. Like Sadeas did.'

'And that is what it will take?' she asked.

'I warned you that I was broken, Syl.'

'No. You've been reforged. It can happen to men.'

'To other men, yes,' Kaladin said, raising his hand, feeling the scars on his forehead. Why had the Stormlight never healed those? 'I'm not certain about myself yet. But I will protect Dalinar Kholin with everything I have. I will learn who he is, who he *really* is. Then, maybe . . . we'll give him his Knights Radiant.'

'And Amaram? What of him?'

Pain. Tien. 'Him I'm going to kill.'

'Kaladin,' she said, hands clasped before her, 'don't let this destroy you.'

'It can't,' he said, Stormlight running out. His uniform coat began to fall backward, toward the ground, as did his hair. 'Amaram already took care of that.'

The ground below fully reasserted itself, and Kaladin fell backward away from her. He sucked in Stormlight, twisting in the air as his veins flared back to life. He landed feet-first in a rush of power and Light.

The other three remained silent for a few moments as he stood up straight.

'That,' Rock said, 'was very fast way to get down. Ha! But it did not include falling on face, which would be fun. So you get only soft clap.' He proceeded to clap. It was indeed soft. Lopen, however, cheered and Sigzil nodded with a wide grin.

Kaladin snorted, grabbing a waterskin. 'The king's railing *was* cut with a Shardblade, Sigzil.' He took a drink. 'And no, it wasn't the Assassin in White. That attempt on Elhokar's life was too crude.'

Sigzil nodded.

'What's more,' Kaladin said, 'the railing must have been cut *after* the highstorm that night. Otherwise, the wind would have blown the railing out of shape. So our saboteur, a Shardbearer, somehow got out onto the balcony after the storm.'

Lopen shook his head, catching the waterskin as Kaladin threw it back. 'We're supposed to believe that one of the camp's Shardbearers snuck through the palace and got onto that balcony, gon? And nobody noticed him?'

'Could someone else do this thing?' Rock said, gesturing to the wall. 'Walk up it?'

'I doubt it,' Kaladin said.

'A rope,' Sigzil said.

They looked to him.

'If I wanted to sneak a Shardbearer in, I'd bribe some servant to let down a rope.' Sigzil shrugged. 'One could be smuggled out onto the railing easily, perhaps wrapped around the servant's body under their clothing. The saboteur and maybe some friends could climb up the rope, cut the railing and dig at the mortar, then climb back down. The accomplice then cuts the rope and goes back inside.'

Kaladin nodded slowly.

'So,' Rock said, 'we find out who went on balcony after storm, and we find accomplice. Easy! Ha. Maybe you are not airsick, Sigzil. No. Probably just a little.'

Kaladin felt unsettled. Moash had been out on that balcony between the storm and the king's near fall.

'I'll ask around,' Sigzil said, rising.

'No,' Kaladin said quickly. 'I'll do it. Don't speak a word of this to anyone else. I want to see what I can find.'

'All right,' Sigzil said. He nodded toward the wall. 'Can you do that again?'

'More tests?' Kaladin asked with a sigh.

'We have time,' Sigzil said. 'Besides, I believe Rock wants to see if you fall on your face.'

'Ha!'

'All right,' Kaladin said. 'But I'm going to have to drain some of those spheres we're using for light.' He glanced toward them sitting in little piles on the too-clean ground. 'By the way, why did you clear away the rubble in this area?'

'Clear it away?' Sigzil asked.

'Yeah,' Kaladin said. 'There was no need to go moving remains around, even if they are just skeletons. It . . .'

He trailed off as Sigzil picked up a sphere and held it up toward the wall, exposing something Kaladin had missed before. Deep gouges where the moss had been scraped off, the rock scored.

Chasmfiend. One of the massive greatshells had passed through the area, and its bulk had scraped everything away.

'I didn't think they came this close to the warcamps,' Kaladin said. 'Maybe we shouldn't train the lads down here for a while, just in case.'

The others nodded.

'Is gone now,' Rock said. 'Otherwise, we'd have been eaten. Is obvious. So, back to training.'

Kaladin nodded, though those gouges haunted him as he practiced.

⋅⋅

A few hours later, they led a tired group of former bridgemen back into their barrack block. Exhausted as they looked, the men of Bridge Seventeen seemed *more* lively than they'd been before going down into the chasm. They perked up even more when they reached their barrack and found one of Rock's apprentice chefs fixing them a big pot of stew.

It was dark by the time Kaladin and Teft got back to Bridge Four's own barrack. Another of Rock's apprentices was fixing the stew here, Rock himself – having gotten back a little earlier than Kaladin – tasting and giving criticism. Shen moved behind Rock, stacking bowls.

Something was wrong.

Kaladin stopped just outside the light of the firepit, and Teft froze beside him. 'Something is off,' Teft said.

'Yeah,' Kaladin agreed, scanning the men. They were clumped together on one side of the fire, some seated, others standing in a group. Their laughter forced, their postures nervous. When you trained men for war, they started to use combat stances whenever they were uncomfortable. Something on the other side of that fire was a threat.

Kaladin stepped into the light and found a man sitting there in a nice uniform, hands down at his side, head bowed. Renarin Kholin. Oddly, he was rocking back and forth with a small motion, staring at the ground.

Kaladin relaxed. 'Brightlord,' Kaladin said, stepping over to him. 'Is there something you need?'

Renarin scrambled to his feet and saluted. 'I would like to serve under your command, sir.'

Inside, Kaladin groaned. 'Let's talk away from the fire, Brightlord.' He took the spindly prince by the arm, leading him away from the ears of the others.

'Sir,' Renarin said, speaking softly, 'I want—'

'You shouldn't call me sir,' Kaladin whispered. 'You're lighteyed. Storms, you're the son of the most powerful man in eastern Roshar.'

'I want to be in Bridge Four,' Renarin said.

Kaladin rubbed his forehead. During his time as a slave, dealing with much larger problems, he had forgotten about the headaches of dealing with highborn lighteyes. Once, he might have assumed he'd heard the most outlandish of their ridiculous demands. Not so, it seemed.

'You can't be in Bridge Four. We're bodyguards for your own family. What are you going to do? Guard yourself?'

'I won't be a liability, sir. I'll work hard.'

'I don't doubt you would, Renarin. Look, *why* do you want to be in Bridge Four?'

'My father and my brother,' Renarin said softly, face shadowed, 'they're warriors. Soldiers. I'm not, if you haven't noticed.'

'Yes. Something about . . .'

'Physical ailments,' Renarin said. 'I've a blood weakness.'

'That's a folk description of many different conditions,' Kaladin said. 'What do you really have?'

'I'm epileptic,' Renarin said. 'It means—'

'Yes, yes. Is it idiopathic or symptomatic?'

Renarin stood absolutely still in the darkness. 'Uh . . .'

'Was it caused by a specific brain injury,' Kaladin asked, 'or is it something that just started happening for no reason?'

'I've had it since I was a kid.'

'How bad are the seizures?'

'They're fine,' Renarin said quickly. 'It's not as bad as everyone says. It's not like I fall to the ground or froth like everyone thinks. My arm will jerk a few times, or I'll twitch uncontrollably for a few moments.'

'You retain consciousness?'

'Yeah.'

'Myoclonic, probably,' Kaladin said. 'You've been given bitterleaf to chew?'

'I . . . Yes. I don't know if it helps. The jerking isn't the whole problem. A lot of times, when it's happening, I get really weak. Particularly along one side of my body.'

'Huh,' Kaladin said. 'I suppose that could fit with the seizures. Have you ever had any persistent relaxation of the muscles, an inability to smile on one side of your face, for example?'

'No. How do you know these things? Aren't you a soldier?'

'I know some field medicine.'

'Field medicine . . . for epilepsy?'

Kaladin coughed into his hand. 'Well, I can see why they didn't want you going into battle. I've seen men with wounds that caused similar symptoms, and the surgeons always dismissed those men from duty. It's no shame to not be fit enough for battle, Brightlord. Not every man is needed for fighting.'

'Sure,' Renarin said bitterly. 'Everyone tells me that. Then they all go back to fighting. The ardents, they claim every Calling is important, but then what do they teach about the afterlife? That it's a big war to reclaim the Tranquiline Halls. That the best soldiers in this life are glorified in the next.'

'If the afterlife really is a big war,' Kaladin said, 'then I hope I end up in Damnation. At least there I might be able to get a wink or two of sleep. Regardless, you're no soldier.'

'I want to be.'

'Brightlord—'

'You don't have to set me to doing anything important,' Renarin said. 'I came to you, instead of one of the other battalions, because most of your men spend their time patrolling. If I'm patrolling, I won't be in much danger, and my fits won't hurt anyone. But at least I can see, I can *feel* what it's like.'

'I—'

He rushed on. Kaladin had never heard so many words from the normally quiet young man.

'I will obey your commands,' Renarin said. 'Treat me like a new recruit. When I'm here, I'm not a prince's son, I'm not a lighteyes. I'm just another soldier. Please. I want to be part of it. When Adolin was young, my father made him serve in a spearman squad for two months.'

'He did?' Kaladin asked, genuinely surprised.

'Father said every officer should serve in the shoes of his men,' Renarin said. 'I have Shards now. I'm going to be in war, but I've never felt what it's like to really be a soldier. I think this is the closest I'll be able to get. *Please.*'

Kaladin folded his arms, looking the youth over. Renarin looked anxious. *Very* anxious. He'd formed his hands to fists, though Kaladin could see no sign of the box Renarin often fiddled with when nervous. He'd begun breathing deeply, but had set his jaw, and kept his eyes forward.

Coming to see Kaladin, to ask this of him, *terrified* the young man for some reason. He'd done it anyway. Could one ask anything more of a recruit?

Am I really considering this? It seemed ludicrous. And yet, one of Kaladin's jobs was to protect Renarin. If he could pound some solid self-defense skills into him, that would go a long way toward helping him survive assassination attempts.

'I should probably point out,' Renarin said, 'how much easier it will be to guard me if I'm spending time training with your men. Your resources are thin, sir. Having one fewer person to protect must be appealing. The only times I'll leave are the days when I practice with my Shards under Swordmaster Zahel.'

Kaladin sighed. 'You really want to be a soldier?'

'Yes, sir!'

'Go take those dirty stew bowls and wash them,' Kaladin said, pointing. 'Then help Rock clean his cauldron and put away the cooking implements.'

'Yes, sir!' Renarin said with an enthusiasm Kaladin had never heard from anyone assigned washing duty. Renarin jogged over and began happily snatching up bowls.

Kaladin folded his arms and leaned against the barrack. The men didn't know how to react to Renarin. They'd hand over bowls of half-finished stew to please him, and conversation hushed when he was too near. But they'd been nervous around Shen too, before eventually coming to accept him. Could they ever do the same for a lighteyes?

Moash had refused to hand his bowl to Renarin, washing it himself, as was their common practice. Once done, he strolled over to Kaladin. 'You're really going to let him join?'

'I'll speak to his father tomorrow,' Kaladin said. 'Get the highprince's read on it.'

'I don't like it. Bridge Four, our nightly conversations ... these things are supposed to be safe from *them*, you know?'

'Yeah,' Kaladin said. 'But he's a good kid. I think if any lighteyes could fit in here, he could.'

Moash turned, raising an eyebrow toward him.

'You disagree, I presume?' Kaladin asked.

'He doesn't act right, Kal. The way he talks, the way he looks at people. He's strange. That's not important, though – he's lighteyed, and that should be enough. It means we can't trust him.'

'We don't need to,' Kaladin said. 'We're just going to keep an eye on him, maybe try to train him to defend himself.'

Moash grunted, nodding. He seemed to accept those as good reasons for letting Renarin stay.

I've got Moash here, Kaladin thought. *Nobody else is close enough to hear. I should ask . . .*

But how did he form the words? *Moash, were you involved in a plot to kill the king?*

'Have you thought about what we're going to do?' Moash asked. 'Regarding Amaram, I mean.'

'Amaram is my problem.'

'You're Bridge Four,' Moash said, taking Kaladin by the arm. 'Your problem *is* our problem. He's the one who made you a slave.'

'He did more than that,' Kaladin growled softly, ignoring Syl's gesturing that he should remain quiet. 'He killed my friends, Moash. Right before my eyes. He's a murderer.'

'Then something has to be done.'

'It does,' Kaladin asked. 'But what? You think I should go to the authorities?'

Moash laughed. 'What are *they* going to do? You have to get the man into a duel, Kaladin. Bring him down, man against man. Until you do it, something's going to feel wrong to you, deep down in your gut.'

'You sound like you know what this feels like.'

'Yeah.' Moash gave a little half smile. 'I have some Voidbringers in my past too. Maybe that's why I understand you. Maybe that's why you understand me.'

'Then what—'

'I don't really want to talk about it,' Moash said.

'We're Bridge Four,' Kaladin said, 'like you said. Your problems are mine.' *What did the king do to your family, Moash?*

'Suppose that's true,' Moash said, turning away. 'I just . . . Not tonight. Tonight, I just want to relax.'

'Moash!' Teft called from nearer the fire. 'You coming?'

'I am,' Moash called back. 'What about you, Lopen? You ready?'

Lopen grinned, standing up and stretching beside the fire. 'I am the Lopen, which means I am ready for anything at any time. You should know this by now.'

Nearby, Drehy snorted and flipped a chunk of stewed longroot at Lopen. It splatted against the Herdazian's face.

Lopen kept right on talking. 'As you can see, I was perfectly ready for that, as shown by the poise I display as I make this decidedly rude gesture.'

Teft chuckled as he, Peet, and Sigzil walked over to join Lopen. Moash moved to go with them, then hesitated. 'You coming, Kal?'

'Where?' Kaladin asked.

'Out,' Moash said, shrugging. 'Visit a few taverns, play some rings, get something to drink.'

Out. The bridgemen had rarely done such things in Sadeas's army, at least not as a group, with friends. At first, they had been too beaten down to care for anything other than sticking their noses in drink. Later, lack of funds and the general prejudice against them among the troops had worked to keep the bridgemen to themselves.

That wasn't the case any longer. Kaladin found himself stammering. 'I . . . probably ought to stay . . . uh, to go look in at the fires of the other crews . . .'

'Come on, Kal,' Moash said. 'You can't *always* work.'

'I'll go with you another time.'

'Fine.' Moash jogged over to join the others.

Syl left the fire, where she'd been dancing with a flamespren, and zipped over to Kaladin. She hung in the air, watching the group walk off into the evening.

'Why didn't you go?' she asked him.

'I can't live that life anymore, Syl,' Kaladin said. 'I wouldn't know what to do with myself.'

'But—'

Kaladin walked away and got himself a bowl of stew.

> *But as for Ishi'Elin, his was the part most important at their inception; he*
> *readily understood the implications of Surges being granted to men, and*
> *caused organization to be thrust upon them; as having too great power,*
> *he let it be known that he would destroy each and every one, unless they*
> *agreed to be bound by precepts and laws.*
>
> —From *Words of Radiance*, chapter 2, page 4

Shallan awoke to humming. She opened her eyes, finding herself snuggled into the luxurious bed in Sebarial's manor. She'd fallen asleep in her clothing.

The humming was Pattern on the comforter beside her. He looked almost like lace embroidery. The window shades had been drawn – she didn't remember doing that – and it was dark outside. The evening of the day she'd arrived at the Plains.

'Did someone come in?' she asked Pattern, sitting up, pushing stray locks of red hair from her eyes.

'Mmm. Someones. Gone now.'

Shallan rose and wandered into her sitting room. Ash's eyes, she almost didn't want to walk on the pristine white carpeting. What if she left tracks and ruined it?

Pattern's 'someones' had left food on the table. Suddenly ravenous,

Shallan sat down on the sofa, lifting the lid off the tray to find flatbread that had been baked with sweet paste in the center, along with dipping sauces.

'Remind me,' she said, 'to thank Palona in the morning. That woman is divine.'

'Mmm. No. I think she is . . . Ah . . . Exaggeration?'

'You catch on quickly,' Shallan said as Pattern became a threedimensional mass of twisting lines, a ball hanging in the air above the seat beside her.

'No,' he said. 'I am too slow. You prefer some food and not others. Why?'

'The taste,' Shallan said.

'I should understand this word,' Pattern said. 'But I do not, not really.'

Storms. How did you describe taste? 'It's like color . . . you see with your mouth.' She grimaced. 'And that was an awful metaphor. Sorry. I have trouble being insightful on an empty stomach.'

'You say you are "on" the stomach,' Pattern said. 'But I know you do not mean this. Context allows me to infer what you truly mean. In a way, the very phrase is a lie.'

'It's not a lie,' Shallan said, 'if everyone understands and knows what it means.'

'Mm. Those are some of the best lies.'

'Pattern,' Shallan said, breaking off a piece of flatbread, 'sometimes you're about as intelligible as a Bavlander trying to quote ancient Vorin poetry.'

A note beside the food said that Vathah and her soldiers had arrived, and had been quartered in a tenement nearby. Her slaves had been incorporated into the manor's staff for the time being.

Chewing on the bread – it was delightful – Shallan went over to her trunks with the intent of unpacking. When she opened the first, however, she was confronted by a blinking red light. Tyn's spanreed.

Shallan stared at it. That would be the person who relayed Tyn's information. Shallan assumed it was a woman, though since the information relay station was in Tashikk, they might not even be Vorin. It could be a man.

She knew so little. She was going to have to be very careful . . . storms, she might get herself killed even if she *was* careful. Shallan was tired, however, of being pushed around.

These people knew something about Urithiru. It was, dangerous or not, Shallan's best lead. She took out the spanreed, prepared its board with paper, and placed the reed. Once she turned the dial to indicate she had set up, the pen remained hanging there, immobile, but did not immediately start writing. The person trying to contact her had stepped away – the pen could have been in there blinking for hours. She'd have to wait until the person on the other side returned.

'Inconvenient,' she said, then smiled at herself. Was she really complaining about waiting a few minutes for instantaneous communication across half the world?

I will need to find a way to contact my brothers, she thought. That would be distressingly slow, without a spanreed. Could she arrange a message through one of these relay stations in Tashikk using a different intermediary, perhaps?

She settled back down on the couch – pen and writing board near the tray of food – and looked through the stack of previous communications that Tyn had exchanged with this distant person. There weren't many. Tyn had probably destroyed them periodically. The ones remaining involved questions regarding Jasnah, House Davar, and the Ghostbloods.

One oddity stood out to Shallan. The way Tyn spoke of this group wasn't like that of a thief and one-off employers. Tyn spoke of 'getting in good' and 'moving up' within the Ghostbloods.

'Pattern,' Pattern said.

'What?' Shallan asked, looking toward him.

'Pattern,' he replied. 'In the words. Mmm.'

'Of this sheet?' Shallan asked, holding up the page.

'There and others,' Pattern said. 'See the first words?'

Shallan frowned, inspecting the sheets. In each one, the first words came from the remote writer. A simple sentence asking after Tyn's health or status. Tyn replied simply each time.

'I don't understand,' Shallan said.

'They form groups of five,' Pattern said. 'Quintets, the letters. Mmm. Each message follows a pattern – first three words start with one each of three of the quintet of letters. Tyn's reply, the two that match.'

Shallan looked it over, though she couldn't see what Pattern meant.

He explained it again, and she *thought* she grasped it, but the pattern was complex.

'A code,' Shallan said. It made sense; you'd want a way to authenticate that the right person was on the other end of the spanreed. She blushed as she realized she had almost ruined this opportunity. If Pattern hadn't seen this, or if the spanreed had started writing immediately, Shallan would have exposed herself.

She couldn't do this. She couldn't infiltrate a group skilled and powerful enough to bring down Jasnah herself. She just *couldn't*.

And yet she had to.

She got out her sketchbook and started to draw, letting her fingers move on their own. She needed to be older, but not too much older. She'd be darkeyed. People would remark upon a lighteyes they didn't know moving through camp. A darkeyes would be more invisible. To the right people, though, she could imply that she was using the eyedrops.

Dark hair. Long, like her real hair, but not red. Same height, same build, but a much different face. Worn features, like Tyn's. A scar across the chin, a more angular face. Not as pretty, but not ugly either. More ... straightforward.

She sucked in Stormlight from the lamp beside her, and that *energy* made her draw more quickly. It wasn't excitement. It was a need to go forward.

She finished with a flourish, and found a face staring back at her from the page, almost alive. Shallan breathed out Light and felt it envelop her, twist about her. Her vision clouded for a moment, and she saw only the glow of that fading Stormlight.

Then it was gone. She didn't feel any different. She prodded at her face. It felt the same. Had she—

The lock of hair hanging down over her shoulder was black. Shallan stared at it, then rose from her seat, eager and timid at the same time. She crossed to the washroom and stepped up to the mirror there, looking at a face transformed, one with tan skin and dark eyes. The face from her drawing, given color and life.

'It works ...' she whispered. This was more than changing scuffs in her dress or making herself look older, as she'd done before. This was a complete transformation. 'What can we do with this?'

'Whatever we imagine,' Pattern said from the wall nearby. 'Or

527

whatever you can imagine. I am not good with what is *not*. But I like it. I like the . . . taste . . . of it.' He seemed very pleased with himself at that comment.

Something was off. Shallan frowned, holding up her sketch, realizing she'd left a spot unfinished on the side of the nose. The Lightweaving there didn't cover up her nose completely, and had a kind of fuzzy gap in the side. It was small; someone else would probably just see it as a strange scar. To her, it seemed glaring, and offended her artistic sense.

She prodded at the rest of the nose. She'd made it slightly larger than her real one, and could reach *through* the image to touch her nose. The image had no substance to it. In fact, if she moved her finger quickly through the tip of the false nose, it fuzzed to Stormlight, like smoke that had been blown away by a gust.

She removed her fingers, and the image snapped back into place, though it still had that gap on the side. Sloppy drawing on her part.

'How long will the image last?' she asked.

'It feeds on Light,' Pattern said.

Shallan dug the spheres from her safepouch. They were all dun – she'd likely used those up in the conversation with the highprinces. She took one from the lamp on the wall, replacing it with a dun sphere of the same denomination, and carried it in her fist.

Shallan went back into the sitting room. She'd need a different outfit, of course. A darkeyed woman wouldn't—

The spanreed was writing.

Shallan hastened over to the sofa, breath catching as she saw the words appear. *I think some information I have today will work.* A simple introduction, but it followed the right pattern for the code.

'Mmm,' Pattern said.

She needed the first two words of her reply to start with the proper letters. *But you said that last time*, she wrote, hopefully completing the code.

Don't worry, the messenger wrote. *You'll like this, though the timing might be tight. They want to meet.*

Good, Shallan wrote back, relaxing – and blessing the time Tyn had spent forcing her to practice forgery techniques. She'd taken to it quickly, as it was a kind of drawing, but Tyn's suggestions now let her imitate the woman's own sloppier writing with demonstrable skill.

They want to meet tonight, Tyn, the reed wrote.

Tonight? What time was it? A clock on the wall read half past first night bell. It was just first moon, right after dark. She picked up the spanreed and started to write, 'I don't know if I'm ready,' but stopped herself. That wasn't how Tyn would say it.

I'm not ready, she wrote instead.

They were insistent, the messenger returned. *It is why I tried to contact you earlier. Apparently, Jasnah's ward arrived today. What happened?*

It is none of your concern, Shallan wrote back, matching the tone Tyn had used previously in these conversations. The person on the other end was a servant, not a colleague.

Of course, the reed wrote. *But they want to meet you tonight. If you refuse, it might mean a severing of ties.*

Stormfather! Tonight? Shallan ran her fingers through her hair, staring at the page. Could she do it tonight?

Would waiting really change anything?

Heart thumping, she wrote, *I thought I had Jasnah's ward captive, but the girl betrayed me. I'm not well. But I will send my apprentice.*

Another one, Tyn? the reed wrote. *After what happened with Si? Anyway, I doubt they'll like meeting with an apprentice.*

They don't have a choice, Shallan wrote.

Perhaps she could have created a Lightweaving around herself that made her look like Tyn, but she doubted she was ready for something like that. Pretending to be someone she'd invented would be tough enough – but imitating a specific person? She'd be discovered for sure.

I'll see, the messenger wrote.

Shallan waited. In distant Tashikk, the messenger would be getting out another spanreed and acting as intermediary to the Ghostbloods. Shallan spent the time checking on the sphere she'd carried in from the washroom.

Its light had faded a small amount. Keeping this Lightweaving going would require her to keep a stock of infused spheres on her person.

The spanreed started writing again. *They'll do it. Can you get to Sebarial's warcamp quickly?*

I think I can, Shallan wrote. *Why there?*

It's one of the few with gates open all night, the messenger wrote. *There is a tenement where your employers will meet your apprentice. I'll draw you a map. Have your apprentice arrive at Salas's moonheight. Good luck.*

A sketch followed, indicating the location. Salas's moonheight? She'd have twenty-five minutes, and she didn't know the camp at all. Shallan leaped to her feet, then froze. She couldn't go like this, dressed as a light-eyed woman. She hurried to Tyn's trunk and dug through clothing.

A few minutes later she stood in front of the mirror, wearing loose brown trousers, a white buttoned shirt, and a thin glove on her safehand. She felt naked with her hand exposed like that. The trousers weren't so bad – darkeyed women wore them when working the plantation back home, though she'd never seen a lighteyed lady in them. But that glove . . .

She shivered, noticing that her false face blushed when she did. The nose moved when she wrinkled her own as well. That was a good thing, though she'd been hoping to be able to hide her embarrassment.

She pulled on one of Tyn's white coats. The stiff thing went all the way down to the top of her boots, and she tied it at the waist with a thick black hogshide belt so that it was mostly closed in front, as Tyn had worn it. She finished by replacing the spheres in the pouch in her pocket with infused ones from the lamps in the room.

That flaw in her nose still bothered her. *Something to shade the face*, she thought, hurrying back to her trunk. There, she dug out Bluth's white hat, the one with the sides that folded upward at a slant. Hopefully it would look better on her than it had on Bluth.

She put it on, and when she returned to the mirror, she was pleased with how it shaded her face. It did look kind of silly. But then, she felt that *everything* about this outfit looked silly. A gloved hand? Trousers? The coat had seemed imposing on Tyn – it indicated experience and a sense of personal style. When Shallan wore it, she looked like she was pretending. She saw through the illusion to the frightened girl from rural Jah Keved.

Authority is not a real thing. Jasnah's words. *It is mere vapors – an illusion. I can create that illusion . . . as can you.*

Shallan stood up taller, straightened the hat, then went to the bedroom and tucked a few things in her pockets, including the map of where to go. She walked to the window and pulled it open. Fortunately, she was on the ground floor.

'Here we go,' she whispered to Pattern.

Out she went, into the night.

*And thus were the disturbances in the Revv toparchy quieted, when, upon
their ceasing to prosecute their civil dissensions, Nalan'Elin betook himself to finally accept the Skybreakers who had named him their master,
when initially he had spurned their advances and, in his own interests,
refused to countenance that which he deemed a pursuit of vanity and
annoyance; this was the last of the Heralds to admit to such patronage.*

—From *Words of Radiance*, chapter 5, page 17

T he warcamp was still busy, despite the hour. She wasn't surprised;
her time in Kharbranth had taught her that not everyone treated
the arrival of night as a reason to stop working. Here, there were
nearly as many people about in the streets as when she'd first ridden
through.

And almost nobody paid attention to her.

For once, she didn't feel conspicuous. Even in Kharbranth, people had
glanced at her – noticed her, considered her. Some had thought of robbing her, others of how to use her. A young lighteyes without proper
escort was distinctive, and possibly an opportunity. However, while wearing straight dark hair and dark brown eyes, she might as well have been
invisible. It was *wonderful*.

Shallan smiled, stuffing her hands in the pockets of her coat – she still felt embarrassed by that gloved safehand, though nobody even *looked* at it. She reached an intersection. In one direction, the warcamp glittered with torches and oil lanterns. A market, busy enough that nobody trusted spheres in their lamps. Shallan walked toward it; she'd be safer on the more traveled streets. Her fingers crinkled on the paper in her pocket, and she drew it out as she stopped to wait for a group of chattering people to move from in front of her.

The map looked easy enough to parse. She just needed to get her bearings. She waited, then finally realized that the group in front of her *wasn't* going to move. She was expecting them to defer to her as they would a lighteyes. Shaking her head at her foolishness, she went around them.

It continued like that; she was forced to squeeze through tight places between bodies, and was jostled as she walked. This market flowed like two rivers passing one another, with shops on either side and vendors peddling food in the center. It was even covered in some places by awnings that stretched across to the buildings on the other side.

Perhaps only ten paces across, it was a claustrophobic, bustling, jabbering mess. And Shallan loved it. She found herself wanting to stop and sketch half the people she passed. They all seemed so full of life, whether haggling or simply walking with a friend and chewing on a snack. Why hadn't she gone out more in Kharbranth?

She stopped, grinning at a man performing a show with puppets and a box. Farther down the way, a Herdazian used a sparkflicker and some kind of oil to make bursts of flame in the air. If she could just stop off a little time and do a sketch of him . . .

No. She had business to be about. Part of her didn't want to go forward with it, obviously, and her mind was trying to distract her. She was becoming increasingly aware of this defense of hers. She used it, she *needed* it, but she couldn't let it control her life.

She did stop at the cart of a woman selling glazed fruit, however. They looked juicy and red, and had been stabbed through with a little stick before being dipped in a glassy melted sugar. Shallan pulled a sphere from her pocket and held it out.

The woman froze, staring at the sphere. Others stopped nearby. What was the problem? It was just an emerald mark. It wasn't like she'd gotten out the broam.

She looked at the glyphs listing prices. A stick of candied fruit was a single clearchip. Denominations of spheres wasn't something she'd often had to think about, but if she remembered . . .

Her mark was worth two hundred and fifty times the cost of the treat. Even in her family's strained state, this wouldn't have been considered much money to them. But that was on the level of houses and estates, not the level of street vendors and working darkeyes.

'Uh, I don't think I can change that,' the woman said. 'Er . . . citizen.' A title given to a wealthy darkeyes of the first or second nahn.

Shallan blushed. How many times was she going to prove just how naive she was? 'It's for one of the treats, and for some help. I'm new to the area. I could use some directions.'

'Expensive way to get directions, miss,' the woman said, but pocketed the sphere with deft fingers nonetheless.

'I need to find Nar Street.'

'Ah. You're going the wrong storming way, miss. Back up the market flow, turn right. You'll need to go, uh, six blocks, I think? It's easy to find; the highprince made everyone lay out their buildings in squares, like in a proper city. Look for the taverns, and you'll be there. But miss, I don't think that's the sort of place one like you should be visiting, if you don't mind me saying.'

Even as a darkeyes, people thought her incapable of taking care of herself. 'Thank you,' Shallan said, plucking out one of the sticks of candied fruit. She hastened away, crossing the flow to join those walking in the opposite direction through the market.

'Pattern?' she whispered.

'Mmm.' He was clinging to the outside of her coat, near the knees.

'Trail behind and watch to see if anyone follows me,' Shallan said. 'Do you think you can do that?'

'They will make a pattern if they come,' he said, dropping to the ground. For a brief moment in the air, between coat and stone, he was a dark mass of twisting lines. Then he vanished like a drop of water hitting a lake.

Shallan hurried along with the flow, safehand securely gripping the sphere pouch in her coat pocket, freehand carrying the stick of fruit. She remembered all too well how Jasnah's deliberate flashing of too much money in Kharbranth had lured thieves like vines to stormwater.

Shallan followed the directions, her sense of liberation replaced by anxiety. The corner she took out of the market led her to a roadway that was much less crowded. Was the fruit vendor trying to direct Shallan into a trap where she could be robbed easily? Head down, she hurried along the road. She couldn't Soulcast to protect herself, not as Jasnah had. Storms! Shallan hadn't even been able to make sticks catch fire. She doubted she'd be able to transform living bodies.

She had Lightweaving, but she was already using that. Could she Lightweave a second image at the same time? How *was* her disguise doing, anyway? It would be draining the Light from her spheres. She almost pulled them out to see how much was gone, then stopped herself. Fool. She was worried about being robbed, and so she considered revealing a handful of money?

She stopped after two blocks. Some people did walk this street, a handful of men in workers' clothing heading home for the night. The buildings here certainly weren't as nice as the ones she'd left behind.

'Nobody follows,' Pattern said from her feet.

Shallan jumped nearly to the rooftops. She raised her freehand to her breast, breathing in and out deeply. She really thought she could infiltrate a group of assassins? Her own *spren* often made her jump.

Tyn said that nothing would teach me, Shallan thought, *but personal experience. I'm just going to have to muddle through these first few times and hope I get used to this before I get myself killed.*

'Let's keep moving,' Shallan said. 'We're running out of time.' She started forward, digging into the fruit. It really was good, though her nerves prevented her from fully enjoying it.

The street with the taverns was actually five blocks away, not six. Shallan's increasingly wrinkled paper showed the meeting place as a tenement building across from a tavern with blue light shining through the windows.

Shallan tossed aside her fruit stick as she stepped up to the tenement building. It couldn't be old – nothing in these warcamps could be more than five or six years old – but it *looked* ancient. The stones weathered, the window shutters hanging askew in places. She was surprised a highstorm hadn't blown the thing over.

Fully aware that she could be striding into the whitespine's den for dinner, she walked up and knocked. The door was opened by a darkeyed man the size of a boulder who had a beard trimmed like a Horneater's. His hair *did* seem to have some red in it.

She resisted the urge to shuffle from one foot to the next as he looked her up and down. Finally, he opened the door all the way, motioning her in with thick fingers. She didn't miss the large axe that leaned against the wall just next to him, illuminated by the single feeble Stormlight lamp – it looked like it only had a chip in it – on the wall.

Taking a deep breath, Shallan entered.

The place smelled moldy. She heard water dripping from somewhere farther inside, stormwater infallibly making its way from a leaking roof down, down, down to the ground floor. The guard did not speak as he led her along the hall. The floor was *wood*. There was something about walking on wood that made her feel as if she were going to fall through. It seemed to groan with every step. Good stone never did anything like that.

The guard nodded toward an opening in the wall, and Shallan stared into the blackness there. Steps. Down.

Storms, what am I doing?

Not being timid. That was what she was doing. Shallan glanced at the brutish guard and raised an eyebrow, forcing her voice to sound calm. 'You really went all-out on the decor. How long did you have to look to find a den in the Shattered Plains that had a creepy staircase in it?'

The guard actually smiled. It didn't make him look any less intimidating.

'The stairs aren't going to collapse under me, are they?' Shallan asked.

'Is fine,' the guard said. His voice was surprisingly high pitched. 'He did not collapse for me, and I had two breakfasts today.' He patted his stomach. 'Go. They wait for you.'

She got out a sphere for light and started down the stairwell. The stone walls here had been cut. Who would go to the trouble to burrow out a basement for a rotting tenement building? The answer came as she noticed several extended crem dribbles on the wall. A little like wax melting down the side of a candle, these had hardened to stone long ago.

This hole was here before the Alethi came, she thought. When settling this warcamp, Sebarial had built this building above an already-existent basement. The warcamp craters must have once held people. There was no other explanation. Who had they been? The Natan people of long ago?

The steps led down into a small, empty room. How odd to find a basement in such a ramshackle building; normally, you found them only in wealthy homes, as the precautions one needed to take to prevent flooding were extensive. Shallan folded her arms, confused, until one corner of the floor opened, bathing the room in light. Shallan stepped back, breath catching. A part of the rock floor was false, hiding a trapdoor.

The basement had a basement. She stepped up to the edge of the hole and saw a ladder heading down toward red carpet and light that seemed almost blinding following the dimness she'd been in. This place must flood something fierce after a storm.

She swung onto the ladder and made her way down, glad for the trousers. The trapdoor closed above – it appeared to have some sort of pulley mechanism.

She hopped off onto the carpet and turned, finding a room that was incongruously palatial. A long dining table ran down the center, and it sparkled with glass goblets that had gemstones set in their sides; their glow sprayed the room with light. Cozy shelves lined the walls, each laden with books and ornaments. Many were in small glass cases. Trophies of some sort?

Of the half-dozen or so people in the room, one drew her attention most. Straight-backed, with jet-black hair, he wore white clothing and stood in front of the room's crackling hearth. He reminded her of someone, a man from her childhood. The messenger with the smiling eyes, the enigma who knew so much. *Two blind men waited at the end of an era, contemplating beauty. . . .*

The man turned around, revealing light violet eyes and a face scarred by old wounds, including a cut that ran down his cheek and deformed his upper lip. Though he looked refined – holding a goblet of wine in his left hand and dressed in the finest of suits – his face and hands told another story. Of battles, of killing, and of strife.

This was not the messenger from Shallan's past. The man raised his right hand, in which he held some kind of long reed. He placed this to his lips. He held it like a weapon, pointed right at Shallan.

She froze in place, unable to move, staring down that weapon across the room. Finally, she glanced over her shoulder. A target hung on the wall in the form of a tapestry with various creatures on it. Shallan yelped and jumped to the side just before the man blew on his weapon, shooting a small dart through the air. It passed within inches of her before embedding itself in one of the figures on the wall hanging.

Shallan raised her safehand to her breast and took a deep breath. *Steady,* she thought at herself. *Steady.*

'Tyn,' the man said, lowering the blowgun, 'is unwell?' The quiet way he spoke made Shallan shiver. She could not place his accent.

'Yes,' Shallan said, finding her voice.

The man set his goblet on the mantel beside him, then slipped another dart from his shirt pocket. He tucked this carefully into the end of the blowgun. 'She does not seem the type to let something so trivial keep her from an important meeting.'

He looked up at Shallan, blowgun loaded. Those violet eyes seemed like glass, his scarred face expressionless. The room seemed to hold its breath.

He'd seen through her lie. Shallan felt a cold sweat.

'You are right,' Shallan said. 'Tyn is well. However, the plan did not go as she promised. Jasnah Kholin is dead, but the implementation of the assassination was sloppy. Tyn felt it prudent to work through an intermediary for now.'

The man narrowed his eyes, then finally raised his reed and blew sharply. Shallan jumped, but the dart did not strike her, instead flying to hit the wall hanging.

'She reveals herself as a coward,' he said. 'You came here willingly, knowing that I might just kill you for her mistakes?'

'Every woman starts somewhere, Brightlord,' Shallan said, voice trembling rebelliously. 'I can't claw my way upward without taking a few chances. If you don't kill me, then I have had a chance to meet people that Tyn probably would never have introduced me to.'

'Bold,' the man said. He gestured with two fingers, and one of the people sitting beside the hearth – a spindly lighteyed man with teeth so large, he might have had some rat in his heritage somewhere – scrambled forward and plunked something down on the long table near Shallan.

A sack of spheres. Inside it must be broams; the sack, though dark brown, glowed brightly.

'Tell me where she is, and you may have that money,' said the scarred man, loading another dart. 'You have ambition. I like that. I will not only pay you for her location, but will attempt to find you a position in my organization.'

'Pardon, Brightlord,' Shallan said. 'But you know I won't sell her out to you.' Surely he could see her fear, sweat dampening the lining of her hat, trickling down her temples. Indeed, fearspren wiggled up through the ground beside her, though his view of them might be blocked by the table. 'If I were willing to betray Tyn for a price, then of what worth would I ever be to you? You'd know that I'd do the same to you, if offered a big enough bounty.'

'Honor?' the man asked, expression still blank, dart pinched between two fingers. 'From a thief?'

'Pardon again, Brightlord,' Shallan said. 'But I am no mere thief.'

'And if I were to torture you? I could get the information that way, I assure you.'

'I don't doubt that you could, Brightlord,' Shallan said. 'But do you really think Tyn would send me with knowledge of her location? What would be the point of torturing me?'

'Well,' the man said, looking down and tucking the dart into place, 'for one thing, it would be fun.'

Breathe, Shallan told herself. *Slowly. Normally.* It was hard to manage. 'I don't think you'll do that, Brightlord.'

He raised the reed and blew with a swift motion. The dart *thumped* as it stuck into the wall. 'And why not?'

'Because you don't seem the type to throw away something useful.' She nodded toward the relics in glass boxes.

'You presume to be of use to me?'

Shallan raised her head, meeting his gaze. 'Yes.'

He held her eyes. The hearth crackled.

'Very well,' he finally said, turning toward his fireplace and picking up his cup again. He continued to hold the reed in one hand, but drank with the other, his back to her.

Shallan felt like a puppet whose strings had been cut. She exhaled in relief, legs wobbling, and sat down on one of the chairs beside the dining table. Fingers trembling, she got out a handkerchief and wiped her brow and temples, pushing back the hat.

When she stopped to put the handkerchief away, she realized that someone had taken the seat beside her. Shallan hadn't even seen him move, and his presence gave her a start. The short, tan-skinned person had some kind of carapace mask tied to his face, pulled tight. In fact, it looked like . . . like the skin had started to grow around the edges of the mask somehow.

The arrangement of red-orange carapace pieces was like a mosaic, giving a hint of eyebrows, of anger and rage. Behind that mask, a pair of dark eyes regarded her, unblinking, and an impassive mouth and chin were also left exposed. The man ... no, the *woman* – Shallan noticed the hint of breasts and shape of the torso. The exposed safehand had thrown her.

Shallan stifled a blush. The woman wore dark brown clothing, simple, tied at the waist with an intricate belt, studded with more carapace. Four other people wearing more traditional Alethi clothing chatted softly beside the fire. The tall man who had questioned her did not speak again.

'Um, Brightlord?' Shallan said, looking toward him.

'I am considering,' the man said. 'I had been expecting to kill you and hunt down Tyn. You can tell her she would have been fine coming to me – I am not angry that she did not retrieve the information from Jasnah. I hired the hunter I felt best for the task, and I understood the risks. Kholin is dead, and Tyn was to achieve that at all other costs. I may not have commended her on the job, but I was satisfied.

'Deciding not to come explain in person, however – that cowardice turns my stomach. She hides, like prey.' He took a sip of his wine. 'You are not a coward. She sent someone she knew I would not kill. She always has been clever.'

Great. What did that mean for Shallan? She hesitantly rose from her seat, wanting to be away from the strange little woman with the unblinking eyes. Instead, Shallan took the chance to inspect the room in greater detail. Where was the smoke from the fire going? Had they cut a flue all the way down here?

The right wall had the greater number of trophies, including several enormous gemhearts. Those were, together, likely worth more than her father's estates. Fortunately, they weren't infused. Even uncut as they were, they'd probably glow enough to blind. There were also shells that Shallan vaguely recognized. That tusk was probably from a whitespine. And that eye socket, that looked frighteningly close to the structure of a santhid's skull.

Other curiosities baffled her. A vial of pale sand. A couple of thick hairpins. A lock of golden hair. The branch of a tree with writing on it she couldn't read. A silver knife. An odd flower preserved in some kind of solution. There were no plaques to explain these mementos. That chunk of pale pink crystal looked like it might be some kind of gemstone, but why was it so delicate? Bits of it had flaked off in its case, as if simply setting it down had almost crushed it.

She stepped, hesitantly, closer to the back of the room. Smoke from the fire rose, then curled and twisted around something hanging at the top of the hearth. A gemstone? . . . No, a fabrial. It gathered the smoke as a spool gathered thread. She'd never seen anything like it.

'Do you know the man named Amaram?' asked the scarred man in white.

'No, Brightlord.'

'I am called Mraize,' the man said. 'You may use that title for me. And you are?'

'I'm called Veil,' Shallan said, using a name she'd been toying with.

'Very well. Amaram is a Shardbearer in the court of Highprince Sadeas. He is also my current prey.'

Hearing it spoken like that sent a shiver through Shallan. 'And what do you wish of me, Mraize?' She tried, but didn't get the pronunciation of the title quite right. It wasn't a Vorin term.

'He owns a manor near Sadeas's palace,' Mraize said. 'Inside, Amaram hides secrets. I would know which ones. Tell your mistress to investigate and return to me with information next week on Chachel. She will know what I seek. If she does this, my disappointment with her will fade.'

Sneaking into the manor of a Shardbearer? Storms! Shallan had no idea how she'd accomplish such a thing. She should leave this place, abandon her disguise, and count herself lucky for having escaped alive.

Mraize set down his empty cup of wine, and she saw that his right hand was scarred, the fingers crooked, as if they had been broken and badly reset. There, glistening and golden on Mraize's middle finger, was a signet ring bearing the same symbol that Jasnah had drawn. The symbol Shallan's steward had carried, the symbol that Kabsal had tattooed on his body.

There was no backing out. Shallan would do whatever she had to in order to find out what these people knew. About her family, about Jasnah, and about the end of the world itself.

'The task will be done,' Shallan said to Mraize.

'No question of payment?' Mraize asked, amused, removing a dart from his pocket. 'Your mistress always asked.'

'Brightlord,' Shallan said, 'one does not haggle at the finest winehouses. Your payment will be accepted.'

For the first time since she'd entered, she saw Mraize smile, though he didn't look toward her. 'Do not harm Amaram, little knife,' he warned. 'His life belongs to another. Do not alert anyone or bring suspicion. Tyn is to investigate and return. Nothing more.'

He turned around and blew a dart into the wall. Shallan glanced at the other four people by the fire and took Memories of them with a quick blink each. Then – sensing she had been dismissed – she walked to the ladder.

She felt Mraize's eyes on her back as he raised his blowgun one last time. The trapdoor opened above. Shallan felt the gaze follow her as she climbed up the ladder.

A dart passed just beneath her, between the rungs, and stabbed the wall. Breathing quickly, Shallan left the hidden chamber, entering the dusty upper basement again. The trapdoor closed, shutting her away into the darkness.

Her poise broke, and she scrambled up the steps and out of the building. She stopped outside, breathing deeply. The street outside had grown *more* busy, not less, with those taverns drawing a crowd. Shallan hurried on her way.

She realized now that she hadn't had much of a plan in coming to meet with the Ghostbloods. What was she going to do? Get information from them somehow? That would require earning their trust. Mraize didn't seem the type to trust anyone. How would she find out what he knew about Urithiru? How to call his people off her brothers? How would she—

'Following,' Pattern said.

Shallan pulled up short. 'What?'

'People follow,' Pattern said, voice pleasant, as if he had no idea how tense this entire experience had been for Shallan. 'You asked me to watch. I watched.'

Of *course* Mraize would send someone to tail her. Her cold sweat returning, Shallan forced herself to move, not looking over her shoulder. 'How many?' she asked Pattern, who had climbed up onto the side of her coat.

'One,' Pattern said. 'The person with the mask, though she now wears a black cloak. Should we go speak with her? You are friends now, right?'

'No. I wouldn't say that.'

'Mmm . . .' Pattern said. She suspected he was trying to figure out the nature of human interactions. Good luck.

What to do? Shallan doubted she could lose her tail. The woman would have practice with this sort of thing, while Shallan . . . well, she had a lot of practice reading books and sketching pictures.

Lightweaving, she thought. *Can I do something with that?* Her disguise was still working – the dark hair trailing down her shoulder proved that. Could she change to a different image overlaying herself?

She drew in Stormlight, and that made her increase her pace. Up ahead, an alley turned between two groups of tenements. Ignoring memories of a similar alleyway in Kharbranth, Shallan turned in to this one with a quick step, then immediately breathed out Stormlight, trying to shape it. Perhaps into the image of a large man, to cover over her coat, and . . .

And the Stormlight just puffed in front of her, doing nothing. She panicked, but forced herself to keep moving down the alleyway.

It didn't work. Why didn't it work? She'd been able to make it work in her rooms!

The only thing she could think that was different was her sketch. In her rooms, she'd drawn a detailed picture. She didn't have that now.

She reached into her pocket, taking out the sheet of paper with the map sketched on it. The back was blank. She fished in the other pocket for the pencil she'd instinctively put there and tried to draw while walking. Impossible. Salas had almost set, and it was too dark. Besides, she couldn't do good detail while moving and with nothing firm to back the paper. If she stopped and sketched, would that arouse suspicion? Storms, she was so nervous, she had trouble keeping the pencil straight.

She needed a place where she could hide, crouch down, and do a solid sketch. Like one of those doorway nooks she'd passed in the alleyway.

She started to draw a wall.

That she *could* do while walking. She turned down a side street, the light from an open tavern spilling across her. She ignored the ruckus of laughter and shouts, though a few of those seemed to be directed at her, and drew a simple stone wall on her sheet.

She had no idea if this would work, but she might as well try. She turned in to another alleyway – almost stumbling over the snoring form of a drunk who was missing his shoes – then took off at a run. A short distance in, she ducked into a doorway recess a couple of feet deep. Breathing out her remaining Stormlight, she imagined the wall she'd drawn covering over the doorway.

Everything went black.

The alley had been dark anyway, but now she couldn't see *anything*. No phantom light of the moon, no glow from the torchlit tavern at the end of the alley. Did that mean her image was working? She pushed back against the door behind her, pulling off her hat, trying to make sure none of her poked through the illusory wall. She heard a faint scrape outside, boots on stone, and a sound like clothing brushing against the wall across from her. Then nothing.

Shallan remained there, frozen, straining her ears but hearing only the thud of her heart. Finally, she whispered, 'Pattern. Are you here?'

'Yes,' he said.

'Go and see if the woman is outside somewhere near.'

He made no sound as he left and then returned. 'She is gone.'

Shallan let out the breath she'd been holding. Then, bracing herself, she stepped through the wall. A glow, like that of Stormlight, filled her vision. Then she was out, standing in the alleyway. The illusion behind her swirled briefly like disturbed smoke, then quickly re-formed.

The imitation was actually pretty good. Examined closely, the joints between her stones didn't align perfectly with the real ones, but that was hard to see at night. Only a few moments later, though, the illusion shattered back to swirling Stormlight and evaporated. She had no Light left to sustain it.

'Your disguise is gone,' Pattern noted.

Red hair. Shallan gasped, then immediately shoved her safehand into her pocket. The darkeyed con woman that Tyn had trained could go about half-clothed, but not Shallan herself. It just wasn't right.

It was also stupid, and she knew that, but she couldn't change her feelings. She hesitated briefly, then took off the coat. With that and the hat removed, and with her hair and face changed, she was a different person. She left out the opposite end of the alley from where she assumed the masked woman had gone.

Shallan hesitated, getting her bearings. Where was the mansion? She tried retracing her route mentally, but had trouble fixing her position. She needed something she could see. She took out her wrinkled paper and drew a quick map of the path she'd taken so far.

'I can lead you back to the mansion,' Pattern said.

'I can manage.' Shallan held up the map and nodded.

'Mmm. It is a pattern. You can see this one?'

'Yes.'

'But not the pattern of letters with the spanreed?'

How could she explain? 'Those were words,' Shallan said. 'The warcamp is a place, something I can draw.' The picture of the path back was clear to her.

'Ah . . .' Pattern said.

She returned to the mansion without incident, but she couldn't be certain she'd cleanly slipped the tail, nor whether someone from Sebarial's staff had seen her crossing the grounds and climbing into the window. That was the problem with sneaking about. If nothing seemed to have gone wrong, you rarely knew if it was because you were safe, or if someone had spotted you and just hadn't done anything. Yet.

After pulling her shutters closed and snapping the drapes into place, Shallan threw herself back onto the plush bed, breathing deeply and trembling.

That was, she thought, *the most ridiculous thing I've ever done.*

And yet she found herself excited, flushed with the thrill of it. Storms! She'd *enjoyed* that. The tension, the sweat, the talking her way out of being killed, even the chase at the end. What was wrong with her? When she'd tried to steal from Jasnah, every part of the experience had made her sick.

I'm not that girl anymore, Shallan thought, smiling and staring at the ceiling. *I haven't been for weeks now.*

She *would* find a way to investigate this Brightlord Amaram, and she would earn the trust of Mraize so she could find out what he knew. *I still need an alliance with the Kholin family,* she thought. *And the path to that is Prince Adolin.* She'd have to find a way to interact with him again as soon as possible, but somehow that didn't make her look desperate.

The part involving him seemed likely to be the most pleasant of her tasks. Still smiling, she threw herself off the bed and went to see if any food remained on that tray she'd been left.

ONE FORM OF JUSTICE

*But as for the Bondsmiths, they had members only three, which number
was not uncommon for them; nor did they seek to increase this by great
bounds, for during the times of Madasa, only one of their order was in
continual accompaniment of Urithiru and its thrones. Their spren was
understood to be specific, and to persuade them to grow to the magnitude of the other orders was seen as seditious.*

—From *Words of Radiance*, chapter 16, page 14

K aladin never felt more uncomfortably conspicuous than when
visiting Dalinar's lighteyed training grounds, where all of the
other soldiers were highborn.

Dalinar mandated that his soldiers wear uniforms during duty hours,
and these men obeyed. In his own blue uniform, Kaladin shouldn't have
felt set off from them, but he did. Theirs were more lavish, with bright
buttons up the sides of the fine coats and gemstones set into the buttons.
Others ornamented their uniforms with embroidery. Colorful scarves
were growing popular.

The lighteyed looked over Kaladin and his men as they entered. As
much as the regular soldiers treated his men like heroes – as much as even
these officers respected Dalinar and his decisions – their postures were
hostile toward him and his.

You are not wanted here, those stares said. *Everyone has a place. You're out of yours. Like a chull in a dining hall.*

'May I be relieved from duty for today's training, sir?' Renarin asked Kaladin. The youth wore a Bridge Four uniform.

Kaladin nodded. His departure made the other bridgemen relax. Kaladin pointed toward three watch positions, and three of his men ran off to stand guard. Moash, Teft, and Yake stayed with him.

Kaladin marched them up to Zahel, who stood at the back of the sandcovered courtyard. Though the other ardents all busied themselves carrying water, towels, or sparring weapons to dueling lighteyes, Zahel had drawn a circle in the sand and was throwing little colored rocks into it.

'I'm taking you up on your offer,' Kaladin said, stepping up to him. 'I brought three of my men to learn with me.'

'Didn't offer to train four of you,' Zahel said.

'I know.'

Zahel grunted. 'Do forty laps around the outside of this building at a jog, then report back. You have until I get tired of my game to return.'

Kaladin gestured sharply, and all four of them took off at a run.

'Wait,' Zahel called.

Kaladin stopped, boots crunching sand.

'I was just testing how willing you were to obey me,' Zahel said, throwing a rock into his circle. He grunted, as if pleased with himself. Finally, he turned to look at them. 'I suppose I don't need to toughen you up. But boy, you've got red on your ears like I've never seen.'

'I – Red on my ears?' Kaladin asked.

'Damnation language. I mean that you feel you've got something to prove, that you are spoiling for a fight. It means you're angry at everything and everyone.'

'Can you blame us?' Moash asked.

'I suppose I can't. But if I'm going to train you lads, I can't have your red ears getting in the way. You're going to listen, and you're going to do what I say.'

'Yes, Master Zahel,' Kaladin said.

'Don't call me master,' Zahel said. He thumbed over his shoulder toward Renarin, who was putting on his Shardplate with the assistance of some ardents. 'I'm his master. For you lads, I'm just an interested party who wants to help you keep my friends alive. Wait here until I get back.'

He turned to walk toward Renarin. As Yake picked up one of the colored stones Zahel had been throwing, the man said, without looking, 'And don't touch my rocks!'

Yake jumped and dropped the stone.

Kaladin settled back, leaning against one of the pillars that held up the roof overhang, watching Zahel give instruction to Renarin. Syl zipped down and began inspecting the little rocks with a curious expression, trying to figure out what was special about them.

A short time later, Zahel walked past with Renarin, explaining the lad's training for today. Apparently, he wanted Renarin to eat lunch. Kaladin smiled as some ardents hurriedly carried out a table, dining ware, and a heavy stool that could support a Shardbearer. They even had a tablecloth. Zahel left the bemused Renarin, who sat in his hulking Shardplate with his faceplate up, regarding a full lunch. He awkwardly picked up a fork.

'You're teaching him to be delicate with his newfound strength,' Kaladin said to Zahel as the man passed back the other way.

'Shardplate is powerful stuff,' Zahel said, not looking at Kaladin. 'Controlling it is about more than punching through walls and jumping off buildings.'

'So when do we—'

'Keep waiting.' Zahel wandered off.

Kaladin glanced at Teft, who shrugged. 'I like him.'

Yake chuckled. 'That's because he's almost as grouchy as you are, Teft.'

'I ain't grouchy,' Teft snapped. 'I just have a low threshold for stupidity.'

They waited until Zahel jogged back toward them. The men grew immediately alert, eyes widening. Zahel carried a Shardblade.

They'd been hoping for it. Kaladin had told them they might be able to hold one as part of this training. Their eyes followed that Blade as they'd follow a gorgeous woman taking off her glove.

Zahel stepped up, then slammed the Blade into the sandy ground in front of them. He took his hand off the hilt and waved. 'All right. Try it out.'

They stared at it. 'Kelek's breath,' Teft finally said. 'You are serious, aren't you?'

Nearby, Syl had turned from the rocks and stared at the Blade.

'The morning after talking to your captain in the middle of the

Damnation night,' Zahel said, 'I went to Brightlord Dalinar and the king and asked permission to train you in sword stances. You don't have to carry swords around or anything, but if you're going to fight an assassin with a Shardblade, you need to know the stances and how to respond to them.'

He looked down, resting his hand on the Shardblade. 'Brightlord Dalinar suggested letting you handle one of the king's Shardblades. Smart man.'

Zahel removed his hand and gestured. Teft reached out to touch the Shardblade, but Moash seized the thing first, taking it by the hilt and yanking it – too hard – out of the ground. He stumbled backward, and Teft backed away.

'Be careful, now!' Teft barked. 'You'll cut off your own storming arm if you act like a fool.'

'I'm no fool,' Moash said, holding the sword up, pointing it outward. A single gloryspren faded into existence near his head. 'It's heavier than I expected.'

'Really?' Yake said. 'Everyone says they're light!'

'Those are people used to a regular sword,' Zahel said. 'If you've trained all of your life with a longsword, then pick up something that looks like it has two or three times as much steel to it, you expect it to weigh more. Not less.'

Moash grunted, delicately swiping with the weapon. 'From the way the stories are told, I thought it wouldn't have any weight at all. Like it would be as light as a breeze.' He hesitantly stuck it into the ground. 'It has more resistance when it cuts than I thought too.'

'Guess it's about expectations again,' Teft said, scratching at his beard and waving Yake to have the weapon next. The stout man pulled it free more carefully than Moash had.

'Stormfather, but it feels strange to hold this,' Yake said.

'It's just a tool,' Zahel said. 'A valuable one, but still just a tool. Remember that.'

'It's more than a tool,' Yake said, swiping it. 'I'm sorry, but it just *is*. I might believe that about a regular sword, but this . . . this is art.'

Zahel shook his head in annoyance.

'What?' Kaladin asked as Yake reluctantly handed the Shardblade over to Teft.

'Men prohibited from using the sword because they're too lowborn,' Zahel said. 'Even after all these years, it strikes me as silly. There's nothing holy about swords. They're better in some situations, worse in others.'

'You're an ardent,' Kaladin said. 'Aren't you supposed to uphold Vorin arts and traditions?'

'Well,' Zahel said, 'if you haven't noticed, I'm not a very good ardent. I just happen to be an excellent swordsman.' He nodded toward the sword. 'You going to take a turn?'

Syl looked at Kaladin sharply.

'I'll pass unless you demand it,' Kaladin said to Zahel.

'Not curious at all how it feels?'

'Those things have killed too many of my friends. I'd rather not have to touch it, if it's all the same to you.'

'Suit yourself,' Zahel said. 'Brightlord Dalinar's suggestion was to get you used to these weapons. To take away some of the awe. Half the time a man dies by one of those, it's because he's too busy staring to dodge.'

'Yeah,' Kaladin said softly. 'I've seen that. Swing it at me. I need practice facing one down.'

'Sure. Let me get the sword's guard.'

'No,' Kaladin said. 'No guard, Zahel. I need to be afraid.'

Zahel studied Kaladin for a moment, then nodded, walking over to take the sword from Moash – who had begun a second turn swinging it.

Syl zipped past, twisting around the heads of the men, who couldn't see her. 'Thank you,' she said, settling onto Kaladin's shoulder.

Zahel walked back and fell into a stance. Kaladin recognized it as one of the lighteyed dueling stances, but he didn't know which one. Zahel stepped forward and swung.

Panic.

Kaladin couldn't keep it from rising. In an instant, he saw Dallet die – the Shardblade shearing through his head. He saw faces with burned-out eyes reflecting on the Blade's too-silvery surface.

The Blade passed a few inches in front of him. Zahel stepped into the swing and brought the Blade around again in a flowing maneuver. This time it would hit, so Kaladin had to step back.

Storms, those monsters were beautiful.

Zahel swung again, and Kaladin had to jump to the side to dodge. *A bit overzealous there, Zahel,* he thought. He dodged again, then reacted to a shadow he'd seen from the corner of his eye. He spun, and came face-to-face with Adolin Kholin.

They stared one another in the eyes. Kaladin waited for a wisecrack. Adolin's eyes flicked toward Zahel and the Shardblade, then turned back to Kaladin. Finally, the prince gave a shallow nod. He turned about and walked toward Renarin.

The implication was simple. The Assassin in White had bested both of them. There was nothing to mock in preparing to fight him again.

Doesn't mean he's not a spoiled blusterer, Kaladin thought, turning back to Zahel. The man had waved over a fellow ardent, and was delivering the Shardblade to him.

'I have to go train Prince Renarin,' Zahel said. 'Can't leave him alone all day for you fools. Ivis here will go through some sparring moves with you and let you each face down a Shardblade, as Kaladin has done. Get comfortable with the sight, so you don't freeze when one comes for you.'

Kaladin and the others nodded. Only after Zahel had trotted away did Kaladin notice that the new ardent, Ivis, was a woman. Though she was an ardent, she kept her hand gloved, so there was some acknowledgment of her gender, even if the flowing ardent clothing and shaved head masked some of the other obvious signs.

A woman with a sword. An odd sight. Of course, was it any odder than darkeyed men holding a Shardblade?

Ivis gave them lengths of wood that, weight and balance wise, were decent approximations of a Shardblade. Like a child's scribble with chalk could be a decent approximation of a person. Then she put them through several routines, demonstrating the ten Shardblade sword stances.

Kaladin had been looking to kill lighteyes from the moment he'd first touched a spear, and during the later years – before being enslaved – he'd gotten pretty good at it. But those lighteyes he'd hunted on the battlefield hadn't been terribly skilled. The majority of men who were truly good with a sword had made their way to the Shattered Plains. So the stances were new to him.

He started to see and understand. Knowing the stances would let him anticipate a swordsman's next move. He didn't have to be wielding a sword himself – he still thought it an inflexible weapon – to make use of that.

An hour or so later, Kaladin set down his practice sword and stepped over to the water barrel. No ardents or parshmen ran drinks to him or his men. He was just fine with that; he wasn't some pampered rich boy. He leaned against the barrel, taking a ladle of water, feeling the good exhaustion deep in his muscles that told him he'd been doing something worthwhile.

He scanned the grounds for Adolin and Renarin. He wasn't on duty watching either of them – Adolin would have come with Mart and Eth, and Renarin was under the watch of the three that Kaladin had assigned earlier. Still, he couldn't help looking to see how they were. An accident here could be—

A woman was on the practice grounds. Not an ardent, but a true light-eyed woman, the one with the vibrant red hair. She had just wandered in, and was scanning the grounds.

He didn't bear a grudge about the incident with his boots. It simply typified how, to a lighteyes, men like Kaladin were playthings. You toyed with darkeyes, took what you needed from them, and gave no thought to having left them far worse for the interaction.

It was how Roshone had been. It was how Sadeas was. It was how this woman was. She wasn't evil, really. She just didn't care.

She's probably a good match for the princeling, he thought as Yake and Teft jogged over for some water. Moash stayed with his practice, intent on his sword forms.

'Not bad,' Yake said, following Kaladin's gaze.

'Not bad at what?' Kaladin asked, trying to figure out what the woman was doing.

'Not bad *looking*, Captain,' Yake said with a laugh. 'Storms! Sometimes, it seems the only thing you think about is who has to be on duty next.'

Nearby, Syl nodded emphatically.

'She's lighteyed,' Kaladin said.

'So?' Yake said, slapping him on the shoulder. 'A lighteyed lady can't be attractive?'

'No.' It was as simple as that.

'You are a strange one, sir,' Yake said.

Eventually, Ivis called for Yake and Teft to stop idling and return to practice. She didn't call for Kaladin. He seemed to intimidate many of the ardents.

Yake jogged back, but Teft lingered for a moment, then nodded toward the girl, Shallan. 'You think we have to worry about her? Foreign woman about whom we know very little, sent in to suddenly be Adolin's betrothed. Sure would make a good assassin.'

'Damnation,' Kaladin said. 'I should have seen that. Good eye, Teft.'

Teft shrugged modestly, then jogged back to his training.

He'd assumed the woman was an opportunist, but could she actually be an assassin? Kaladin picked up his practice sword and wandered toward her, passing Renarin, who was training in some of the same stances that Kaladin's men were practicing.

As Kaladin walked toward Shallan, Adolin clanked up beside him in Shardplate.

'What is she doing here?' Kaladin asked.

'Come to watch me while I spar, presumably,' Adolin said. 'I usually have to kick them out.'

'Them?'

'You know. Girls who want to gawk at me while I fight. I wouldn't mind, but if we allowed it, they'd clog the entire grounds every time I came. Nobody would be able to get any sparring done.'

Kaladin raised an eyebrow at him.

'What?' Adolin asked. 'You don't get women coming to watch while you spar, bridgeboy? Little darkeyed ladies, missing seven teeth and afraid of bathing . . .'

Kaladin looked away from Adolin, drawing his lips to a line. *Next time*, he thought, *I let the assassin have* this one.

Adolin chuckled for a moment, though his laughter trailed off awkwardly. 'Anyway,' he continued, 'she probably has a better reason to be here than others, considering our relationship. We'll still have to kick her out. Can't set a bad precedent.'

'You really let this happen?' Kaladin asked. 'A betrothal to a woman you'd never met?'

Adolin shrugged armored shoulders. 'Things always go so well at first, and then . . . they fall apart on me. I can never figure out where I go wrong. I thought, maybe if there were something more formal in place . . .'

He scowled, as if remembering who he was talking to, and tromped forward at a faster pace to get away from Kaladin. Adolin reached Shallan, who – humming to herself – passed him right by without looking.

Adolin raised a hand, mouth opened to speak, as he turned and watched her walk farther across the courtyard. Her eyes were on Nall, head ardent of the practice grounds. Shallan bowed to her in reverence.

Adolin scowled, turning to jog after Shallan, passing Kaladin, who smirked at him.

'Come to watch you, I see,' Kaladin said. 'Completely fascinated by you, obviously.'

'Shut up,' Adolin growled.

Kaladin strolled after Adolin, reaching Shallan and Nall in the middle of a conversation.

'. . . visual records of these suits are *pathetic*, Sister Nall,' Shallan was saying, handing Nall a bound leather portfolio. 'We need new sketches. Though much of my time will be spent clerking for Brightlord Sebarial, I would like a few projects of my own during my time at the Shattered Plains. With your blessing, I wish to proceed.'

'Your talent is admirable,' Nall said, flipping through pages. 'Art is your Calling?'

'Natural History, Sister Nall, though sketching is a priority for me in that line of study as well.'

'As well it should be.' The ardent turned another page. 'You have my blessing, dear child. Tell me, which devotary do you call your own?'

'That is . . . a subject of some consternation on my part,' Shallan said, taking the portfolio back. 'Oh! Adolin. I didn't notice you there. My, but you *do* loom when you wear that armor, don't you?'

'You're letting her stay?' Adolin asked Nall.

'She wishes to update the royal record of Shardplate and Shardblades in the warcamps with new sketches,' Nall said. 'This seems wise. The king's current accounting of the Shards includes many rough sketches, but few detailed drawings.'

'So you're going to need me to pose for you?' Adolin asked, turning to Shallan.

'Actually, the sketches of your Plate are quite complete,' Shallan said, 'thanks to your mother. I'll focus first on the King's Plate and Blades, which nobody has thought to sketch in any detail.'

'Just stay out of the way of the men sparring, child,' Nall said as someone called for her. She walked off.

'Look,' Adolin said, turning to Shallan. 'I can see what you're up to.'

'Five foot six inches,' Shallan said. 'I suspect that's all I will ever be up to, unfortunately.'

'Five foot . . .' Adolin said, frowning.

'Yes,' Shallan said, scanning the practice grounds. 'I thought it was a good height, then I came here. You Alethi really are freakishly tall, aren't you? I'd guess everyone here is a good two inches taller than the Veden average.'

'No, that's not . . .' Adolin frowned. 'You're here because you want to watch me spar. Admit it. The sketching is a ruse.'

'Hmmm. Someone has a high opinion of himself. Comes with being royalty, I suppose. Like funny hats and a fondness for beheadings. Ah, and it's our captain of the guard. Your boots are on the way to your barracks via courier.'

Kaladin started as he realized she was talking to him. 'Is that so?'

'I had the soles replaced,' Shallan said. 'They were terribly uncomfortable.'

'I liked how they fit!'

'Then you must have stones for feet.' She glanced down, then cocked an eyebrow.

'Wait,' Adolin said, frowning more deeply. 'You wore the bridgeboy's *boots*? How did that happen?'

'Awkwardly,' Shallan replied. 'And with three pairs of socks.' She patted Adolin's armored arm. 'If you really want me to sketch you, Adolin, I will. No need to act jealous, though I do still want that walk you promised me. Oh! I *need* to get that. Excuse me.'

She strode toward where Renarin was taking hits on his armor from Zahel, presumably to get him used to taking a beating while wearing Plate. Shallan's green gown and red hair were vibrant slashes of color on the grounds. Kaladin inspected her, wondering just how far she could be trusted. Probably not far.

'Insufferable woman,' Adolin growled. He glanced at Kaladin. 'Stop leering at her backside, bridgeboy.'

'I'm *not* leering. And what do you care? You just said she was insufferable.'

'Yeah,' Adolin said, looking back toward her with a wide grin. 'She all but ignored me, didn't she?'

'I suppose.'

'Insufferable,' Adolin said, though he seemed to mean something completely different. His smile widened and he strode after her, moving with the grace of Shardplate that was so discordant with its apparent bulk.

Kaladin shook his head. Lighteyes and their games. How had he found himself in such a position that he had to spend so much time around them? He walked back to the barrel and got another drink. Soon after, a practice sword crunching to the sand announced Moash joining him.

Moash nodded gratefully as Kaladin handed over the ladle. Teft and Yake were having a turn facing down the Shardblade.

'She let you go?' Kaladin asked, nodding toward their trainer.

Moash shrugged, gulping water. 'I didn't flinch.'

Kaladin nodded appreciatively.

'What we're doing here is good,' Moash said. '*Important*. After the way you trained us in those chasms, I thought I didn't have anything left to learn. Shows how much I knew.'

Kaladin nodded, folding his arms. Adolin displayed several dueling stances for Renarin, Zahel nodding approvingly. Shallan had settled down to sketch them. Was this all an excuse to get her close, so she could wait for the right time to slide a knife into Adolin's gut?

A paranoid way to think, perhaps, but that *was* his job. So he kept an eye on Adolin as the man turned and began sparring with Zahel, to give Renarin some perspective on how to use the stances.

Adolin *was* a good swordsman. Kaladin would give him that much. So was Zahel, for that matter.

'It was the king,' Moash said. 'He had my family executed.'

It took Kaladin a moment to realize what Moash was talking about. The person that Moash wanted to kill, the person he had a grudge against. It *was* the king.

Kaladin felt a shock spike through him, as if he'd been punched. He turned on Moash.

'We're Bridge Four,' Moash continued, staring off to the side at nothing in particular. He took another drink. 'We stick together. You should know about . . . why I am the way I am. My grandparents were the only family I ever knew. Parents died when I was a child. Ana and Da, they raised me. The king . . . he killed them.'

'How did it happen?' Kaladin asked softly, checking to make sure none of the ardents were close enough to hear.

'I was away,' Moash said, 'working a caravan that ran out here, to this wasteland. Ana and Da, they were second nahn. Important for darkeyes, you know? Ran their own shop. Silversmiths. I never picked up on the trade. Liked to be out walking. Going somewhere.

'Well, a lighteyed man owned two or three silversmith shops in Kholinar, one of which was across from my grandparents. He never did like the competition. This was a year or so before the old king died, and Elhokar was left in charge of the kingdom while Gavilar was out at the Plains. Anyway, Elhokar was good friends with the lighteyes who was in competition with my grandparents.

'So, he did his friend a favor. Elhokar had Ana and Da dragged in on some charge or another. They were important enough to demand a right to trial, an inquest before magistrates. I think it surprised Elhokar that he couldn't completely ignore the law. He pled lack of time and sent Ana and Da to the dungeons to wait until an inquest could be arranged.' Moash dipped the ladle back into the barrel. 'They died there a few months later, still waiting for Elhokar to approve their paperwork.'

'That's not exactly the same as killing them.'

Moash met Kaladin's eyes. 'You doubt that sending a seventy-five-year-old couple to the palace *dungeons* is a death sentence?'

'I guess . . . well, I guess you're right.'

Moash nodded sharply, tossing the ladle into the barrel. 'Elhokar knew they'd die in there. That way, the hearing would never go before the magistrates, exposing his corruption. That bastard killed them – murdered them to keep his secret. I came home from my trip with the caravan to an empty house, and the neighbors told me my family was already two months dead.'

'So now you're trying to assassinate King Elhokar,' Kaladin said softly, feeling a chill to be speaking it. Nobody was close enough to hear, not over the sounds of weapons and shouting common to sparring grounds. Still, the words seemed to hang in front of him, as loud as a trumpeter's call.

Moash froze, looking him in the eye.

'That night on the balcony,' Kaladin said, 'did you make it look like a Shardblade cut the railing?'

Moash took him by the arm in a tight grip, looking about. 'We shouldn't talk about this here.'

'Stormfather, Moash!' Kaladin said, the depth of it sinking in. 'We've been hired to *protect* the man!'

'Our *job*,' Moash said, 'is to keep Dalinar alive. I can agree with that. He doesn't seem too bad, for a lighteyes. Storms, this kingdom would be a lot better off if he were king instead. Don't tell me you think differently.'

'But killing the king—'

'Not here,' Moash hissed through clenched teeth.

'I can't just let it go. Nalan's hand! I'm going to have to tell—'

'You'd do that?' Moash demanded. 'You'd turn on a member of Bridge Four?'

They locked gazes.

Kaladin turned away. 'Damnation. No, I won't. At least, not if you'll agree to stop. You may have a grudge with the king, but you can't just try to . . . you know . . .'

'And what else am I supposed to do?' Moash asked softly. By now, he'd pulled right up to Kaladin. 'What kind of justice can a man like me get on a *king*, Kaladin? Tell me.'

This can't be happening.

'I'll stop for now,' Moash said. 'If you'll agree to meet with someone.'

'Who?' Kaladin asked, looking back to him.

'This plan wasn't my idea. Some others are involved. All I had to do was throw them a rope. I want you to listen to them.'

'Moash . . .'

'Listen to what they have to say,' Moash said, grip tightening on Kaladin's arm. 'Just *listen*, Kal. That's all. If you don't agree with what they tell you, I'll back out. Please.'

'You promise not to do anything else against the king until we've had this meeting?'

'On my grandparents' honor.'

Kaladin sighed, but nodded. 'All right.'

Moash relaxed visibly. He nodded, scooping up his mock sword, then ran back to do some more practice with the Shardblade. Kaladin sighed, turning to grab his sword, and came face-to-face with Syl hovering behind him. Her tiny eyes had gone wide, hands as fists to her sides.

'What did you just do?' she demanded. 'I only heard the last part.'

'Moash *was* involved,' Kaladin whispered. 'I need to follow this through, Syl. If someone is trying to kill the king, it's my job to investigate them.'

'Oh.' She frowned. 'I felt something. Something else.' She shook her head. 'Kaladin, this is dangerous. We should go to Dalinar.'

'I promised Moash,' he said, kneeling and untying his boots and removing his socks. 'I can't go to Dalinar until I know more.'

Syl followed him as a ribbon of light as he took the fake Shardblade and walked out into the sands of the dueling grounds. The sand was cold under his bare feet. He wanted to feel it.

He fell into Windstance and practiced a few of the swings that Ivis had taught them. Nearby, a group of lighteyed men nudged one another, nodding toward him. One said something soft, making the others laugh, though several others continued frowning. The image of a darkeyed man with even a practice Shardblade was not something they found amusing.

This is my right, Kaladin thought, swinging, ignoring them. *I defeated a Shardbearer. I belong here.*

Why weren't darkeyes encouraged to practice like this? The darkeyed men in history who had won Shardblades were praised in song and story. Evod Markmaker, Lanacin, Raninor of the Fields . . . These men were revered. But modern darkeyes, well, they were told not to think beyond their station. Or else.

But what was the purpose of the Vorin church? Of ardents and Callings and the arts? Improve yourself. Be better. Why *shouldn't* men like him be expected to dream big dreams? None of it seemed to fit. Society and religion, they just flat-out contradicted each other.

Soldiers are glorified in the Tranquiline Halls. But without farmers, soldiers can't eat – so being a farmer is probably all right too.

Better yourself with a Calling in life. But don't get *too* ambitious or we'll lock you away.

Don't get revenge upon the king for ordering the death of your grandparents. But do get revenge on the Parshendi for ordering the death of someone you never met.

Kaladin stopped swinging, sweating but feeling unfulfilled. When he fought or trained, it wasn't supposed to be like this. It was supposed to be Kaladin and the weapon, as one, not all of these problems bouncing around in his head.

'Syl,' he said, trying a thrust with the sword, 'you're honorspren. Does that mean you can tell me the right thing to do?'

'Definitely,' she said, hanging nearby in the form of a young woman, legs swinging off an invisible ledge. She wasn't zipping around him in a ribbon, as she often did when he sparred.

'Is it wrong for Moash to try to kill the king?'

'Of course.'

'Why?'

'Because killing is wrong.'

'And the Parshendi I killed?'

'We've talked about this. It had to be done.'

'And what if one of them was a Surgebinder,' Kaladin said. 'With his own honorspren?'

'Parshendi can't become Surgebin—'

'Just pretend,' Kaladin said, grunting as he tried another thrust. He wasn't getting it right. 'I'd guess all the Parshendi want to do at this point is survive. Storms, the ones involved in Gavilar's death, they might not even still be alive. Their leaders were executed back in Alethkar, after all. So you tell me, if a common Parshendi who is protecting his people comes up against me, what would his honorspren say? That he's doing the right thing?'

'I . . .' Syl hunched down. She hated questions like this. 'It doesn't matter. You said you won't kill the Parshendi anymore.'

'And Amaram? Can I kill him?'

'Is that justice?' Syl asked.

'One form.'

'There's a difference.'

'What?' Kaladin demanded, thrusting. Storm it! Why couldn't he make the stupid weapon go where it should?

'Because of what it does to you,' Syl said softly. 'Thinking about him changes you. Twists you. You're supposed to *protect*, Kaladin. Not kill.'

'You have to kill to protect,' he snapped. 'Storms. You're starting to sound as bad as my father.'

He tried a few more stances, until finally Ivis came over and gave him some corrections. She laughed at his frustration as he held the sword wrong again. 'You expected to pick this up in one day?'

He kind of had. He knew the spear; he'd trained long and hard. He thought that maybe, this would all just *click*.

It didn't. He kept on anyway, going through the motions, kicking up cold sand, mixing among the lighteyes sparring and practicing their own forms. Eventually, Zahel wandered by.

'Keep at it,' the man said without even inspecting Kaladin's forms.

'I was under the impression you'd be training me personally,' Kaladin called after him.

'Too much work,' Zahel called back, digging a canteen of something from a bundle of cloth beside one of the pillars. Another ardent had piled his colored rocks there, which made Zahel scowl.

Kaladin jogged up to him. 'I saw Dalinar Kholin, while unarmed and unarmored, catch a Shardblade in midair with the flats of his palms.'

Zahel grunted. 'Old Dalinar pulled off a lastclap, eh? Good for him.'

'Can you teach me?'

'It's a stupid maneuver,' Zahel said. 'When it works, it's only because most Shardbearers learn to swing their weapons without as much force as they would a regular blade. And it *doesn't* usually work; it usually fails, and you're dead when it does. Better to focus your time practicing things that will actively help you.'

Kaladin nodded.

'Not going to push me on it?' Zahel asked.

'Your argument is good,' Kaladin said. 'Solid soldier's logic. Makes sense.'

'Huh. Might be hope for you after all.' Zahel took a swig from his canteen. 'Now go get back to practicing.'

FIRESTORM
The Blade of
King Gavilar

SUNRAISER
The Blade of
King Elhokar

sigh

45

MIDDLEFEST

THREE AND A HALF YEARS AGO

Shallan poked at the cage, and the colorful creature inside shifted on its perch, cocking its head at her.

It was the most bizarre thing she'd ever seen. It stood on two feet like a person, though its feet were clawed. It was only about as tall as two fists atop one another, but the way it turned its head as it looked at her showed unmistakable personality.

The thing only had a little bit of shell – on the nose and mouth – but the strangest part was its hair. It had *bright green* hair that covered its entire body. The hair lay flat, as if manicured. As she watched, the creature turned and began to pick at the hair – a large flap of it lifted up, and she could see it grew out of a central spine.

'What does the young lady think of my chicken?' the merchant said proudly, standing with hands clasped behind his back, ample stomach thrust forward like the prow of a ship. Behind, people moved through the fair in a throng. There were so many. Five hundred, perhaps even *more*, people in the same place.

'Chicken,' Shallan said, poking at the cage with a timid finger. 'I've eaten chicken before.'

'Not this breed!' the Thaylen man said with a laugh. 'Chickens for eating are stupid – this one is smart, almost as smart as a man! It can speak. Listen. Jeksonofnone! Say your name!'

'Jeksonofnone,' the creature said.

Shallan jumped back. The word was mangled by the creature's inhuman voice, but it was recognizable. 'A Voidbringer!' she hissed, safehand to her chest. 'An animal that speaks! You'll bring the eyes of the Unmade upon us.'

The merchant laughed. 'These things live all over Shinovar, young lady. If their speech drew the Unmade, the entire country would be cursed!'

'Shallan!' Father stood with his bodyguards where he had been speaking to another merchant across the way. She hurried toward him, looking over her shoulder at the strange animal. Deviant though the thing was, if it could talk, she felt sorry for its being trapped in that cage.

The Middlefest Fair was a highlight of the year. Set during the midpeace – a period opposite the Weeping when there were no storms – it drew people from hamlets and villages all around. Many of the people here were from lands her father oversaw, including lesser lighteyes from families who had ruled the same villages for centuries.

The darkeyes came too, of course, including merchants – citizens of the first and second nahns. Her father didn't speak of it often, but she knew he found their wealth and station inappropriate. The Almighty had chosen the lighteyes to rule, not these merchants.

'Come along,' Father said to her.

Shallan followed him and his bodyguards through the busy fair, which was laid out on her father's estates about a half day's travel from the mansion. The basin was fairly well sheltered, the slopes nearby covered in jella trees. Their strong branches grew spindly leaves – long spikes of pink, yellow, and orange, and so the trees looked like explosions of color. Shallan had read in one of her father's books that the trees drew in crem, then used it to make their wood hard, like rock.

In the basin itself, most of the trees had been broken down, though some were instead used to hold up canopies dozens of yards wide, tied in place high above. They passed a merchant cursing as a windspren darted through his enclosure, making objects stick together. Shallan smiled, pulling her satchel out from under her arm. There wasn't time to sketch, however, as her father barreled on toward the dueling grounds where – if this was like previous years – she would spend most of the fair.

'Shallan,' he said, causing her to scurry to catch up. At fourteen, she felt horribly gangly and far too boyish in figure. As womanhood had begun to come upon her, she had learned that she should be embarrassed by her red hair and freckled skin, as they were a mark of an impure heritage. They were traditional Veden colorings, but that was because – in their past – their lines had mixed with the Horneaters up in the peaks.

Some people were proud of the coloring. Not her father, so neither was Shallan.

'You are coming to an age where you must act more like a lady,' Father said. The darkeyes gave them plenty of room, bowing as her father passed. Two of Father's ardents trailed after them, hands behind their backs, contemplative. 'You will need to stop gawking so often. It will not be long before we will want to find a husband for you.'

'Yes, Father,' she said.

'I may need to stop bringing you to events like these,' he said. 'All you do is run around and act like a child. You need a new tutor, at the very least.'

He'd scared off the last tutor. The woman had been an expert in languages, and Shallan had been picking up Azish quite well – but she'd left soon after one of Father's . . . episodes. Shallan's stepmother had appeared the next day with bruises on her face. Brightness Hasheh, the tutor, had packed her things and fled without giving notice.

Shallan nodded to her father's words, but secretly hoped that she'd be able to sneak away and find her brothers. Today she had work to do. She and her father approached the 'dueling arena,' which was a grandiose term for a section of roped-off ground where parshmen had dumped half a beach's worth of sand. Canopied tables had been erected for the lighteyes to sit at, dine, and converse.

Shallan's stepmother, Malise, was a young woman less than ten years older than Shallan herself. Short of stature with buttonlike features, she sat straight-backed, her black hair brightened by a few streaks of blond. Father settled in beside her in their box; he was one of four men of his rank, fourth dahn, who would be attending the fair. The duelists would be the lesser lighteyes from the surrounding region. Many of them would be landless, and duels would be one of their only ways to gain notoriety.

Shallan sat in the seat reserved for her, and a servant handed her chilled water in a glass. She had barely taken a single sip before someone approached the box.

Brightlord Revilar might have been handsome, if his nose hadn't been removed in a youthful duel. He wore a wooden replacement, painted black – a strange mixture of covering up the blemish and drawing attention to it at the same time. Silver-haired, well-dressed in a suit of a modern design, he had the distracted look of someone who had left his hearth burning untended back at home. His lands bordered Father's; they were two of the ten men of similar rank who served under the highprince.

Revilar approached with not one, but two master-servants at his side. Their black-and-white uniforms were a distinction that ordinary servants were denied, and Father eyed them hungrily. He'd tried to hire masterservants. Each had cited his 'reputation' and had refused.

'Brightlord Davar,' Revilar said. He did not wait for permission before climbing up the steps into the box. Father and he were the same rank, but everyone knew the allegations against Father – and that the highprince saw them as credible.

'Revilar,' Father said, eyes forward.

'May I sit?' He took a seat beside Father – the one that Helaran, as heir, would have used if he'd been there. Revilar's two servants took up places behind him. They somehow managed to convey a sense of disapproval of Father without saying anything.

'Is your son going to duel today?' Father asked.

'Actually, yes.'

'Hopefully he can keep all of his parts. We wouldn't want your experience to become a tradition.'

'Now, now, Lin,' Revilar said. 'That is no way to speak to a business associate.'

'Business associate? We have dealings of which I am not aware?'

One of Revilar's servants, the woman, set a small sheaf of pages on the table before Father. Shallan's stepmother took them hesitantly, then began to read them out loud. The terms were for an exchange of goods, Father trading some of his breachtree cotton and raw shum to Revilar in exchange for a small payment. Revilar would then take the goods to market for sale.

Father stopped the reading three-quarters of the way through. 'Are you delusional? One clearmark a bag? A tenth of what that shum is worth! Considering patrols of roadways and maintenance fees paid back to the villages where the materials are harvested, I would *lose* spheres on this deal.'

'Oh, it is not so bad,' Revilar said. 'I think you will find the arrangement quite agreeable.'

'You're insane.'

'I'm popular.'

Father frowned, growing red-faced. Shallan could remember a time when she'd rarely, if ever, seen him angry. Those days were long, long dead. 'Popular?' Father demanded. 'What does—'

'You may or may not know,' Revilar said, 'that the highprince himself recently visited my estates. It seems he likes what I have been doing for this princedom's textiles. That, added to my son's dueling prowess, has drawn attention to my house. I have been invited to visit the highprince in Vedenar one week out of ten, starting next month.'

At times, Father was not the cleverest of men, but he did have a mind for politics. So Shallan thought, at least, though she did so want to believe the best about him. Either way, he saw this implication immediately.

'You rat,' Father whispered.

'You have very few options open to you, Lin,' Revilar said, leaning toward him. 'Your house is on the decline, your reputation in shambles. You need allies. _I_ need to look the part of a financial genius to the highprince. We can assist one another.'

Father bowed his head. Outside the box, the first duelists were announced, an inconsequential bout.

'Everywhere I step, I find only corners,' Father whispered. 'Slowly, they trap me.'

Revilar pushed the papers toward Shallan's stepmother once more. 'Would you start again? I suspect your husband was not listening carefully the last time.' He glanced at Shallan. 'And does the child need to be here?'

Shallan left without a word. It was what she'd wanted anyway, though she did feel bad leaving Father. He didn't often speak with her, let alone ask for her opinion, but he did seem to be stronger when she was near.

He was so disconcerted that he didn't even send one of the guards with her. She slipped out of the box, satchel under her arm, and passed through the Davar servants who were preparing her father's meal.

Freedom.

Freedom was as valuable as an emerald broam to Shallan, and as rare as a larkin. She hurried away, lest her father realize he had given no orders for her to be accompanied. One of the guards at the perimeter – Jix – stepped toward her anyway, but then looked back at the box. He went that way instead, perhaps intending to ask if he should follow.

Best to not be easily found when he returned. Shallan took a step toward the fair, with its exotic merchants and wonderful sights. There would be guessing games and perhaps a Worldsinger telling tales of distant kingdoms. Over the polite clapping of the lighteyes watching the duel behind her, she could hear drums from the common darkeyes along with singing and merriment.

Work first. Darkness lay over her house like a storm's shadow. She would find the sun. She *would*.

That meant turning back to the dueling grounds, for now. She rounded the back of the boxes, weaving between parshmen who bowed and darkeyes who gave her nods or bows, depending on their rank. She eventually found a box where several lesser lighteyed families shared space in the shade.

Eylita, daughter of Brightlord Tavinar, sat on the end, just within the sunlight shining through the side of the box. She stared at the duelists with a vapid expression, head slightly cocked, a whimsical smile on her face. Her long hair was a pure black.

Shallan stepped up beside the box and hissed at her. The older girl turned, frowning, then raised hands to her lips. She glanced at her parents, then leaned down. 'Shallan!'

'I told you to expect me,' Shallan whispered back. 'Did you think about what I wrote you?'

Eylita reached into the pocket of her dress, then slipped out a small note. She grinned mischievously and nodded.

Shallan took the note. 'You'll be able to get away?'

'I'll need to take my handmaid, but otherwise I can go where I want.'

What would that be like?

Shallan ducked away quickly. Technically, she outranked Eylita's parents, but age was a funny thing among the lighteyes. Sometimes, the higher-ranked child didn't seem nearly as important when speaking to adults of a lower dahn. Besides, Brightlord and Brightness Tavinar had been there on *that* day, when the bastard had come. They were not fond of Father, or his children.

Shallan backed away from the boxes, then turned toward the fair itself.

Here, she paused nervously. The Middlefest Fair was an intimidating collage of people and places. Nearby, a group of tenners drank at long tables and placed bets on the matches. The lowest rank of lighteyes, they were barely above darkeyes. They not only had to work for their living, they weren't even merchants or master craftsmen. They were just ... people. Helaran had said there were many of them in the cities. As many as there were darkeyes. That seemed very odd to her.

Odd and fascinating at the same time. She itched to find a corner to watch where she would not be noticed, her sketchpad out and her imagination boiling. Instead, she forced herself to move around the edge of the fair. The tent that her brothers had spoken of would be on the outer perimeter, wouldn't it?

Darkeyed fairgoers gave her a wide berth, and she found herself afraid. Her father spoke of how a young lighteyed girl could be a target for the brutish people of the lower classes. Surely nobody would harm her here in the open, with so many people about. Still, she clutched her satchel to her chest and found herself trembling as she walked.

What would it be like, to be brave like Helaran? As her mother had been.

Her mother ...

'Brightness?'

Shallan shook herself. How long had she been standing there, on the path? The sun had moved. She turned sheepishly to find Jix the guard standing behind her. Though he had a gut and rarely kept his hair combed, Jix was strong – she had once seen him pull a cart out of the way when the chull's hitch broke. He'd been one of her father's guards for as long as she could remember.

'Ah,' she said, trying to cover her nervousness, 'you're here to accompany me?'

'Well, I was *gonna* bring you back. ...'

'Did my father order you to?'

Jix chewed on the yamma root, called cussweed by some, in his cheek. 'He was busy.'

'Then you will accompany me?' She shook from the nervousness of saying it.

'I suppose.'

She breathed out a sigh of relief and turned around on the pathway, stone where rockbuds and shalebark had been scraped away. She turned one way, then the other. 'Um . . . We need to find the gambling pavilion.'

'That's not a place for a lady.' Jix eyed her. 'Particularly not one of your age, Brightness.'

'Well, I suppose you can go tell my father what I'm doing.' She shuffled from one foot to the other.

'And in the meantime,' Jix said, 'you'll try to find it on your own, won't you? Go in by yourself if you find it?'

She shrugged, blushing. That was exactly what she'd do.

'Which means I'd have left you wandering around in a place like that without protection.' He groaned softly. 'Why do you defy him like this, Brightness? You're just going to make him angry.'

'I think . . . I think he will anger no matter what I or anyone does,' she said. 'The sun will shine. The highstorms will blow. And Father will yell. That's just how life is.' She bit her lip. 'The gambling pavilion? I promise that I will be brief.'

'This way,' Jix said. He didn't walk particularly quickly as he led her, and he frequently glared at darkeyed fairgoers who passed. Jix was light-eyed, but only of the eighth dahn.

'Pavilion' turned out to be too grand a term for the patched and ripped tarp strung up at the edge of the fairgrounds. She'd have found it on her own soon enough. The thick canvas, with sides that hung down a few feet, made it surprisingly dark inside.

Men crowded together in there. The few women that Shallan saw had the fingers cut out of the gloves on their safehands. Scandalous. She found herself blushing as she stopped at the perimeter, looking in at the dark, shifting forms. Men shouted inside with raw voices, any sense of Vorin decorum left out in the sunlight. This was, indeed, not a place for someone like her. She had trouble believing it was a place for *anyone*.

'How about I go in for you,' Jix said. 'Is it a bet you're wanting to—'

Shallan pushed forward. Ignoring her own panic, her discomfort, she moved into the darkness. Because if she did not, then it meant that none of them were resisting, that nothing would change.

Jix stayed at her side, shoving her some space. She had trouble breathing inside; the air was dank with sweat and curses. Men turned and glanced at her. Bows – even nods – were slow in coming, if they were offered at all. The implication was clear. If she wouldn't obey social conventions by staying out, they didn't have to obey them by showing her deference.

'Is there something specific you're searching for?' Jix asked. 'Cards? Guessing games?'

'Axehound fights.'

Jix groaned. 'You're gonna end up stabbed, and I'm gonna end up on a roasting spit. This is crazy. . . .'

She turned, noting a group of men cheering. That sounded promising. She ignored the increasing trembling in her hands, and also tried to ignore a group of drunk men sitting in a ring on the ground, staring at what appeared to be vomit.

The cheering men sat on crude benches with others crowded around. A glimpse between bodies showed two small axehounds. There were no spren. When people crowded about like this, spren were rare, even though the emotions seemed to be very high.

One set of benches was not crowded. Balat sat here, coat unbuttoned, leaning on a post in front of him with arms crossed. His disheveled hair and stooped posture gave him an uncaring look, but his eyes . . . his eyes lusted. He watched the poor animals killing one another, fixated on them with the intensity of a woman reading a powerful novel.

Shallan stepped up to him, Jix remaining a little ways behind. Now that he'd seen Balat, the guard relaxed.

'Balat?' Shallan asked timidly. 'Balat!'

He glanced at her, then nearly toppled off his bench. He scrambled up to his feet. 'What in the . . . Shallan! Get out of here. What are you doing?' He reached for her.

She cringed down despite herself. He sounded like Father. As he took her by the shoulder, she held up the note from Eylita. The lavender paper, dusted with perfume, seemed to glow.

Balat hesitated. To the side, one axehound bit deeply into the leg of the other. Blood sprayed the ground, deep violet.

'What is it?' Balat asked. 'That is the glyphpair of House Tavinar.'

'It's from Eylita.'

'Eylita? The daughter? Why . . . what . . .'

Shallan broke the seal, opening the letter to read for him. 'She wishes to walk with you along the fairgrounds stream. She says she'll be waiting there, with her handmaid, if you want to come.'

Balat ran a hand through his curling hair. 'Eylita? She's here. Of course she's here. Everyone is here. You talked to her? Why – But—'

'I know how you've looked at her,' Shallan said. 'The few times you've been near.'

'So you talked to her?' Balat demanded. 'Without my permission? You said I'd be interested in something like' – he took the letter – 'like this?'

Shallan nodded, wrapping her arms around herself.

Balat looked back toward the fighting axehounds. He bet because it was expected of him, but he didn't come here for the money – unlike Jushu would.

Balat ran his hand through his hair again, then looked back at the letter. He wasn't a cruel man. She knew it was a strange thing to think, considering what he sometimes did. Shallan knew the kindness he showed, the strength that hid within him. He hadn't acquired this fascination with death until Mother had left them. He could come back, stop being like that. He *could*.

'I need . . .' Balat looked out of the tent. 'I need to go! She'll be waiting for me. I shouldn't make her wait.' He buttoned up his coat.

Shallan nodded eagerly, following him from the pavilion. Jix trailed along behind, though a couple of men called out to him. He must be known in the pavilion.

Balat stepped out into the sunlight. He seemed a changed man, just like that.

'Balat?' Shallan asked. 'I didn't see Jushu in there with you.'

'He didn't come to the pavilion.'

'What? I thought—'

'I don't know where he went,' Balat said. 'He met some people right after we arrived.' He looked toward the distant stream that ran down from the heights and through a channel around the fairgrounds. 'What do I say to her?'

'How should I know?'

'You're a woman too.'

'I'm fourteen!' She wouldn't spend time courting, anyway. Father would choose her a husband. His only daughter was too precious to be wasted on something fickle, like her own powers of decision.

'I guess . . . I guess I'll just talk to her,' Balat said. He jogged off without another word.

Shallan watched him go, then sat down on a rock and trembled, arms around herself. That place . . . the tent . . . it had been *horrible*.

She sat there for an extended time, feeling ashamed of her weakness, but also proud. She'd done it. It was small, but she'd done something.

Eventually, she rose and nodded to Jix, letting him lead the way back toward their box. Father should be finished with his meeting by now.

It turned out that he had finished that meeting only to start another. A man she did not know sat next to Father with a cup of chilled water in one hand. Tall, slender, and blue-eyed, he had deep black hair without a hint of impurity and wore clothing the same shade. He glanced at Shallan as she stepped up into the box.

The man started, dropping his cup to the table. He caught it with a swift lunge, keeping it from tipping over, then turned to stare at her with a slack jaw.

It was gone in a second, replaced with an expression of practiced indifference.

'Clumsy fool!' Father said.

The newcomer turned away from Shallan, speaking softly to Father. Shallan's stepmother stood to the side, with the cooks. Shallan slipped over to her. 'Who is that?'

'Nobody of consequence,' Malise said. 'He claims to have brought word from your brother, but is of low enough dahn that he can't even produce a writ of lineage.'

'My brother? Helaran?'

Malise nodded.

Shallan turned back to the newcomer. She caught, with a subtle movement, the man slipping something from his coat pocket and moving it up toward the drinks. A shock coursed through Shallan. She raised a hand. Poison—

The newcomer covertly dumped the pouch's contents into his *own* drink, then raised it to his lips, gulping down the powder. What had it been?

Shallan lowered her hand. The newcomer stood up a moment later. He didn't bow to Father as he left. He gave Shallan a smile, then was down the steps and out of the box.

Word from Helaran. What had it been? Shallan timidly moved to the table. 'Father?'

Father's eyes were on the duel in the center of the ring. Two men with swords, no shields, harking back to classical ideals. Their sweeping methods of fighting were said to be an imitation of fighting with a Shardblade.

'Word from Nan Helaran?' Shallan prodded.

'You will not speak his name,' Father said.

'I—'

'You will *not* speak of that one,' Father said, looking to her, thunder in his expression. 'Today I declare him disinherited. Tet Balat is officially now Nan Balat, Wikim becomes Tet, Jushu becomes Asha. I have only three sons.'

She knew better than to push him when he was like this. But how would she discover what the messenger had said? She sank into her chair, shaken again.

'Your brothers avoid me,' Father said, watching the duel. 'Not one chooses to dine with their father as would be proper.'

Shallan folded her hands in her lap.

'Jushu is probably drinking somewhere,' Father said. 'The Stormfather only knows where Balat has run off to. Wikim refuses to leave the carriage.' He downed the wine in his cup. 'Will you speak with him? This has not been a good day. If I went to him, I . . . worry what I would do.'

Shallan rose, then rested a hand on her father's shoulder. He slumped, leaning forward, one hand around the empty wine flagon. He raised his other hand and patted hers on his shoulder, his eyes distant. He *did* try. They all did.

Shallan sought out their carriage, which stood parked with a number of others near the western slope of the fairgrounds. Jella trees here rose high, their hardened trunks colored the light brown of crem. The needles sprouted like a thousand tongues of fire from each limb, though the nearest ones pulled in as she approached.

She was surprised to see a mink slinking in the shadows; she'd expected all those in the area to have been trapped by now. The coachmen played cards in a ring nearby; some of them had to stay and watch the carriages, though Shallan had heard Ren speaking of some kind of rotation so that they all got a chance at the fair. In fact, Ren wasn't there at the moment, though the other coachmen bowed as she passed.

Wikim sat in their carriage. The slender, pale youth was only fifteen months older than Shallan. He shared some resemblance to his twin, but few people mistook them for one another. Jushu looked older, and Wikim was so thin he looked sickly.

Shallan climbed in to sit across from Wikim, setting her satchel on the seat beside her.

'Did Father send you,' Wikim asked, 'or did you come on one of your new little missions of mercy?'

'Both?'

Wikim turned away from her, looking out the window toward the trees, away from the fair. 'You can't fix us, Shallan. Jushu will destroy himself. It's only a matter of time. Balat is becoming Father, step by step. Malise spends one night in two weeping. Father will kill her one of these days, like he did Mother.'

'And you?' Shallan asked. It was the wrong thing to say, and she knew it the moment it came out of her mouth.

'Me? I won't be around to see any of it. I'll be dead by then.'

Shallan wrapped her arms around herself, pulling her legs up beneath her on the seat. Brightness Hasheh would have chided her for the un-ladylike posture.

What did she do? What did she say? *He's right*, she thought. *I can't fix this. Helaran could have. I can't.*

They were all slowly unraveling.

'So what was it?' Wikim said. 'Out of curiosity, what did you come up with to "save" me? I'm guessing you used the girl on Balat.'

She nodded.

'You were obvious about that,' Wikim said. 'With the letters you sent her. Jushu? What of him?'

'I have a list of the day's duels,' Shallan whispered. 'He so wishes he could duel. If I show him the fights, maybe he'll want to come watch them.'

'You'll have to find him first,' Wikim said with a snort. 'And what about me? You have to know that neither swords nor pretty faces will work for me.'

Feeling a fool, Shallan dug in her satchel and came out with several sheets of paper.

'Drawings?'

'Math problems.'

Wikim frowned and took them from her, absently scratching the side of his face as he looked them over. 'I'm no ardent. I'll not be boxed up and forced to spend my days convincing people to listen to the Almighty – who suspiciously has nothing to say for himself.'

'That doesn't mean you can't study,' Shallan said. 'I gathered those from Father's books, equations for determining highstorm timing. I translated and simplified the writing to glyphs, so you could read them. I figured you could try to guess when the next ones would come....'

He shuffled through the papers. 'You copied and translated it all, even the drawings. Storms, Shallan. How long did this take you?'

She shrugged. It had taken weeks, but she had nothing but time. Days sitting in the gardens, evenings sitting in her room, the occasional visit to the ardents for some peaceful tutoring about the Almighty. It was good to have things to do.

'This is stupid,' Wikim said, lowering the papers. 'What do you think you'll accomplish? I can't believe you wasted so much time on this.'

Shallan bowed her head and then, blinking tears, scrambled out of the carriage. It felt horrible – not just Wikim's words, but the way her emotions betrayed her. She couldn't hold them in.

She hastened away from the carriages, hoping the coachmen wouldn't see her wiping her eyes with her safehand. She sat down on a stone and tried to compose herself, but failed, tears flowing freely. She turned her head aside as a few parshmen trotted past, running their master's axehounds. There would be several hunts as part of the festivities.

'*Axehound*,' a voice said from behind her.

Shallan jumped, safehand to breast, and spun.

He rested up on a tree limb, wearing his black outfit. He moved as she saw him, and the spiky leaves around him retreated in a wave of vanishing red and orange. It was the messenger who had spoken to Father earlier.

'I have wondered,' the messenger said, 'if any of you find the term odd. You know what an *axe* is. But what is a *hound*?'

'Why does that matter?' Shallan asked.

'Because it is a word,' the messenger replied. 'A simple word with a world embedded inside, like a bud waiting to open.' He studied her. 'I did not expect to find you here.'

'I . . .' Her instincts told her to back away from this strange man. And yet, he had news of Helaran – news her father would never share. 'Where did you expect to find me? At the dueling grounds?'

The man swung around the branch and dropped to the ground.

Shallan stepped backward.

'No need for that,' the man said, settling onto a rock. 'You needn't fear me. I'm terribly ineffective at hurting people. I blame my upbringing.'

'You have news of my brother Helaran.'

The messenger nodded. 'He is a very determined young man.'

'Where is he?'

'Doing things he finds very important. I would fault him for it, as I find nothing more frightening than a man trying to do what he has decided is important. Very little in the world has ever gone astray – at least on a grand scale – because a person decided to be frivolous.'

'He *is* well, though?' she asked.

'Well enough. The message for your father was that he has eyes nearby, and is watching.'

No wonder it had put Father in a bad mood. 'Where is he?' Shallan said, timidly stepping forward. 'Did he tell you to speak to me?'

'I'm sorry, young one,' the man said, expression softening. 'He gave me only that brief message for your father, and that only because I mentioned I would be traveling this direction.'

'Oh! I assumed he'd sent you here. I mean, that coming to us was your primary purpose.'

'Turns out that it was. Tell me, young one. Do spren speak to you?'

The lights going out, life drained from them.

Twisted symbols the eye should not see.

Her mother's soul in a box.

'I . . .' she said. 'No. Why would a spren speak to me?'

'No voices?' the man said, leaning forward. 'Do spheres go dark when you are near?'

'I'm sorry,' Shallan said, 'but I should be getting back to my father. He will be missing me.'

'Your father is slowly destroying your family,' the messenger said. 'Your brother was right on that count. He was wrong about everything else.'

'Such as?'

'Look.' The man nodded back toward the carriages. She was at the right angle to see into the window of her father's carriage. She squinted.

Inside, Wikim leaned forward, using a pencil taken from her satchel

– which she'd left behind. He scribbled at the mathematical problems she'd left.

He was smiling.

Warmth. That warmth she felt, a deep glow, was like the joy she had known before. Long ago. Before everything had gone wrong. Before Mother.

The messenger whispered. 'Two blind men waited at the end of an era, contemplating beauty. They sat atop the world's highest cliff, overlooking the land and seeing nothing.'

'Huh?' She looked to him.

' "Can beauty be taken from a man?" the first asked the second.

' "It was taken from me," the second replied. "For I cannot remember it." This man was blinded in a childhood accident. "I pray to the God Beyond each night to restore my sight, so that I may find beauty again."

' "Is beauty something one must see, then?" the first asked.

' "Of course. That is its nature. How can you appreciate a work of art without seeing it?"

' "I can hear a work of music," the first said.

' "Very well, you can hear some kinds of beauty – but you cannot know full beauty without sight. You can know only a small portion of beauty."

' "A sculpture," the first said. "Can I not feel its curves and slopes, the touch of the chisel that transformed common rock into uncommon wonder?"

' "I suppose," said the second, "that you can know the beauty of a sculpture."

' "And what of the beauty of food? Is it not a work of art when a chef crafts a masterpiece to delight the tastes?"

' "I suppose," said the second, "that you can know the beauty of a chef's art."

' "And what of the beauty of a woman," the first said. "Can I not know her beauty in the softness of her caress, the kindness of her voice, the keenness of her mind as she reads philosophy to me? Can I not know this beauty? Can I not know most kinds of beauty, even without my eyes?"

' "Very well," said the second. "But what if your ears were removed, your hearing taken away? Your tongue taken out, your mouth forced shut, your sense of smell destroyed? What if your skin were burned so that you could no longer feel? What if all that remained to you was pain? You could not know beauty then. It *can* be taken from a man."'

The messenger stopped, cocking his head at Shallan.

'What?' she asked.

'What think you? Can beauty be taken from a man? If he could not touch, taste, smell, hear, see . . . what if all he knew was pain? Has that man had beauty taken from him?'

'I . . .' What did this have to do with anything? 'Does the pain change day by day?'

'Let us say it does,' the messenger said.

'Then beauty, to that person, would be the times when the pain lessens. Why are you telling me this story?'

The messenger smiled. 'To be human is to seek beauty, Shallan. Do not despair, do not end the hunt because thorns grow in your way. Tell me, what is the most beautiful thing you can imagine?'

'Father is probably wondering where I am. . . .'

'Indulge me,' the messenger said. 'I will tell you where your brother is.'

'A wonderful painting, then. That is the most beautiful thing.'

'Lies,' the messenger said. 'Tell me the truth. What is it, child? Beauty, to you.'

'I . . .' What was it? 'Mother still lives,' she found herself whispering, meeting his eyes.

'And?'

'And we are in the gardens,' Shallan continued. 'She is speaking to my father, and he is laughing. Laughing and holding her. We are all there, including Helaran. He never left. The people my mother knew . . . Dreder . . . never came to our home. Mother loves me. She teaches me philosophy, and she shows me how to draw.'

'Good,' the messenger said. 'But you can do better than that. What is that place? What does it *feel* like?'

'It's spring,' Shallan shot back, growing annoyed. 'And the mossvines bloom a vigorous red. They smell sweet, and the air is moist from the morning's highstorm. Mother whispers, but there is music to her tone, and Father's laugh doesn't echo – it rises high into the air, bathing us all.

'Helaran is teaching Jushu swords, and they spar nearby. Wikim laughs as Helaran is struck on the side of the leg. He is studying to be an ardent, as Mother wanted. I am sketching them all, charcoal scratching paper. I feel warm, despite the slight chill to the air. I have a steaming cup of cider beside me, and I taste the sweetness in my mouth from the sip I just took. It is beautiful because it *could* have been. It *should* have been. I . . .'

She blinked tears. She saw it. Stormfather, but she *saw* it. She heard her mother's voice, saw Jushu giving up spheres to Balat as he lost the duel, but laughing as he paid, uncaring of the loss. She could feel the air, smell the scents, hear the sounds of songlings in the brush. Almost, it became real.

Wisps of Light rose before her. The messenger had gotten out a handful of spheres and held them toward her while staring into her eyes. The steamy Stormlight rose between them. Shallan lifted her fingers, the image of her ideal life wrapped around her like a comforter.

No.

She drew back. The misty light faded.

'I see,' the messenger said softly. 'You do not yet understand the nature of lies. I had that trouble myself, long ago. The Shards here are very strict. You will have to see the truth, child, before you can expand upon it. Just as a man should know the law before he breaks it.'

Shadows from her past shifted in the depths, surfacing just briefly toward the light. 'Could you help?'

'No. Not now. You aren't ready, for one, and I have work to be about. Another day. Keep cutting at those thorns, strong one, and make a path for the light. The things you fight aren't completely natural.' He stood up, then bowed to her.

'My brother,' she said.

'He is in Alethkar.'

Alethkar? 'Why?'

'Because that is where he feels he is needed, of course. If I see him again, I will give him word of you.' The messenger walked away on light feet, his steps smooth, almost like moves in a dance.

Shallan watched him go, the deep things within her settling again, returning to the forgotten parts of her mind. She realized she had not even asked the man his name.

When Simol was informed of the arrival of the Edgedancers, a concealed consternation and terror, as is common in such cases, fell upon him; although they were not the most demanding of orders, their graceful, limber movements hid a deadliness that was, by this time, quite renowned; also, they were the most articulate and refined of the Radiants.

—From *Words of Radiance*, chapter 20, page 12

Kaladin reached the end of the line of bridgemen. They stood at attention, spears to shoulders, eyes forward. The transformation was marvelous. He nodded under the darkening sky.

'Impressive,' he said to Pitt, the sergeant of Bridge Seventeen. 'I've rarely seen such a fine platoon of spearmen.'

It was the kind of lie that commanders learned to give. Kaladin didn't mention how some of the bridgemen shuffled while they stood, or how their maneuvers in formation were sloppy. They were trying. He could sense it in their earnest expressions, and in the way they had begun taking pride in their uniforms, their identity. They were ready to patrol, at least close to the warcamps. He made a mental note to have Teft start taking them out in a rotation with the other two crews that were ready.

Kaladin was proud of them, and he let them know it as the hour stretched long and night arrived. He then dismissed them to their evening meal, which smelled quite different from Rock's Horneater stew. Bridge Seventeen considered their nightly bean curry to be part of their identity. Individuality through meal choice; Kaladin found that amusing as he moved off into the night, shouldering his spear. He had three more crews to look in on.

The next, Bridge Eighteen, was one of those having problems. Their sergeant, though earnest, didn't have the presence necessary for a good officer. Or, well, none of the bridgemen had *that*. He was just particularly weak. Prone to begging instead of ordering, awkward in social situations.

It couldn't all be blamed on Vet, however. He'd also been given a particularly discordant group of men. Kaladin found the soldiers of Eighteen sitting in isolated bunches, eating their evening meal. No laughter, no camaraderie. They weren't as solitary as they'd been as bridgemen. Instead, they'd splintered into little cliques who didn't mingle.

Sergeant Vet called them to order and they rose sluggishly, not bothering to stand in a straight line or salute. Kaladin saw the truth in their eyes. What could he do to them? Surely nothing as bad as their lives had been as bridgemen. So why make an effort?

Kaladin spoke to them of motivation and unity for a time. *I'll need to do another training session in the chasms with this lot*, he thought. And if that didn't work either . . . well, he'd probably have to break them up, stick them in other platoons that were working.

He eventually left Eighteen, shaking his head. They didn't seem to want to be soldiers. Why had they taken Dalinar's offer then, instead of leaving?

Because they don't want to make choices anymore, he thought. *Choices can be hard.*

He knew how that felt. Storms, but he did. He remembered sitting and staring at a blank wall, too morose to even get up and go kill himself.

He shivered. Those were not days he wanted to remember.

As he made his way toward Bridge Nineteen, Syl floated past on a current of wind in the form of a small patch of mist. She melded into a ribbon of light and zipped around him in circles before coming to rest on his shoulder.

'Everyone else is eating their dinners,' Syl said.

'Good,' Kaladin said.

'That wasn't a status report, Kaladin,' she said. 'It was a point of contention.'

'Contention?' He stopped in the darkness near the barrack of Bridge Nineteen, whose men were doing well, eating around their fire as a group.

'You're working,' Syl said. 'Still.'

'I need to get these men ready.' He turned his head to look at her. 'You know something is coming. Those countdowns on the walls . . . Have you seen more of those red spren?'

'Yes,' she admitted. 'I think so, at least. In the corners of my eyes, watching me. Very infrequently, but there.'

'Something is coming,' Kaladin said. 'That countdown points right toward the Weeping. Whatever happens then, I'll have the bridgemen ready to weather it.'

'Well, you won't if you drop dead from exhaustion first!' Syl hesitated. 'People really can do that, right? I heard Teft saying he felt like he was going to do so.'

'Teft likes to exaggerate,' Kaladin said. 'It's one mark of a good sergeant.'

Syl frowned. 'And that last part . . . was a joke?'

'Yes.'

'Ah.' She looked into his eyes. 'Rest anyway, Kaladin. Please.'

Kaladin looked toward Bridge Four's barrack. It was a distance away, down the rows, but he thought he could hear Rock's laughter echoing through the night.

Finally, he sighed, acknowledging his exhaustion. He could check on the last two platoons tomorrow. Spear in hand, he turned and hiked back. The advent of darkness meant it would be about two hours before men started turning in for the night. Kaladin arrived to the familiar scent of Rock's stew, though Hobber – sitting on a tall stump the men had fashioned for him, a blanket across his grey, useless legs – was doing the serving. Rock stood nearby, arms folded, looking proud.

Renarin was there, taking and washing the dishes of those who'd finished. He did that every night, kneeling quietly beside the washbasin in his bridgeman uniform. The lad certainly was earnest. He didn't display any of the spoiled temperament of his brother. Though he had insisted on joining them, he often sat at the edges of the group, near the back of the bridgemen at night. Such an odd young man.

Kaladin passed Hobber and gripped the man's shoulder. He nodded, meeting Hobber's eyes, raising a fist. *Fight on.* Kaladin reached for some stew, then froze.

Sitting nearby on a log were not one, but *three* beefy, thick-armed Herdazians. All wore Bridge Four uniforms, and Kaladin only recognized Punio out of the three.

Kaladin found Lopen nearby, staring at his hand – which he held before himself in a fist for some reason. Kaladin had long since given up on understanding Lopen.

'Three?' Kaladin demanded.

'Cousins!' Lopen replied, looking up.

'You have too many of those,' Kaladin said.

'That's impossible! Rod, Huio, say hello!'

'Bridge Four,' the two men said, raising their bowls.

Kaladin shook his head, accepting his own stew and then walking past the cauldron into the darker area beside the barrack. He peeked into the storage room, and found Shen stacking sacks of tallew grain there, lit only by a single diamond chip.

'Shen?' Kaladin said.

The parshman continued stacking bags.

'Fall in and attention!' Kaladin barked.

Shen froze, then stood up, back straight, at attention.

'At ease, soldier,' Kaladin said softly, stepping up to him. 'I spoke to Dalinar Kholin earlier today and asked if I could arm you. He asked if I trusted you. I told him the truth.' Kaladin held out his spear to the parshman. 'I do.'

Shen looked from the spear to Kaladin, dark eyes hesitant.

'Bridge Four doesn't have slaves,' Kaladin said. 'I'm sorry for being frightened before.' He urged the man to take the spear, and Shen finally did so. 'Leyten and Natam practice in the mornings with a few men. They're willing to help you learn so that you don't have to train with the greenvines.'

Shen held the spear with what seemed to be reverence. Kaladin turned to leave the storage room.

'Sir,' Shen said.

Kaladin paused.

'You are,' Shen said, speaking in his slow way, 'a good man.'

'I've spent my life being judged for my eyes, Shen. I won't do something similar to you because of your skin.'

'Sir, I—' The parshman seemed troubled by something.

'Kaladin!' Moash's voice came from outside.

'Was there something you wanted to say?' Kaladin asked Shen.

'Later,' the parshman said. 'Later.'

Kaladin nodded, then stepped out to see what the disturbance was. He found Moash looking for him near the cauldron.

'Kaladin!' Moash said, spotting him. 'Come on. We're going out, and you're coming with us. Even Rock is coming tonight.'

'Ha! Stew is in good hands,' Rock said. 'I will go do this thing. Will be good to get away from stink of little bridgemen.'

'Hey!' Drehy said.

'Ah. And stink of big bridgemen too.'

'Come on,' Moash said, waving to Kaladin. 'You promised.'

He'd done no such thing. He just wanted to settle down by the fire, eat his stew, and watch the flamespren. Everyone was looking at him, though. Even the ones who weren't going with Moash tonight.

'I . . .' Kaladin said. 'Fine. Let's go.'

They cheered and clapped. Storming fools. They cheered to see their commander go out drinking? Kaladin slurped down a few bites of stew, then handed the rest to Hobber. With reluctance, he then walked over to join Moash, as did Lopen, Peet, and Sigzil.

'You know,' Kaladin growled under his breath to Syl, 'if this had been one of my old spearman crews, I'd assume they wanted me out of the camp so they could get away with something while I'm gone.'

'I doubt it's that,' Syl said, frowning.

'No,' Kaladin said. 'These men just want to see me as human.' He *did* need to go, for that reason. He was already too separate from the men. He didn't want them thinking of him as they would a lighteyes.

'Ha!' Rock said, jogging up to join them. 'These men, they claim they can drink more than Horneater. Airsick lowlanders. Is not possible.'

'A drinking contest?' Kaladin said, groaning inwardly. What was he getting into?

'None of us are on duty until the late morning,' Sigzil said with a shrug. Teft was watching the Kholins overnight, along with Leyten's team.

'Tonight,' Lopen said, finger to the air, 'I will be victorious. It is said you should never bet against the one-armed Herdazian in a drinking contest!'

'It is?' Moash asked.

'It *will be* said,' Lopen continued, 'you should never bet against the one-armed Herdazian in a drinking contest!'

'You weigh about as much as a starved axehound, Lopen,' Moash said skeptically.

'Ah, but I have *focus*.'

They continued, turning down a pathway that led toward the market. The warcamp was laid out with blocks of barracks forming a large circle around the lighteyed buildings closer to the center. On the way out toward the market, which was in the outer ring of camp followers beyond the soldiers, they passed plenty of other barracks manned by ordinary soldiers – and the men there were busy in tasks that Kaladin had rarely seen in Sadeas's army. Sharpening spears, oiling breastplates, before their dinner call came.

Kaladin's men weren't the only ones going out for the night, though. Other groups of soldiers had already eaten, and these strolled toward the market, laughing. They were recovering, slowly, from the slaughter that had left Dalinar's army crippled.

The market was aglow with life, torches and oil lanterns shining from most buildings. Kaladin wasn't surprised. An ordinary army would have had camp followers aplenty, and that was for a moving army. Here, merchants showed off wares. Criers sold news they claimed had come via spanreed, reporting events in the world. What was that about a war in Jah Keved? And a new emperor in Azir? Kaladin had only a vague idea of where that was.

Sigzil jogged over to get an earful of news, paying the crier a sphere while Lopen and Rock argued which tavern was the best to visit for the night. Kaladin watched the flow of life. Soldiers passing on the night watch. A group of chatting darkeyed women moving from spice merchant to spice merchant. A lighteyed courier posting projected highstorm dates and times on a board, her husband yawning nearby and looking bored – as if he'd been forced to come along to keep her company. The Weeping was coming up soon, the time of constant rain with no highstorms – the only break was Lightday, right in the middle. It was an off year in the thousandday cycle of two years, which meant the Weeping would be a calm one this time.

'Enough arguing,' Moash said to Rock, Lopen, and Peet. 'We're going to the Ornery Chull.'

'Aw!' Rock said. 'But they do not have Horneater lagers!'

'That's because Horneater lagers melt your teeth,' Moash said. 'Anyway, it's my pick tonight.' Peet nodded eagerly. That tavern had been his choice as well.

Sigzil got back from hearing the news, and he'd apparently stopped somewhere else as well, as he carried something steaming and wrapped in paper.

'Not you too,' Kaladin said, groaning.

'It's good,' Sigzil said defensively, then took a bite of the chouta.

'You don't even know what it is.'

'Of course I do.' Sigzil hesitated. 'Hey, Lopen. What's *in* this stuff?'

'Flangria,' Lopen said happily as Rock ran off to the street vendor to get himself some chouta too.

'Which is?' Kaladin asked.

'Meat.'

'What kind of meat?'

'The meaty kind.'

'Soulcast,' Kaladin said, looking at Sigzil.

'You ate Soulcast food every night as a bridgeman,' Sigzil said, shrugging and taking a bite.

'Because I had no choice. Look. He's *frying* that bread.'

'You fry the flangria too,' Lopen said. 'Make little balls of it, mixed with ground lavis. Batter it up and fry it, then stuff it in fried bread and pour on gravy.' He made a satisfied sound, licking his lips.

'It's cheaper than *water*,' Peet noted as Rock jogged back.

'That's probably because even the grain is Soulcast,' Kaladin said. 'It will all taste like mold. Rock, I'm disappointed in you.'

The Horneater looked sheepish, but took a bite. His chouta crunched.

'Shells?' Kaladin asked.

'Cremling claws.' Rock grinned. 'Deep-fried.'

Kaladin sighed, but they finally struck out again through the crowd, eventually reaching a wooden building built on the leeward side of a larger stone structure. Everything here was, of course, arranged so that as many doorways as possible could point away from the Origin, streets designed so that they could run east to west and provide a way for winds to blow.

Warm, orange light spilled from the tavern. Firelight. No tavern would use spheres for light. Even with locks on the lanterns, the rich glow of spheres might be just a little too tempting for the intoxicated patrons. Shouldering their way inside, the bridgemen were confronted by a low roar of chatter, yelling, and singing.

'We'll never find seats,' Kaladin said over the din. Even with the reduced population of Dalinar's warcamp, this place was packed.

'Of course we will find seat,' Rock said, grinning. 'We have secret weapon.' He pointed to where Peet, oval-faced and quiet, was working his way through the room toward the front bar. A pretty darkeyed woman stood polishing a glass there, and she smiled brightly when she saw Peet.

'So,' Sigzil said to Kaladin, 'have you given thought to where you're going to house the married men of Bridge Four?'

Married men? Looking at Peet's expression as he leaned across the bar, chatting with the woman, it seemed that might not be far off. Kaladin *hadn't* given any thought to it. He should have. He knew that Rock was married – the Horneater had already sent letters to his family, though the Peaks were so far away, news had not yet returned. Teft had been married, but his wife was dead, as was much of his family.

Some of the others might have families. When they'd been bridgemen, they hadn't spoken much of their pasts, but Kaladin had teased out hints here and there. They would slowly reclaim normal lives, and families would be part of that, particularly here with the stable warcamp.

'Storms!' Kaladin said, raising a hand to his head. 'I'll have to ask for more space.'

'There are many barracks partitioned to allow families,' Sigzil noted. 'And some of the married soldiers rent places in the market. Men could move to one of those choices.'

'This thing would break up Bridge Four!' Rock said. 'It cannot be allowed.'

Well, married men tended to make better soldiers. He'd have to find a way to make it work. There *were* a lot of empty barracks around in Dalinar's camp now. Maybe he should ask for a few more.

Kaladin nodded toward the woman at the bar. 'She doesn't own the place, I assume.'

'No, Ka is just barmaid,' Rock said. 'Peet is quite taken with her.'

'We'll need to see if she can read,' Kaladin said, stepping aside as a semi-drunk patron pushed out into the night. 'Storms, but it would be good to have someone around to do that.' In a normal army, Kaladin would be lighteyed, and his wife or sister would act as the battalion's scribe and clerk.

Peet waved them over, and Ka led them through to a table set off to the side. Kaladin settled himself with his back to the wall, near enough to a window that he could look out if he wanted, but where he wouldn't be silhouetted. He spared some pity for Rock's chair as the Horneater settled down. Rock was the only one in the crew who had a few inches' height on Kaladin, and he was practically twice as broad.

'Horneater lager?' Rock asked hopefully, looking at Ka.

'It melts our cups,' she said. 'Ale?'

'Ale,' Rock said with a sigh. 'This thing should be a drink for women, not for large Horneater men. At least he is not wine.'

Kaladin told her to bring whatever, barely paying attention. This place was not *inviting*, really. It was loud, obnoxious, smoky, and smelly. It was also alive. Laughing. Boasts and calls, mugs clanking. This ... this was what some people lived for. A day of honest labor, followed by an evening at the tavern with friends.

That was not so bad a life.

'It's loud tonight,' Sigzil noticed.

'Is always loud,' Rock replied. 'But tonight, maybe more.'

'The army won a plateau run along with Bethab's army,' Peet said.

Good for them. Dalinar hadn't gone, but Adolin had, along with three men from Bridge Four. They hadn't been required to go into battle, though – and any plateau run that didn't endanger Kaladin's men was a good one.

'So many people is nice,' Rock said. 'Makes tavern warmer. Is too cold outside.'

'Too cold?' Moash said. 'You're from the storming Horneater Peaks!'

'And?' Rock asked, frowning.

'And those are *mountains*. It's got to be colder up there than anything down here.'

Rock actually sputtered, an amusing mixture of indignation and incredulity, bringing a red cast to his light Horneater skin. 'Too much air! Hard for you to think. Cold? Horneater Peaks is warm! Wonderfully warm.'

'Really?' Kaladin asked, skeptical. This could be one of Rock's jokes. Sometimes, those didn't make much sense to anyone but Rock himself.

'It's true,' Sigzil said. 'The peaks have hot springs to warm them.'

'Ah, but these are not springs,' Rock said, wagging a finger at Sigzil. 'This is lowlander word. The Horneater oceans are waters of life.'

'Oceans?' Peet asked, frowning.

'Very small oceans,' Rock said. 'One for every peak.'

'The top of each mountain forms a kind of crater,' Sigzil explained, 'which is filled with a large lake of warm water. The heat is enough to create a pocket of livable land, despite the altitude. Walk too far from one of the Horneater towns, though, and you'll end up in freezing temperatures and ice fields left by the highstorms.'

'You are telling story wrong,' Rock said.

'These are facts, not a story.'

'Everything is story,' Rock said. 'Listen. Long ago, the Unkalaki – my people, ones you call Horneaters – did not live in peaks. They lived down where air was thick and thinking was difficult. But we were hated.'

'Who would hate Horneaters?' Peet said.

'Everyone,' Rock replied as Ka brought the drinks. More special attention. Most everyone else was having to go to the bar to pick up drinks. Rock smiled at her and grabbed his large mug. 'Is first drink. Lopen, you are trying to beat me?'

'I'm at it, mancha,' Lopen said, raising his own mug, which was not quite so large.

The large Horneater took a pull on his drink, which left froth on his lip. 'Everyone wanted to kill Horneaters,' he said, thumping his fist on the table. 'They were frightened of us. Stories say we were too good at fighting. So we were hunted and nearly destroyed.'

'If you were so good at fighting,' Moash said, pointing, 'then how come you were nearly destroyed?'

'There are few of us,' Rock said, hand proudly to his chest. 'And very many of you. You are all over down here in lowlands. Man cannot step without finding toes of Alethi beneath his boot. So the Unkalaki, we were nearly destroyed. But our *tana' kai* – is like a king, but more – went to the gods to plead for help.'

'Gods,' Kaladin said. 'You mean spren.' He sought out Syl, who had chosen a perch on a rafter up above, watching a couple of little insects climb on a post.

'These are gods,' Rock said, following Kaladin's gaze. 'Yes. Some gods, though, they are more powerful than others. The *tana' kai*, he sought the strongest among them. He went first to gods of the trees. 'Can you hide us?' he asked. But gods of the trees could not. 'Men hunt us too,' they said. 'If you hide here, they will find you, and will use you for wood just like they use us."

'Use Horneaters,' Sigzil said blandly, 'as wood.'

'Hush,' Rock replied. 'Next, *tana' kai*, he visited gods of the waters. "Can we live in your depths?" he pled. "Give to us power to breathe as fish, and we will serve you beneath oceans." Alas, waters could not help. "Men dig into our hearts with hooks, and bring forth those we protect. If you were to live here, you would become their meals." So we could not live there.

'Last, *tana' kai* – desperate – visited most powerful of gods, gods of the mountains. "My people are dying," he pled. "Please. Let us live on your slopes and worship you, and let your snows and ice provide our protection."

'Gods of the mountains thought long. "You cannot live upon our slopes," they said, "for is no life here. This is place of spirits, not of men. But if you can find way to make him a place of men *and* of spirits, we will protect you." And so, *tana' kai* returned to gods of the waters and said, "Give to us your water, that we may drink and live upon mountains." And he was promised. *Tana' kai* went to gods of the trees and said, "Give to us your fruit in bounty, that we may eat and live upon the mountains." And he was promised. Then, *tana' kai* returned to mountains, and said, "Give to us your heat, this thing that is in your heart, that we may live upon your peaks."

'And this thing, he pleased gods of mountains, who saw that Unkalaki would work hard. They would not be burden upon the gods, but would solve problems on their own. And so, gods of mountains withdrew their peaks into themselves, and made open place for waters of life. The oceans were created of gods of the waters. Grass and fruit to give life were had of promise of gods of trees. And heat from heart of the mountains gave a place that we may live.'

He sat back, taking a deep drink of his mug, then slammed it down on the table, grinning.

'So the gods,' Moash said, nursing his own drink, 'were pleased that you solved problems on your own . . . by going to other gods and begging them for help instead?'

'Hush,' Rock said. 'Is good story. And is truth.'

'But you did call the lakes up there water,' Sigzil said. 'So they're hot springs. Just like I said.'

'Is different,' Rock replied, raising his hand and waving toward Ka, then smiling very deeply and wagging his mug in a supplicating way.

'How?'

'Is not just water,' Rock said. 'Is water of life. It is connection to gods. If Unkalaki swim in it, sometimes they see place of gods.'

Kaladin leaned forward at that. His mind had been drifting toward how to help Bridge Eighteen with their discipline problems. This struck him. 'Place of the gods?'

'Yes,' Rock said. 'Is where they live. The waters of life, they let you see place. In it, you commune with gods, if you are lucky.'

'Is that why you can see spren?' Kaladin asked. 'Because you swam in these waters, and they did something to you?'

'Is not part of story,' Rock said as his second mug of ale arrived. He grinned at Ka. 'You are very wonderful woman. If you come to the Peaks, I will make you family.'

'Just pay your tab, Rock,' Ka said, rolling her eyes. As she moved off to collect some empty mugs, Peet jumped up to help her, surprising her by gathering some from another table.

'You can see the spren,' Kaladin pressed, 'because of what happened to you in these waters.'

'Is not part of story,' Rock said, eyeing him. 'It is . . . involved. I will say no more of this thing.'

'I'd like to visit,' Lopen said. 'Go for a dip myself.'

'Ha! Is death to one not of our people,' Rock said. 'I could not let you swim. Even if you beat me at drinking tonight.' He raised an eyebrow at Lopen's drink.

'Swimming in the emerald pools is death to outsiders,' Sigzil said, 'because you execute outsiders who touch them.'

'No, this is not true. Listen to story. Stop being boring.'

'They're just hot springs,' Sigzil grumbled, but returned to his drink.

Rock rolled his eyes. 'On top, is water. Beneath, is not. Is something else. Water of life. The place of the gods. This thing is true. I have met a god myself.'

'A god like Syl?' Kaladin asked. 'Or maybe a riverspren?' Those were somewhat rare, but supposedly able to speak at times in simple ways, like windspren.

'No,' Rock said. He leaned in, as if saying something conspiratorial. 'I saw Lunu'anaki.'

'Uh, great,' Moash said. 'Wonderful.'

'Lunu'anaki,' Rock said, 'is god of travel and mischief. Very powerful god. He came from depths of peak ocean, from realm of gods.'

'What did he look like?' Lopen asked, eyes wide.

'Like person,' Rock said. 'Maybe Alethi, though skin was lighter. Very angular face. Handsome, perhaps. With white hair.'

Sigzil looked up sharply. 'White hair?'

'Yes,' Rock said. 'Not grey, like old man, but white – yet he is young man. He spoke with me on shore. Ha! Made mockery of my beard. Asked what year it was, by Horneater calendar. Thought my name was funny. Very powerful god.'

'Were you scared?' Lopen asked.

'No, of course not. Lunu'anaki cannot hurt man. Is forbidden by other gods. Everyone knows this.' Rock downed the rest of his second mug and raised it to the air, grinning and wagging it toward Ka *again* as she passed.

Lopen hurriedly drank the rest of his first mug. Sigzil looked troubled, and had only touched half of his drink. He stared at it, though when Moash asked him what was wrong, Sigzil made an excuse about being tired.

Kaladin finally took a sip of his own drink. Lavis ale, sudsy, faintly sweet. It reminded him of home, though he'd only started drinking it once in the army.

The others moved on to a conversation about plateau runs. Sadeas had apparently been disobeying orders to go on plateau runs in teams. He'd gone on one a bit back on his own, seizing the gemheart before anyone got there, then tossing it away as if it was unimportant. Just a few days back, though, Sadeas and Highprince Ruthar had gone on another run together – one they weren't supposed to go on. They claimed to have failed to get the gemheart, but it was open knowledge they'd won and hidden the winnings.

These overt slaps in Dalinar's face were the buzz of the warcamps. More so because Sadeas seemed outraged that he wasn't being allowed to put investigators into Dalinar's warcamp to search for 'important facts' he said related to the safety of the king. It was all a game to him.

Someone needs to put Sadeas down, Kaladin thought, sipping his drink, swishing the cool liquid in his mouth. *He's as bad as Amaram – tried to get me and mine killed repeatedly. Don't I have reason, even right, to return the favor?*

Kaladin was learning how to do what the assassin did – how to run up walls, maybe reach windows that were thought inaccessible. He could visit Sadeas's camp in the night. Glowing, violent . . .

Kaladin could *bring* justice to this world.

His gut told him that there was something wrong with that reasoning, but he had trouble producing it logically. He drank a little more, and looked around the room, noticing again how relaxed everyone seemed. This was their life. Work, then play. That was enough for them.

Not for him. He needed something more. He got out a glowing sphere – just a diamond chip – and began to idly roll it on the table.

After about an hour of conversation, Kaladin taking part only sporadically, Moash nudged him in the side. 'You ready?' he whispered.

'Ready?' Kaladin frowned.

'Yeah. Meeting is in the back room. I saw them come in a bit ago. They'll be waiting.'

'Who . . .' He trailed off, realizing what Moash intended. Kaladin had said he'd meet with Moash's friends, the men who had tried to kill the king. Kaladin's skin went cold, the air suddenly seeming chill. 'That's why you wanted me to come tonight?'

'Yeah,' Moash said. 'I thought you'd figured it out. Come on.'

Kaladin looked down into his mug of yellow-brown liquid. Finally, he downed the rest and stood up. He needed to know who these men were. His duty demanded it.

Moash excused them, saying he'd noticed an old friend he wanted to introduce to Kaladin. Rock, looking not the least bit drunk, laughed and waved them on. He was on his . . . sixth drink? Seventh? Lopen was already tipsy after his third. Sigzil had only barely finished his second, and didn't seem inclined to continue.

So much for the contest, Kaladin thought, letting Moash lead him. The place was still busy, though not quite as packed as it had been earlier. Tucked away in the back of the tavern was a hallway with private dining rooms, the type used by wealthy merchants who didn't want to be subjected to the crudeness of the common room. A swarthy man lounged outside of one. He might have been part Azish, or maybe just a very tan Alethi. He carried very long knives at his belt, but didn't say anything as Moash pushed open the door.

'Kaladin . . .' Syl's voice. Where was she? Vanished, apparently, from even his eyes. Had she done that before? 'Be careful.'

He stepped into the room with Moash. Three men and a woman drank wine at a table inside. Another guard stood at the back, wrapped in a cloak, a sword at his waist and his head down, as if he were barely paying attention.

Two of the seated people, including the woman, were lighteyes. Kaladin should have expected this, considering the fact that a Shardblade was involved, but it still gave him pause.

The lighteyed man stood up immediately. He was perhaps a little older than Adolin, and he had jet-black Alethi hair, styled crisply. He wore an open jacket and an expensive-looking black shirt underneath, embroidered with white vines running between the buttons, and a stock at his throat.

'So this is the famous Kaladin!' the man exclaimed, stepping forward and reaching out to clasp Kaladin's hand. 'Storms, but it is a pleasure to meet you. Embarrassing Sadeas while saving the Blackthorn himself? Good show, man. Good *show*.'

'And you are?' Kaladin asked.

'A patriot,' the man said. 'Call me Graves.'

'And are you the Shardbearer?'

'Straight to the point, are you?' Graves said, gesturing for Kaladin to sit at the table.

Moash took a seat immediately, nodding to the other man at the table – he was darkeyed, with short hair and sunken eyes. *Mercenary,* Kaladin guessed, noting the heavy leathers he was wearing and the axe beside his seat. Graves continued to gesture, but Kaladin delayed, inspecting the young woman at the table. She sat primly and sipped her cup of wine held in two hands, one covered in her buttoned sleeve. Pretty, with pursed red lips, she wore her hair up and stuck through with sundry metal decorations.

'I recognize you,' Kaladin said. 'One of Dalinar's clerks.'

She watched him, careful, though she tried to appear relaxed.

'Danlan is a member of the highprince's retinue,' Graves said. 'Please, Kaladin. Sit. Have some wine.'

Kaladin sat down, but did not pour a drink. 'You are trying to kill the king.'

'He *is* direct, isn't he?' Graves asked Moash.

'Effective, too,' Moash said. 'It's why we like him.'

Graves turned to Kaladin. 'We are patriots, as I said before. Patriots of Alethkar. The Alethkar that *could* be.'

'Patriots who wish to murder the kingdom's ruler?'

Graves leaned forward, clasping his hands on the table. A bit of the humor left him, which was fine. He'd been trying too hard anyway. 'Very well, we shall be on with it. Elhokar is a supremely *bad* king. Surely you've noticed this.'

'It's not my place to pass judgment on a king.'

'Oh please,' Graves said. 'You're telling me you haven't seen the way he acts? Spoiled, petulant, paranoid. He squabbles instead of consulting, he makes childish demands instead of leading. He is blowing this kingdom to the ground.'

'Have you any idea the kinds of policies he put into place before Dalinar got him under control?' Danlan asked. 'I spent the last three years in Kholinar helping the clerks there sort through the mess he made of the royal codes. There was a time when he'd sign practically *anything* into law if he was cajoled the right way.'

'He is incompetent,' said the darkeyed mercenary, whose name Kaladin didn't know. 'He gets good men killed. Lets that bastard Sadeas get away with high treason.'

'So you try to assassinate him?' Kaladin demanded.

Graves met Kaladin's eyes. 'Yes.'

'If a king is destroying his country,' the mercenary said, 'is it not the right – the duty – of the people to see him removed?'

'If he *were* removed,' Moash said, 'what would happen? Ask yourself that, Kaladin.'

'Dalinar would probably take the throne,' Kaladin said. Elhokar had a son back in Kholinar, a child, barely a few years old. Even if Dalinar only proclaimed himself regent in the name of the rightful heir, he would rule.

'The kingdom would be far better off with him at the head,' Graves said.

'He practically rules the place anyway,' Kaladin said.

'No,' Danlan said. 'Dalinar holds himself back. He knows he should take the throne, but hesitates out of love for his dead brother. The other highprinces interpret this as weakness.'

'We need the Blackthorn,' Graves said, pounding the table. 'This kingdom is going to fall otherwise. The death of Elhokar would spur Dalinar to action. We would get back the man we had twenty years ago, the man who unified the highprinces in the first place.'

'Even if that man didn't fully return,' the mercenary added, 'we certainly couldn't be worse off than we are now.'

'So yes,' Graves said to Kaladin. 'We're assassins. Murderers, or would be ones. We don't want a coup, and we don't want to kill innocent guards. We just want the king removed. Quietly. Preferably in an accident.'

Danlan grimaced, then took a drink of wine. 'Unfortunately, we have not been particularly effective so far.'

'And that's why I wanted to meet with you,' Graves said.

'You expect me to *help* you?' Kaladin asked.

Graves raised his hands. 'Think about what we've said. That is all I ask. Think about the king's actions, watch him. Ask yourself, "How much longer will the kingdom last with this man at its head?"'

'The Blackthorn must take the throne,' Danlan said softly. 'It *will* happen eventually. We want to help him along, for his own good. Spare him the difficult decision.'

'I could turn you in,' Kaladin said, meeting Graves's eyes. To the side, the cloaked man – who had been leaning against the wall and listening – shuffled, standing up straighter. 'Inviting me here was a risk.'

'Moash says you were trained as a surgeon,' Graves said, not looking at all concerned.

'Yes.'

'And what do you do if the hand is festering, threatening the entire body? Do you wait and hope it gets better, or do you act?'

Kaladin didn't reply.

'You control the King's Guard now, Kaladin,' Graves said. 'We will need an opening, a time when no guards will be hurt, to strike. We didn't want the actual blood of the king on our hands, wanted to make this seem an accident, but I have realized this is cowardly. I will do the deed myself. All I want is an opening, and Alethkar's suffering will be over.'

'It will be better for the king this way,' Danlan said. 'He is dying a slow death on that throne, like a drowning man far from land. Best to be done with it quickly.'

Kaladin stood up. Moash rose hesitantly.

Graves looked at Kaladin.

'I will consider,' Kaladin said.

'Good, good,' Graves said. 'You can get back to us through Moash. Be the surgeon this kingdom needs.'

'Come on,' Kaladin said to Moash. 'The others will be wondering where we got to.'

He walked out, Moash following after making a few hasty farewells. Kaladin, honestly, expected one of them to try to stop him. Didn't they worry that he'd turn them in, as he'd threatened?

They let him go. Back out into the clattering, chattering common room. *Storms*, he thought. *I wish their arguments hadn't been so good.* 'How did you meet them?' Kaladin asked as Moash jogged up to join him.

'Rill, that's the fellow who was sitting at the table, he was a mercenary on some of the caravans I worked before ending up in the bridge crews. He came to me once we were free of slavery.' Moash took Kaladin by the arm, halting him before they got back to their table. 'They're right. You know they are, Kal. I can see it in you.'

'They're traitors,' Kaladin said. 'I want nothing to do with them.'

'You said you'd consider!'

'I said that,' Kaladin said softly, 'so that they'd let me leave. We have a *duty*, Moash.'

'Is it greater than the duty to the country itself?'

'You don't care about the country,' Kaladin snapped. 'You just want to pursue your grudge.'

'All right, fine. But Kaladin, did you notice? Graves treats all men the same, regardless of eye color. He doesn't care that we're darkeyed. He married a darkeyed woman.'

'Really?' Kaladin had heard of wealthy darkeyes marrying lowborn lighteyes, but never anyone as high-dahn as a Shardbearer.

'Yeah,' Moash said. 'One of his sons is even a one-eye. Graves doesn't give a storm about what other people think of him. He does what is right. And in this case, it's – ' Moash glanced around. They were now surrounded by people. 'It's what he said. Someone has to do it.'

'Don't speak of this to me again,' Kaladin said, pulling his arm free and walking back toward the table. 'And don't meet with them anymore.'

He sat back down, Moash slinking into his place, annoyed. Kaladin tried to get himself to rejoin the conversation with Rock and Lopen, but he just couldn't.

All around him, people laughed or shouted.

Be the surgeon this kingdom needs. . . .

Storms, what a mess.

Yet, were the orders not disheartened by so great a defeat, for the Lightweavers provided spiritual sustenance: they were enticed by those glorious creations to venture on a second assault.

—From *Words of Radiance*, chapter 21, page 10

'It doesn't make sense,' Shallan said. 'Pattern, these maps are baffling.'

The spren hovered nearby in his three-dimensional form full of twisting lines and angles. Sketching him had proven difficult, as whenever she looked closely at a section of his form, she found that it had so much detail as to defy proper depiction.

'Mmm?' Pattern asked in his humming voice.

Shallan climbed off her bed and tossed the book onto her white-painted writing desk. She knelt beside Jasnah's trunk, digging through it before coming out with a map of Roshar. It was ancient, and not terribly accurate; Alethkar was depicted as far too large and the world as a whole was misshapen, with trade routes emphasized. It clearly predated modern methods of survey and cartography. Still, it was important, for it showed the Silver Kingdoms as they had supposedly existed during the time of the Knights Radiant.

'Urithiru,' Shallan said, pointing toward a shining city depicted on the map as the center of everything. It wasn't in Alethkar, or Alethela as it had been known at the time. The map put it in the middle of the mountains near what might have been modern Jah Keved. However, Jasnah's annotations said other maps from the time placed it elsewhere. 'How could they not *know* where their capital was, the center of the orders of knights? Why does every map argue with its fellows?'

'Mmmmmm . . .' Pattern said, thoughtful. 'Perhaps many had heard of it, but never visited.'

'Cartographers as well?' Shallan asked. 'And the kings who commissioned these maps? Surely *some* of them had been to the place. Why on Roshar would it be so difficult to pinpoint?'

'They wished to keep its location secret, perhaps?'

Shallan stuck the map to the wall using some weevilwax from Jasnah's supplies. She backed away, folding her arms. She hadn't dressed for the day yet, and wore her dressing gown, hands uncovered.

'If that's the case,' Shallan said, 'they did too good a job of it.' She dug out a few other maps from the time, created by other kingdoms. In each, Shallan noted, the country of origin was presented far larger than it should have been. She stuck these to the wall too.

'Each shows Urithiru in a different location,' Shallan said. 'Notably close to their own lands, yet not *in* their lands.'

'Different languages on each,' Pattern said. 'Mmm . . . There are patterns here.' He started to try sounding them out.

Shallan smiled. Jasnah had told her that several of them were thought to have been written in the Dawnchant, a dead language. Scholars had been trying for years to—

'Behardan King . . . something I do not understand . . . order, perhaps . . .' Pattern said. 'Map? Yes, that would likely be map. So the next is perhaps to draw . . . draw . . . something I do not understand . . .'

'You're *reading* it?'

'It is a pattern.'

'You're *reading the Dawnchant*.'

'Not well.'

'You're reading the *Dawnchant*!' Shallan exclaimed. She scrambled up to the map beside which Pattern hovered, then rested her fingers on the script at the bottom. 'Behardan, you said? Maybe Bajerden . . . Nohadon himself.'

'Bajerden? Nohadon? Must people have so many names?'

'One is honorific,' Shallan said. 'His original name wasn't considered symmetrical enough. Well, I guess it wasn't really symmetrical at all, so the ardents gave him a new one centuries ago.'

'But . . . the new one isn't symmetrical either.'

'The *h* sound can be for any letter,' Shallan said absently. 'We write it as the symmetrical letter, to make the word balance, but add a diacritical mark to indicate it sounds like an *h* so the word is easier to say.'

'That – One can't just *pretend* that a word is symmetrical when it isn't!'

Shallan ignored his sputtering, instead staring at the alien script of what was supposedly the Dawnchant. *If we do find Jasnah's city,* Shallan thought, *and if it does have records, they might be in this language.* 'We need to see how much of the Dawnchant you can translate.'

'I did not read it,' Pattern said, annoyed. 'I postulated a few words. The name I could translate because of the sounds of the cities above.'

'But those aren't written in the Dawnchant!'

'The scripts are derived from one another,' Pattern said. 'Obviously.'

'So obvious that no human scholar has ever figured it out.'

'You are not as good with patterns,' he said, sounding smug. 'You are abstract. You think in lies and tell them to yourselves. That is fascinating, but it is not good for patterns.'

You are abstract . . . Shallan rounded the bed and slipped a book from the pile there, one written by the scholar Ali-daughter-Hasweth of Shinovar. The Shin scholars were among the most interesting to read, as their perspectives on the rest of Roshar could be so frank, so different.

She found the passage she wanted. Jasnah had highlighted it in her notes, so Shallan had sent out for the full book. Sebarial's stipend to her – which he *was* paying – came in very handy. Vathah and Gaz, by her request, had spent the last few days visiting book merchants asking after *Words of Radiance,* the book Jasnah had given her just before dying. So far no luck, though one merchant had claimed he might be able to order it in from Kholinar.

'Urithiru was the connection to all nations,' she read from the Shin writer's work. 'And, at times, our only path to the outside world, with its stones unhallowed.' She looked up at Pattern. 'What does that mean to you?'

'It means what it says,' Pattern replied, still hovering beside the maps. 'That Urithiru was well connected. Roads, perhaps?'

'I've always read the phrase metaphorically. Connected in purpose, in thought, and scholarship.'

'Ah. Lies.'

'What if it's not a metaphor? What if it's like what you say?' She rose and crossed the room toward the maps, resting her fingers on Urithiru at the center. 'Connected . . . but not by roads. Some of these maps don't have any roads leading to Urithiru at all. They all place it in the mountains, or at least the hills. . . .'

'Mmm.'

'How do you reach a city if not by roads?' Shallan asked. 'Nohadon could walk there, or so he claimed. But others do not speak of riding, or walking, to Urithiru.' True, there were few accounts of people visiting the city. It was a legend. Most modern scholars considered it a myth.

She needed more information. She scrambled over to Jasnah's trunk, digging out one of her notebooks. 'She said that Urithiru wasn't on the Shattered Plains,' Shallan said, 'but what if the *pathway* to it is here? Not an ordinary pathway, though. Urithiru was the city of Surgebinders. Of ancient wonders, like Shardblades.'

'Mm . . .' Pattern said softly. 'Shardblades are no wonder . . .'

Shallan found the reference she was searching for. It wasn't the quote she found curious, but Jasnah's annotation of it. *Another folktale, this one recorded in* Among the Darkeyed, *by Calinam. Page 102. Stories of instantaneous travel and the Oathgates pervade these tales.*

Instantaneous travel. Oathgates.

'That's what she was coming here for,' Shallan whispered. 'She thought she could find a passageway here, on the Plains. But they're barren stormlands, just stone, crem, and greatshells.' She looked up at Pattern. 'We *really* need to get out there, onto the Shattered Plains.'

Her announcement was accompanied by an ominous chime from the clock. Ominous in that it meant the hour was far later than she'd assumed. Storms! She needed to meet Adolin by noon. She had to leave in a half hour if she was going to meet him on time.

Shallan yelped and ran for the washroom. She turned the spigot for water to fill the tub. After a moment of it spitting out dirty cremwater, clean, warm water began to flow, and she put in the stopper. She put her hand underneath it, marveling yet again. Flowing warm water. Sebarial said that artifabrians had visited recently, arranging to set up a fabrial that would keep the water in the cistern above perpetually warm, like the ones in Kharbranth.

'I,' she said, shucking off her dressing gown, 'am going to allow myself to grow very, very accustomed to this.'

She climbed into the tub as Pattern moved along the wall above her. She had decided not to be bashful around him. True, he had a male voice, but he wasn't *really* a man. Besides, there were spren everywhere. The tub probably had one in it, as did the walls. She'd seen for herself that everything had a soul, or a spren, or whatever. Did she care if the walls watched her? No. So why should she care about Pattern?

She did have to repeat this line of reasoning every time he saw her undress. It would help if he weren't so blasted *curious* about everything.

'The anatomical differences between genders are so slight,' Pattern said, humming to himself. 'Yet so profound. And you augment them. Long hair. Blush on the cheeks. I went and watched Sebarial bathe last night and—'

'Please tell me you didn't,' Shallan said, blushing as she grabbed some pasty soap from the jar beside the iron tub.

'But . . . I just told you that I did. . . . Anyway, I wasn't seen. I would not need to do this if you'd be more accommodating.'

'I am *not* doing nude sketches for you.'

She had made the mistake of mentioning that many of the great artists had trained themselves this way. After much pleading back home, she'd gotten several of the maids to pose for her, so long as she promised to destroy the sketches. Which she had. She'd never sketched men that way. Storms, that would be embarrassing!

She didn't let herself linger in the bath. A quarter hour later – by the clock – she stood dressed and combing her damp hair before the mirror.

How would she ever go back to Jah Keved and a placid, rural life again? The answer was simple. She probably would never return. Once, that thought would have horrified her. Now it thrilled her – though she was determined to bring her brothers to the Shattered Plains. They would be far safer here than at her father's estates, and what would they be leaving behind? Barely anything at all. She'd begun to think it was a far better solution than anything else, and let them dodge the issue of the missing Soulcaster, to an extent.

She'd gone to one of the information stations connected to Tashikk – there was one in every warcamp – and paid to have a letter, along with a spanreed, sent by messenger from Valath to her brothers. It would take weeks to arrive, unfortunately. If it even did. The merchant she'd talked to at the information station had warned her that moving through Jah Keved was difficult these days, with the succession war. To be careful, she'd sent a second letter from Northgrip, which was as far from the battlefields as one could get. Hopefully at least one of the two would arrive safely.

When she established contact again, she'd make a single argument to her brothers. Abandon the Davar estates. Take the money Jasnah had sent and flee to the Shattered Plains. For now, she'd done what she could.

She rushed through the room, hopping on one foot as she pulled on a slipper, and passed the maps. *I'll deal with you later.*

It was time to go woo her betrothed. Somehow. The novels she'd read made it seem easy. A batting of eyelashes, blushes at appropriate times. Well, she had that last one down in good measure. Except maybe the appropriate part. She buttoned up the sleeve over her safehand, then paused at the door as she looked back and saw her sketchbook and pencil lying on the table.

She didn't want to leave without those ever again. She tucked both in her satchel and rushed out. On the way through the white-marbled house, she passed Palona and Sebarial in a room with enormous glass windows, facing leeward over the gardens. Palona lay facedown, getting a massage – completely bare-backed – while Sebarial reclined and ate sweets. A young woman stood at a lectern in the corner, reciting poetry to them.

Shallan had a difficult time judging those two. Sebarial. Was he a clever civil planner or an indolent glutton? Both? Palona certainly did like the luxuries of wealth, but she didn't seem the least bit arrogant. Shallan had spent the last three days poring over Sebarial's house ledgers, and had found them an absolute *mess*. He seemed so smart in some areas. How could he have let his ledgers get so overgrown?

Shallan wasn't especially good with numbers, not compared to her art, but she did enjoy math on occasion and was determined to tackle those ledgers.

Gaz and Vathah waited for her outside the doors. They followed her toward Sebarial's coach, which waited for her to use, along with one of her slaves to act as footman. En said he'd done the job before, and he smiled at her as she stepped up. That was good to see. She couldn't remember any of the five smiling on their trip out, even when she'd released them from the cage.

'You are being treated well, En?' she asked as he opened the coach door for her.

'Yes, mistress.'

'You'd tell me if you weren't?'

'Er, yes, mistress.'

'And you, Vathah?' she asked, turning to him. 'How are you finding your accommodations?'

He grunted.

'I assume that means they're accommodating?' she asked.

Gaz chuckled. The short man had an ear for wordplay.

'You've kept your bargain,' Vathah said. 'I'll give you that. The men are happy.'

'And you?'

'Bored. All we do every day is sit around, collect what you pay us, and go drinking.'

'Most men would consider that an ideal profession.' She smiled at En, then climbed into the coach.

Vathah shut the door for her, then looked in the window. 'Most men are idiots.'

'Nonsense,' Shallan said, smiling. 'By the law of averages, only half of them are.'

He grunted. She was learning to interpret those, which was essential to speaking Vathahese. This one roughly meant, 'I'm not going to acknowledge that joke because it would spoil my reputation as a complete and utter dunnard.'

'I suppose,' he said, 'we have to ride up top.'

'Thank you for offering,' Shallan said, then pulled down the window shade. Outside, Gaz chuckled again. The two climbed into the guard positions on the top back of the carriage, and En joined the coachman up front. It was a true proper coach, pulled by horses and everything. Shallan had originally felt bad about asking to use it, but Palona had laughed. 'Take the thing whenever you want! I have my own, and if Turi's coach is gone, he'll have an excuse to not go when people ask him to visit. He loves that.'

Shallan closed the other window shade as the coachman started the vehicle rolling, then got out her sketchbook. Pattern waited on the first blank white page. 'We are going to find out,' Shallan whispered, 'just what we can do.'

'Exciting!' Pattern said.

She got out her pouch of spheres and breathed in some of the Stormlight. Then, she puffed it out in front of her, trying to shape it, meld it.

Nothing.

Next, she tried holding a very specific image in her head – herself, with one small change: black hair instead of red. She puffed out the Stormlight, and this time it shifted around her and hung for a moment. Then it too vanished.

'This is silly,' Shallan said softly, Stormlight trailing from her lips. She did a quick sketch of herself with dark hair. 'What does it matter if I draw it first or not? The pencils don't even show color.'

'It shouldn't matter,' Pattern said. 'But it matters to you. I do not know why.'

She finished the sketch. It was very simple – it didn't show her features, only really her hair, everything else indistinct. Yet when she used Stormlight this time, the image took and her hair darkened to black.

Shallan sighed, Stormlight leaking from her lips. 'So, how do I make the illusion vanish?'

'Stop feeding it.'

'How?'

'I am supposed to know this?' Pattern asked. 'You are the expert on feeding.'

Shallan gathered all of her spheres – several were now dun – and set them on the seat across from her, out of reach. That wasn't far enough, for as her Stormlight ran out, she breathed in using instincts she hadn't realized she had. Light streamed from across the carriage and into her.

'I'm quite good at that,' Shallan said sourly, 'considering how short a time I've been doing it.'

'Short time?' Pattern said. 'But we first . . .'

She stopped listening until he was done.

'I really need to find another copy of *Words of Radiance*,' Shallan said, starting another sketch. 'Maybe it talks about how to dismiss the illusions.'

She continued to work on her next sketch, a picture of Sebarial. She'd taken a Memory of him while dining the night before, just after returning from a session scouting Amaram's compound. She wanted to get the details of this sketch right for her collection, so it took some time. Fortunately, the level roadway meant no big bumps. It wasn't ideal, but she seemed to have less and less time these days, with her research, her work for Sebarial, infiltrating the Ghostbloods, and meetings with Adolin Kholin. She'd had so much more time when she was younger. She couldn't help thinking she'd wasted much of it.

She let the work consume her. The familiar sound of pencil on paper, the focus of creation. Beauty was out there, all around. To create art was not to capture it, but to *participate* in it.

When she finished, a glance out the window showed them approaching the Pinnacle. She held up the sketch, studying it, then nodded to herself. Satisfactory.

Next she tried using Stormlight to create an image. She breathed out a lot of it, and it formed immediately, snapping into an image of Sebarial sitting across from her in the carriage. He held the same position as he did in her sketch, hands out to slice food that was not included in her image.

Shallan smiled. The detail was *perfect*. Folds in skin, individual hairs. She hadn't drawn those – no sketch could capture all the hairs on a head, all the pores in skin. Her image had these things, so it didn't create exactly what she drew, but the drawing was a focus. A model that the image built from.

'Mmm,' Pattern said, sounding satisfied. 'One of your most truthful lies. Wonderful.'

'He doesn't move,' Shallan said. 'Nobody would mistake this for something living, never mind the unnatural pose. The eyes are lifeless; the chest doesn't rise and fall with breath. The muscles don't shift. It's detailed – but like a statue can be detailed yet still dead.'

'A statue of light.'

'I didn't say it isn't impressive,' Shallan said. 'But the images will be much harder to use unless I can give them life.' How strange that she should feel that her sketches were alive, but this thing – which was so much more realistic – was dead.

She reached out to wave her hand through the image. If she touched it slowly, the disturbance was minor. Waving her hand disturbed it like smoke. She noticed something else. While her hand was in the image . . .

Yes. She sucked in a breath and the image dissolved to glowing smoke, drawn into her skin. She could reclaim Stormlight from the illusion. *One question answered,* she thought, settling back and making notes about the experience in the back of the notebook.

She began packing up her satchel as the carriage arrived at the Outer Market, where Adolin would be waiting for her. They'd gone on their promised walk the day before, and she felt things were going well. But she also knew she needed to impress him. Her efforts with Highlady Navani had not been fruitful so far, and she really *did* need an alliance with the Kholin house.

That made her consider. Her hair had dried, but she tended to keep it long and straight down her back, with only its natural curl to give it body. The Alethi women favored intricate braids instead.

Her skin was pale and dusted lightly with freckles, and her body was nowhere near curvaceous enough to inspire envy. She could change all of this with an illusion. An augmentation. Since Adolin had seen her without, she couldn't change anything dramatic – but she could enhance herself. It would be like wearing makeup.

She hesitated. If Adolin came to agree to the marriage, would it be because of her, or the lies?

Foolish girl, Shallan thought. *You were willing to change your appearance to get Vathah to follow you and to gain a place with Sebarial, but not now?*

But capturing Adolin's attention with illusions would lead her down a difficult path. She couldn't wear an illusion always, could she? In married life? Better to see what she could do without one, she thought as she climbed out of the carriage. She'd have to rely, instead, upon her feminine wiles.

She wished she knew if she had any.

48

NO MORE
WEAKNESS

THREE YEARS AGO

'These are really good, Shallan,' Balat said, leafing through pages of her sketches. The two of them sat in the gardens, accompanied by Wikim, who sat on the ground tossing a cloth-wrapped ball for his axehound Sakisa to catch.

'My anatomy is off,' Shallan said with a blush. 'I can't get the proportions right.' She needed models to pose for her so she could work on that.

'You're better than Mother ever was,' Balat said, flipping to another page, where she had sketched Balat on the sparring grounds with his swordsmanship tutor. He tipped it toward Wikim, who raised an eyebrow.

Her middle brother was looking better and better these last four months. Less scrawny, more solid. He almost constantly had mathematical problems with him. Father had once railed at him for that, claiming it was feminine and unseemly – but, in a rare show of dissension, Father's ardents had approached him and told him to calm himself, and that the Almighty approved of Wikim's interest. They hoped Wikim might find his way into their ranks.

'I heard that you got another letter from Eylita,' Shallan said, trying to distract Balat from the sketchbook. She couldn't keep herself from blushing as he turned page after page. Those weren't meant for others to look at. They weren't any good.

'Yeah,' he said, grinning.

'You going to have Shallan read it to you?' Wikim asked, throwing the ball.

Balat coughed. 'I had Malise do it. Shallan was busy.'

'You're embarrassed!' Wikim said, pointing. 'What is *in* those letters?'

'Things my fourteen-year-old sister doesn't need to know about!' Balat said.

'That racy, eh?' Wikim asked. 'I wouldn't have figured that for the Tavinar girl. She seems too proper.'

'No!' Balat blushed further. 'They aren't racy; they are merely private.'

'Private like your—'

'Wikim,' Shallan cut in.

He looked up, and then noticed that angerspren were pooling underneath Balat's feet. 'Storms, Balat. You are getting so touchy about that girl.'

'Love makes us all fools,' Shallan said, distracting the two.

'Love?' Balat asked, glancing at her. 'Shallan, you're barely old enough to pin up your safehand. What do you know about love?'

She blushed. 'I . . . never mind.'

'Oh, look at that,' Wikim said. 'She's thought up something clever. You're going to have to say it now, Shallan.'

'No use keeping something like that inside,' Balat agreed.

'Ministara says I speak my mind too much. That it's not a feminine attribute.'

Wikim laughed. 'That hasn't seemed to stop any women *I've* known.'

'Yeah, Shallan,' Balat said. 'If you can't say the things you think of to us, then who can you say them to?'

'Trees,' she said, 'rocks, shrubs. Basically anything that can't get me in trouble with my tutors.'

'You don't have to worry about Balat, then,' Wikim said. 'He couldn't manage something clever even in repetition.'

'Hey!' Balat said. Though, unfortunately, it wasn't far from the truth.

'Love,' Shallan said, though partially just to distract them, 'is like a pile of chull dung.'

'Smelly?' Balat asked.

'No,' Shallan said, 'for even as we try to avoid both, we end up stepping in them anyway.'

'Deep words for a girl who hit her teens precisely fifteen months ago,' Wikim said with a chuckle.

'Love is like the sun,' Balat said, sighing.

'Blinding?' Shallan asked. 'White, warm, powerful – but also capable of burning you?'

'Perhaps,' Balat said, nodding.

'Love is like a Herdazian surgeon,' Wikim said, looking at her.

'And how is that?' Shallan asked.

'You tell me,' Wikim said. 'I'm seeing what you can make of it.'

'Um … Both leave you uncomfortable?' Shallan said. 'No. Ooh! The only reason you'd want one was if you'd taken a sharp blow to the head!'

'Ha! Love is like spoiled food.'

'Necessary for life on one hand,' Shallan said, 'but also expressly nauseating.'

'Father's snoring.'

She shuddered. 'You have to experience it to believe just how distracting it can be.'

Wikim chuckled. Storms, but it was good to see him doing that.

'Stop it, you two,' Balat said. 'That kind of talk is disrespectful. Love … love is like a classical melody.'

Shallan grinned. 'If you end your performance too quickly, your audience is disappointed?'

'Shallan!' Balat said.

Wikim, however, was rolling on the ground. After a moment, Balat shook his head, and gave an agreeable chuckle. For her own part, Shallan was blushing. *Did I really just say that?* That last one had actually been somewhat witty, far better than the others. It had also been improper.

She got a guilty thrill from it. Balat looked embarrassed, and he blushed at the double meaning, collecting shamespren. Sturdy Balat. He wanted so much to lead them. So far as she knew, he'd given up his habit of killing cremlings for fun. Being in love strengthened him, changed him.

The sound of wheels on stone announced a carriage arriving at the house. No hoof beats – father owned horses, but few other people in the area did. Their carriages were pulled by chulls or parshmen.

Balat rose to go see who had come, and Sakisa followed after, trumping in excitement. Shallan picked up her sketchpad. Father had recently forbidden her from drawing the manor's parshmen or darkeyes – he found it unseemly. That made it hard for her to find practice figures.

'Shallan?'

She started, realizing that Wikim hadn't followed Balat. 'Yes.'

'I was wrong,' Wikim said, handing her something. A small pouch. 'About what you're doing. I see through it. And . . . and still it's working. Damnation, but it's working. Thank you.'

She moved to open the pouch he'd given her.

'Don't,' he said.

'What is it?'

'Blackbane,' Wikim said. 'A plant, the leaves at least. If you eat them, they paralyze you. Your breathing stops too.'

Disturbed, she pulled the top tight. She didn't even want to know how Wikim could recognize a deadly plant like this.

'I've carried those for the better part of a year,' Wikim said softly. 'The longer you have them, the more potent the leaves are supposed to become. I don't feel like I need them any longer. You can burn them, or whatever. I just thought you should have them.'

She smiled, though she felt unsettled. Wikim had been carrying this poison around? He felt he needed to give it to her?

He jogged after Balat, and Shallan stuffed the pouch in her satchel. She'd find a way to destroy it later. She picked up her pencils and went back to drawing.

Shouting from inside the manor distracted her a short time later. She looked up, uncertain even how much time had passed. She rose, satchel clutched to her chest, and crossed the yard. Vines shook and withdrew before her, though as her pace sped up, she stepped on more and more of them, feeling them writhe beneath her feet and try to yank back. Cultivated vines had poor instincts.

She reached the house to more shouting.

'Father!' Asha Jushu's voice. 'Father, please!'

Shallan pushed open the slatted wood doors, silk dress rustling against the floor as she stepped in and found three men in old-style clothing – skirtlike ulatu to their knees, bright loose shirts, flimsy coats that draped to the ground – standing before Father.

Jushu knelt on the floor, hands bound behind his back. Over the years, Jushu had grown plump from his periods of excess.

'Bah,' Father said. 'I will not suffer this extortion.'

'His credit is your credit, Brightlord,' one of the men said in a calm, smooth voice. He was darkeyed, though he didn't sound it. 'He promised us you would pay his debts.'

'He lied,' Father said, Ekel and Jix – house guards – at his sides, hands on weapons.

'Father,' Jushu whispered through his tears. 'They'll take me—'

'You were supposed to be riding our outer holdings!' Father bellowed. 'You were supposed to be checking on our lands, not dining with thieves and gambling away our wealth and our good name!'

Jushu hung his head, sagging in his bonds.

'He's yours,' Father said, turning and storming from the chamber.

Shallan gasped as one of the men sighed, then gestured toward Jushu. The other two grabbed him. They didn't seem pleased to be leaving without payment. Jushu trembled as they towed him away, past Balat and Wikim, who watched nearby. Outside, Jushu cried for mercy and begged the men to let him speak to Father again.

'Balat,' Shallan said, walking to him, taking his arm. 'Do something!'

'We all knew where the gambling would take him,' Balat said. 'We told him, Shallan. He wouldn't listen.'

'He's still our brother!'

'What do you expect me to do? Where would I get spheres enough to pay his debt?'

Jushu's weeping grew softer as the men left the manor.

Shallan turned and dashed after her father, passing Jix scratching his head. Father had gone into his study two rooms over; she hesitated in the doorway, looking in at her father slumped in his chair beside the hearth. She stepped in, passing the desk where his ardents – and sometimes his wife – tallied his ledgers and read him reports.

Nobody stood there now, but the ledgers were open, displaying a brutal truth. She raised a hand to her mouth, noticing several letters of debt. She'd helped with minor accounts, but never seen so much of the full picture, and was stunned by what she saw. How could the family owe that much money?

'I'm not going to change my mind, Shallan,' Father said. 'Leave. Jushu prepared this pyre himself.'

'But—'

'Leave me!' Father roared, standing.

Shallan cringed back, eyes widening, heart nearly stopping. Fearspren wriggled up around her. He never yelled at her. *Never.*

Father took a deep breath, then turned to the room's window. His back to her, he continued, 'I can't afford the spheres.'

'Why?' Shallan asked. 'Father, is this because of the deal with Brightlord Revilar?' She looked at the ledgers. 'No, it's bigger than that.'

'I will finally make something of myself,' Father said, 'and of this house. I will stop them from whispering about us; I will end the questioning. House Davar will become a *force* in this princedom.'

'By bribing favor from supposed allies?' Shallan asked. 'Using money we don't have?'

He looked at her, face shadowed but eyes reflecting light, like twin embers in the dark of his skull. In that moment, Shallan felt a terrifying hatred from her father. He strode over, grabbing her by the arms. Her satchel dropped to the floor.

'I've done this for *you*,' he growled, holding her arms in a tight, painful grip. 'And you *will* obey. I've gone wrong, somewhere, in letting you learn to question me.'

She whimpered at the pain.

'There will be changes in this house,' Father said. 'No more weakness. I've found a way . . .'

'Please, stop.'

He looked down at her and seemed to see the tears in her eyes for the first time.

'Father . . .' she whispered.

He looked upward. Toward his rooms. She knew he was looking toward Mother's soul. He dropped her then, causing her to tumble to the floor, red hair covering her face.

'You are confined to your rooms,' he snapped. 'Go, and do not leave until I give you permission.'

Shallan scrambled to her feet, snatching her satchel, then left the room. In the hallway, she pressed her back against the wall, panting raggedly, tears dripping from her chin. Things had been going better . . . her father had been better . . .

She squeezed her eyes shut. Emotion stormed inside of her, twisting about. She couldn't control it.

Jushu.

Father actually looked like he wanted to hurt me, Shallan thought, shivering. *He's changed so much.* She started to sink down toward the floor, arms wrapped around herself.

Jushu.

Keep cutting at those thorns, strong one . . . Make a path for the light . . .

Shallan forced herself to her feet. She ran, still crying, back into the feast hall. Balat and Wikim had taken seats, Minara quietly serving them drinks. The guards had left, perhaps to their post at the manor grounds.

When Balat saw Shallan, he stood, eyes widening. He rushed to her, knocking over his cup in his haste, spilling wine to the floor.

'Did he hurt you?' Balat asked. 'Damnation! I'll kill him! I'll go to the highprince and—'

'He didn't hurt me,' Shallan said. 'Please. Balat, your knife. The one Father gave you.'

He looked to his belt. 'What of it?'

'It's worth good money. I'm going to try to trade it for Jushu.'

Balat lowered his hand protectively to the knife. 'Jushu built his pyre himself, Shallan.'

'That's exactly what Father said to me,' Shallan replied, wiping her eyes, then meeting those of her brother.

'I . . .' Balat looked over his shoulder in the direction Jushu had been taken. He sighed, then unhooked the sheath from his belt and handed it to her. 'It won't be enough. They say he owes almost a hundred emerald broams.'

'I have my necklace too,' Shallan said.

Wikim, silently drinking his wine, reached to his belt and took off his knife. He set it at the edge of the table. Shallan scooped it up as she passed, then ran from the room. Could she catch the men in time?

Outside, she spotted the carriage only a short way down the road. She hurried as best she could on slippered feet down the cobbled drive and out the gates onto the road. She wasn't fast, but neither were chulls. As she drew closer, she saw that Jushu had been tied to walk behind the carriage. He didn't look up as Shallan passed him.

The carriage stopped, and Jushu dropped to the ground and curled up. The darkeyed man with the haughty air pushed open his door to look at Shallan. 'He sent the child?'

'I came on my own,' she said, holding up the daggers. 'Please, they are very fine work.'

The man raised an eyebrow, then gestured for one of his companions to step down and fetch them. Shallan unhooked her necklace and dropped it into the man's hands with the two knives. The man took out one of the knives, inspecting it as Shallan waited, apprehensive, shifting from foot to foot.

'You've been weeping,' said the man in the carriage. 'You care for him that much?'

'He is my brother.'

'So?' the man asked. 'I killed my brother when he tried to cheat me. You shouldn't let relations cloud your eyes.'

'I love him,' Shallan whispered.

The man looking over the daggers slid them both back in their sheaths. 'They are masterworks,' he admitted. 'I'd value them at twenty emerald broams.'

'The necklace?' Shallan asked.

'Simple, but of aluminum, which can only be made by Soulcasting,' the man said to his boss. 'Ten emerald.'

'Together half what your brother owes,' said the man in the carriage.

Shallan's heart sank. 'But . . . what would you do with him? Selling him as a slave cannot redeem so great a debt.'

'I'm often in the mood to remind myself that lighteyes bleed the same as darkeyes,' the man said. 'And sometimes it is useful to have a deterrent for others, a way to remind them not to take loans they cannot repay. He may save me more than he cost, if I display him prudently.'

Shallan felt small. She clasped her hands, one covered, one not. Had she lost, then? The women from Father's books, the women she was coming to admire, would not have made pleas to win this man's heart. They would have tried logic.

She wasn't good at that. She didn't have the training for it, and she certainly didn't currently have the temperament. But as the tears began again, she forced out the first thing that came to mind.

'He may save you money that way,' Shallan said. 'But he may not. It is a gamble, and you do not strike me as the kind of man who gambles.'

The man laughed. 'What makes you say that? Gambling is what brought me here!'

'No,' she said, blushing at her tears. 'You are the type of man who profits from the gambling of others. You know that it usually leads to loss. I give you items of real value. Take them. Please?'

The man considered. He held out his hands for the daggers, and his man passed them over. He unsheathed one of the daggers and inspected it. 'Name for me one reason I should show this man pity. In my house, he was an arrogant glutton, acting without thought for the difficulty he would cause you, his family.'

'Our mother was murdered,' Shallan said. 'That night, as I cried, Jushu held me.' It was all she had.

The man considered. Shallan felt her heart pounding. Finally, he tossed the necklace back to her. 'Keep that.' He nodded to his man. 'Cut the little cremling free. Child, if you are wise, you will teach your brother to be more . . . conservative.' He pulled the door closed.

Shallan stepped back as the servant cut Jushu free. The man then climbed onto the back of the vehicle and knocked. It pulled away.

Shallan knelt beside Jushu. He blinked one eye – the other was bruised and beginning to swell shut – as she untied his bloodied hands. It had not been a quarter hour since Father had declared that the men could have him, but they had obviously taken that time to show Jushu what they thought of not being paid.

'Shallan?' he asked, lips bloodied. 'What happened?'

'You weren't listening?'

'My ears ring,' he said. 'Everything is spinning. I . . . am I free?'

'Balat and Wikim traded their knives for you.'

'Mill took so little in trade?'

'Obviously, he did not know your true worth.'

Jushu smiled a toothy smile. 'Always quick with your tongue, aren't you?' He climbed to his feet with Shallan's help and began to limp back toward the house.

Halfway there, Balat joined them, taking Jushu under his arm. 'Thank you,' Jushu whispered. 'She says you saved me. Thank you, Brother.' He started weeping.

'I . . .' Balat looked to Shallan, then back to Jushu. 'You're my brother. Let's get you back and cleaned up.'

Content that Jushu would be cared for, Shallan left them and entered the manor house. She climbed the stairs, passed Father's glowing room, and entered her chambers. She sat down on the bed.

There, she waited for the highstorm.

Shouts rose from below. Shallan squeezed her eyes shut.

Finally, the door to her rooms opened.

She opened her eyes. Father stood outside. Shallan could make out a crumpled form beyond him, lying on the floor of the hallway. Minara, the serving maid. Her body didn't lie right, one arm bent at the wrong angle. Her figure stirred, whimpering, leaving blood on the wall as she tried to crawl away.

Father entered Shallan's room and shut the door behind him. 'You know I would never hurt you, Shallan,' he said softly.

She nodded, tears leaking from her eyes.

'I've found a way to control myself,' her father said. 'I just have to let the anger out. I can't blame myself for that anger. Others create it when they disobey me.'

Her objection – that he hadn't told her to go *immediately* to her room, only that she shouldn't leave it once she was there – died on her lips. A foolish excuse. They both knew she'd intentionally disobeyed.

'I would not want to have to punish anyone else because of you, Shallan,' Father said.

This cold monster, was this really her father?

'It is time.' Father nodded. 'No more indulgences. If we are to be important in Jah Keved, we cannot be seen as weak. Do you understand?'

She nodded, unable to stop the tears.

'Good,' he said, resting his hand on her head, then running his fingers through her hair. 'Thank you.'

He left her, shutting the door.

This folio page shows contemporary designs out of Azir, using local models. Though these are specifically male civil servant outfits, the styles have deeply influenced all Azish fashion

These Lightweavers, by no coincidence, included many who pursued the arts; namely: writers, artists, musicians, painters, sculptors. Considering the order's general temperament, the tales of their strange and varied mnemonic abilities may have been embellished.

—From *Words of Radiance*, chapter 21, page 10

After leaving her carriage at a stable in the Outer Market, Shallan was led to a stairwell carved into the stone of a hillside. She climbed this, then stepped hesitantly out onto a terrace that had been cut from the side of the hill here. Lighteyes wearing stylish clothing chatted over cups of wine at the patio's numerous ironwork tables.

They were high enough here to look out over the warcamps. The perspective was eastward, toward the Origin. What an unnatural arrangement; it made her feel exposed. Shallan was accustomed to balconies, gardens, and patios all facing away from the storms. True, nobody was likely to be out here when a highstorm was expected, but it just felt *off* to her.

A master-servant in black and white arrived and bowed, calling her Brightness Davar without need of an introduction. She'd have to get used to that; in Alethkar she was a novelty, and an easily recognizable one. She let the servant lead her among the tables, sending her guards for the day off toward a larger room cut farther into the stone to the right. This one had a proper roof and walls, so it could be completely closed off, and a group of other guards waited here upon the whims of their masters.

Shallan drew the eyes of the other patrons. Well, good. She had come here to upset their world. The more people spoke of her, the better her chances of persuading them, when the time came, to listen to her regarding the parshmen. Those were everywhere in camp, even here in this luxurious winehouse. She spotted three in the corner, moving wine bottles from wall-mounted racks to crates. They moved at a plodding yet implacable pace.

A few more steps brought her to the marble balustrade right at the edge of the terrace. Here Adolin had a table set off by itself with an unobstructed view directly east. Two members of Dalinar's house guard stood by the wall a short distance away; Adolin was important enough, apparently, that his guards didn't need to wait with the others.

Adolin browsed a folio, oversized by design so it wouldn't be mistaken for a woman's book. Shallan had seen some folios containing battle maps, others with designs for armor or pictures of architecture. She was amused as she caught sight of the glyphs for this one, with women's script underneath for further clarification. Fashions out of Liafor and Azir.

Adolin looked as handsome as he had before. Maybe more so, now that he was obviously more relaxed. She would *not* let him muddle her mind. She had a purpose to this meeting: an alliance with House Kholin to help her brothers and give her resources for exposing the Voidbringers and discovering Urithiru.

She couldn't afford to come off as weak. She had to control the situation, could not act like a sycophant, and she couldn't—

Adolin saw her and closed the portfolio. He stood up, grinning.

– oh, *storms*. That *smile*.

'Brightness Shallan,' he said, holding out a hand toward her. 'You are settling well in Sebarial's camp?'

'Yeah,' she said, grinning at him. That mop of unruly hair just made her want to reach out and run her fingers through it. *Our children would have the strangest hair ever,* she thought. *His gold and black Alethi locks, my red ones, and . . .*

And was she really thinking about their *children*? Already? Foolish girl.

'Yes,' she continued, trying to de-melt a little. 'He has been quite kind to me.'

'It's probably because you're family,' Adolin said, letting her sit, then pushing in her chair. He did it himself, rather than allowing the master-servant to do so. She would not have expected that of someone so highborn. 'Sebarial only does what he feels he's forced to.'

'I think he may surprise you,' Shallan said.

'Oh, he's already done *that* on several occasions.'

'Really? When?'

'Well,' Adolin said, sitting, 'he once produced a very, um, loud and inappropriate noise at a meeting with the king. . . .' Adolin smiled, shrugging as if embarrassed, but he didn't blush as Shallan might have in a similar situation. 'Does that count?'

'I'm not sure. Knowing what I do of Uncle Sebarial, I doubt that such a thing is particularly *surprising* from him. Expected is more like it.'

Adolin laughed, tossing his head back. 'Yes, I suppose you're right. That you are.'

He seemed so *confident*. Not in a particularly conceited way, not like her father had been. In fact, it occurred to her that her father's attitude had been caused not by confidence, but the opposite.

Adolin seemed perfectly at ease both with his station and those around him. When he waved for the master-servant to bring him a list of wines, he smiled at the woman, though she was darkeyed. That smile was enough to produce a blush even in a master-servant.

Shallan was supposed to get this man to court her? Storms! She'd felt far more capable when trying to scam the leader of the Ghostbloods. *Act refined*, Shallan told herself. *Adolin has moved with the elite, and has been in relationships with the most sophisticated ladies of the world. He will expect that from you.*

'So,' he said, flipping through the list of wines, described by glyphs, 'we are supposed to get *married*.'

'I would lighten that phrasing, Brightlord,' Shallan said, choosing her words carefully. 'We aren't *supposed* to get married. Your cousin Jasnah merely wanted us to consider a union, and your aunt seemed to agree.'

'The Almighty save a man when his female relatives collude about his future,' Adolin said with a sigh. 'Sure, it's all right for *Jasnah* to run about into her middle years without a spouse, but if I reach my twenty-third

622

birthday without a bride, it's like I'm some kind of menace. Sexist of her, don't you think?'

'Well, she wanted me to get married too,' Shallan said. 'So I wouldn't call her sexist. Merely . . . Jasnah-ist?' She paused. 'Jasnagynistic? No, drat. It would have to be Misjasnahistic, and that doesn't work nearly as well, does it?'

'You're asking me?' Adolin asked, turning around the menu so she could see it. 'What do you think we should order?'

'Storms,' she breathed. 'Those are *all* different kinds of wine?'

'Yeah,' Adolin said. He leaned toward her, as if conspiratorial. 'Honestly, I don't pay a lot of attention. Renarin knows the difference between them – he'll drone on if you let him. Me, I order something that sounds important, but I'm really just choosing based on color.' He grimaced. 'We're technically at war. I won't be able to take anything too intoxicating, just in case. Kind of silly, as there won't be any plateau runs today.'

'You're sure? I thought they were random.'

'Yeah, but my warcamp isn't up. They almost never come too close before a highstorm, anyway.' He leaned back, scanning the menu, before pointing at one of the wines and winking at the serving woman.

Shallan felt cold. 'Wait. *Highstorm?*'

'Yeah,' Adolin said, checking the clock in the corner. Sebarial had mentioned that those were growing more and more common around here. 'Should come any time now. You didn't know?'

She sputtered, looking eastward, across the cracked landscape. *Act poised!* she thought. *Elegant!* Instead, a primal part of her wanted to scramble for a hole and hide. Suddenly she imagined she could sense the pressure dropping, as if the air itself were trying to escape. Could she see it out there, starting? No, that was nothing. She squinted anyway.

'I didn't look at the list of storms Sebarial keeps,' Shallan forced herself to say. In all honesty, it was probably outdated, knowing him. 'I've been busy.'

'Huh,' Adolin said. 'I wondered why you didn't ask about this place. I just assumed you'd heard of it already.'

This place. The open balcony, facing east. The lighteyes drinking wine now seemed anticipatory to her, with an air of nervousness. The second room – the large one for bodyguards she'd seen with the substantial doors – made far more sense now.

'We're here to watch?' Shallan whispered.

'It's the new fad,' Adolin said. 'Apparently we're supposed to sit here until the storm is almost upon us, then run into that other room and take shelter. I've wanted to come for weeks now, and only just managed to convince my minders that I'd be safe here.' He said that last part somewhat bitterly. 'We can go move into the safe room now, if you want.'

'No,' Shallan said, forcing herself to pry her fingers from the table edge. 'I'm fine.'

'You look pale.'

'It's natural.'

'Because you're Veden?'

'Because I'm always at the edge of panic these days. Oh, is that our wine?'

Poised, she reminded herself yet again. She pointedly did not look eastward.

The servant had brought them two cups of brilliant blue wine. Adolin picked his up and studied it. He smelled it, sipped it, then nodded in satisfaction and dismissed the servant with a parting smile. He watched the woman's backside as she retreated.

Shallan raised an eyebrow at him, but he didn't seem to notice that he'd done anything wrong. He looked back at Shallan and leaned in again. 'I know you're supposed to swish the wine about and taste it and things,' he whispered, 'but nobody has ever explained to me what I'm looking for.'

'Bugs floating in the liquid, perhaps?'

'Nah, my new food taster would have spotted one of those.' He smiled, but Shallan realized he probably wasn't joking. A thin man who didn't wear a uniform had walked over to chat with the bodyguards. Probably the food taster.

Shallan sipped her wine. It was good – slightly sweet, a tad spicy. Not that she could spare much thought for its taste, with that storm—

Stop it, she told herself, smiling at Adolin. She needed to make sure this meeting went well for him. *Get him to talk about himself.* That was one piece of advice she remembered from books.

'Plateau runs,' Shallan said. 'How *do* you know when to begin one, anyway?'

'Hmm? Oh, we have spotters,' Adolin said, lounging back in his chair.

'Men who stand atop towers with these enormous spyglasses. They inspect every plateau we can reach in a reasonable time, watching for a chrysalis.'

'I hear you've captured your share of those.'

'Well, I probably shouldn't talk about it. Father doesn't want it to be a competition anymore.' He looked at her, expectant.

'But surely you can talk about what happened before,' Shallan said, feeling as if she were filling an expected role.

'I suppose,' Adolin said. 'There was one run a few months back where I seized the chrysalis basically by myself. You see, Father and I, we would usually jump the chasm first and clear the way for the bridges.'

'Isn't that dangerous?' Shallan asked, dutifully looking at him with widened eyes.

'Yes, but we're Shardbearers. We have strength and power granted by the Almighty. It's a great responsibility, and it's our duty to use it for the protection of our men. We save hundreds of lives by going across first. Lets us lead the army, firsthand.'

He paused.

'So brave,' Shallan said, in what she hoped was a breathy, adoring voice.

'Well, it's the right thing to do. But it *is* dangerous. That day, I leaped across, but my father and I got pushed too far apart by the Parshendi. He was forced to jump back across, and a blow to his leg meant that when he landed, his greave – that's a piece of armor on the leg – cracked. That made it dangerous for him to jump back again. I was left alone while he waited for the bridge to lock down.'

He paused again. She was probably supposed to ask what happened next.

'What if you need to poop?' she asked instead.

'Well, I put my back to the chasm and laid about me with my sword, intending to . . . Wait. What did you say?'

'Poop,' Shallan said. 'You're out there on the battlefield, encased in metal like a crab in its shell. What do you do if nature calls?'

'I . . . er . . .' Adolin frowned at her. 'That is not something any woman has ever asked me before.'

'Yay for originality!' Shallan said, though she blushed as she said it. Jasnah would have been displeased. Couldn't Shallan mind her tongue

625

for a single conversation? She'd gotten him talking about something he liked; everything had been going well. Now this.

'Well,' Adolin said slowly, 'every battle has breaks in the flow, and men rotate in and out of the front lines. For every five minutes you're fighting, you often have almost as many resting. When a Shardbearer pulls back, men inspect his armor for cracks, give him something to drink or eat, and help him with . . . what you just mentioned. It's not something that makes a good topic of conversation, Brightness. We don't really talk about it.'

'That's precisely *what* makes it a good topic of conversation,' she said. 'I can find out about wars and Shardbearers and glorious killing in the official accounts. The grimy details, though – nobody writes those down.'

'Well, it *does* get grimy,' Adolin said with a grimace, taking a drink. 'You can't really . . . I can't believe I'm saying this . . . you can't really wipe yourself in Shardplate, so someone has to do it for you. Makes me feel like an infant. Then, sometimes, you just don't have time . . .'

'And?'

He inspected her, narrowing his eyes.

'What?' she asked.

'Just trying to determine if you're secretly Wit wearing a wig. This is something he would do to me.'

'I'm not doing anything to you,' she said. 'I'm just curious.' And honestly, she was. She'd thought about this. Perhaps more than it deserved consideration.

'Well,' Adolin said, 'if you must know, an old adage on the battlefield teaches that it's better to be embarrassed than dead. You can't let anything draw your attention from fighting.'

'So . . .'

'So yes, I, Adolin Kholin – cousin to the king, heir to the Kholin princedom – have shat myself in my Shardplate. Three times, all on purpose.' He downed the rest of his wine. 'You are a very strange woman.'

'If I must remind you,' Shallan said, 'you are the one who opened our conversation today with a joke about Sebarial's flatulence.'

'I guess I did at that.' He grinned. 'This is not exactly going the way it's supposed to, is it?'

'Is that a bad thing?'

'No,' Adolin said, then his grin widened. 'Actually, it's kind of refreshing.

Do you know how many times I've told that story about saving the plateau run?'

'I'm sure you were quite brave.'

'Quite.'

'Though probably not as brave as the poor men who have to clean your armor.'

Adolin bellowed out a laugh. For the first time it seemed like something genuine – an emotion from him that wasn't scripted or expected. He pounded his fist on the table, then waved for more wine, wiping a tear from his eye. The grin he gave her threatened to bring out another blush.

Wait, Shallan thought, *did that just . . . work?* She was supposed to be acting feminine and delicate, not asking men what it's like to have to defecate in battle.

'All right,' Adolin said, taking the cup of wine. He didn't even glance at the serving woman this time. 'What other dirty secrets do you want to know? You've got me laid bare. There are tons of things the stories and official histories don't mention.'

'The chrysalises,' Shallan said, eager. 'What do they look like?'

'That's what you want to know?' Adolin said, scratching his head. 'I thought for sure you'd want to know about the chafing. . . .'

Shallan got out her satchel, setting a piece of paper on the table and starting a sketch. 'From what I've been able to determine, nobody has done a solid study on the Chasmfiends. There are some sketches of dead ones, but that's it, and the anatomy on those is dreadful.

'They must have an interesting life cycle. They haunt these chasms, but I doubt they actually live here. There's not enough food to support creatures of their size. That means they come here as part of some migratory pattern. They come here to *pupate*. Have you ever seen a juvenile? Before they form the chrysalis?'

'No,' Adolin said, scooting his chair around the table. 'It often happens at night, and we don't spot them until morning. They're hard to see out there, colored like rock. Makes me think that the Parshendi must be watching us. We end up fighting over plateaus so often. It might mean they spot us mobilizing, then use the direction we're going to judge where to find the chrysalis. We get a head start, but they move faster over the Plains, so we arrive near the same time. . . .'

He trailed off, cocking his head to get a better look at her sketch. 'Storms! That's really good, Shallan.'

'Thanks.'

'No, I mean *really* good.'

She'd done a quick sketch of several types of chrysalises she had read about in her books, along with quick depictions of a man beside them for size reference. It wasn't very good – she'd done it for speed. Yet Adolin seemed genuinely impressed.

'The shape and texture of the chrysalis,' Shallan said, 'could help place the chasmfiends in a family of similar animals.'

'It looks most like this one,' Adolin said, scooting closer and pointing at one of the sketches. 'When I've touched one, they've been hard as rock. It's hard to dig into one without a Shardblade. It can take men with hammers forever to break into one.'

'Hmmm,' Shallan said, making a note. 'You're sure?'

'Yeah. That's how they look. Why?'

'That's the chrysalis of a yu-nerig,' Shallan said. 'A greatshell from the seas around Marabethia. The people there feed criminals to them, I'm told.'

'Ouch.'

'This might be a false positive, a coincidence. The yu-nerig are an aquatic species. The only time they come onto land is to pupate. Seems tenuous to assume a relationship to the chasmfiends . . .'

'Sure,' Adolin said, taking a drink of wine. 'If you say so.'

'This is probably important,' Shallan said.

'For research. Yeah, I know. Aunt Navani is always talking about things like that.'

'This could be of more practical import than that,' Shallan said. 'About how many of these things total are killed by your armies and the Parshendi each month?'

Adolin shrugged. 'One every three days or so, I'd guess. Sometimes more, sometimes less. So . . . fifteen or so a month?'

'You see the problem?'

'I . . .' Adolin shook his head. 'No. Sorry. I'm kind of useless at anything that doesn't involve someone getting stabbed.'

She smiled at him. 'Nonsense. You proved skilled at choosing wine.'

'I did that basically at random.'

'And it tastes delicious,' Shallan said. 'Empirical proof of your methodology. Now, you probably don't see the problem because you don't have the proper facts. Greatshells, generally, are slow to breed and slow to grow. This is because most ecosystems can only support a small population of apex predators of this size.'

'I've heard some of those words before.'

She looked to him, raising an eyebrow. He'd gotten a lot closer to her, in order to look at her drawing. He wore a faint cologne, a brisk woody scent. *Oh my . . .*

'All right, all right,' he said, chuckling as he inspected her drawings. 'I'm not as dense as I feign. I see what you're saying. You really think we could kill enough of them that it could be a problem? I mean, people have been doing greatshell hunts for generations, and the beasts are still around.'

'You're not hunting them here, Adolin. You're *harvesting* them. You're systematically destroying their juvenile population. Have fewer of them been pupating lately?'

'Yeah,' he said, though he sounded reluctant. 'We think it might be the season.'

'It might be. Or, it might be that, after over five years of harvesting, the population is starting to dwindle. Animals like the chasmfiends don't normally have predators. Suddenly losing a hundred and fifty or more of their numbers a year could be catastrophic to their population.'

Adolin frowned. 'The gemhearts we get feed the people of the warcamps. Without a constant flow of new stones of reasonable size, the Soulcasters will eventually crack the ones we have, and we won't be able to support the armies here.'

'I'm not telling you to stop your hunts,' Shallan said, blushing. This probably wasn't the point she should be making. Urithiru and the parshmen, that was the immediate problem. Still, she needed to gain Adolin's trust. If she could provide useful help regarding the chasmfiends, perhaps he'd listen when she approached him with something even more revolutionary.

'All I'm saying,' Shallan continued, 'is that it's worth thinking about and studying. What would it be like if you could start raising chasmfiends, growing them to juveniles in batches like men raise chulls? Instead of hunting three a week, what if you could breed and harvest hundreds?'

'That *would* be useful,' Adolin said thoughtfully. 'What would you need in order to make it happen?'

'Well, I wasn't saying … I mean …' She stopped herself. 'I need to get out onto the Shattered Plains,' she said more firmly. 'If I'm going to try to figure out how to breed them, I'd need to see one of these chrysalises before it's been cut into. Preferably, I get to see an adult chasmfiend, and – ideally – I'd like a captured juvenile to study.'

'Just a small list of impossibilities.'

'Well, you *did* ask.'

'I might be able to get you onto the Plains,' Adolin said. 'Father promised that he'd show Jasnah a dead chasmfiend, so I think he was planning to take her out after a hunt. Seeing a chrysalis, though … those rarely appear close to camp. I'd have to take you dangerously close to Parshendi territory.'

'I'm sure you can protect me.'

He looked at her, expectant.

'What?' Shallan asked.

'I'm waiting for a wisecrack.'

'I was serious,' Shallan said. 'With you there, I'm certain the Parshendi wouldn't dare get close.'

Adolin smiled.

'I mean,' she said, 'the stench alone—'

'I suspect I'm never going to live down telling you about that.'

'Never,' Shallan agreed. 'You were honest, detailed, and engaging. Those aren't the sorts of things I let myself forget about a man.'

His smile broadened. Storms, those eyes …

Careful, Shallan told herself. *Careful! Kabsal took you in easily. Don't repeat that.*

'I'll see what I can do,' Adolin said. 'The Parshendi might not be an issue in the near future.'

'Really?'

He nodded. 'It's not widely known, though we've told the highprinces. Father is going to be meeting with some of the Parshendi leaders tomorrow. It could end up starting a peace negotiation.'

'That's *fantastic*!'

'Yeah,' Adolin said. 'I'm not hopeful. The assassin … anyway, we'll see what happens tomorrow, though I'll have to do this between the other work Father has for me.'

'The duels,' Shallan said, leaning in. 'What is going on there, Adolin?'

He seemed hesitant.

'Whatever is going on in the camps now,' she said, speaking more softly, 'Jasnah didn't know about it. I feel woefully ignorant about politics here, Adolin. Your father and Highprince Sadeas had a falling-out, I've gathered. The king has changed the nature of these plateau runs, and everyone is talking about how you're dueling now. But from what I've been able to gather, you never *stopped* dueling.'

'It's different,' he said. 'Now I'm dueling to win.'

'And you didn't before?'

'No, then I dueled to punish.' He glanced about, then met her eyes. 'It began when my father started seeing visions . . .'

He continued. He poured out a surprising story, one with far greater detail than she'd anticipated. A story of betrayal, and of hope. Visions of the past. A unified Alethkar, prepared to weather a coming storm.

She didn't know what to make of it all, though she gathered that Adolin was telling her of it because he knew the rumors in camp. She'd heard of Dalinar's fits, of course, and had an inkling of what Sadeas had done. When Adolin mentioned that his father wanted the Knights Radiant to return, Shallan felt a chill. She glanced about for Pattern – he'd be close – but couldn't find him.

The meat of the story, at least in Adolin's estimation, was the betrayal by Sadeas. The young prince's eyes grew dark, face flushed, as he talked of being abandoned on the Plains, surrounded by enemies. He seemed embarrassed when he spoke of salvation by a lowly bridge crew.

He's actually confiding in me, Shallan thought, feeling a thrill. She rested her freehand on his arm as he spoke, an innocent gesture, but it seemed to spur him forward as he quietly explained Dalinar's plan. She wasn't certain he should be sharing all of this with her. They barely knew one another. But speaking of it seemed to lift a weight from Adolin's back, and he grew more relaxed.

'I guess,' Adolin said, 'that's the end of it. I'm supposed to win Shardblades off the others, taking away their bite, embarrassing them. But I don't know if it will work.'

'Why not?' Shallan asked.

'The ones who agree to duel me aren't important enough,' he said, forming a fist. 'If I win too much from them, the real targets – the highprinces – will get scared of me and refuse duels. I need matches that are more high profile. No, what I *need* is to duel Sadeas. Pound that grinning face of his into the stones and take back my father's Blade. He's too oily, though. We'll never get him to agree.'

She found herself wishing desperately to do something, anything, to help. She felt herself melting at the intense concern in those eyes, the passion.

Remember Kabsal . . . she reminded herself again.

Well, Adolin wasn't likely to try to assassinate her – but then, that didn't mean she should let her brain turn to curry paste around him. She cleared her throat, tearing her eyes away from his and looking down at her sketch.

'Bother,' she said. 'I've left you upset. I'm not very good at this wooing thing.'

'Could have fooled me . . .' Adolin said, resting his hand on her arm.

Shallan covered another blush by ducking her head and digging into her satchel. 'You,' she said, 'need to know what your cousin was working on before she died.'

'Another volume in her father's biography?'

'No,' Shallan said, getting out a sheet of paper. 'Adolin, Jasnah thought that the Voidbringers were going to return.'

'What?' he said, frowning. 'She didn't even believe in the Almighty. Why would she believe in the Voidbringers?'

'She had evidence,' Shallan said, tapping the paper with one finger. 'A lot of that sank in the ocean, I'm afraid, but I do have some of her notes, and . . . Adolin, how hard do you think it would be to convince the highprinces to get rid of their parshmen?'

'Get rid of *what*?'

'How hard would it to be to make everyone stop using parshmen as slaves? Give them away, or . . .' Storms. She didn't want to start a genocide here, did she? But these were the *Voidbringers*. '. . . or set them free or something. Get them out of the warcamps.'

'How difficult would it be?' Adolin said. 'Off the cuff, I'd say impossible. That, or *really* impossible. Why would we even want to do something like that?'

632

'Jasnah thought they might be related to the Voidbringers and their return.'

Adolin shook his head, looking bemused. 'Shallan, we can barely get the highprinces to fight this war properly. If my father or the king were to require everyone to get rid of their parshmen ... Storms! It would break the kingdom in a heartbeat.'

So Jasnah was right on that count as well. Unsurprising. Shallan *was* interested to see how violently Adolin himself opposed the idea. He took a big gulp of wine, seeming utterly floored.

Time to pull back, then. This meeting had gone very well; she wouldn't want to end it on a sour note. 'It was something Jasnah said,' Shallan said, 'but really, I'd rather that Brightlady Navani judge how important a suggestion it was. She would know her daughter, her notes, better than anyone.'

Adolin nodded. 'So go to her.'

Shallan tapped the paper in her fingers. 'I've tried. She's not been very accommodating.'

'Aunt Navani can be overbearing sometimes.'

'It's not that,' Shallan said, scanning the words on the letter. It was a reply she'd gotten after requesting to meet the woman and discuss her daughter's work. 'She doesn't want to meet with me. She barely seems to want to acknowledge I exist.'

Adolin sighed. 'She doesn't want to believe. About Jasnah, I mean. You represent something to her – the truth, in a way. Give her time. She just needs to grieve.'

'I'm not certain if this is something that should wait, Adolin.'

'I'll talk to her,' he said. 'How about that?'

'Wonderful,' she said. 'Much like you yourself.'

He grinned. 'It's nothing. I mean, if we're going to halfway-almost-kind-of-maybe-get-married, we should probably look out for one another's interests.' He paused. 'Don't mention that parshman thing to anyone else, though. That's not something that will go over well.'

She nodded absently, then realized she'd been staring at him. She was going to kiss those lips of his someday. She let herself imagine it.

And, Ash's eyes ... he had a very friendly way about him. She hadn't expected that in someone so highborn. She'd never actually met anyone of his rank before coming to the Shattered Plains, but all the men she knew near his level had been stiff and even angry.

Not Adolin. Storms, but being with him was something else she could get very, very used to.

People began to stir on the patio. She ignored them for a moment, but then many began to stand up from their seats, looking eastward.

Highstorm. Right.

Shallan felt a spike of alarm as she looked toward the Origin of Storms. The wind picked up, leaves and bits of refuse fluttering across the patio. Down below, the Outer Market had been packed up, tents folded away, awnings withdrawn, windows closed. The entirety of the warcamps braced itself.

Shallan stuffed her things into her satchel, then rose to her feet, stepping to the edge of the terrace, freehand fingers on the stone railing there. Adolin joined her. Behind them, people whispered and gathered. She heard iron grinding across stone; the parshmen had begun pulling away the tables and chairs, stowing them to both protect them and make a path for the lighteyes to retreat to safety.

The horizon had bled from light to dark, like a man flushing with anger. Shallan gripped the railing, watching the entire world transform. Vines withdrew, rockbuds closed. Grass hid in its holes. They knew, somehow. They all knew.

The air grew chill and wet, and prestorm winds gusted against her, blowing her hair back. Below and just to the north, the warcamps had piled refuse and waste to be blown away with the storm. It was a forbidden practice in most civilized areas, where that waste could blow into the next town. Out here, there was no next town.

The horizon grew even darker. A few people on the balcony fled to the back room's safety, their nerves getting the better of them. Most stayed, silent. Windspren zipped in tiny rivers of light overhead. Shallan took Adolin by the arm, staring eastward. Minutes passed until finally, she saw it.

The stormwall.

A huge sheet of water and debris blown before the storm. In places, it flashed with light from behind, revealing movement and shadows within. Like the skeleton of a hand when light illuminated the flesh, there was something *inside* this wall of destruction.

Most of the people fled the balcony, though the stormwall was still distant. In moments, only a handful remained, Shallan and Adolin among them. She watched, transfixed, as the storm approached. It took longer than she'd expected. It was moving at a terrible speed, but it was so large, they'd been able to spot it from quite a distance.

It consumed the Shattered Plains, one plateau at a time. Soon, it loomed over the warcamps, coming on with a roar.

'We should go,' Adolin eventually said. She barely heard him.

Life. Something *lived* inside that storm, something that no artist had ever drawn, no scholar had ever described.

'Shallan!' Adolin began to tow her toward the protected room. She grabbed the railing with her freehand, remaining in place, clutching her satchel to her chest with her safehand. That humming, that was Pattern.

She'd never been so close to a highstorm. Even when she'd been only inches away from one, separated by a window shutter, she had not been as close as she was now. Watching that darkness descend upon the warcamps . . .

I need to draw.

'Shallan!' Adolin said, pulling her away from the railing. 'They'll close the doors if we don't go now!'

With a start, she realized that everyone else had left the balcony. She allowed Adolin to get her moving, and she joined him in a dash across the empty patio. They reached the room at the side, packed with huddled lighteyes who watched in terror. Adolin's guards entered right after her, and several parshmen slammed the thick doors. The bar *thumped* in place, locking out the sky, leaving them to the light of spheres on the walls.

Shallan counted. The highstorm hit – she could *feel* it. Something beyond the thumping of the door and the distant sound of thunder.

'Six seconds,' she said.

'What?' Adolin asked. His voice was hushed, and others in the room spoke in whispers.

'It took six seconds after the servants closed the doors until the storm hit. We could have spent that much longer out there.'

Adolin regarded her with an incredulous expression. 'When you first realized what we were doing on that balcony, you seemed *terrified.*'

'I was.'

'Now you wish you'd stayed out until the last moment before the storm hit?'

'I . . . yeah,' she said, blushing.

'I have no idea what to make of you.' Adolin regarded her. 'You're not like anyone I've met.'

'It's my air of feminine mystique.' He raised an eyebrow.

'It's a term we use,' she said, 'when we're feeling particularly erratic. It's considered polite not to point out that you know this. Now, do we just . . . wait in here?'

'In this box of a room?' Adolin asked, sounding amused. 'We're light-eyes, not livestock.' He gestured to the side, where several servants had opened doors leading to places burrowed deeper into the mountain. 'Two sitting rooms. One for men, the other for women.'

Shallan nodded. Sometimes during a highstorm, the genders would retire to separate rooms to chat. It looked like the winehouse followed this tradition. They'd probably have finger food. Shallan walked toward the indicated room, but Adolin rested a hand on her arm, making her pause.

'I'll see about getting you out onto the Shattered Plains,' he said. 'Amaram wants to go explore more, he's said, than he gets to during a plateau run. I think he and Father are having dinner to talk about it to-morrow night, and I can ask then if I can bring you. I'll also talk to Aunt Navani. Maybe we can discuss what I've come up with at the feast next week?'

'There's a feast next week?'

'There's always a feast next week,' Adolin said. 'We just have to figure out who's throwing it. I'll send to you.'

She smiled, and then they separated. *Next week is not soon enough,* she thought. *I' ll have to find a way to drop in on him when it's not too awkward.*

Had she really promised to help him breed chasmfiends? As if she needed something *else* to take her time. Still, she felt good about the day as she entered the women's sitting room, her guards taking their places in the appropriate waiting room.

Shallan strolled through the women's room, which was well lit with gemstones gathered in goblets – cut stones, but not in spheres. An expensive display.

She felt that, if her teachers had been watching, both would have been disappointed at her conversation with Adolin. Tyn would have wanted her to manipulate the prince more; Jasnah would have wanted Shallan to be more poised, more in control of her tongue.

It seemed that Adolin liked her anyway. That made her want to cheer.

The looks of the women about her washed away that emotion. Some turned backs toward Shallan, and others pressed their lips together and looked her up and down skeptically. Courting the kingdom's most eligible bachelor was not going to make her popular, not when she was an outsider.

That didn't bother Shallan. She didn't need acceptance from these women; she just needed to find Urithiru and the secrets it contained. Gaining Adolin's trust was a big step in that direction.

She decided to reward herself by stuffing her face with sweets and thinking further on her plan to sneak into Brightlord Amaram's house.

And now, if there was an uncut gem among the Radiants, it was the Willshapers; for though enterprising, they were erratic, and Invia wrote of them, 'capricious, frustrating, unreliable,' as taking it for granted that others would agree; this may have been an intolerant view, as often Invia expressed, for this order was said to be most varied, inconsistent in temperament save for a general love of adventure, novelty, or oddity.

—From *Words of Radiance*, chapter 7, page 1

Adolin sat in a high-backed chair, cup of wine in his hand, listening to the highstorm rumble outside. He should have felt safe in this bunker of rock, but there was something about storms that undercut any sense of security, no matter how rational. He'd be glad for the Weeping, and the end of the highstorms for a few weeks.

Adolin raised his cup toward Elit, who stomped past. He hadn't seen the man above, on the winehouse terrace, but this chamber also served as a highstorm bunker for several shops in the Outer Market.

'Are you ready for our duel?' Adolin asked. 'You've made me wait an entire week so far, Elit.'

The short, balding man took a drink of wine, then lowered his cup, not looking at Adolin. 'My cousin is planning to kill you for challenging me,' he said. 'Right after he kills me for agreeing to the challenge.' He finally turned toward Adolin. 'But when I stomp you into the sands and claim all of your family's Shards, I'll be the rich one and he'll be forgotten. Am I ready for our duel? I *long* for it, Adolin Kholin.'

'You're the one who wanted to wait,' Adolin noted.

'The more time to savor what I'm going to do to you.' Elit smiled with white lips, then moved on.

Creepy fellow. Well, Adolin would deal with him in two days, the date of their duel. Before that, though, was tomorrow's meeting with the Parshendi Shardbearer. It loomed over him like a thunderhead. What would it mean, if they finally found peace?

He mulled over that thought, regarding his wine and listening with half an ear to Elit chatting behind him with someone. Adolin recognized that voice, didn't he?

Adolin sat upright, then looked over his shoulder. How long had *Sadeas* been back there, and why hadn't Adolin spotted him when first entering?

Sadeas turned to him, a calm smile on his face.

Maybe he'll just . . .

Sadeas strolled up to Adolin, hands clasped behind his back, wearing a fashionable open-fronted short brown coat and an embroidered green stock. The buttons along the front of the coat were gemstones. Emeralds to match the stock.

Storms. He did *not* want to deal with Sadeas today.

The highprince took the seat beside Adolin, their backs to a hearth that a parshman had begun stoking. The room contained a low hum of nervous conversation. You could never quite be comfortable, no matter how pretty the decor, when a highstorm raged outside.

'Young Adolin,' Sadeas said. 'What do you think of my coat?'

Adolin took a gulp of wine, not trusting himself to reply. *I should just get up and walk away.* But he didn't. A small part of him wished for Sadeas to provoke him, push away his inhibitions, drive him to do something stupid. Killing the man right here, right now, would likely earn Adolin an execution – or at least an exile. It might be worth either punishment.

'You've always been so keen-eyed when it comes to style,' Sadeas continued. 'I'd know your opinion. I do think the coat is splendid, but I worry that the short cut might be trending out of fashion. What is the latest from Liafor?'

Sadeas pulled out the front of his jacket, moving his hand to display a ring that matched the buttons. The ring's emerald, like those on the jacket, was uncut. They glowed softly with Stormlight.

Uncut emeralds, Adolin thought, then looked up to meet Sadeas's eyes. The man smiled.

'The gemstones are recent acquisitions,' Sadeas noted. 'I am fond of them.'

Gained from doing a plateau run with Ruthar that he wasn't supposed to have been on. Racing ahead of the other highprinces, like this was the old days, where each prince tried to be first and claim their winnings.

'I hate you,' Adolin whispered.

'As well you should,' Sadeas said, letting go of his coat. He nodded toward Adolin's bridgeman guards, watching with overt hostility nearby. 'My former property is treating you well? I've seen their like patrolling the market here. I find that amusing for reasons I doubt I could ever properly express.'

'They patrol,' Adolin said, 'to create a better Alethkar.'

'Is that what Dalinar wants? I am surprised to hear it. He talks of justice, of course, but he doesn't allow justice to take its course. Not properly.'

'And I know where you're going, Sadeas,' Adolin snapped. 'You're annoyed that we haven't been letting you put judges into our warcamp as Highprince of Information. Well, I'll have you know that Father has decided to let—'

'Highprince of . . . Information? You didn't hear? I recently renounced the title.'

'*What?*'

'Yes,' Sadeas said. 'I fear I was never a good match for the position. My Shalashian temperament, perhaps. I wish Dalinar good fortune in finding a replacement – though from what I've heard, the other highprinces have come to an agreement that none of us are . . . suited to these kinds of appointments.'

He renounces the king's authority, Adolin thought. Storms, this was bad. He gritted his teeth, and found himself reaching his hand to the side to summon his Blade. No. He pulled the hand back. He'd find a way to force this man into the dueling ring. Killing Sadeas now – no matter how much he deserved it – would undermine the very laws and codes Adolin's father was working so hard to uphold.

But storms . . . Adolin was tempted.

Sadeas smiled again. 'Do you think me an evil man, Adolin?'

'That's too simple a term,' Adolin snapped. 'You're not just evil, you're a selfish, crem-crusted eel who is trying to strangle this kingdom with his bulbous, bastard hand.'

'Eloquent,' Sadeas said. 'You realize I *created* this kingdom.'

'You only helped my father and uncle.'

'Men who are both gone,' Sadeas said. 'The Blackthorn is as dead as old Gavilar. Instead, two *idiots* rule this kingdom, and each one is – in a way – a shadow of a man I loved.' He leaned forward, looking Adolin straight in the eyes. 'I'm not strangling Alethkar, son. I'm trying with everything I have to keep a few chunks of it strong enough to weather the collapse your father is bringing.'

'Don't call me son,' Adolin hissed.

'Fine,' Sadeas said, standing. 'But I'll tell you one thing. I'm glad you survived the events on the Tower that day. You'll make a fine highprince in the coming months. I have a feeling that in ten years or so – following an extended civil war between the two of us – our alliance will be a strong one. By then, you'll understand why I did what I did.'

'I doubt it. I'll have rammed my sword through your gut long before that, Sadeas.'

Sadeas raised his cup of wine, then walked off, joining a different group of lighteyes. Adolin let out a long sigh of exhaustion, then leaned back against the chair. Nearby, his short bridgeman guard – the one with the silver at his temples – gave Adolin a nod of respect.

Adolin slumped there, feeling drained, until long after the highstorm ended and people started to depart. Adolin preferred to wait until the rain stopped completely before leaving, anyway. He never had liked how his uniform looked when it got wet.

Eventually, he rose, collected his two guards, and stepped out of the winehouse to a grey sky and a deserted Outer Market. He was mostly over the conversation with Sadeas, and kept reminding himself that up to that point the day had been going very well.

Shallan and her carriage had already gone, of course. He could have ordered a ride for himself, but after being locked away for so long, it felt good to be walking in the open air; chill, wet, and fresh from the storm.

Hands in the pockets of his uniform, he started along a pathway through the Outer Market, strolling around puddles. Gardeners had begun growing ornamental shalebark along the sides of the path, though it wasn't very high yet, just a few inches. A good shalebark ridge could take years to grow properly.

Those two insufferable bridgemen followed along behind him. Not that Adolin minded the men personally – they seemed like amiable enough fellows, particularly when away from their commander. Adolin just didn't like needing minders. Though the storm had passed into the west, the afternoon felt gloomy. Clouds obscured the sun, which had moved from its zenith and was drooping slowly toward the distant horizon. He didn't pass many people, so his only companions were the bridgemen – well, those and a legion of cremlings that had emerged to feast upon plants that lapped at water in pools.

Why did plants spend so much more time in their shells out here than they did back home? Shallan probably knew. He smiled, forcing thoughts of Sadeas into the back of his mind. This thing with Shallan, it was working. It always worked at first though, so he contained his enthusiasm.

She *was* marvelous. Exotic, witty, and not smothered in Alethi propriety. She was smarter than he was, but she didn't make him feel stupid. That was a large point in her favor.

He passed out of the market, then crossed the open ground beyond it, eventually reaching Dalinar's warcamp. The guards let him through with crisp salutes. He idled in the warcamp market, comparing the wares he saw here with those in the market near the Pinnacle.

What will happen to this place, Adolin thought, *when the war stops?* It would end someday. Perhaps tomorrow, with the negotiations with the Parshendi Shardbearer.

The Alethi presence wouldn't end here, not with the chasmfiends to hunt, but surely this large a population couldn't continue, could it? Could he really be witnessing a permanent shift of the king's seat?

Hours later – after spending some time at jewelry shops looking for something for Shallan – Adolin and his guards reached his father's complex. By then, Adolin's feet were starting to ache and the camp had grown dark. He yawned, making his way through the cavernous guts of his father's bunkerish dwelling. Wasn't it about time they built a proper mansion? Being an example for the men was all well and good, but there were certain standards a family like theirs should uphold. Particularly if the Shattered Plains were going to remain as important as they had been. It was . . .

He hesitated, stopping at an intersection and looking right. He'd been intending to visit the kitchens for a snack, but a group of men moved and threw shadows in the other direction. Hushed whispers.

'What is this?' Adolin demanded, marching toward the gathering, his two guards following. 'Soldiers? What have you found?'

The men scrambled to turn and salute, spears to shoulders. They were more bridgemen from Kaladin's unit. Just beyond them were the doors to the wing where Dalinar, Adolin, and Renarin all made their quarters. Those doors lay open, and the men had set spheres on the ground.

What was going on? Normally, two or maybe four men would be on guard here. Not eight. And . . . why was there a *parshman* wearing a guardsman uniform, holding a spear with the others?

'Sir!' said a lanky, long-armed man at the front of the bridgemen. 'We were just heading in to check on the highprince, when . . .'

Adolin didn't hear the rest. He pushed through the bridgemen, finally seeing what the spheres illuminated on the floor of the sitting room.

More scratched glyphs. Adolin knelt down, trying to read them. Unfortunately, they hadn't been drawn in any kind of picture to help. He thought they were numbers . . .

'Thirty-two days,' said one of the bridgemen, a short Azish man. 'Seek the center.'

Damnation. 'Have you told anyone of this?' Adolin asked.

'We just found it,' the Azish man said.

'Post guards at either end of the hallway,' Adolin said. 'And send for my aunt.'

⁎

Adolin summoned his Blade, then dismissed it, then summoned it again. A nervous habit. The white fog appeared – manifesting as little vines sprouting in the air – before *snapping* into the form of a Shardblade, which suddenly weighed down his hand.

He stood in the sitting room, those foreboding markings staring up at him, as if in silent challenge. The closed door kept the bridgemen out so only he, Dalinar, and Navani would be privy to the discussion. Adolin wanted to use the Blade to cut those cursed glyphs away. Dalinar had *proven* that he was sane. Aunt Navani almost had an entire document of the Dawnchant translated, using the words of Father's visions as a guide!

The visions were from the Almighty. It all made sense.

Now this.

'They were made with a knife,' Navani said, kneeling beside the glyphs. The sitting room was a large open area, used for receiving callers or holding meetings. Doors beyond led to the study and the bedrooms.

'This knife,' Dalinar replied, holding up a side knife of the style most lighteyes wore. 'My knife.'

The edge was blunted and still bore flecks of stone from the gouges. The scratches matched the size of the blade. They'd found it just in front of the door to Dalinar's study, where he'd spent the highstorm. Alone. Navani's carriage had been delayed, and she'd been forced to return to the palace or risk being caught in the storm.

'Someone else could have taken it and done this,' Adolin snapped. 'They could have sneaked into your study, grabbed it while you were consumed by the visions, and come out here . . .'

The other two looked at him.

'Often,' Navani said, 'the simplest answer is the right one.'

Adolin sighed, dismissing his Blade and slumping down in a chair beside the offending glyphs. His father stood tall. In fact, Dalinar Kholin never seemed to have stood as tall as he did now, hands clasped behind his back, eyes away from the glyphs, toward the wall – eastward.

Dalinar was a rock, a boulder too big for even storms to move. He seemed so *sure*. It was something to cling to.

'You don't remember anything?' Navani asked Dalinar, rising.

'No.' He turned to Adolin. 'I think it's obvious now that I was behind each of these. Why does that bother you so, son?'

'It's the idea of you scribbling on the ground,' Adolin said, shivering. 'Lost in one of those visions, not in control of yourself.'

'The Almighty's path for me is a strange one,' Dalinar said. 'Why do I need to get the information this way? Scratches on the ground or the wall? Why not say it to me plainly in the visions?'

'It's foretelling, you realize,' Adolin said softly. 'Seeing the future. A thing of the Voidbringers.'

'Yes.' Dalinar narrowed his eyes. 'Seek the center. What do you think, Navani? The center of the Shattered Plains? What truths hide there?'

'The Parshendi, obviously.'

They talked about the center of the Shattered Plains as if they knew of the place. But no man had been there, only Parshendi. To the Alethi, the word 'center' just referred to the vast open expanse of unexplored plateaus beyond the scouted rims.

'Yes,' Adolin's father said. 'But where? Maybe they move around? Maybe there is no Parshendi city in the center.'

'They would only be able to move if they had Soulcasters,' Navani said, 'which I personally doubt. They'll have entrenched somewhere. They aren't a nomadic people, and there's no reason for them to move.'

'If we can make peace,' Dalinar mused, 'reaching the center would be a lot easier. . . .' He looked to Adolin. 'Have the bridgemen fill those scratches with crem, then have them pull the rug over that section of floor.'

'I'll see it done.'

'Good,' Dalinar said, seeming distant. 'After that, get some sleep, son. Tomorrow is a big day.'

Adolin nodded. 'Father. Were you aware that there is a *parshman* among the bridgemen?'

'Yes,' Dalinar said. 'There has been one among their numbers from the beginning, but they didn't arm him until I gave them permission.'

'Why would you do such a thing?'

'Out of curiosity,' Dalinar said. He turned and nodded toward the glyphs on the floor. 'Tell me, Navani. Assuming these numbers are counting toward a date, is it a day when a highstorm will come?'

'Thirty-two days?' Navani asked. 'That will be in the middle of the Weeping. Thirty-two days won't even be the exact end of the year, but two days ahead of it. I can't fathom the significance.'

'Ah, it was too convenient an answer anyway. Very well. Let's allow the guards back in and swear them to secrecy. Wouldn't want to inspire a panic.'

In short, if any presume Kazilah to be innocent, you must look at the facts and deny them in their entirety; to say that the Radiants were destitute of integrity for this execution of one their own, one who had obviously fraternized with the unwholesome elements, indicates the most slothful of reasoning; for the enemy's baleful influence demanded vigilance on all occasions, of war and of peace.

—From *Words of Radiance*, chapter 32, page 17

The next day, Adolin stomped his feet into his boots, hair still damp from a morning bath. It was amazing the difference a little hot water and some time to reflect could make. He'd come to two decisions.

He wasn't going to worry about his father's disconcerting behavior during the visions. The whole of it – the visions, the command to refound the Knights Radiant, the preparation for a disaster that might or might not come – was a package. Adolin had already decided to believe that his father wasn't mad. Further worry was pointless.

The other decision might get him into trouble. He left his quarters, entering the sitting room, where Dalinar was already planning with Navani, General Khal, Teshav, and Captain Kaladin. Renarin, frustratingly, guarded the door wearing a Bridge Four uniform. He'd refused to give up on that decision of his, despite Adolin's insistence.

'We'll need the bridgemen again,' Dalinar said. 'If something goes wrong, we may need a quick retreat.'

'I'll prepare Bridges Five and Twelve for the day, sir,' Kaladin said. 'Those two seem nostalgic for their bridges, and talk about the bridge runs with fondness.'

'Weren't those *bloodbaths*?' Navani asked.

'They were,' Kaladin said, 'but soldiers are a strange lot, Brightness. A disaster unifies them. These men would never want to go back, but they still identify as bridgemen.'

Nearby, General Khal nodded in understanding, though Navani still seemed baffled.

'I'll take my position here,' Dalinar said, holding up a map of the Shattered Plains. 'We can scout the meeting plateau first, while I wait. It apparently has some odd rock formations.'

'That sounds good,' Brightness Teshav said.

'It does,' Adolin said, joining the group, 'except for one thing. You won't be there, Father.'

'Adolin,' Dalinar said with a suffering tone. 'I know you think this is too dangerous, but—'

'It *is* too dangerous,' Adolin said. 'The assassin is still out there – and he attacked us last on the very *day* the Parshendi messenger came to camp. Now, we have a meeting with the enemy out on the Shattered Plains? Father, you can't go.'

'I have to,' Dalinar said. 'Adolin, this could mean an end to the war. It could mean answers – why they attacked in the first place. I will not give up this opportunity.'

'We're not going to give it up,' Adolin said. 'We're just going to do things a little differently.'

'How?' Dalinar asked, narrowing his eyes.

'Well for one thing,' Adolin said, 'I'm going to go in your place.'

'Impossible,' Dalinar said, 'I won't risk my son on—'

'Father!' Adolin snapped. 'This is *not* subject to discussion!'

The room fell silent. Dalinar lowered his hand from the map. Adolin stuck out his jaw, meeting his father's eyes. Storms, it was difficult to deny Dalinar Kholin. Did his father realize the presence he had, the way he moved people about by sheer force of expectation?

Nobody contradicted him. Dalinar did what he wanted. Fortunately, these days those motives had a noble purpose. But in many ways he was the same man he had been twenty years ago, when he'd conquered a kingdom. He was the Blackthorn, and he got what he wanted.

Except today.

'You are too important,' Adolin said, pointing. 'Deny that. Deny that your visions are vital. Deny that if you die, Alethkar would fall apart. Deny that every single person in this room is less important than you are.'

Dalinar drew in a deep breath, then exhaled slowly. 'It shouldn't be so. The kingdom needs to be strong enough to survive the loss of one man, no matter who.'

'Well, it's not there yet,' Adolin said. 'To get it there, we're going to need you. And that means you need to let us watch out for you. I'm sorry, Father, but once in a while you just have to let someone else do their job. You can't fix every problem with your own hands.'

'He's right, sir,' Kaladin said. 'You really shouldn't be risking yourself out on those Plains. Not if there's another option.'

'I fail to see that there is one,' Dalinar said, his tone cool.

'Oh, there is,' Adolin said. 'But I'm going to need to borrow Renarin's Shardplate.'

∴

The strangest thing about this experience, in Adolin's estimation, wasn't wearing his father's old armor. Despite the outward stylistic differences, suits of Shardplate all tended to fit similarly. The armor adapted, and within a short time after donning it, the Plate felt exactly like Adolin's own.

It also wasn't strange to ride at the front of the force, Dalinar's banner flapping over his head. Adolin had been leading them to battle on his own for six weeks now.

No, the strangest part was riding his father's horse.

Gallant was a large black animal, bulkier and squatter than Sureblood, Adolin's horse. Gallant looked like a warhorse even when compared to other Ryshadium. So far as Adolin knew, no man had ever ridden him but Dalinar. Ryshadium were finicky that way. It had taken a lengthy explanation from Dalinar to even get the horse to allow Adolin to hold the reins, let alone climb into the saddle.

It had eventually worked, but Adolin wouldn't dare ride Gallant into battle; he was pretty sure the beast would throw him off and run away, looking to protect Dalinar. It did feel odd climbing on a horse that wasn't Sureblood. He kept expecting Gallant to move differently than he did, turn his head at the wrong times. When Adolin patted his neck, the horse's mane felt off to him in ways he couldn't explain. He and his Ryshadium were more than simply rider and horse, and he found himself oddly melancholy to be out on a ride without Sureblood.

Foolishness. He had to stay focused. The procession approached the meeting plateau, which had a large, oddly shaped mound of rock near the center. This plateau was close to the Alethi side of the Plains, but much farther south than Adolin had ever gone. Early patrols had said chasmfiends were more common out in this region, but they never spotted a chrysalis here. Some kind of hunting ground, but not a place for pupating?

The Parshendi weren't there yet. When the scouts reported that the plateau was secure, Adolin urged Gallant across the mobile bridge. He felt warm in his Plate; the seasons, it seemed, had finally decided to inch through spring and maybe even toward summer.

He approached the rock mound at the center. It really *was* odd. Adolin circled it, noticing its shape, ridged in places, almost like . . .

'It's a chasmfiend,' Adolin realized. He passed the face, a hollowed-out piece of stone that evoked the exact feeling of a chasmfiend's head. A statue? No, it was too natural. A chasmfiend had died here centuries ago, and instead of being blown away, had slowly crusted over with crem.

The result was eerie. The crem had duplicated the creature's form, clinging to the carapace, entombing it. The hulking rock seemed like a creature born of stone, like the ancient stories of Voidbringers.

Adolin shivered, nudging the horse away from the stone corpse and toward the other side of the plateau. Shortly, he heard alarms from the outrunners. Parshendi coming. He steeled himself, ready to summon his Shardblade. Behind him arrayed a group of bridgemen, ten in number, including that parshman. Captain Kaladin had remained with Dalinar back in the warcamp, just in case.

Adolin was the one more exposed. Part of him *wished* for the assassin to come today. So Adolin could try himself again. Of all the duels he hoped to fight in the future, this one – against the man who had killed his uncle – would be the most important, even more than taking down Sadeas. The assassin did not make an appearance as a group of two hundred Parshendi crossed from the next plateau, jumping gracefully and landing on the meeting plateau. Adolin's soldiers stirred, armor clanking, spears lowering. It had been years since men and Parshendi had met without blood being spilled.

'All right,' Adolin said in his helm. 'Fetch my scribe.'

Brightness Inadara was carried up through the ranks in a palanquin. Dalinar wanted Navani with him – ostensibly because he wanted her advice, but probably also to protect her.

'Let's go,' Adolin said, nudging Gallant forward. They crossed the plateau, just him and Brightness Inadara, who rose from her palanquin to walk. She was a wizened matron, with grey hair she cut short for simplicity. He'd seen sticks with more flesh on them than she had, but she was keen-minded and as trustworthy a scribe as they had.

The Parshendi Shardbearer emerged from the ranks and strode forward on the rocks alone. Uncaring, unworried. This was a confident one.

Adolin dismounted and went the rest of the way on foot, Inadara at his side. They stopped a few feet from the Parshendi, the three of them alone on an expanse of rock, the fossilized chasmfiend staring at them from the left.

'I am Eshonai,' the Parshendi said. 'Do you remember me?'

'No,' Adolin said. He pitched his voice down to try and match the voice of his father, and hoped that – with the helm in place – it would be enough to fool this woman, who couldn't know well what Dalinar sounded like.

'Not surprising,' Eshonai said. 'I was young and unimportant when we first met. Barely worth remembering.'

Adolin had originally expected Parshendi conversation to be singsongish, from what he'd heard said of them. That wasn't the case at all. Eshonai had a rhythm to her words, the way she emphasized them and where she paused. She changed tones, but the result was more of a chant than a song.

Inadara took out a writing board and spanreed, then started writing down what Eshonai said.

'What is this?' Eshonai demanded.

'I came alone, as you asked,' Adolin said, trying to project his father's air of command. 'But I *will* record what is said and send it back to my generals.'

Eshonai did not raise her faceplate, so Adolin had a good excuse not to raise his. They stared at each other through eye slits. This was not going as well as his father had hoped, but it was about what Adolin had expected.

'We are here,' Adolin said, using the words his father had suggested he begin with, 'to discuss the terms of a Parshendi surrender.'

Eshonai laughed. 'That is not the point at all.'

'Then what?' Adolin demanded. 'You seemed eager to meet with me. Why?'

'Things have changed since I spoke with your son, Blackthorn. Important things.'

'What things?'

'Things you cannot imagine,' Eshonai said.

Adolin waited, as if pondering, but actually giving Inadara time to correspond with the warcamps. Inadara leaned up to him, whispering what Navani and Dalinar had written for him to say.

'We tire of this war, Parshendi,' Adolin said. 'Your numbers dwindle. We know this. Let us make a truce, one that would benefit us both.'

'We are not as weak as you believe,' Eshonai said.

Adolin found himself frowning. When she'd spoken to him before, she'd seemed passionate, inviting. Now she was cold and dismissive. Was that right? She was Parshendi. Perhaps human emotions didn't apply to her.

Inadara whispered more to him.

'What do you want?' Adolin asked, speaking the words his father sent. 'How can there be peace?'

'There will be peace, Blackthorn, when one of us is dead. I came here because I wanted to see you with my own eyes, and I wanted to warn you. We have just changed the rules of this conflict. Squabbling over gemstones no longer matters.'

No longer matters? Adolin started to sweat. *She makes it sound like they were playing their own game all this time. Not desperate at all.* Could the Alethi have misjudged everything so profoundly?

She turned to go.

No. All of this, just to have the meeting puff into smoke? Storm it!

'Wait!' Adolin cried, stepping forward. 'Why? Why are you acting like this? What is wrong?'

She looked back at him. 'You really want to end this?'

'Yes. Please. I want peace. Regardless of the cost.'

'Then you will have to destroy us.'

'Why?' Adolin repeated. 'Why did you kill Gavilar, all those years ago? Why betray our treaty?'

'King Gavilar,' Eshonai said, as if mulling over the name. 'He should not have revealed his plans to us that night. Poor fool. He did not know. He bragged, thinking we would welcome the return of our gods.' She shook her head, then turned again and jogged off, armor clinking.

Adolin stepped back, feeling useless. If his father had been there, would he have been able to do more? Inadara still wrote, sending the words to Dalinar.

A reply from him finally came. 'Return to the warcamps. There is nothing you, or I myself, could have done. Clearly, her mind is already made up.'

Adolin spent the return ride brooding. When he finally reached the warcamps a few hours later, he found his father in conference with Navani, Khal, Teshav, and the army's four battalionlords.

Together, they pored over the words that Inadara had sent. A group of parshman servants quietly brought wine and fruit. Teleb – wearing the Plate that Adolin had won from his duel with Eranniv – watched from the side of the room, Shardhammer on his back, faceplate up. His people had once ruled Alethkar. What did he think of all this? The man usually kept his opinions to himself.

Adolin stomped into the room, pulling off his father's – well, Renarin's – helm. 'I should have let you go,' Adolin said. 'It wasn't a trap. Perhaps you could have talked sense to her.'

'These are the people who murdered my brother on the very night they signed a treaty with him,' Dalinar said, inspecting maps on the table. 'It seems they have not changed at all from that day. You did perfectly, son; we know everything we need to.'

'We do?' Adolin said, walking up to the table, helm under arm.

'Yes,' Dalinar said, looking up. 'We know that they will not agree to peace, no matter what. My conscience is clear.'

Adolin looked over the outspread maps. 'What is this?' he asked, noting troop movement symbols. They were all pointed across the Shattered Plains.

'A plan of assault,' Dalinar said quietly. 'The Parshendi will not deal with us, and they are planning something big. Something to change the war. The time has come to bring the fight directly to them and end this war, one way or another.'

'Stormfather,' Adolin said. 'And if we're surrounded while we're out there?'

'We will take everyone,' Dalinar said, 'our whole army, and as many of the highprinces as will join me. Soulcasters for food. The Parshendi won't be able to surround that large a force, and even if they did, it wouldn't matter. We'd be able to stand against them.'

'We can leave right after the final highstorm before the Weeping,' Navani said, writing some numbers on the side of the map. 'It is the Light Year, and so we'll have steady rains, but no highstorms for weeks. We won't be exposed to one while out on the Plains.'

It would also put them out on the Shattered Plains, alone, within days of the date that had been scratched on the walls and floor. . . . Adolin's spine crawled.

'We have to beat them to it,' Dalinar said softly, scanning the maps. 'Interrupt whatever it is they are planning. Before the countdown ends.' He looked up at Adolin. 'I need you to duel more. High-profile matches, as high profile as you can manage. Win Shards for me, son.'

'I'm dueling Elit tomorrow,' Adolin said. 'From there, I have a plan for my next target.'

'Good. To succeed out on the Plains, we will need Shardbearers – and we will need the loyalty of as many highprinces as will follow me. Focus your dueling on the Shardbearers of the faction loyal to Sadeas, and beat them with as much fanfare as you can manage. I will go to the neutral highprinces, and will remind them of their oaths to fulfill the Vengeance Pact. If we can take Shards from those who follow Sadeas and use them to end the war, it will go a long way toward proving what I've been saying all along. That unity is the path to Alethi greatness.'

Adolin nodded. 'I'll see it done.'